Dick Francis has written forty books, all of them best-sellers. He has published thirty-seven novels and is widely acclaimed as one of the world's finest thriller writers; the first book was his autobiography, *The Sport of Queens*, and the twenty-sixth book was the official biography of Lester Piggott. His most recent is *Second Wind*.

He has received many awards, amongst them the prestigious Crime Writers' Association's Cartier Diamond Dagger for his outstanding contribution to the genre. The Mystery Writers of America have given him three Edgar Allen Poe awards for the best novel of the year and in 1996 made him a Grand Master for a lifetime's achievement.

Dick Francis and his wife, Mary, divide their time between England and an island in the Caribbean Sea.

Dick Francis Omnibus Three

SLAY-RIDE
BANKER
PROOF

PAN BOOKS

Slay-Ride first published 1973 by Michael Joseph Ltd
and published by Pan Books in 1974
Banker first published 1982 by Michael Joseph Ltd
and published by Pan Books in 1983
Proof first published 1984 by Michael Joseph Ltd
and published by Pan Books in 1985

This omnibus edition published 2000 by Pan Books
an imprint of Macmillan Publishers Ltd
25 Eccleston Place, London SW1W 9NF
Basingstoke and Oxford
Associated companies throughout the world
www.macmillan.com

ISBN 0 330 48483 4

1 3 5 7 9 8 6 4 2

A CIP catalogue record for this book is available from
the British Library.

Phototypeset by Intype London Ltd
Printed and bound in Great Britain by
Mackays of Chatham plc, Chatham, Kent

SLAY-RIDE

CHAPTER ONE

Cold grey water lapped the flimsy-looking sides of the fibre-glass dinghy, and I shivered and thought of the five hundred feet straight down to the sea-bed underneath.

An hour out of Oslo with the outboard motor stilled and my friend Arne Kristiansen taking all afternoon to answer some simple questions.

A grey day, damp, not far from rain. The air sang in my ears with stinging chill. My feet were congealing. The October temperature down the fjord was giving the land a twenty degree lead towards zero, and of the two of us only Arne was dressed for it.

Where I had a showerproof jacket over an ordinary suit and no hat, he had come equipped with the full bit: a red padded cap with ear flaps fastened with a strap under his chin, blue padded trousers tucked into short wide-legged gumboots, and a red padded jacket fastened up the front with silver coloured press studs. A glimpse of black and yellow at the neck spoke of other warm layers underneath.

He had arranged on the telephone to meet me at

the statue in the Radhusplassen by the harbour, brushing aside my suggestion that he should come to the Grand Hotel, where I was staying. Even in those wide open spaces he had gone muttering on about being overheard by long range bugging machines (his words) and had finally insisted on taking to the dinghy. Knowing from past experience the quickest way in the end to deal with his perennial mild persecution complex was to go along with it, I had shrugged and followed him along the quay to where the small pale green craft bobbed beside a flight of steps.

I had forgotten that it is always very much colder out on open water. I flexed the stiffening fingers inside my pockets and repeated my last question.

'How would you smuggle sixteen thousand stolen kroner out of the country?'

For the second time, I got no answer. Arne produced answers as prodigally as tax collectors offer rebates.

He blinked slowly, the dropping of the eyelids marking some intermediary stage in the chess-like permutations going on in his head. He was no doubt, as always, considering every foreseeable consequence: if answer A might produce any one of five responses, and answer B lead on to six subsidiary questions, wouldn't it be wiser to answer C, in which case, though . . .

It made conversation with him a trifle slow.

I tried a little prompting. 'You said it was all in coins

4

and used notes of small denominations. How bulky? Enough to fit in a small sized suitcase?'

He blinked.

'Do you think he just walked out with it through the customs?'

He blinked.

'Or do you think he is still somewhere in Norway?'

Arne opened his mouth and said grudgingly, 'No one knows.'

I tried some more. 'When a foreigner stays in one of your hotels, he has to fill in a form and show his passport. These forms are for the police. Have your police checked those forms?'

Pause.

'Yes,' he said.

'And?'

'Robert Sherman did not fill in any form.'

'None at all? What about when he arrived from England?'

'He did not stay in an hotel.'

Patience, I thought. Give me patience.

'Where, then?'

'With friends.'

'What friends?'

He considered. I knew he knew the answer. He knew he was eventually going to tell me. I suppose he couldn't help the way his mind worked, but this, God help us, was supposed to be an investigator.

What was more, I had taught him myself. 'Think

before you answer any question,' I'd said. So now he did.

In the three months he had spent in England learning how the Jockey Club ran its investigation department we had grown to know each other well. Some of the time he had stayed in my flat, most of the time we had travelled together to the races, all of the time he had asked and listened and blinked as he thought. That had been three years ago. Two minutes had been enough to resuscitate the old warm feelings of tolerant regard. I liked him, I thought, more because of the mild eccentric kinks than despite.

'He stayed with Gunnar Holth,' he said.

I waited.

After ten seconds he added, 'He is a racehorse trainer.'

'Did Bob Sherman ride for him?'

This dead simple question threw him into a longer than ever session of mental chess, but finally he said, 'Bob Sherman rode the ones of his horses which ran in hurdle races while Bob Sherman was in Norway. *Ja*. He did not ride the horses of Gunnar Holth which ran in flat races while he was in Norway.'

God give me strength.

Arne hadn't actually finished. 'Robert Sherman rode horses for the racecourse.'

I was puzzled. 'How do you mean?'

He consulted his inner man again, who evidently said it was OK to explain.

'The racecourse pays appearance money to some foreign jockeys, to get them to come to Norway. It makes the racing more interesting for the racegoers. So the racecourse paid Robert Sherman to ride.'

'How much did they pay him?'

A rising breeze was stirring the fjord's surface into proper little wavelets. The fjord just below Oslo is not one of those narrow canyon jobs on the Come-To-Scenic-Norway posters, but a wide expanse of sea dotted with rocky islands and fringed by the sprawling suburbs of the city. A coastal steamer surged past half a mile away and tossed us lightly in its wake. The nearest land looked a lot further off.

'Let's go back,' I said abruptly.

'No, no . . .' He had no patience for such weak suggestions. 'They paid him fifteen hundred kroner.'

'I'm cold,' I said.

He looked surprised. 'It is not winter yet.'

I made a noise which was half laugh and half teeth beginning to chatter. 'It isn't summer either.'

He looked vaguely all around. 'Robert Sherman had made six visits to race in Norway,' he said. 'This was his seventh.'

'Look, Arne, tell me about it back at the hotel, huh?'

He attended to me seriously. 'What is the matter?'

'I don't like heights,' I said.

He looked blank. I took one frozen mitt out of its pocket, hung it over the side of the boat, and pointed straight down. Arne's face melted into comprehension

7

and a huge grin took the place of the usual tight careful configuration of his mouth.

'David, I am sorry. The water to me, it is home. Like snow. I am sorry.'

He turned at once to start the outboard, and then paused to say, 'He could simply have driven over the border to Sweden. The customs, they would not search for kroner.'

'In what car?' I asked.

He thought it over. 'Ah yes.' He blinked a bit. 'Perhaps a friend drove him . . .'

'Start the engine,' I said encouragingly.

He shrugged and gave several small nods of the head, but turned to the outboard and pressed the necessary knobs. I had half expected it to prove as lifeless as my fingers, but the spark hit the gas in an orderly fashion and Arne pointed the sharp end back towards hot coffee and radiators.

The dinghy slapped busily through the little waves and the crosswind flicked spray on to my left cheek. I pulled my jacket collar up and made like a tortoise.

Arne's mouth moved as he said something, but against the combined noises of the engine and the sea and the rustle of gaberdine against my ears, I couldn't hear any words.

'What?' I shouted.

He started to repeat whatever it was, but louder. I caught only snatches like 'ungrateful pig' and 'dirty thief', which I took to be his own private views of

Robert Sherman, British steeplechase jockey. Arne had had a bad time since the said Bob Sherman disappeared with the day's take from the turnstiles of Øvrevoll, because Arne Kristiansen, besides being the Norwegian Jockey Club's official investigator, was also in charge of racecourse security.

The theft, he had told me on the outward chug, was an insult, first to himself, and secondly to Norway. Guests in a foreign country should not steal. Norwegians were not criminals, he said, and quoted jail statistics per million of population to prove it. When the British were in Norway, they should keep their hands to themselves.

Commiserating, I refrained from drawing his country's raids on Britain to his attention: they were, after all, a thousand or so years in the past, and the modern Vikings were less likely to burn, rape, pillage and plunder than to take peaceable photographs of Buckingham Palace. I felt moreover a twinge of national shame about Bob Sherman: I had found myself apologizing, of all things, for his behaviour.

Arne was still going on about it: on that subject unfortunately he needed no prompting. Phrases like 'put me in an intolerable position' slid off his tongue as if he had been practising them for weeks – which, on reflection, of course he had. It was three weeks and four days since the theft: and forty-eight hours since the Chairman of the racecourse had telephoned and asked me to send over a British Jockey Club

investigator to see what he could do. I had sent (you
will have guessed) myself.

I hadn't met the Chairman yet, nor seen the racecourse, nor ever before been to Norway. I was down
the fjord with Arne because Arne was the devil I knew.

Three years earlier the hair now closely hidden
under the red padded hood had been a bright blond
fading at the temples to grey. The eyes were as fierce
a blue as ever, the wrinkles around them as deep, and
the bags below a good deal heavier. The spray blew on
to skin that was weather-beaten but not sunburned;
thick-looking impervious yellowish-white skin lumped
and pitted by forty-something winters.

He was still breaking out in bursts of aggrieved half-
heard monologue, trudging along well-worn paths of
resentment. I gave up trying to listen. It was too cold.

He stopped in mid-sentence and looked with raised
eyebrows at some distant point over my left shoulder.
I turned. A large speedboat, not very far away, was
slicing down the fjord in our general direction with its
bow waves leaping out like heavy silver wings.

I turned back to Arne. He shrugged and looked
uninterested, and the outboard chose that moment to
splutter and cough and choke to silence.

'*Fanden*,' said Arne loudly, which was nothing at all
to what I was saying in my head.

'Those people will help us,' he announced, pointing
at the approaching speedboat, and without hesitation

he stood up, braced his legs, and waved his scarlet clad arms in wide sweeps above his head.

Twisting on my bench seat, I watched the speedboat draw near.

'They will take us on board,' Arne said.

The speedboat did not seem to be slowing down. I could see its shining black hull and its sharp cutting bow, and the silver wings of wave looked as high and full as ever.

If not higher and fuller.

I turned to Arne with the beginnings of apprehension.

'They haven't seen us,' I said.

'They must have.' Arne waved his arms with urgent acceleration, rocking the dinghy precariously.

'Hey!' Arne shouted to the speedboat. And after that he screamed at it, in Norwegian.

The wind blew his words away. The helmsman of the speedboat didn't hear, didn't see. The sharp hard shining black prow raced straight towards us at forty knots.

'Jump!' yelled Arne; and he jumped. A flash of scarlet streaking into the sea.

I was slow. Thought perhaps that the unimaginable wouldn't happen, that the bow wave would toss the dinghy clear like it would a swan, that the frail craft would bob away as lightly as a bird.

I tumbled over the side into the water about one second before the bow split the fibre-glass open like an eggshell. Something hit me a colossal bang on the shoulder while I was still gasping from the shock of immersion and I went down under the surface into a roaring buffeting darkness.

People who fall off boats die as often from the propellers as from drowning, but I didn't remember that until the twin screws had churned past and left me unsliced. I came stuttering and gulping to the daylight in the jumbled frothing wake and saw the back of the speedboat tearing away unconcernedly down the fjord.

'Arne,' I shouted, which was about as useless as dredging for diamonds in the Thames. A wave slapped me in the open mouth and I swallowed a double salt water, neat.

The sea seemed much rougher at face level than it had done from above. I floundered in high choppy waves with ruffles of white frothing across their tops and blowing into my eyes, and I shouted again for Arne. Shouted with intensifying concern for him and with fear for myself: but the wind tore the words away and battered them to bits.

There was no sign of the dinghy. My last impression was that it had been cut clean into two pieces, which were now, no doubt, turning over and over in a slow sink down to the far away sea-bed.

I shuddered as much from imagination as from cold.

There was no sight anywhere of Arne. No red-padded head, no red waving arms above the waves, no cheerful smile coming to tell me that the sea was home to him and that safety and hot muffins were *this* way, just over here.

Land lay visible all around me in greyish misty heights. None of it was especially near. About two miles away, I guessed, whichever way I looked.

Treading water, I began to pull my clothes off, still looking desperately for Arne, still expecting to see him.

There was nothing but the rough slapping water. I thought about the speedboat's propellers and I thought about Arne's wide legged gumboots which would fill with water in the first few seconds. I thought finally that if I didn't accept that Arne was gone and get started shorewards I was very likely going to drown on that spot.

I kicked off my shoes and struggled with the zip of my raincoat. Ripped open the buttons of my suit jacket underneath and shrugged out of both coats together. I let go of them, then remembered my wallet, and although it seemed crazy I took it out of my jacket pocket and shoved it inside my shirt.

The two coats, waterlogged, floated briefly away and started to go down out of sight. I slid out of my trousers, and let them follow.

Pity, I thought. Nice suit, that had been.

The water was very cold indeed.

I began to swim. Up the fjord. Towards Oslo. Where else?

*

I was thirty-three and hardy and I knew more statistics than I cared to. I knew for instance that the average human can live less than an hour in water of one degree centigrade.

I tried to swim unhurriedly in long undemanding strokes, postponing the moment of exhaustion. The water in Oslo fjord was not one degree above freezing, but at least five. Probably not much colder than the stuff buffeting the English beach at Brighton at that very moment. In water five degrees above freezing, one could last . . . well, I didn't actually know *that* statistic. Had to take it on trust. Long enough anyway to swim something over two miles.

Bits of distant geography lessons made no sense. 'The Gulf Stream warms the coast of Norway . . .' Good old Gulf Stream. Where had it gone?

Cold had never seemed a positive force to me before. I supposed I had never really been *cold*, just chilled. This cold dug deep into every muscle and ached in my gut. Feeling had gone from my hands and feet, and my arms and legs felt heavy. The best long-distance swimmers had a nice thick insulating layer of subcutaneous fat: I hadn't. They also covered themselves with water-repelling grease and swam alongside comfort boats which fed them hot cocoa through tubes on demand. The best long-distance swimmers were, of course, usually going twenty miles or so further than I was.

I swam.

The waves seemed frighteningly big: and I couldn't see where I was aiming unless I lifted my head right up and trod water, and that wasted time and energy.

The nearest-looking land seemed to my salt-stinging eyes to be as far away as ever. And surely Oslo fjord should be a Piccadilly Circus of boats? But I couldn't see a single one.

Dammit, I thought. I'm bloody well not going to drown. I'm bloody well *not*.

I swam.

Daylight was slowly fading. Sea, sky, and distant mountains were all a darker grey. It began to rain.

I travelled, it seemed, very slowly. The land I was aiming for never appeared to be nearer. I began to wonder if some current was cancelling out every yard I swam forward: but when I looked back, the land behind was definitely receding.

I swam mechanically, growing tired.

Time passed.

A long way off, straight ahead, pinpricks of light sprang out against the fading afternoon. Every time I looked, there were more. The city was switching on in the dusk.

Too far, I thought. They are too far for me. Land and life all around me, and I couldn't reach them.

An awful depth beneath. And I never did like heights. A cold lonely death, drowning.

I swam. Nothing else to do.

When another light shone out higher up and to the left, it took at least a minute for the news to reach my sluggish brain. I trod water and wiped the rain and sea out of my eyes as best I could and tried to make out where it came from: and there, a great deal nearer than when I'd last looked, was the solid grey shape of land.

Houses, lights, and people. All there, somewhere, on that rocky hump.

Gratefully I veered fifteen degrees left and pressed on faster, pouring out the carefully hoarded reserves of stamina like a penitent miser. And that was stupid, because no shelving beach lay ahead. The precious land, when I reached it, proved to be a smooth sheer cliff dropping perpendicularly into the water. Not a ledge, not a cranny, to offer even respite from the effort of staying afloat.

The last quarter mile was the worst. I could *touch* the land if I wanted to, and it offered nothing to cling to. There had to be a break somewhere, if I went far enough, but I had practically nothing left. I struggled feebly forward through the slapping waves, wishing in a hazy way that I could surge through warm calm water like Mark Spitz and make a positive touchdown against a nice firm rail, with my feet on the bottom. What I actually did was a sort of belly-flop on to a small boat slipway bordered with large rock slabs.

I lay half in and half out of the water, trying to get

back breath I didn't know I'd lost. My chest heaved. I coughed.

It wasn't dark; just the slow northern twilight. I wouldn't have minded if it had been three in the morning: the cold wet concrete beneath my cheek felt as warm and welcoming goose feathers.

Footsteps crunched rhythmically along the quay at the head of the slipway and then suddenly stopped.

I did a bit towards lifting my head and flapping a numb hand.

'*Hvem er der?*' he said; or something like it.

I gave a sort of croak and he walked carefully, crabwise, down the slipway towards me, a half seen, well-wrapped figure in the rainy gloom.

He repeated his question, which I still didn't understand.

'I'm English,' I said. 'Can you help me?'

Nothing happened for a few seconds. Then he went away.

So what, I thought tiredly. At least from the waist up I was safe in Norway. Didn't seem to have the energy to drag myself uphill till my feet were out, not just for a minute or two. But I would, I thought, given time.

The man came back, and brought a friend. Ungrateful of me to have misjudged him.

The companion peered through the rain and said, 'You are English? Did you say you are English?' His tone seemed to suggest that being English automatically explained such follies as swimming in October in shirt and underpants and lying about on slipways.

'Yes,' I said.

'You fell off a ship?'

'Sort of.'

I felt his hand slide under my armpit.

'Come. Out of the water.'

I scraped myself on to the slipway and with their help more or less crawled to the top. The quay was edged with railings and posts. I sat on the ground with my back against one of the posts and wished for enough strength to stand up.

They consulted in Norwegian. Then the English speaking one said, 'We will take you to my house, to dry and get warm.'

'Thank you,' I said, and by God I meant it.

One of them went away again and came back with a battered old van. They gave me the front passenger seat though I offered to drip in the back, and whisked me about a quarter of a mile to a small wooden house, standing near two or three others. There was no village, no shops, no telephone.

'This is an island,' my rescuer explained. 'One kilometre long, three hundred metres across.' He told me its name, which seemed to me like 'gorse'.

His living-room was small and bright, and warmed by the huge stove which took up at least a sixth of the floorspace. Seen clearly in the light he himself was a short friendly man of middle age with hands that were

used for work. He shook his head over me and produced first a blanket and then, after some rummaging,
a thick woollen shirt and a pair of trousers.

'You are not a sailor,' he said matter of factly,
watching me fumble off my shirt and pants.

'No,' I agreed.

My wallet fell on the floor. I was surprised it was still
there; had forgotten it. The Norwegian-only rescuer
politely picked it up and handed it to me, smiling
broadly. He looked very like his friend.

Between hopeless bouts of shivering I told them
what had happened and asked them how I could get
back to the city. They talked to each other about it
while I dressed, first with a lot of shaking of heads but
finally with a few nods.

'When you are warmer we will take you by boat,'
said the English-speaker. He looked at the wallet which
lay now on a polished pine table. 'We ask only that
you will pay for the fuel. If you can.'

Together we took out my sodden money and spread
it on the table. I asked them to take whatever they
liked, and after debate they chose a fifty kroner note.
I urged them to double it. It wouldn't cost so much,
they protested, but in the end they put two notes aside
and dried the rest for me quickly on the stove so that
the edges curled. After more consultation they dug in
a cupboard and brought out a bottle of pale gold liquid.
One small glass followed, and a moderate tot was
poured into it. They handed it to me.

'*Skol!*' they said.

'*Skol!*' I repeated.

They watched interestedly while I drank. Smooth fire down the throat, heat in the stomach, and soon a warm glow along all the frozen veins.

They smiled.

'Aquavit,' said my host, and stored the precious bottle away ready for the next needy stranger who swam to their doorstep.

They suggested I should sit for a while on the one comfortable-looking chair. Since various muscles were still trembling with weakness this seemed a good idea, so I rested while they busied themselves putting out businesslike sets of oilskins, and by the time they were kitted up my skin had returned from a nasty bluish purplish white to its more usual shade of sallow.

'D'you feel better?' my host observed, smiling.

'I do.'

They nodded, pleased, and held out a spare set of oilskins for me to put on. They took me in a big smelly fishing boat back up the twinkle-edged fjord to the city, and it rained all the way. I spent the journey calculating that I had been in the water for about two hours, which didn't prove anything in particular about the current in the fjord or the inefficiency of my swimming or the distance I had travelled, but did prove pretty conclusively that the temperature was more than one degree above freezing.

CHAPTER TWO

They waited while I changed at the Grand, so that they could take back the lent clothes. We parted with warm handshakes and great camaraderie, and it was only after they had gone that I realized that I didn't know their names.

I would have liked nothing better than to go to bed and sleep for half a century, but the thought of Arne's wife waiting for him to come home put a damper on that. So I spent the next couple of hours with various Norwegian authorities, reporting what had happened.

When the police finished taking notes and said they would send someone to tell Mrs Kristiansen, I suggested that I should go too. They agreed. We went in an official car and rang the bell of Flat C on the first floor of a large timber house in a prosperous road not far from the city centre.

The girl who opened the door looked inquiringly out at us from clear grey eyes in a firm, friendly, thirtyish face. Behind her the flat looked warm and colourful, and the air was thick with Beethoven.

21

'Is Mrs Kristiansen in?' I asked.

'Yes,' she said. 'I am Mrs Kristiansen.'

Not in the least what I would have expected. Oddballs like Arne shouldn't turn out to have slender young wives with thick pale blonde hair falling in loose curls on their shoulders. She looked away from my own less striking face to the policeman behind me, and the eyes widened.

'I'm David Cleveland,' I said. 'I was with Arne this afternoon . . .'

'Oh were you?' she exclaimed. 'Oh, do come in . . . I'm *so* glad . . .'

She held the door wider and turned to call over her shoulder.

'Arne,' she said. 'Arne, see who's here.'

He stepped into the hall. Very much alive.

We stared at each other in consternation. My own face must have mirrored the surprise and shock I saw on his, and then he was striding forward with his hand outheld and his face creasing into the most gigantic smile of all time.

'David! I don't believe it. I have reported you drowned.' He clasped both my hands in both of his and shook them warmly. 'Come in, come in, my dear fellow, and tell me how you were saved. I have been so grieved . . . I was telling Kari . . .'

His wife nodded, as delighted as he was.

The policeman behind me said, 'It would seem Mr Kristiansen wasn't drowned after all, then,' which

22

seemed in our high state of relief to be extremely funny. We all laughed. Even the policeman smiled.

'I was picked up by some fisherman near Nesodden,' Arne told him. 'I reported the accident to the police there. They said they would send a boat to look for Mr Cleveland, but they weren't very hopeful of finding him. I'd better call them . . .'

'Thank you,' said the policeman. 'That would be helpful,' and he smiled once more at us all and went away.

Kari Kristiansen shut the front door and said 'Do come in, we must celebrate,' and led me through into the living-room. Beethoven was thundering away in there, and Kari switched him off. 'Arne always plays loud music when he's upset,' she said.

Out in the hall Arne busied himself with the telephone, and among his explanatory flow of Norwegian I caught my own name spoken with astonishment and relief.

'It is wonderful,' he said, coming into the room and rubbing his hands together. 'Wonderful.' He gestured to me to sit on a deep comfortable sofa near a cheerful wood-burning fire. 'The Nesodden police say they sent a boat out to search for you, but it was too dark and raining and they could see nothing.'

'I'm sorry they had the trouble,' I said.

'My dear fellow . . .' He spread his fingers. 'It was nothing. And now, a drink, eh? To celebrate.'

He filled glasses of red wine from a bottle standing already open on a side-table.

'Arne has been so depressed all evening,' Kari said. 'It is truly a miracle that you were both saved.'

We exchanged stories. Arne had torn off the red clothes and kicked his boots off instantly (I suppose I should have known that a man at home on the sea would wear *loose* gumboots), but although he had called my name and searched around for some minutes he had caught no sign of me.

'When I last saw you,' he said apologetically, 'you were still in the dinghy, and I thought the speedboat must have hit you directly, so when I could not see you I thought that you must be already dead.'

He had started swimming, he said; and knowing a lot more than I did about tides and winds, had taken almost the opposite direction. He had been picked up near the coast by a small home-going fishing boat which was too low on fuel to go out into the fjord to look for me. It had however landed him in the small town where he reported my loss, and from there he had returned by hired boat to the city.

My story was so much the same that it could be told in two sentences: I swam to an island. Two men brought me back in a boat.

Arne searched among an untidy pile of papers and triumphantly produced a map. Spreading it out, he pointed to the widest part of the fjord and showed both Kari and me where we had sunk.

'The worst possible place,' Kari exclaimed. 'Why did you go so far?'

'You know me,' said Arne, folding the map up again. 'I like to be moving.'

She looked at him indulgently. 'You don't like to be followed, you mean.'

Arne looked a little startled, but that complex of his stood out like Gulliver in Lilliput.

I said, 'The police asked me if I saw the name of that speedboat.'

'Did you?' asked Arne.

I shook my head. 'No. Did you?'

He blinked through one of those maddening pauses into which the simplest question seemed to throw him, but in the end all he said was 'No, I didn't.'

'I don't think there was any name to see,' I said.

They both turned their faces to me in surprise.

'There must have been,' Kari said.

'Well . . . I've no impression of one . . . no name, no registration number, no port of origin. Perhaps you don't have things like that in Norway.'

'Yes we do,' Kari said, puzzled. 'Of course we do.'

Arne considered lengthily, then said, 'It was going too fast . . . and straight towards us. It must have had a name. We simply didn't see it.' He spoke with finality, as if the subject could hold no more interest. I nodded briefly and let it go, but I was certain that on that thundering black hull there had been nothing to see but black paint. How were they off for smugglers, I wondered, in this neck of the North Sea?

'It's a pity,' I said. 'Because you might have got compensation for your dinghy.'

'It was insured,' he said. 'Do not worry.'

Kari said, 'It's disgraceful he did not stop. He must have felt the bump . . . even a big heavy speedboat, like Arne says it was, could not crush a dinghy without feeling it.'

Hit and run, I thought flippantly. Happens on the roads, why not on the water?

'Arne was afraid you could not swim.'

'Up and down a pool or two,' I said. 'Never tried such long-distance stuff before.'

'You were lucky,' she said seriously.

'Arne too.' I looked at him thoughtfully, for I was younger by a good ten years and I had been near to exhaustion.

'Oh no. Arne's a great swimmer. A great sportsman, all round. Very fit and tough.' She smiled ironically, but the wifely pride was there. 'He used to win across-country ski races.'

There had been several sets of skis stacked casually in an alcove in the hall, along with squash rackets, fishing rods, mountain walking boots and half a dozen anoraks like the lost red one. For a man who liked to keep moving, he had all the gear.

'Have you eaten?' Kari asked suddenly. 'Since your swim, I mean? Did you think of eating?'

I shook my head.

'I suppose I was worried about Arne.'

She stood up, smiling. 'Arne had no appetite for his supper.' She looked at the clock. Ten minutes before ten. 'I will bring something for you both,' she said.

Arne fondly watched her backview disappearing towards the kitchen.

'What do you think of her, eh? Isn't she beautiful?'

Normally I disliked men who invited admiration for their wives as if they were properties like cars, but I would have forgiven Arne a great deal that evening.

'Yes,' I said, more truthfully than on many similar occasions; and Arne positively smirked.

'More wine,' he said, getting up restlessly and filling both our glasses.

'Your house, too, is beautiful,' I said.

He looked over his shoulder in surprise. 'That is Kari as well. She ... it is her job. Making rooms for people. Offices, hotels. Things like that.'

Their own sitting-room was a place of natural wood and white paint, with big parchment-shaded table lamps shedding a golden glow on string-coloured upholstery and bright scattered cushions. A mixture of the careful and haphazard, overlaid with the comfortable debris of a full life. Ultra-tidy rooms always oppressed me: the Kristiansens' was just right.

Arne brought back my filled glass and settled himself opposite, near the fire. His hair, no longer hidden, was now more grey than blond; longer than before, and definitely more distinguished.

'Tomorrow,' I said, 'I'd like to see the racecourse Chairman, if I could.'

He looked startled, as if he had forgotten the real purpose of my visit.

'Yes.' He blinked a bit. 'It is Saturday tomorrow. It is the Grand National meeting on Sunday. He will be at the racecourse on Sunday.'

Don't let a thieving jockey spoil the man's day off, Arne was meaning, so I shrugged and said Sunday would do.

'I'll maybe call on Gunnar Holth tomorrow, then.'

For some reason that didn't fill Arne with joy either, but I discovered, after a long pause on his part, that this was because he, Arne, wished to go fishing all day and was afraid I would want him with me, instead.

'Does Gunnar Holth speak English?' I asked.

'Oh yes.'

'I'll go on my own, then.'

He gave me the big smile and jumped up to help Kari, who was returning with a laden tray. She had brought coffee and open sandwiches of prawns and cheese and pineapple which we ate to the last crumb.

'You must come another evening,' Kari said. 'I will make you a proper dinner.'

Arne agreed with her warmly and opened some more wine.

'A great little cook,' he said proprietorially.

The great little cook shook back her heavy blonde hair and stretched her elegant neck. She had a jaw-line in the same class and three small brown moles like dusty freckles high on one cheekbone.

'Come any time,' she said.

I got back to the Grand by taxi at one in the morning, slept badly, and woke at seven feeling like Henry Cooper's punchbag.

Consultation with the bathroom looking-glass revealed a plate-sized bruise of speckled crimson over my left shoulder-blade, souvenir of colliding boats. In addition every muscle I possessed was groaning with the morning-after misery of too much strain. David Cleveland, it seemed, was no Matthew Webb.

Bath, clothes and breakfast didn't materially improve things, nor on the whole did a telephone call to Gunnar Holth.

'Come if you like,' he said. 'But I can tell you nothing. You will waste your time.'

As all investigators waste a lot of time listening to people with nothing to tell, I naturally went. He had a stable yard adjoining the racecourse and a belligerent manner.

'Questions, questions,' he said. 'There is nothing to tell.'

I paid off my taxi driver.

29

'You shouldn't have sent him away,' Gunnar Holth said. 'You will be going soon.'

I smiled. 'I can go back on a tram.'

He gave me a grudging stare. 'You don't look like a Jockey Club official.'

'I would appreciate it very much,' I said, 'if you would show me your horses. Arne Kristiansen says you have a good lot . . . that they've been winning big prizes this year.'

He loosened, of course. He gestured towards a large barn on the other side of an expanse of mud. We made our way there, him in his boots showing me I shouldn't have come in polished shoes. He was short, wiry, middle-aged and a typical stableman, more at home with his horses, I guessed, than with their owners; and he spoke English with an Irish accent.

The barn contained two rows of boxes facing into a wide central passage. Horses' heads showed over most of the half doors and three or four lads were carrying buckets of water and haynets.

'They've just come in from exercise,' Holth said. 'We train on the sand track on the racecourse.' He turned left and opened the door of the first box. 'This fellow runs tomorrow in the Grand National. Would you look at his shoulders now, isn't that a grand sort of horse?'

'Bob Sherman won a race on him the day he disappeared,' I said.

He gave me a sharp wordless glance and went in to pat a strong-looking character with more bone than breeding. He felt the legs, looked satisfied, and came back to join me.

'How do you know?' he said.

No harm in telling him. 'Arne Kristiansen gave me a list of Bob Sherman's last rides in Norway. He said that this horse of yours was likely to win the National, and if Sherman had had any sense he would have come back for that race and then stolen the National day takings, which would have been a better haul all round.'

Holth allowed himself a glint of amusement. 'That's true.'

We continued round the barn, admiring every inmate. There were about twenty altogether, three-quarters of them running on the flat, and although they seemed reasonable animals, none of them looked likely to take Epsom by storm. From their coats, though, and general air of well-being, Holth knew his trade.

One end of the barn was sectioned off to form living quarters for the lads, and Holth took me through to see them. Dormitory, washroom, and kitchen.

'Bob stayed here, most times,' he said.

I glanced slowly round the big main room with its half dozen two-tiered bunk beds, its bare board floor, its wooden table, wooden chairs. A big brown-tiled stove and double-glazed windows with curtains like blankets promised comfort against future snow, and a couple of mild girlie calendars brightened the walls, but it was a far cry from the Grand.

'Always?' I asked.

31

Holth shrugged. 'He said it was good enough here, and he saved the expense of a hotel. Nothing wrong there now, is there?'

'Nothing at all,' I agreed.

He paused. 'Sometimes he stayed with an owner.'

'Which owner?'

'Oh ... the man who owns Whitefire. Per Bjørn Sandvik.'

'How many times?'

Holth said with irritation, 'What does it matter? Twice, I suppose. Yes, twice. Not the last time. The two times before that.'

'How often did he come over altogether?'

'Six perhaps. Or seven ... or eight.'

'All this summer?'

'He didn't come last year, if that's what you mean.'

'But he liked it?'

'Of course he liked it. All British jockeys who are invited, they like it. Good pay, you see.'

'How good?'

'Well,' he said, 'They get their fare over here, and a bit towards expenses. And the fees for riding. And the appearance money.'

'The racecourse pays the appearance money?'

'Not exactly. Well ... the racecourse pays the money to the jockey but collects it from the owners who the jockey rode for.'

'So an owner, in the end, pays everything, the riding

fees, the winning percentage, a share of the fares, and a share of the appearance money?'

'That is right.'

'What happens if after all that the jockey rides a stinking race?'

Holth answered with deadly seriousness. 'The owner does not ask the jockey to come again.'

We stepped out of the barn back into the mud. It hadn't actually rained that day, but the threat still hung in the cold misty air.

'Come into my house,' suggested Holth. 'Have some coffee before you catch the tram.'

'Great,' I said.

His house was a small wooden bungalow with lace curtains and geraniums in pots on every window sill. The stove in the living-room was already lit, with an orange metal coffee pot heating on top. Gunnar dug into a cupboard for two earthenware mugs and some sugar in a packet.

'Would the owners have asked Bob Sherman to come again?' I said.

He poured the coffee, stirring with a white plastic spoon.

'Per Bjørn Sandvik would. And Sven Wangen; that's the owner of that dappled mare on the far side.' He pondered. 'Rolf Torp, now. Bob lost a race the day he went. Rolf Torp thought he should have walked it.'

'And should he?'

Holth shrugged. 'Horses aren't machines,' he said.

'Mind you, I don't train Rolf Torp's horses, so I don't really know, do I?'

'Who trains them?'

'Paul Sundby.'

'Will Rolf Torp be at the races tomorrow?'

'Naturally,' Holth said. 'He has the favourite in the National.'

'And you,' I said. 'Would you have asked him to ride for you again?'

'Certainly,' he said without hesitation. 'Bob is a good jockey. He listens to what you say about a horse. He rides with his head. He would not have been asked so many times if he had not been good.'

The door from the yard opened without warning and one of the lads poked his head in: he was about twenty-five, cheerful, and wore a woollen cap with a pompom.

'Gunny,' he said, 'will ye be takin' a look at that bleedin' mare now? She's a right cow, that one.'

The trainer said he would look in a minute, and the head withdrew.

'He's Irish,' I said surprised.

'Sure. I've three Irish lads and one from Yorkshire. And three from here. There's a lot of British lads in Norwegian racing.'

'Why is that?'

'They get a chance of riding in races here, see? More than they do at home.'

We drank the coffee which was well boiled and all the stronger for it.

I said, 'What did Bob do for transport? Did he ever hire a car?'

'No. I don't think so. When he stayed here he used to go with me over to the course.'

'Did he ever borrow your car? Or anyone's?'

'He didn't borrow mine. I don't think he ever drove, when he came.'

'Did you take him anywhere except to the races, the day he disappeared?'

'No.'

I knew from a file of statements which had been awaiting my arrival at the hotel that Bob Sherman had been expected to leave the racecourse by taxi to catch the late flight to Heathrow. He had not caught it. The taxi driver who had been engaged for the trip had simply shrugged when his passenger didn't show, and had taken some ordinary race-goers back to the city instead.

That left public transport, all the taxi drivers who didn't know Bob by sight, and other people's cars. Plus, I supposed, his own two feet. It would have been all too easy to leave the racecourse without being seen by anyone who knew him, particularly if, as the collected notes implied, the last race had been run after dark.

I put down my empty coffee mug and Gunnar Holth abruptly said, 'Could you be doing something about Bob's wife, now?'

'His wife? I might see her when I go back, if I find out anything useful.'

'No,' he shook his head. 'She is here.'

'Here?'

He nodded. 'In Oslo. And she won't go home.'

'Arne didn't mention it.'

Holth laughed. 'She follows him round like a dog. She asks questions, like you. Who saw Bob go, who did he go with, why does no one find him? She comes to every race meeting and asks and asks. Everyone is very tired of it.'

'Do you know where she's staying?'

He nodded vigorously and picked up a piece of paper lying near on a shelf.

'The Norsland Hotel. Second class, away from the centre. This is her telephone number. She gave it to me in case I could think of anything to help.' He shrugged. 'Everyone is sorry for her. But I wish she would go away.'

'Will you telephone her?' I said. 'Say I would like to ask her some questions about Bob. Suggest this afternoon.'

'I've forgotten your name,' he said without apology.

I smiled and gave him one of the firm's official cards. He looked at it and me in disbelief, but got the Norsland Hotel on the line. Mrs Emma Sherman was fetched.

Holth said into the receiver, 'A Mr David Cleveland . . . come from England to try to find your husband.' He read from the card, 'Chief Investigator, Investigation Office, Jockey Club, Portman Square, London. He wants to see you this afternoon.'

He listened to the reaction, then looked at me and said 'Where?'

'At her hotel. Three o'clock.'

He relayed the news.

'She'll be waiting for you,' he said, putting the receiver down.

'Good.'

'Tell her to go home,' he said.

CHAPTER THREE

She was waiting in the small lobby of the Norsland, sitting on the edge of a chair and anxiously scanning the face of every passing male. I watched her for a while through the glass doors to the street, before going in. She looked small and pale and very very jumpy. Twice she half stood up, and twice, as the man she had focused on walked past without a sign, subsided more slowly back to her seat.

I pushed through the doors into air barely warmer than the street, which in a totally centrally heated city spoke poorly of the management. Emma Sherman looked at me briefly and switched her gaze back to the door. I was not what she expected: the next man through, sixtyish and military-looking, had her again halfway to her feet.

He passed her without a glance on his way to collect his room key at the desk. She sat slowly down, looking increasingly nervous.

I walked over to her.

'Mrs Sherman?'

'Oh.' She stood up slowly. 'Is there a message from Mr Cleveland?'

'I am,' I said, 'David Cleveland.'

'But,' she said, and stopped. The surprise lingered on her face among the strain and tiredness, but she seemed past feeling anything very clearly. At close quarters the nervousness resolved itself into a state not far from total breakdown.

Her skin looked almost transparent from fatigue, dark shadows round her eyes emphasizing the pebbly dullness of the eyes themselves. She was about twenty-two and should have been pretty: she had the bones and the hair for it, but they hadn't a chance. She was also, it seemed to me, pregnant.

'Where can we talk?' I asked.

She looked vaguely round the lobby which contained three chairs, no privacy, and a rubber plant.

'Your room?' I suggested.

'Oh no,' she said at once, and then more slowly, in explanation, 'It is small . . . not comfortable . . . nowhere to sit.'

'Come along, then,' I said. 'We'll find a coffee shop.'

She came with me out into the street and we walked in the general direction of the Grand.

'Will you find him?' she said. 'Please find him.'

'I'll do my best.'

'He never stole that money,' she said. 'He didn't.'

I glanced at her. She was trembling perceptibly and looking paler than ever. I stopped walking and put my hand under her elbow. She looked at me with glazing eyes, tried to say something else, and fell forward against me in a thorough-going swoon.

Even seven stone nothing of fainting girl is hard to support without letting her lie on a cold city pavement. Two passing strangers proved to have friendly faces but no English, and the third, who had the tongue, muttered something about the disgrace of being drunk at four in the afternoon and scurried away. I held her up against me with my arms under hers and asked the next woman along to call a taxi.

She too looked disapproving and backed away, but a boy of about sixteen gave her a withering glance and came to the rescue.

'Is she ill?' he asked. His English was punctilious stuff, learned in school.

'She is. Can you get a taxi?'

'*Ja*. I will return. You will . . .' he thought, then found the word . . . 'Wait?'

'I will wait,' I agreed.

He nodded seriously and darted away round the nearest corner, a slim figure in the ubiquitous uniform of the young, blue jeans and a padded jacket. He came back, as good as his word, with a taxi, and helped me get the girl into it.

'Thank you very much,' I said.

He beamed. 'I learn English,' he said.

'You speak it very well.'

He waved as the taxi drew away: a highly satisfactory encounter to both parties.

She began to wake up during the short journey, which seemed to reassure the taxi driver. He spoke no English except one word which he repeated at least ten times with emphasis, and which was 'doctor'.

'*Ja*,' I agreed. '*Ja*. At the Grand Hotel.'

He shrugged, but drove us there. He also helped me support her through the front doors and accepted his fare after she was safely sitting down.

'Doctor,' he said as he left, and I said, '*Ja*.'

'No,' said Bob Sherman's wife, in little more than a whisper. 'What . . . happened?'

'You fainted,' I said briefly. 'And doctor or no doctor, you need to lie down. So up you come . . .' I more or less lifted her to her feet, walked her to the lift, and took her up the one floor to my room. She flopped full length on the bed without question and lay there with her eyes closed.

'Do you mind if I feel your pulse?' I asked.

She gave no answer either way, so I put my fingers on her wrist and found the slow heartbeat. Her arm was slippery with sweat though noticeably cold, and all in all she looked disturbingly frail.

'Are you hungry?' I said.

She rolled her head on the pillow in a slow negative, but I guessed that what was really wrong with her, besides strain, was simple starvation. She had been too

41

worried to take care of herself, and besides, eating came expensive in Norway.

A consultation on the telephone with the hotel restaurant produced a promise of hot meat soup and some bread and cheese.

'And brandy,' I said.

'No brandy, sir, on Saturday. Or on Sunday. It is the rule.'

I had been warned, but had forgotten. Extraordinary to find a country with madder licensing laws than Britain's. There was a small refrigerator in my room, however, which stocked, among the orangeade and mineral waters, a quarter bottle of champagne. It had always seemed to me that bottling in quarters simply spoiled good fizz, but there's an occasion for everything. Emma said she couldn't, she shouldn't; but she did, and within five minutes was looking like a long-picked flower caught just in time.

'I'm sorry,' she said, leaning on one elbow on my bed and sipping the golden bubbles from my tooth mug.

'You're welcome.'

'You must think me a fool.'

'No.'

'It's just . . . No one seems to care any more. Where he's gone. They just say they can't find him. They aren't even looking.'

'They've looked,' I began, but she wasn't ready to listen.

'Then Gunnar Holth said . . . the Jockey Club had sent their chief investigator . . . so I've been hoping so hard all day that at last someone would find him, and then . . . and then . . . you . . .'

'I'm not the father-figure you were hoping for,' I said.

She shook her head. 'I didn't think you'd be so young.'

'Which do you want most,' I asked. 'A father-figure, or someone to find Bob?' But it was too soon to expect her to see that the two things didn't necessarily go together. She needed the comfort as much as the search.

'He didn't steal that money,' she said.

'How do you know?'

'He just wouldn't.' She spoke with conviction, but I wondered if the person she most wanted to convince was herself.

A waiter knocked on the door, bringing a tray, and Emma felt well enough to sit at the table and eat. She started slowly, still in a weak state, but by the end it was clear she was fiercely hungry.

As she finished the last of the bread I said, 'In about three hours we'll have dinner.'

'Oh no.'

'Oh yes. Why not? Then you'll have plenty of time to tell me about Bob. Hours and hours. No need to hurry.'

She looked at me with the first signs of connected

thought and almost immediately glanced round the room. The awareness that she was in my bedroom flashed out like neon in the North Pole. I smiled. 'Would you prefer the local nick? One each side of a table in an interview room?'

'Oh! I . . . suppose not.' She shuddered slightly. 'I've had quite a lot of that, you see. In a way. Everyone's been quite kind, really, but they think Bob stole that money and they treat me as if my husband was a crook. It's . . . it's pretty dreadful.'

'I understand that,' I said.

'Do you?'

The meal had done nothing for her pallor. The eyes still looked as hollowed and black-smudged, and the strain still vibrated in her manner. It was going to take more than champagne and soup to undo the knots.

'Why don't you sleep for a while?' I suggested. 'You look very tired. You'll be quite all right here, and I've some reports which I ought to write. I'd be glad to get them out of the way.'

'I can't sleep,' she said automatically, but when I determinedly took papers out of my briefcase, spread them on the table and switched on a bright lamp to see them by, she stood up and hovered a bit and finally lay down again on the bed. After five minutes I walked over to look and she was soundly asleep with sunken cheeks and pale blue veins in her eyelids.

She wore a camel coloured coat, which she had relaxed as far as unbuttoning, and a brown and white checked dress underneath. With the coat falling open, the bulge in her stomach showed unmistakably. Five months, I thought, give or take a week or two.

I pushed the papers together again and returned them to the briefcase. They were the various statements and accounts relating to her husband's disappearance, and I had no report to write on them. I sat instead in one of the Grand's comfortable armchairs and thought about why men vanished.

In the main they either ran *to* something or *from* something: occasionally a combination of both. To a woman; from a woman. To the sunshine; from the police. To political preference; from political oppression. To anonymity; from blackmail.

Sometimes they took someone else's money with them to finance the future. Bob Sherman's sixteen thousand kroner didn't seem, at first sight, to be worth what he'd exchanged for it. He earned five times as much every year.

So what had he gone *to*?

Or what had he gone *from*?

And how was I to find him by Monday afternoon?

She slept soundly for more than two hours with periods of peaceful dreaming, but after that went into a session which was distressing her. She moved restlessly and sweat appeared on her forehead, so I touched her hand and called her out of it.

'Emma. Wake up. Wake up, now, Emma.'

She opened her eyes fast and wide with the night-mare pictures still in them. Her body began to tremble.

'Oh,' she said. 'Oh God . . .'

'It's all right. You were dreaming. It was only a dream.'

Her mind finished the transition to consciousness, but she was neither reassured nor comforted.

'I dreamed he was in jail . . . there were bars . . . and he was trying to get out . . . frantically . . . and I asked him why he wanted to get out, and he said they were going to execute him in the morning . . . and then I was talking to someone in charge and I said what had he done, why were they going to execute him, and this man said . . . he'd stolen the racecourse . . . and the law said that if people stole racecourses they had to be executed . . .'

She rubbed a hand over her face.

'It's so silly,' she said. 'But it seemed so real.'

'Horrid,' I said.

She said with desolation, 'But where is he? Why doesn't he write to me? How can he be so cruel?'

'Perhaps there's a letter waiting at home.'

'No. I telephone . . . every day.'

I said, 'Are you . . . well . . . are you happy together?'

'Yes,' she said firmly, but after five silent seconds the truer version came limping out. 'Sometimes we have rows. We had one the day he came here. All morning. And it was over such a little thing . . . just that he'd

46

spent a night away when he didn't have to . . . I'd not been feeling well and I told him he was selfish and thoughtless . . . and he lost his temper and said I was too damn demanding . . . and I said I wouldn't go with him to Kempton then, and he went silent and sulky because he was going to ride the favourite in the big race and he always likes to have me there after something like that, it helps him unwind.' She stared into a past moment she would have given the world to change. 'So he went on his own. And from there to Heathrow for the six-thirty to Oslo, same as usual. Only usually I went with him, to see him off and take the car home.'

'And meet him again Sunday night?'

'Yes. On Sunday night when he didn't come back at the right time I was worried sick that he'd had a fall in Norway and hurt himself and I telephoned to Gunnar Holth . . . but he said Bob hadn't fallen, he'd ridden a winner and got round in the other two races, and as far as he knew he'd caught the plane as planned. So I rang the airport again . . . I'd rung them before, and they said the plane had landed on time . . . and I begged them to check and they said there was no Sherman on the passenger list . . .' She stopped and I waited, and she went on in a fresh onslaught of misery. 'Surely he knew I didn't really mean it? I love him . . . Surely he wouldn't just leave me, without saying a word?'

It appeared, however, that he had.

'How long have you been married?'

'Nearly two years.'

'Children?'

She glanced down at the brown and white checked mound and gestured towards it with a flutter of slender fingers. 'This is our first.'

'Finances?'

'Oh . . . all right, really.'

'How really?'

'He had a good season last year. We saved a bit then. Of course he does like good suits and a nice car . . . All jockeys do, don't they?'

I nodded. I knew also more about her husband's earnings than she seemed to, as I had access to the office which collected and distributed jockeys' fees; but it wasn't so much the reasonable income that was significant as the extent to which they lived within it.

'He does get keen on schemes for making money quickly, but we've never lost much. I usually talk him out of it. I'm not a gambler at all, you see.'

I let a pause go by. Then, 'Politics?'

'How do you mean?'

'Is he interested in communism?'

She stared. 'Good heavens, no.'

'Militant in any way?'

She almost laughed. 'Bob doesn't give a damn for politics or politicians. He says they're all the same, hot air and hypocrisy. Why do you ask such an extra-ordinary question?'

I shrugged. 'Norway has a common frontier with Russia.'

Her surprise was genuine on two counts: she didn't know her geography and she did know her husband. He was not the type to exchange good suits and a nice car and an exciting job for a dim existence in a totalitarian state.

'Did he mention any friends he had made here?'

'I've seen nearly everyone I can remember him talking about. I've asked them over and over ... Gunnar Holth, and his lads, and Mr Kristiansen, and the owners. The only one I haven't met is one of the owner's sons, a boy called Mikkel. Bob mentioned him once or twice ... he's away at school now, or something.'

'Was Bob in any trouble before this?'

She looked bewildered. 'What sort?'

'Bookmakers?'

She turned her head away and I gave her time to decide on her answer. Jockeys were not allowed to bet, and I worked for the Jockey Club.

'No,' she said indistinctly.

'You might as well tell me,' I said. 'I can find out. But you would be quicker.'

She looked back at me, perturbed. 'He only bets on himself, usually,' she said defensively. 'It's legal in a lot of countries.'

'I'm only interested in his betting if it's got anything to do with his disappearance. Was anyone threatening him for payment?'

'Oh.' She sounded forlorn, as if the one thing she

did not want to be given was a good reason for Bob to steal a comparatively small sum and ruin his life for it.

'He never said . . . I'm sure he would have told . . .' She gulped. 'The police asked me if he was being black-mailed. I said no, of course not . . . but if it was to keep me from knowing something . . . how can I be sure? Oh, I do wish, I do wish he'd write to me . . .'

Tears came in a rush and spilled over. She didn't apologize, didn't brush them away, and in a few seconds they had stopped. She had wept a good deal, I guessed, during the past three weeks.

'You've done all you can here,' I said. 'Better come back with me on Monday afternoon.'

She was surprised and disappointed. 'You're going back so soon? But you won't have found him.'

'Probably not. But I've a meeting in London on Tuesday that I can't miss. If it looks like being useful I'll come back here afterwards, but for you, it's time now to go home.'

She didn't answer at once, but finally, in a tired, quiet, defeated voice, said 'All right.'

CHAPTER FOUR

Arne was having difficulty with his complex, constantly looking over his shoulder to the extent of making forward locomotion hazardous. Why he should find any threat in the cheerful frost-bitten looking crowd which had turned up at Øvrevoll for the Norsk Grand National was something between him and his psychiatrist, but as usual his friends were suffering from his affliction.

He had refused, for instance, to drink a glass of wine in a comfortable available room with a king-sized log fire. Instead we were marching back and forth outside, him, me, and Per Bjørn Sandvik, wearing out shoe leather and turning blue at the ears, for fear of bugging machines. I couldn't see how overhearing our present conversation could possibly benefit anyone, but then I wasn't Arne. And at least this time, I thought philosophically, we would not be mown down by a speedboat.

As before, he was ready for the outdoor life: a blue padded hood joined all in one to his anorak. Per Bjørn

Sandvik had a trilby. I had my head. Maybe one day I would learn.

Sandvik, one of the Stewards, was telling me again at first hand what I'd already read in the statements: how Bob Sherman had had access to the money.

'It's collected into the officials' room, you see, where it is checked and recorded. And the officials' room is in the same building as the jockeys' changing-room. Right? And that Sunday, Bob Sherman went to the officials' room to ask some question or other, and the money was stacked there, just inside the door. Arne saw him there himself. He must have planned at once to take it.'

'What was the money contained in?' I asked.

'Canvas bags. Heavy double canvas.'

'What colour?'

He raised his eyebrows. 'Brown.'

'Just dumped on the floor?'

He grinned. 'There is less crime in Norway.'

'So I've heard,' I said. 'How many bags?'

'Five.'

'Heavy?'

He shrugged. 'Like money.'

'How were they fastened?'

'With leather straps and padlocks.'

Arne cannoned into a blonde who definitely had the right of way. She said something which I judged from his expression to be unladylike, but it still didn't persuade him to look where he was going. Some enemy lay behind, listening: he was sure of it.

Sandvik gave him an indulgent smile. He was a tall pleasant unhurried man of about fifty, upon whom authority sat as lightly as fluff. Arne had told me he was 'someone at the top in oil', but he had none of the usual aura of big business: almost the reverse, as if he derived pleasure from leaving an impression of no power, no aggression. If so, he would be a board-room opponent as wicked as a mantrap among the daisies. I looked at him speculatively. He met my eyes. Nothing in his that shouldn't be.

'What was it intended to do with the bags, if Sherman hadn't nicked them?' I asked.

'Lock them in the safe in the officials' room until Monday morning, when they would go to the bank.'

'Guarded,' Arne said, eyes front for once, 'By a night watchman.'

But by the time the night watchman had clocked in, the booty had vanished.

'How did the officials all happen to desert the room at once, leaving the money so handy?' I asked.

Sandvik spread his thickly gloved hands. 'We have discussed this endlessly. It was accidental. The room can only have been empty for five minutes or less. There was no special reason for them all being out at one time. It just happened.'

He had a high-register voice with beautifully distinct enunciation, but his almost-perfect English sounded quite different from the home-grown variety. I worked it out after a while: it was his 'l's. The British pronounced 'l' with their tongue lolling back in the throat, the Norwegians said theirs with the tongue tight up behind the teeth. Retaining the Norwegian 'l' gave Sandvik's accent a light, dry, clear-vowelled quality which made everything he said sound logical and lucid.

'No one realized, that evening, that the money had been stolen. Each of the officials took it for granted that another had put the bags in the safe as they were no longer to be seen. It was the next day, when the safe was opened for the money to be banked, that it was found to be missing. And then, of course, we heard from Gunnar Holth that Sherman had disappeared as well.'

I thought. 'Didn't Gunnar Holth tell me that Bob Sherman stayed with you once or twice?'

'Yes, that's right.' Sandvik briefly pursed his well-shaped mouth. 'Twice. But not the time he stole the money, I'm glad to say.'

'You liked him, though?'

'Oh yes, well enough, I suppose. I asked him out of politeness. He had ridden several winners for me, and I know what Gunnar's bunk room is like . . .' He grinned slightly. 'Anyway, he came. But we had little of common interest except horses, and I think he really preferred Gunnar's after all.'

'Would you have expected him to steal?'

'It never crossed my mind. I mean, it doesn't does it? But I didn't know him well.'

Arne could not bear the close quarters of the crowd on the stands, so we watched the first race, a hurdle, from rising ground just past the winning post. The race-course, forming the floor of a small valley, was overlooked on all sides by hillsides of spruce and birch, young trees growing skywards like the Perpendicular period come to life. The slim, dark evergreens stood in endless broken vertical stripes with the yellow-drying leaves and silver trunks of the birch, and the whole backdrop, that afternoon, was hung along the skyline with fuzzy drifts of misty low cloud.

The light was cold grey, the air cold damp. The spirits of the crowd, sunny Mediterranean. An English jockey won the race on the favourite and the crowd shouted approval.

It was time, Sandvik said, to go and see the Chairman, who had not been able to manage us sooner on account of lunching a visiting ambassador. We went into the Secretariat building adjoining the grandstand, up some sporting print-lined stairs, and into a large room containing not only the Chairman but five or six supporting Stewards. Per Bjørn Sandvik walked in first, then me, then Arne pushing his hood back, and the Chairman went on looking inquiringly at the door, still waiting for me, so to speak, to appear. I sometimes wondered if it would help if I were fat, bald and bespec-tacled: if premature ageing might produce more confidence and belief than the thin-six-feet-with-brown-hair job did. I'd done a fair amount of living, one way or another, but it perversely refused to show.

'This is David Cleveland,' Sandvik said, and several pairs of eyes mirrored the same disappointment.

'How do you do,' I murmured gently to the Chairman, and held out my hand.

'Er . . .' He cleared his throat and recovered manfully. 'So glad you have come.'

I made a few encouraging remarks about how pleasant I found it in Norway and wondered if any of them knew that Napoleon was promoted General at twenty-four.

The Chairman, Lars Baltzersen, was much like his letters to my office, brief, polite and effective. It took him approximately ten seconds to decide I wouldn't have been given my job if I couldn't do it, and I saw no need to tell him that my boss had died suddenly, eighteen months earlier, and left the manager-elect in charge a lot sooner than anyone intended.

'You sound older on the telephone,' he said simply, and I said I'd been told so before, and that was that.

'Go anywhere you like on the racecourse,' he said. 'Ask anything . . . Arne can interpret for those who do not speak English.'

'Thank you.'

'Do you need anything else?'

Second sight, I thought; but I said, 'Perhaps, if possible, to see you again before I go at the end of the afternoon.'

'Of course. Of course. We all want to hear of your progress. We'll all gather here after the last race.'

Heads nodded dubiously, and I fully expected to justify their lowly expectations. Either briefed or bored or merely busy, they drifted away through the door, leaving only Arne and the Chairman behind.

'Some beer?' suggested Baltzersen.

Arne said yes and I said no. Despite the glow from a huge stove it was a cold day for hops.

'How far is it to the Swedish border?' I asked.

'By road, about eighty kilometres,' Baltzersen said.

'Any formalities there?'

He shook his head. 'Not for Scandinavians in their own cars. There are few inspections or customs. But none of the frontier posts remember an Englishman crossing on that evening.'

'I know. Not even as a passenger in a Norwegian car. Would he have been spotted if he'd gone across crouching under a rug on the floor behind the driver's seat?'

They pondered. 'Very probably not,' Baltzersen said, and Arne agreed.

'Can you think of anyone who might have taken him? Anyone he was close to here, either in business or friendship?'

'I do not know him well enough,' the Chairman said

regretfully, and Arne blinked a little and said Gunnar Holth, or maybe some of the lads who worked for him.

'Holth says he drove him only round to the races,' I said: but he would have had plenty of time to drive into Sweden and back before Emma Sherman had rung him up.

'Gunnar tells lies whenever it suits him,' Arne said.

Lars Baltzersen sighed. 'I'm afraid that is true.'

He had grey hair, neatly brushed, with a tidy face and unimaginative clothes. I was beginning to get the feel of Norwegian behaviour patterns, and he came into the very large category of sober, slightly serious people who were kind, efficient, and under little stress. Get-up-and-go was conspicuously absent, yet the job would clearly be done. The rat race taken at a walk. Very civilized.

There were other types, of course.

'The people I hate here,' Emma Sherman had said, 'are the drunks.'

I'd taken her to dinner in the hotel the evening before, and had listened for several hours, in the end, to details of her life with Bob, her anxieties, and her experiences in Norway.

'When I first came,' she said, 'I used to have dinner in the dining-room, and all these men used to come and ask if they could share my table. They were quite polite, but very very persistent. They wouldn't go away. The head waiter used to get rid of them for me. He told me they were drunk. They didn't really look it. They weren't rolling or anything.'

I laughed. 'Considering the price of alcohol here, you wouldn't think they could.'

'No,' she said. 'Anyway I stopped having dinner. I needed to make my money go as far as possible and I hated eating on my own.'

Arne said, 'Where do you want to go first?'

Arne came into a third group: the kinks. You find them everywhere.

'Weighing room, I should think.'

They both nodded in agreement. Arne pulled his hood back over his head and we went down into the raw outdoors. The crowd had swelled to what Arne described as 'very big', but there was still plenty of room. One of the greatest advantages of life in Norway, I guessed, was the small population. I had not so far in its leisurely capital seen a queue or a crush or anyone fighting to get anywhere first. As there always seemed to be room for all, why bother?

The officials checking tickets at the gates between different enclosures were all keen young men of about twenty, most of them blond also, all with blue armbands on their anoraks. They knew Arne, of course, but they checked my pass even though I was with him, the serious faces hardly lightening as they nodded me through. Lars Baltzersen had given me a five-by-three-inch card stamped all over with *adgang paddock, adgang stallomradet, adgang indre bane* and one or two other *adgangs*, and it looked as if I wouldn't get far if I lost it.

The weighing room, black wood walls, white paint, red tiled roof, lay on the far side of the parade ring, where the jockeys were already out for the second race. Everything looked neat, organized and pleasing, and despite an eye trained to spot trouble at five hundred paces in a thick fog, I couldn't see any. Even in racing, good nature prevailed. Several of the lads leading the horses round wore sweaters in the owner's colours, matching the jockey's; a good and useful bit of display I'd seen nowhere else. I commented on it to Arne.

'*Ja*,' he said. 'Many of the private stables do that now. It helps the crowd to know their colours.'

Between the paddock and the U-shaped weighing room buildings, and up into the U itself, there was a grassy area planted thickly with ornamental bushes. Everyone walking between weighing room and paddock had to detour either to one side or the other, along comparatively narrow paths: it made a change from the rolling acres of concrete at home but took up a lot of apology time.

Once inside the weighing room Arne forgot about bugging machines and introduced me rapidly to a stream of people, like the secretary, clerk of the course, clerk of the scales, without once looking over his shoulder. I shook hands and chatted a bit, but although they all knew I was looking for Bob Sherman, I couldn't see anyone feeling twitchy about my presence.

'Come this way, David,' Arne said, and took me down a side passage with an open door at the end leading out to the racecourse. A step or two before this door, Arne turned smartly right, and we found ourselves in the officials' room from which the money had been stolen. It was just an ordinary businesslike room, wooden walls, wooden floor, wooden tables acting as desks, wooden chairs. (With all those forests, what else?) There were pleasant, red checked curtains, first-class central heating, and in one corner, a no-nonsense safe.

Apart from us, there was no one there.

'That's all there is,' Arne said. 'The money bags were left on the floor . . .' he pointed, 'and the lists of totals from each collecting point were put on that desk, same as usual. We still have the lists.'

It had struck me several times that Arne felt no responsibility for the loss of the money, nor did anyone seem in the remotest way to blame him, but by even the most elementary requirements of a security officer, he'd earned rock bottom marks.

'Do you still have the same system,' I asked, 'with the bags?'

Arne gave me a look somewhere between amusement and hurt.

'No. Since that day, the bags are put immediately into the safe.'

'Who has the keys?'

'I have some, and the secretary, and the clerk of the course.'

'And each of you three thought one of the other two had stowed the money away safely?'

'That is right.'

We left the room and stepped out into the open air. Several jockeys, changed into colours for later races but with warm coats on at the moment, came along the passage and out through the same door, and they, Arne, and I climbed an outside staircase on to a small open stand attached to the side of the weighing room buildings. From there, a furlong or more from the winning post, we watched the second race.

Arne had begun looking apprehensively around again, though there were barely twenty on the stand. I found I had begun doing it myself: it was catching. It netted, however, the sight of an English jockey who knew me, and as everyone after the finish poured towards the stairs I arranged to fetch up beside him. Arne went on down the steps, but the jockey stopped when I touched his arm, and was easy to keep back.

'Hallo,' he said in surprise. 'Fancy seeing you here.'

'Came about Bob Sherman,' I explained.

I'd found that if I said straight out what I wanted to know, I got better results. No one wasted time wondering what I suspected them of, and if they weren't feeling on the defensive they talked more.

'Oh. I see. Found the poor bugger, then?'

'Not yet,' I said.

'Let him go, why don't you?'

Rinty Ranger knew Bob Sherman as well as anyone who'd been thrown together in the same small professional group for five years, but they were not especially close friends. I took this remark to be a general statement of sympathy for the fox and asked if he didn't think stealing the money had been a bloody silly thing to do.

'Too right,' he said. 'I'll bet he wished he hadn't done it, five minutes after. But that's Bob all over, smack into things without thinking.'

'Makes him a good jockey,' I said, remembering how he flung his heart over fences regardless.

Rinty grinned, his thin, sharp face looking cold above his sheepskin coat. 'Yeah. Done him no good this time, though.'

'What else has he done that was impulsive?'

'I don't know... Always full of get-rich-quick schemes like buying land in the Bahamas or backing crazy inventors, and I even heard him on about pyramid selling once, only we told him not to be such a bloody fool. I mean, it's hard enough to earn the stuff, you don't actually want to throw it down the drain.'

'Were you surprised when he stole the money?' I asked.

'Well of course I was, for Chrissakes. And even more by him doing a bunk. I mean, why didn't he just stash away the loot and carry on with business as usual?'

'Takes nerve,' I said, but of course that was just

what Bob Sherman had. 'Also the money was in heavy canvas bags which would take a lot of getting into. He wouldn't have had time to do that and catch his flight home.'

Rinty thought a bit but came up with nothing useful.

'Stupid bugger,' he said. 'Nice wife, kid coming, good job. You'd think he'd have more sense.' And I'd got as far as that myself.

'Anyway, he's done me a favour,' Rinty said. 'I've got his ride in this here Grand National.' He opened his sheepskin a fraction to show me the colours underneath. 'The owner, fellow called Torp, isn't best pleased with Bob on any account. Says he should've won at a canter that last day he was here. Says he threw it away, left it too late, came through too soon, should've taken the outside, didn't put him right at the water, you name it, Bob did it wrong.'

'He got another English jockey, though.'

'Oh sure. D'you know how many home-bred jump jocks there are here? About fifteen, that's all, and some of those are English or Irish. Lads they are mostly. You don't get many self-employed chaps, like us. There isn't enough racing here for that. You get them going to Sweden on Saturdays, they race there on Saturdays. Here Thursdays and Sundays. That's the lot. Mind you, they don't keep the jumpers to look at. They all run once a week at least, and as there are only four or five jump races a week – all the rest are flat – it makes life interesting.'

'Were you and Bob often over here together?'

'This year, three or four trips, I suppose. But I came last year too, which he didn't.'

'How long is a trip?'

He looked surprised. 'Only a day usually. We race in England Saturday afternoon, catch the six-thirty, race here Sunday, catch the late plane back if we can, otherwise the eight-fifteen Monday morning. Sometimes we fly here Sunday morning, but it's cutting it a bit fine. No margin for hold-ups.'

'Do you get to know people here well, in that time?'

'I suppose it sort of accumulates. Why?'

'Has Bob Sherman made any friendships here, would you say?'

'Good God. Well, no, not that I know of, but then likely as not I wouldn't know if he did. He knows a lot of trainers and owners, of course. Do you mean girls?'

'Not particularly. Were there any?'

'Shouldn't think so. He likes his missus.'

'Do you mind thinking fairly hard about it?'

He looked surprised. 'If you like.'

I nodded. He lengthened the focus of his gaze in a most satisfactory manner and really concentrated. I waited without pressure, watching the crowd. Young, it was, by British standards: at least half under thirty, half blond, all the youth dressed in anoraks of blue, red, orange and yellow in the sort of colourful haphazard uniformity that stage designers plan for the chorus.

65

Rinty Ranger stirred and brought his vision back to the present.

'I don't know ... He stayed with Mr Sandvik a couple of times, and said he got on better with his son than the old man ... I met him once, the son, that is, with Bob when they were chatting at the races ... but I wouldn't say they were great friends or anything ...'

'How old is he, roughly?'

'The son? Sixteen, seventeen. Eighteen maybe.'

'Anyone else?'

'Well ... One of the lads at Gunnar Holth's. An Irish lad, Paddy O'Flaherty. Bob knows him well, because Paddy used to work for old Tasker Mason, where Bob was apprenticed. They were lads together, one time, you might say. Bob likes staying at Gunnar Holth's on account of Paddy, I think.'

'Do you know if Paddy has a car?'

'Haven't a clue. Why don't you ask him? He's bound to be here.'

'Were you here,' I asked, 'the day Bob disappeared?'

''Fraid not.'

'Well ... Mm ... anything you can think of which is not what you'd've expected?'

'What bloody questions! Let's see ... can't think of anything ... except that he left his saddle here.'

'Bob?'

'Yes. It's in the changing-room. And his helmet. He must have known, the silly sod, that he'd never be able to race anywhere in the world again, otherwise he'd never have left them.'

I moved towards the stairs. Rinty hadn't told me a great deal, but if there had been much to tell the police of one country or the other would have found Bob long ago. He followed me down, and I wished him good luck in the National.

'Thanks,' he said. 'Can't say I wish you the same, though. Let the poor bastard alone.'

At the bottom of the steps, Arne was talking to Per Bjørn Sandvik. They turned to include me with smiles, and I asked the offensive question with as much tact as possible.

'Your son Mikkel, Mr Sandvik. Do you think he could've driven Bob Sherman away from the races? Without knowing, of course, that he had the money with him?'

Per Bjørn reacted less violently than many a father would to the implication that his son, having entertained a thief even if unawares, had nonetheless kept quiet about it. Scarcely a ripple went through him.

He said smoothly, 'Mikkel cannot drive yet. He is still at school . . . his seventeenth birthday was six weeks ago.'

'That's good,' I said in apology; and I thought, that's that.

Per Bjørn said 'Excuse me,' without noticeable resentment and walked away. Arne, blinking furiously, asked where I wanted to go next. To see Paddy

O'Flaherty, I said, so we went in search and found him in the stables getting Gunnar Holth's runner ready for the Grand National. He turned out to be the lad in the woolly cap with uncomplimentary opinions of a mare, and described himself as Gunny's head lad, so I am.

'What did I do after the races?' he repeated. 'Same as I always do. Took the runners home, squared 'em up and saw to their scoff.'

'And after that?'

'After that, same as always, down to the local hop. There's a good little bird there, d'you see?'

'Do you have a car?' I asked.

'Well, sure I have now, but the tyres are as thin as a stockpot on Thursday and I wouldn't be after driving on them any more at all. And there's the winter coming on, so there's my car up on bricks, d'you see?'

'When did you put it on bricks?'

'The police stopped me about those tyres, now . . . well, there's the canvas peeping through one or two, if you look close. Sure it's all of six weeks ago now.'

After that we drifted around while I took in a general view of what went on, and then walked across the track to watch a race from the tower. This looked slightly like a small airfield control tower, two storeys high with a glass-walled room at the top. In this eyrie during races sat two keen-eyed men with fierce race-glasses clamped to their eyes: they were non-automatic patrol cameras, and never missed a trick.

Arne introduced me. Feel free, they said, smiling, to

come up into the tower at any time. I thanked them and stayed to watch the next race from there, looking straight down the narrow elongated oval of the track. Sixteen hundred metres for staying two-year-olds: they started almost level with the tower, scurried a long way away, rounded the fairly sharp bottom bend, and streamed up the long straight to finish at the winning post just below where we stood. There was a photo-finish. The all-seeing eyes unstuck themselves from their raceglasses, nodded happily, and said they would be back for the next race.

Before following them down the stairs I asked Arne which way the Grand National went, as there seemed to be fences pointing in every direction.

'Round in a figure of eight,' he said, sweeping a vague arm. 'Three times round. You will see when they go.' He seemed to want to be elsewhere fairly promptly, but when we had hurried back over to the paddock it appeared merely that he was hungry and had calculated enough eating time before the Norsk St Leger. He magicked some huge open sandwiches on about a foot of french loaf, starting at one end with prawns and proceeding through herring, cheese, pâté and egg to beef at the far end, adorned throughout by pickled cucumber, mayonnaise and scattered unidentified crispy bits. Arne stayed the course, but I blew up in the straight.

We drank wine: a bottle. We would come back later, Arne said, and finish it. We were in the big warm room he had shunned earlier, but the listeners weren't troubling him at that moment.

'If you're going home tomorrow, David,' he said, 'come to supper with us tonight.'

I hesitated. 'There's Emma Sherman,' I said.

'That girl,' he exclaimed. He peered around, though there were barely six others in the room. 'Where is she? She's usually on my heels.'

'I talked to her yesterday. Persuaded her not to come today and to go back to England tomorrow.'

'Great. Great, my friend.' He rubbed his hands together. 'She'll be all right, then. You come to supper with us. I will telephone to Kari.'

I thought of Kari's hair and Kari's shape. Everything stacked as I liked it best. I imagined her in bed. Very likely I should have allowed no such thoughts but you might as well forbid fish to swim. A pity she was Arne's, I thought. To stay away would make it easier on oneself.

'Come,' Arne said.

Weak, that's what I am. I said, 'I'd love to.'

He bustled off instantly to do the telephoning and soon returned beaming.

'She is very pleased. She says we will give you cloud-berries, she bought some yesterday.'

We went out to the raw afternoon and watched the big flat race together, but then Arne was whisked off on official business and for a while I wandered around alone. Though its organization and upkeep were clearly first class, it was not on British terms a big racecourse.

Plenty of room, but few buildings. Everyone could see: no one was pushed, rushed or crushed. Space was the ultimate luxury, I thought, as I strolled past a small oblong ornamental pond with a uniformed military band playing full blast beside it. Several children sat in bright little heaps around the players' feet and one or two were peering interestedly into the quivering business ends of trombones.

Øvrevoll, someone had told me, was a fairly new racecourse, the only one in Norway to hold ordinary flat and jump races. Most racing, as in Germany, was trotting, with sulkies.

For the Grand National itself I went back up the tower, which I found stood in the smaller top part of the figure of eight, with the larger part lying in the main part of the course, inside the flat track. Twenty runners set off at a spanking pace to go three and a half times round, which set the binocular men in the tower rotating like gyros. Soon after the start the horses circled the tower, cut closer across beside it and sped towards the water jump and the farther part of the course, took the bottom bend, and returned towards the start. In the top part of the course, near the tower, lay a large pond with a couple of swans swimming in stately unison across from two small devoted black and white ducks. Neither pair took the slightest notice of the throng of horses thundering past a few feet from home.

Rinty Ranger won the race, taking the lead at the

beginning of the last circuit and holding off all challengers, and I saw the flash of his triumphant teeth as he went past the post.

The misty daylight had already faded to the limit for jumping fences safely, but the two races still to come, in a card of ten altogether, were both on the flat. The first was run in peering dusk and the second in total darkness, with floodlights from the tower illuminating just the winning line, bright enough to activate the photo-finish. Eleven horses sped up the dark track, clearly seen only for the seconds it took them to flash through the bright patch, but cheered nonetheless by a seemingly undiminished crowd.

So they literally did race in the dark. I walked thoughtfully back towards the officials' room to meet up with Arne. It really had been night-black when Bob Sherman left the racecourse.

There was bustle in the officials' room and a lot of grins and assurances that the takings this day were safe in the safe. Arne reminded several of them that the Chairman had said they could come to the progress-report meeting if they liked: he said it in English in deference to me, and in English they answered. They would come, except for one or two who would wait for the night watchman. A right case of bolting stable doors.

The Chairman's room had too many people in it, as far as I was concerned. Fifteen besides myself. Every chair filled up, coffee and drinks circulated, and the eyes waited. Lars Baltzersen raised his eyebrows in my direction to tell me I was on, and shushed the low-key chatter with a single smooth wave of his hand.

'I think you've all met Mr Cleveland at some time today . . .' He turned directly to me and smiled forgivingly. 'I know we have asked the impossible. Sherman left no traces, no clues. But is there any course of action you think we might take which we have not so far done?'

He made it so easy.

'Look for his body,' I said.

CHAPTER FIVE

It seemed that that was not what they expected.

Per Bjørn Sandvik said explosively in his high, distilled English, 'We know he is a thief. Why should he be dead?' and someone else murmured, 'I still think he is in the south of France, living in the sun.'

Rolf Torp, owner of the Grand National winner, lit a cigar and said, 'I do not follow your reasoning.' Arne sat shaking his head and blinking as if he would never stop.

Lars Baltzersen gave me a slow stare and then invited me to explain.

'Well,' I said. 'Take first the mechanics of that theft. Everyone agrees that the officials' room was empty for a very few minutes, and that no one could have predicted when it would be empty, or that it would be empty at all. Everyone agrees that Bob Sherman simply saw the money lying handy, was overcome with sudden temptation, and swiped it. Sorry . . .' I said as I saw their puzzlement, ' . . . stole it.'

Heads nodded all round. This was well worn ground.

'After that,' I said, 'we come to a few difficulties. That money was enclosed in five hefty . . . er, bulky . . . canvas bags fastened with straps and padlocks. Now a hundred-and-thirty-three-pound jockey couldn't stow five such bags out of sight under his coat. Anyone, however big, would have found it awkward to pick all of them up at once. To my mind, if Sherman's first impulse was to steal, his second would instantly be to leave well alone. He had no way of knowing how much the bags contained. No way of judging whether the theft would be worthwhile. But in fact there is no evidence at all to suggest that he even felt any impulse to steal, even if he saw the bags on the floor when he went in earlier to ask some question or other. There is no evidence whatsoever to prove that Bob Sherman stole the money.'

'Of course there is,' Rolf Torp said. 'He disappeared.'

'How?' I asked.

There were several puzzled frowns, one or two blank faces, and no suggestions.

'This must have been a spur-of-the-moment theft,' I said, 'so he could have made no preparations. Well, say for argument he had taken the bags, there he is staggering around with the swag . . . the stolen goods . . . in full view. What does he do? Even with a sharp knife it would have taken some time to slit open those bags and remove the money. But we can discount that he did this on the racecourse, because the bags in fact have never been found.'

Some heads nodded. Some were shaken.

'Bob Sherman had a small overnight grip with him, which I understand from his wife was not big enough to contain five canvas bags, let alone his clothes as well. No one has found his clothes lying around, so he could not have packed the money in his grip.'

Lars Baltzersen looked thoughtful.

'Take transport,' I said. 'He had ordered a taxi to take him to Fornebu airport, but he didn't turn up. The police could find no taxi driver who took one single Englishman anywhere. Gunnar Holth says he drove him round to the racecourse at midday, but not away. Because the theft has to be unpremeditated, Sherman could not have hired himself a getaway car, and the police anyway could trace no such hiring. He did not steal a car to transport the money: no cars were stolen from here that day. Which leaves friends . . .' I paused. 'Friends who could be asked to take him say to Sweden, and keep quiet afterwards.'

'They would be also guilty,' said Rolf Torp disbelievingly.

'Yes. Well . . . he had been to Norway seven times but only for a day or two each time. The only friends I can find who might conceivably have known or liked him well enough to get themselves into trouble on his account are Gunnar Holth's head lad, Paddy O'Flaherty, and perhaps . . . if you'll forgive me, sir . . . Mikkel Sandvik.'

He was much more annoyed this time, but protested no further than a grim stare.

'But Paddy O'Flaherty's car has been up on bricks for six weeks,' I said. 'And Mikkel Sandvik cannot drive yet. Neither of them had wheels . . . er, transport . . . ready and waiting for Sherman's unexpected need.'

'What you are saying,' Baltzersen said, 'is that once he'd stolen the money, he couldn't have got it away. But suppose he hid it, and came back for it later?'

'He would still have much the same transport problem, and also the night watchmen to contend with. No . . . I think if he had stolen and hidden the money, he would not have gone back for it, but just abandoned it. Sense would have prevailed. Because there are other things about that cash . . . To you, it is familiar. It is *money*. To Bob Sherman, it was foreign currency. All British jockeys riding abroad have enough trouble changing currency as it is; they would not leap at stealing bagfuls of something they could not readily spend. And don't forget, a large proportion of it was in coins, which are both heavy and even more difficult to exchange in quantity than notes, once they are out of Norway.'

Per Bjørn Sandvik was studying the floor and looking mild again. Arne had blinked his eyes to a standstill and was now holding them shut. Rolf Torp puffed his cigar with agitation and Lars Baltzersen looked unhappy.

'But that still does not explain why you think Sherman is dead,' he said.

'There has been no trace of him from that day to this . . . No one even thinks they might have seen him. There have been no reports from anywhere. His pregnant wife has had no word of reassurance. All this is highly unusual in the case of a thief on the run, but entirely consistent with the man being dead.'

Baltzersen took his bottom lip between his teeth.

I said, 'It is usually fairly easy to account for a man's abrupt disappearance . . . during an investigation his motive emerges pretty strongly. But there seems to have been no factor in Bob Sherman's life likely to prompt him into impulsive and irreversible flight. No one would exchange a successful career for an unknown but not huge amount of foreign currency unless some secondary force made it imperative. Neither your police, nor the British police, nor his wife, nor Arne Kristiansen, nor I, have found any suggestion, however faint or unlikely, that there was such force at work.'

Arne opened his eyes and shook his head.

'Suppose,' I said, 'that someone else stole the money, and Bob Sherman saw him.'

The Stewards and officials looked startled and intensely gloomy. No one needed to have it spelled out that anyone caught red-handed might have had too much to lose, and from there it was a short step to imagine the thief desperate enough to kill Bob Sherman to keep him quiet.

'Murder?' Baltzersen spoke the word slowly as if it were strange on his tongue. 'Is that what you mean?'

'It's possible,' I said.

'But not certain.'

'If there were any clear pointers to murder,' I said, 'your police would have already found them. There is no clarity anywhere. But if there are no answers at all to the questions where he went, why he went, and how he went, I think one should then ask *whether* he went.'

Baltzersen's strained voice mirrored their faces: they did not want me to be right. 'You surely don't think he is still *here*? On the racecourse?'

Rolf Torp shook his head impatiently. He was a man most unlike the Chairman, as quick tempered as Baltzersen was steady. 'Of course he doesn't. There are people here every day training their horses, and we have held eight race meetings since Sherman disappeared. If his body had been here, it would have been found at once.'

Heads nodded in unanimous agreement, and Baltzersen said regretfully, 'I suppose he could have been driven away from here unconscious or dead, and hidden . . . buried . . . later, somewhere else.'

'There's a lot of deep water in Norway,' I said.

My thoughts went back to our little junket in the fjord, and I missed some lightning reaction in someone in that room. I knew that a shift had been made, but because of that gap in concentration I couldn't tell who had made it. Fool, I thought, you got a tug on the line and you didn't see which fish, and even the certainty that a fish was there was no comfort.

The silence lengthened, until finally Per Bjørn Sandvik looked up from the floor with a thoughtful frown. 'It would seem, then, that no one can ever get to the truth of it. I think David's theory is very plausible. It fits all the facts . . . or rather, the lack of facts . . . better than any explanation we have discussed before.'

The heads nodded.

'We will tell our police here what you have suggested,' Baltzersen said in a winding-up-the-meeting voice, 'but I agree with Per . . . After so long a time, and after so much fruitless investigation, we will never really know what happened either to Sherman or to the money. We are all most grateful that you took the trouble to come over, and I know that for most of us, on reflection, your answer to the puzzle will seem the one most likely to be right.'

They gave me a lot of worried half-smiles and some more nods. Rolf Torp stubbed out his cigar vigorously and everyone shifted on their chairs and waited for Baltzersen to stand up.

I thought about the two graceful swans and the two little black and white ducks swimming around quietly out there on the dark side of the tower.

'You could try the pond,' I said.

*

80

The meeting broke up half an hour later, after it had been agreed with a certain amount of horror that the peaceful little water should be dragged the following morning.

Arne had some security jobs to see to, which he did with painstaking slowness. I wandered aimlessly around, listening to the Norwegian voices of the last of the crowd going home. A good hour after the last race, and still a few lights, still a few people. Not the most private place for committing murder.

I went back towards the weighing room and stood beside the clump of ornamental bushes on the grass outside. Well . . . they were thick enough and dark enough to have hidden a body temporarily, until everyone had gone. A jockey and his overnight grip, and five bags of stolen money. Plenty of room, in these bushes, for the lot. There were lights outside the weighing room, but the bushes threw heavy shadows and one could not see to their roots.

Arne found me there and exclaimed with passionate certainty, 'He can't be in those, you know. Someone would have seen him long ago.'

'And smelled him,' I said.

Arne made a choking noise and, 'Christ.'

I turned away. 'Have you finished now?'

He nodded, one side of his face brightly lit, the other in shadow. 'The night watchman is here and everything is as it should be. He will make sure all the gates are locked for the night. We can go home.'

He drove me in his sturdy Swedish Volvo back towards the city and round to his leafy urban street. Kari greeted us with roaring logs on the fire and tall glasses of frosty thirst-quenching white wine. Arne moved restlessly round the apartment like a bull and switched Beethoven on again, *fortissimo*.

'What's the matter?' Kari asked him, raising her voice. 'For God's sake turn it down.'

Arne obliged, but the sacrifice of his emotional safety valve clearly oppressed him.

'Let him rip,' I told her. 'We can stand it for five minutes.'

Kari gave me a gruesome look and vanished into the kitchen as Arne with great seriousness took me at my word. I sat resignedly on the sofa while the stereophonics shook the foundations, and admired the forebearance of his neighbours. The man who lived alone below my own flat in London had ears like stethoscopes and was up knocking on my door at every dropped pin.

The five minutes stretched to nearly twenty before Arne stopped pacing around and turned down the volume.

'Great stuff, great stuff,' he said.

'Sure,' I agreed because it was, in its place, which was somewhere the size of the Albert Hall.

Kari returned from exile with little wifely indulgent shakes of the head. She looked particularly disturbing in a copper-coloured, silky trouser suit which did fantastic things for the hair, the colouring and the eyes and nothing bad for the rest of her. She refilled our glasses and sat on some floor cushions near the fire.

'How did you enjoy the races?' she asked.

'Very much,' I said.

Arne blinked a bit, said he had some telephone calls to make, and removed himself to the hall. Kari said she had watched the Grand National on television but rarely went to the races herself.

'I'm an indoors person,' she said. 'Arne says the outdoor life is healthier, but I don't enjoy being cold or wet or cut up by the wind, so I let him go off doing all those rugged things like skiing and sailing and swimming, and me, I just make a warm room for him to come back to.'

She grinned, but I caught the faintest of impressions that wifely though she might thoroughly appear to be, she had feelings for Arne which were not wholehearted love. Somewhere deep lay an attitude towards the so-called manly pursuits which was far from admiration; and a basic antipathy to an activity nearly always extended, in my experience, to anyone who went in for it.

Arne's voice floated in from the hall, speaking Norwegian.

'He is talking about dragging a pond,' Kari said, looking puzzled. 'What pond?'

I told her what pond.

'Oh dear ... his poor little wife ... I hope he isn't in there ... how would she bear it?'

Better, I thought, on the whole, than believing he was a thief who had deserted her. I said, 'It's only a possibility. But it's as well to make sure.'

She smiled. 'Arne has a very high opinion of you. I expect you are right. Arne said when he came back from England that he would never want to be invest-igated by you, you seemed to know what people were thinking. When the Chairman asked for someone to find Bob Sherman and Arne heard that you were coming yourself, he was very pleased. I heard him telling someone on the telephone that you had the eyes of a hawk and a mind like a razor.' She grinned ironic-ally, the soft light gleaming on her teeth. 'Are you flattered?'

'Yes,' I said. 'I wish it were true.'

'It must be true if you are in charge when you are so young.'

'I'm thirty-three,' I said. 'Alexander the Great had conquered the world from Greece to India by that time.'

'You look twenty-five,' she said.

'It's a great drawback.'

'A ... what?'

'A disadvantage.'

'No woman would think so.'

Arne came back from the hall looking preoccupied. 'Everything all right?'

'Oh . . . er . . . *ja.*' He blinked several times. 'It is all arranged. Nine o'clock tomorrow morning, they drag the pond.' He paused. 'Will you be there, David?'

I nodded. 'And you?'

'*Ja.*' The prospect did not seem to please him; but then I was not wildly excited about it myself. If Bob Sherman were indeed there, he would be the sort of unforgettable object you wished you had never seen, and my private gallery of those was already too extensive.

Arne piled logs on the fire as if to ward off demons, and Kari said it was time to eat. She gave us reindeer steaks in a rich dark sauce and after that the promised cloudberries, which turned out to be yellowy-brown and tasted of caramel.

'They are very special,' Arne said, evidently pleased to be able to offer them. 'They grow in the mountains, and are only in season for about three weeks. There is a law about picking them. One can be prosecuted for picking them before the right date.'

'You can get them in tins,' Kari said. 'But they don't taste the same as these.'

We ate in reverent silence.

'No more until next year,' Arne said regretfully, putting down his spoon. 'Let's have some coffee.'

Kari brought the coffee and with amusement declined half-hearted offers from me to help with the dishes.

'You do not want to. Be honest.'

'I do not want to,' I said truthfully.

She laughed. A highly feminine lady with apparently no banners to wave about equality in the kitchen. Between her and Arne the proposition that everything indoors was her domain, and everything outside, his, seemed to lead only to harmony. In my own sister it had led to resentment, rows, and a broken marriage. Kari, it seemed to me, expected less, settled for less, and achieved more.

I didn't stay late. I liked looking at Kari just a shade too much, and Arne, for all his oddnesses, was an investigator. I had taught him myself how to notice where people were looking, because where their eyes were, their thoughts were, as often as not. Some men felt profound gratification when others lusted after their wives, but some felt a revengeful anger. I didn't know what Arne's reaction would be, and I didn't aim to find out.

CHAPTER SIX

Monday morning. Drizzle. Daylight slowly intensifying over Øvrevoll racecourse, changing anthracite clouds to flannel grey. The dark green spruce and yellow birch stood around in their dripping thousands and the paper debris from the day before lay soggily scattered across the wet tarmac.

Round the lower end of the track, Gunnar Holth and one or two other trainers were exercising their strings of racehorses, but the top part, by and above the winning post, had been temporarily railed off.

Shivering from depression more than cold, I was sitting up in the observation tower with Lars Baltzersen, watching the dragging of the pond down below. Hands in pockets, shoulders hunched, rain dripping off hat brims, Arne and two policemen stood at the water's edge, peering morosely at the small boat going slowly, methodically, backwards and forwards from bank to bank.

The pond was more or less round, approximately thirty yards in diameter, and apparently about six feet deep. The boat contained two policemen with grappling hooks and a third, dressed in a black rubber scuba suit, who was doing the rowing. He wore flippers, gloves, hood and goggles, and had twice been over the side with an underwater torch to investigate when the grapples caught. Both times he had returned to the surface and shaken his head.

The swans and the black and white ducks swam around in agitated circles. The water grew muddier and muddier. The boat moved slowly on its tenth traverse, and Lars Baltzersen said gloomily. 'The police think this is a waste of time.'

'Still,' I said, 'they did come.'

'They would, of course.'

'Of course,' I said.

We watched in silence.

A grapple caught. The swimmer went over the side, submerged for a full minute, came up, shook his head, and was helped back into the boat. He took up the oars; rowed on. One each side of the boat, the two men swung the three pronged grapples into the water again, dragging them slowly across the bottom.

'They considered emptying the pond,' Baltzersen said. 'But the technical difficulties are great. Water drains into it from all the top part of the racecourse. They decided on dragging.'

'They are being thorough enough,' I said.

He looked at me soberly. 'If they do not find

Sherman, then, will you be satisfied that he is not there?'

'Yes,' I said.

He nodded. 'That is reasonable.'

We watched for another hour. The swimmer made two more trips into the water, and came up with nothing. The boat finished its journey, having missed not an inch. There was no body. Bob Sherman was not in the pond.

Beside me, Baltzersen stood up stiffly and stretched, his chair scraping loudly on the wooden boards.

'That is all, then,' he said.

'Yes.'

I stood and followed him down the outside staircase, to be met at the bottom by Arne and the policeman in charge.

'No one is there,' he said to me in English, implying by his tone that he wasn't surprised.

'No. But thank you for finding out.'

He, Baltzersen and Arne spoke together for some time in Norwegian, and Baltzersen walked across to thank the boatmen personally. They nodded, smiled, shrugged, and began to load their boat on to a trailer.

'Never mind, David,' said Arne with sympathy. 'It was a good idea.'

'One more theory down the drain,' I agreed philosophically. 'Not the first, by a long way.'

'Will you go on looking?'

I shook my head. The fjords were too deep. Someone

in the Chairman's room had reacted strongly to my mention of water, and if Bob Sherman wasn't in the pond he was somewhere just as wet.

Baltzersen, Arne, the senior policeman and I trudged back across the track and into the paddock enclosure, on our way to the cars parked beside the main entrance. Baltzersen frowned at the rubbish lying around in the shape of dropped race-cards and old tote tickets and said something to Arne. Arne replied in Norwegian and then repeated it in English.

'The manager thought it better that the refuse collectors should not be here to see the police drag the pond. Just in case, you see . . . Anyway, they are coming tomorrow instead.'

Baltzersen nodded. He had taken the morning off from his timber business and looked as though he regretted it.

'I'm sorry,' I said, 'to have wasted your time.'

He made a little movement of his head to acknowledge that I was more or less forgiven. The persistent drizzle put a damper on anything warmer.

In silence we passed the stands, the ornamental pond (too shallow) and secretariat, and it was probably because the only noise was the crunch of our feet that we heard the child.

He was standing in a corner of the Tote building, sobbing. About six, soaked to the skin, with hair plastered to his forehead in forlorn-looking spikes. The policeman looked across to him and beckoned, and in a kind enough voice said what must have been, 'Come here.'

The boy didn't move, but he said something which halted my three companions in mid-step. They stood literally immobile, as if their reflexes had all stopped working. Their faces looked totally blank.

'What did he say?' I asked.

The boy repeated what he had said before, and if anything the shock of my companions deepened.

Baltzersen loosened his jaw with a visible effort, and translated.

'He said, "I have found a hand".'

The child was frightened when we approached, his big eyes looking frantically around for somewhere to run to, but whatever the policeman said reassured him, and when we reached him he was just standing there, wet, terrified, and shivering.

The policeman squatted beside him, and they went into a longish quiet conversation. Eventually the policeman put out his hand, and the child gripped it, and after that the policeman stood up and told us in English what he'd said.

'The boy came to look for money. The racing crowd often drop coins and notes, especially after dark. This boy says he always squeezes through a hole in the fence, before the rubbish collectors come, to see if he can find money. He says he always finds some. This

91

morning he found twenty kroner before the men came. He means before the police came. But he is not supposed to be here, so he hid. He hid behind the stands up there.' The policeman nodded across the tarmac. 'He says that behind the stands he found a hand lying on the ground.'

He looked down at the child clutching his own hand like a lifeline, and asked Arne to go across to his men, who had packed up all their gear and were on the point of leaving, to ask them to come over at the double. Arne gave the child a sick look and did as he was asked, and Baltzersen himself slowly returned to businesslike efficiency.

The policeman had difficulty transferring the boy's trust to one of his men, but finally disengaged himself, and he, two of his men, Baltzersen, Arne and I walked up to and around the stands to see the hand which was lying on the ground.

The child was not mistaken. Waxy white and horrific, it lay back downwards on the tarmac, fingers laxly curled up to meet the rain.

What the child had not said, however, was that the hand was not alone.

In the angle between the wall and the ground lay a long mound covered by a black tarpaulin. Halfway along its length, visible to the wrist, the hand protruded.

Wordlessly the senior policeman took hold of a corner of the tarpaulin and pulled it back.

Arne took one look, bolted for the nearest bushes,

and heaved up whatever Kari had given him for breakfast. Baltzersen turned grey and put a shaking hand
over his mouth. The policemen themselves looked sick,
and I added another to the unwanted memories.

He was unrecognizable really: it was going to be a
teeth job for the inquest. But the height and clothes
were right, and his overnight grip was lying there beside
him, still with the initials R. T. S. stamped on in black.

A piece of nylon rope was securely knotted round
the chest, and another halfway down the legs, and from
each knot, one over the breastbone, one over the knees,
led a loose piece of rope which finished in a frayed
end.

One of the policemen said something to his chief,
and Baltzersen obligingly translated for me.

'That is the policeman who was diving,' he said, 'and
he says that in the pond the grapples caught on a
cement block. He did not think anything of it at the
time, but he says there were frayed ends of rope coming
from the cement. He says it looked like the same rope
as this.'

The policeman in charge pulled the tarpaulin back
over the tragic bundle and started giving his men
instructions. Arne stood several yards away, mopping
his face and mouth with a large white handkerchief
and looking anywhere but at the black tarpaulin. I
walked over and asked if he was all right. He was
trembling, and shook his head miserably.

'You need a drink,' I said. 'You'd better go home.'

'No.' He shuddered. 'I'll be all right. So stupid of me. Sorry, David.'

He came with me round to the front of the stands and we walked over to where Baltzersen and the top policeman had rejoined the little boy. Baltzersen adroitly drew me aside a pace or two, and said quietly, 'I don't want to upset Arne again . . . The child says the hand was not showing at first. He lifted the tarpaulin a little to see what was underneath . . . you know what children are like . . . and he saw something pale and tried to pull it out. It was the hand. When he saw what it was . . . he ran away.'

'Poor little boy,' I said.

'He shouldn't have been here,' he said, meaning by his tone, serve him right.

'If he hadn't been, we wouldn't have found Bob Sherman.'

Lars Baltzersen looked at me thoughtfully. 'I suppose whoever took him out of the pond meant to return with transport and get rid of him somewhere else.'

'No, I shouldn't think so,' I said.

'He must have done. If he didn't mind him being found, he would have left him in the pond.'

'Oh sure. I just meant . . . why take him anywhere else? Why not straight back into the pond . . . as soon as it was dark? That's the one place no one would ever look for Bob Sherman again.'

He gave me a long considering stare, and then unexpectedly, for the first time that morning, he smiled.

'Well . . . you've done what we asked,' he said.

I smiled faintly back and wondered if he yet understood the significance of that morning's work. But catching murderers was a matter for the police, not for me. I was only catching the two-five to Heathrow, with little enough margin for what I still had to do first.

I said, 'Any time I can help . . .' in the idle way that one does, and shook hands with him, and with Arne, and left them there with their problem, in the drizzle.

I picked up Emma Sherman at her hotel as I had arranged, and took her up to my room in the Grand. I had been going to give her lunch before we set off to the airport, but instead I asked the restaurant to bring hot soup upstairs. Still no brandy. Not until three o'clock, they said. Next time, I thought, I'd pack a gallon.

Champagne was emotionally all wrong for the news I had to give her, so I stirred it around with some orange juice and made her drink it first. Then I told her, as gently as I could that Bob had died at the time of his disappearance. I told her he was not a thief and had not deserted her. I told her he had been murdered.

The desperately frail look came back to her face, but she didn't faint.

'You did . . . find him, then.'

'Yes.'

'Where . . . is he?'

'At the racecourse.'

She stood up, swaying a bit. 'I must go and see him.'

'No,' I said firmly, holding her elbow. 'No, Emma, you must not. You must remember him alive. He doesn't look the same now, and he would hate you to see him. He would beg you not to see him.'

'I must see him . . . of course I must.'

I shook my head.

'Do you mean . . .' It began to dawn on her . . . 'That he looks . . . *horrible*?'

'I'm afraid so. He's been dead a month.'

'Oh God.'

She sat down with weak knees and began to cry. I told her about the pond, the ropes, the cement. She had to know some time, and it couldn't be much worse than the agony of spirit she had suffered through four long weeks.

'Oh my poor Bob,' she said. 'Oh darling . . . oh darling . . .'

The floodgates of all that misery were opened and she wept with a fearful outpouring intensity, but at least and at last it was a normal grief, without the self doubt and humiliating shame.

After a while, still shaking with sobs, she said, 'I'll have to get my room back, at the hotel.'

'No,' I said. 'You're coming home to England today, with me, as we planned.'

'But I can't . . .'

'Indeed you can, and indeed you will. The last place for you now is here. You need to go home, to rest, recover, and look after that baby. The police here will do everything necessary, and I'll see that the Jockey Club, and the Injured Jockeys' Fund perhaps, organizes things from the English end. In a little while we can have Bob brought home to England, if that's what you would like . . . But for today, it's you that matters. If you stay here, you will be ill.'

She listened, took in barely half, but in fact raised no more objections. Maybe the police would not be overjoyed at her leaving, I thought, but they'd had her around for a month, and there couldn't be much she hadn't already told them. We caught the flight on schedule, and she stared out of the window all the way home with exhausted tears running intermittently down her cheeks.

Her grandfather, alerted from Oslo, met her at Heathrow. Tall, thin, stooping and kind, he greeted her with a small kiss and many affectionate pats: her parents, she had told me, had died during her school days, leaving her and a brother to be shuttled between relays of other relations. She liked her mother's widowed father best, and wanted him most in her troubles.

He shook my hand.

97

'I'll see she's looked after,' he said.

He was a nice scholarly man. I gave him my private address and telephone number, in case she needed an inside edge on official help.

CHAPTER SEVEN

Tuesday morning from nine to ten I spent in the office finding out that everyone had been doing just great in my absence and would undoubtedly continue to do so if I disappeared altogether. On my desk lay neat reports of finished inquiries: the man we had suspected of running a retired high-class 'chaser under a hunter's name in a point-to-point had in fact done so and was now in line for a fraud prosecution, and an applicant for a trainer's licence in the Midlands had been found to have totally unsuitable training facilities.

Nothing to make the hair curl. Nothing like weighted bodies in Norwegian ponds.

The whole of the rest of the day was spent with two opposite numbers from the New York Racing Commission who had come to discuss the viability of a world-wide racing investigatory link-up, something along the lines of Interpol. It was one of a series of talks I'd had with officials of many countries and the idea seemed very slowly to be staggering towards achievement. As usual the chief stumbling block to any rapid progress seemed to be my own apparent youth: I supposed that by the time I was sixty, when I'd run out of steam, they would begin to nod while they listened.

I talked my throat dry, gave away sheaves of persuasive literature, took them to dinner at Inigo Jones, and hoped the seed hadn't fallen on stony ground. At farewell time the older of them asked a question I was by then well used to.

'If you succeed in setting this thing up, do you have it in mind to be head of it yourself?'

I smiled. I knew very well that if the baby was born it would very smartly be found to be not mine after all.

'Once it's set up,' I said, 'I'll move on.'

He looked at me curiously.

'Where to?'

'Don't know yet.'

They shook their heads and tut-tutted slightly, but gripped hands with cordiality as we separated into a couple of homeward taxis. It was after midnight when I reached the house where I lived behind the Brompton Road, but as usual the lights were still on in the rooms below my own small flat. The street door banged if you let it go, reverberating through the walls, and perhaps that, I thought, as I shut it gently, explained the ground floor tenant's hypersensitivity. He was a self-contained man, greyish, fiftyish, very neat and precise. Our acquaintanceship after six months of living stacked one over the other extended simply to his trips to my door urging an instant lessening of decibels on the television. Once I had asked him in for a drink, but he politely declined, preferring solitude downstairs. Hardly the *entente cordiale* of the century.

I went up, opened my own door, and shut that quietly also. The telephone bell, starting suddenly in all that noble silence, made me jump.

'Mr Cleveland?' The voice was hurried, practically incoherent. 'Thank goodness you're back at last ... This is William Romney ... Emma's grandfather ... She didn't want me to ring you so late, but I must ... Two men were searching her house when she went in and they hit her ... Mr Cleveland ... she needs your help ...'

'Stop a minute,' I said. 'First thing you need is the police.'

He calmed down a fraction. 'They've been here. Just left. I called them.'

'And a doctor for Emma?'

'Yes, yes. He's gone, too.'

'What time did all this happen?'

'About seven this evening ... we drove over from my house just to fetch some things for her ... and there was a light on ... and she went in first and they jumped on her ... they hit us both ... I do wish ... well ... tell you the truth ... I think we're both still frightened.'

I stifled a sigh. 'Where exactly are you?'

'At Emma's house, still.'

'Yes, but ...'

'Oh, I see. Near Newbury. You go down the M4 . . .' He gave me details of the journey, certain in his own mind that I would hurry to their aid. He made it impossible for me to say take a tranquillizer and I'll come in the morning, and anyway, by the sound of his voice, nothing short of a full anaesthetic was going to give him any rest.

At least at night it was a fast straightforward journey, so I took the MGB down there in fifty minutes flat. The Shermans' house proved to be a modernized pair of farm cottages down an uninhabited lane, a nerve-testing isolation at the best of times.

Lights were on in every window, and at the sound of my car William Romney's anxious figure appeared in the doorway.

'Thank goodness, thank goodness,' he said agitatedly, coming down the short path to meet me. 'I don't know what we would have done . . . if you hadn't been coming . . .'

I refrained from saying that I thought they should have gone back to his house or otherwise stayed in a hotel, and once through the door I was glad I hadn't, because it wouldn't have helped. Shock prevents people from leaving the scene of personal disaster of their own accord, and of the scope and depth of their shock there could be no doubt.

The house was a shambles. Pictures had been torn from the walls, curtains from the windows, carpets from the floor. Furniture was not merely turned inside out, but smashed. Lamps, vases, ornaments lay in pieces. Papers and books scattered the wreckage like autumn leaves.

'It's all like this,' Romney said. 'The whole house. All except the spare bedroom. That's where they were when we interrupted them. The police say so . . .'

Emma herself was in the spare bedroom, lying awake with eyes like soot smudges. Both of her cheeks were swollen and puffy, with red marks showing where blows had landed. Her lower lip had been split, and one eyebrow ended in a raw skinned patch.

'Hullo,' I said inadequately, and pulled up a chair so that I could sit beside her. Her grandfather hovered around making fussing noises, obviously freshly worried by the darkening bruises but tiring Emma beyond bearing. He looked more upset than ever when I asked him if I could speak to her alone, but in the end he reluctantly returned to the devastation below.

I held her hand.

'David . . .'

'Wait a bit,' I said. 'Then tell me.'

She nodded slightly. She was lying on the blankets of the unmade bed, still wearing the brown and white checked dress, her head supported by two coverless pillows and with a flowered quilt over her from the waist down.

The room was hot with a pulsating gas fire, but Emma's hand was cold.

'I told the police,' she said, 'I think they were Norwegians.'

103

'The two men?'

She nodded. 'They were big . . . They had thick sweaters and rubber gloves . . . They talked with accents . . .'

'Start at the beginning,' I said.

She loosened her mouth, obviously troubled by the split and swelling lip.

'We came over to get me some different clothes. I was beginning to feel better . . . There was a light on upstairs but I thought Mrs Street who has been looking after the house had left it on . . . but when I unlocked the front door and went into the hall they jumped on me . . . they switched all the lights on . . . I saw the mess . . . One of them hit me in the face and I screamed for Grandad . . . When he came in they knocked him over . . . so easily, it was awful . . . and they kicked him . . . One of them asked me where Bob would hide papers . . . and when I didn't answer at once he just went on . . . punching me in the face . . . with his fists . . . I didn't answer because I didn't know . . . Bob doesn't hide things . . . didn't . . . oh God . . .'

Her fingers curled tight round mine.

'All right, all right, Emma,' I said, meaning nothing except that I understood. 'Wait a bit.'

We waited until some of the tension left her body; then she swallowed and tried again.

'The telephone rang then, and it seemed to worry them. They talked to each other, and then suddenly they just threw me into a chair . . . and they went away ... through the front door ... Grandad got up off the floor but the telephone stopped before he reached it ... but anyway he called the police ...'

The tired voice stopped. I said, 'Did the men wear masks of any sort?'

'No.'

'Would you know them again?'

'The police asked ... they want me to look at photographs ... but I don't know ... I was trying to avoid being hurt ... I tried to put my hands in front of my face ... and I shut my eyes ...'

'How about your grandfather?'

'He says he might know them ... but it was over so quickly, really.'

'I suppose they didn't tell you what papers they were looking for?'

She shook her head miserably. 'The police asked me that, over and over.'

'Never mind,' I said. 'How does your face feel now?'

'Awfully stiff. Dr West gave me some pills, though. He says he'll look in again tomorrow.'

'Here?'

'Yes ... I didn't want to go back to Grandad's. This ... this is ... home.'

'Do you want the bed made properly?'

'No thank you. I'm comfortable like this ... too tired to move.'

'I'll go down, then, and give your grandfather a hand.'

'All right . . .' Anxiety flooded her suddenly. 'But you won't go, will you?'

I promised her, and in fact I slept in trousers and shirt on the sofa in the sitting-room on a cleared oasis amid the rubble. William Romney, taxed almost too far, snored gently with a strong sedative on the double bed in the Shermans' own room, and from three o'clock to five the cottage was dark and quiet.

I awoke suddenly with a soft wail in my ears like the sound of a lamb in a snowstorm.

'David . . .'

It was Emma's voice from upstairs, urgent and quavery.

I tossed off the rug, stood up, and beat it up there fast. I'd left her door open and the fire on, and as I went in I could see the ultimate disaster looking out of her great dark eyes.

'David . . .' Her voice filled with inconsolable desolation. 'David . . . I'm bleeding.'

She lost the baby and very nearly her life. I went to see her three days after she'd been whisked away in a bell-ringing ambulance (three days because no one was allowed in sooner) and was surprised to discover that she could and did look even paler than she had in Oslo. The swellings had gone down in her face, though the bruises showed dark in patches. Her eyes were dulled, which seemed a mercy.

The five minutes visit passed on the surface.

'Nice of you to come,' she said.

'Brought you some grapes.'

'Very kind.'

'Sorry about the baby.'

She nodded vaguely, but some sort of drug was dealing with that pain also.

'Hope you'll soon be better.'

'Oh yes. Yes, I will.'

William Romney shook with fury, stamping up and down my office with outrage.

'Do you realize that it is a week tomorrow since we were attacked and no one has done *anything*? People can't just vanish into thin air ... those men must be somewhere ... why can't the police find them? It isn't right that thugs should just walk into a defenceless girl's house and tear things to pieces and hurt her so much that she nearly dies of it ... It's *disgraceful* that the police haven't found those despicable *bastards* ...'

The word was a strong one for him: he looked almost surprised that he'd used it, and nothing could have more clearly stated the fierceness of his feelings.

'I believe neither you nor Emma could identify the men from police photographs,' I said, having checked via a friendly police contact that this was so.

'They weren't there. There weren't any pictures of them. Can't say that's surprising ... why don't the police get photographs of *Norwegian* crooks for us to look at?'

'It would probably mean your going to Norway,' I said. 'And Emma's in no state, physical or emotional, to do that.'

'I'll go then,' he said belligerently. 'I'll go, at my own expense. Anything . . . *anything* to see those men punished for what they've done to Emma.'

His thin face was flushed with the strength of his resentment. I wondered if part of his fury sprang from unnecessary guilt that he hadn't been young and strong enough to defend or rescue her from two aggressive toughs. Amends in the shape of effort and expense were what he was offering, and I saw no reason to dissuade him from a journey which would bring him mental ease even if no concretely helpful results.

'I'll fix it for you, if you like,' I said.

'What . . .?'

'To go to Norway and look at the mug-shots.'

His resolution took shape and hardened. He straightened his stooping shoulders, calmed his voice, and stopped wearing out so much of the Jockey Club's carpet.

'Yes. Please do that. I'll go as soon as I can.'

I nodded. 'Sit down,' I said. 'Do you smoke? And how's Emma?'

He sat down, declined a desk-box of cigarettes, and said that last evening, when he'd seen her, Emma was very much stronger.

'She says she'll be out of hospital in two or three days.'

'Good.'

He didn't look as if it were good. He said in recurring worried anger, 'What on earth is that poor girl going to do? Her husband murdered . . . her home wrecked . . . I suppose she can live with me, but . . .'

'I'm sure she'll live in her own house,' I said. 'For a while, at least. Best if she does. Get her grieving done properly.'

'What an extraordinary thing to say.'

'When can you go?' I said, reaching for the telephone.

'At once.'

'Right.'

Øvrevoll racecourse answered in the shape of the manager who gave me the home and office telephone numbers of Lars Baltzersen. He answered from his office, and I explained the situation. Of course, he said in dismay, of course he could arrange it with the police. For tomorrow? Certainly. Poor Mrs Sherman, he said, please give her my condolences. I said I would, and asked if there had been any recent progress.

'None at all, I'm afraid,' he said. He hesitated for several seconds, and then went on, 'I have been thinking . . . I suppose . . . if the police don't solve this crime . . . that you wouldn't come back yourself, and see what you can do?'

I said, 'I'm not experienced in murder investigation.'

'It must in essence be the same as any other sort.'

'Mm . . . My masters here might not be willing for me to take the time.'

'If I asked them myself, as an international favour? After all, Bob Sherman was a British jockey.'

'Wouldn't Norway prefer to ship him home and forget about the whole nasty incident?'

'No, Mr Cleveland,' he said severely. 'A murder has been done, and justice should follow.'

'I agree.'

'Then . . . you'll come?'

I thought. 'Wait another week. Then if neither your police nor ours have found any new leads, and if you still want me to, well, maybe I can. But . . . don't expect too much, will you?'

'No more than before,' he said dryly, and disconnected.

William Romney had adjusted by then to the prospect of travelling the next day, and began to fuss mildly about tickets, currency and hotels. I shooed him out because he could do all that for himself, and I had a good deal of work on hand to start with, and more still if I had to clear time for another trip to Oslo. The police, I hoped, would quickly dig down to the roots themselves and save me from proving to the world that I couldn't.

*

110

William Romney went to Norway, spent two full days there and returned depressed. The Norwegian police did not have photographs of the intruders, or if they did, Romney did not recognize them.

Emma left hospital and went home to put her house straight. An offer from me to help her do that was declined; one to come down and take her out to lunch was accepted.

'Sunday?' I suggested.

'Fine.'

Sunday found the carpets flat on the floors, the pictures back on the walls, the broken mess cleared away, and the curtains bundled up for the cleaners. The house looked stark and unlived-in, but its mistress had come a long way back to life. For the first time since I had known her, she was wearing lipstick. Her hair was newly washed, her clothes neat, her manner composed. The pretty girl lurked not far away now, just below the still over-pale skin, just behind the still unhappy eyes.

'It's his funeral on Thursday,' she said.

'Here?'

She nodded. 'In the church in the village. Thank you for doing everything about bringing him home.'

I had delegated the whole job. 'I only got it done,' I said.

'Anyway . . . thanks.'

The October day was calm and sunny and crisp round the edges. I took her to a Thames-side pub where pointed yellow willow leaves floated slowly past on

111

grey water and anglers flicked maggots on hooks to wily fish. We walked along the bank; slowly, because she was still weak from haemorrhage.

'Have you any plans?' I asked.

'I don't know . . . I've thought a lot, of course, while I've been in hospital. I'll go on living in the cottage for a while, I think. It feels right, somehow. In the end I suppose I'll sell it, but not yet.'

'How are the finances?'

She produced a flicker of smile. 'Everyone is being fantastic. Really marvellous. Did you know, the owners Bob rode for in Norway clubbed together and sent me a cheque? How kind people are.'

Conscience money, I thought sourly, but I didn't say so.

'Those two men who burst into your house, do you mind if we talk about them?'

She sighed. 'I don't mind.'

'Describe them.'

'But . . .'

'Yes, I've read what you told the police. You didn't look at them, you shut your eyes, you only saw their sweaters and their rubber gloves.'

'That's right.'

'No. What you told the police was all you could bear to remember, and you would have shut out even that if they hadn't pressed you for answers.'

'That's nonsense.'

'Try it another way. Which one hit you?'

She said instantly, 'The bigger one with the . . .' Her voice stopped uncertainly.

'With the what?'

'I was going to say, with the reddish hair. How odd. I didn't remember until now that one of them had reddish hair.'

'What about the other?'

'Brown. Brown hair. He was kicking Grandad.'

'The one who was hitting you . . . what was he saying?'

' "Where does your husband keep secret papers? Where does he hide things? Tell us where he hides things." '

'Good English?'

'Ye-es. Pretty good. He had an accent.'

'What were his eyes like, while he was hitting you?'

'Fierce . . . frightful . . . like an eagle . . . sort of black and yellow . . . very angry.'

There was a small silence, then she said, 'Yes, I do remember, like you said. I shut it out.'

After a few seconds, 'He was quite young, about the same as you. His mouth was very tight . . . his lips were stiff . . . his face looked hard . . . very angry.'

'How tall?'

'Same as you, about. Broader, though. Much heavier. Big thick shoulders.'

'Big shoulders in a thick sweater. What sort of thick sweater? Did it have a pattern?'

'Well, yes, that was why . . .' She stopped again.

'Why what?'

'Why I thought at once that he was Norwegian . . . before he even spoke. Because of the patterns in his sweater. They were sort of white patterns . . . two colours, though, I think . . . all over a brown sweater. I'd seen dozens like it in the shops in Oslo.' She looked puzzled. 'Why didn't I think of that before?'

'Memories often work like that. Sort of delayed action.'

She smiled. 'I must say it's easier remembering things quietly here by the river than in all that mess with my face hurting and policemen asking me questions from all sides and bustling about . . .'

We went indoors for a drink and a good lunch, and over coffee I asked her other things.

'You said Bob never hid papers. Are you sure?'

'Oh yes. He wasn't secretive. Never. He was more careless, really, than anything else, when it came to papers and documents and things like that.'

'It seems quite extraordinary that two men should come all the way from Norway to search your house for papers.'

She frowned. 'Yes, it does.'

'And to search it so violently, so destructively, so thoroughly.'

'And they were so angry, too.'

'Angry, I expect, because they'd worked hard and hadn't found what they'd come for.'

'But what *did* they come for?'

'Well . . .' I said slowly. 'Something to do with Norway. What papers did Bob ever have that had anything to do with Norway?'

She shook her head. 'Nothing much. A few receipts, for the accounts. Race-cards, sometimes. A cutting from a Norwegian paper with a picture of him winning a race. Nothing, honestly, that anyone could want.'

I drank my coffee, considering. I said, 'Look at it the other way round . . . Did he ever take any papers *to* Norway?'

'No. Why should he?'

'I don't know. I just wondered. Because those men might have been looking for something he hadn't taken to Norway, not for something he had brought away.'

'You do think some weird things.'

'Mm . . .'

I paid the bill and drove her home. She was silent most of the way, but thoughtful, and the fruit of that was a plum.

'I suppose . . . well, it's stupid, really . . . but it couldn't have anything to do with blue pictures?'

'What sort of blue pictures?' I asked.

'I don't know. I didn't see them. Only Bob said that's what they were.'

I pulled up outside her gate but made no move to leave the car.

'Did he get them in Norway?'

She was surprised. 'Oh no. It was like you said. He was taking them over there with him. In a brown envelope. It came by hand the night before he went. He said they were blue pictures which a chap in Oslo wanted him to bring over.'

'Did he say what chap?'

She shook her head. 'No. I hardly listened. I'd forgotten all about it until you said . . .'

'Did you see the brown envelope? How big was it?'

'I must have seen it. I mean, I know it was brown.' She frowned, concentrating. 'Fairly big. Not an ordinary letter. About the size of a magazine.'

'Was it marked "photographs", or anything like that?'

'I don't think so. I can't remember. It's more than six weeks ago.' Her eyes filled suddenly with tears. 'He put it in his overnight grip at once, so as not to forget to take it.' She sniffed twice, and found a handkerchief. 'So he did take it to Norway. It wasn't in the house for those men to find. If that's what they were looking for . . . they did all that for nothing.' She put the handkerchief to her mouth and stifled a sob.

'Was Bob interested in blue pictures?' I asked.

'Like any other man, I suppose,' she said through the handkerchief. 'He'd look at them.'

'But he wouldn't collect them himself?'

She shook her head.

I got out of the car, opened the door her side, and went with her into the cottage. She looked at the racing pictures of Bob which hung in the hall.

'They tore all those photographs out of the frames,' she said. 'Some of them were ruined.'

Many of the prints were about ten inches by eight. A magazine-sized brown envelope would have held them easily.

I stayed another hour simply to keep her company, but for the evening ahead she insisted that she would be all right alone. She looked round the barenesses of the sitting-room and smiled to herself. She obviously found the place friendly, and maybe Bob was there too.

When I went she gave me a warm kiss on the cheek and said, 'I can't thank you enough . . .' and then broke off and opened her eyes wide.

'Golly,' she said. 'That was the second lot.'

'What of?'

'Blue pictures. He took some before. Oh . . . months ago. Back in the summer.' She shook her head in fresh frustration. 'I can't remember. I just remember him saying . . . blue pictures.'

I kissed her in return.

'Take care of yourself,' I said.

'You, too.'

CHAPTER EIGHT

A little matter of doping-to-win took me to Plumpton races in Sussex the following day but I saw no harm in some extra spadework on the side. Rinty Ranger, busy in second and fifth races, was comparatively easy to pin down between the third and the fourth.

'What did you say?' he repeated in exaggerated amazement. 'Take pornography to Scandinavia? Christ, that's like wasting pity on bookmakers. They don't need it, mate. They don't bloody need it.'

'Bob Sherman told his wife he was taking blue pictures to Norway.'

'And she believed it?'

'The point is, did he?'

'He never said a word about it to me.'

'Do me a favour,' I said. 'Find out in the changing-room here today if anyone ever asked any jockey to act as a messenger ... a carrier ... of any papers of any sort from Britain to Norway.'

'Are you serious?'

'Bob Sherman's dead.'

118

'Yes.' He thought. 'OK.'

He gave me a noncommittal wave as he walked out to the fifth, in which he rode a bright, tight, tactical race to be beaten half a length by a better horse, but came straight out of the weighing room after he had changed and put an end to my easy theory.

'None of them who have ridden in Norway has ever been asked to take over any papers or pictures or anything like that.'

'Would they say, if they had?'

He grinned. 'Depends how much they'd been paid to forget.'

'What do you think yourself?'

'Hard to tell. But they all seemed surprised. There weren't any knowing looks, sort of, if you see what I mean.'

'Carry on asking, would you? Tomorrow and so on. Say they can tell me hush hush, if they like. No kick backs if they've been fiddling currency.'

He grinned again. 'Some copper you are. Bend the rules like curling tongs.'

That evening I telephoned Baltzersen at his home. There was no news, he said. He had consulted his friends in the police, and they would raise no objections if I joined the hunt. On the contrary, they would, as before, let me see what they'd got, to save me reploughing their furrows.

'So, Mr Cleveland, will you come?'

'I guess so,' I said.

With flattering relief he said, 'Good, good,' explosively, and added, 'come tomorrow.'

''Fraid I can't. I have to give evidence in court tomorrow, and the case may last two days. Soonest would be Thursday morning.'

'Come straight to the racecourse then. We have a meeting on Thursday and another on Sunday, but I fear they may be the last this year. It's a little colder now, and we have had frost.'

I wrote 'warm clothes' in large letters on my memo pad and said I'd see him at the races.

'By the way,' I said. 'You know I told you the people who broke into the Shermans' house were looking for papers? Mrs Sherman now remembers that Bob took with him to Norway a packet which had been entrusted to him, which he believed contained blue pictures. Did anyone mention to you, or to the police, or to Arne in all those preliminary investigations into his disappearance, anything at all about his bringing such a packet with him, or delivering it?'

There was an unexpectedly long silence on the other end of the line, but in the end he only said uncertainly, 'Blue pictures . . . what are those?'

'Pornography.'

'I see.' Another pause. 'Please explain a little.'

I said, 'If the package reached its destination, then it cannot be that particular package that the men were searching for. So I could stop chasing after innocent blue pictures and start looking elsewhere.'

'*Ja*. I see.' He cleared his throat. 'I haven't heard of any such package, but perhaps Arne or the police have done. I will ask them. Of course you know it is unlikely that anyone would need to bring pornography secretly into this country?'

'It would have to be special,' I said, and left it at that.

All Tuesday and Wednesday morning I spent in court giving evidence for the prosecution in an insurance swindle involving grievous cruelty to horses, and Wednesday afternoon I sat in the office juggling six jobs at once like some multi-armed Siva. Looking for Bob Sherman's murderer had meant advancing myself a week's leave when I was too busy to take one, and by seven o'clock when I locked up and left, I was wishing he'd got himself bumped off at any other time.

I went home on tube and feet, thinking comforting thoughts about a large scotch indoors followed by a stroll round to a local grill for a steak. I shut the street door without letting it bang, put one foot in front of the other up the carpeted stairs, unlocked the door to my own flat and switched on the lights; and it was at that point that the day stopped operating according to schedule.

I heard, felt, maybe assimilated by instinct, a change

121

in the air behind me. Nothing as definite as a noise. More a current. Undoubtedly a threat.

All those useful dormant jungle reactions came to my rescue before a thought process based on reason had time to get off the ground. So I was already whipping round to face the stairs and pushing further through my own doorway when the man with the knife did his best to send me early to the cemetery.

He did not have reddish hair, angry yellow eagle eyes or a Norwegian sweater. He did have rubber gloves, a stocky muscular body, a lot of determination and a very sharp blade.

The stab which had been supposed to stop my heart from the back ripped instead through some decent Irish tweed, through a blue cotton shirt below that, and down half a dozen inches of skin on my chest.

He was surprised and fed up that at first he hadn't succeeded, but he'd heard all about try try again. He crowded through my door after me with the knife already rising for another go. I backed through the tiny hall and into the sitting-room, unable to take my eyes off his intentions long enough to find any household object to fight him off with.

He came on with a feint and a slice at my middle regions and I got another rip in my jacket and a closer look at some narrowed and murderous eyes.

He tried next a sort of lunging jump, the point of the knife coming in fast and upward. I tried to leap away backwards, tripped on a rug, fell on my back and found my hand hitting the base of the standard lamp. One wild clutch and I'd pulled it over, knocking him off his aim just when he thought he finally had me. The lamp hit him with a crash and while he was off balance I got both my hands on his knife arm; but it was then that I discovered the rock-like muscles. And also, unfortunately, that he was more or less ambidexterous.

He shifted the knife like lightning from his right hand to his left and I avoided the resulting stab only by a sort of swinging jump over an armchair, using his arm as a lever. The blade hit a cushion and feathers floated up like snowflakes.

I threw a cigarette box at him and missed, and after that a vase which hit but made no difference. As long as I kept the armchair between us he couldn't reach me, but neither did he give me much chance of getting past him to the still open door to the stairs.

Behind me on a wide shelf stood my portable television. I supposed it might stop him if I threw it at him, but on the other hand . . . I stretched out backwards without losing sight of his knife, found the on-off switch, and turned the volume up to maximum.

The din when it started took him totally by surprise and gave me a fractional chance. I pushed the armchair viciously forward at his knees and he overbalanced, twisting as he tried to get his feet under him. He went down as far as one knee, partially recovered, and toppled altogether when I shoved again with the chair. But it was nothing permanent. He was rolling back to his feet like a cat before I had time to get round the big chair and step on some of his tender bits.

Up until that point he had said not a word and now if he did I wouldn't hear: the television literally vibrated with the intense noise of some pop star or other's Special Spectacular; and if that didn't bring the US cavalry, nothing would.

He came. Looking cross. Ready to blow like a geyser. And stood there in consternation in my open door.

'Fetch the police,' I yelled, but he didn't hear. I slapped the off switch.

'Fetch the police,' I yelled again, and my voice bounced off the walls in the sudden silence.

The man with the knife turned to see, gave himself fresh instructions, and went for my friend from downstairs. I did a sort of sliding rugger tackle, throwing myself feet first at his legs. He stumbled over my shoes and ankles and went down on his side. I swept one leg in an arc and by sheer good luck kicked him on the wrist. The knife flew out of his hand at least ten feet, and fell nearer to me than him, and only at that point did he think of giving up.

He scrambled to his feet, looked at me with the first sign of uncertainty, then made up his mind, turned on his heel, crashed past my neighbour and jumped down the stairs in two giant strides. The front door slammed behind him with a force that shook the building, and from the window I saw him running like the Olympics under the street lamps.

I looked breathlessly at the mess in my sitting-room and at my man from downstairs.

'Thanks,' I said.

He took a tentative step into the sitting-room.

'You're bleeding,' he said.

'But not dying.'

I picked up the standard lamp.

'Was he a burglar?' he asked.

'A murderer,' I said. 'Enter a murderer.'

We looked at each other in what was no doubt professional curiosity on both sides, because all he said next was, 'Sit down, you're suffering from shock.'

It was advice I'd given pretty often to others, and it made me smile. All the same there was a perceptible tremble somewhere around my knees, so I did as he said.

He looked around the room, looked at the knife still lying where it had fallen, and took it all in quietly.

'Shall I carry out your instructions, or were they principally a diversion?'

'Hm?'

'Fetch the police.'

'Oh . . . It can wait a bit.'

He nodded, considered a moment, and then said, 'If you'll excuse me asking, why was he trying to kill you?'

'He didn't say.'

My neighbour's name was Stirling. C. V. Stirling, according to the neat white card beside his bell push. He had grey patches neatly brushed back over his ears and nostrils pinched into an expression of distaste for bad smells. His hands looked excessively clean and well manicured, and even in these bizarre circumstances he wore a faint air of exasperated patience. A man used to being the brightest person around, I guessed, with the power to make it felt.

'Did he need to?'

'It would have been helpful,' I said.

He came a pace nearer.

'I could do something about that bleeding, if you like.'

I looked down at the front of my shirt, which had changed colour pretty thoroughly from blue to red.

'Could you?'

'I'm a surgeon,' he said. 'Ear, nose and throat, actually. Other areas by arrangement.'

I laughed. 'Stitch away, then.'

He nodded, departed downstairs, and returned with a neat flat case containing the tools of his trade. He used clips not needles. The slice through my skin was more gory than deep, bleeding away persistently like a shaving nick. When he'd finished, it was a thin red line under a sticking plaster.

'You were lucky,' he said.

'Yes, I was.'

'Do you do this sort of thing often? Fight for your life, I mean.'

'Very rarely.'

'My fee for professional services rendered is a little more chat.'

I smiled wryly.

'OK. I'm an investigator. I don't know why I was attacked unless there's someone around who particularly does not want to be investigated.'

'Good God.' He stared at me curiously. 'A private eye? Philip Marlowe, and all that?'

'Nothing so fancy. I work in racing; for the Jockey Club. Looking into small frauds, most of the time.'

'This,' he waved at my chest and the knife and the scattered cushion feathers, 'doesn't look like a small fraud.'

It didn't. It didn't look, either, even like a severe warning off. It looked like a ruthless all-out push for a final solution.

I changed my clothes and took him round to the grill for the overdue steak. His name was Charles, he said, and we walked home as friends. When I let myself in upstairs and reviewed the general untidiness it occurred to me that in the end I had never called in the police. It seemed a little late to bother, so I didn't.

CHAPTER NINE

I caught the eleven twenty-five to Norway the next morning with the knife wrapped in polythene in my sponge-bag; or rather the black, zipped-leather case which did that duty. It was a hunter's knife, the sort of double-sided blade used for skinning and disjointing game. The cutting edges had been sharpened like razors and the point would have been good as a needle. A professional job: no amateur could have produced that result with a few passes over a carborundum.

The handle was of horn of some sort, but workman-like not tourist-trap stuff. Between handle and blade protruded a short silver bar for extra leverage with fingers. There were no fingerprints on it anywhere, and no blood. Punched into the blade near the hilt were the words *Norsk Stål*.

Its owner hadn't, of course, intended to leave it behind. Just one dead body neatly disposed inside its own front door, out of sight and undiscovered for a minimum of twenty-four hours.

He hadn't followed me into the house: he'd been

there before I came, waiting higher up the stairs for me to come home.

At breakfast time I'd knocked on the doors of the other three tenants, the one in the basement, the one above me, and the one above that, and asked them if they'd seen my visitor on the stairs or let him in through the front door. I got negatives all round, but as one of them said, we were hardly a matey lot, and if the visitor entered boldly while one of the tenants was leaving, no one would have stopped him. None of them remembered him, but the basement man observed that as the laundry van had called that day, a stranger could easily have walked in with the man who collected and delivered the boxes from the hall.

There had been nothing suspicious or memorable about my visitor's appearance. His face was a face; hair brown, skin sallow, eyes dark. Age, about thirty. Clothes, dark grey trousers, navy close-fitting sweater, neat shirt and tie showing at the neck. Entirely the right rig for the neighbourhood. Even a little formal.

BEA landed on time at Fornebu and I took a taxi straight out to the racecourse. Nothing much had changed in the two and a half weeks I'd been away, not even the weather or the runners in the races, and within the first half hour I had spotted all the same faces, among them Gunnar Holth, Paddy O'Flaherty, Per Bjørn Sandvik, Rolf Torp and Lars Baltzersen. Arne greeted me with a beaming smile and an invitation to spend as much time with Kari and himself as I could.

I walked around with him for most of the afternoon, partly from choice, partly because Baltzersen was busy being Chairman. Arne said that whereas he personally was pleased to see me, many of the racecourse committee had opposed Baltzersen in the matter of bringing me back.

'Lars told us at the Tuesday committee meeting that you were definitely coming today, and that caused quite a row. You should have heard it. Lars said that the racecourse would be paying your fare and expenses like last time, and half of them said it was unjustifiable to spend so much.'

He broke off rather suddenly as if he had decided not to repeat what had actually been said.

'I could easily have been persuaded to stay at home,' I said. But by words, I reflected. Not knives.

'Several of the committee said Lars had no right to act without taking a vote.'

'And Lars?'

Arne shrugged. 'He wants Bob Sherman's death explained. Most of them just want to forget.'

'And you?' I asked.

He blinked. 'Well,' he said, 'I would give up more easily than Lars or you. Which is no doubt why,' he grinned, 'Lars is Chairman and you are the chief investigator, and I am only a security officer who lets the racecourse takings be stolen from under his nose.'

I smiled. 'No one blames you.'

'Perhaps they should.'

I thought in my intolerant way that they definitely should, but I shook my head and changed the subject.

'Did Lars tell you all about the attack on Emma Sherman, and about her losing her baby?'

'Yes,' he said. 'Poor girl.' There was more lip-service in his voice than genuine regret. I supposed that no one who hadn't seen her as I had could properly understand all that she'd suffered; and I knew that it was in great part because of Emma that I was back in Norway. No one should be allowed to inflict such hurt on another human being, and get away with it. The fact that the same agency had murdered Bob and tried to see me off was in a curious way secondary: it was possible future victims who had to be saved. If you don't dig ground elder out of the flower beds it can strangle the garden.

Rolf Torp was striding about in a bad temper. His horse, he said, had knocked itself that morning and his trainer had omitted to tell him it couldn't run. He had taken the afternoon off from his mining office, which he wouldn't have done if he'd known, on account of being indispensable and nothing constructive ever being achieved in his absence.

After he had delivered himself of that little lot he adjusted his sights more specifically on me.

'I was against bringing you back. I'll tell you that myself. I told the committee. It is a waste of our money.'

131

His name was on the list Emma had given me of the contributors to the solidly worthwhile cheque the Norwegian owners had sent. If he thought that any available cash should only be spent on the living, perhaps it was a valid point of view; but he wasn't paying my expenses out of his own private pocket.

He was a man of less than average height and more than average aggressiveness: a little bull of a man with a large black moustache that was more a statement than an adornment. Difficult to please and difficult to like, I thought, but sharp of eye and brain as well as tongue.

His voice boomed as heavily as a bittern in the reed beds, and although his English was as comprehensive as most well-educated Norwegians', he spoke it unlovingly, as if he didn't care too much for the taste.

I said without heat, 'As a miner, you'll understand that surveys are a legitimate expense even when they don't strike ore.'

He gave me a hard look. 'As a miner I understand that I would not finance a survey to find slime.'

Klonk. One over the head for D. Cleveland. I grinned appreciatively, and slowly, unwillingly, the corners of his mouth twitched.

I made the most of it. 'May I come and see you in your office?' I asked. 'Just for a few questions. I might as well try my best to earn what you're paying me, now that I'm here.'

132

'Nothing I can tell you will be of any help,' he said, as if believing made it so.

'Still . . .'

The vestiges of smile disappeared, but finally, grudgingly, he nodded.

'Very well. Tomorrow afternoon. Four o'clock.' And he went so far as to tell me how to find him.

As he walked away Arne said, 'What are you going to ask him?'

'Don't know yet. I just want to see his background. You can't tell what people are really like if you only meet them at the races.'

'But,' he said, blinking furiously, 'why Rolf Torp?'

'Not especially Rolf Torp,' I said. 'Everyone who knew Bob Sherman.'

'David!' He looked staggered. 'It will take you months.'

I shook my head. 'Several days, that's all. Bob didn't know so many people here as all that.'

'But he could have been killed by a total stranger. I mean, if he saw someone stealing the money and didn't know him . . .'

'It's possible,' I said, and asked him if he had ever heard Bob talking about bringing any sort of package from England to Norway.

Arne wrinkled his forehead and darted a compulsive look over his shoulder. No one there, of course.

'Lars mentioned this mysterious package on Tuesday night. No one knew anything about it.'

'What did Lars actually ask?'

'Just said you wanted to know if anyone had received a package from Bob Sherman.'

'And no one had?'

'No one who was there, anyway.'

'Could you write me a list of those who were there?'

'Yes,' he said with surprise. 'If you want it. But I can't see what it could possibly have to do with Bob's death.'

'I'm a great one for collecting useless information,' I said, smiling, and Arne gave me a look which said, oh yeah, plain as plain.

The races proceeded the same as before, except that the watching crowd was a good deal thinner than on Grand National day. The birch trees had dropped most of their yellow leaves and looked silver, the daylight was colder and greyer than ever, and a sharp wind whipped round every corner. But this time I had come prepared with a skiing cap with ear flaps and only my nose, like everyone else's, was turning blue.

Gunnar Holth saddled two for the hurdle race, hurrying busily from one to the other and juggling both sets of owners with anxious dexterity. One of his runners was the dappled mare with the uncertain temper, whose owner, Sven Wangen, was on Emma's list. Arne confirmed that the big young man assiduously hopping out of the way every time the mare presented her heels was indeed Sven Wangen, and added that the brunette sneering at him from a safe distance was his wife.

The jockey mounted warily and the mare bucked and kicked every inch to the start. Arne said that like all mean, bad-tempered females she would get her own way in the end, and went off to invest a little something on the Tote.

Wise move. She won. Arne beamed and said what did I tell you, when she comes here bitching she always wins. Was she ever docile? I asked, and Arne said sure, but those were her off days. We watched her being unsaddled in the winner's enclosure, with Gunnar Holth and Sven Wangen both tangoing smartly out of her way.

I told Arne I would like to meet Sven Wangen because Bob had ridden a winner for him on that last day. Arne showed reservations, so I asked him why.

He pursed his mouth. 'I don't like him. That's why.'

'What's wrong with him?'

'Too much money,' Arne said reprovingly. 'He behaves as if everyone ought to go on their knees when they talk to him. He has done nothing himself. The money was his father's. His father was a rich man. Too rich.'

'In what way too rich?'

Arne raised his eyebrows at what evidently seemed to him a nonsensical question, because from the tone of his reply it seemed he held great wealth to be morally wrong.

'He was a millionaire.'

'Don't you have millionaires in Norway?'

'Very few. They are not popular.'

I persuaded him, however, to introduce me to the unpopular Sven Wangen, whose father had made a million out of ships: and I saw at once why Arne didn't like him.

Perhaps two inches taller than I, he looked down his nose as if from a great height: and it was clear that this was no accidental mannerism but the manifestation of deep self-importance. Still probably in his twenties, he was bulky to the point of fatness and used his weight for throwing about. I didn't take to his manner, his small mouth, or his unfriendly light-amber eyes: nor, in fact, to his wife, who looked as if she could beat the difficult mare's temper by a couple of lengths.

Arne introduced me, and Sven Wangen saw no reason at all why I should call upon him at any time to ask him questions. He had heavy, rust-brown hair growing long over his ears, and a small flat cap which made his big head look bigger.

I said I understood he was a member of the racecourse committee which had asked me to come.

'Lars Baltzersen asked you,' he said brusquely. 'I was against it. I said so on Tuesday.'

'The sooner I get the questions answered, the sooner I'll go home,' I said. 'But not until.'

He looked at me with intense disfavour. 'What do you want, then?'

'Half an hour in your house,' I said. 'Any time that would suit you except for tomorrow afternoon.'

He settled in irritation for Sunday morning. His elegantly thin wife manufactured a yawn and they turned away without any pretence of politeness.

'See what I mean?' Arne said.

'I do indeed. Very unusual, wouldn't you say?'

'Unusual?'

'The rich don't usually behave like that.'

'Do you know so many rich people?' Arne asked with a touch of sarcasm.

'Meet them every day of the week,' I said. 'They own racehorses.'

Arne conceded that the rich weren't necessarily all beastly and went off on some official tasks. I tracked down Paddy O'Flaherty and found him with five minutes to spare between races.

'Brown envelope of blue pictures?' he repeated. 'He never said a dicky bird to me, now, about any blue pictures.' He grinned, and then an uncertain memory floated back. 'Wait now, I tell a lie. Back in the summer, now, he told me he had a good little tickle going for him, do you see? Always one for a chance at easy money, so he was. And there was this day, he winked at me like, and showed me the corner of an envelope in his overnight bag, and he said it would make our hair curl, so it would. So then I asked him for a look, do you see, but he said it was sealed some way so he couldn't steam it. I remember that, sure now I do.'

'The last time he came, did he say anything about bringing an envelope?'

Paddy shook his head. 'Like I said. Not a word.'

I thought. 'Did he come straight to your stable from the airport? Did he arrive on time, for instance?'

'I'll tell you something now. No, he didn't.' He concentrated. 'He was that late I thought he'd missed the flight and would come in the morning. Then, sure, a taxi rolls up and out he hops, large as life. He'd bought a bottle of brandy on the plane and there wasn't much left of that, now, before we went to bed.'

'What did he talk about?'

'Bejasus, how do I know, after all this time?'

'You must have thought often about that night.'

'Well, so I have, then.' He sighed at my perseverance, but thought some more. 'Horses, of course. We talked about horses. I don't remember him saying why he was late, or anything like that. And sure now I'd have thought it was the flight that was late, that was all.'

'I'll check,' I said:

'Look now, there was only one thing he said . . . Late on, when we'd maybe had a skinful, he said "Paddy, I think I've been conned." That's what he said now. "Paddy I think I've been conned." So I asked him what he meant, but he didn't tell me.'

'How insistently did you ask?'

'Insist . . .? Bejasus, of course I didn't. Uh . . . there

he was putting his finger over his mouth and nodding ... he was a bit tight, do you see? So I just put my finger over my mouth like him and I nodded just the same. Well now, it seemed sensible enough at the time do you see?'

I did see. It was a miracle Paddy remembered that evening at all.

The afternoon ambled on. Gunnar Holth won the steeplechase with Per Bjørn Sandvik's Whitefire, which displeased Rolf Torp, who was second. Per Bjørn, it appeared, had not come to the meeting: he rarely did on Thursdays, because it showed a bad example to his staff.

It was Lars Baltzersen who told me this, with warm approval in his voice. He himself, he said, had to leave his work only because he was Chairman, and all his employees understood. As one who had played lifelong truant at the drop of a starter's flag I found such noble standards a bit stifling, but one had to admire them.

Lars and I crossed the track and climbed the tower and looked down at the pond below. With its surface ruffled by the breeze it was far less peaceful than when I'd first seen it and just as brownly muddy as the day it gave up its dead. The swans and the ducks had gone.

'It will freeze soon,' Lars said. 'And snow will cover the racecourse for three or four months.'

'Bob Sherman is being buried today,' I said. 'In England.'

He nodded. 'We have sent a letter of regret to Mrs Sherman.'

'And a cheque,' I said; because his name too was on the list. He made a disclaiming movement with his hands but seemed genuinely pleased when I told him how much Emma had appreciated their kindness.

'I'm afraid we were all a little annoyed with her while she was here. She was so persistent. But perhaps it was partly because of her that we asked you to come. Anyway, I am glad she is not bitter about the way we tried to avoid her continual questions. She would have a right to be.'

'She isn't that sort of person.'

He turned his head to look at me. 'Do you know her well?' he asked.

'Only since all this started.'

'I regret the way we treated her,' he said. 'I think of it often. Giving her money does not buy us off.'

I agreed with him and offered no comfort. He looked away down the racecourse and I wondered if it was his guilty conscience that had driven him to persuade me back.

After the next race, a long distance flat race, we walked across together to the weighing room.

I said, 'You were in the officials' room that day when Bob Sherman poked his head in and could have seen the money lying on the floor.'

'That's right,' Lars said.

'Well . . . what was the question?'

He was puzzled. 'What question?'

'Everyone's statement to the police was the same. You all said "Bob Sherman came to the door asking some question or other." So . . . what was the question?'

He looked deeply surprised. 'It can't have had anything to do with his disappearance.'

'What was it?'

'I can't remember. Nothing of the slightest importance, I assure you, or of course we would have told the police.'

We rejoined Arne, and Lars asked him if he by any chance remembered what Bob had wanted. Arne looked just as surprised and said he had no idea, he'd been busy anyway and probably hadn't even heard. The racecourse manager however knew that he had known once, because it was he who had answered.

'Let me think,' he said, frowning. 'He came in . . . not his feet, just his head and shoulders. He looked down at the money, which was lying in front of him. I remember that distinctly. I told the police. But the question . . . it was nothing.'

I shrugged. 'Tell me if you ever remember?'

He said he would as if he thought it unlikely, but an hour later he sought me out.

'Bob Sherman asked if Mikkel Sandvik had already gone home, and I said I didn't know.'

'Oh.'

He laughed. 'Well, we did tell you it was nothing important.'

'And you were right.' I sighed resignedly. 'It was just a chance.'

At the end of the afternoon Lars took me up to his Chairman's room to give me the copies the police had provided of their Bob Sherman file. He stood in front of the big stove, a neat, substantial figure in his heavy, dark blue overcoat and ear-flapped astrakhan hat, blowing on his fingers.

'Cold today,' he said.

I thought I probably knew him better than anyone I'd met in Norway, but all the same I said, 'May I call to see you in your office?'

He'd heard about my appointments and smiled wryly at being included. 'Saturday, if you like. I'll be there until noon.'

Declining a pressing invitation from Arne to dine with him and Kari, I ate early at the Grand and went upstairs to do my homework.

The police had been painstaking, but the net result, as Lars had said, was nil.

A long and immensely detailed autopsy report, filled with medical terms I only half understood, concluded that the deceased had died of three overlapping depressed fractures of the skull. Unconsciousness would have been immediate. Death followed a few minutes later: the exact interval could not be specified. Immersion was subsequent to death.

The nylon rope found on the deceased had been unravelled strand by strand, and an analysis had indicated it to be part of a batch manufactured the previous spring and distributed during the summer to countless shops and ships' chandlers throughout greater Oslo.

The nylon rope found embedded in a concrete block in the Øvrevoll pond was of identical composition.

The cement block itself was a sort of sandbag in widespread use for sea-walling. The type in the pond was very common, and none of the contractors currently using it could remember having one stolen. The writer of the report added his own personal opinion that no contractor would ever miss one single bag out of hundreds.

The properties of the bag were such that its ingredients were crumbly when dry, but solidified like rock under water. The nylon rope had been tied tightly round the cement bag while it had still been dry.

Extensive inquiries had dug up no one who had heard or seen any activity round the pond on either the night of the deceased's disappearance or the night he had been removed from the water. The night watchman had proved a dead loss. There were lists of everything they had found in Bob Sherman's pockets and in his overnight bag. Clothes, watch, keys were all as they should be: it was papers I was interested in, and they, after a month submerged, were in a pretty pulpy state.

Passport and air ticket had been identified. Currency notes had been nearly all British: total value fifteen pounds sterling. There had been no Norwegian money to speak of, and certainly not five canvas bags of it.

The report made no mention of any papers or ruins of papers being found in the overnight bag. Nor of photographs: and photographic paper fared better than most under water.

I read everything through twice and drew no conclusions which the police hadn't. Bob Sherman had had his head bashed in, and later he'd been roped to a cement bag and dumped in the pond. By person or persons unknown.

By person or persons who were doing their damndest, also, to remain unknown.

I lifted the polythene-wrapped knife from my sponge case and propped it against the reading lamp; and immediately the slice down my chest took up throbbing where it had left off that morning. Why was it, I wondered irritably, that cuts only throbbed at night?

It was as well though to have that to remind me not to walk trustingly into hotel rooms or hail the first taxi that offered. Business had been meant in London, and I saw no safety in Oslo.

I smiled ruefully to myself. I was getting as bad as Arne at looking over my shoulder.

But there could be a lot more knives where that one came from.

CHAPTER TEN

In the morning I took the knife along to the police and told them how I'd come by it. The man in charge of the case, the same policeman who had been overseeing the dragging of the pond, looked at me in a sort of startled dismay.

'We will try to trace it, as you ask. But this knife is not rare. There are many knives of this kind. In English those words *Norsk Stål* on the blade merely mean Norwegian steel.'

His name was Lund. His air that of long-term policemen everywhere: cautious, watchful, friendly with reservations. It seemed to me that many policemen were only completely at ease with criminals; and certainly the ex-policemen who worked for the investigation branch of the Jockey Club always spoke of petty crooks more affectionately than of the general public.

Dedicated to catching them, policemen also admired criminals. They spoke the same language, used the same jargon. I knew from observation that if a crook and a detective who didn't know each other turned up at the same social gathering, they would unerringly seek each other out. Unless one of them happened to be chasing the other at that moment, they would get on well together; a fact which explained the apparently extraordinary shared holidays which occasionally scandalized the press.

Lund treated me with scrupulous fairness as a temporary colleague. I thanked him warmly for letting me use his files, and he offered help if I should need it.

I said at once that I needed a car with a driver I could trust, and could he recommend one.

He looked at the knife lying on his desk.

'I cannot lend you a police car.' He thought it over, then picked up a telephone, gave some Norwegian instructions, put down the receiver, and waited.

'I will ask my brother to drive you,' he said. 'He is an author. His books make little money. He will be pleased to earn some for driving, because he likes driving.'

The telephone buzzed and Lund evidently put forward his proposition. I gathered that it met with the author's approval because Lund asked when I would like him to start.

'Now,' I said. 'I'd like him to collect me here.'

Lund nodded, put down the receiver, and said, 'He will be here in half an hour. You will find him helpful. He speaks English very well. He worked once in England.'

I spent the half hour looking through mug-shots, but my London assailant was nowhere to be seen.

Lund's brother Erik was a bonus in every way.

He met me in the front hall with a vague distracted grin as if he had been waiting for someone else. A tallish man of about fifty-five, he had sparse, untidy blond hair, a shapeless old sports jacket, and an air of being totally disorganized: and he drove, I soon discovered, as if other cars were invisible.

He waved me from the police building to a small-sized cream Volvo waiting at the kerb. Dents and scratches of varying rust vintages bore witness to long and sturdy service, and the boot was held shut by string. Upon opening the passenger-side door I found that most of the interior was already occupied by a very large Great Dane.

'Lie down, Odin,' Erik said hopefully, but the huge dog understood no English, remained on his feet, and slobbered gently down my neck.

'Where first?' Erik asked. His English, as his brother had said, was splendid. He settled himself in the driver's seat and looked at me expectantly.

'What did your brother tell you?' I asked.

'To drive you around and if possible make sure no one bumps you off.' He said it as casually as if he'd been entrusted to see me on to the right train.

'What are you good at?' I said curiously.

148

'Driving, boxing and telling tales out of school.'

He had a long face, deeply lined round the eyes, smoother round mouth and chin: evidence of a nature more at home with a laugh than a scowl. In the course of the next few days I learnt that if it hadn't been for his highly developed sense of the ludicrous, he would have been a dedicated communist. As it was he held good radical left wing views, but found himself in constant despair over the humourlessness of his fellow travellers. He had worked on the gossip pages of newspapers throughout his youth, and had spent two years in Fleet Street; and he told me more about the people he was driving me to visit than I would have dug out in six weeks.

'Per Bjørn Sandvik?' he repeated, when I told him our first destination. 'The upright man of the oil fields?'

'I guess so,' I said.

He took off into the traffic without waiting for a gap. I opened my mouth and shut it again: after all, if his brother was trusting him to keep me alive, the least I could do was let him get on with it. We swung round some hair-raising corners on two wheels but pulled up unscathed outside the main offices of Norsk Oil Imports Ltd. The Great Dane licked his great chops and looked totally unmoved.

'There you are,' Erik said, pointing to an imposing double-door entrance into a courtyard. 'Through there, turn left, big entrance with pillars.'

'You know it?'

He nodded. 'I know most places in Oslo. And most people.' And he told me about his years on the newspapers.

'Tell me about Per Bjørn, then.'

He smiled. 'He is stuffy, righteous, and has given himself to big business. During the war he wasn't like that at all. When we were all young, he was a great fighter against the Nazis, a great planner and saboteur. But the years go by and he has solidified into a dull lump, like the living core of a volcano pouring out and dying to dry, grey pumice.'

'He must have some fire left,' I objected. 'To be the head of an oil company.'

He blew down his nostrils in amusement. 'All the oil companies in Norway are tied hand and foot by government regulations, which is as it should be. There is no room for private speculation. Per Bjørn can only make decisions within a small area. For anything above ordering new ashtrays he has to have permission from the government.'

'You approve of that?'

'Naturally.'

'What do you know about his family?' I asked.

His eyes glimmered. 'He married a thoroughly boring plain girl called Ragnhild whose dad just happened at that time to be the head man in Norsk Oil Imports.'

I grinned and climbed out of the car, and told him I would be half an hour at least.

'I brought a book,' he said equably, and pulled a tattered paperback of *The Golden Notebook* out of his jacket pocket.

The courtyard, tidily paved, had a stone-edged bed of frostbitten flowers in the centre and distinguished pale yellow buildings all round the edge. The main entrance to the left was imposing, and opposite, to the right, stood a similar entrance on a much smaller scale. The wall facing the entrance from the street was pierced with tall windows and decorated with shutters, and the whole opulent little square looked more like a stately home than an oil company's office.

It was, I found, both.

Per Bjørn's secretary fielded me from the main entrance, shovelled me up one flight of carpeted stairs and into his office, told me Mr Sandvik was still at a meeting but would not be long, and went away.

Although the building was old the head man's room was modern, functional, and highly Scandinavian, with thickly double-glazed windows looking down into the courtyard. On the wall hung a simple chart of a rock formation with layers labelled impermeable, source, permeable and reservoir; a list saying things like spudded Oct 71, plugged and abandoned Jan 72; and three brightly coloured maps of the North Sea, each of them showing a different aspect of the oil drilling operations going on there.

In each map the sea area was subdivided along lines of latitude and longitude into small squares which were labelled 'Shell', 'Esso', 'Conoco', and so on, but although I looked carefully I could see none marked Norsk Oil Imports.

The door opened behind me and Per Bjørn Sandvik came in, as pleasant and easy as ever and giving every impression of having got to the top without pushing.

'David,' he said in his high clear diction, 'sorry to keep you waiting.'

'Just looking at your maps,' I said.

He nodded, crossing to join me. 'We're drilling there . . . and there.' He pointed to two areas which bore an entirely different name. I commented on it, and he explained.

'We are part of a consortium. There are no private oil companies in Norway.'

'What did Norsk Oil Imports do before anyone discovered oil under the North Sea?'

'Imported oil, of course.'

'Of course.'

I smiled and sat down in the square armchair he indicated.

'Fire away,' he said, 'with the questions.'

'Did Bob Sherman bring you any papers or photographs from England?'

He shook his head. 'No. Lars asked us this on Tuesday. Sherman did not bring any papers for anyone.' He stretched out a hand towards his desk intercom. 'Would you like some coffee?'

'Very much.'

He nodded and asked his secretary to arrange it.

'All the same,' I said, 'he probably did bring a package of some sort with him, and he probably did pass it on. If anyone would admit to having received it we might be able to take it out of consideration altogether.'

He stared vaguely at his desk.

'For instance,' I said, 'if what he brought was straight pornography, it probably had nothing to do with his death.'

He looked up.

'I see,' he said. 'And because no one has said they received it, you think it did not contain pornography?'

'I don't know what it contained,' I said. 'I wish I did.'

The coffee arrived and he poured it carefully into dark brown crusty mugs.

'Have you discarded the idea that Bob Sherman was killed by whoever stole the money?'

'It's in abeyance,' I said, refusing the offered cream and sugar. 'Could you give me your impression of Bob Sherman as a man?'

He bunched his lips assessingly.

'Not over-intelligent,' he said. 'Honest, but easily influenced. A good rider, of course. He always rode well for me.'

'I gather Rolf Torp thought he rode a bad race for him that last day.'

Sandvik delicately shrugged. 'Rolf is sometimes hard to please.'

We drank the coffee and talked about Bob, and after a while I said I would like very much to meet Per Bjørn's son, Mikkel.

He frowned. 'To ask him questions?'

'Well ... some. He knew Bob comparatively well, and he's the one good contact I've not yet met.'

He didn't like it. 'I can't stop you, of course. Or at least, I won't. But he has been very upset by the whole affair, first by thinking his friend was a thief, and now more since he knows he was murdered.'

'I'll try not to worry him too much. I've read his short statement to the police. I don't expect to do much more than cover the same ground.'

'Then why bother him at all?'

After a pause to consider it, I said, 'I think I need to see him, to get the picture of Bob's visits complete.'

He slowly sucked his lower lip but finally made no more objections.

'He's at boarding school now,' he said. 'But he'll be home here for the afternoon tomorrow. If you come at three, he'll be here.'

'Here ... in your office?'

He shook his head. 'In my house. The other side of the courtyard.'

I stood up to go and thanked him for his time.

'I haven't been of much use,' he said. 'We've given you a pretty hopeless job.'

'Oh well . . .' I said, and told myself that things some-times broke if one hammered on long enough. 'I'll do my best to earn your money.'

He saw me to the top of the stairs and shook hands. 'Let me know if there's anything I can do.'

'I will,' I said. 'And thank you.'

I walked down the quiet stairs to the large empty hall. The only sounds of life seemed to come from behind a door at the back of the hall, so I walked over and opened it.

It led, I found, straight into the next door building, one dedicated not to front offices but to getting the paper work done. Even there, however, things were going at a gentle pace without any feeling of pressure, and in the doorways of the row of small offices stretch-ing away from me stood relaxed people in sweaters drinking coffee and smoking and generally giving no impression that commercial life was rushing by.

I retreated through the hall, through the courtyard, and back to Erik Lund. He withdrew his eyes from his Golden Notes as I climbed into his car and appeared to be wondering who I was.

Recognition of sorts awoke.

'Oh yes . . .' he said.

'Lunch, then?' I suggested.

He had few definite views on where to eat, but once we were installed in a decent restaurant he lost no time in ordering something he called *gravlaks*. The price made me wince on behalf of the racecourse, but I had some too, and it proved to be the most exquisite form of salmon, cured instead of smoked.

'Are you from Scotland Yard?' he asked after the last of the pink heaven had been dispatched.

'No. From the Jockey Club.'

It surprised him, so I explained briefly why I was there.

'What's all this about being bumped off, then?'

'To stop me finding out what happened.'

He gazed past me in thought.

'Makes my brother Knut a dumb cluck, doesn't it? No one's tried to get rid of *him*.'

'Knock down one policeman and six more pop up,' I said.

'And there aren't six more of you?' he asked dryly.

'The racing cupboard's pretty bare.'

He drank coffee thoughtfully. 'Why don't you give it up while you're still whole?'

'Natural bloody obstinacy,' I said. 'What do you know about Rolf Torp?'

'Rolf Torp the terror of the ski slopes or Rolf Torp who designs glass houses for pygmies?'

'Rolf Torp who owns racehorses and does something in mines.'

'Oh. Him.' He frowned, sniffed, and grimaced. 'Another goddam capitalist exploiting the country's natural resources for private gain.'

'Do you know anything about him personally?'

'Isn't that personal enough?'

'No.'

He laughed. 'You don't think money-grubbing says anything about a man's soul?'

'Everything any man does says something about his soul.'

'You wriggle out of things,' he said.

'And things out of people.'

'Well,' he said smiling, 'I can't actually tell you much about that Rolf Torp. For one thing I've never met him, and for another, capitalists make dull copy for gossip columns unless they're caught in bed with their secretaries and no pyjamas.'

Blue pictures for blackmail, I thought irrelevantly. Or black and white pictures for blackmail. Why not?

'Do you know anyone called Lars Baltzersen?' I asked.

'Sure. The Chairman of Øvrevoll? Every man's idea of a respectable pillar of society. Entertains ambassadors and presents prizes. Often a picture on the sports pages, always beside the man of the moment. Mind you, our Lars was a live wire once himself. Did a lot of motor racing, mostly in Sweden. That was before banking finally smothered him, of course.'

'Family?'

'Dutch wife, lots of solid children.'

I paid the bill and we strolled back to the car. Odin stared out of the front window with his huge head close to the glass and his eyes unblinking. Some people who stopped to try 'isn't-he-a-nice-boy' noises got a big yawn and a view down a cavernous throat.

Erik opened his door, gave the dog a shove and said, '*Fanden ta dig*.' The Dane shifted his bulk towards the back seat without taking offence, and the journey continued.

'What did Lars do in the war?'

'He wasn't here,' he said promptly. 'He was in London, reading the news in Norwegian on the radio.'

'He didn't tell me he'd lived in London.'

'He's quiet now. Another dead volcano. More pumice.'

Erik crossed some traffic lights three seconds after they turned red and genuinely didn't seem to hear six other motorists grinding their brake drums to screaming point. Odin gave him an affectionate nudge in the neck and Erik put out the hand he needed on the gear lever and fondled the huge wet nose.

He pulled up in front of a modern square-built glass and slab affair a mile out of the city centre, a far cry from Sandvik's architectural elegance.

'This is the address you gave me,' Erik said dubiously.

'Fine,' I said. 'Would you like to wait inside?'

He shook his head, though the afternoon was cold and rapidly growing dark. 'Odin gives off heat like a nuclear reactor and I don't like sitting in plastic lobbies being stared at.'

'OK.'

I left them to their companionship and rode a lift up to Rolf Torp's office, where again as I was early I was asked to wait. This time not in Torp's own office, but a small purpose-decorated room overflowing with useful handouts about 'Torp-Nord Associates'.

The walls here also were hung with diagrams of rock formations, charts of progress and maps showing areas being worked. These maps were not of the North Sea but of the mainland, with the thickest cluster of work-tags to the west of Oslo, in the mountains.

Someone had told me Rolf Torp's business was silver, but it wasn't or no longer chiefly. His associates had switched to titanium.

Before he finally turned up (at four twenty) for his four o'clock appointment I had learnt a good deal I didn't especially want to know about titanium. For example that it weighed only 0.163 lb per cubic inch and in alloy form could reach a tensile strength of 200,000 lb per square inch. Bully for titanium, I thought.

Rolf Torp was much like his product in tensile strength but couldn't match it for lightness. He made no effort to conceal that my visit was a nuisance, bursting into the waiting room saying, 'Come on, come on then. I can give you ten minutes, that's all,' and stomping off to his own office without waiting to see if I followed.

I did, of course. His office was much like Sandvik's: same type of furniture, fabrics and carpet, a reflection of prevailing style but no clue to the occupant. The walls here were dotted with framed photographs of various stages of metal production, and another large map with thumb tacks took pride of place.

'How do you mine titanium?' I asked, and sat in the visitors' chair without being invited. Irritably he took his own place behind half an acre of tidy desk and lit a cigarette.

'Like one?' he said belatedly, pushing a box towards me.

'No, thank you.'

He flicked a lighter and deeply inhaled the smoke.

'You don't find titanium lying around like coal,' he said. 'Are you sure you want to use your ten minutes on this?'

'Might as well.'

He gave me a puzzled look over the heavy black moustache, but seemed to find his own subject a lot less temper-disturbing than mine.

'Titanium is the ninth most common element on earth. It is found in ninety-eight per cent of rocks and also in oil, coal, water, plants, animals, and stars.'

'You can hardly dig it out of people.'

'No. It is mostly mined as a mineral called ilmenite . . . which is one third titanium.'

'Does your firm do the actual mining?'

He shook his head. 'We survey, do first drillings, advise and establish.'

I looked vaguely at the photographs on the walls.

'Apart from high speed aircraft, what's the stuff used for?'

He reeled off technical uses as if he'd been asked that one once or twice before. Towards the end, slowing down, he included paint, lipstick and smokescreens. There was little you couldn't do, it seemed, with the strength of the Titans.

'Did Bob Sherman bring you any photographs?'

I asked him casually without looking at him directly, but if it jerked him at all I couldn't tell, as he swept any involuntary movement into a quick gesture to flick off ash.

'No, he didn't.'

'Did he ask your advice about anything?'

'Why should he?'

'People do need advice sometimes,' I said.

He gave a laugh that was half a scowl. 'I gave him some. He didn't ask. I told him to ride races better or stay in England.'

'He didn't please you?'

'He should have won on my good horse. He went to sleep. He stopped trying to win, and he was beaten. Also he did not ride as I told him, all the way round.'

'Do you think someone bribed him to lose?'

He looked startled. For all his bad-tempered criticism it hadn't occurred to him, and to be fair, he didn't pounce on the idea.

'No,' he said heavily. 'He wanted to ride that horse in the Grand National. It started favourite and it won.'

I nodded. 'I saw the race.'

'That's right. Bob Sherman wanted to ride it, but I would have got someone else anyway. He rode it very badly.'

I imagined that any time Rolf Torp's jockey didn't win, he had automatically ridden badly. I stood up to go, which puzzled him again, and shook his hand.

'Coming here has been a waste of your time,' he said.

'Of course not . . . I'll let myself out.'

He didn't stop me. I closed his door and did a brief exploration. More offices. More bustle than at Sandvik's. More impression of work being done, but nothing so earthy as a lump of ore.

Erik was not parked out front where I had left him. I went through the big glass entrance doors, peered briefly into the darkness, and ignominiously retreated. One thing I did not plan to do was walk around at night alone, making everything easy for assassins.

After ten minutes I began to wonder if he'd simply forgotten about me and gone home, but he hadn't. The small cream Volvo returned at high speed and stopped outside in its own length. Its owner extricated himself from the quivering metal and strolled towards the building.

'Hullo,' he said, as I met him. 'Hope you haven't

been waiting. I had to get Odin's dinner. Forgot all about it.'

In the car, Odin loomed hungrily over my head, dribbling. Just as well, I thought, that he was about to be fed.

Erik returned us to the Grand at tar-melting speed and seemed disappointed that I hadn't wanted any longer journeys.

CHAPTER ELEVEN

The receptionists of the Grand considered me totally mad because I was insisting on changing my room every day, but they would have thought me even madder if I'd told them the reason. I asked them just to allocate me the last empty room, or if there were several, to give me a random choice at bed time. They did it with politely glazed eyes while I thankfully put my trust in unpredictability.

When Erik dropped me at the door and took his big friend home I telephoned to Arne and Kari and asked them to dinner.

'Come here,' Kari demanded warmly, but I said it was time I repaid their kindness, and after much demur they agreed to the Grand. I sat in the bar and read a newspaper until they arrived, and thought about growing old.

It was strange, but away from her chosen setting, Kari looked a different person. Not so young, not so domesticated, not so tranquil. This Kari, walking with assurance into the bar in a long black skirt and white ruffled shirt was the woman who designed interiors as a business. This Kari, wearing perfect make-up, diamonds in her ears and hair smoothly pinned up, looked at once cooler and more mature than the casual homegirl. When she put a smooth sweet-smelling cheek forward for a kiss and gave me a pretty look from under her lashes I found I both liked her less and wanted her more; both of which reactions were disconcerting and no good.

Arne was Arne, the antithesis of a chameleon, his personality so concretely formed that it retained its own shape whatever the environment. He swept foursquare into the bar and gave it a quick suspicious survey to make sure no one could listen at his shoulder.

'Hallo David,' he said, shaking my hand vigorously. 'What have you been doing all day?'

'Wasting time,' I said smiling, 'and wondering what to do next.'

We sat in a comfortable corner and drank (as for once it was the right hour on the right day) whisky.

Arne wanted to know what progress I had made.

'Not much,' I said. 'You might practically say none.'

'It must be very difficult,' Kari said sympathetically, with Arne nodding in agreement. 'How do you know what to look for?'

'I don't often look for things. I look at what's there.'

'All detectives look for things. Look for clues and follow trails. Of course they do.'

'And trudge up dead ends and find red herrings,' I said.

'Herrings are not red,' Kari said in puzzlement.

Fifty-seven varieties of herring in Norway, and not one of them red.

'A red herring is something that doesn't exist,' Arne said, but had to explain it again to her in Norwegian.

She laughed, but returned to her questions. 'How do you solve a crime?'

'Um . . . you think what you might have done if you'd been the crook, and then you look to see if that's what he did. And sometimes it is.'

'No one else solves crimes like David,' Arne said.

'Believe me,' I said. 'They do.'

'What do you think the crook did this time?' Kari asked.

I looked at her clear grey eyes, asking the question I couldn't answer without freezing the evening in its tracks.

'There's more than one,' I said neutrally. 'Emma Sherman saw two.'

We talked about Emma for a while. Arne had met her grandfather during his brief visit, and knew he had not been able to identify either of the intruders.

'And nobody knows what they were looking for,' Kari said thoughtfully.

'The men knew,' I said.

Arne's eyes stretched suddenly wide, which made a change from blinking. 'So they did,' he said.

'Of course they did,' she said. 'I don't see the point.'

'It isn't really a point. Only that someone somewhere does know what is missing. Or what was missing, because it may have been found now.'

Kari thought it over. 'Why do you think they didn't search the Shermans' house at once, as soon as they'd killed Bob Sherman? Why wait a month?'

Arne went back to blinking fit to bust, but he left it to me to answer.

'I think,' I said, 'it was because Bob Sherman was found, and whatever it was that was missing wasn't found with him.' I paused. 'Say Mr X kills Bob and dumps him in the pond, for a reason as yet unknown. Suppose this was after Bob delivered a package he had been bringing with him. Suppose also that Bob had opened the package and taken out some of the contents, but that Mr X did not discover this until after he'd killed Bob and put him in the pond. OK so far? So then he has to guess whether Bob had the missing contents in his pockets or his overnight bag, in which case they too are safely in the pond, or whether he passed them on to someone else, or even posted them home to himself in England, before he was killed. Short of getting Bob out of the pond, Mr X can't find out for certain, but the longer the missing contents don't turn up, the surer Mr X becomes that they are with Bob. Right. But then Bob is found, and the missing contents are still missing. So a search party is sent out to find out if Bob took them out of the package at home before he even left England, and Emma was unfortunate enough to choose just that moment to go back for some fresh clothes.'

Kari's mouth had slowly opened. 'Wow,' she said. 'And it seemed such a simple little question.'

'I told you,' Arne said. 'Give him one fact and he guesses the rest.'

'And a guess is all it is.' I smiled. 'I don't know why they took a month to start searching. Do you?'

Kari said 'But you must be right. It sounds so reasonable.'

'Like the earth is flat.'

'What?'

'Sounds reasonable until you know different.'

We went in to dinner. There was an orchestra playing, and dancing, and later, with the coffee, a singer. It was all too much in the end for Arne who stood up abruptly, said he needed some air, and made a compulsive dash for the door.

We watched his retreating back.

'Has he always been like that?' I asked.

'Always since I've known him. Though lately, perhaps, it has been worse. He used not to worry about bugging machines.'

'He used not to know they existed.'

'Well . . . that's true.'

'How did it start? His persecution complex, I mean.'

'Oh . . . the war, I suppose. When he was a child. I wasn't born until after, but Arne was a child then. His grandfather was shot as a hostage, and his father was in the resistance. Arne says he was always frightened when he was a child, but he wasn't always sure what he was frightened of. Sometimes his father sent him to run with messages and told him to be sure not to be followed. Arne says he was always terrified those times that he would turn round and find a big man behind him.'

'Poor Arne,' I said.

'He has been to psychiatrists,' Kari said. 'He knows . . . but he still can't help it.' She looked away from me, at the couples slowly circling on the square of polished floor. 'He can't bear dancing.'

After a few seconds I said, 'Would you like to?'

'I don't suppose he'd mind.'

She stood up without hesitation and danced with natural rhythm. She also knew quite well that I liked having her close: I could see it in her eyes. I wondered if she'd ever been unfaithful to Arne, or ever would be. I wondered about the age-old things. One can't help it, I find.

She smiled and moved forward until our bodies were touching at more points than not, and no woman ever did that unless she meant to. What we were engaged in from that moment on was an act of sex: upright, dancing, public and fully clothed, but an act of sex none the less. I knew theoretically that a woman could reach a vivid orgasm without actual intercourse, that in fact some could do it when all alone simply by thinking erotic thoughts, but I had never before seen it happen.

It happened to Kari because she wanted it to. Because she rubbed closely against me with every turn of the dance. Because I didn't expect it. Because I didn't push her off.

Her breathing grew slower and deeper and her eyes lost their brightness. Her mouth was closed, half smiling. Head up, neck straight, she looked more withdrawn and absent-minded than passionately aroused. Then quite suddenly her whole body flushed with heat, and behind her eyes and right through her very deep I was for almost twenty seconds aware of a gentle intense throbbing.

After that she took a great deep gulping breath as if her lungs had been cramped. Her mouth opened, the smile broadened, and she unplastered herself from my front.

Her eyes grew bright as stars, and she laughed into mine.

'Thank you,' she said.

She had finished with dancing. She broke away and walked back to the table, sitting down sociably as if nothing had happened. Oh thanks very much, I thought, and where does that leave me? Dealing with an unscratchable itch and without the later comfort of doing it on my own like she had, because I'd never found that much fun.

'More coffee?' I said. One had to say something, I

supposed. How about 'Damn your eyes you selfish little pig'?

'Thank you,' she said.

The waiter brought more coffee. Civilization won the day.

Arne returned looking windblown and a little happier. Kari put her hand on his with wifely warmth and understanding, and I remembered ironically that I had wondered if she were ever unfaithful to him. She was and she wasn't: the perfect recipe for having it both ways.

They left shortly afterwards, pressing me to spend another evening at their flat before I went home.

'See you on Sunday at Øvrevoll,' Arne said. 'If not before.'

When they had gone I collected my suitcase from the hall porter and took myself to the reception desk. There were five empty rooms to choose from, so I took a key at random and got myself a spacious double room with a balcony looking out towards the parliament building. I opened the well-closed double doors and let a blast from the Arctic play havoc with the central heating. Then I shut them again and went coldly to bed, and lay awake for a long time thinking about a lot of things but hardly at all about Kari.

Erik came to breakfast the next morning. He joined me with a grin, helped himself to half a ton of assorted pickled fish from the buffet, and ate as if there were no tomorrow.

'Where to?' he asked after two further bread rolls, four slices of cheese and several cups of coffee.

'Øvrevoll,' I said.

'But there's no racing today.'

'I know.'

'Well, if that's what you want, let's go.'

Odin, in a friendly mood, sat centrally with his rump wedged against the rear seat and his front paws and huge head burying the handbrake. When Erik gave him a nudge with his elbow the dog lifted his chin long enough for his master to release the wheels. A double act of long standing, it seemed.

The journey was a matter of staring death in the face, but we got there. The main gates of the racecourse stood open with various trade vans standing inside on the tarmac, so we simply drove in and stopped near the weighing room. Erik and Odin unfolded themselves and stretched their legs while I went on my short and abortive mission.

There were cleaners, a man and two women, in the weighing room building, and none of them spoke English. I went outside and cajoled Erik, the easiest task on earth, to do my talking.

He asked, listened, and passed on the bad news.

'They say Bob Sherman's saddle was here for a long time. In the changing room, on the peg nearest the corner.'

I had just looked all round the changing room. No saddles on any pegs and no trace of Bob Sherman's.

'They say it went at about the time the body was found in the pond. They don't know who took it.'

'That's that, then.'

We left the weighing room building and strolled the few yards to the racecourse rails. The morning was icy, the wind fresh, the trees sighing. Winter on the doorstep, snow on the way.

Down the sand track Gunnar Holth's string was starting a canter, and as we watched they came up fast towards us and swept past along to the winning post and round the top of the course where the pond lay. Paddy O'Flaherty in his brilliant woollen cap rode in front, giving a lead and setting the pace. With racing the next day, it was little more than a pipe-opener, and the string presently slowed to walk home.

'Next stop,' I said, 'is Gunnar Holth's stable.'

We drew up in the yard as the horses came back from the track, steaming like kettles under their rugs. Gunnar Holth himself jumped down from Sandvik's Whitefire, patted him vigorously, and waited for me to open the game.

'Morning,' I said.

'Morning.'

'Can we talk?'

He nodded resignedly, led Whitefire off into the barn, returned, jerked his head towards his bungalow and opened his door. Erik this time chose to stay in the car for which Gunnar Holth, having spotted Odin, looked thankful.

'Coffee?'

Same orange pot on the stove. Same coffee, I dared say.

'I am looking for Bob Sherman's saddle,' I said.

'His saddle? Didn't he leave it behind? I heard he did . . .'

'I wondered if you knew who had it. I want to find it . . . It belongs to his wife now.'

'And saddles are worth money,' he said, nodding. 'I haven't seen it. I don't know who has it.'

I asked him obliquely twice more in different ways but in the end was satisfied that he knew nothing helpful.

'I'll ask Paddy,' I said. But Paddy too had few ideas.

'It was there, so it was, until they pulled the poor devil out of the water. Sure I saw it there myself on Grand National day. Then the next meeting, on the Thursday, it was gone.'

'Are you sure of that?'

'As sure as I'm standing here.'

I said mildly, 'Why? Why are you so sure?'

His eyes flickered. 'Well . . . as to that, now . . .'

'Paddy,' I said. 'Come clean.'

'Uh . . .'

'Did you take it?'

'No,' he said positively. 'That I did not.' The idea apparently outraged him.

'What, then?'

'Well now then, do you see, he was after being a real mate of mine, Bob was . . . Well I was sure now, in my own mind, that he would want me to do it . . .' He ran down and stopped.

'To do what?'

'Look now, it wasn't stealing or anything like that.'

'Paddy, what did you do?'

'Well . . . there was my helmet, see, and there was his helmet, hanging there with his saddle. Well now, my helmet had a strap broken, so it had, and Bob's was there, good as new, so I just swapped them over, do you see . . .'

'And that was on Grand National day?'

'That's right. And the next race day, after Bob was found, his saddle was gone. And my helmet was gone with it, do you see.'

'So Bob's helmet is . . . here?'

'It is so. In my box, now, under my bunk.'

'Will you lend it to me for a while?'

'Lend it?' He was surprised. 'I thought you'd be taking it away altogether, now, as by rights it belongs to his missus.'

'I expect she'd be glad for you to keep it.'

'It's a good helmet, so it is.'

He went and fetched it and handed it over, an ordinary regulation jockey helmet with a chin strap. I thanked him, told him I'd let him have it back, waved goodbye to Gunnar Holth, and set off on the perilous passage back to central Oslo.

In between bounces I pulled out the padded lining of the helmet and looked underneath. No photographs, papers or other missing objects. Nothing but black regulation padding. I put it back into place.

'No good?' Erik said sympathetically, peering round Odin.

'All stones have to be turned.'

'Which stone next, then?'

'Lars Baltzersen.'

The route to his bank lay past the front door of the Grand, so I stopped off there and left Bob Sherman's helmet with the hall porter, who was already sheltering my newly re-packed suitcase. He told me he would take good care of anything I left with him. I left three ten-kroner notes with him, and with a smile he took good care of those.

Lars had almost given up.

'Thought you'd changed your mind,' he said, showing me into his office.

'Had to make a detour,' I said, apologizing.

'Well, now that you are here . . .' He produced a bottle of red wine and two small glasses from a discreet cupboard, and poured for us both.

His room, like Sandvik's and Torp's, was standard Scandinavian, modern vintage. Commerce, I supposed, must be seen to be up to date, but as a source of personal information these interiors were a dead loss.

No maps on his walls. Pictures of houses, factories, office blocks, distant ports. When I asked him, he told me that his banking firm was chiefly concerned with the financing of industrial projects.

'Merchant banking,' he said. 'Also we run a building scheme very like an English building society. Except that here, of course, we lend at a much lower interest rate, so that mortgages are cheaper.'

'Don't the investors complain?'

'They get almost the same return as British investors. It is just that Norwegian societies don't have to pay big taxes. It is the tax which puts up the British mortgage rate.'

He told me that there were many small private banks in Norway running building schemes, but that his own was one of the largest.

'There is a terrible shortage of building land round Oslo,' he said. 'Young couples find it very difficult to find a house. Yet far out in the country there are whole farms standing empty and derelict. The old people have died or are too weak to work the fields, and the young people have left the hard life and gone to the towns.'

'Same everywhere,' I said.

He liked wooden houses best, he said. 'They breathe.'

'How about fire?' I asked.

'It always used to be a fearful risk. Cities were burnt sometimes. But now our fire services are so fast, so expert, that I am told if you want to burn your house for the insurance, you have to hose it down with petrol. Otherwise the fire will be put out at the first puff of smoke.'

We drank the wine and Lars smoked a cigarette. I asked him about his years in London and about his motor racing in Sweden, but he seemed to have no interest left in them.

'The past is over,' he said. 'It is banking and Øvrevoll which I think about now.'

He asked me if I yet knew who killed Bob Sherman. Such faith in the way he put it.

'Not yet,' I said. 'What's my limit on expenses?'

I couldn't pin him to an amount. It seemed that if I succeeded there was no limit. If I failed, I had already overspent.

'Have you any ideas?' he asked.

'Ideas aren't enough.'

'You need proof as well, I suppose.'

'Mm . . . have to make like a poacher.'

'What do you mean?'

'Set traps,' I said. 'And keep my feet out of other poachers' snares.'

I stood up to go. He too said my visit had been a waste of time because he had told me nothing useful.

'You never know,' I said.

Erik and I had lunch in a café not far from his brother's headquarters because I wanted to call in afterwards to see him. He would be off duty at two o'clock, he said on the telephone; if that would do, he could see me before he went home.

Erik spent most of lunch explaining with chapter and verse why all revolutions ended in gloom because all revolutionaries were incapable of humour.

'If the activists knew how to be funny,' he said, 'the workers would have ruled the world long ago.'

'Jokes should be taught in school,' I suggested.

He looked at me suspiciously. 'Are you taking the micky?'

'I thought that was the point.'

'Oh God, yes.' He laughed. 'So it is. What makes you spend your life detecting?'

'Curiosity.'

'Killed the cat.'

'Shut up.'

'Sorry,' he said, grinning. 'Anyway, you're still alive. How did you train for it? Is there a school for detectives?'

'Don't think so. I went to university. Tried industry, didn't like it. Didn't want to teach. Liked going racing ... so got a job going racing.'

'That's as smart a canter over the course as I've ever heard, and as a gossip columnist I've heard a lot. What did you read at which university?'

'Psychology at Cambridge.'

'Ah-hah,' he said. 'Ah absolutely *Hah*.'

He came with me up to Knut's office, leaving Odin

179

in charge of the car. Knut was tired after an apparently frustrating spell of duty, yawning and rubbing his eyes when we walked in.

'I am sorry,' he said. 'But I have been awake since two o'clock this morning.' He shook his head to clear it. 'Never mind. How can I help you?'

'Not in detail today. Tell me if your terms of reference would let you catch a rabbit if I enticed one out of a hole.' I turned to Erik. 'Explain to him. If I set a trap, can he help me to spring it? Is he allowed to, and would he personally want to?'

The brothers consulted in their own language, Knut neat, restrained, over-tired, and Erik with undisciplined gestures, bohemian clothes and wild, wispy hair. Erik was older, but in him the life force still flowed with generous vigour.

In the end they both nodded. Knut said, 'As long as it is not against the regulations, I will help.'

'I'm very grateful.'

He smiled faintly. 'You are doing my work.'

He collected his coat and cap and came down to the street with us. His car, it appeared, was along with Erik's in the side road running down beside a small railed public garden.

Erik's car was a centre of attention.

About ten feet away from it, ranged round in a semi-circle, stood about a dozen children and one uncertain looking policeman. His face changed thankfully at the sight of Knut, and he saluted and began to shift his anxiety on to someone else.

Erik translated for me, looking puzzled.

'One of the children says a man told her not on any account to go near my car. He told her to run home as fast as she could.'

I looked at the car. Odin was not facing out of the front window as usual, but out of the back and he was looking down, not interestedly at the crowd. Something in the great dog's world seemed wrong to him. He was standing rigidly. Much too tense. And the boot was no longer tied up with string.

'Oh Christ,' I said. 'Get those children out of here. Make them run.'

They simply stared at me and didn't move. But they hadn't been near the Old Bailey in London on 8 March 1973.

'It could be a bomb,' I said.

181

CHAPTER TWELVE

The children recognized the word but of course they didn't believe it. The people in London hadn't believed it until the flying glass ripped their faces.

'Tell them to run,' I said to Knut.

He decided to take it seriously, even if it were a false alarm. He said something unequivocal to the policeman, and he grabbed hold of Erik's arm.

He knew his brother. He must have loved him more than most. He grabbed him tight just as Erik took his first step towards the car, saying 'Odin,' half under his breath.

They more or less fought. Knut wouldn't let go and Erik grew frantic. Knut put a lock on Erik's arm which would have arrested a twenty stone boxer with a skinful, and Erik's face crumpled into despair. The two of them, step by contested step, retreated from the car.

The policeman had chased the children away to a safe distance and was yelling to approaching pedestrians to get behind cover. No one paid any attention to me, so I nipped smartly along the pavement, put my hand on the handle, wrenched the door open, and sprinted.

Even then the wretched dog didn't come out at once. It took a screeching whistle from Erik to get results, and Odin came bounding after me down the pavement as if it were playtime.

The bomb went off just as he drew level, twenty feet from the car. The blast slammed us both down in a heap, hitting like a fierce blow in the back, knocking all breath out, leaving one limp, weak, and shaken.

Not a big bomb by Irish standards. But this one had presumably not been meant to destroy the neighbourhood. Just the occupants of a car. Two men and a dog.

Knut helped me to my feet and Erik took hold of Odin's collar, kneeling down and patting him solicitously. Odin slobbered all over him, as good as new.

'That was stupid,' Knut said.

'Yes,' I said.

'Are you hurt?'

'No.'

'You deserve to be.'

'It might not have gone off for hours.'

'It might have gone off while you were beside it.'

Erik's car was gutted. Windows blown out, interior torn to shreds, boot burst wide open. I picked splinters of glass out of the hair on the back of my head and asked him if it was insured.

'I don't know,' he said vaguely. He rubbed his arm where Knut had locked it. 'Knut wanted me to wait for an expert to come to see if it was a bomb, and if it was, to dismantle it.'

'Knut was quite right.'

'He didn't stop you.'

'I'm not his brother. He had his hands full with you, and the bomb probably had my name on it in the first place.'

'What a bloody awful way to die.' He stood up and grinned suddenly, his whole face lighting up. 'Thanks anyway,' he said. Which was pretty generous, considering the state of his Volvo.

Once the fireworks were over the children came back, staring at the wreck with wide eyes. I asked Knut to find the little girl who'd been told to run home, and he said he'd already sent his policeman to bring her.

Apart from the car, there was little damage. The windows had been broken in a severe-looking building on the far side of the road, but neither the railings nor the shivering bushes in the little public garden nearest the Volvo seemed to have suffered. Cars parked several yards away fore and aft were slightly scratched with glass splinters but otherwise undamaged. If the bomb had gone off while we had been driving along a busy street, there would have been a lot more mess.

The little girl was blonde, solemn, hooded and zipped into a red anorak, and accompanied now by a scolding older child of about thirteen who had fallen down on the job of looking after her and was busy justifying herself. Knut, as with the boy on the racecourse, won the smaller girl's confidence by squatting down to her level and chatting along quietly.

I leant against the railings and felt cold, and watched Erik smoothing Odin's sand-coloured skin over and over, seeing him dissipate an overwhelming build-up of tension in small, self-controlled gestures. Odin himself seemed to be enjoying it.

Knut stood up, holding the little girl's hand.

'Her name is Liv. She is four. She lives about half a mile away and she was playing in the park with her big sister. She came out of the gate down there and walked up the road here. Her sister had told her not to, but Liv says she doesn't do what her sister says.'

'The sister's too damn bossy,' Erik said unexpectedly. 'Little Fascist.'

'Liv says there was a man cutting some string at the back of the car and the big dog looking at him out of the window. She stopped to watch. She was behind the man. He didn't see her or hear her. She says he took something out of his coat and put it inside the boot, but she didn't see what shape it was. She says the man tried to shut the back of the car, but it wouldn't shut. Then he tried to tie the string where it had been before, but it was too short because he had cut it. He put the string in his pocket, and that was when he saw Liv. He told her to go away, but she seems to be a child who does the opposite of what she's told. She says she went up to the car and looked through the side window at the dog, but the dog went on looking out of the back.

Then the man shook her and told her to run home at once and not to play near the car. Then he went away.'

Knut looked at the small crowd of children beginning to cluster again round Liv.

'She is one of those children who draws others to her. Like now. They came out of the park to join her, and she told them about the man cutting the string and trying to tie the boot shut again. It was that which interested her most, it seemed. Then my policeman came along, on his way to start his afternoon duty, and he asked the children why they were standing there.'

'Then we came?'

'Right.'

'Has Liv said what the man looked like?'

'Big, she said. But all men are big to little girls.'

'Could she see his hair?'

Knut asked her. She answered. Knut said, 'He was wearing a woollen cap, like a sailor.'

'What did his eyes look like?'

Knut asked. Her little voice rose clear, high, definite, and all the children looked interested.

'He had yellow eyes. Sharp, like a bird.'

'Did he have gloves?'

Knut asked. 'Yes,' he reported.

'What sort of shoes?'

Back came the answer: big, soft, squashy shoes, like on a boat.

Children were the best witnesses on earth. Their eyes saw clearly, their memories were accurate, and their impressions weren't interpreted by probability or prejudice. So when Liv added something which made Knut and Erik and the older children laugh, I asked what she'd said.

'She must have been mistaken,' Knut said.

'What did she say?'

'She said he had a butterfly on his neck.'

'Ask her what sort of butterfly,' I said.

'It's too late for butterflies,' Knut said patiently. 'Too cold.'

'Ask her what it was like,' I urged.

He shrugged, but he asked. The reply surprised him, because Liv described it with sharp positive little nods. She knew she'd seen a butterfly.

Knut said, 'She says it was on the back of his neck. She saw it because his head was bent forward. It was between his woolly cap and his collar and it didn't move.'

'What colour?'

He consulted. 'Dark red.'

'Birth mark?'

'Could be,' he agreed. He asked her one or two more questions and nodded to me. 'I should think so,' he said. 'She says it had two wings lying open flat, but one was bigger than the other.'

'So all we need now is a big man with yellow eyes and a butterfly birthmark.'

'Or a small man,' Erik said, 'With the sun in his eyes and a dirty neck.'

'No sun,' I said. The iron grey sky pressed down like an army blanket, without warmth. The shivers in my gut, however, had little to do with the cold.

Knut sent his policeman to fetch experts in fingerprints and explosives and took the names and addresses of half the children. The crowd of watchers grew a bit, and Erik restively asked Knut when he could go home.

'What in?' said Knut pointedly, so we stamped around on the pavement for nearly another hour.

With darkness we returned to Knut's office. He took his coat and cap off and looked wearier than ever.

I borrowed his telephone and rang the Sandviks to apologize for my non-arrival. I spoke, in the event, to Mrs Per Bjørn, who explained that her husband was out.

'Mikkel did wait for you, Mr Cleveland,' she said in heavily accented English. 'But after one hour he went away with some friends.'

'Please tell him I'm very sorry.'

'I will tell him.'

'What school does he go to?'

'College of Gol,' she said, and then thought better of it. 'But I do not think that my husband would like . . .'

I interrupted, 'I just wondered if I could see him this evening before he goes back.'

'Oh . . . He is going straight back with the friends. They will have started by now.'

'Never mind, then.'

I put down the receiver. Knut was organizing coffee.

'Where is the College of Gol?' I asked.

'Gol is in the mountains, on the way to Bergen. It is a holiday ski town, in the winter. The college is a boarding school for rich boys. Are you going all the way out there to see Mikkel Sandvik? He knows nothing about Bob Sherman's death. When I saw him he was very upset about his friend dying like that. He would have helped me if he could.'

'How upset? Crying?'

'No, not crying. Pale. Very shocked. Trembling. *Upset.*'

'Angry?'

'No. Why should he be angry?'

'People are usually furious when their friends are murdered. They feel like strangling the murderer, don't they?'

'Oh, that,' he said, nodding. 'No, I don't remember that Mikkel was especially angry.'

'What is he like?' I asked.

'Just a boy. Sixteen. No, seventeen. Intelligent, but not outstanding. Average height, slim build, light brown hair, good manners. Nothing unusual about him. A nice boy. A little nervous, perhaps.'

We sat around and drank the coffee. Odin had some too, in a bowl, with a lot of sugar. Erik had recovered from the nearness of losing his companion and was beginning to think about his car.

'I'll need to hire one, I suppose,' he said. 'For driving David around.'

'You're not driving David any more,' Knut said positively.

'Of course I am.'

'No,' said Knut. 'It's too dangerous.'

There was a small meaningful silence. Anyone in future who drove me must be presumed to be at risk. Which put me high in the unpopularity stakes as a passenger.

'I'll manage,' I said.

Erik said, 'Where do you plan to go?'

'Tomorrow, to call on Sven Wangen, then to Øvrevoll. On Monday . . . I don't know yet.'

'I could do with another of those Grand breakfasts,' he said.

'No,' said Knut. They argued heatedly in private, and Knut lost. He turned a grim face and a compressed mouth to me. 'Erik says he never leaves a job unfinished.'

Erik grinned and rubbed a hand over his straggly blond hair. 'Only dull ones.'

Knut said crossly, 'I suppose you realize that one of these attempts will be successful? Two have failed, but . . .'

'Three,' I said. 'Someone tried to drown me in the fjord the first day I came to Norway.'

I told them about the black speedboat. Knut frowned and said, 'But that could have been an accident.'

I nodded. 'At the time, I thought it was. I don't think

so any longer.' I got up to pour myself some more hot strong black coffee. 'I do rather agree with you that they will succeed in the end, but I don't know what to do about it.'

'Give up and go back to England,' Knut said.

'Would you?'

He didn't answer. Nor did Erik. There wasn't an answer to give.

Knut sent me back in a police car to the Grand, where as the bar was again shut (Saturday) I ate an early dinner, collected my suitcases and Bob Sherman's helmet from the porter, picked a room at random from those available, and spent the evening upstairs alone, sitting in an armchair and contemplating several unpalatable facts.

Such as, there was a limit to luck and little girls.

Such as, next time they could use a rifle, because sniping was the surest way of killing.

Such as, tomorrow if I went to the races I would be scared to death the whole bloody day.

Not much comfort in the hope that old yellow eyes with the birthmark might be a lousy shot.

There were various other thoughts, chiefly that somewhere there existed a particular way of discovering who had killed Bob Sherman, and why. There had to be such a way, for if there wasn't, no one would need to kill me. Knut hadn't found it. Maybe he had looked the solution in the face and not recognized it, which was easy enough to do. Maybe I had, also, but could be expected to understand later what I had heard or seen.

Yellow eyes must have followed Erik's car, I thought. Erik's breakneck driving and red light jumping made it exceedingly unlikely that anything bar a fire engine could have tailed us to Øvrevoll: but then I'd considerately returned to the Grand to dump the helmet, and made it easy for a watcher to pick us up again.

I hadn't spotted a follower, nor had Erik. But our trip to Baltzersen's and from there to where we parked for lunch had been comparatively short and, in retrospect, almost legal. Anyone risking a couple of head-on crashes could have kept us in sight.

Yellow eyes was the man who had attacked Emma; and it seemed likely that the man who kicked her grandfather was the man who'd tried to knife me. Both, it seemed to me, were mercenaries, paid to do a violent job but not the instigators. They hadn't the aura of principals.

To my mind there were at least two others, one of whom I knew, one or more I didn't. To bring out the unknown, I had to bamboozle the known. The big snag was that when it came to setting traps, the only bait at present available was myself, and this cheese could find itself eaten if it wasn't extremely careful.

It was easy to see that to bring out the big boys, yellow eyes and brown eyes would have to be decoyed away while at the same time a situation needing instant action was temptingly arranged elsewhere. How to do it was another matter. I stared at the carpet for ages and came up with nothing foolproof.

I wished there was a way of knowing what Bob Sherman had been bringing to Norway. Unlikely to be straight pornography, because Bob had told Paddy O'Flaherty that he, Bob, had been conned. If he had opened the packet and found that it did not contain ordinary pornography, he might well have thought that.

Suppose . . . he had opened the packet and reckoned he was not being paid enough for what he was carrying.

Suppose . . . he had removed something from the packet, meaning to use it to up the stakes.

But . . . he couldn't have used it, because, if he had, the enemy would have known he had taken it, and would not have killed him without getting it back.

So suppose . . . simply opening the packet and seeing the contents was in itself a death warrant.

Suppose . . . the enemy killed him for knowing the contents, and only discovered afterwards that he had removed some of them.

It came back to that every time.

So . . . what the *hell* was in that packet?

Start another way.

When had he opened the packet?

Probably not at home. Emma had seen him put it in

193

his overnight bag so as not to risk forgetting it. Yellow eyes and friend had subsequently smashed the place up looking for things from it, and hadn't found any. So it seemed reasonable to suppose that he had set off from home with the envelope intact.

He had had all day at Kempton races. Time enough if he'd urgently wanted to open it: but if he'd felt like that, he'd already had it available all night.

Not much time at Heathrow between arriving from Kempton and boarding the aeroplane. Hardly the opportunity for an impulsive bit of snooping.

He had turned up at Gunnar Holth's an hour or so later than expected. So he could have done his lethal bit of nosey-parkering either on the flight or in the first hour after he'd landed.

On the flight, I thought, was most likely of all.

A couple of drinks under his belt, an hour or so to while away, and a packet of blue pictures temptingly to hand.

Open the packet and see . . . what?

Suppose he had had perhaps half an hour before landing to come up with the idea of demanding a larger freight fee. Suppose he took something out of the envelope and hid it . . . where had he hidden it?

Not in his pockets or his overnight bag. Perhaps in his saddle, but doubtful, because for one thing his racing saddle was tiny, and for another he'd ridden three races on it the following day.

Not in his helmet: no papers or photographs lurked inside the padded headband.

Which left one unaccounted-for hour, during which he could have left any object at the reception desk of any hotel in Oslo, with a request to keep it for him until he returned.

In one hour he could have hidden something anywhere.

I sighed. It was hopeless.

I stood up, stretched, unpacked a few things, undressed, brushed my teeth.

Bob's helmet lay on my bed. I picked it up and dangled it by the chin strap as I pulled back the quilt and pushed up the pillows as a back-rest for reading before sleep. Sitting between the sheets I turned the helmet idly over in my hands, scarcely looking at it, thinking about Bob and the last day he'd worn it.

I thought seriously about wearing it myself to Øvrevoll to protect my head, and buying a bullet-proof vest besides. I thought ungenerous thoughts about Emma's husband because I too could still die for what he'd done.

No papers. No photographs. I pulled the soft black padding out again. Nothing, still nothing tucked behind it.

In the crown there was just the small round centre-piece of black-covered padding suspended by straps fixed into the shell itself. A marvellous piece of engineering, designed to prevent a man falling on his nut at thirty miles an hour off a galloping horse from bashing his skull in. The central suspended piece of padding shielded the top of the head and stopped it crashing into the shell itself at concussion speed.

Underneath the central piece of padding there was no room at all for any papers or photographs or anything out of magazine-sized packets. I put my hand below it, just to make sure.

And there, in the roof of his helmet, Bob had left the key.

Literally, the key.

I felt it there with complete disbelief.

Fixed to the hard outer casing by two crossed strips of sellotape, unseen until one deliberately pushed the central piece of padding sideways out of position, was a key.

I unstuck it from the helmet and pulled off the sticky tape. It was a yale-type key, but with a small black tag bonded on instead of the usual round metal thumb plate. A small white number, C14, was stamped on the black plastic on the side which had been against the helmet's wall. The key itself, at first, second, third glance, had been unnoticeable: and Bob certainly could have ridden his races with it firmly and invisibly in place.

C14.

It looked like a locker key. Very like those from the left-luggage lockers of any big airport or railway station in the world. Nothing at all to show to which city, country or continent it belonged.

I thought.

If the key had been in the package, one would have expected it to be of extreme importance. Vital enough to be worth dragging the pond for, when it was found to be missing. Or searching for at once in the house in England.

The men searching the house in England had specifically mentioned papers. They had been looking for papers, not a key.

So, suppose Bob had left the papers somewhere in a locker, and this was the key to it.

Much easier. It cut out New York, Nairobi and outer Mongolia and narrowed the search to most of southern England or anywhere in Oslo.

The harmless-looking little key promised to be everything I needed. I closed my hand over it, with an illogical instinct to hide it, to keep it safe.

Bob too must have felt like that. The care with which he'd hidden it revealed the strength of his instinct. And he hadn't known at the time how true that instinct had been.

Smiling at myself I nevertheless followed his example.

There was in my suitcase a fresh unopened dressing for the cut on my chest, thoughtfully provided by Charles Stirling in case I needed it: but since the intermittent throbbing had faded to an intermittent itch, I'd left his original handiwork undisturbed.

Laying the key on the bedside table I pulled off the old dressing to take a look: and dark, dry and healthy, the slit was healing fast.

I fetched the new plaster and stuck it on, with Bob Sherman's precious key snug inside it against my skin.

CHAPTER THIRTEEN

Erik came to breakfast looking almost as depressed as the freezing wet day outside. He brought two plates heaped like the Matterhorn over from the buffet, sat opposite me, and toyed with the foothills.

'Did you sleep well?' he asked.

'No.'

'Nor did I. Kept hearing the bang of that bloody bomb.' He looked at the smoked fish I had acquired before his arrival. 'Aren't you eating?'

'Not madly hungry.'

He raised a grin. 'The condemned man syndrome?'

'Thanks.'

He sighed, adjusted his mind to the task and began proving his stomach was as big as his eyes. When both plates were empty of all but a trace of oil and six dorsal fins he patted his mouth with a napkin and resurfaced to the dangerous Sunday.

'Are you seriously going to the races?' he said.

'Don't know yet.'

'I didn't bring Odin today. Left him with a

neighbour.' He drank his coffee. 'I hired a bigger Volvo. A fast one. Here's the bill.' He dug in his pocket and produced a receipt.

I took out my wallet and paid him. He didn't say leave it until later.

A party of English racing people came into the restaurant in ones and twos and sat together at a table near the window. I knew most of them: a top amateur jump rider, a pro from the flat, an assistant trainer, an owner and his wife. When they'd chosen their food and begun to eat I drifted over to them and pulled up a chair.

'Hi,' they said. 'How's things?'

Things, meaning mostly their chances that afternoon, were relaxedly discussed, and after a while I asked the question I had joined them for.

'Remember the weekend Bob Sherman disappeared? Did any of you happen to come over with him on the same flight?'

The top amateur rider had. Glory be.

'Did you sit next to each other?'

He explained delicately that he had travelled first class, Bob tourist.

'But,' he said, 'I gave him a lift into Oslo in my taxi.'

'Where did you drop him?'

'Oh ... here. I was staying here, but he was going on to that trainer feller he rode for. He thanked me for the ride ... and I think he said he would catch the Lijordet tram if there was one. Anyway, I remember him standing on the pavement with his bag and saddle and stuff. But does it matter? After all, he rode next day, all right.'

'Was the flight on time?'

'Don't remember that it wasn't.'

I asked a few more questions, but the amateur remembered nothing else of much significance.

'Thanks anyway,' I said.

'Hope you get whoever did it,' he said. He smiled. 'I expect you will.'

If he didn't get me, I thought with a twinge, and went back to collect Erik.

'Where first?'

'All the railway stations.'

'All the *what*?'

'The nearest railway station,' I amended.

'Whatever for?'

'I want a time-table.'

'They have them here at the hotel desk.'

I grinned at him. 'Which is the nearest station?'

He said doubtfully, 'The Østbanen, I suppose.'

'Off we go, then.'

He shook his head in exasperation, but off we went.

From the Østbanen, I discovered, trains ran through Gol on the line to Bergen. Trains ran also to Lille-hammer, Trondheim, and the Arctic circle. Østbanen was the main long-distance terminus in Oslo.

It had left-luggage lockers and it even had a C14.

But the locker was empty, the key was in the open door, and the tag was different.

I took time-tables which included Gol, where Mikkel Sandvik's school was.

One never knew.

'What now?' Erik said.

'The other railway stations,' I said, and we went there, but without finding any matching black tags.

'Where else would you find lockers like those?'

'Besides railway stations? At the airport. In factories, offices, schools. Lots of places.'

'Available to a foreign traveller at eight-thirty on a Saturday evening.'

'Ah . . . Fornebu. Where else?' Where else indeed. 'Shall we go there?'

'Later,' I said. 'After Sven Wangen.'

Erik objected. 'He lives in the opposite direction, further out than the racecourse.'

'All the same,' I said. 'Sven Wangen first.'

'You're the boss.'

He looked carefully several times in the driving mirror as we set off, but said he was sure we were not being followed. I believed him. Nothing could have stayed with Erik when he was really trying.

'Tell me about Sven Wangen,' I said.

He pursed his mouth in much the same disapproving way that Arne had.

'His father was a collaborator,' he said.

'And no one forgets it?'

He sniffed. 'Officially, the past is past. But after the war, the collaborators didn't thrive. If some town wanted a bridge built or a school, for instance, it would happen that an architect or a builder who had worked well with the Nazis would just not be the one to get the contract.'

'But Sven Wangen's father was already rich . . . from shipping.'

He looked at me sideways while taking a sharp turn to the left and missed a lamp post by millimetres.

'Arne Kristiansen told me,' I said.

'Inherited wealth is immoral,' Erik said. 'All estates should be distributed among the masses.'

'Especially the estates of collaborators?'

He grinned. 'I suppose so.'

'Was the father like the son?' I asked.

Erik shook his head. 'A hard-headed greedy businessman. He made a lot of money out of the Nazis.'

'Surely that was patriotic of him?'

Erik wouldn't have it. 'He did nothing for his fellow-countrymen. He made money only for himself.'

'The father destroyed the son,' I said.

'Destroyed him?' He shook his head. 'Sven Wangen is an overpowering boor who always gets his way. He's nowhere near destroyed.'

'He's an empty person. Because of his father, I shouldn't think he ever had a chance to be normally liked, and people who are spurned for no fault of their own can become terribly aggressive.'

He thought it over. 'Guess you may be right. But I still don't like him.'

Sven Wangen lived in the style to which he had been born in a huge country house built mostly of wood, partly of stone. Even on a cold wet early winter morning it looked neat, clean and prosperous. Everything growing was sharply clipped into geometric precision, a regimentation totally uncongenial to Erik's casual, generous and untidy mind. He stared around in distaste, his give-everything-to-the-masses expression much in evidence.

'All this for two people,' he said. 'It's wrong.'

The place oppressed me as well, but for a different reason. There were too many windows all looking with black eyes towards the car. If I got out and stood away from its protection I would be a sitting target for anyone in that house with a gun.

Erik got out of the car. I had to force myself to follow him.

And of course, no one shot. If I'd really thought they would I wouldn't have gone. But it was one thing telling myself that Sven Wangen wasn't going to kill me on his own doorstep and another getting my nerves to believe it. Something, I thought grimly, was going to have to be done about those stupid nerves, or I'd never complete the course.

A middle-aged woman came to open the front door and show me down the hall to a small sitting-room with windows facing the drive. Through them I could see

Erik pacing up and down in the rain radiating Marxist disapproval and stamping the undeserving bourgeoisie into the gravel with each crunch of his heel.

Sven Wangen strolled into the room eating a sugary pastry and staring with cold eyes down from a great height.

'I'd forgotten you were coming,' he said. 'Have you solved everything yet?' A slight sneer. No friendliness.

'Not everything.'

A small bad-tempered flash in the supercilious eyes.

'I've nothing to tell you. You are wasting your time.'

They'd all told me that, and they were all mistaken.

Without a hat, Sven Wangen was revealed as going prematurely bald, the russet hair as thick as ever round the back and sides, but almost as thin as Erik's on top. He took a large sticky bite, chewed, swallowed: added another fraction to his overweight.

'The last day Bob Sherman rode for you, did he say anything unexpected?'

'No, he did not.' He hadn't bothered to think about it.

'Did you take him for a drink to celebrate the winner he rode for you?'

'Certainly not.' He started another mouthful.

'Did you talk to him at all . . . either before or after the race?'

He chewed. Swallowed. Looked closely at the pastry, prospecting the next area.

'In the parade ring, I gave him his orders. I told him

I expected better than he'd just done for Rolf Torp. He said he understood.'

Bite. Munch. Swallow.

'After the race, he unsaddled the horse and went to weigh in. I didn't see him again.'

'While he was unsaddling, did he tell you how the mare had run?'

'No. I was telling Holth she needed a good thrashing to quieten her down. Holth disagreed. I didn't speak to Sherman.'

'Didn't you congratulate him?' I asked curiously.

'No.'

'Do you wish you had?'

'Why should I?'

You might need to eat less, I thought, but refrained from saying so. His psychological hang-ups weren't in this instance my affair.

'Did he mention delivering a package which he had brought from England?'

'No.' He stuffed the rest of the gooey goody into his mouth and had difficulty closing his lips.

'Did you ask him to ride the mare next time he came?'

He stared, then spoke round the dough and currants. 'He didn't come again.'

'I mean, that last day, did you ask him to ride for you again?'

'Oh. No.' He shrugged. 'Holth always engages the jockeys. I just say who I want.'

'You never telephoned to Sherman in England personally to discuss his rides for you?'

'Certainly not.'

'Some owners do talk to their jockeys,' I said.

'I pay Holth to do that sort of thing.'

What a lot you miss, I thought. Poor fat unloved deprived rich young man. I thanked him for his time and went back to Erik. Sven Wangen watched us through the window, licking the sugar off his fingers.

'Well?' Erik said.

'He might have issued the orders, but he never killed anyone himself.'

Erik grunted as he started the hired Volvo towards the gate. 'Where now?'

'You're wet,' I said. 'Why did you stay out in the rain?'

He was almost embarrassed. 'Oh . . . I thought I'd hear you better if you yelled.'

We went in silence for five miles down the road and then he pulled up at a fork.

'You'll have to decide here,' he said. 'That way to Øvrevoll, and that way to the airport. The racecourse is much nearer.'

'The airport.'

'Right.'

He blasted off down the road to Fornebu as if trying to fly there.

'Mind we aren't followed,' I said.

'You're joking.'

The thirty mile journey, from one side of Oslo to the other, took just over half an hour.

No one followed.

C14 was locked and C13 next to it had a key in its door with a black tag, just the same. Both were large lockers in the bottom row of a three-high tier.

Erik, who had allotted himself full bodyguard status, stood at my elbow and peered at the ranks of metal doors.

'Are these the lot you're looking for?'

I nodded. 'I think so.'

'What do we do now, then?'

'We walk around for a bit to make sure there's no one here we know.'

'A sensible idea.'

We walked around and stood in corners to watch, but as far as I could see every person in the airport was a complete stranger. Drifting gently back to the lockers, Erik stood stalwartly with his back to C13 and looked ready to repel boarders while I inconspicuously fished out the hidden key and tried it in the lock next door.

The right key, no mistake. The locker door swung open revealing a space big enough for two large suitcases: and on the scratched metal floor, looking lost and inappropriate, lay a folded piece of paper.

I bent down, picked it up, and tucked it into my inside jacket pocket.

'See anyone?' I asked Erik, straightening again.

'Not a soul we know.'

'Let's grab some coffee.'

'What about the locker?'

I looked down at C14 with its key in the lock and its door open.

'We don't need it any more.'

Erik steered us to the airport buffet and bought coffee for both of us and a couple of open sandwiches for himself. We sat at a plastic-topped table amid travellers with untidy hand luggage and children running about doing what they were told not to, and with an almost fluttery feeling of expectation I took out the paper Bob Sherman had left.

I had supposed it would prove to be a base for blackmail: incriminating letters or photographs no one dared show his wife. But it proved to be neither of those things. It proved to be something I didn't recognize at all.

For one thing, the paper was thinner than I had at first supposed, and only seemed to be thick because it was folded several times. Unfolded, it turned out to be a strip six inches across but nearly three feet long, and it was divided into three columns which were intended to be read downwards. One could not, however, actually read them, as each inch and a half wide column seemed to be composed of variously shaded blocks and squares, not letters or figures. Down the long left-hand edge of the paper were numbers at regular intervals, starting with 3 at the top and ending with 14 at the bottom. Across the top in hand-written capitals was a single heading: Data Summary.

I refolded the strip and put it back in my pocket.

'What is it?' Erik asked.

I shook my head. 'Don't know.'

He stirred his coffee. 'Knut will find out.'

I considered that and didn't especially like it.

'No,' I said. 'This paper came from England. I think I'll take it back there to find out what it is.'

'It's Knut's case,' he said with a certain amount of quiet obstinacy.

'Mine as well.' I hesitated. 'Tell Knut I found the paper if you must, but I'd rather you didn't mention it to anyone at all. I don't want it leaking out round Oslo, and if you tell Knut he will have to record it, and if he records it, you never know who will see it. I'd much rather tell him myself when I get back. We can't anyway make a useful plan of campaign until we know what we're dealing with, so nothing can really be gained by telling him now.'

He looked unconvinced, but after a while all he said was, 'Where did you find the key to the locker?'

'In Bob Sherman's helmet.'

His obstinacy slowly melted to resignation.

'All right,' he said. 'I won't tell Knut. He could have found the key first.'

As logic it hardly stood up, but I was grateful. I looked at my watch and said, 'I can catch the two five to Heathrow.'

'Right now?' He sounded surprised.

I nodded. 'Don't tell anyone I've gone. I don't want any friend of yellow eyes waiting at the other end.'

He grinned. 'David Cleveland? Who's he?' He stood up and turned to go. 'I'll give your regards to Odin.'

I watched his untidy back depart forthwith through the scattered crowd towards the distant exit and felt unexpectedly vulnerable without him. But nothing dire happened. I caught the flight and landed safely at Heathrow, and, after thought, left my car where it was in the car park and took myself by train to Cambridge.

Sunday evening in mid-term was as good a time as any to beard professors in their dens, but the first one I backed was a loser. He lectured in Computer Science: but my Data Summary, he said, had nothing to do with computers. Why didn't I try Economics? I tried Economics who said why didn't I try Geology.

Although it was by then getting on for ten o'clock I tried Geology, who took one brief glance at the paper and said, 'Christ, where did you get this, they guard these things like gold dust.'

'What is it?' I asked.

'A core. A chart of a core. From a drilling. See those numbers down the left-hand side? I'd say they refer to the depth of each section. Might be in hundreds of feet. Might be in thousands.'

'Can you tell where the drilling was done?'

He shook his head, a youngish earnest man with a mass of reddish hair merging into an undisciplined beard.

'Could be anywhere in the world. You'd need the key to the shadings even to guess what they were looking for.'

I said in depression, 'Isn't there any way of finding out where it came from?'

'Oh Lord, yes,' he said cheerfully. 'Depends how important it is.'

'It's a long story,' I said doubtfully, with a look at his clock.

'Sleep is a waste of time,' he said like a true scholar, so I told him more or less exactly why I wanted to know.

'Have a beer?' he suggested, when I'd finished.

'Thanks.'

He found two cans under a heap of uncorrected essays and ripped off the rings.

'Cheers!' he said, dispensing with a glass. 'All right. You convinced me. I'll pass you on to the people who drew that chart.'

I was astonished. 'How do you know who drew it?'

He laughed. 'It's like knowing a colleague's hand-writing. Any research geologist could probably tell you where that chart came from. It's a research lab job. I'll give the managing director a ring in the morning and explain, and see if he'll help you. They're awfully touchy about these charts.' He eyed it thoughtfully. 'I shouldn't be surprised if there'll be an unholy row, because from what you've said I should think it was stolen.'

The seeds of the unholy row were plain to see, next day, on the face of Dr William Leeds, managing director of the Wessex-Wells Research Laboratory. An impressive man, small, calm and decisive, he looked deeply disturbed at what I'd brought him.

'Sit down, Mr Cleveland,' he said.

We sat one each side of his managerial desk.

'Tell me where you got this.'

I told him. He listened intently, without interrupting. At the end he said, 'What do you want to know?'

'What this chart is about. Who could benefit from getting hold of it, and how.'

He smiled. 'Fairly comprehensive.' He looked out of his big first floor office window for a while at a row of leaf-dropping willows across a stretch of lawn. Deep in the heart of Dorset, the laboratory stood in ancient parkland, a Victorian country residence sitting easily beside new low flat-topped workaday workshops. Dr Leeds's window overlooked the main artery of pathways linking the complex, a neat finger on the pulse if ever I saw one.

'Almost anyone could benefit from getting hold of

it,' he said. 'If they were unscrupulous. This chart cost perhaps half a million pounds.'

My mouth fell open. He laughed.

'Well . . . you have to remember that drill rigs are enormously sophisticated and expensive. You don't get a core by digging a hole with a spade. This one . . .' he tapped the paper, 'is only five inches in diameter but about fourteen thousand feet in depth. A fourteen thousand foot drilling costs a lot of money.'

'I can see,' I said, 'that it does.'

'Of course you couldn't sell it for that, but I should think this particular chart might be worth a hundred thousand, if you had a market.'

I asked if he would explain in more detail.

'A chart like this is information. You can always sell information illegally if you know someone ready to buy. Well . . . suppose this core showed a deposit of nickel, which it doesn't, incidentally, and you knew exactly from which particular drilling it came, you would know whether it was worth investing money in the drilling company, or not. For instance, during the Poseidon nickel boom in Australia, you'd have been able to make literally millions on the stock market through knowing infallibly in advance which of the dozens of prospecting companies had made the drilling that was richest in ore.'

'Good grief,' I said.

'It can work the other way too,' he said. 'If you know that a concession which has been expected to give a high yield is in fact not going to be good, you can sell out while the share price is still high.'

'So it wouldn't only be people engaged in mining who would be ready to buy such a chart.'

'Certainly not. The people who make most out of the earth probably don't know what a drill looks like.'

I said, 'Why sell the chart to someone else? Why not make millions on the stock market yourself?'

He smiled. 'It's much safer to be paid a lump sum into a nice anonymous Swiss bank account than to start dealing in shares. Any geologist dealing much in significant shares would be detected at once.'

'Do people approach geologists, asking them to sell information?'

'They do. We try to protect our geologists here by not letting them know exactly where the material they're working on has come from. But obviously we have not been entirely successful.' He looked bleak. 'We know from past experience that a working geologist is usually approached by a middle man, an entrepreneur who buys information from the research source and then sells it to a bigger fish who operates in the world markets.'

'Am I dealing with the middle man or the big fish?'

He smiled and shook his head. 'Can't tell. But the middle man, I suspect, as you found the chart so close to source.'

'What exactly do these columns mean?' I asked.

He picked up the chart and showed me. 'The first

column is lithology ... the composition of the rock layers. The second is the original particle type ... that means micro- and macrofossils and micrite. The third ...' He compressed his lips, clearly most upset by this one. 'The third is a fairly new and highly secret process, scanning electron microscopy. Our clients will be particularly furious that this finding has been leaked. They paid a mint for it. We can stay in business here only as long as every client remains convinced that the analysis he is paying for will never be seen by anyone except himself.'

I said, 'This chart wouldn't be much use, though, without the key to the various shadings.'

'No.' He thought. 'If I had to guess, I'd say that this might be used as a sort of appetizer, or a proof that the middle man had the real goods to sell. We don't normally make up charts in this form. This is an abbreviation. A condensed, composite edition. Specially made.'

'But would the rest of Bob Sherman's package be worth anything without this chart?'

'Oh, sure. It depends what else was in it. A written analysis would be just as good as a chart. If they had a written analysis it wouldn't matter all that much if they lost the chart.'

I thanked him for his help. 'Could you tell me where that drilling was made ... and what for?'

He glanced at it. 'I can tell you in general just by

looking at it. But do you want to know precisely, to the half mile?'

'Please,' I said.

'Then come with me.'

He led me along a wide passage, through some swing doors, and into a modern wing tacked on to the back of the original house. We were bound, it seemed, for the records department, but to get in there even the managing director had to announce himself to the inmates and get the door unlocked electronically from inside.

He smiled wryly at my surprise.

'We usually pride ourselves on our security. We're going to have a great upheaval sorting out which of our people sold the information on this chart.' A thought struck him. 'I suppose you wouldn't like to come back and work on it yourself?'

I wouldn't have minded, but explained about the Jockey Club.

'Pity,' he said.

He unerringly sorted out one particular folder from the thousands in the filing cupboards which lined the walls. He knew exactly which company had commissioned the analysis, and he knew roughly from where the core had been taken.

He turned a few pages, comparing the chart with the notes.

'There,' he said finally, pointing with his finger. 'Those are the coordinates you want.'

I looked over his arm. Read the coordinates.
Read the name of the company.
I'd never heard of it.
'Thank you very much,' I said.

CHAPTER FOURTEEN

I called to see Emma.

The cottage was warm and welcoming in the cold afternoon, alive with a glowing log fire and a huge vase of bronze chrysanthemums. None of the furniture had been replaced and the curtains were still at the cleaners, but Emma herself during the past week had made strides. There was at last a shade of colour in her cheeks and the faintest of sparkles in the eyes. The pretty girl had come back to life.

'David! How great to see you. Have a hot scone. They're just out of the oven.'

We sat in front of the fire eating the scones with butter and jam and concentration.

'Golly, you must have been hungry,' she said later, eyeing the almost-empty dish. 'I really made them to take over to Grandfather.' She laughed. 'Guess I'd better make some more.'

'They were lovely.' What with bombs and general

chasing around I had missed a lot of meals and picked at others. With Emma, for the first time in days, my stomach nerves felt safe enough to encourage intake.

'I don't know whether to ask,' she said, 'but have you found out anything about Bob?'

'Not enough.' I looked at my watch. 'May I use your telephone?'

'Of course.'

I called a stockbroker I knew who owned racehorses and asked him about the share movements of the company which had commissioned the analysis of the core.

'That's easy,' he said. 'About two months ago the share price started to soar. Someone had a hot tip, bought at the bottom and made a real packet.'

'Who?' I said.

'Impossible to tell, but probably a syndicate, considering the huge sums involved. All done through nominees, mostly on overseas markets.'

I thanked him and rang off; and after that I called SAS, who made warm noises and said sure there was a free seat on the six-thirty. A lot of my mind persisted in telling me that there was another flight in the morning and widows were meant for consoling: well, maybe, but not this one, not yet.

I kissed her goodbye.

'Come again,' she said, and I said, 'I will.'

*

I handed in at Heathrow the car I'd hired that morning in Cambridge, and squeezed into the six-thirty at the last call.

I didn't seem able to help the tension screwing up again as we began the descent into Oslo, but a harmless taxi took me uneventfully to the hotel, where the reception desk resignedly let me choose my own room.

I telephoned to Erik.

'Where are you?' he demanded.

'At the Grand.'

'For God's sake . . . didn't you go?'

'There and back.'

'Did you find out . . .?'

'Up to a point. I know what it is, but not who it belongs to. Look . . . could you give me Knut's home number?'

He told me. 'Do you want any more driving done?'

'I'm afraid so, if you can face it.'

'Count,' he said, 'on me.'

I rang Knut who yawned and said he'd just come off duty and wouldn't be back until two o'clock the following afternoon.

'Do you know a place called Lillehammer?' I asked.

'*Ja*. Of course.'

'What's it like?'

'How do you mean? It is a big town. A tourist town in the summer, and a ski place in the winter. No visitors go there in October and November.'

'If you wanted to meet someone secretly in Lillehammer, within fairly easy walking distance of the railway station, where would you suggest?'

'Not in a public place?'

'No. Somewhere quiet.'

There was a pause. Then he said, 'It might be better to walk away from the town itself. Down towards the lake. There is a road going down to the bridge over the lake. It is the main road to Gjøvik, but there is not much traffic, and there are some small side roads down to the houses round the lakeside. Is that what you want?'

'Sounds perfect.'

'Who are you going to meet?'

I told him at considerable length. Somewhere along the way he shed his fatigue, because when he next spoke his voice was alert and even eager.

'*Ja*. I understand. I will arrange everything.'

'I'll see you in the morning, then.'

'*Ja*. Agreed. And . . . er . . . take good care, David.'

'You bet,' I said.

I rang Erik again, who said certainly he would come to breakfast, drive me to Knut's office, and get me to the station in time to catch the ten o'clock to Lillehammer.

'Is that all?'

'No . . . Would you meet me again when I get back? Four thirty, I think.'

'All right.' He sounded almost disappointed.

'Bring knuckledusters,' I said, which cheered him.

Next, Lars Baltzersen.

'Of course I've heard of that company,' he said. 'Their shares are booming. I bought some myself a few weeks ago and already they show a good profit.'

'Do you know anyone else who bought any while the price was still low?'

A pause, then he said, 'Rolf Torp did. I believe it was Rolf who told me about them, but I can't be sure.' He cleared his throat. 'I have heard worrying rumours, though, that the really big buyers were in the Middle East. One cannot be sure. There is much secrecy. But it seems likely.'

'Why would that be worrying?' I asked, and he told me.

Last of all I telephoned Arne. Kari answered, her voice warm, amused, and full of memory from our last meeting.

'Haven't seen you since Friday,' she said. 'Why don't you come to dinner here tomorrow?'

'Love to,' I said, 'but I don't think I can.'

'Oh. Well . . . how's the case going?'

'That's really what I wanted to talk about with Arne.'

She said she would fetch him, and he came on the line. He sounded glad that I'd called.

'David . . . haven't seen you for days,' he said. 'What have you been doing?'

'Ferreting,' I said. 'Look, Arne, I've had a piece of luck. Some man in a place called Lillehammer telephoned and said he could tell me something about Bob Sherman being killed. He said he almost saw it happen.

He wouldn't say any more on the phone, but I'm going to meet him tomorrow. The thing is . . . I wondered if you'd like to come with me. I'd be glad of your company, if you could spare the time. And he didn't speak very good English . . . so you could interpret for me, if you would.'

'Tomorrow?'

'Yes. I'm catching the ten o'clock train in the morning.'

'Where in Lillehammer are you meeting this man?'

'On the road to Gjøvik, down near the bridge over the lake. He's going to be there at midday.'

He said doubtfully, 'I suppose I could . . .'

'Please do come, Arne,' I said.

He made up his mind. '*Ja*. I'll come. Are you still staying at the Grand?'

'Yes,' I said. 'But you are nearer the station. I'll meet you there.'

'Right.' He hesitated again. 'I hope he isn't some lunatic, making up stories.'

'So do I,' I said.

I slept with my bed pushed right across the door, but nobody tried to get in.

Erik had brought Odin again to assist with the guard duty, although I now knew from longer acquaintance that the Dane's fierce appearance was only a front. A right great softy lived inside the sandy skin.

Together nonetheless they conveyed me safely to the police station where Knut met us, keenly awake a good five hours before he was due on duty. Up in his office I gave him the geological chart, which he inspected curiously.

'Don't lose it,' I said.

He smiled. 'Better to lose my life, I suspect.'

'You'll get it photo-copied?'

He nodded. 'Straight away.'

'See you this evening, then.'

We shook hands.

'Be careful,' he said.

Erik and Odin stuck beside me while I bought my ticket and walked to the barrier. It was the worst morning yet for jumpy nerves, with me far outstripping Arne in the matter of looking over my shoulder. By this evening, I thought grimly, I'd either be safe or dead. It seemed an awful long time to the evening.

Arne, already waiting on the platform, greeted me with a big smile.

'What number is your ticket?' he asked.

I hadn't realized that each ticket bore a seat number on the train, but it was so.

'I'll see if I can change mine to be next to you,' he said, and vanished on his errand at high speed. While he was gone I found my allotted number, a window seat facing forward, halfway up one of the large, airy coaches. With only a few minutes to go to departure time about half the seats were filled with respectable-looking citizens, and I managed to look over my shoulder only twice.

Arne returned with an air of satisfaction and the ticket for the seat beside mine.

'That's better,' he said, and gave all the worthy fellow travellers a severe inspection before sitting down. 'I should have waited for you at the ticket office . . . didn't think of it in time.'

Erik, with Odin still beside him, suddenly appeared on the platform outside the window, rapping to attract my attention and vigorously beckoning me to talk to him. I pointed to the rear of the carriage, excused myself past Arne, and went to the door to hear what Erik wanted to tell.

'I saw him,' he said, almost stuttering with urgency. 'Get off the train and come with me.'

'Who?'

'It'll go if you don't get off quickly. The man who planted the bomb. Big, with a butterfly birth-mark. I saw it. He was buying a ticket . . . he dropped some change and bent to pick it up. I saw his neck . . . and I saw his eyes. They really are a sort of yellow. Very light and bright and odd. Do hurry, David. There was another man with him. They got on this train, in the rear carriage. Three carriages back from here.'

A whistle blew. He practically danced with frustration.

'Get off. Get off . . .'

I shook my head. 'I'll find a way of avoiding them.' The train began to move. 'Thanks a lot. See you this afternoon. Mind you come.'

'Of course I'll come.'

The train gathered speed, diminishing my protectors second by second until I could no longer see the bewilderment on Erik's face or the patient lack of comprehension on Odin's.

'Who was that?' Arne asked as I returned to my place.

'Someone I hired to drive me around.'

'Extraordinary looking chauffeur, isn't he?'

I smiled. 'His driving is pretty hair-raising as well.'

'Tell me about this man we're going to see.'

'I don't know much, really. He said his name was Johan Petersen . . .'

Arne grunted. 'There are dozens of Johan Petersens.'

'He said he was at the races the day Bob Sherman disappeared. He said he would like to tell me something about that. He said he lived at Lillehammer and worked there in the timber yard. I asked him to come to Oslo, but he said he couldn't take the day off. He said he'd meet me during his lunch break today. It was very difficult to understand him clearly, as he spoke so little English. It'll be fine with you there.'

Arne nodded, blinking away as usual. The train took things easily, sliding quietly through the outer suburbs in a typically unhurried Norwegian fashion.

'How will you know him?'

'He said he would know me. All I have to do is walk down towards the bridge carrying an English news-paper.'

'Did you bring one?'

I nodded. 'In my coat pocket.'

The train was well heated. Coats were expected to be shed, and there was a rail at the rear equipped with hangers, where Arne's coat and mine hung side by side.

The line ran north through farmland and woods and alongside an extensive lake. On any other day I would have enjoyed the journey but it was extraordinary how a little fear could keep the mind focused close at hand. Old yellow eyes and his pal were a sight too near for comfort, and I'd developed an even worse over-the-shoulder compulsion through passengers walking up the centre aisle through the train. Every bang of the door from one carriage to the next had me looking to make sure.

A woman in a blue overall pushed a trolley into the carriage, selling from it hot drinks, biscuits and sweets. Arne bought me coffee. The trolley trundled away, and bang went the door behind her.

We stopped lengthily at a largish town, Hamar, a

junction with masses of open windswept platforms and no air of shunting or bustle. Then on again, moving faster, on towards Lillehammer. Two and a half hours, altogether, on the train.

'I missed you at the races on Sunday,' Arne said.

'Yes. I meant to go, but it was so cold.'

He gave me a look of friendly contempt.

'I might be going home soon,' I said.

'Are you?' He was surprised. 'I thought . . . you'd never leave us without finding out . . .'

'Well, after this trip today we should know a lot more. With a bit of luck. And then there's the key . . .'

'What key?'

'I found a luggage-locker key stuck in Bob Sherman's riding helmet.'

'You didn't!'

I nodded and told him about the trail to Paddy O'Flaherty's. 'So you see, although I'll go home soon, we should have most of the answers.'

Arne was enthusiastic. 'That's great,' he said. 'All we have to do now is find what's in the locker which the key fits.' A thought struck him. 'Perhaps it's that money. In the canvas bags . . . you know, the money that was stolen.'

'It's a thought,' I said. I didn't launch into explaining what actually had been in the locker; time enough for that later, as from the way the other passengers were standing up and putting on their coats it was clear we had nearly arrived. The train ran beside Lake Mjøsa

229

and in the distance I could see the timber yard, with acres of pine tree logs floating in the water.

Arne held my coat for me, and I his for him. He smiled a little sadly.

'Kari and I will miss you.'

'I'll be back one day. I like Norway very much.'

He nodded. The train passed the end of the bridge to Gjøvik, climbed a hill slowly, inched into Lillehammer station, and sighed to a stop. We stepped out into a stinging wind under a grey cloud-filled sky. So much, I thought, for all those happy holiday posters of sun and snow and people on skis showing their suntans and teeth. It was odd, too, how none of the far frozen north railway stations had sheltering roofs over the platforms. Perhaps no one ever stood waiting in the open air, so that roofs were redundant and there was some point in them all still looking like the last scene in *Anna Karenina*.

'Are you coming, David?' Arne said.

'Yeah.' I stopped looking around vaguely and followed him through the main doors into the booking hall. At the far end of the platform two men, by-passing the station buildings, had set off quickly in the general direction of the road to the bridge. One was big. The other, of the same build as my attacker in the flat. They were too far away for me to swear to it in court.

But I was sure, just the same.

The small booking hall was scattered with prospective travellers wearing limbo expressions, waiting for time to pass. There were seats round the walls, doors to washrooms, a window for buying tickets: all the amenities in one central area. Arne said he wanted to make a telephone call before we set off to the meeting with our informer down the road.

'Carry on,' I said amiably.

I watched him through the glass wall of the booth feeding money into the slot and talking earnestly into the mouthpiece. He talked for a good long time, and came out smiling.

'All done. Let's go,' he said.

'Arne . . .' I hesitated. 'I know this is going to sound silly, but I don't want to go.'

He looked dumbstruck. 'But why not? This man might have seen who killed Bob Sherman.'

'I know. But . . . I can't explain it. I have . . . the weirdest feeling of premonition. I've had it before . . . I can't . . . I can't ignore it. Something tells me not to go. So I'm not going.'

'But David,' he said. 'That's crazy.'

'I can't help it. I'm not going.'

'But what about the man?'

I said helplessly, 'I don't know.'

Arne grew impatient. He tried insults. He tried persuasion. I wouldn't budge.

In the end he said, 'Give me the newspaper. I'll go and meet him myself.'

'But,' I objected, 'if my premonition means there is some danger down that road, it must be dangerous for you as well. I had a premonition about a street once before . . . I wouldn't go down it, and a few seconds later several tons of scaffolding collapsed on to where I would have been. Ever since then, when I've a strong feeling against doing something, I don't do it.'

He blinked at me earnestly. 'If I see any scaffolding, I'll keep away from it. But we must see this Johan Petersen and hear his story. Give me the newspaper.'

Reluctantly I handed him the previous day's *Express*.

'I'll wait for you here,' I said.

He nodded, still not pleased, and set off on his own. I chose a place to sit at one end of one of the bench seats, with solid wall at my back and on one side. On my other side sat a plump teenage girl in a shaggy sheepskin coat eating herring sandwiches noisily.

A few people came. A train arrived and took most of them away, including my neighbour. Time passed very slowly.

An hour and a half between our arrival and the train back to Oslo. An hour and a half to kill. Correction, I thought wryly. To stay alive. I wished I smoked or bit my nails or went in for yoga. I wished my heart wouldn't jump every time people walked past the window in pairs. I wished I knew what views yellow eyes and brown eyes held on murdering in public, because if only I was sure they wouldn't risk it I could save myself a lot of fretting. As it was I sat and waited and slowly sweated, hoping I'd judged their limit right.

When passengers for the Oslo train started arriving

and buying tickets I bought two myself for Arne and me. I asked particularly for the most public pair of seats in the carriage, as observed on the way up, and although I had difficulty explaining what I wanted as the ticket seller spoke little English, I got them.

Back in my careful corner I found myself flanked by an elderly man with an ear-flapped cap topping cream-coloured skin over an elongated skull. He had heard me speak English at the ticket window and was eager to tell me that he'd been in England the year before on holiday with his son and daughter-in-law. I encouraged him a bit, and got in return a minute by minute conducted tour from Tower Hill via Westminster Abbey to the National Gallery. By the time Arne came back, a quarter of an hour before train time, we were chatting away like old friends.

Arne was looking anxious. I stood up to meet him, gesturing to the elderly man and saying, 'We've been talking about London . . .'

Arne glanced at the man without really seeing him and abruptly interrupted. 'He didn't come.'

'Oh no,' I said.

Arne shook his head. 'I waited. I walked down to the bridge twice. I showed the newspaper. No one spoke to me. No one even walked past looking as if they were looking for anyone.'

I made frustrated noises. 'What a bloody nuisance. I'm so sorry, Arne, to have wasted a whole day for you . . . but he sounded so definite. Perhaps he was delayed and couldn't help it. Perhaps we could telephone the timber yard . . .'

'I did,' he said. 'They haven't any Johan Petersen working there.'

We stared at each other.

I said depressedly, 'I banked so much on his giving us some really vital information.'

He looked at me uncertainly.

'My premonition was all wrong then,' I said.

'I told you.'

'Yes, you did.'

He began to fish out his wallet.

'I've got the tickets,' I said, producing them. 'Two seats together.'

'Oh . . . good.'

The train arrived, dark red and silver, and we climbed aboard. The seats were all I'd hoped, right down at one end, with their backs to the wardrobe end but facing every other seat in the coach. By a stroke of luck my elderly friend of the London holiday took his place on the aisle three seats down. He had a clear view of Arne and me, and waved and smiled. I told Arne how friendly he had been. Like all Norwegians, I said.

Arne jerked a look over his shoulder. Only a row of hangers with coats; but he didn't look happy.

Two bright-eyed young girls came and sat in the two seats directly facing us. I moved my feet out of the way of theirs, and smiled at them. They smiled back and said something in their own language.

'I'm English,' I said, and they repeated 'English' and nodded and smiled again. 'And this is my friend Arne Kristiansen.' They put the introduction down to the eccentricity of foreigners, saying hello to him with giggles. Arne said hello back, but he was old enough to be their father and not interested in their girlish chat.

The train started back towards Oslo. We talked for a while about the non-appearance of Johan Petersen and I said we would just have to hope that he would telephone again.

'You'll let me know if he does?'

'Of course,' I said.

The lady in blue overalls arrived, pushing her comforts trolley down the aisle. I said it was my turn to buy the coffee, and despite Arne's protestations I did so. I also offered drinks to the two girls who thought it a great lark and went pink. They asked Arne to see if it was all right for them to have orangeade, as they didn't like coffee. The lady in blue overalls patiently attended to all Arne's translations and finally with a smile gave him my change.

Arne began to wear the hunted look he often did in crowds.

'Let's go somewhere quieter,' he said.

'You go,' I said. 'But I rather like it here.'

He shook his head, but he stayed.

To his relief and my regret the two young girls got off at Hamar, giggling goodbye with backward glances. No one embarked to take their empty places, but after the train had started again my elderly friend got to his feet and came inquiringly towards us.

'May I sit here with you?' he said. 'It is so interesting to talk about England.'

Too much for Arne. He rose abruptly to his feet and dived through to the next carriage. The door banged behind him.

'Have I upset your friend?' asked the elderly man anxiously. 'I am sorry.'

'He has problems,' I said. 'But not of your making.'

Relieved, he launched into more reminiscences which bored me to death but quite likely kept me alive. He was still there, talking inexhaustibly, as we drew into Oslo. And on the platform, flanked by Odin, stood Erik anxiously looking out for me, just as promised.

There wasn't much time left. If they were going to make an attempt now they were going to have to do it in the open.

I stepped off the train and turned towards Erik. And there between us, looking sickeningly businesslike, stood the two men I least wanted to see.

CHAPTER FIFTEEN

Battle never commenced.

Erik saw them at the same moment I did, and yelled 'Police' at the top of his lungs.

Every person within earshot stopped to look.

'Police,' he yelled again, pointing at yellow eyes and brown eyes. 'These are thieves. Fetch the police.' And he repeated it in Norwegian, very loudly.

It broke their nerve. They looked round at the growing circle staring at them wide-eyed, and suddenly made a bolt for the exit. No one made much effort to stop them, and the chief expression on every beholder's face was astonishment.

Erik strode up to me and pumped my hand.

'Just putting your theory into practice,' he said.

I looked blank.

He explained. 'Knut told me you didn't think they'd kill you while people were looking. So I just got a few people to look.'

'Thanks.'

'Call it quits,' he said with a grin, and patted Odin.

I discovered that the palms of my hands were wet and a lot of me was quietly shaking.

'I need a telephone,' I said.

'You need a good stiff drink.'

'That too.'

I rang Knut. 'I'm back at the terminus,' I said.

'Thank God for that.'

'Did it work?'

I asked with some intensity, because I'd risked my skin for nearly seven shivery hours and no one could be entirely objective after that.

'Yes,' he said, but there was an odd note of reservation in his voice. 'At least . . . *Ja.*'

'What's the matter?'

'You had better come here, to the police station. It will be easier to explain.'

'All right.'

I stepped outside the box and almost fell over Odin who was lying across the door like a medieval page. He gave me a reproachful look, stood nonchalantly up, and yawned.

I asked Erik, 'Did you see Arne Kristiansen anywhere?'

'Who?'

I scanned the crowd without success. 'Never mind. I expect he's gone home.'

In gathering dusk Erik drove sedately (only one near-miss) to the police building, where I went upstairs and found Knut sitting alone and chewing a pencil. He gestured me to the visitors' chair and produced only the vestige of a smile.

'Well . . . we did everything you suggested,' he said. 'We planted the chart in a locker at Fornebu and put the key loose in the helmet in your room at the Grand. We sprinkled anthracene dust over every surface an intruder would touch and we waited at Fornebu to see if anyone would come.'

He rattled the pencil along his teeth.

'Someone did come,' he said.

'Who?'

He sighed. 'You'd better come and see.'

He led the way out of his meagre office and down an uncarpeted corridor, and stopped outside a cream painted door. Bright light from inside shone through a small glass panel let into the wood at viewing height.

'Look,' Knut said.

I looked.

The room was small and bare, containing only a simple table and three chairs. One chair was occupied by a young uniformed policeman looking stolid. On another, smoking quietly and as calm as if he were back in his own boardroom, sat Per Bjørn Sandvik.

I pulled my head away from the glass and stared at Knut.

'Come back to my office,' he said.

We went back and sat down as before.

'He came to Fornebu and opened the locker,' Knut said. 'That was at . . .' he consulted a note-pad, ' . . . fourteen thirty-five hours precisely. He removed the chart from the locker and put it in an inside pocket. I myself and two other officers went up to him as he was walking away from the lockers and asked him to accompany us to this police station. He seemed surprised but not . . . not deeply disturbed. I have arrested so many people . . . Per Bjørn Sandvik did not behave like a guilty man.'

He rubbed thumb and finger down his nose.

'I don't know what to make of him, David. He shrugged and said he would come with us if we liked, but he said almost nothing else until we got back here. He was completely calm. No sign of stress. None at all. He has been here now for about an hour and a half, and he has been calm and courteous the whole time.'

'What explanation did he give?'

'We went into that interview room and sat on the chairs, with a constable to take notes. Mr Sandvik offered me a cigarette. He said he had only been trying to help the investigation into Bob Sherman's death. He said Arne Kristiansen had telephoned to say that you had found a key which might lead to useful information, so he went to the Grand Hotel to fetch the key, which he recognized as having come from Fornebu, as he has often used those lockers in the past. So he went to the airport . . . to see what Bob Sherman had left there. He said he thought it might have been the

240

missing money, but it was only a paper. He hadn't done more than glance at it when we stopped him.'

'Did he give any reason for doing all this himself and not waiting for Arne or me to get back or enlisting the help of the police?'

'*Ja.*' He smiled a small tight smile to mock me. 'He said Arne asked him to do it. Arne wanted to prove to the racecourse committee that he was worth his salary as an investigator, so he telephoned to Sandvik as a member of the racecourse committee to tell him about the key. Arne apparently said that if he and Mr Sandvik helped with the case, the committee would not be able to give all the praise to you.'

'What do you think?'

He looked depressed. 'Per Bjørn Sandvik is a leader of industry. He is much respected. He is being very reasonable, but if we keep him here much longer he will be angry.'

'And your superiors will lean on you?'

'Er . . . *ja.*'

I thought.

'Don't worry, Knut,' I said. 'We've got the right man.'

'But he is so confident.'

I nodded. 'He's working on a false assumption.'

'What's that?'

'He thinks I'm dead.'

*

Per Bjørn Sandvik got a very nasty shock indeed when I walked into the interview room.

Muscles round his eyes and mouth contracted sharply, and his pale skin went perceptibly paler. But his resilience was extraordinary. Within three seconds he was smiling pleasantly with the deceptive lack of agitation which was so confusing Knut.

'David!' he said as if in welcome, yet I could almost hear and certainly sense the alarm bells going at panic strength.

'I'm afraid this isn't the happiest of meetings,' I said.

He was making such an urgent reappraisal that the muscles round his eyes were moving in tiny rhythmical spasms: which booted out of me any hint of complacency, because people who could think as quickly and intently as that in such adverse circumstances had brains to beware of.

Knut followed me into the room and told the young policeman to fetch another chair. While he went to get it I watched Per Bjørn finish reorganizing his thoughts. Infinitesimally, he relaxed. Too soon, I reckoned; and I couldn't afford to be wrong.

The extra chair came, and we all sat down round the bare table as if to a simple business discussion.

I said, 'It must have occurred to you by now that there was no Johan Petersen at Lillehammer.'

'I don't understand,' he said pleasantly in his high, distinct diction. 'I thought we were talking about the locker key and Fornebu airport.'

242

'We're talking about Arne Kristiansen,' I said.

A pause. I waited. But he was too cautious now to take any step without prospecting for quicksand, and after some time, when he said nothing, I invited him a little further along the path.

'You shouldn't rely on Arne,' I said. 'Arne is deep in, up to the neck.'

No response.

'Come to think of it,' I said. 'Up to his neck and over his head, considering the amount of swimming he's done.'

No reaction.

'All that messing around in the fjord,' I said. 'There was me thinking Arne had drowned, while all the time he had a scuba suit on under his red anorak. Nice snug black rubber with yellow seams, fitting right up over his head to keep him warm.' I'd seen the black-and-yellow under his anorak. It had taken me days to realize it had been rubber. But then that chug down the fjord happened before I'd begun to be sure that Arne was on the other side.

'A strong swimmer, Arne,' I said. 'A tough all-round sportsman. So there he is standing up in the dinghy waving his arms about as if to warn the speedboat not to run us down while all the time signalling to it that yes, this was the dinghy it was supposed to be sinking. This dinghy, not some other poor innocent slob out on a fishing trip. Arne swam ashore, reported an accident, reported me drowned.'

A pause.

'I don't know what you're talking about,' Per Bjørn said, and patiently sighed.

'I'm talking about Arne putting on his scuba suit and diving into the pond at Øvrevoll to get Bob Sherman out of it.'

Silence.

Arne had been sick when he saw the month-dead body. At night, when he'd fished Bob out and wrapped him in tarpaulin it couldn't have seemed so bad: but in the light of a drizzly day it had hit him a bull's-eye in the stomach.

'I'm talking about Arne being the one person who could be sure no one saw him putting bodies into ponds, taking them out again, and later putting them back again. Arne was security officer. He could come and go on that racecourse as he pleased. No one would think it odd if he were on the racecourse first, last, and during the night. But he could also make sure that the night watchman saw nothing he shouldn't, because the night watchman would carry out any attention-distracting task Arne gave him.'

Nothing.

'This is speculation,' he said.

Knut sat still and quiet, keeping his promise that he would make no comment, whatever I said. The young policeman's pencil had made scarcely a mark on the page.

'Arne stole the money himself,' I said. 'To provide a reason for Bob Sherman's disappearance.'

'Nonsense.'

'The impression of most people in the officials' room was that the money had been put in the safe. And so it had. Arne himself had put it there, as he usually does. He has keys to every gate, every building, every door on the place. He didn't take the money during the five minutes that the room happened to be empty. He had all night to do it in.'

'I don't believe it. Arne Kristiansen is a respected servant of the racecourse.'

He sat there listening to me with long-suffering courtesy as if I were a rather boring guest he was stuck with.

'Bob Sherman brought a packet of papers with him from England,' I said.

'Yes, you've already asked about that. I told you I couldn't help you.'

'Unfortunately for him, he was curious. He opened the package and saw what he had no business to see. He must have done this on the flight over, as he left some of the contents in a locker at Fornebu.'

Per Bjørn slowly turned his good-looking head until he was facing Knut, not me, and he spoke to him in Norwegian. Knut made gestures of regret and helplessness, and said nothing at all.

'Bob Sherman was too fond of schemes for getting rich quickly,' I said. 'He was being paid for bringing

245

the envelope, but it seemed to him that he could push the price up a bit. Very much his mistake, of course. He got bonked on the head for his pains. And no one discovered until long after he was dead and in the pond that when he'd opened the envelope he'd taken something out.'

Per Bjørn sat impassively, waiting for the annoying gnat to stop buzzing around him.

I buzzed a bit more.

'Because what he took out was in a way a duplication of what he left in.'

That one hit home. His eye muscles jumped. He knew that I'd noticed. He smiled.

I said, 'Bob Sherman took the precaution of hiding the key to the Fornebu locker in his racing helmet. By the time he was brought out of the pond it had been discovered that he had removed a paper from the envelope, but a search of his waterlogged clothes and overnight bag failed to produce any sign of it. So did a search of his house in England. By the time I realized what must be going on, and came to wonder if Bob had somehow hidden the missing object in his racing saddle or helmet, others had had the same idea. His saddle, which had stayed on its peg in the changing room for a month after he disappeared, was suddenly nowhere to be found.'

He sat. Quiet.

'However, the helmet with the saddle was no longer

246

Bob's but Paddy O'Flaherty's. I told Arne about the exchange. I told him I'd found the key.'

Per Bjørn crossed one leg over the other and took out his cigarettes. He offered them round, then when no one accepted, returned his case to his pocket and lit his own with a practised flick on a gas lighter. The hand which held the lighter was rock steady.

'I didn't tell him that we had already opened the locker and seen what it contained,' I said. 'We wanted to find out who else besides Arne was looking for the missing paper, so we gave that person an opportunity of finding it.'

'Ingenious,' he said. 'What a pity you had made the fundamental mistake of believing Arne Kristiansen to be connected with Bob Sherman's death. If he had been guilty of all you say, of course it would have been an excellent trap. As it is, of course . . .'

He delicately shrugged. Knut looked worried.

'There was the problem of the two men who searched Bob Sherman's house,' I said. 'If we didn't decoy them away they would be available to fetch the key and open the locker. So we provided an urgent reason for them to leave Oslo. We invented, in fact, a possible eye-witness to the killing of Bob Sherman. I told only Arne Kristiansen that I was going to Lillehammer to meet this man, and I asked Arne to come with me. On the train I told him about the key and said that as soon as I got back I was going to give it to the police. I told him that the police were expecting me to report to them at once on my return, to tell them what the man in Lillehammer had said. This meant to Arne that if I didn't return the hunt would be on immediately and there might be no later opportunity to get into my room for the key. It had to be done quickly. A risk had to be taken.'

I paused.

'You took it,' I said.

'No.'

'You believed no one knew of the existence of the key except Arne and myself. You were wrong. You believed there was a possible eye-witness to Bob's murder and you sent your two assassins to deal with him. You expected them also to kill me as well. They aren't very successful at that. You should sack them.'

'This is ridiculous,' he said.

I said, 'I asked the reception desk at the Grand not to worry if anyone asked for my room number or my door key.' And extremely odd they'd thought it, after all the hide and seek of the previous days. 'We made it as easy as we could.'

He said nothing.

Knut had sprinkled the room with anthracene dust, which clung invisibly to any clothes or flesh which touched it and showed up with fluorescence under a strong ultra-violet light. Anyone denying he'd been in my room would have been proved to be lying. But Per Bjørn had out-thought that one and hadn't denied it. He must have done a great deal of fast figuring during his non-speaking ride from Fornebu to the police station. He couldn't have known about the anthracene, but he must have guessed that a trap so complicated in some respects wasn't likely to be naïve in others.

I said, 'The paper you were looking for is a chart of a core taken from area twenty-five/six of the North Sea.'

He absorbed that shock as if he were made throughout of expanded polystyrene.

I gave him some more. 'It was stolen from the Wessex-Wells Research Laboratory in Dorset, England, and the information it contains was the property of the Interpetro Oil Company. It is a chart showing exceptionally rich oil-bearing rock of high porosity and good permeability at a depth of thirteen thousand feet.'

It seemed to me that he had almost stopped breathing. He sat totally without movement, smoke from the cigarette between his fingers rising in a column as straight as honesty.

I said, 'The Interpetro Oil Company isn't part of the consortium to which your own company belongs, but it is or was mainly Norwegian owned, and the well in question is in the Norwegian area of the North Sea. Immediately after Bob Sherman brought his package to Norway, the Interpetro shares started an upward movement on the world stock markets. Although a great deal of secrecy surrounds the buying, I'm told that the most active purchasers were in the Middle

East. You would know far better than I do whether it is to Norway's advantage to have one of her most promising oil fields largely bought up by oil-producing rivals.'

Not a flicker.

I said, 'Norway has never really forgiven the citizens who collaborated with the Nazis. How would they regard one of their most respected businessmen who sold advance news of their best oil field to the Middle East for his own personal gain?'

He uncrossed his legs and recrossed them the other way. He tapped the ash off his cigarette on to the floor, and inhaled a deep lungful of smoke.

'I wish,' he said, 'to telephone to my lawyer. And to my wife.'

CHAPTER SIXTEEN

Knut and I went back to his office and sat one each side of his desk.

'Can you prove it?' he said.

'We can prove he went to the Grand, fetched the key and opened the locker.'

'Anything else?'

I said gloomily, 'It's circumstantial. A good defence lawyer could turn everything inside out.'

Knut chewed his pencil.

'The scandal will ruin him,' he said.

I nodded. 'I'll bet he's got a fortune tucked away somewhere safe, though.'

'But,' Knut said, 'he must care more for his reputation than for just money, otherwise he would simply have left the country instead of having Bob Sherman killed.'

'Yes.'

We sat in silence.

'You are tired,' Knut said.

'Yeah. So are you.'

He grinned and looked suddenly very like Erik.

I said, 'Your brother told me Per Bjørn Sandvik was in the Resistance during the war.'

'*Ja*. He was.'

'Nothing wrong with his nerve,' I said. 'Nothing then, nothing now.'

'And we are not the Gestapo,' Knut said. 'He knows we will not torture him. We must seem feeble to him, after what he risked when he was young. He is not going to give in and confess. Not ever.'

I agreed.

'These two men,' I said. 'Yellow eyes and brown eyes. They're too young to have been in the Resistance themselves. But . . . is there a chance their fathers were? Arne's father was. Could you run a check on the group Per Bjørn belonged to, and see if any of them fathered yellow eyes?'

'You ask such impossible things.'

'And it's a very long shot indeed,' I sighed.

'I'll start tomorrow,' he said.

Some coffee arrived, very milky. I could have done with a treble scotch and a batch of Emma's scones.

'You know,' I said after another silence, 'there's something else. Some other way . . . There has to be.'

'What do you mean?'

'I mean . . . It was just luck finding that key. If Paddy hadn't swapped the helmets we would never have found the paper at Fornebu.' I drank the coffee. It wasn't strong enough to deal with anything but thirst.

'But ... they tried to kill me before they knew the chart wasn't in the pond with Bob Sherman. So there must be something else which they couldn't afford for me to find.'

I put down the cup with a grimace.

'But what?' Knut asked.

'God knows.'

'Something I missed,' he said with gloom.

'Why would they think I would see it if you didn't?'

'Because you do,' he said. 'And Arne knows it.'

Arne ... My friend Arne.

'Why didn't he kill you himself, out on the fjord?' Knut asked. 'Why didn't he just bang you on the head and push you overboard?'

'It isn't that easy to bang someone on the head when you're sitting at opposite ends of a small dinghy. And besides ... leading a beast to the abattoir and slitting its neck are two different things.'

'I don't understand.'

'Arne was keen for me to die but wouldn't do it himself.'

'How do you know?'

'Because he didn't. Over the last few weeks he's had more chance than anybody, but he didn't do it.'

'You couldn't be sure he wouldn't.'

'He's a complex person but his attitudes are all fixed ... if he didn't do it the first time he wouldn't do it afterwards.'

A few more minutes dawdled by while I tried to concentrate on what I hadn't discovered.

Useless, I thought.

Yesterday, I thought, I didn't know who had manipulated Interpetro Oil. Today I did. Did that make any difference?

'Oh my Christ,' I said, and nearly fell out of my chair.

'What is it?' Knut said.

'I'm bloody mad.'

'What do you mean?'

'You remember that bomb . . .'

'Well, of course I do.'

'It was such a sloppy way to kill someone,' I said. 'It might have gone off before we got back to the car . . . It didn't kill us, so we thought of it as a failure. But it didn't fail. Not a bit. It was a roaring success. It did just what it was meant to.'

'David . . .'

'Do you remember where I was going that afternoon? I didn't go, because the bomb stopped me. I'm so damned stupid . . . it isn't *what* I haven't seen, it's *who.*'

He just stared.

'*It's Mikkel Sandvik.*'

I telephoned to the College of Gol and spoke to the headmaster.

'Oh, but Mikkel isn't here,' he said. 'His father telephoned on Sunday morning to say that Mikkel must go and visit his aunt, who was dying and asking for him.'

'Where does the aunt live?'

'I don't know. Mr Sandvik talked to Mikkel himself.' There was some speaking in the background, and then he said, 'My wife says Mikkel told her his Aunt Berit was dying. He went to catch the Bergen train. We don't know where he went after that . . . Why don't you ask his father?'

'Good idea,' I said.

'What now?' Knut said, when I told him.

'I think . . . I'll go and see Mrs Sandvik, and see if she'll tell me where Mikkel is.'

'All right. And I will do what I must about keeping Mr Sandvik here all night.' He sighed. 'A man like that . . . it doesn't seem right to put him in a cell.'

'Don't let him go,' I said.

'Oh no.'

Erik had gone home long ago but Knut reckoned I was on police business and sent me to the Sandvik house in a police car. I walked through the arch into the courtyard, turned right, and rang the bell outside the well-lit imposing front door.

A heavy middle-aged woman opened it. She wore frumpy clothes and no make-up, and had a positive, slightly forbidding manner.

'*Ja?*' she said inquiringly.

255

I explained who I was and asked to see Mrs Sandvik.

'I am Mrs Sandvik. I spoke to you on the telephone a few days ago.'

'That's right.' I swallowed my surprise. I had thought she would already have known about her husband being at the police station, but apparently he hadn't yet made his two calls. When we had left him, Knut had said he would arrange for a telephone to be taken to the interview room and plugged into the socket there, which I supposed took time. No one was positively rushing to provide facilities for a suspect, not even for Per Bjørn Sandvik.

It made it easier, however, for me to ask questions.

'Come inside,' she said. 'It is cold with the door open.'

I stepped into the hall. She invited me no farther.

'Mikkel?' she said in surprise. 'He is at school. I told you.'

I explained about his Aunt Berit.

'He has no Aunt Berit.'

Wow.

'Er . . .' I said. 'Does he know anyone at all called Berit?'

She raised her eyebrows. 'Is this important?'

'I cannot go home until I have seen Mikkel. I am sorry.'

She shrugged. After a longish pause for thought she said, 'Berit is the name of an old nurse of my husband.

256

I do not know if Mikkel knows any other person called Berit. I expect so.'

'Where does your husband's old nurse live?'

'I don't know.'

She couldn't remember the old nurse's surname, and she wasn't sure if she was still alive. She said her husband would be able to tell me, when he came home. She opened the door with finality for me to leave, and with a distinct feeling of cowardice, I left. Per Bjørn had smashed up her secure world and he would have to tell her about it himself.

'He might be with his father's old nurse,' I told Knut. 'And he might not.'

He reflected. 'If he caught the Bergen train, perhaps the Gol ticket office would remember him.'

'Worth a try. But he could be anywhere by now. Anywhere in the world.'

'He's barely seventeen,' Knut said.

'That's old, these days.'

'How did Mrs Sandvik take the news of her husband's arrest?'

'I didn't tell her. I thought Per Bjørn should do that.'

'But he has!'

'She didn't know,' I said blankly.

'But,' Knut said, 'I am sure he made his two calls almost half an hour ago.'

'Bloody hell,' I said.

He steamed out of the office at twenty knots and yelled at several unfortunate subordinates. When he returned he was carrying a piece of paper and looking grim, worried and apologetic all at once.

'They find it difficult not to obey a man with such prestige,' he said. 'He told them to wait outside the door while he spoke to his wife and his lawyer, as both calls were of a private nature. They did what he said.' He looked at the paper in his hand. 'At least they had the sense to dial the numbers for him, and to write them down. They are both Oslo numbers.'

He handed the paper over for me to see. One of the numbers meant nothing. The other meant too much.

'He talked to Arne,' I said.

I pressed the bell outside Arne's flat and after a long interval Kari opened the door.

'David.' She seemed neither surprised nor pleased to see me. She seemed drained.

'Come in,' she said.

The flat seemed somehow colder, less colourful, much quieter than before.

'Where's Arne?' I said.

'He's gone.'

'Where to?'

'I don't know.'

'Tell me everything he did since he came home.'

She gave me an empty stare, then turned away and

walked through to the sitting-room. I followed her. She
sat on the cream-coloured sofa and shivered. The stove
no longer glowed with warmth and welcome and the
stereo record player was switched off.

'He came home upset. Well . . . he's been upset ever
since this Bob Sherman thing started. But today he was
very worried and puzzled and disturbed. He played two
long records and marched about . . . he couldn't keep
still.'

Her voice had the calmness of shock. The reality of
whatever had happened had not yet tipped her into
anger or fear or despair: but tomorrow, I thought, she
might suffer all three.

'He rang Per Bjørn Sandvik's house twice, but they
said he wasn't in. It seemed to worry him very much.'

There was a tray on the coffee table in front of her
laden with an untouched dish of open sandwiches. They
made me feel frantically hungry as I hadn't eaten since
a pin-sized breakfast, but she gave them an indifferent
glance and said, 'He left them. He said he couldn't . . .'

Try me, I thought: but hostessing was far out of her
mind.

'Then Per Bjørn Sandvik rang here. Only a little
while ago . . . but it seems hours and hours . . . Arne
was relieved at first, but then . . . he went so quiet . . . I
knew something was wrong.'

'What did he say to Per Bjørn? Can you remember?'

'He said Ja, and No. He listened a long time. He
said . . . I think he said . . . don't worry, I'll find him.'

'That was all?'

She nodded. 'Then he went into the bedroom and he was so quiet . . . I went to see what was the matter. He was sitting on the bed, looking at the floor. He looked up at me when I came. His eyes were . . . I don't know . . . dead.'

'And then?'

'He got up and began packing a suitcase. I asked him . . . he said don't worry me . . . so I just stood there. He packed . . . he threw things into the case . . . and he was muttering away, mostly about you.'

She looked at me intently but still with the numb lack of emotion.

'He said . . . "I told him, I told him David would beat him . . . I told him at the beginning . . . he still says David hasn't beaten him but he has, he has . . ." I asked Arne what he was talking about but I don't think he even heard me.' She pressed her fingers against her forehead, rubbing the smooth skin. 'Arne said . . . "David . . . David knew all day . . . he made the trap and put himself into it as bait . . . he knew all day." Then he said something about you using some girls and an old man, and something about orangeade . . . and a premonition you invented. He said he knew you would be the end of everything; he said so before you came.'

She looked at me with the sudden awakening of awareness and the beginnings of hostility.

'What did you do?' she asked.

'I'm sorry, Kari. I gave Arne and Per Bjørn Sandvik

a chance to show they knew more than they ought about Bob Sherman's death, and they took it.'

'More than they ought . . .?' she repeated vaguely: then overwhelmingly understood. 'Oh no. Oh no. Not Arne.' She stood up abruptly. 'I don't believe it.' But she already did.

'I still don't know who killed Bob Sherman,' I said. 'I think Arne does know. I want to talk to him.'

'He's not coming back. He said . . . he would write, and send for me. In a few weeks.' She looked forlorn. 'He took the car.' She paused. 'He kissed me.'

'I wish . . .' I said uselessly, and she caught the meaning in my voice though the words weren't spoken.

'Yes,' she said. 'In spite of everything . . . he likes you too.'

It was still not yet eight o'clock and Per Bjørn was still in the interview room when I got back to the police station.

'His lawyer is with him,' Knut said morosely. 'We won't get a word out of him now.'

'We haven't had so many already.'

'No.' He flicked the paper with the telephone numbers which was lying on his desk. 'This other number . . . it isn't the lawyer's.'

'Whose, then?'

'It's a big second-class hotel near the docks. Dozens of incoming calls; they couldn't remember one more than any other. I have sent a policeman down there with a description of the man with yellow eyes.'

'Mm. Whoever he spoke to at the hotel then telephoned the lawyer.'

'*Ja*,' he said. 'It must be so. Unless Arne did.'

'I don't think so, from what his wife said.'

'He had gone?'

I nodded. 'In his car.'

He put his hand again on the telephone. 'We will find the number and put out an alert: and also check with the airport and the frontier posts with Sweden.'

'I know the number.' I told it to him. He looked surprised, but I said, 'I've been in his car . . . and I've a memory for numbers. Don't know why.'

He put out his alerts and sat tapping his pencil against his teeth.

'And now we wait,' he said.

We waited precisely five seconds before the first call came through. He scooped up the receiver with a speed which betrayed his inner pressure, and listened intently.

'*Ja*,' he said eventually. '*Ja . . . takk*. Thank you.'

He put down the receiver and relayed the news.

'That was the policeman I sent to the hotel. He says the man with yellow eyes has been staying there for a week, but this evening he paid his bill and left. He gave no address. He was known to the hotel as L. Horgen. My policeman says that unfortunately the room has already been cleaned because the hotel is busy, but he has directed them to leave it empty until we've searched it and tried for fingerprints. Excuse me while I send a team to do that.'

He went out of the office and was gone a fair time, but when he came back he had more to tell.

'We've found Arne's car. It is parked not far from the quay of the Nansen shipping line, and one of their ships left for Copenhagen an hour ago. We are radioing to the ship and to Copenhagen to pick him up.'

'Don't let them relax at Fornebu,' I said.

He looked at me.

I grinned faintly. 'Well . . . If I wanted to slip out by air I'd leave my car beside a shipping line and take a taxi to the airport. And Arne and I once discussed quite a lot of things like that.'

'He'd know you'd guess, then.'

'I'd pin more hope on the ship if he'd left his car at the airport.'

He shook his head and sighed. 'A good thing you're not a crook,' he said.

A young policeman knocked, came in, and spoke to Knut.

He translated for me. 'Mr Sandvik's lawyer wants to see me, with his client. I'll go along to the interview room . . . Do you want to come?'

'Please,' I said.

With Per Bjørn, his lawyer, Knut, me, and a note-taking policeman all inside with the door shut, the small interview room looked overcrowded with dark suits and solemnity. The other four sat on the hard chairs round the plain table and I stood leaning against the door, listening to a long conversation of which I understood not a word.

Per Bjørn pushed back his chair, crossed his legs and set fire to a cigarette, much as before. His lawyer, a heavy self-possessed man of obvious worldly power, was speaking in an authoritative voice and making Knut perceptibly more nervous minute by minute. But Knut survived uncracked and although when he answered he sounded friendly and apologetic, the message he got across was 'No.'

It angered the lawyer more than the client. He stood up, towering over Knut, and delivered a severe caution. Knut looked worried, stood up in his turn, and shook his head. After that the young policeman was sent on an errand, presently returning with a sergeant and an escort.

Knut said, 'Mr Sandvik . . .', and waited.

Per Bjørn stood up slowly and stubbed out his filter tip. He looked impassively at the escort and walked calmly towards them. When he drew level with me at the doorway he stopped, turned his head, and stared very deliberately at my face.

But whatever he was thinking, nothing at all showed in his eyes, and he spoke not a word.

Knut went home, but I spent the night in his office sleeping on the floor on blankets and pillows borrowed from the cells; and I daresay I was less comfortable than the official guest downstairs.

'What's wrong with the Grand?' Knut said, when I asked him to let me stay.

'Yellow eyes is on the loose,' I said. 'And who knows what instructions Per Bjørn gave him?'

Knut looked at me thoughtfully. 'You think there's more to come?'

'Per Bjørn is still fighting.'

'*Ja*,' he sighed. 'I think so too.'

He sent a policeman out to bring me a hot meal from a nearby restaurant, and in the morning at eight o'clock he came back with a razor. He himself, trim in his uniform, seemed to have shed yesterday like a skin and arrived bright eyed and awake to the new day. I shivered blearily in my crumpled clothes and felt like a reject from a doss house.

At eight forty-five the telephone rang. Knut picked up the receiver, listened, and seemed pleased with what he heard.

'*Ja. Ja. Takk*,' he said.

'What is it?'

He put the receiver back. 'We've had a message from Gol. The man who was on duty in the ticket office on Sunday remembers that a boy from the College bought a ticket to Finse.'

'Finse . . .' I thought back to my time-tables. 'On the Bergen line?'

'*Ja*. Finse is the highest town on the line. Up in the

265

mountains. I will find out if he is remembered at the station there. I will find out if anyone has seen him in the streets or knows if he is staying.'

'How long will that take?'

'One can't tell.'

'No.' I thought it over. 'Look . . . the train for Bergen leaves at ten, if I remember right. I'll catch it. Then if you hear that Mikkel is or isn't at Finse, perhaps you could get a message to me at one of the stops up the line.'

'Have you forgotten yellow eyes?'

'Unfortunately not,' I said.

He smiled. 'All right. I will send you to the station in a police car. Do you want a policeman to go with you?'

I thought. 'I might get further with Mikkel if I go alone.'

On the train I sat next to a total stranger, a cheerful young man with little English, and spent an uneventful journey looking out at peaceful fields and bright little dolls' houses scattered haphazardly on hillsides.

At Gol there was a written message.

'Young man disembarkation to Finse the Sunday. One knows not until where he gone. The questions is continue.'

'Thank you very much,' I said.

The train climbed slowly above the tree line into a landscape of blue-grey rock and green-grey water. Snow scattered the ground, at first in patches, then in profusion, and finally as a thin white rug over every sloping surface, with sharp rock edges like hatchets showing through.

'Is small snow,' said my companion. 'In winter in Finse is two metres.'

'Two metres deep?' I asked.

He nodded. '*Ja*. Is good for ski.'

The railway ran for a time alongside a fiercely cold-looking wind-ruffled grey-green lake and slowed with a sigh of relief into Finse.

'Is hot summer,' my friend said, looking around in surprise. 'Is snow gone.'

He might think so, but I didn't. Snow still covered everything worth mentioning, hot summer gone by or not; and icicles dangled from every roof like stiff, glittering fringes. Once out of the warmth of the train the cold bit sharply and even in my ear-covering cap and padded jacket I wrapped my arms round my chest in a futile attempt to hold on to my body heat.

I was met by the bulk of the Finse police force in the shape of a broadly smiling officer of turnstile-blocking size.

'Mr Cleveland.' He shook my hand. 'We do not know where is this boy Mikkel Sandvik. We have not seen him in the village. There are not many strangers here now. In the summer, and in the winter, we have very many strangers. We have the big hotel, for the ski. But now, not many. We have look for an old woman who is called Berit. There are two. It is not one, because she is in bed in the house of her son and she is . . . er . . . she is . . . old.'

'Senile?' I suggested.

He didn't know the word. 'Very old,' he repeated.

'And the other Berit?'

'She lives in a house beside the lake. One and a half kilometres out of Finse. She goes away in the winter. Soon, now. She is a strong old woman. In the summer, she takes people who come to fish, but they have all gone now. Usually on Wednesdays she comes for food, so we have not gone to see her. But she is late today. She comes in the mornings.'

'I'll go there,' I said, and listened to directions.

The way to the house of Berit-by-the-lake turned out to be merely a path which ran between the railway line and the shore, more a matter of small stones and pebbles through an area of boulders than any recognizable beaten track. With its roughnesses still half-covered with crusty ice, it was easy to imagine that once the new snows fell it would be entirely obliterated.

CHAPTER SEVENTEEN

I looked back.

A bend had taken Finse out of sight.

I looked forward. Nothing but the sketchy path picking its uncertain way through the snow-strewn boulders. Only on my right could be seen any evidence of humanity, and that was the railway. And then that too ran straight ahead behind a hill while the shore curved to the left, so that in the end there was just me and the stark unforgiving landscape, just me trudging through an energetic wind on a cold, wild and lonely afternoon.

The path snaked its way round two small bays and two small headlands, with the hillside on my right rising ever more steeply the farther I went, and then all of a sudden the house lay before me, standing alone on a flat stony area spread out like an apron into the lake.

The house was red. A strong crimson. Roof, walls, door, the lot. The colour stood out sharply against the grey and white of the shore and the darker grey-green of the water; and rising beyond it at the head of the lake stood dark towering cliffs, thrown up like a sudden mountain against the northern sky.

Maybe it was a grand, extraordinary, awe-inspiring sight. Maybe it should have swelled my spirit, uplifted my soul. Actually it inspired in me nothing more noble than a strong desire to retreat.

I stopped.

Surely Sandvik wouldn't have sent his son to this threatening place, even if he did urgently want to hide him. Surely Mikkel was half the world away by now, with Arne cantering post haste in his wake to look after him.

Damned bloody silly place to build a house, I thought. Enough to give anyone the creeps, living with a mountain on the doorstep.

I went on. The house had a landing stage with a motor boat tied to a post like a hitched horse in a Western. It also had looped up lace curtains and geraniums on the window sills. Red geraniums. Naturally.

I looked in vain for smoke from the chimney, and no one stared out at me as I approached.

I banged the knocker. The door was opened straight away by a ramrod-backed old woman, five feet tall, sharp eyed, entirely self possessed. Far, very far, from dying.

'*Ja?*' she said enquiringly.

'I'd like to talk to Mikkel,' I said.

She took a very brief pause to change languages,

and then in a pure near-Scots accent said, 'Who are you?'

'I am looking for Mikkel.'

'Everyone is looking for Mikkel.' She inspected me from head to foot. 'Come in. It is cold.'

She showed me into the living-room, where everything was in process of being packed away in crates. She gestured round with a fine-boned hand. 'I am leaving now for the winter. It is beautiful here in the summer, but not in winter.'

'I have a message from his father,' I said.

'Another one?'

'What do you mean?'

'Already one man came this morning. Then another. Both of them said they had a message from his father. And now you.' She looked at me straightly. 'That is very many messages.'

'Yes . . . I have to find him.'

She put her head on one side. 'I told the others. I cannot judge which of you I should not tell. So I will tell you. He is on the mountain.'

I looked through the window to the wall of rock and the end of the lake.

'Up there?'

'*Ja*. There is a cabin up there. I rent it to visitors in the summer, but in the winter the snow covers it. Mikkel went up there this morning to bring down the things I do not want to leave there. He is a kind boy.'

'Who were the other men who came?'

271

'I don't know. The first one said his name was Kristian-sen. They both said they would go up and help Mikkel bring down the things, although I said it was not necessary, there are not many things and he took the sleigh.'

'The sleigh?'

'*Ja*. Very light. You can pull it.'

'Perhaps I had better go up there as well.'

'You have bad shoes.'

I looked down. City casuals, not built for snowy mountains, and already darkly wet round the edges.

'Can't be helped,' I said.

She shrugged. 'I will show you the path. It is better than the one round the lake.' She smiled faintly. 'I do not walk to Finse. I go in the boat.'

'The second man,' I said. 'Did he have extraordinary yellow eyes?'

'No.' She shook her head decisively. 'He was ordinary. Very polite. Like you.' She smiled and pointed through the window. 'The path starts over there behind that big rock. It is not steep. It winds away from the lake and then comes back. You will see it easily.'

I thanked her and set off, and found almost at once that she was right about the shoes. One might be able to see the path easily, but that was because it was a well-worn track through the snow, patterned widely on either side by the marks of skis, like a sort of mini highway.

I slithered along in the brisk wind, working round

the hillside in a wide, ever upward-sloping U. But it proved to be not as far as I'd feared, because, long before I expected it, I came to the top of a small rise and found below me, suddenly only a few yards away, a sturdy little log hut, built to the traditional Norwegian pattern like a roofed box standing on a slightly smaller plinth.

It was already too late to make a careful inconspicuous approach. I stood there in full view of a small window: so I simply walked straight up and looked through it.

The cabin was dark inside and at first I thought it was empty. Then I saw him. Huddled in a corner, with his head bent over his knees, slowly rocking as if in pain.

There was only one small room. Only one door. I put my hand on its latch and opened it.

The movement galvanized the figure inside into action, and it was only something half seen, half instinctive, which had me leaping sideways away from the entrance with adrenalin scorching down to my toes. Blast from a shotgun roared through the doorway, and I pressed myself against the heavy log wall alongside and hoped to God it was impervious to pellets.

A voice shouted something hysterically from inside.

Not Arne's voice. Young. Stretched to breaking.

'Mikkel,' I said. 'I will not harm you. I am David Cleveland.'

Silence.

'Mikkel . . .'

'If you come in, I will shoot you.' His voice was naturally high pitched like his father's, and the tension in it had strung it up another octave.

'I only want to talk to you.'

'No. No. No.'

'Mikkel . . . You can't stay here for ever.'

'If you come in, I'll shoot.'

'All right . . . I'll talk from here.' I shivered with cold and wholeheartedly cursed him.

'I will not talk to you. Go away. Go away.'

I didn't answer. Five minutes passed with no sound except the blustering wind. Then his voice from inside, tight and frightened. 'Are you still there?'

'Yes,' I said.

'Go away.'

'We have to talk sometime. Might as well be now.'

'No.'

'Where is Arne Kristiansen?' I asked.

His reply was a high keening wail which raised goose-bumps up my spine. What followed it was a thoroughly normal sob.

I crouched down low and risked a quick look through the door. The gun lay in one hand on the floor and with the other he was trying to wipe away tears. He looked up and saw me, and again immediately began to aim.

I retreated smartly and stood up outside against the wall, as before.

'Why don't you tell me?' I said.

A long pause of several minutes.

'You can come in.'

I took another quick look. He was sitting straight legged on the floor with the gun pointing at the door.

'Come in,' he said. 'I won't shoot.'

'Put the gun on the floor and slide it away.'

'No.'

More time passed.

'The only way I'll talk,' he said, 'is if you come in. But I will keep the gun.'

I swallowed. 'All right.'

I stepped into the doorway. Looked down the double barrels. He sat with his back against the wall, holding the gun steady. A box of cartridges lay open beside him, with one or two scattered around.

'Shut the door,' he said. 'Sit down opposite me, against the wall. On the floor.'

I did as he said.

He was slight and not full grown. Brown hair, dark frightened eyes. Cheeks still round from childhood; the jaw line of an adult. Half boy, half man, with tear stains on his face and his finger on the trigger.

Everything movable in the bare little cabin had been stacked in a neat pile to one side. A heavy table and two solid chairs were the total to be left. No curtains at the single small window. No rugs on the bare wood floor. Two collapsible camp beds, folded and strapped together for transport, leaned against a wall. A pair of skis stood beside them.

No logs by the cold stove, and no visible food.

'It'll be dark soon,' I said. 'Within an hour.'

'I don't care.' He stared at me with burning eyes and unnerving intensity.

'We should go down to Berit's house while we can still see the way.'

'No.'

'We'll freeze up here.'

'I don't care.'

I believed him. Anyone as distracted as he was tended to blot even extreme discomforts out of his mind: and although he had allowed me into the hut he was far from coming down off the high wire. Little tremors of tension ran in his body and twitched his feet. Occasionally the gun shook in his hands. I tried not to think gloomy thoughts.

'We must go,' I said.

'Sit still,' he said fiercely, and the right forefinger curled convulsively. I looked at it. And I sat.

Daylight slowly faded and the cold crept in inexorably. The wind outside whined like a spoilt child, never giving up. I thought I might as well face it: the prospect of the night ahead made the fjord water seem in retrospect as cosy as a heated pool. I put my padded mitts inside my padded pockets and tried to kid myself that my fingers were warm. And it was a minor disaster that the jacket wasn't really long enough for sitting on.

'Mikkel,' I said. 'Just tell me. You'll explode if you don't talk to someone. And I'm here. So just . . . tell me. Whatever you like.'

He stared fixedly through the gathering dusk. I waited a long time.

'I killed him,' he said.

Oh God.

A long pause. Then on a rising note he said it again, 'I killed him.'

'Who?' I said.

Silence.

'How?' I said.

The question surprised him. He took his gaze for one moment off my face and glanced down at the gun.

'I . . . shot . . .'

With an effort I said, 'Did you shoot . . . Arne?'

'Arne . . .' The hysteria rose again. 'No. No. No. Not Arne. I didn't kill Arne. I didn't. I didn't.'

'All right,' I said. 'All right, Mikkel. Let's wait a bit . . . until you can tell me. Until you feel it is the right time to tell me.' I paused. 'Is that OK?'

After a while he said, '*Ja*. OK.'

We waited.

It got darker until it seemed that the only light left was the reflection from the window in his eyes. I could see them long after the rest of him dissolved into one amorphous shadow, two live agonized signals of a mind desperately afraid of the help it desperately needed.

It must have occurred to him as to me that after

total darkness I would be able to jump his gun, because he stirred restlessly on the floor and muttered something in Norwegian, and finally in a much more normal voice said, 'There is a lamp in a box. On top of the things.'

'Shall I find it and light it?'

'*Ja.*'

I stood up stiffly, glad of the chance to move, but sensing him lift the gun to keep me where it mattered.

'I won't try to take the gun away,' I said.

No answer.

The heap of gear was to my right, near the window. I moved carefully, but with many small noises so that he should know where I was and not be alarmed, and felt around for the box on top. Nothing wrong with his memory: the box was there, and the lamp in it, and also a box of matches.

'I've found the lamp,' I said. 'Shall I strike a match?'

A pause.

'*Ja.*'

It proved to be a small gas lamp. I lit it and put it on the table from where it cast a weak white light into every corner. He blinked twice as his irises adjusted, but his concentration never wavered.

'Is there any food?' I asked.

'I'm not hungry.'

'I am.'

'Sit down,' he said. 'Where you were.'

I sat. The gun barrels followed. In the new light I could see down them a lot too well.

Time passed. I lit the lamp at four thirty in the afternoon and it was eight before he began to talk.

By then, if I was anything to go by, he had lost all feeling from the waist down. He wore no gloves and his hands had turned blue-white, but he still held the gun ready, with his finger inside the trigger guard. His eyes still watched. His face, his whole body, were still stiff with near-unbearable tension.

He said suddenly, 'Arne Kristiansen told me that my father was arrested. He told me he was arrested because of you.'

His voice came out high and his breath condensed into a frosty plume.

Once started, he found it easier.

'He said . . . my father wanted us to go to Bergen . . . and on a boat to Stavanger . . . and fly . . .' He stopped.

'And you didn't go,' I said. 'Why didn't you go?'

The gun shook.

'They came in . . .' he said.

I waited.

He said, 'I was talking to him. Outside. About going away.' A pause. 'They came over the hill. On skis, with goggles.' Another pause. 'One of them told Arne to step away from me.' After a longer pause and with an even sharper burst of remembered terror he said, 'He had a knife.'

'Oh Mikkel,' I said.

He talked faster, tumbling it out.

'Arne said, "You can't. You can't. He wouldn't send you to kill his own son. Not Mikkel." He pushed me behind him. He said, "You're crazy. I talked to his father myself. He told me to come here to take Mikkel away." '

He stared across at me with stretched eyes, reliving it.

'They said . . . my father had changed his mind about Arne going. They said they were to take me themselves on a ship to Denmark and wait until my father sent money and instructions. Arne said it was not true. They said . . . it was true . . . and they said . . . Arne was going no further than right here . . . He didn't believe it . . . he said not even my father would do that. He watched only the one with the knife and the other one swung a ski stick and hit him on the head . . . He fell down in the snow . . . I tried to stop them . . . they just pushed me off . . . and they put him on the sleigh . . . they strapped him on . . . and pulled him up the path.'

The panic he had felt then came crowding back into his face. He said painfully, 'I remembered the gun in the cabin . . . I went inside and loaded it . . . and put on my skis and went after them . . . to stop them . . . but when I found them they were coming back . . . without the sleigh . . . and I thought . . . I thought . . . they were going to . . . they were going to . . .'

He took a deep shuddering breath. 'I fired the gun. The one with the knife . . . he fell down . . .'

'I fired again,' he said. 'But the other one was still on his skis ... So I came back to the cabin because I thought he would come after me ... I came back to reload the gun. But he didn't come ... He didn't come ...

'You came,' he said. 'I thought it was him.'

He stopped.

'Did you know the two men?' I asked. 'Had you ever seen them before?'

'No.'

'How long was it before I came?' I said.

'I don't know. A long time.'

'Hours?'

'I think so.'

I hadn't seen any of them on my way up.

'Killing is wrong,' he said jerkily.

'It depends.'

'No.'

'To defend your life, or someone else's life, it would be all right,' I said.

'I ... I believe ... I *know* it is wrong. And yet I ... when I was so afraid ...' His high voice cracked. 'I have done it. I despise killing and I've done it. And I would have killed you too. I know I would. If you hadn't jumped.'

'Never mind,' I said; but the horrors were still there in his eyes. Making it deliberately an emotion-reducing question I asked, 'Have you known Arne Kristiansen long?'

'What . . .?' His own voice came down a bit. 'About three years, I suppose.'

'And how well do you know him?'

'Not very well. On the racecourse. That's all.'

'Has your father known him long?'

'I don't think so . . . The same as me. At the races.'

'Are they close friends?'

He said with sudden extreme bitterness, 'My father has no close friends.'

'Will you put the gun down now?' I said.

He looked at it.

'All right.'

He put it beside him on the floor. A relief not to be looking down those two round holes.

The lamp chose that moment to give notice it was running out of gas. Mikkel switched his gaze from me to the table, but the message of fading light didn't seem to pierce through the inner turmoil.

'The lamp is going out,' I said. 'Is there a spare gas cylinder?'

He slowly shook his head.

'Mikkel,' I said. 'It is freezing and it will soon be dark. If we are to survive the night we must keep warm.'

No response.

'Are you listening?'

'What?'

'You are going to have to face life as it is.'

'I . . . can't . . .'

'Are there any blankets?'

'There is one.'

I began to try to stand up and he reached immediately for the gun.

'Don't be silly,' I said. 'I won't hurt you. And you won't shoot me. So let's just both relax, huh?'

He said uncertainly. 'You had my father arrested.'

'Do you know why?'

'Not . . . not really.'

I told him about the oil transaction, playing down the disloyalty, to put it no higher, that Per Bjørn had shown to his country, but there was, it seemed, nothing basically wrong with Mikkel's brains. He was silent for some time after I'd finished and the muscles slowly relaxed limb by limb.

'Once he had been found out,' he said, 'he would lose his job. He would lose the respect of everyone. He wouldn't be able to live like that . . . not my father.'

His voice at last was sane and controlled; and almost too late. The lamp was going out.

'The blanket,' he said, 'is in the beds.'

He tried to stand up and found his legs were as numb and useless as mine, if not more so. It kicked him straight back to practical sense.

'I'm cold!'

'So am I.'

He looked across, seeing our predicament squarely for the first time.

'Stand up,' he said. 'Walk about.'

Easier said, but it had to be done.

'Can we light the stove?' I said. 'There are four more matches, the cardboard boxes, and the table and chairs, if we can break them up.'

We had both by then tottered to our feet. The lamp shone with one candle power, sadly.

'There is no axe,' Mikkel said.

The lamp went out.

'I'm sorry,' he said.

'Never mind.'

We jumped up and down in total darkness. Funny if it hadn't been urgent. Blood started circulating again, though, to the places where it was needed, and after half an hour or so we were both warm enough to give it a rest.

'I can find the blanket,' Mikkel said, and did so. 'Shall we share it?'

'We certainly shall.'

We both wore warm jackets and he, when he remembered where he'd put them, had a cap and mitts like my own. We laid the folded canvas beds on an insulating foundation of cardboard boxes, and wrapped ourselves from the waist down in one cocoon in the single blanket, sitting close together to share every scrap of warmth. It was too dark to see what he was thinking, but there were faint tremors still, occasionally, through his body.

'I took the rest of the bedding down to Berit's house yesterday,' he said. 'On the sleigh.'

'Pity.'

The word switched his thoughts. He said abruptly, 'Do you think Arne is dead?'

'I don't know,' I said. But I did think so.

'What will happen to me, for killing that man?'

'Nothing. Just tell it as you told me. No one will blame you.'

'Are you sure?'

'Yes.'

'I am as bad as anyone else who kills,' he said, but this time there was adult acceptance and despair in his voice, not hysteria. I wondered if it were possible for a boy to age ten years in one night, because it would be better for him if he could.

'Tell me about Bob Sherman,' I said; and felt the jolt that went through him at the name.

'I . . . can't . . .'

'Mikkel . . . I know that Bob brought the stolen surveys from England to give to your father . . .'

'No,' he interrupted.

'What, then?'

'He had to deliver them to Arne. I didn't know they were for my father when I . . .' He stopped dead.

'When you what?'

'I mustn't tell you. I can't.'

In the darkness I said calmly, almost sleepily, 'Did Bob tell you he had brought a package?'

He said unwillingly, 'Yes.'

I yawned. 'When?'

285

'When I met him in Oslo. The night he came.'

I wondered if he felt in his turn the thud with which that news hit me.

'Where in Oslo?' I said casually.

'He was outside the Grand with his saddle and his overnight bag. I was walking home from a friend's house, and I stopped. He said he might go and catch the tram. I asked him if he would like some coffee first, so we walked along to our house. I carried his saddle.' He paused. 'I liked Bob. We were friends.'

'I know,' I said.

'My father was out. He usually is. Mother was watching television. Bob and I went into the kitchen, and I made the coffee. We ate some cake my mother had made.'

'What did you talk about?'

'At first about the horses he was riding the next day . . . Then he said he had brought a package from England, and he'd opened it, and it didn't contain what he'd been told. He said he had to give it to Arne Kristiansen at the races but he was going to ask for a bit more money before he handed it over.'

His body trembled against mine within the blanket.

'He was laughing about it, really. He said they'd told him it was pornography, but it wasn't, and he didn't know what it was even though he'd seen it. Then he took the package out of his case and told me to look.'

He stopped.

'And,' I said, 'when you saw what was in the package, you knew what it was?'

'I'd seen papers like that before . . . I mean . . . I knew it was an oil survey. Yes.'

'Did you tell Bob what it was?'

'Yes. I did. We talked about it a bit.'

'And then?'

'It was late. Too late for the tram. Bob took a taxi out to Gunnar Holth's stable, and I went to bed.'

'What happened the next day?'

'I promised . . . I promised I wouldn't tell anybody. I didn't tell the police. I mustn't tell you. Especially not you. I know that.'

'All right,' I said.

Time passed. It was almost too cold to think.

'I told my father about Bob Sherman's package on the way to the races,' he said. 'He took me in the car. I only told him for something to say. Because I thought he might be interested. But he didn't say much. He never does. I never know what he's thinking.'

'Nor do I,' I said.

'I have heard people say he looks kindest when he is being most cruel. When I was small, I heard it first.'

'Is he cruel to you?'

'No. Just . . . cold. But he is my father.'

'Yes.'

'I think I want to tell you . . . but I can't.'

'All right.'

A long time passed. His breath and body movements

betrayed his wakefulness and the churning thoughts in his mind.

'Mr Cleveland? Are you awake?'

'David,' I said.

'David ... Do you think he meant those men to kill me?'

'No, I don't.'

'He told them where to come. He told me to come to Finse. He told Arne Kristiansen to come to Finse. And those men.'

'He did,' I said. 'But I should think they spoke the truth. I should think he meant them to take you out of the country, after they had dealt with Arne. I should think they were very clumsy to let you see them actually attack Arne, but then they have more strength than brains, those two. Arne is the only one who could go into court and give conclusive evidence against your father, and I do think that your father is ruthless enough to have him killed to prevent that.'

'Why ... why do you think so?'

'Because he sent those two men after me, too.'

I told him about the boat in the fjord, the knife in Chelsea, the bomb in Erik's car.

'They're terrible men,' he said. 'They frightened me the instant I saw them.'

He relapsed into silence. I could almost feel him thinking, suffering, working it all out.

'David?'

'Yes?'

'It was my fault Bob died.'

'Certainly not.'

'But if I hadn't told my father that Bob knew he'd brought an oil survey . . .'

'Arne would have told him,' I said flatly. 'You can go on saying if for ever. If Bob hadn't opened the package. If your father hadn't been ruthless enough to get rid of him. But all these things happened. They all happened because your father is both greedy and proud, which is always a pretty deadly combination. But also he learned how to live a secret life when he was young. Against the Nazis, it was good. Everyone admired him. I should think he's never lost the feeling that anything anti-authority is daring and therefore all right. I should think he put the police into the place of the Nazis, as the enemy to be outwitted. He thinks like lightning, he gives away nothing under questioning, he coolly takes tremendous risks, he arranges without mercy for people to die. He's still acting the way he did when he was twenty. He always will.'

Time passed.

'David . . .'

'Yes?'

'I'll have to tell you,' he said.

I took a deep breath. It felt icy in my lungs.

'Go on,' I said.

He paused again. Then he said, 'I was talking to Bob at the races. He laughed and told me it was all fixed,

Arne was going to drive him to the airport afterwards and pay him extra for the package.'

He stopped.

I waited.

His voice went on, hesitant but at last committed.

'By the end of the races it was dark. I went out to the car to wait for my father. He is often late because of being on the committee. I sat in the car and waited for him. I hadn't talked to him at all at the races. I usually don't see him much there. He's always busy.'

He stopped again. His breathing grew heavier, more disturbed.

'Most of the cars went. Then two people came past and in some passing headlights I saw they were Bob and Arne. I was going to call out to them . . . I wish I had . . . but I couldn't get the window down fast enough . . . and then they were over by Arne's car. They were talking face to face. I could only see them now and then, you see, when car lights pointed that way as people went home. But I saw another man walk up behind Bob and raise his arm. He held something shiny . . . Then he brought it down . . .'

He stopped. Gulped a bit. Went on. 'The next time I could see, there were only two people there. I thought . . . I couldn't *believe* . . . And then one of them turned and came towards our car. I was scared . . .'

He shuddered violently.

'But he just opened the boot and threw into it something which clinked, and then he got into the driving seat, and he was smiling.'

A long pause.

'Then he saw me sitting there, and he looked absolutely astonished. And he said . . . he said . . . "Mikkel! I'd forgotten you were at the races." '

His voice was full of pain.

'He'd forgotten me. Forgotten me.'

He was trying not to cry.

'My father,' he said. 'My father killed Bob Sherman.'

CHAPTER EIGHTEEN

We went down to Finse at first light, him sliding easily on his skis, me scrunching and slipping in my city shoes. If I looked anything like he did I had blue grey circles round my eyes, hollows at the corners of my mouth, and a certain overall air of extreme weariness.

He had said little more during the night. He had rolled his head on to my shoulder at one point and fallen exhaustedly asleep, and in the early morning, when he stirred, he had been calm and apparently untroubled, as if the final unburdening of the horror he'd lived with through eight long weeks had set him quietly free.

I left him with the warm comforting people of Finse, and went up the mountain again with several local men. This time I went on skis, shuffling along inexpertly up the slope. They waited for me, making jokes. They had cheerful faces, carefree smiles. And the sun came wanly through the clouds, the first time I'd seen it in Norway.

We reached the hut and went on past it, up beyond where the path petered out into a flat field of snow.

Two of the men were pulling a sleigh, a lightweight affair sliding easily on ski-like runners; just like the one old Berit has, they said.

Brown eyes was lying face down in the snow.

Dead.

But he hadn't died from gunshot wounds: or not primarily. He'd died from exposure and cold.

The men from Finse looked in silence at the trail leading away behind his body. He'd been pulling himself along, crawling. The snow where he'd been was streaked black with his blood.

They wrapped him in canvas, put him on the sleigh, and turned to go to Finse.

'I'll go that way,' I said, pointing to where brown eyes had come from.

They nodded, consulted, and sent a man with me, as they didn't trust my rudimentary ability on skis.

We followed the blood-stained trail up a shallow slope and on to a sort of plateau whose far edge was a smooth horizon against a pale grey sky. The trail ended in a jumble of tracks which the man from Finse rapidly interpreted.

'This is where he was shot. See the blood. There was another man with him.' He pointed to a set of ski marks setting off at a tangent across virgin snow. 'That man is an expert cross-country skier. He went fast. He left the other man lying wounded in the snow. He did not come back with help. If he had, he could have followed the trail of blood.'

Yellow eyes had just upped and left. But Knut would find him in the end.

'The two men came across to here skiing fast and easily,' my guide said, and pointed to tracks stretching away across the plateau.

'There are other tracks over there,' he said, turning to his right and stretching out a well gloved hand.

'Let's look,' I said.

We went over.

'Two men,' he said, 'pulling a loaded sleigh.'

Although I expected it, it hit in my gut.

'They came that way,' I said, pointing back towards the hut.

He nodded. We went back along the trail until we found the marks of Mikkel's skis beside it.

'The boy came to here. Stopped. Then he turned and went back. You can see from his tracks that he was disturbed when he came. And panic stricken when he left. Look at the depth and the sharpness and the small steps.'

'We might find the cartridges,' I said.

He nodded. We looked for a while and found both of them, bright orange cylinders on the snow.

'And now . . .' I gestured ahead along the trail which Mikkel had been following: two men and a loaded sleigh.

The marks ran regularly across the plateau towards the horizon. We followed.

The horizon proved to be not the end of the world,

but the brow of a hill. Down the other side the slope was steep, short, and sharp edged, and far beyond it, mile upon mile, lay a vista of snow-scattered peaks. We were standing at the top of the cliffs above the lake where Berit lived.

The marks of the two men on skis stopped at the brow of the hill, and turned back.

The sleigh marks ran on straight and true to the edge.

'I want to go down there,' I said, and unclipped my skis.

My guide didn't like it, but produced a rope from round his waist. He tied me to it, and paid it out foot by foot, standing four square and solid at the top of the slope.

I went down slowly in my borrowed boots, finding the snow surprisingly glassy and having to be careful not to slide. Having to concentrate, too, on not feeling giddy, and finding it as difficult as ever. When I stood at length on the edge I could see all the lake stretching away, with Berit's house a crimson blob far down to the left.

Beside my feet the marks of the runners looked shallow and crisp, speaking of speed. And they ran on without pity, pointing straight out into space.

The drop in front was six hundred feet, perpendicular. The ruffled green water lay secretively below. Nothing else. Nothing to see.

Arne, I thought. Flying through the air on a sleigh, down to his death.

Arne ... who didn't look over his shoulder the one time the enemy was really there.

Arne, my treacherous friend.

You would have sworn that round the snowy cliffs you could hear crashing chords of Beethoven echoing in the wind.

BANKER

My sincere thanks for the
generous help of
JEREMY H. THOMPSON MD FRCPI
Professor of Pharmacology
University of California
Los Angeles
and of
MICHAEL MELLUISH
and JOHN COOPER

The First Year

MAY

Gordon Michaels stood in the fountain with all his clothes on.

'My God,' Alec said. 'What is he doing?'

'Who?'

'Your boss,' Alec said. 'Standing in the fountain.'

I crossed to the window and stared downwards: down two floors to the ornamental fountain in the forecourt of the Paul Ekaterin merchant bank. Down to where three entwining plumes of water rose gracefully into the air and fell in a glittering circular curtain. To where, in the bowl, calf-deep, stood Gordon in his navy pin-striped suit . . . in his white shirt and sober silk tie . . . in his charcoal socks and black shoes . . . in his gold cufflinks and onyx ring . . . in his polished City persona . . . soaking wet.

It was his immobility, I thought, which principally alarmed. Impossible to interpret this profoundly uncharacteristic behaviour as in any way an expression of lightheartedness, of celebration or of joy.

I whisked straight out of the deep-carpeted office,

303

through the fire doors, down the flights of gritty stone staircase and across the marbled expanse of entrance hall. The uniformed man at the security desk was staring towards the wide glass front doors with his fillings showing and two arriving visitors were looking stunned. I went past them at a rush into the open air and slowed only in the last few strides before the fountain.

'Gordon!' I said.

His eyes were open. Beads of water ran down his forehead from his dripping black hair and caught here and there on his lashes. The main fall of water slid in a crystal sheet just behind his shoulders with scatterings of drops spraying forwards onto him like rain. Gordon's eyes looked at me unblinkingly with earnest vagueness as if he were not at all sure who I was.

'Get into the fountain,' he said.

'Er . . . why, exactly?'

'They don't like water.'

'Who don't?'

'All those people. Those people with white faces. They don't like water. They won't follow you into the fountain. You'll be all right if you're wet.'

His voice sounded rational enough for me to wonder wildly whether this was not after all a joke: but Gordon's jokes were normally small, civilized, glinting commentaries on the stupidities of mankind, not whooping, gusty, practical affairs smacking of the surreal.

'Come out of there, Gordon,' I said uneasily.

'No, no. They're waiting for me. Send for the police. Ring them up. Tell them to come and take them all away.'

'But *who*, Gordon?'

'All those people, of course. Those people with white faces.' His head slowly turned from side to side, his eyes focused as if at a throng closely surrounding the whole fountain. Instinctively I too looked from side to side, but all I could see were the more distant stone and glass walls of Ekaterin's, with, now, a growing chorus of heads appearing disbelievingly at the windows.

I clung still to a hope of normality. 'They work here,' I said. 'Those people work here.'

'No, no. They came with me. In the car. Only two or three of them, I thought. But all the others, they were here, you know. They want me to go with them, but they can't reach me here, they don't like the water.'

He had spoken fairly loudly throughout so that I should hear him above the noise of the fountain, and the last of these remarks reached the chairman of the bank who came striding briskly across from the building.

'Now, Gordon, my dear chap,' the chairman said authoritatively, coming to a purposeful halt at my side, 'what's all this about, for God's sake?'

'He's having hallucinations,' I said.

The chairman's gaze flicked to my face, and back to Gordon, and Gordon seriously advised him to get into the fountain, because the people with white faces couldn't reach him there, on account of disliking water.

'Do something, Tim,' the chairman said, so I stepped into the fountain and took Gordon's arm.

'Come on,' I said. 'If we're wet they won't touch us. We don't have to stay in the water. Being wet is enough.'

'Is it?' Gordon said. 'Did they tell you?'

'Yes, they did. They won't touch anyone who's wet.'

'Oh. All right. If you're sure.'

'Yes, I'm sure.'

He nodded understandingly and with only slight pressure from my arm took two sensible-seeming paces through the water and stepped over the knee-high coping onto the paving slabs of the forecourt. I held onto him firmly and hoped to heaven that the people with white faces would keep their distance; and although Gordon looked around apprehensively, it appeared that they were not so far trying to abduct him.

The chairman's expression of concern was deep and genuine, as he and Gordon were firm and long-time friends. Except in appearance they were much alike; essentially clever, intuitive, and with creative imaginations. Each in normal circumstances had a manner of speaking which expressed even the toughest commands in gentle politeness and both had a visible appetite for their occupation. They were both in their fifties, both at the top of their powers, both comfortably rich.

Gordon dripped onto the paving stones.

'I think,' the chairman said, casting a glance at the inhabited windows, 'that we should go indoors. Into the boardroom, perhaps. Come along, Gordon.'

He took Gordon Michaels by his other sodden sleeve, and between us one of the steadiest banking brains in London walked obediently in its disturbing fog.

'The people with white faces,' I said as we steered a calm course across the marble entrance hall between clearly human open-mouthed watchers, 'are they coming with us?'

'Of course,' Gordon said.

It was obvious also that some of them came up in the lift with us. Gordon watched them dubiously all the time. The others, as we gathered from his reluctance to step out into the top-floor hallway, were waiting for our arrival.

'It's all right,' I said to Gordon encouragingly. 'Don't forget, we're still wet.'

'Henry isn't,' he said, anxiously eyeing the chairman.

'We're all together,' I said. 'It will be all right.'

Gordon looked doubtful, but finally allowed himself to be drawn from the lift between his supporters. The white faces apparently parted before us, to let us through.

The chairman's personal assistant came hurrying along the corridor but the chairman waved him conclusively to a stop and said not to let anyone disturb us in the boardroom until he rang the bell; and Gordon and I in our wet shoes sloshed across the deep-piled green carpet to the long glossy mahogany boardroom table. Gordon consented to sit in one of the comfortable leather armchairs which surrounded it with me and the chairman alongside, and this time it was the chairman who asked if the people with white faces were still there.

'Of course,' Gordon said, looking around. 'They're sitting in all the chairs round the table. And standing behind them. Dozens of them. Surely you can see them?'

'What are they wearing?' the chairman asked.

Gordon looked at him in puzzlement, but answered simply enough. 'White suits of course. With black buttons. Down the front, three big black buttons.'

'All of them?' the chairman asked. 'All the same?'

'Oh yes, of course.'

'Clowns,' I exclaimed.

'What?'

'White-faced clowns.'

'Oh no,' Gordon said. 'They're not clowns. They're not funny.'

'White-faced clowns are sad.'

Gordon looked troubled and wary, and kept a good eye on his visitations.

'What's best to do?' wondered the chairman; but he was talking principally to himself. To me directly, after a pause, he said, 'I think we should take him home.

He's clearly not violent, and I see no benefit in calling in a doctor here, whom we don't know. I'll ring Judith and warn her, poor girl. I'll drive him in my car as I'm perhaps the only one who knows exactly where he lives. And I'd appreciate it, Tim, if you'd come along, sit with Gordon on the back seat, keep him reassured.'

'Certainly,' I agreed. 'And incidentally his own car's here. He said that when he drove in he thought there were two or three of the white faces with him. The rest were waiting here.'

'Did he?' The chairman pondered. 'He can't have been hallucinating when he actually left home. Surely Judith would have noticed.'

'But he seemed all right in the office when he came in,' I said. 'Quiet, but all right. He sat at his desk for nearly an hour before he went out and stood in the fountain.'

'Didn't you talk with him?'

'He doesn't like people to talk when he's thinking.'

The chairman nodded. 'First thing, then,' he said, 'see if you can find a blanket. Ask Peter to find one. And ... er ... how wet are you, yourself?'

'Not soaked, except for my legs. No problem, honestly. It's not cold.'

He nodded, and I went on the errand. Peter, the assistant, produced a red blanket with Fire written across one corner for no good reason that I could think of, and with this wrapped snugly round his, by now, naked chest Gordon allowed himself to be conveyed discreetly to the chairman's car. The chairman himself slid behind the wheel and with the direct effectiveness which shaped his whole life drove his still half-damp passengers southwards through the fair May morning.

Henry Shipton, chairman of Paul Ekaterin Ltd, was physically a big-framed man whose natural bulk was kept short of obesity by raw carrots, mineral water and will power. Half visionary, half gambler, he habitually subjected every soaring idea to rigorous analytic test: a man whose powerful instinctive urges were everywhere harnessed and put to work.

I admired him. One had to. During his twenty-year stint (including ten as chairman) Paul Ekaterin Ltd had grown from a moderately successful banking house into one of the senior league, accepted world-wide with respect. I could measure almost exactly the spread of public recognition of the bank's name, since it was mine also: Timothy Ekaterin, great-grandson of Paul the founder. In my schooldays people always said 'Timothy who? E-kat-erin? How do you spell it?' Quite often now they simply nodded – and expected me to have the fortune to match, which I hadn't.

'They're very peaceful, you know,' Gordon said after a while.

'The white faces?' I asked.

He nodded. 'They don't say anything. They're just waiting.'

'Here in the car?'

He looked at me uncertainly. 'They come and go.'

At least they weren't pink elephants, I thought irreverently; but Gordon, like the chairman, was abstemious beyond doubt. He looked pathetic in his red blanket, the sharp mind confused with dreams, the well-groomed businessman a pre-fountain memory, the patina stripped away. This was the warrior who dealt confidently every day in millions, this huddled mass of delusions going home in wet trousers. The dignity of man was everywhere tissue-paper thin.

He lived, it transpired, in leafy splendour by Clapham Common, in a late Victorian family pile surrounded by head-high garden walls. There were high cream-painted wooden gates which were shut, and which I opened, and a short gravelled driveway between tidy lawns.

Judith Michaels erupted from her opening front door to meet the chairman's car as it rolled to a stop, and the first thing she said, aiming it variously between Henry Shipton and myself was, 'I'll throttle that bloody doctor.'

After that she said, 'How is he?' and after that, in compassion, 'Come along, love, it's all right, come along in, darling, we'll get you warm and tucked into bed in no time.'

She put sheltering arms round the red blanket as her child of a husband stumbled out of the car, and to me and to Henry Shipton she said again in fury, 'I'll kill him. He ought to be struck off.'

'They're very bad these days about house calls,' the chairman said doubtfully, 'but surely . . . he's coming?'

'No, he's not. Now you lambs both go into the kitchen – there's some coffee in the pot – and I'll be down in a sec. Come on Gordon, my dear love, up those stairs . . .' She helped him through the front door, across a Persian-rugged hall and towards a panelled wood staircase, with me and the chairman following and doing as we were told.

Judith Michaels, somewhere in the later thirties, was a brown-haired woman in whom the life-force flowed strongly and with whom I could easily have fallen in love. I'd met her several times before that morning (at the bank's various social gatherings) and had been freshly conscious each time of the warmth and glamour which were as normal to her as breathing. Whether I in return held the slightest attraction for her I didn't know and hadn't tried to find out, as entangling oneself emotionally with one's boss's wife was hardly best for one's prospects. All the same I felt the same old tug, and wouldn't have minded taking Gordon's place on the staircase.

With these thoughts, I hoped, decently hidden, I went with Henry Shipton into the friendly kitchen and drank the offered coffee.

'A great girl, Judith,' the chairman said with feeling, and I looked at him in rueful surprise and agreed.

She came to join us after a while, still more annoyed than worried. 'Gordon says there are people with white faces sitting all round the room and they won't go away. It's really too bad. It's infuriating. I'm so angry I could *spit*.'

The chairman and I looked bewildered.

'Didn't I tell you?' she said, observing us. 'Oh no, I suppose I didn't. Gordon hates anyone to know about his illness. It isn't very bad, you see. Not bad enough for him to have to stop working, or anything like that.'

'Er . . .' said the chairman. 'What illness?'

'Oh, I suppose I'll have to tell you, now this has happened. I could kill that doctor, I really could.' She took a deep breath and said, 'Gordon's got mild Parkinson's disease. His left hand shakes a bit now and then. I don't expect you've noticed. He tries not to let people see.'

We blankly shook our heads.

'Our normal doctor's just retired, and this new man, he's one of those frightfully bumptious people who think they know better than everyone else. So he's taken Gordon off the old pills, which were fine as far as I could see, and put him on some new ones. As of the day before yesterday. So when I rang him just now in an absolute *panic* thinking Gordon had suddenly gone raving mad or something and I'd be spending the rest of my life visiting mental hospitals he says lightheartedly not to worry, this new drug quite often causes hallucinations, and it's just a matter of getting the dosage right. I tell you, if he hadn't been at the other end of a telephone wire, I'd have *strangled* him.'

Both Henry Shipton and I, however, were feeling markedly relieved.

'You mean,' the chairman asked, 'that this will all just . . . wear off?'

She nodded. 'That bloody doctor said to stop taking the pills and Gordon would be perfectly normal in thirty-six hours. I *ask* you! And after that he's got to start taking them again, but only half the amount, and to see what happens. And if we were *worried*, he said pityingly, as if we'd no right to be, Gordon could toddle along to the surgery in a couple of days and discuss it with him, though as Gordon would be perfectly all right by tomorrow night we might think there was no need.'

She herself was shaking slightly with what still looked like anger but was more probably a release of tension, because she suddenly sobbed, twice, and said, 'Oh God,' and wiped crossly at her eyes.

'I was so frightened, when you told me,' she said, half apologetically. 'And when I rang the surgery I got that damned obstructive receptionist and had to argue for ten minutes before she let me even *talk* to the doctor.'

After a brief sympathetic pause the chairman, going as usual to the heart of things, said, 'Did the doctor say how long it would take to get the dosage right?'

She looked at him with a defeated grimace. 'He said that as Gordon had reacted so strongly to an average dose it might take as much as six weeks to get him thoroughly stabilized. He said each patient was different, but that if we would persevere it would be much the best drug for Gordon in the long run.'

Henry Shipton drove me pensively back to the City.

'I think,' he said, 'that we'll say – in the office – that Gordon felt flu coming on and took some pills which proved hallucinatory. We might say simply that he imagined that he was on holiday, and felt the need for a dip in a pool. Is that agreeable?'

'Sure,' I said mildly.

'Hallucinatory drugs are, after all, exceedingly common these days.'

'Yes.'

'No need, then, Tim, to mention white-faced clowns.'

'No,' I agreed.

'Nor Parkinson's disease, if Gordon doesn't wish it.'

'I'll say nothing,' I assured him.

The chairman grunted and lapsed into silence; and perhaps we both thought the same thoughts along the well-worn lines of drug-induced side-effects being more disturbing than the disease.

It wasn't until we were a mile from the bank that Henry Shipton spoke again, and then he said, 'You've been in Gordon's confidence for two years now, haven't you?'

'Nearly three,' I murmured, nodding.

'Can you hold the fort until he returns?'

It would be dishonest to say that the possibility of this offer hadn't been in my mind since approximately

315

ten-fifteen, so I accepted it with less excitement than relief.

There was no rigid hierarchy in Ekaterin's. Few explicit ranks: to be 'in so and so's confidence', as house jargon put it, meant one would normally be on course for more responsibility, but unlike the other various thirty-two-year-olds who crowded the building with their hopes and expectations I lived under the severe disadvantage of my name. The whole board of directors, consistently afraid of accusations of nepotism, made me double-earn every step.

'Thank you,' I said neutrally.

He smiled a shade. 'Consult,' he said, 'whenever you need help.'

I nodded. His words weren't meant as disparagement. Everyone consulted, in Ekaterin's, all the time. Communication between people and between departments was an absolute priority in Henry Shipton's book, and it was he who had swept away a host of small-room offices to form opened-up expanses. He himself sat always at one (fairly opulent) desk in a room that contained eight similar, his own flanked on one side by the vice-chairman's and on the other by that of the head of Corporate Finance. Further senior directors from other departments occupied a row of like desks opposite, all of them within easy talking earshot of each other.

As with all merchant banks, the business carried on by Ekaterin's was different and separate from that conducted by the High Street chains of clearing banks. At Ekaterin's one never actually saw any money. There were no tellers, no clerks, no counters, no paying-ins, no withdrawals and hardly any chequebooks.

There were three main departments, each with its separate function and each on its own floor of the building. Corporate Finance acted for major clients on mergers, takeovers and the raising of capital. Banking, which was where I worked with Gordon, lent money to enterprise and industry. And Investment Management, the oldest and largest department, aimed at producing the best possible returns for the vast investment funds of charities, companies, pensions, trusts and trade unions.

There were several small sections like Administration, which did everyone's paperwork; like Property, which bought, sold, developed and leased; like Research, which dug around; like Overseas Investments, growing fast; and like Foreign Exchange, where about ten frenetic young wizards bought and sold world currencies by the minute, risking millions on decimal point margins and burning themselves out by forty.

The lives of all the three hundred and fifty people who worked for Ekaterin's were devoted to making money work. To the manufacture, in the main, of business, trade, industry, pensions and jobs. It wasn't a bad thing to be convinced of the worth of what one did, and certainly there was a tough basic harmony in the place which persisted unruffled by the surface tensions and jealousies and territorial defences of everyday office life.

Events had already moved on by the time the chairman and I returned to the hive. The chairman was pounced upon immediately in the entrance hall by a worriedly waiting figure from Corporate Finance, and upstairs in Banking Alec was giggling into his blotter.

Alec, my own age, suffered, professionally speaking, from an uncontrollable bent for frivolity. It brightened up the office no end, but as court jesters seldom made it to the throne his career path was already observably sideways and erratic. The rest of us were probably hopelessly stuffy. Thank God, I often thought, for Alec.

He had a well-shaped face of scattered freckles on cream-pale skin; a high forehead, a mat of tight tow-coloured curls. Stiff blond eyelashes blinked over alert blue eyes behind gold-framed spectacles, and his mouth twitched easily as he saw the funny side. He was liked on sight by almost everybody, and it was only gradually that one came to wonder whether the examiner who had awarded him a First in Law at Oxford had been suffering from critical blindness.

'What's up?' I said, instinctively smiling to match the giggles.

'We've been leaked.' He lifted his head but tapped the paper which lay on his desk. 'My *dear*,' he said with mischievous pleasure, 'this came an hour ago and it seems we're leaking all over the place like a punctured bladder. Like a baby. Like the *Welsh*.'

Leeking like the Welsh . . . ah well.

He lifted up the paper, and all, or at least a great deal, was explained. There had recently appeared a slim bi-monthly publication called *What's Going On Where It Shouldn't*, which had fast caught the attention of most of the country and was reportedly read avidly by the police. Descendant of the flood of investigative journalism spawned by the tidal wave of Watergate, *What's Going On . . .* was said to be positively bombarded by informers telling *precisely* what was going on, and all the investigating the paper had to do was into the truth of the information: which task it had been known to perform less than thoroughly.

'What does it say?' I asked; as who wouldn't?

'Cutting out the larky innuendo,' he said, 'it says that someone at Ekaterin's has been selling inside information.'

'*Selling . . .*'

'Quite so.'

'About a takeover?'

'How did you guess?'

I thought of the man from Corporate Finance hopping from leg to leg with impatience while he waited for the chairman to return and knew that nothing but extreme urgency would have brought him down to the doorstep.

'Let's see,' I said, and took the paper from Alec.

The piece headed merely 'Tut tut' was only four paragraphs long, and the first three of those were taken up with explaining with seductive authority that in merchant banks it was possible for the managers of investment funds to learn at an early stage about a takeover being organized by their colleagues. It was strictly illegal, however, for an investment manager to act on this private knowledge, even though by doing so he might make a fortune for his clients.

The shares of a company about to be taken over were likely to rise in value. If one could buy them at a low price before even a rumour of takeover started, the gain could be huge.

Such unprofessional behaviour by a merchant bank would be instantly recognized simply *because* of the profits made, and no investment manager would invite personal disaster in that way.

However, [asked the article] What's Going On in the merchant bank of Paul Ekaterin Ltd? Three times in the past year takeovers managed by this prestigious firm have been 'scooped' by vigorous buying beforehand of the shares concerned. The buying itself cannot be traced to Ekaterin's investment managers, but we are informed that the information did come from within Ekaterin's, and that someone there has been selling the golden news, either for straight cash or a slice of the action.

'It's a guess,' I said flatly, giving Alec back the paper. 'There are absolutely no facts.'

'A bucket of cold water,' he complained, 'is a sunny day compared with you.'

'Do you *want* it to be true?' I asked curiously.

'Livens the place up a bit.'

And there, I thought, was the difference between Alec and me. For me the place was alive all the time, even though when I'd first gone there eight years earlier it had been unwillingly; a matter of being forced into it by my uncle. My mother had been bankrupt at that point, her flat stripped to the walls by the bailiffs of everything except a telephone (property of the Post Office) and a bed. My mother's bankruptcy, as both my uncle and I well knew, was without doubt her own fault, but it didn't stop him applying his blackmailing pressure.

'I'll clear her debts and arrange an allowance for her if you come and work in the bank.'

'But I don't want to.'

'I know that. And I know you're stupid enough to try to support her yourself. But if you do that she'll ruin you like she ruined your father. Just give the bank a chance, and if you hate it after three months I'll let you go.'

So I'd gone with mulish rebellion to tread the path of my great-grandfather, my grandfather and my uncle, and within three months you'd have had to prise me loose with a crowbar. I suppose it was in my blood. All the snooty teenage scorn I'd felt for 'money-grubbing', all the supercilious disapproval of my student days, all the negative attitudes bequeathed by my failure of a father, all had melted into comprehension, interest and finally delight. The art of money-management now held me as addicted as any junkie, and my working life was as fulfilling as any mortal could expect.

'Who do you think did it?' Alec said.

'If anyone did.'

'It must have happened,' he said positively. 'Three times in the last year . . . that's more than a coincidence.'

'And I'll bet that that coincidence is all the paper's working on. They're dangling a line. Baiting a hook. They don't even say which takeovers they mean, let alone give figures.'

True or not, though, the story itself was bad for the bank. Clients would back away fast if they couldn't trust, and *What's Going On* . . . was right often enough to instil disquiet. Henry Shipton spent most of the afternoon in the boardroom conducting an emergency meeting of the directors, with ripples of unease spreading outwards from there through all departments. By going-home time that evening practically everyone in the building had read the bombshell, and although some took it as lightheartedly as Alec, it had the effect of almost totally deflecting speculation from Gordon Michaels.

I explained only twice about flu and pills: only two people asked. When the very reputation of the bank was being rocked, who cared about a dip in the ornamental fountain, even if the bather had had all his clothes on and was a director in Banking.

On the following day I found that filling Gordon's job was no lighthearted matter. Until then he had gradually given me power of decision over loans up to certain amounts, but anything larger was in his own domain entirely. Within my bracket, it meant that I could arrange any loan if I believed the client was sound and could repay principal and interest at an orderly rate: but if I judged wrong and the client went bust, the lenders lost both their money and their belief in my common sense. As the lenders were quite often the bank itself, I couldn't afford for it to happen too often.

With Gordon there, the ceiling of my possible disasters had at least been limited. For him, though, the ceiling hardly existed, except that with loans incurring millions it was normal for him to consult with others on the board.

These consultations, already easy and informal because of the open-plan layout, also tended to stretch over lunch, which the directors mostly ate together in their own private dining room. It was Gordon's habit to look with a pleased expression at his watch at five to one and take himself amiably off in the direction of a tomato juice and roast lamb; and he would return an hour later with his mind clarified and made up.

I'd been lent Gordon's job but not his seat on the

board, so I was without the benefit of the lunches; and as he himself had been the most senior in our own green pasture of office expanse, there was no one else of his stature immediately at hand. Alec's advice tended to swing between the brilliantly perceptive and the maniacally reckless, but one was never quite sure which was which at the time. All high-risk Cinderellas would have gone to the ball under Alec's wand; the trick was in choosing only those who would keep an eye on the clock and deliver the crystal goods.

Gordon tended therefore to allocate only cast-iron certainties to Alec's care and most of the Cinderella-type to me, and he'd said once with a smile that in this job one's nerve either toughened or broke, which I'd thought faintly extravagant at the time. I understood, though, what he meant when I faced without him a task which lay untouched on his desk: a request for financial backing for a series of animated cartoon films.

It was too easy to turn things down . . . and perhaps miss Peanuts or Mickey Mouse. A large slice of the bank's profits came from the interest paid by borrowers. If we didn't lend, we didn't earn. A toss-up. I picked up the telephone and invited the hopeful cartoonist to bring his proposals to the bank.

Most of Gordon's projects were halfway through, his biggest at the moment being three point four million for an extension to a cake factory. I had heard him working on this one for a week, so I merely took on where he had left off, telephoning people who sometimes had funds to lend and asking if they'd be interested in underwriting a chunk of Home-made Heaven. The bank itself, according to Gordon's list, was lending three hundred thousand only, which made me wonder whether he privately expected the populace to go back to eating bread.

There was also, tucked discreetly in a folder, a glossy prospectus invitation to participate in a multi-million project in Brazil, whereon Gordon had doodled in pencil an army of question marks and a couple of queries: *Do we or don't we? Remember Brasilia! Is coffee enough??* On the top of the front page, written in red, was a jump-to-it memo: *Preliminary answer by Friday.*

It was already Thursday. I picked up the prospectus and went along to the other and larger office at the end of the passage, where Gordon's almost-equal sat at one of the seven desks. Along there the carpet was still lush and the furniture still befitting the sums dealt with on its tops, but the view from the windows was different. No fountain, but the sunlit dome of St Paul's Cathedral rising like a Fabergé egg from the white stone lattice of the City.

'Problem?' asked Gordon's almost-equal. 'Can I help?'

'Do you know if Gordon meant to go any further with this?' I asked. 'Did he say?'

Gordon's colleague looked the prospectus over and shook his head. 'Who's along there with you today?'

'Only Alec. I asked him. He doesn't know.'

'Where's John?'

'On holiday. And Rupert is away because of his wife.'

The colleague nodded. Rupert's wife was imminently dying: cruel at twenty-six.

'I'd take it around,' he said. 'See if Gordon's put out feelers in Research, Overseas, anywhere. Form a view yourself. Then if you think it's worth pursuing you can take it to Val and Henry.' Val was head of Banking and Henry was Henry Shipton. I saw that to be Gordon was a big step up indeed, and was unsure whether to be glad or sorry that the elevation would be temporary.

I spent all afternoon drifting round with the prospectus and in the process learned less about Brazil than about the tizzy over the report in *What's Going On* . . . Soul-searching appeared to be fashionable. Long faces enquired anxiously, 'Could one possibly . . . without knowing . . . have mentioned a takeover to an interested party?' And the short answer to that, it seemed to me, was No, one couldn't. Secrecy was everywhere second nature to bankers.

If the article in the paper were true there had to be three people involved: the seller, the buyer and the informant; and certainly neither the buyer nor the informant could have acted in ignorance or by chance. Greed and malice moved like worms in the dark. If one were infested by them, one knew.

Gordon seemed to have asked no one about Brazil,

and for me it was make-up-your-mind time. It would have been helpful to know what the other merchant banks thought, the sixteen British accepting houses like Schroder's, Hambro's, Morgan Grenfell, Kleinwort Benson, Hill Samuel, Warburg's, Robert Fleming, Singer and Friedlander . . . all permitted, like Paul Ekaterin's, to assume that the Bank of England would come to their aid in a crisis.

Gordon's opposite numbers in those banks would all be pursing mouths over the same prospectus, committing millions to a fruitful enterprise, pouring millions down the drain, deciding not to risk it either way.

Which?

One could hardly directly ask, and finding out via the grapevine took a little time.

I carried the prospectus finally to Val Fisher, head of Banking, who usually sat at one of the desks facing Henry Shipton, two floors up.

'Well, Tim, what's your own view?' he said. A short man, very smooth, very charming, with nerves like toughened ice.

'Gordon had reservations, obviously,' I said. 'I don't know enough, and no one else here seems to. I suppose we could either make a preliminary answer of cautious interest and then find out a bit more, or just trust to Gordon's instinct.'

He smiled faintly. 'Which?'

Ah, which?

'Trust to Gordon's instinct, I think,' I said.

'Right.'

He nodded and I went away and wrote a polite letter to the Brazil people expressing regret. And I wouldn't know for six or seven years, probably, whether that decision was right or wrong.

The gambles were all long term. You cast your bread on the waters and hoped it would float back in the future with butter and jam.

Mildew . . . too bad.

JUNE

Gordon telephoned three weeks later sounding thoroughly fit and well. I glanced across to where his desk stood mute and tidy, with all the paper action now transferred to my own.

'Judith and I wanted to thank you . . .' he was saying.

'Really no need,' I said. 'How are you?'

'Wasting time. It's ridiculous. Anyway, we've been offered a half-share in a box at Ascot next Thursday. We thought it might be fun . . . We've six places. Would you like to come? As our guest, of course. As a thank you.'

'I'd love it,' I said. 'But . . .'

'No buts,' he interrupted. 'If you'd like to, Henry will fix it. He's coming himself. He agreed you'd earned a day off, so all you have to do is decide.'

'Then I'd like to, very much.'

'Good. If you haven't a morning coat, don't worry. We're not in the Royal Enclosure.'

'If you're wearing one . . . I inherited my father's.'

'Ah. Good. Yes, then. One o'clock Thursday, for

lunch. I'll send the entrance tickets to you in the office. Both Judith and I are very pleased you can come. We're very grateful. Very.' He sounded suddenly half-embarrassed, and disconnected with a click.

I wondered how much he remembered about the white faces, but with Alec and Rupert and John all in earshot it had been impossible to ask. Maybe at the races he would tell me. Maybe not.

Going racing wasn't something I did very often now-adays, although as a child I'd spent countless afternoons waiting around the Tote queues while my mother in pleasurable agony backed her dozens of hunches and bankers and third strings and savers and lost money by the ton.

'I've won!' she would announce radiantly to all about her, waving an indisputably winning ticket: and the bunch of losses on the same race would be thrust into a pocket and later thrown away.

My father at the same time would be standing drinks in the bar, an amiable open-fisted lush with more good nature than sense. They would take me home at the end of the day giggling happily together in a hired chauffeur-driven Rolls, and until I was quite old I never questioned but that this contented affluence was built on rock.

I had been their only child and they'd given me a very good childhood to the extent that when I thought of holidays it was of yachts on warm seas or Christmas in the Alps. The villain of those days was my uncle who descended on us occasionally to utter Dire Warnings about the need for his brother (my father) to find a job.

My father, however, couldn't shape up to 'money-grubbing' and in any case had no real ability in any direction; and with no habit of working he had quietly scorned people who had. He never tired of his life of aimless ease, and if he earned no one's respect, few detested him either. A weak, friendly, unintelligent man. Not bad as a father. Not good at much else.

He dropped dead of a heart attack when I was nineteen and it was then that the point of the Dire Warnings became apparent. He and mother had lived on the capital inherited from grandfather, and there wasn't a great deal left. Enough just to see me through college; enough, with care, to bring mother a small income for life.

Not enough to finance her manner of betting, which she wouldn't or couldn't give up. A lot more of the Dire Warnings went unheeded, and finally, while I was trying to stem a hopeless tide by working (of all things) for a bookmaker, the bailiffs knocked on the door.

In twenty-five years, it seemed, my mother had gambled away the best part of half a million pounds; all gone on horses, fast and slow. It might well have sickened me altogether against racing, but in a curious way it hadn't. I remembered how much she and father had enjoyed themselves; and who was to say that it was a fortune ill spent?

'Good news?' Alec said, eyeing my no doubt ambivalent expression.

'Gordon's feeling better.'

'Hm,' he said judiciously, 'so he should be. Three weeks off for flu . . .' He grinned. 'Stretching it a bit.'

I made a non-committal grunt.

'Be glad, shall we, when he comes back?'

I glanced at his amused, quizzical face and saw that he knew as well as I did that when Gordon reappeared to repossess his kingdom, I wouldn't be glad at all. Doing Gordon's job, after the first breath-shortening initial plunge, had injected me with great feelings of vigour and good health; had found me running up stairs and singing in the bath and showing all the symptoms of a love affair; and like many a love affair it couldn't survive the return of the husband. I wondered how long I'd have to wait for such a chance again, and whether next time I'd feel as high.

'Don't think I haven't noticed,' Alec said, the eyes electric blue behind the gold-rimmed specs.

'Noticed what?' Rupert asked, raising his head above papers he'd been staring blindly at for ninety minutes.

Back from his pretty wife's death and burial poor Rupert still wore a glazed otherwhere look and tended too late to catch up with passing conversations. In the two days since his return he had written no letters, made no telephone calls, reached no decisions. Out of compassion one had had to give him time, and Alec and I continued to do his work surreptitiously without him realizing.

'Nothing,' I said.

Rupert nodded vaguely and looked down again, an automaton in his living grief. I'd never loved anyone, I thought, as painfully as that. I think I hoped that I never would.

John, freshly returned also, but from his holidays, glowed with a still-red sunburn and had difficulty in fitting the full lurid details of his sexual adventures into Rupert's brief absences to the washroom. Neither Alec nor I ever believed John's sagas, but at least Alec found them funny, which I didn't. There was an element lurking there of a hatred of women, as if every boasted possession (real or not) was a statement of spite. He didn't actually use the word possession. He said 'made' and 'screwed' and 'had it off with the little cow'. I didn't like him much and he thought me a prig: we were polite in the office and never went together to lunch. And it was he alone of all of us who actively looked forward to Gordon's return, he who couldn't disguise his dismay that it was I who was filling the empty shoes instead of himself.

'Of course, if I'd been here . . .' he said at least once a day; and Alec reported that John had been heard telling Gordon's almost-equal along the passage that now he, John, was back, Gordon's work should be transferred from me to him.

'Did you hear him?' I asked, surprised.

'Sure. And he was told in no uncertain terms that it was the Old Man himself who gave you the green light, and there was nothing John could do about it. Proper miffed was our Lothario. Says it's all because you are who you are, and all that.'

'Sod him.'

'Rather you than me.' He laughed gently into his blotter and picked up the telephone to find backers for a sewage and water purification plant in Norfolk.

'Did you know,' he said conversationally, busy dialling a number, 'that there are so few sewage farms in West Berlin that they pay the East Berliners to get rid of the extra?'

'No, I didn't.' I didn't especially want to know, either, but as usual Alec was full of useless information and possessed by the urge to pass it on.

'The East Berliners take the money and dump the stuff out in the open fields. Untreated, mind you.'

'Do shut up,' I said.

'I saw it,' he said. 'And smelled it. Absolutely disgusting.'

'It was probably fertilizer,' I said, 'and what were you doing in East Berlin?'

'Calling on Nefertiti.'

'She of the one eye?'

'My God, yes, isn't it a shock? Oh . . . hello . . .' He got through to his prospective money-source and for far too long and with a certain relish explained the need for extra facilities to reverse the swamp of effluent which had been killing off the Broads. 'No risk involved, of course, with a water authority.' He listened. 'I'll put you in, then, shall I? Right.' He scribbled busily and in due course disconnected. 'Dead easy, this one. Ecology and all that. Good emotional stuff.'

I shuffled together a bunch of papers of my own that were very far from dead easy and went up to see Val Fisher, who happened to be almost alone in the big office. Henry Shipton, it seemed, was out on one of his frequent walkabouts through the other departments.

'It's a cartoonist,' I said. 'Can I consult?'

'Pull up a chair.' Val nodded and waved hospitably, and I sat beside him, spread out the papers, and explained about the wholly level-headed artist I had spent three hours with two weeks earlier.

'He's been turned down by his own local bank, and so far by three other firms like ourselves,' I said. 'He's got no realizable assets, no security. He rents a flat and is buying a car on HP. If we financed him, it would be out of faith.'

'Background?' he asked. 'Covenant?'

'Pretty solid. Son of a sales manager. Respected at art school as an original talent: I talked to the Principal. His bank manager gave him a clean bill but said that his head office wouldn't grant what he's asking. For the past two years he's worked for a studio making animated commercials. They say he's good at the job; understands it thoroughly. They know he wants to go it alone, they think he's capable and they don't want to lose him.'

'How old?'

'Twenty-four.'

Val gave me an 'Oh ho ho' look, knowing, as I did, that it was the cartoonist's age above all which had invited negative responses from the other banks.

'What's he asking?' Val said, but he too looked as if he were already deciding against.

'A studio, properly equipped. Funds to employ ten copying artists, with the expectation that it will be a year before any films are completed and can expect to make money. Funds for promotion. Funds for himself to live on. These sheets set out the probable figures.'

Val made a face over the pages, momentarily re-arranging the small neat features, slanting the tidy dark moustache, raising the arched eyebrows towards the black cap of hair.

'Why haven't you already turned him down?' he asked finally.

'Um,' I said. 'Look at his drawings.' Opened another file and spread out the riotously coloured progression of pages which established two characters and told a funny story. I watched Val's sophisticated world-weary face as he leafed through them: saw the awakening interest, heard the laugh.

'Exactly,' I said.

'Hmph.' He leaned back in his chair and gave me

an assessing stare. 'You're not saying you think we should take him on?'

'It's an unsecured risk, of course. But yes, I am. With a string or two, of course, like a cost accountant to keep tabs on things and a first option to finance future expansion.'

'Hm.' He pondered for several minutes, looking again at the drawings which still seemed funny to me even after a fortnight's close acquaintance. 'Well, I don't know. It's too like aiming at the moon with a bow and arrow.'

'They might watch those films one day on space shuttles,' I said mildly, and he gave me a fast amused glance while he squared up the drawings and returned them to their folder.

'Leave these all here, then, will you?' he said. 'I'll have a word with Henry over lunch.' And I guessed in a swift uncomfortable moment of insight that what they would discuss would be not primarily the cartoonist but the reliability or otherwise of my judgement. If they thought me a fool I'd be back behind John in the promotion queue in no time.

At four-thirty, however, when my inter-office telephone rang, it was Val at the other end.

'Come up and collect your papers,' he said. 'Henry says this decision is to be yours alone. So sink or swim, Tim, it's up to you.'

*

337

One's first exposure to the Royal Ascot meeting was, according to one's basic outlook, either a matter of surprised delight or of puritanical disapproval. Either the spirits lifted to the sight of emerald grass, massed flowers, bright dresses, fluffy hats and men elegant in grey formality, or one despised the expenditure, the frivolity, the shame of champagne and strawberries while some in the world starved.

I belonged, without doubt, to the hedonists, both by upbringing and inclination. The Royal meeting at Ascot was, as it happened, the one racing event from which my parents had perennially excluded me, children in any case being barred from the Royal Enclosure for three of the four days, and mother more interested on this occasion in socializing than betting. School, she had said firmly every year, must come first: though on other days it hadn't, necessarily. So it was with an extra sense of pleasure that I walked through the gates in my father's resurrected finery and made my way through the smiling throng to the appointed, high-up box.

'Welcome to the charade,' Gordon said cheerfully, handing me a bubbling glass, and 'Isn't this *fun*?' Judith exclaimed, humming with excitement in yellow silk.

'It's great,' I said, and meant it; and Gordon, looking sunburned and healthy, introduced me to the owner of the box.

'Dissdale, this is Tim Ekaterin. Works in the bank. Tim – Dissdale Smith.'

We shook hands. His was plump and warm, like his body, like his face. 'Delighted,' he said. 'Got a drink? Good. Met my wife? No? Bettina, darling, say hello to Tim.' He put an arm round the thin waist of a girl less than half his age whose clinging white black-dotted dress was cut low and bare at neck and armholes. There was also a wide black hat, beautiful skin and a sweet and practised smile.

'Hello, Tim,' she said. 'So glad you could come.' Her voice, I thought, was like the rest of her: manufactured, processed, not natural top drawer but a long way from the gutter.

The box itself was approximately five yards by three, most of the space being filled by a dining table laid with twelve places for lunch. The far end wall was of windows looking out over the green course, with a glass door opening to steps going down to the viewing balcony. The walls of the box were covered as if in a house with pale blue hessian, and a soft blue carpet, pink flowers and pictures lent an air of opulence far greater than the actual expense. Most of the walls of the boxes into which I'd peered on the way along to this one were of builders' universal margarine colour, and I wondered fleetingly whether it was Dissdale or Bettina who had the prettying mind.

Henry Shipton and his wife were standing in the doorway to the balcony, alternately facing out and in, like a couple of Januses. Henry across the room lifted his glass to me in a gesture of acknowledgement, and Lorna as ever looked as if faults were being found.

Lorna Shipton, tall, over-assured, and dressed that frilly day in repressive tailored grey, was a woman from whom disdain flowed outward like a tide, a woman who seemed not to know that words could wound and saw no reason not to air each ungenerous thought. I had met her about the same number of times as I'd met Judith Michaels and mostly upon the same occasions, and if I smothered love for the one, it was irritation I had to hide for the other. It was, I suppose, inevitable, that of the two it was Lorna Shipton I was placed next to at lunch.

More guests arrived behind me, Dissdale and Bettina greeting them with whoops and kisses and making the sort of indistinct introductions that one instantly forgets. Dissdale decided there would be less crush if everyone sat down and so took his place at the top of the table with Gordon, his back to the windows, at the foot. When each had arranged their guests around them there were two empty places, one next to Gordon, one up Dissdale's end.

Gordon had Lorna Shipton on his right, with me beside her: the space on his left, then Henry, then Judith. The girl on my right spent most of her time leaning forward to speak to her host Dissdale, so that although I grew to know quite well the blue chiffon back of her shoulder, I never actually learned her name.

Laughter, chatter, the study of race cards, the

refilling of glasses; Judith with yellow silk roses on her hat and Lorna telling me that my morning coat looked a size too small.

'It was my father's,' I said.

'Such a stupid man.'

I glanced at her face, but she was merely expressing her thoughts, not positively trying to offend.

'A beautiful day for racing,' I said.

'You should be working. Your Uncle Freddie won't like it, you know. I'm certain that when he bailed you out he made it a condition that you and your mother should both stay away from racecourses. And now look at you. It's really too bad. I'll have to tell him, of course.'

I wondered how Henry put up with it. Wondered, as one does, why he'd married her. He, however, his ear attuned across the table in a husbandly way, said to her pleasantly, 'Freddie knows that Tim is here, my dear. Gordon and I obtained dispensation, so to speak.' He gave me a glimmer of a smile. 'The wrath of God has been averted.'

'Oh.' Lorna Shipton looked disappointed and I noticed Judith trying not to laugh.

Uncle Freddie, ex-vice-chairman, now retired, still owned enough of the bank to make his unseen presence felt, and I knew he was in the habit of telephoning Henry two or three times a week to find out what was going on. Out of interest, one gathered, not from a desire to meddle; as certainly, once he had set his terms, he never meddled with mother and me.

Dissdale's last guest arrived at that point with an unseen flourish of trumpets, a man making an entrance as if well aware of newsworthiness. Dissdale leapt to his feet to greet him and pumped him warmly by the hand.

'Calder, this is great. Calder Jackson, everybody.'

There were yelps of delight from Dissdale's end and polite smiles round Gordon's. 'Calder Jackson,' Dissdale said down the table, 'you know, the miracle-worker. Brings dying horses back to life. You must have seen him on television.'

'Ah yes,' Gordon responded. 'Of course.'

Dissdale beamed and returned to his guest who was lapping up adulation with a show of modesty.

'Who did he say?' Lorna Shipton asked.

'Calder Jackson,' Gordon said.

'Who?'

Gordon shook his head, his ignorance showing. He raised his eyebrows in a question to me, but I fractionally shook my head also. We listened, however, and we learned.

Calder Jackson was a shortish man with a head of hair designed to be noticed. Designed literally, I guessed. He had a lot of dark curls going attractively grey, cut short towards the neck but free and fluffy on top of his head and over his forehead; and he had let his beard grow in a narrow fringe from in front of his ears round the line of his jaw, the hairs of this being also bushy and curly but grey to white. From in front his weathered face was thus circled with curls: from the side he looked as if he were wearing a helmet. Or a coal-scuttle, I thought unflatteringly. Once seen, in any case, never forgotten.

'It's just a gift,' he was saying deprecatingly in a voice that had an edge to it more compelling than loudness: an accent very slightly of the country but of no particular region; a confidence born of acclaim.

The girl sitting next to me was ecstatic. 'How *divine* to meet you. One has heard so *much* . . . Do tell us, now do tell us your secret.'

Calder Jackson eyed her blandly, his gaze sliding for a second beyond her to me and then back again. Myself he quite openly discarded as being of no interest, but to the girl he obligingly said, 'There's no secret, my dear. None at all. Just good food, good care and a few age-old herbal remedies. And, of course . . . well . . . the laying on of hands.'

'But *how,*' asked the girl, 'how do you do that to horses?'

'I just . . . touch them.' He smiled disarmingly. 'And then sometimes I feel them quiver, and I know the healing force is going from me into them.'

'Can you do it infallibly?' Henry asked politely, and I noted with interest that he'd let no implication of doubt sound in his voice: Henry, whose gullibility could be measured in micrograms, if at all.

Calder Jackson took his seriousness for granted and

slowly shook his head. 'If I have the horse in my care for long enough, it usually happens in the end. But not always. No, sadly, not always.'

'How fascinating,' Judith said, and earned another of those kind bland smiles. Charlatan or not, I thought, Calder Jackson had the mix just right: an arresting appearance, a modest demeanour, no promise of success. And for all I knew, he really could do what he said. Healers were an age-old phenomenon, so why not a healer of horses?

'Can you heal people too?' I asked in a mirror-image of Henry's tone. No doubts. Just enquiry.

The curly head turned my way with more civility than interest and he patiently answered the question he must have been asked a thousand times before. Answered in a sequence of words he had perhaps used almost as often. 'Whatever gift it is that I have is especially for horses. I have no feeling that I can heal humans, and I prefer not to try. I ask people not to ask me, because I don't like to disappoint them.'

I nodded my thanks, watched his head turn away and listened to him willingly answering the next question, from Bettina, as if it too had never before been asked. 'No, the healing very seldom happens instantaneously. I need to be near the horse for a while. Sometimes for only a few days. Sometimes for a few weeks. One can never tell.'

Dissdale basked in the success of having hooked his celebrity and told us all that two of Calder's ex-patients were running that very afternoon. 'Isn't that right, Calder?'

The curly head nodded. 'Cretonne, in the first race, she used to break blood vessels, and Molyneaux, in the fifth, he came to me with infected wounds. I feel they are my friends now. I feel I know them.'

'And shall we back them, Calder?' Dissdale asked roguishly. 'Are they going to win?'

The healer smiled forgivingly. 'If they're fast enough, Dissdale.'

Everyone laughed. Gordon refilled his own guests' glasses. Lorna Shipton said apropos of not much that she had occasionally considered becoming a Christian Scientist and Judith wondered what colour the Queen would be wearing. Dissdale's party talked animatedly among themselves, and the door from the corridor tentatively opened.

Any hopes I might have had that Gordon's sixth place was destined for a Bettina-equivalent for my especial benefit were immediately dashed. The lady who appeared and whom Judith greeted with a kiss on the cheek was nearer forty than twenty-five and more solid than lissom. She wore a brownish pink linen suit and a small white straw hat circled with a brownish pink ribbon. The suit, I diagnosed, was an old friend; the hat, new in honour of the occasion.

Judith in her turn introduced the newcomer: Penelope Warner – Pen – a good friend of hers and Gordon's. Pen Warner sat where invited, next to

Gordon, and made small-talk with Henry and Lorna. I half listened, and took in a few desultory details like no rings on the fingers, no polish on the nails, no grey in the short brown hair, no artifice in the voice. Worthy, I thought. Well intentioned; slightly boring. Probably runs the church.

A waitress appeared with an excellent lunch, during which Calder could from time to time be heard extolling the virtues of watercress for its iron content and garlic for the treatment of fever and diarrhoea.

'And of course in humans,' he was saying, 'garlic is literally a life saver in whooping cough. You make a poultice and bind it onto the bottom of the feet of the child every night, in a bandage and a sock, and in the morning you'll smell the garlic on the breath of the child, and the cough will abate. Garlic, in fact, cures almost anything. A truly marvellous life-giving plant.'

I saw Pen Warner lift her head to listen and I thought that I'd been wrong about the church. I had missed the worldliness of the eyes, the long sad knowledge of human frailty. A magistrate, perhaps? Yes, perhaps.

Judith leaned across the table and said teasingly, 'Tim, can't you forget you're a banker even at the races?'

'What?' I said.

'You look at everyone as if you're working out just how much you can lend them without risk.'

'I'd lend you my soul,' I said.

'For me to pay back with interest?'

'Pay in love and kisses.'

Harmless stuff, as frivolous as her hat. Henry, sitting next to her, said in the same vein, 'You're second in the queue, Tim. I've a first option, eh, Judith? Count on me, dear girl, for the last drop of blood.'

She patted his hand affectionately and glowed a little from the deep truth of our idle protestations; and Calder Jackson's voice came through with, 'Comfrey heals tissues with amazing speed and will cause chronic ulcers to disappear in a matter of days, and of course it mends fractures in half the time considered normal. Comfrey is miraculous.'

There was a good deal of speculation after that all round the table about a horse called Sandcastle that had won the 2,000 Guineas six weeks earlier and was hot favourite for the King Edward VII Stakes, the top Ascot race for three-year-old colts, due to be run that afternoon.

Dissdale had actually seen the Guineas at New-market and was enthusiastic. 'Daisy-cutter action. Positively eats up the ground.' He sprayed his opinions good naturedly to the furthest ear. 'Big rangy colt, full of courage.'

'Beaten in the Derby, though,' Henry said, judiciously responding.

'Well, yes,' Dissdale allowed. 'But fourth, you know. Not a total disgrace, would you say?'

'He was good as a two-year-old,' Henry said, nodding.

'Glory, yes,' said Dissdale fervently. 'And you can't fault his breeding. By Castle out of an Ampersand mare. You can't get much better than that.'

Several heads nodded respectfully in ignorance.

'He's my banker,' Dissdale said and then spread his arms wide and half laughed. 'OK, we've got a roomful of bankers. But Sandcastle is where I'm putting my money today. Doubling him with my bets in every other race. Trebles. Accumulators. The lot. You all listen to your Uncle Dissdale. Sandcastle is the soundest banker at Ascot.' His voice positively shook with evangelical belief. 'He simply can't be beaten.'

'Betting is out for you, Tim,' Lorna Shipton said severely in my ear.

'I'm not my mother,' I said mildly.

'Heredity,' Lorna said darkly. 'And your father drank.'

I smothered a bursting laugh and ate my strawberries in good humour. Whatever I'd inherited from my parents it wasn't an addiction to their more expensive pleasures; rather a firm intention never again to lose my record collection to the bailiffs. Those stolid men had taken even the rocking horse on which at the age of six I'd ridden my fantasy Grand Nationals. They'd taken my books, my skis and my camera. Mother had fluttered around in tears saying those things were mine, not hers, and they should leave them, and the men had gone on marching out with all our stuff as if they were deaf. About her own disappearing treasures she had been distraught, her distress and grief hopelessly mixed with guilt.

I had been old enough at twenty-four to shrug off our actual losses and more or less replace them (except for the rocking horse) but the fury of that day had affected my whole life since; and I had been silent when it happened, white and dumb with rage.

Lorna Shipton removed her disapproval from me long enough to tell Henry not to have cream and sugar on his strawberries or she would have no sympathy if he put on weight, had a heart attack, or developed pimples. Henry looked resignedly at the forbidden delights which he wouldn't have eaten anyway. God preserve me, I thought, from marrying a Lorna Shipton.

By the coffee-brandy-cigar stage the tranquil seating pattern had broken up into people dashing out to back their hopes in the first race and I, not much of a gambler whatever Mrs Shipton might think, had wandered out onto the balcony to watch the Queen's procession of sleek horses, open carriages, gold, glitter and fluttering feathers trotting like a fairy tale up the green course.

'Isn't it *splendid*,' said Judith's voice at my shoulder, and I glanced at the characterful face and met the straight smiling eyes. Damn it to hell, I thought, I'd like to live with Gordon's wife.

'Gordon's gone to bet,' she said, 'so I thought I'd take the opportunity... He's appalled at what happened ... and we're really grateful to you, you know, for what you did that dreadful day.'

I shook my head. 'I did nothing, believe me.'

'Well, that's half the point. You *said* nothing. In the bank, I mean. Henry says there hasn't been a whisper.'

'But ... I wouldn't.'

'A lot of people *would*,' she said. 'Suppose you had been that Alec.'

I smiled involuntarily. 'Alec isn't unkind. He wouldn't have told.'

'Gordon says he's as discreet as a town-crier.'

'Do you want to go down and see the horses?' I asked.

'Yes. It's lovely up here, but too far from life.'

We went down to the paddock, saw the horses walk at close quarters round the ring and watched the jockeys mount ready to ride out onto the course. Judith smelled nice. Stop it, I told myself. Stop it.

'That horse over there,' I said, pointing, 'is the one Calder Jackson said he cured. Cretonne. The jockey in bright pink.'

'Are you going to back it?' she asked.

'If you like.'

She nodded the yellow silk roses and we queued up in good humour to make the wager. All around us in grey toppers and frothy dresses the Ascot crowd swirled, a feast to the eye in the sunshine, a ritual in make-believe, a suppression of gritty truth. My father's whole life had been a pursuit of the spirit I saw in these Royal Ascot faces; the pursuit and entrapment of happiness.

'What are you thinking,' Judith said, 'so solemnly?'

'That lotus-eaters do no harm. Let terrorists eat lotus.'

'As a steady diet,' she said, 'it would be sickening.'

'On a day like this one could fall in love.'

'Yes, one could.' She was reading her racecard over-intently. 'But should one?'

After a pause I said, 'No, I don't think so.'

'Nor do I.' She looked up with seriousness and understanding and with a smile in her mind. 'I've known you six years.'

'I haven't been faithful,' I said.

She laughed and the moment passed, but the declaration had quite plainly been made and in a way accepted. She showed no awkwardness in my continued presence but rather an increase of warmth, and in mutual contentment we agreed to stay in the paddock for the first short race rather than climb all the way up and find it was over by the time we'd reached the box.

The backs of the jockeys disappeared down the course as they cantered to the start, and I said, as a way of conversation, 'Who is Dissdale Smith?'

'Oh.' She looked amused. 'He's in the motor trade. He loves to make a splash, as no doubt you saw, but I don't think he's doing as well as he pretends. Anyway, he told Gordon he was looking for someone to share the expense of this box here and asked if Gordon would

be interested in buying half the box for today. He's
sold halves for the other days as well. I don't think he's
supposed to, actually, so better say nothing to anyone
else.'

'No.'

'Bettina's his third wife,' she said. 'She's a model.'

'Very pretty.'

'And not as dumb as she looks.'

I heard the dryness in her voice and acknowledged
that I had myself sounded condescending.

'Mind you,' Judith said forgivingly, 'his second wife
was the most gorgeous thing on earth, but without two
thoughts to rub together. Even Dissdale got tired of
the total vacancy behind the sensational violet eyes. It's
all very well to get a buzz when all men light up on
meeting your wife, but it rather kicks the stilts away
when the same men diagnose total dimness within five
minutes and start pitying you instead.'

'I can see that. What became of her?'

'Dissdale introduced her to a boy who'd inherited
millions and had an IQ on a par with hers. The last I
heard they were in a fog of bliss.'

From where we stood we couldn't see much of the
race, only a head-on view of the horses as they came
up to the winning post. In no way did I mind that, and
when one of the leaders proved to carry bright pink
Judith caught hold of my arm and shook it.

'That's Cretonne, isn't it?' She listened to the
announcement of the winner's number. 'Do you realize,

Tim, that we've damned well won?' She was laughing with pleasure, her face full of sunshine and wonder.

'Bully for Calder Jackson.'

'You don't trust him,' she said. 'I could see it in all your faces, yours and Henry's and Gordon's. You all have the same way of peering into people's souls: you too, though you're so young. You were all being incredibly polite so that he shouldn't see your reservations.'

I smiled. 'That sounds disgusting.'

'I've been married to Gordon for nine years,' she said.

There was again a sudden moment of stillness in which we looked at each other in wordless question and answer. Then she shook her head slightly, and after a pause I nodded acquiescence; and I thought that with a woman so straightforwardly intelligent I could have been content for ever.

'Do we collect our winnings now or later?' she asked.

'Now, if we wait awhile.'

Waiting together for the jockeys to weigh-in and the all-clear to be given for the pay-out seemed as little hardship for her as for me. We talked about nothing much and the time passed in a flash; and eventually we made our way back to the box to find that everyone there too had backed Cretonne and was high with the same success. Calder Jackson beamed and looked modest, and Dissdale expansively opened more bottles of excellent Krug, champagne of Kings.

Escorting one's host's wife to the paddock was not merely acceptable but an expected civility, so that it was with a benign eye that Gordon greeted our return. I was both glad and sorry, looking at his unsuspecting friendliness, that he had nothing to worry about. The jewel in his house would stay there and be his alone. Unattached bachelors could lump it.

The whole party, by now markedly carefree, crowded the box's balcony for the big race. Dissdale said he had staked his all on his banker, Sandcastle; and although he said it with a laugh I saw the tremor in his hands which fidgeted with the raceglasses. He's in too deep, I thought. A bad way to bet.

Most of the others, fired by Dissdale's certainty, happily clutched tickets doubling Sandcastle every which-way. Even Lorna Shipton, with a pink glow on each bony cheekbone, confessed to Henry that just for once, as it was a special day, she had staked five pounds in forecasts.

'And you, Tim?' Henry teased. 'Your shirt?'

Lorna looked confused. I smiled. 'Buttons and all,' I said cheerfully.

'No, but . . .' Lorna said.

'Yes, but,' I said, 'I've dozens more shirts at home.'

Henry laughed and steered Lorna gently away, and I found myself standing next to Calder Jackson.

'Do you gamble?' I asked, for something to say.

'Only on certainties.' He smiled blandly in the way

354

that scarcely warmed his eyes. 'Though on certainties it's hardly a gamble.'

'And is Sandcastle a certainty?'

He shook his curly head. 'A probability. No racing bet's a certainty. The horse might feel ill. Might be kicked at the start.'

I glanced across at Dissdale who was faintly sweating, and hoped for his sake that the horse would feel well and come sweetly out of the stalls.

'Can you tell if a horse is sick just by looking at him?' I enquired. 'I mean, if you just watched him walk round the parade ring, could you tell?'

Calder answered in the way that revealed it was again an often-asked question. 'Of course sometimes you can see at once, but mostly a horse as ill as that wouldn't have been brought to the races. I prefer to look at a horse closely. To examine for instance the colour inside the eyelid and inside the nostril. In a sick horse, what should be a healthy pink may be pallid.' He stopped with apparent finality, as if that were the appointed end of that answer, but after a few seconds, during which the whole huge crowd watched Sandcastle stretch out in the sun in the canter to the post, he said almost with awe, 'That's a superb horse. Superb.' It sounded to me like his first spontaneous remark of the day and it vibrated with genuine enthusiasm.

'He looks great,' I agreed.

Calder Jackson smiled as if with indulgence at the shallowness of my judgement compared with the weight of his inside knowledge. 'He should have won the Derby,' he said. 'He got shut in on the rails, couldn't get out in time.'

My place at the great man's side was taken by Bettina, who threaded her arm through his and said, 'Dear Calder, come down to the front, you can see better than here at the back.' She gave me a photogenic little smile and pulled her captive after her down the steps.

In a buzz that rose to a roar the runners covered their mile and a half journey; longer than the 2,000 Guineas, the same length as the Derby. Sandcastle in scarlet and white was making no show at all to universal groans and lay only fifth as the field swept round the last bend, and Dissdale looked as if he might have a heart attack.

Alas for my shirt, I thought. Alas for Lorna's forecasts. Bang goes the banker that can't lose.

Dissdale, unable to watch, collapsed weakly onto one of the small chairs which dotted the balcony, and in the next-door boxes people were standing on top of theirs and jumping up and down and screaming.

'Sandcastle making his move . . .' the commentator's voice warbled over the loudspeakers, but the yells of the crowd drowned the rest.

The scarlet and white colours had moved to the outside. The daisy-cutter action was there for the world to see. The superb horse, the big rangy colt full of courage was eating up his ground.

Our box in the grandstand was almost a furlong down the course from the winning post, and when he reached us Sandcastle still had three horses ahead. He was flying, though, like a streak, and I found the sight of this fluid valour, this all-out striving, most immensely moving and exciting. I grabbed Dissdale by his despairing shoulder and hauled him forcefully to his feet.

'Look,' I shouted in his ear. 'Watch. Your banker's going to win. He's a marvel. He's a dream.'

He turned with a gaping mouth to stare in the direction of the winning post and he saw ... he saw Sandcastle among the tumult going like a javelin, free now of all the others, aiming straight for the prize.

'He's won,' Dissdale's mouth said slackly, though amid the noise I could hardly hear him. 'He's bloody won.'

I helped him up the steps into the box. His skin was grey and damp and he was stumbling.

'Sit down,' I said, pulling out the first chair I came to, but he shook his head weakly and made his shaky way to his own place at the head of the table. He almost fell into it, heavily, and stretched out a trembling hand to his champagne.

'My God,' he said, 'I'll never do that again. Never on God's earth.'

'Do what?'

He gave me a flickering glance over his glass and said, 'All on one throw.'

All. He'd said it before. 'All on the banker . . .' He

surely couldn't, I thought, have meant literally *all*; but yet not much else could have produced such physical symptoms.

Everyone else piled back into the room with ballooning jollity. Everyone without exception had backed Sandcastle, thanks to Dissdale. Even Calder Jackson, when pressed by Bettina, admitted to 'a small something on the Tote. I don't usually, but just this once.' And if he'd lost, I thought, he wouldn't have confessed.

Dissdale, from near fainting, climbed rapidly to a pulse-throbbing high, the colour coming back to his plump cheeks in a hectic red. No one seemed to have noticed his near-collapse, certainly not his wife, who flirted prettily with the healer and got less than her due response. More wine easily made its way down every throat, and there was no doubt that for the now commingled party the whole day was a riotous success.

In a while Henry offered to take Judith to the paddock. Gordon to my relief invited Lorna, which left me with the mystery lady, Pen Warner, with whom I'd so far exchanged only the thrilling words 'How do you do.'

'Would you like to go down?' I asked.

'Yes, indeed. But you don't need to stay with me if it's too much bother.'

'Are you so insecure?'

There was a quick widening of the eyes and a visible mental shift. 'You're damned rude,' she said. 'And Judith said you were nice.'

I let her go past me out onto the landing and smiled as she went. 'I should like to stay with you,' I said, 'if it's not too much bother.'

She gave me a dry look, but as we more or less had to walk in single file along the narrow passageway owing to people going in the opposite direction she said little more until we had negotiated the lifts, the escalators and the pedestrian tunnel and had emerged into the daylight of the paddock.

It was her first time at Ascot, she said. Her first time, in fact, at the races.

'What do you think of it?'

'Very beautiful. Very brave. Quite mad.'

'Does sanity lie in ugliness and cowardice?' I asked.

'Life does, pretty often,' she said. 'Haven't you noticed?'

'And some aren't happy unless they're desperate.'

She quietly laughed. 'Tragedy inspires, so they say.'

'They can stick it,' I said. 'I'd rather lie in the sun.'

We stood on the raised tiers of steps to watch the horses walk round the ring, and she told me that she lived along the road from Judith in another house fronting the common. 'I've lived there all my life, long before Judith came. We met casually, as one does, in the local shops, and just walked home together one day several years ago. Been friends ever since.'

'Lucky,' I said.

'Yes.'

'Do you live alone?' I asked conversationally.

Her eyes slid my way with inner amusement. 'Yes, I do. Do you?'

I nodded.

'I prefer it,' she said.

Her skin was clear and still girlish, the thickened figure alone giving an impression of years passing. That and the look in the eyes, the 'I've seen the lot' sadness.

'Are you a magistrate?' I asked.

She looked startled. 'No, I'm not. What an odd thing to ask.'

I made an apologetic gesture. 'You just look as if you might be.'

She shook her head. 'Wouldn't have time, even if I had the urge.'

'But you do do good in the world.'

She was puzzled. 'What makes you say so?'

'I don't know. The way you look.' I smiled to take away any seriousness and said, 'Which horse do you like? Shall we choose one and bet?'

'What about Burnt Marshmallow?'

She liked the name, she said, so we queued briefly at a Tote window and invested some of the winnings from Cretonne and Sandcastle.

During our slow traverse of the paddock crowds on our way back towards the box we came upon Calder Jackson, who was surrounded by respectful listeners and didn't see us.

'Garlic is as good as penicillin,' he was saying. 'If you scatter grated garlic onto a septic wound it will kill all the bacteria . . .' We slowed a little to hear. ' . . . and comfrey is miraculous,' Calder said. 'It knits bones and cures intractable skin ulcers in half the time you'd expect.'

'He said all that upstairs,' I said.

Pen Warner nodded, faintly smiling. 'Good sound herbal medicine,' she said. 'You can't fault him. Comfrey contains allantoin, a well-known cell proliferant.'

'Does it? I mean . . . do you know about it?'

'Mm.' We walked on, but she said nothing more until we were high up again in the passageway to the box. 'I don't know whether you'd think I do good in the world . . . but basically I dole out pills.'

'Er . . .?' I said.

She smiled. 'I'm a lady in a white coat. A pharmacist.'

I suppose I was in a way disappointed, and she sensed it.

'Well,' she sighed, 'we can't all be glamorous. I told you life was ugly and frightening, and from my point of view that's often what it is for my customers. I see fear every day . . . and I know its face.'

'Pen,' I said, 'forgive my frivolity. I'm duly chastened.'

We reached the box to find Judith alone there, Henry having loitered to place a bet.

'I told Tim I'm a pharmacist,' Pen said. 'He thinks it's boring.'

I got no further than the first words of protestation when Judith interrupted.

'She's not just "a" pharmacist,' she said. 'She owns her own place. Half the medics in London recommend her. You're talking to a walking gold-mine with a heart like a wet sponge.'

She put her arm round Pen's waist and the two of them together looked at me, their eyes shining with what perhaps looked like liking, but also with the mischievous feminine superiority of being five or six years older.

'Judith!' I said compulsively. 'I ... I ...' I stopped. 'Oh *damn* it,' I said. 'Have some Krug.'

Dissdale's friends returned giggling to disrupt the incautious minute and shortly Gordon, Henry and Lorna crowded in. The whole party pressed out onto the balcony to watch the race, and because it was a time out of reality Burnt Marshmallow romped home by three lengths.

The rest of the afternoon slid fast away. Henry at some point found himself alone out on the balcony beside me while inside the box the table was being spread with a tea that was beyond my stretched stomach entirely and a temptation from which the ever-hungry Henry had bodily removed himself.

'How's your cartoonist?' he said genially. 'Are we staking him, or are we not?'

'You're sure ... I have to decide ... all alone?'

'I said so. Yes.'

'Well . . . I got him to bring some more drawings to the bank. And his paints.'

'His *paints*?'

'Yes. I thought if I could see him at work, I'd know . . .' I shrugged. 'Anyway, I took him into the private interview room and asked him to paint the outline of a cartoon film while I watched; and he did it, there and then, in acrylics. Twenty-five outline sketches in bright colour, all within an hour. Same characters, different story, and terrifically funny. That was on Monday. I've been . . . well . . . dreaming about those cartoons. It sounds absurd. Maybe they're too much on my mind.'

'But you've decided?'

After a pause I said, 'Yes.'

'And?'

With a sense of burning bridges I said, 'To go ahead.'

'All right.' Henry seemed unalarmed. 'Keep me informed.'

'Yes, of course.'

He nodded and smoothly changed the subject. 'Lorna and I have won quite a bit today. How about you?'

'Enough to give Uncle Freddie fits about the effect on my unstable personality.'

Henry laughed aloud. 'Your Uncle Freddie,' he said, 'knows you better than you may think.'

*

363

At the end of that splendid afternoon the whole party descended together to ground level and made its way to the exit; to the gate which opened onto the main road, and across that to the car park and to the covered walk which led to the station.

Calder just ahead of me walked in front, the helmet of curls bent kindly over Bettina, the strong voice thanking her and Dissdale for 'a most enjoyable time'. Dissdale himself, not only fully recovered but incoherent with joy as most of his doubles, trebles and accumulators had come up, patted Calder plumply on the shoulder and invited him over to 'my place' for the weekend.

Henry and Gordon, undoubtedly the most sober of the party, were fiddling in their pockets for car keys and throwing their racecards into wastebins. Judith and Pen were talking to each other and Lorna was graciously unbending to Dissdale's friends. It seemed to be only I, with unoccupied eyes, who saw at all what was about to happen.

We were out on the pavement, still in a group, half-waiting for a chance to cross the road, soon to break up and scatter. All talking, laughing, busy; except me.

A boy stood there on the pavement, watchful and still. I noticed first the fixed, burning intent in the dark eyes, and quickly after that the jeans and faded shirt which contrasted sharply with our Ascot clothes, and then finally with incredulity the knife in his hand.

I had almost to guess at whom he was staring with

such deadly purpose, and had no time even to shout a warning. He moved across the pavement with stunning speed, the stab already on its upward travel.

I jumped almost without thinking; certainly without assessing consequences or chances. Most unbankerlike behaviour.

The steel was almost in Calder's stomach when I deflected it. I hit the boy's arm with my body in a sort of flying tackle and in a flashing view saw the weave of Calder's trousers, the polish on his shoes, the litter on the pavement. The boy fell beneath me and I thought in horror that somewhere between our bodies he still held that wicked blade.

He writhed under me, all muscle and fury, and tried to heave me off. He was lying on his back, his face just under mine, his eyes like slits and his teeth showing between drawn-back lips. I had an impression of dark eyebrows and white skin and I could hear the breath hissing between his teeth in a tempest of effort.

Both of his hands were under my chest and I could feel him trying to get space enough to up-end the knife. I pressed down onto him solidly with all my weight and in my mind I was saying, 'Don't do it, don't do it, you bloody fool'; and I was saying it *for his sake*, which seemed crazy to me at the time and even crazier in retrospect. He was trying to do me great harm and all I thought about was the trouble he'd be in if he succeeded.

We were both panting but I was taller and stronger

and I could have held him there for a good while longer but for the two policemen who had been out on the road directing traffic. They had seen the mêlée; seen as they supposed a man in morning dress attacking a pedestrian, seen us struggling on the ground. In any case the first I knew of their presence was the feel of vice-like hands fastening onto my arms and pulling me backwards.

I resisted with all my might. I didn't know they were policemen. I had eyes only for the boy: his eyes, his hands, his knife.

With peremptory strength they hauled me off, one of them anchoring my upper arms to my sides by encircling me from behind. I kicked furiously backwards and turned my head, and only then realized that the new assailants wore navy blue.

The boy comprehended the situation in a flash. He rolled over onto his feet, crouched for a split second like an athlete at the blocks and without lifting his head above waist-height slithered through the flow of the crowds still pouring out of the gates and disappeared out of sight inside the racecourse. Through there they would never find him. Through there he would escape to the cheaper rings and simply walk out of the lower gate.

I stopped struggling but the policemen didn't let go. They had no thought of chasing the boy. They were incongruously calling me 'sir' while treating me with contempt, which if I'd been calm enough for reflection I would have considered fairly normal.

'For God's sake,' I said finally to one of them, 'what do you think that knife's doing on the pavement?'

They looked down to where it lay; to where it had fallen when the boy ran. Eight inches of sharp steel kitchen knife with a black handle.

'He was trying to stab Calder Jackson,' I said. 'All I did was stop him. Why do you think he's gone?'

By this time Henry, Gordon, Laura, Judith and Pen were standing round in an anxious circle continually assuring the law that never in a million years would their friend attack anyone except out of direst need, and Calder was looking dazed and fingering a slit in the waistband of his trousers.

The farce slowly resolved itself into duller bureaucratic order. The policemen relinquished their hold and I brushed the dirt off the knees of my father's suit and straightened my tangled tie. Someone picked up my tumbled top hat and gave it to me. I grinned at Judith. It all seemed such a ridiculous mixture of death and bathos.

The aftermath took half of the evening and was boring in the extreme: police station, hard chairs, polystyrene cups of coffee.

No, I'd never seen the boy before.

Yes, I was sure the boy had been aiming at Calder specifically.

Yes, I was sure he was only a boy. About sixteen, probably.

Yes, I would know him again. Yes, I would help with an Identikit picture.

No. My fingerprints were positively not on the knife. The boy had held onto it until he ran.

Yes, of course they could take my prints, in case.

Calder, wholly mystified, repeated over and over that he had no idea who could want to kill him. He seemed scandalized, indeed, at the very idea. The police persisted: most people knew their murderers, they said, particularly when as seemed possible in this case the prospective killer had been purposefully waiting for his victim. According to Mr Ekaterin the boy had known Calder. That was quite possible, Calder said, because of his television appearances, but Calder had *not* known *him*.

Among some of the police there was a muted quality, among others a sort of defiant aggression, but it was only Calder who rather acidly pointed out that if they hadn't done such a good job of hauling me off, they would now have the boy in custody and wouldn't need to be looking for him.

'You could have asked first,' Calder said, but even I shook my head.

If I had indeed been the aggressor I could have killed the boy while the police were asking the onlookers just who was fighting whom. Act first, ask questions after

368

was a policy full of danger, but getting it the wrong way round could be worse.

Eventually we both left the building, Calder on the way out trying his best with unrehearsed words. 'Er . . . Tim . . . Thanks are in order . . . If it hadn't been for you . . . I don't know what to say.'

'Say nothing,' I said. 'I did it without thinking. Glad you're OK.'

I had taken it for granted that everyone else would be long gone, but Dissdale and Bettina had waited for Calder, and Gordon, Judith and Pen for me, all of them standing in a group by some cars and talking to three or four strangers.

'We know you and Calder both came by train,' Gordon said, walking towards us, 'but we decided we'd drive you home.'

'You're extraordinarily kind,' I said.

'My dear Dissdale . . .' Calder said, seeming still at a loss for words. 'So grateful, really.'

They made a fuss of him; the endangered one, the lion delivered. The strangers round the cars turned out to be gentlemen of the press, to whom Calder Jackson was always news, alive or dead. To my horror they announced themselves, producing notebooks and a camera, and wrote down everything anyone said, except they got nothing from me because all I wanted to do was shut them up.

As well try to stop an avalanche with an outstretched palm. Dissdale and Bettina and Gordon and Judith and

Pen did a diabolical job, which was why for a short time afterwards I suffered from public notoriety as the man who had saved Calder Jackson's life.

No one seemed to speculate about his assailant setting out for a second try.

I looked at my photograph in the papers and wondered if the boy would see it, and know my name.

OCTOBER

Gordon was back at work with his faintly trembling left hand usually out of sight and unnoticeable.

During periods of activity, as on the day at Ascot, he seemed to forget to camouflage, but at other times he had taken to sitting forwards in a hunched way over his desk with his hand anchored down between his thighs. I thought it a pity. I thought the tremor so slight that none of the others would have remarked on it, either aloud or to themselves, but to Gordon it was clearly a burden.

Not that it seemed to have affected his work. He had come back in July with determination, thanked me briskly in the presence of the others for my stop-gapping and taken all major decisions off my desk and back to his.

John asked him, also in the hearing of Alec, Rupert and myself, to make it clear to us that it was he, John, who was the official next-in-line to Gordon, if the need should occur again. He pointed out that he was older

371

and had worked much longer in the bank than I had. Tim, he said, shouldn't be jumping the queue.

Gordon eyed him blandly and said that if the need arose no doubt the chairman would take every factor into consideration. John made bitter and audible remarks under his breath about favouritism and unfair privilege, and Alec told him ironically to find a merchant bank where there *wasn't* a nephew or some such on the force.

'Be your age,' he said. 'Of *course* they want the next generation to join the family business. Why shouldn't they? It's natural.' But John was unplacated, and didn't see that his acid grudge against me was wasting a lot of his time. I seemed to be continually in his thoughts. He gave me truly vicious looks across the room and took every opportunity to sneer and denigrate. Messages never got passed on, and clients were given the impression that I was incompetent and only employed out of family charity. Occasionally on the telephone people refused to do business with me, saying they wanted John, and once a caller said straight out, 'Are you that playboy they're shoving ahead over better men's heads?'

John's gripe was basically understandable: in his place I'd have been cynical myself. Gordon did nothing to curb the escalating hate campaign and Alec found it funny. I thought long and hard about what to do and decided simply to work harder. I'd see it was very difficult for John to make his allegations stick.

His aggression showed in his body, which was roundedly muscular and looked the wrong shape for a city suit. Of moderate height, he wore his wiry brown hair very short so that it bristled above his collar, and his voice was loud, as if he thought volume equated authority: and so it might have done in schoolroom or on barrack square, instead of on a civilized patch of carpet.

He had come into banking via business school with high ambitions and good persuasive skills. I sometimes thought he would have made an excellent export salesman, but that wasn't the life he wanted. Alec said that John got his kicks from saying 'I am a merchant banker' to pretty girls and preening himself in their admiration.

Alec was a wicked fellow, really, and a shooter of perceptive arrows.

There came a day in October when three whirlwind things happened more or less simultaneously. The cartoonist telephoned; *What's Going On Where It Shouldn't* landed with a thud throughout the City; and Uncle Freddie descended on Ekaterin's for a tour of inspection.

To begin with the three events were unconnected, but by the end of the day, entwined.

I heard the cartoonist's rapid opening remarks with a sinking heart. 'I've engaged three extra animators and I need five more,' he said. 'Ten isn't nearly enough.

I've worked out the amount of increased loan needed to pay them all.'

'Wait,' I said.

He went right on. 'I also need more space, of course, but luckily that's no problem, as there's an empty warehouse next to this place. I've signed a lease for it and told them you'll be advancing the money, and of course more furniture, more materials . . .'

'*Stop*,' I said distractedly. 'You *can't*.'

'What? I can't what?' He sounded, of all things, bewildered.

'You can't just keep on borrowing. You've a limit. You can't go beyond it. Look for heaven's sake come over here quickly and we'll see what can be undone.'

'But you said,' his voice said plaintively, 'that you'd want to finance later expansion. That's what I'm doing. Expanding.'

I thought wildly that I'd be licking stamps for a living as soon as Henry heard. Dear *God* . . .

'*Listen*,' the cartoonist was saying, 'we all worked like hell and finished one whole film. Twelve minutes long, dubbed with music and sound effects, everything, titles, the lot. And we did some rough-cuts of three others, no music, no frills, but enough . . . and I've sold them.'

'You've what?'

'Sold them.' He laughed with excitement. 'It's solid, I promise you. That agent you sent me to, he's fixed the sale and the contract. All I have to do is sign. It's a major firm that's handling them, and I get a big perpetual royalty. Worldwide distribution, that's what they're talking about, and the BBC are taking them. But we've got to make twenty films in a year from now, not seven like I meant. Twenty! And if the public like them, that's just the start. Oh heck, I can't believe it. But to do twenty in the time I need a lot more money. Is it all right? I mean . . . I was so sure . . .'

'Yes,' I said weakly. 'It's all right. Bring the contract when you've signed it, and new figures, and we'll work things out.'

'Thanks,' he said. 'Thanks, Tim Ekaterin, God bless your darling bank.'

I put the receiver down feebly and ran a hand over my head and down the back of my neck.

'Trouble?' Gordon asked, watching.

'Well no, not exactly . . .' A laugh like the cartoonist's rose in my throat. 'I backed a winner. I think perhaps I backed a bloody geyser.' The laugh broke out aloud. 'Did you ever do that?'

'Ah yes.' Gordon nodded. 'Of course.'

I told him about the cartoonist and showed him the original set of drawings, which were still stowed in my desk; and when he looked through them, he laughed.

'Wasn't that application on my desk,' he said, wrinkling his forehead in an effort to remember, 'just before I was away?'

I thought back. 'Yes, it probably was.'

He nodded. 'I'd decided to turn it down.'

'Had you?'

'Mm. Isn't he too young, or something?'

'That sort of talent strikes at birth.'

He gave me a brief assessing look and handed the drawings back. 'Well,' he said. 'Good luck to him.'

The news that Uncle Freddie had been spotted in the building rippled through every department and stiffened a good many slouching backbones. Uncle Freddie was given to growling out devastatingly accurate judgements of people in their hearing, and it was not only I who'd found the bank more peaceful (if perhaps also more complacent) when he retired.

He was known as 'Mr Fred' as opposed to 'Mr Mark' (grandfather) and 'Mr Paul', the founder. No one ever called me 'Mr Tim'; sign of the changing times. If true to form Uncle Freddie would spend the morning in Investment Management, where he himself had worked all his office life, and after lunch in the boardroom would put at least his head into Corporate Finance, to be civil, and end with a march through Banking. On the way, by some telepathic process of his own, he would learn what moved in the bank's collective mind; sniff, as he had put it, the prevailing scent on the wind.

He had already arrived when the copies of *What's Going On . . .* hit the fan.

Alec as usual slipped out to the local paper shop at about the time they were delivered there and returned with the six copies which the bank officially sanctioned. No one in the City could afford not to know about What Was Going On on their own doorstep.

Alec shunted around delivering one copy to each floor and keeping ours to himself to read first, a perk he said he deserved.

'Your uncle,' he reported on his return, 'is beating the shit out of poor Ted Lorrimer in Investments for failing to sell Winkler Consolidated when even a squint-eyed baboon could see it was overstretched in its Central American operation, and a neck sticking out asking for the comprehensive chop.'

Gordon chuckled mildly at the verbatim reporting, and Alec sat at his desk and opened the paper. Normal office life continued for perhaps five more minutes before Alec shot to his feet as if he'd been stung.

'Jes-us *Christ*,' he said.

'What is it?'

'Our leaker is at it again.'

'What?' Gordon said.

'You'd better read it.' He took the paper across to Gordon whose preliminary face of foreboding turned slowly to anger.

'It's disgraceful,' Gordon said. He made as if to pass the paper to me, but John, on his feet, as good as snatched it out of his hand.

'I should come first,' he said forcefully, and took the paper over to his own desk, sitting down methodically and spreading the paper open on the flat surface to read. Gordon watched him impassively and I said nothing to provoke. When John at his leisure had finished, showing little reaction but a tightened mouth, it was to Rupert he gave the paper, and Rupert, who read it with small gasps and widening eyes, who brought it eventually to me.

'It's bad,' Gordon said.

'So I gather.' I lolled back in my chair and lifted the offending column to eye level. Under a heading of 'Dinky Dirty Doings' it said:

It is perhaps not well known to readers that in many a merchant bank two thirds of the annual profits come from interest on loans. Investment and Trust management and Corporate Finance departments are the public faces and glamour machines of these very private banks. Their investments (of other people's money) in the stock market and their entrepreneurial role in mergers and takeovers earn the spotlight year by year in the City Pages.

Below stairs, so to speak, lies the tail that wags the dog, the secretive Banking department which quietly lends from its own deep coffers and rakes in vast profits in the shape of interest at rates they can set to suit themselves.

These rates are not necessarily high.

Who in Paul Ekaterin Ltd has been effectively lending to himself small fortunes from these coffers at FIVE per cent? Who in Paul Ekaterin Ltd has set up private companies which are NOT carrying on the business for which the money has ostensibly been lent? Who has not declared that these companies are his?

The man-in-the-street (poor slob) would be delighted to get unlimited cash from Paul Ekaterin Ltd at five per cent so that he could invest it in something else for more.

Don't Bankers have a fun time?

I looked up from the damaging page and across at Alec, and he was, predictably, grinning.

'I wonder who's had his hand in the cookie jar,' he said.

'And who caught it there,' I asked.

'Wow, yes.'

Gordon said bleakly, 'This is very serious.'

'If you believe it,' I said.

'But this paper . . .' he began.

'Yeah,' I interrupted. 'It had a dig at us before, remember? Way back in May. Remember the flap everyone got into?'

'I was at home . . . with flu.'

'Oh, yes. Well, the furore went on here for ages and no one came up with any answers. This column today is just as unspecific. So . . . supposing all it's designed to do is stir up trouble for the bank? Who's got it in for us? To what raving nut have we for instance refused a loan?'

379

Alec was regarding me with exaggerated wonder. 'Here we have Sherlock Holmes to the rescue,' he said admiringly. 'Now we can all go out to lunch.'

Gordon, however, said thoughtfully, 'It's perfectly possible, though, to set up a company and lend it money. All it would take would be paperwork. I could do it myself. So could anyone here, I suppose, up to his authorized ceiling, if he thought he could get away with it.'

John nodded. 'It's ridiculous of Tim and Alec to make a joke of this,' he said importantly. 'The very reputation of the bank is at stake.'

Gordon frowned, stood up, took the paper off my desk, and went along to see his almost-equal in the room facing St Paul's. Spreading consternation, I thought; bringing out cold sweats from palpitating banking hearts.

I ran a mental eye over everyone in the whole department who could possibly have had enough power along with the opportunity, from Val Fisher all the way down to myself; and there were twelve, perhaps, who could theoretically have done it.

But . . . not Rupert, with his sad mind still grieving, because he wouldn't have had the appetite or energy for fraud.

Not Alec, surely; because I liked him.

Not John: too self-regarding.

Not Val, not Gordon, unthinkable. Not myself.

That left the people along in the other pasture, and

I didn't know them well enough to judge. Maybe one of them did believe that a strong fiddle on the side was worth the ruin of discovery, but all of us were already generously paid, perhaps for the very reason that temptations would be more likely to be resisted if we weren't scratching around for the money for the gas.

Gordon didn't return. The morning limped down to lunchtime, when John bustled off announcing he was seeing a client, an Alec encouraged Rupert to go out with him for a pie and pint. I'd taken to working through lunch because of the quietness, and I was still there alone at two o'clock when Peter, Henry's assistant, came and asked me to go up to the top floor, because I was wanted.

Uncle Freddie, I thought. Uncle Freddie's read the rag and will be exploding like a warhead. In some way he'll make it out to be my fault. With a gusty sigh I left my desk and took the lift to face the old warrior with whom I had never in my life felt easy.

He was waiting in the top-floor hallway, talking to Henry. Both of them at six foot three over-topped me by three inches. Life would never have been as ominous, I thought, if Uncle Freddie had been small.

'Tim,' Henry said when he saw me, 'go along to the small conference room, will you?'

I nodded and made my way to the room next to the boardroom where four or five chairs surrounded a square polished table. A copy of *What's Going On . . .* lay there, already dog-eared from many thumbs.

'Now, Tim', said my uncle, coming into the room behind me, 'do you know what all this is about?'

I shook my head and said, 'No.'

My uncle growled in his throat and sat down, waving Henry and myself to seats. Henry might be chairman, might indeed in office terms have been Uncle Freddie's boss, but the white-haired old tyrant still personally owned the leasehold of the building itself and from long habit treated everyone in it as guests.

Henry absently fingered the newspaper. 'What do you think?' he said to me. '*Who* ... do you think?'

'It might not be anyone.'

He half smiled. 'A stirrer?'

'Mm. Not a single concrete detail. Same as last time.'

'Last time,' Henry said, 'I asked the paper's editor where he got his information from. Never reveal sources, he said. Useless asking again.'

'Undisclosed sources,' Uncle Freddie said, 'never trust them.'

Henry said, 'Gordon says you can find out, Tim, how many concerns, if any, are borrowing from us at five per cent. There can't be many. A few from when interest rates were low. The few who got us in the past to agree to a long-term fixed rate.' The few, though he didn't say so, from before his time, before he put an end to such unprofitable straitjackets. 'If there are more recent ones among them, could you spot them?'

'I'll look,' I said.

We both knew it would take days rather than hours

and might produce no results. The fraud, if it existed, could have been going on for a decade. For half a century. Successful frauds tended to go on and on unnoticed, until someone tripped over them by accident. It might almost be easier to find out who had done the tripping, and why he'd told the paper instead of the bank.

'Anyway,' Henry said, 'that isn't primarily why we asked you up here.'

'No,' said my uncle, grunting. 'Time you were a director.'

I thought: I didn't hear that right.

'Er . . . what?' I said.

'A director. A director,' he said impatiently. 'Fellow who sits on the board. Never heard of them, I suppose.'

I looked at Henry, who was smiling and nodding.

'But,' I said, 'so soon . . .'

'Don't you want to, then?' demanded my uncle.

'Yes, I do.'

'Good. Don't let me down. I've had my eye on you since you were eight.'

I must have looked as surprised as I felt.

'You told me then,' he said, 'how much you had saved, and how much you would have if you went on saving a pound a month at four per cent compound interest for forty years, by which time you would be very old. I wrote down your figures and worked them out, and you were right.'

'It's only a formula,' I said.

'Oh sure. You could do it now in a drugged sleep. But at *eight*? You'd inherited the gift, all right. You were just robbed of the inclination.' He nodded heavily. 'Look at your father. My little brother. Got drunk nicely, never a mean thought, but hardly there when the brains were handed out. Look at the way he indulged your mother, letting her gamble like that. Look at the life he gave you. All pleasure, regardless of cost. I despaired of you at times. Thought you'd been ruined. But I knew the gift was there somewhere, might still be dormant, might grow if forced. So there you are, I was right.'

I was pretty well speechless.

'We all agree,' Henry said. 'The whole board was unanimous at our meeting this morning that it's time another Ekaterin took his proper place.'

I thought of John, and of the intensity of rage my promotion would bring forth.

'Would you,' I said slowly, 'have given me a director-ship if my name had been Joe Bloggs?'

Henry levelly said, 'Probably not this very day. But soon, I promise you, yes. You're almost thirty-three, after all, and I was on the board here at thirty-four.'

'Thank you,' I said.

'Rest assured,' Henry said. 'You've earned it.' He stood up and formally shook hands. 'Your appointment officially starts as of the first of November, a week today. We will welcome you then to a short meeting in the boardroom, and afterwards to lunch.'

They must both have seen the depth of my pleasure, and they themselves looked satisfied. Hallelujah, I thought, I've made it. I've got there . . . I've barely started.

Gordon went down with me in the lift, also smiling.

'They've all been dithering about it on and off for months,' he said. 'Ever since you took over from me when I was ill, and did OK. Anyway I told them this morning about your news from the cartoonist. Some of them said it was just lucky. I told them you'd now been lucky too often for it to be a coincidence. So there you are.'

'I can't thank you . . .'

'It's your own doing.'

'John will have a fit.'

'You've coped all right so far with his envy.'

'I don't like it, though,' I said.

'Who would? Silly man, he's doing his career no good.'

Gordon straightaway told everyone in the office, and John went white and walked rigidly out of the room.

I went diffidently a week later to the induction and to the first lunch with the board, and then in a few days, as one does, I got used to the change of company and to the higher level of information. In the departments one heard about the decisions that had been made; in the dining room one heard the decisions being reached.

'Our daily board meeting,' Henry said. 'So much easier this way when everyone can simply say what they think without anyone taking notes.'

There were usually from ten to fifteen directors at lunch, although at a pinch the elongated oval table could accommodate the full complement of twenty-three. People would vanish at any moment to answer telephone calls, and to deal. Dealing, the buying and selling of stocks, took urgent precedence over food.

The food itself was no great feast, though perfectly presented. 'Always lamb on Wednesdays,' Gordon said at the buffet table as he took a couple from a row of trimmed lean cutlets. 'Some sort of chicken on Tuesdays, beef wellington most Thursdays. Henry never eats the crust.' Each day there was a clear soup before and fruit and cheese after. Alcohol if one chose, but most of them didn't. No one should deal in millions whose brain wanted to sleep, Henry said, drinking Malvern water steadily. Quite a change, all of it, from a rough-hewn sandwich at my desk.

They were all polite about my failure to discover 'paper' companies to whom the bank had been lending at five per cent, although Val and Henry, I knew, shared my own view that the report originated from malice and not from fact.

I had spent several days in the extra-wide office at the back of our floor, where the more mechanical parts of the banking operation were carried on. There in the huge expanse (grey carpet, this time) were row upon

row of long desks whose tops were packed with telephones, adding machines and above all computers.

From there went out our own interest cheques to
the depositors who had lent us money for us to lend
to things like 'Home-made Heaven cakes' and 'Water
Purification' plants in Norfolk. Into there came the
interest paid *to* us by cakes and water and cartoonists
and ten thousand such. Machines clattered, phone bells
rang, people hurried about.

Many of the people working there were girls, and it
had often puzzled me why there were so few women
among the managers. Gordon said it was because few
women wanted to commit their whole lives to making
money and John (in the days when he was speaking to
me) said with typical contempt that it was because they
preferred to spend it. In any case, there were no female
managers in banking, and none at all on the board.

Despite that, my best helper in the fraud search
proved to be a curvy redhead called Patty who had
taken the *What's Going On* . . . article as a personal
affront, as had many of her colleagues.

'No one could do that under our noses,' she
protested.

'I'm afraid they could. You know they could. No
one could blame any of you for not spotting it.'

'Well . . . where do we start?'

'With all the borrowers paying a fixed rate of five
per cent. Or perhaps four per cent, or five point seven
five, or six or seven. Who knows if five is right?'

She looked at me frustratedly with wide amber eyes. 'But we haven't got them sorted like that.'

Sorted, she meant, on the computer. Each loan transaction would have its own agreement, which in itself could originally range from one single slip of paper to a contract of fifty pages, and each agreement should say at what rate the loan interest was to be levied, such as two above the current accepted base. There were thousands of such agreements typed onto and stored on computer discs. One could retrieve any one transaction by its identifying number, or alphabetically, or by the dates of commencement, or full term, or by the date when the next interest payment was due, but if you asked the computer who was paying at what per cent you'd get a blank screen and the microchip version of a raspberry.

'You can't sort them out by rates,' she said. 'The rates go up and down like see-saws.'

'But there must still be some loans being charged interest at a fixed rate.'

'Well, yes.'

'So when you punch in the new interest rate the computer adjusts the interest due on almost all the loans but doesn't touch those with a fixed rate.'

'I suppose that's right.'

'So somewhere in the computer there must be a code which tells it when not to adjust the rates.'

She smiled sweetly and told me to be patient, and

half a day later produced a cheerful-looking computer programmer to whom the problem was explained.

'Yeah, there's a code,' he said. 'I put it there myself. What you want, then, is a programme that will print out all the loans which have the code attached. That right?'

We nodded. He worked on paper for half an hour with a much-chewed pencil and then typed rapidly onto the computer, pressing buttons and being pleased with results.

'You leave this programme on here,' he said, 'then feed in the discs, and you'll get the results on that line-printer over there. And I've written it all out for you tidily in pencil, in case someone switches off your machine. Then just type it all in again, and you're back in business.'

We thanked him and he went away whistling, the aristocrat among ants.

The line-printer clattered away on and off for hours as we fed through the whole library of discs, and it finally produced a list of about a hundred of the ten-digit numbers used to identify an account.

'Now,' Patty said undaunted, 'do you want a complete print-out of all the original agreements for those loans?'

'I'm afraid so, yes.'

'Hang around.'

It took two days even with her help to check through all the resulting paper and by the end I couldn't spot any companies there that had no known physical exist-ence, though short of actually tramping to all the addresses and making an on-the-spot enquiry, one couldn't be sure.

Henry, however, was against the expenditure of time. 'We'll just be more vigilant,' he said. 'Design some more safeguards, more tracking devices. Could you do that, Tim?'

'I could, with that programmer's help.'

'Right. Get on with it. Let us know.'

I wondered aloud to Patty whether someone in her own department, not one of the managers, could set up such a fraud, but once she'd got over her instinctive indignation she shook her head.

'Who would bother? It would be much simpler – in fact it's almost dead easy – to feed in a mythical firm who has lent *us* money, and to whom we are paying interest. Then the computer goes on sending out interest cheques for ever, and all the crook has to do is cash them.'

Henry, however, said we had already taken advice on that one, and the 'easy' route had been plugged by systematic checks by the auditors.

The paper-induced rumpus again gradually died down and became undiscussed if not forgotten. Life in our plot went on much as before with Rupert slowly recovering, Alec making jokes and Gordon stuffing his left hand anywhere out of sight. John continued to suffer from his obsession, not speaking to me, not looking at me if he could help it, and apparently telling clients outright that my promotion was a sham.

'Cosmetic of course,' Alec reported him of saying on the telephone. 'Makes the notepaper heading look impressive. Means nothing in real terms, you know. Get through to me, I'll see you right.'

'He said all that?' I asked.

'Word for word.' Alec grinned. 'Go and bop him on the nose.'

I shook my head, however, and wondered if I should get myself transferred along to the St Paul's-facing office. I didn't want to go, but it looked as if John wouldn't recover his balance unless I did. If I tried to get John himself transferred, would it make things that much worse?

I was gradually aware that Gordon, and behind him Henry, were not going to help, their thought being that I was a big boy now and should be able to resolve it myself. It was a freedom which brought responsibility, as all freedoms do, and I had to consider that for the bank's sake John needed to be a sensible member of the team.

I thought he should see a psychiatrist. I got Alec to say it to him lightly as a joke, out of my hearing ('what you need, old pal, is a friendly shrink'), but to John his own anger appeared rational, not a matter for treatment.

I tried saying to him straight, 'Look, John, I know how you feel. I know you think my promotion isn't fair. Well, maybe it is, maybe it isn't, but either way I can't help it. You'll be a lot better off if you just face things and forget it. You're good at your job, we all know it, but you're doing yourself no favours with all this bellyaching. So shut up, accept that life's bloody, and let's lend some money.'

It was a homily that fell on a closed mind, and in the end it was some redecorating which came to the rescue. For a week while painters re-whitened our walls the five of us in the fountain-facing office squeezed into the other one, desks jammed together in every corner, phone calls made with palms pressed to ears against the noise and even normally placid tempers itching to snap. Overcrowd the human race, I thought, and you always got a fight. In distance lay peace.

Anyway, I used the time to do some surreptitious persuasion and shuffling, so that when we returned to our own patch both John and Rupert stayed behind. The two oldest men from the St Paul's office came with Gordon, Alec and myself, and Gordon's almost-equal obligingly told John that it was great to be working again with a younger team of bright energetic brains.

NOVEMBER

Val Fisher said at lunch one day, 'I've received a fairly odd request.' (It was a Friday: grilled fish.)

'Something new?' Henry asked.

'Yes. Chap wants to borrow five million pounds to buy a racehorse.'

Everyone at the table laughed except Val himself.

'I thought I'd toss it at you,' he said. 'Kick it around some. See what you think.'

'What horse?' Henry said.

'Something called Sandcastle.'

Henry, Gordon and I all looked at Val with sharpened attention; almost perhaps with eagerness.

'Mean something to you three, does it?' he said, turning his head from one to the other of us.

Henry nodded. 'That day we all went to Ascot. Sandcastle ran there, and won. A stunning performance. Beautiful.'

Gordon said reminiscently, 'The man whose box we were in saved his whole business on that race. Do you remember Dissdale, Tim?'

'Certainly do.'

'I saw him a few weeks ago. On top of the world. God knows how much he won.'

'Or how much he staked,' I said.

'Yes, well,' Val said. 'Sandcastle. He won the 2,000 Guineas, as I understand, and the King Edward VII Stakes at Royal Ascot. Also the "Diamond" Stakes in July, and the Champion Stakes at Newmarket last month. This is, I believe, a record second only to winning the Derby or the Arc de Triomphe. He finished fourth, incidentally, in the Derby. He could race next year as a four-year-old, but if he flopped his value would be less than it is at the moment. Our prospective client wants to buy him now and put him to stud.'

The rest of the directors got on with their fillets of sole while listening interestedly. A stallion made a change, I suppose, from chemicals, electronics and oil.

'Who is our client?' Gordon asked. Gordon liked fish. He could eat it right handed with his fork, in no danger of shaking it off between plate and mouth.

'A man called Oliver Knowles,' Val said. 'He owns a stud farm. He got passed along to me by the horse's trainer, whom I know slightly because of our wives being distantly related. Oliver Knowles wants to buy, the present owner is willing to sell. All they need is the cash.' He smiled. 'Same old story.'

'What's your view?' Henry said.

Val shrugged his well-tailored shoulders. 'Too soon to have one of any consequence. But I thought, if it

interested you at all, we could ask Tim to do a preliminary look-see. He has a background, after all, a lengthy
acquaintance, shall we say, with racing.'

There was a murmur of dry amusement round the
table.

'What do you think?' Henry asked me.

'I'll certainly do it if you like.'

Someone down the far end complained that it would
be a waste of time and that merchant banks of our
stature should not be associated with the Turf.

'Our own dear Queen,' someone said ironically, 'is
associated with the Turf. And knows the Stud Book
backwards, so they say.'

Henry smiled. 'I don't see why we shouldn't at least
look into it.' He nodded in my direction. 'Go ahead,
Tim. Let us know.'

I spent the next few working days alternately chewing
pencils with the computer programmer and joining us
to a syndicate with three other banks to lend twelve
point four million pounds short term at high interest
to an international construction company with a gap in
its cash-flow. In between those I telephoned around for
information and opinions about Oliver Knowles, in the
normal investigative preliminaries to any loan for anything, not only for a hair-raising price for a stallion.

Establishing a covenant, it was called. Only if the

covenant was sound would any loan be further considered.

Oliver Knowles, I was told, was a sane, sober man of forty-one with a stud farm in Hertfordshire. There were three stallions standing there with ample provision for visiting mares, and he owned the one hundred and fifty acres outright, having inherited them on his father's death.

When talking to local bank managers one listened attentively for what they left out, but Oliver Knowles' bank manager left out not much. Without in the least discussing his client's affairs in detail he said that occasional fair-sized loans had so far been paid off as scheduled and that Mr Knowles' business sense could be commended. A rave notice from such a source.

'Oliver Knowles?' a racing acquaintance from the long past said. 'Don't know him myself. I'll ask around.' And an hour later called back with the news. 'He seems to be a good guy but his wife's just buggered off with a Canadian. He might be a secret wife-beater, who can tell? Otherwise the gen is that he's as honest as any horse-breeder, which you can take as you find it, and how's your mother?'

'She's fine, thanks. She remarried last year. Lives in Jersey.'

'Good. Lovely lady. Always buying us ice creams. I adored her.'

I put the receiver down with a smile and tried a

credit rating agency. No black marks, they said: the Knowles credit was good.

I told Gordon across the room that I seemed to be getting nothing but green lights, and at lunch that day repeated the news to Henry. He looked around the table, collecting a few nods, a few frowns and a great deal of indecision.

'We couldn't carry it all ourselves, of course,' Val said. 'And it isn't exactly something we could go to our regular sources with. They'd think us crackers.'

Henry nodded. 'We'd have to canvass friends for private money. I know a few people here or there who might come in. Two million, I think, is all we should consider ourselves. Two and a half at the outside.'

'I don't approve,' a dissenting director said. 'It's madness. Suppose the damn thing broke its leg?'

'Insurance,' Henry said mildly.

Into a small silence I said, 'If you felt like going into it further I could get some expert views on Sandcastle's breeding, and then arrange blood and fertility tests. And I know it's not usual with loans, but I do think someone like Val should go and personally meet Oliver Knowles and look at his place. It's too much of a risk to lend such a sum for a horse without going into it extremely carefully.'

'Just listen to who's talking,' said the dissenter, but without ill-will.

'Mm,' Henry said, considering. 'What do you think, Val?'

Val Fisher smoothed a hand over his always smooth face. 'Tim should go,' he said. 'He's done the groundwork, and all I know about horses is that they eat grass.'

The dissenting director almost rose to his feet with the urgency of his feelings.

'Look,' he said, 'all this is ridiculous. How can we possibly finance a *horse*?'

'Well, now,' Henry answered. 'The breeding of thoroughbreds is big business, tens of thousands of people round the world make their living from it. Look upon it as an industry like any other. We gamble here on shipbuilders, motors, textiles, you name it, and all of those can go bust. And none of them,' he finished with a near-grin, 'can procreate in their own image.'

The dissenter heavily shook his head. 'Madness. Utter madness.'

'Go and see Oliver Knowles, Tim,' Henry said.

Actually I thought it prudent to bone up on the finances of breeding in general before listening to Oliver Knowles himself, on the basis that I would then have a better idea of whether what he was proposing was sensible or not.

I didn't myself know anyone who knew much on the subject, but one of the beauties of merchant banking was the ramification of people who knew people who knew people who could find someone with the information that was wanted. I sent out the question mark smoke signal and from distant out-of-sight mountain tops the answer puff-puffed back.

Ursula Young, I was told, would put me right. 'She's a bloodstock agent. Very sharp, very talkative, knows her stuff. She used to work on a stud farm, so you've got it every which way. She says she'll tell you anything you want, only if you want to see her in person this week it will have to be at Doncaster races on Saturday, she's too busy to spend the time else.'

I went north to Doncaster by train and met the lady at the racecourse, where the last Flat meeting of the year was being held. She was waiting as arranged by the entrance to the Members' Club and wearing an identifying red velvet beret, and she swept me off to a secluded table in a bar where we wouldn't be interrupted.

She was fifty, tough, good-looking, dogmatic and inclined to treat me as a child. She also gave me a patient and invaluable lecture on the economics of owning a stallion.

'Stop me,' she said to begin with, 'if I say something you don't understand.'

I nodded.

'All right. Say you own a horse that's won the Derby and you want to capitalize on your gold-mine. You judge what you think you can get for the horse, then you divide that by forty and try to sell each of the forty shares at that price. Maybe you can, maybe you can't.

399

It depends on the horse. With Troy, now, they were queuing up. But if your winner isn't frightfully well bred or if it made little show *except* in the Derby you'll get a cool response and have to bring the price down. OK so far?'

'Um,' I said. 'Why only forty shares?'

She looked at me in amazement. 'You don't know a *thing* do you?'

'That's why I'm here.'

'Well, a stallion covers forty mares in a season, and the season, incidentally, lasts roughly from February to June. The mares come to *him*, of course. He doesn't travel, he stays put at home. Forty is just about average; physically I mean. Some can do more, but others get exhausted. So forty is the accepted number. Now, say you have a mare and you've worked out that if you mate her with a certain stallion you might get a top-class foal, you try to get one of those forty places. The places are called nominations. You apply for a nomination, either directly to the stud where the stallion is standing, or through an agent like me, or even by advertising in a breeders' newspaper. Follow?'

'Gasping.' I nodded.

She smiled briefly. 'People who invest in stallion shares sometimes have broodmares of their own they want to breed from.' She paused. 'Perhaps I should have explained more clearly that everyone who owns a share automatically has a nomination to the stallion every year.'

'Ah,' I said.

'Yes. So say you've got your share and consequently your nomination but you haven't a mare to send to the stallion, then you sell your nomination to someone who *has* a mare, in the ways I already described.'

'I'm with you.'

'After the first three years the nominations may vary in price and in fact are often auctioned, but of course for the first three years the price is fixed.'

'Why of course?'

She sighed and took a deep breath. 'For three years no one knows whether the progeny on the whole are going to be winners or not. The gestation period is eleven months, and the first crop of foals don't race until they're two. If you work it out, that means that the stallion has stood for three seasons, and therefore covered a hundred and twenty mares, before the crunch.'

'Right.'

'So to fix the stallion fee for the first three years you divide the price of the stallion by one hundred and twenty, and that's it. That's the fee charged for the stallion to cover a mare. That's the sum you receive if you sell your nomination.'

I blinked.

'That means,' I said, 'that if you sell your nomination for three years you have recovered the total amount of your original investment?'

'That's right.'

'And after that ... every time, every year you sell your nomination, it's clear profit?'

'Yes. But taxed, of course.'

'And how long does that go on?'

She shrugged. 'Ten to fifteen years. Depends on the stallion's potency.'

'But that's ...'

'Yes,' she said. 'One of the best investments on earth.'

The bar had filled up behind us with people crowding in, talking loudly, and breathing on their fingers against the chill of the raw day outside. Ursula Young accepted a warmer in the shape of whisky and ginger wine, while I had coffee.

'Don't you drink?' she asked with mild disapproval.

'Not often in the daytime.'

She nodded vaguely, her eyes scanning the company, her mind already on her normal job. 'Any more questions?' she asked.

'I'm bound to think of some the minute we part.'

She nodded. 'I'll be here until the end of racing. If you want me, you'll see me near the weighing room after each race.'

We were on the point of standing up to leave when a man whose head one could never forget came into the bar.

'Calder Jackson!' I exclaimed.

Ursula casually looked. 'So it is.'

'Do you know him?' I asked.

'Everyone does.' There was almost a conscious neutrality in her voice as if she didn't want to be caught with her thoughts showing. The same response, I reflected, that he had drawn from Henry and Gordon and me.

'You don't like him?' I suggested.

'I feel nothing either way.' She shrugged. 'He's part of the scene. From what people say, he's achieved some remarkable cures.' She glanced at me briefly. 'I suppose you've seen him on television, extolling the value of herbs?'

'I met him,' I said, 'at Ascot, back in June.'

'One tends to.' She got to her feet, and I with her, thanking her sincerely for her help.

'Think nothing of it,' she said. 'Any time.' She paused. 'I suppose it's no use asking what stallion prompted this chat?'

'Sorry, no. It's on behalf of a client.'

She smiled slightly. 'I'm here if he needs an agent.'

We made our way towards the door, a path, I saw, which would take us close to Calder. I wondered fleetingly whether he would know me, remember me after several months. I was after all not as memorable as himself, just a standard issue six foot with eyes, nose and mouth in roughly the right places, dark hair on top.

'Hello Ursula,' he said, his voice carrying easily through the general din. 'Bitter cold day.'

'Calder.' She nodded acknowledgement.

His gaze slid to my face, dismissed it, focused again on my companion. Then he did a classic double-take, his eyes widening with recognition.

'Tim,' he said incredulously. 'Tim . . .' he flicked his fingers to bring the difficult name to mind, '. . . Tim Ekaterin!'

I nodded.

He said to Ursula, 'Tim, here, saved my life.'

She was surprised until he explained, and then still surprised I hadn't told her. 'I read about it, of course,' she said, 'and congratulated you, Calder, on your escape.'

'Did you ever hear any more,' I asked him. 'From the police, or anyone?'

He shook his curly head. 'No, I didn't.'

'The boy didn't try again?'

'No.'

'Did you really have no idea where he came from?' I said. 'I know you told the police you didn't know, but . . . well . . . you just might have done.'

He shook his head very decisively, however, and said, 'If I could help to catch the little bastard I'd do it at once. But I don't know who he was. I hardly saw him properly, just enough to know I didn't know him from Satan.'

'How's the healing?' I said. 'The tingling touch.'

There was a brief flash in his eyes as if he had found the question flippant and in bad taste, but perhaps mindful that he owed me his present existence he answered civilly. 'Rewarding,' he said. 'Heartwarming.'

Standard responses, I thought. As before.

'Is your yard full, Calder?' Ursula asked.

'Always a vacancy if needed,' he replied hopefully. 'Have you a horse to send me?'

'One of my clients has a two-year-old which looks ill and half dead all the time, to the despair of the trainer, who can't get it fit. She – my client – was mentioning you.'

'I've had great success with that sort of general debility.'

Ursula wrinkled her forehead in indecision. 'She feels Ian Pargetter would think her disloyal if she sent you her colt. He's been treating him for weeks, I think, without success.'

Calder smiled reassuringly. 'Ian Pargetter and I are on good terms, I promise you. He's even persuaded owners himself sometimes to send me their horses. Very good of him. We talk each case over, you know, and act in agreement. After all, we both have the recovery of the patient as our prime objective.' Again the swift impression of a statement often needed.

'Is Ian Pargetter a vet?' I asked incuriously.

They both looked at me.

'Er . . . yes,' Calder said.

'One of a group practice in Newmarket,' Ursula

added. 'Very forward-looking. Tries new things. Dozens of trainers swear by him.'

'Just ask him, Ursula,' Calder said. 'Ian will tell you he doesn't mind owners sending me their horses. Even if he's a bit open-minded about the laying on of hands, at least he trusts me not to make the patient worse.' It was said as a self-deprecating joke, and we all smiled. Ursula Young and I in a moment or two walked on and out of the bar, and behind us we could hear Calder politely answering another of the everlasting questions.

'Yes,' he was saying, 'one of my favourite remedies for a prolonged cough in horses is liquorice root boiled in water with some figs. You strain the mixture and stir it into the horse's normal feed . . .'

The door closed behind us and shut him off.

'You'd think he'd get tired of explaining his methods,' I said. 'I wonder he never snaps.'

The lady said judiciously, 'Calder depends on television fame, good public relations and medical success, roughly in that order. He owns a yard with about thirty boxes on the outskirts of Newmarket – it used to be a regular training stables before he bought it – and the yard's almost always full. Short-term and long-term crocks, all sent to him either from true belief or as a last resort. I don't pretend to know anything about herbalism, and as for supernatural healing powers . . .' She shook her head. 'But there's no doubt that whatever his methods, horses do usually seem to leave his yard in a lot better health than when they went in.'

'Someone at Ascot said he'd brought dying horses back to life.'

'Hmph.'

'You don't believe it?'

She gave me a straight look, a canny businesswoman with a lifetime's devotion to thoroughbreds.

'Dying,' she said, 'is a relative term when it doesn't end in death.'

I made a nod into a slight bow of appreciation.

'But to be fair,' she said, 'I know for certain that he totally and permanently cured a ten-year-old brood-mare of colitis X, which has a habit of being fatal.'

'They're not all horses in training, then, that he treats?'

'Oh no, he'll take anybody's pet from a pony to an event horse. Showjumpers, the lot. But the horse has to be worth it, to the owner, I mean. I don't think Calder's hospital is terribly cheap.'

'Exorbitant?'

'Not that I've heard. Fair, I suppose, if you consider the results.'

I seemed to have heard almost more about Calder Jackson than I had about stallion shares, but I did after all have a sort of vested interest. One tended to want a life one had saved to be of positive use in the world. Illogical, I dare say, but there it was. I was pleased that it was true that Calder cured horses, albeit in his own mysterious unorthodox ways; and if I wished that I could warm to him more as a person, that was unrealistic and sentimental.

Ursula Young went off about her business, and although I caught sight of both her and Calder during the afternoon, I didn't see them again to speak to. I went back to London on the train, spent two hours of Sunday morning on the telephone, and early Sunday afternoon drove off to Hertfordshire in search of Oliver Knowles.

He lived in a square hundred-year-old stark redbrick house which to my taste would have been friendlier if softened by trailing creeper. Blurred outlines, however, were not in Oliver Knowles' soul: a crisp bare tidiness was apparent in every corner of his spread.

His land was divided into a good number of paddocks of various sizes, each bordered by an immaculate fence of white rails; and the upkeep of those, I judged, as I pulled up on the weedless gravel before the front door, must alone cost a fortune. There was a scattering of mares and foals in the distance in the paddocks, mostly heads down to the grass, sniffing out the last tender shoots of the dying year. The day itself was cold with a muted sun dipping already towards distant hills, the sky quiet with the greyness of coming winter, the damp air smelling of mustiness, wood smoke and dead leaves.

There were no dead leaves as such to be seen. No

flower beds, no ornamental hedges, no nearby trees. A barren mind, I thought, behind a business whose aim was fertility and the creation of life.

Oliver Knowles himself opened his front door to my knock, proving to be a pleasant lean man with an efficient, cultured manner of authority and politeness. Accustomed to command, I diagnosed. Feels easy with it; second nature. Positive, straightforward, self-controlled. Charming also, in an understated way.

'Mr Ekaterin?' He shook hands, smiling. 'I must confess I expected someone . . . older.'

There were several answers to that, such as 'time will take care of it' and 'I'll be older tomorrow', but nothing seemed appropriate. Instead I said 'I report back' to reassure him, which it did, and he invited me into his house.

Predictably the interior was also painfully tidy, such papers and magazines as were to be seen being squared up with the surface they rested on. The furniture was antique, well polished, brass handles shining, and the carpets venerably from Persia. He led me into a sitting room which was also office, the walls thickly covered with framed photographs of horses, mares and foals, and the window giving on to a view of, across a further expanse of gravel, an archway leading into an extensive stable yard.

'Boxes for mares,' he said, following my eyes. 'Beyond them, the foaling boxes. Beyond those, the breeding pen, with the stallion boxes on the far side of that again. My stud groom's bungalow and the lads' hostel, those roofs you can see in the hollow, they're just beyond the stallions.' He paused. 'Would you care perhaps to look round?'

'Very much,' I said.

'Come along, then.' He led the way to a door at the back of the house, collecting an overcoat and a black retriever from a mud room on the way. 'Go on then, Squibs, old fellow,' he said, fondly watching his dog squeeze ecstatically through the opening outside door. 'Breath of fresh air won't hurt you.'

We walked across to the stable arch with Squibs circling and zig-zagging nose down to the gravel.

'It's our quietest time of year,' Oliver Knowles said. 'We have our own mares here, of course, and quite a few at livery.' He looked at my face to see if I understood and decided to explain anyway. 'They belong to people who own broodmares but have nowhere of their own to keep them. They pay us to board them.'

I nodded.

'Then we have the foals born to the mares this past spring, and of course the three stallions. Total of seventy-eight at the moment.'

'And next spring,' I said, 'the mares coming to your stallions will arrive?'

'That's right.' He nodded. 'They come here a month or five weeks before they're due to give birth to the foals they are already carrying, so as to be near the stallion within the month following. They have to

foal here, because the foals would be too delicate
straight after birth to travel.'

'And . . . how long do they stay here?'

'About three months altogether, by which time we
hope the mare is safely in foal again.'

'There isn't much pause then,' I said. 'Between . . .
er . . . pregnancies?'

He glanced at me with civil amusement. 'Mares
come into use nine days after foaling, but normally we
would think this a bit too soon for breeding. The
oestrus – heat you would call it – lasts six days, then
there's an interval of fifteen days, then the mare comes
into use again for six days, and this time we breed her.
Mind you,' he added, 'nature being what it is, this cycle
doesn't work to the minute. In some mares the oestrus
will last only two days, in some as much as eleven. We
try to have the mare covered two or three times while
she's in heat, for the best chance of getting her in foal.
A great deal depends on the stud groom's judgement,
and I've a great chap just now, he has a great feel for
mares, a sixth sense, you might say.'

He led me briskly across the first big oblong yard
where long dark equine heads peered inquisitively from
over half-open stable doors, and through a passage on
the far side which led to a second yard of almost the
same size but whose doors were fully shut.

'None of these boxes is occupied at the moment,' he
said, waving a hand around. 'We have to have the
capacity, though, for when the mares come.'

Beyond the second yard lay a third, a good deal smaller and again with closed doors.

'Foaling boxes,' Oliver Knowles explained. 'All empty now, of course.'

The black dog trotted ahead of us, knowing the way. Beyond the foaling boxes lay a wide path between two small paddocks of about half an acre each, and at the end of the path, to the left, rose a fair-sized barn with a row of windows just below its roof.

'Breeding shed,' Oliver Knowles said economically, producing a heavy key ring from his trouser pocket and unlocking a door set into a large roll-aside entrance. He gestured to me to go in, and I found myself in a bare concrete-floored expanse surrounded by white walls topped with the high windows, through which the dying sun wanly shone.

'During the season of course the floor in here is covered with peat,' he said.

I nodded vaguely and thought of life being generated purposefully in that quiet place, and we returned prosaically to the outer world with Oliver Knowles locking the door again behind us.

Along another short path between two more small paddocks we came to another small stable yard, this time of only six boxes, with feed room, tack room, hay and peat storage alongside.

'Stallions,' Oliver Knowles said.

Three heads almost immediately appeared over the

412

half-doors, three sets of dark liquid eyes turning inquisitively our way.

'Rotaboy,' my host said, walking to the first head and producing a carrot unexpectedly. The black mobile lips whiffled over the outstretched palm and sucked the goodie in: strong teeth crunched a few times and Rotaboy nudged Oliver Knowles for a second helping. Oliver Knowles produced another carrot, held it out as before, and briefly patted the horse's neck.

'He'll be twenty next year,' he said. 'Getting old, eh, old fella?'

He walked along to the next box and repeated the carrot routine. 'This one is Diarist, rising sixteen.'

By the third box he said, 'This is Parakeet,' and delivered the treats and the pat. 'Parakeet turns twelve on January first.'

He stood a little away from the horse so that he could see all three heads at once and said, 'Rotaboy has been an outstanding stallion and still is, but one can't realistically expect more than another one or two seasons. Diarist is successful, with large numbers of winners among his progeny, but none of them absolutely top rank like those of Rotaboy. Parakeet hasn't proved as successful as I'd hoped. He turns out to breed better stayers than sprinters, and the world is mad nowadays for very fast two-year-olds. Parakeet's progeny tend to be better at three, four, five and six. Some of his first crops are now steeplechasing and jumping pretty well.'

413

'Isn't that good?' I asked, frowning, since he spoke with no great joy.

'I've had to reduce his fee,' he said. 'People won't send their top flat-racing mares to a stallion who breeds jumpers.'

'Oh.'

After a pause he said, 'You can see why I need new blood here. Rotaboy is old, Diarist is middle rank, Parakeet is unfashionable. I will soon have to replace Rotaboy, and I must be sure I replace him with something of at least equal quality. The *prestige* of a stud farm, quite apart from its income, depends on the drawing-power of its stallions.'

'Yes,' I said, 'I see.'

Rotaboy, Diarist and Parakeet lost interest in the conversation and hope in the matter of carrots, and one by one withdrew into the boxes. The black retriever trotted around smelling unimaginable scents and Oliver Knowles began to walk me back towards the house.

'On the bigger stud farms,' he said, 'you'll find stallions which are owned by syndicates.'

'Forty shares?' I suggested.

He gave me a brief smile. 'That's right. Stallions are owned by any number of people between one and forty. When I first acquired Rotaboy it was in partnership with five others. I bought two of them out – they needed the money – so now I own half. This means I have twenty nominations each year, and I have no trouble in selling all of them, which is most satisfactory.' He looked at me enquiringly to make sure I understood, which, thanks to Ursula Young, I did.

'I own Diarist outright. He was as expensive in the first place as Rotaboy, and as he's middle rank, so is the fee I can get for him. I don't always succeed in filling his forty places, and when that occurs I breed him to my own mares, and sell the resulting foals as yearlings.'

Fascinated, I nodded again.

'With Parakeet it's much the same. For the last three years I haven't been able to charge the fee I did to begin with, and if I fill his last places these days it's with mares from people who *prefer* steeplechasing, and this is increasingly destructive of his flat-racing image.'

We retraced our steps past the breeding shed and across the foaling yard.

'This place is expensive to run,' he said objectively. 'It makes a profit and I live comfortably, but I'm not getting any further. I have the capacity here for another stallion – enough accommodation, that is to say, for the extra forty mares. I have a good business sense and excellent health, and I feel underextended. If I am ever to achieve more I must have more capital . . . and capital in the shape of a world-class stallion.'

'Which brings us,' I said, 'to Sandcastle.'

He nodded. 'If I acquired a horse like Sandcastle this stud would immediately be more widely known and more highly regarded.'

Understatement, I thought. The effect would be galvanic. 'A sort of overnight stardom?' I said.

'Well, yes,' he agreed with a satisfied smile. 'I'd say you might be right.'

The big yard nearest the house had come moderately to life, with two or three lads moving about carrying feed scoops, hay nets, buckets of water and sacks of muck. Squibs with madly wagging tail went in a straight line towards a stocky man who bent to fondle his black ears.

'That's Nigel, my stud groom,' Oliver Knowles said. 'Come and meet him.' And as we walked across he added, 'If I can expand this place I'll up-rate him to stud manager; give him more standing with the customers.'

We reached Nigel, who was of about my own age with crinkly light-brown hair and noticeably bushy eyebrows. Oliver Knowles introduced me merely as 'a friend' and Nigel treated me with casual courtesy but not as the possible source of future fortune. He had a Gloucestershire accent but not pronounced, and I would have placed him as a farmer's son, if I'd had to.

'Any problems?' Oliver Knowles asked him, and Nigel shook his head.

'Nothing except that Floating mare with the discharge.'

His manner to his employer was confident and without anxiety but at the same time diffident, and I had a strong impression that it was Nigel's personality which suited Oliver Knowles as much as any skill he might have with mares. Oliver Knowles was not a man, I judged, to surround himself with awkward, unpredictable characters: the behaviour of everyone around him had to be as tidy as his place.

I wondered idly about the wife who had 'just buggered off with a Canadian', and at that moment a horse trotted into the yard with a young woman aboard. A girl, I amended, as she kicked her feet from the stirrups and slid to the ground. A noticeably curved young girl in jeans and heavy sweater with her dark hair tied in a pony tail. She led her horse into one of the boxes and presently emerged carrying the saddle and bridle, which she dumped on the ground outside the box before closing the bottom half of the door and crossing the yard to join us.

'My daughter,' Oliver Knowles said.

'Ginnie,' added the girl, holding out a polite brown hand. 'Are you the reason we didn't go out to lunch?'

Her father gave an instinctive repressing movement and Nigel looked only fairly interested.

'I don't know,' I said. 'I wouldn't think so.'

'Oh, I would,' she said. 'Pa really doesn't like parties. He uses any old excuse to get out of them, don't you Pa?'

He gave her an indulgent smile while looking as if his thoughts were elsewhere.

'I didn't mind missing it,' Ginnie said to me, anxious not to embarrass. 'Twelve miles away and people all Pa's age . . . but they do have frightfully good canapés, and also a lemon tree growing in their greenhouse. Did you know that a lemon tree has everything all at once – buds, flowers, little green knobbly fruit and big fat lemons, all going on all the time?'

'My daughter,' Oliver Knowles said unnecessarily, 'talks a lot.'

'No,' I said, 'I didn't know about lemon trees.'

She gave me an impish smile and I wondered if she was even younger than I'd first thought: and as if by telepathy she said, 'I'm fifteen.'

'Everyone has to go through it,' I said.

Her eyes widened. 'Did you hate it?'

I nodded. 'Spots, insecurity, a new body you're not yet comfortable in, self-consciousness . . . terrible.'

Oliver Knowles looked surprised. 'Ginnie isn't self-conscious, are you, Ginnie?'

She looked from him to me and back again and didn't answer. Oliver Knowles dismissed the subject as of no importance anyway and said he ought to walk along and see the mare with the discharge. Would I care to go with him?

I agreed without reservation and we all set off along one of the paths between the white-railed paddocks, Oliver Knowles and myself in front, Nigel and Ginnie following, Squibs sniffing at every fencing post and marking his territory. In between Oliver Knowles explaining that some mares preferred living out of doors permanently, others would go inside if it snowed, others went in at nights, others lived mostly in the boxes, I could hear Ginnie telling Nigel that school this term was a dreadful drag owing to the new head-mistress being a health fiend and making them all do jogging.

'How do you know what mares prefer?' I asked.

Oliver Knowles looked for the first time nonplussed. 'Er . . .' he said. 'I suppose . . . by the way they stand. If they feel cold and miserable they put their tails to the wind and look hunched. Some horses never do that, even in a blizzard. If they're obviously unhappy we bring them in. Otherwise they stay out. Same with the foals.' He paused. 'A lot of mares are miserable if you keep them inside. It's just . . . how they are.'

He seemed dissatisfied with the loose ends of his answer, but I found them reassuring. The one thing he had seemed to me to lack had been any emotional contact with the creatures he bred: even the carrots for the stallions had been slightly mechanical.

The mare with the discharge proved to be in one of the paddocks at the boundary of the farm, and while Oliver Knowles and Nigel peered at her rump end and made obscure remarks like 'With any luck she won't slip,' and 'It's clear enough, nothing yellow or bloody,' I spent my time looking past the last set of white rails to the hedge and fields beyond.

The contrast from the Knowles land was dramatic. Instead of extreme tidiness, a haphazard disorder. Instead of short green grass in well-tended rectangles, long unkempt brownish stalks straggling through an army of drying thistles. Instead of rectangular brick-built stable yards, a ramshackle collection of wooden boxes, light grey from old creosote and with tarpaulins tied over patches of roof.

Ginnie followed my gaze. 'That's the Watcherleys' place,' she said. 'I used to go over there a lot but they're so grimy and gloomy these days, not a laugh in sight. And all the patients have gone, practically, and they don't even have the chimpanzees any more, they say they can't afford them.'

'What patients?' I said.

'Horse patients. It's the Watcherleys' hospital for sick horses. Haven't you heard of it?'

I shook my head.

'It's pretty well known,' Ginnie said. 'Or at least it was until that razzamatazz man Calder Jackson stole the show. Mind you, the Watcherleys were no great shakes, I suppose, with Bob off to the boozer at all hours and Maggie sweating her guts out carrying muck sacks, but at least they used to be fun. The place was *cosy*, you know, even if bits of the boxes were falling off their hinges and weeds were growing everywhere, and all the horses went home blooming, or most of them, even if Maggie had her knees through her jeans and wore the same jersey for weeks and weeks on end. But Calder Jackson, you see, is the *in* thing, with all those chat shows on television and the publicity and such, and the Watcherleys have sort of got elbowed out.'

Her father, listening to the last of these remarks, added his own view. 'They're disorganized,' he said. 'No business sense. People liked their gypsy style for a while, but, as Ginnie says, they've no answer to Calder Jackson.'

'How old are they?' I asked, frowning.

Oliver Knowles shrugged. 'Thirties. Going on forty. Hard to say.'

'I suppose they don't have a son of about sixteen, thin and intense, who hates Calder Jackson obsessively for ruining his parents' business?'

'What an extraordinary question,' said Oliver Knowles, and Ginnie shook her head. 'They've never had any children,' she said. 'Maggie can't. She told me. They just lavish all that love on animals. It's really grotty, what's happening to them.'

It would have been so neat, I thought, if Calder Jackson's would-be assassin had been a Watcherley son. Too neat, perhaps. But perhaps also there were others like the Watcherleys whose star had descended as Calder Jackson's rose. I said, 'Do you know of any other places, apart from this one and Calder Jackson's, where people send their sick horses?'

'I expect there *are* some,' Ginnie said. 'Bound to be.'

'Sure to be,' said Oliver Knowles, nodding. 'But of course we don't send away any horse which falls ill here. I have an excellent vet, great with mares, comes day or night in emergencies.'

We made the return journey, Oliver Knowles

pointing out to me various mares and foals of interest and distributing carrots to any head within armshot. Foals at foot, foals in utero; the fertility cycle swelling again to fruition through the quiet winter, life growing steadily in the dark.

Ginnie went off to see to the horse she'd been riding and Nigel to finish his inspections in the main yard, leaving Oliver Knowles, the dog and myself to go into the house. Squibs, poor fellow, got no further than his basket in the mud room, but Knowles and I returned to the sitting room office from which we'd started.

Thanks to my telephone calls of the morning I knew what the acquisition and management of Sandcastle would mean in the matter of taxation, and I'd also gone armed with sets of figures to cover the interest payable should the loan be approved. I found that I needed my knowledge not to instruct but to converse: Oliver Knowles was there before me.

'I've done this often, of course,' he said. 'I've had to arrange finance for buildings, for fencing, for buying the three stallions you saw, and for another two before them. I'm used to repaying fairly substantial bank loans. This new venture is of course huge by comparison, but if I didn't feel it was within my scope I assure you I shouldn't be contemplating it.' He gave me a brief charming smile. 'I'm not a nut case, you know. I really do know my business.'

'Yes,' I said. 'One can see.'

I told him that the maximum length of an Ekaterin

loan (if one was forthcoming at all) would be five years, to which he merely nodded.

'That basically means,' I insisted, 'that you'd have to receive getting on for eight million in that five years, even allowing for paying off some of the loan every year with consequently diminishing interest. It's a great deal of money . . . Are you sure you understand how much is involved?'

'Of course I understand,' he said. 'Even allowing for interest payments and the ridiculously high insurance premiums on a horse like Sandcastle, I'd be able to repay the loan in five years. That's the period I've used in planning.'

He spread out his sheets of neatly written calculations on his desk, pointing to each figure as he explained to me how he'd reached it. 'A stallion fee of forty thousand pounds will cover it. His racing record justifies that figure, and I've been most carefully into the breeding of Sandcastle himself, as you can imagine. There is absolutely nothing in the family to alarm. No trace of hereditary illness or undesirable tendencies. He comes from a healthy blue-blooded line of winners, and there's no reason why he shouldn't breed true.' He gave me a photocopied genealogical table. 'I wouldn't except you to advance a loan without getting an expert opinion on this. Please do take it with you.'

He gave me also some copies of his figures, and I packed them all into the briefcase I'd taken with me.

'Why don't you consider halving your risk to twenty-one shares?' I asked. 'Sell nineteen. You'd still outvote the other owners – there'd be no chance of them whisking Sandcastle off somewhere else – and you'd be less stretched.'

With a smile he shook his head. 'If I found for any reason that the repayments were causing me acute difficulty, I'd sell some shares as necessary. But I hope in five years time to own Sandcastle outright, and also as I told you to have attracted other stallions of that calibre, and to be numbered among the world's top-ranking stud farms.'

His pleasant manner took away any suggestion of megalomania, and I could see nothing of that nature in him.

Ginnie came into the office carrying two mugs with slightly anxious diffidence.

'I made some tea. Do you want some, Dad?'

'Yes, please,' I said immediately, before he could answer, and she looked almost painfully relieved. Oliver Knowles turned what had seemed like an incipient shake of the head into a nod, and Ginnie, handing over the mugs, said that if I wanted sugar she would go and fetch some. 'And a spoon, I guess.'

'My wife's away,' Oliver Knowles said abruptly.

'No sugar,' I said. 'This is great.'

'You won't forget, Dad, will you, about me going back to school?'

'Nigel will take you.'

'He's got visitors.'

'Oh . . . all right.' He looked at his watch. 'In half an hour, then.'

Ginnie looked even more relieved, particularly as I could clearly sense the irritation he was suppressing. 'The school run,' he said as the door closed behind his daughter, 'was one of the things my wife always did. Does . . .' He shrugged. 'She's away indefinitely. You might as well know.'

'I'm sorry,' I said.

'Can't be helped.' He looked at the tea mug in my hand. 'I was going to offer you something stronger.'

'This is fine.'

'Ginnie comes home on four Sundays a term. She's a boarder, of course.' He paused. 'She's not yet used to her mother not being here. It's bad for her, but there you are, life's like that.'

'She's a nice girl,' I said.

He gave me a glance in which I read both love for his daughter and a blindness to her needs. 'I don't suppose,' he said thoughtfully, 'that you go anywhere near High Wycombe on your way home?'

'Well,' I said obligingly, 'I could do.'

I consequently drove Ginnie back to her school, listening on the way to her views on the new head-mistress's compulsory jogging programme ('all our bosoms flopping up and down, bloody uncomfortable and absolutely *disgusting* to look at') and to her opinion of Nigel ('Dad thinks the sun shines out of his you-know-what and I dare say he is pretty good with the mares, they all seem to flourish, but what the lads get up to behind his back is nobody's business. They smoke in the feed sheds, I ask you! All that hay around ... Nigel never notices. He'd make a rotten school prefect.') and to her outlook on life in general ('I can't wait to get out of school uniform and out of dormitories and being bossed around, and I'm no good at lessons; the whole thing's a *mess*. Why has everything *changed*? I used to be happy, or at least I wasn't *unhappy*, which I mostly seem to be nowadays, and no, it isn't because of Mum going away, or not especially, as she was never a lovey-dovey sort of mother, always telling me to eat with my mouth shut and so on ... and you must be bored silly hearing all this.').

'No,' I said truthfully. 'I'm not bored.'

'I'm not even *beautiful*,' she said despairingly. 'I can suck in my cheeks until I faint but I'll never look pale and bony and interesting.'

I glanced at the still rounded child-woman face, at the peach-bloom skin and the worried eyes.

'Practically no one is beautiful at fifteen,' I said. 'It's too soon.'

'How do you mean – too soon?'

'Well,' I said, 'say at twelve you're a child and flat and undeveloped and so on, and at maybe seventeen or eighteen you're a full-grown adult, just think of the terrific changes your body goes through in that time. Appearance, desires, mental outlook, everything. So at fifteen, which isn't much more than halfway, it's still too soon to know exactly what the end product will be like. And if it's of any comfort to you, you do now look as if you may be beautiful in a year or two, or at least not unbearably ugly.'

She sat in uncharacteristic silence for quite a distance, and then she said, 'Why did you come today? I mean, who are you? If it's all right to ask?'

'It's all right. I'm a sort of financial adviser. I work in a bank.' ·

'Oh.' She sounded slightly disappointed but made no further comment, and soon after that gave me prosaic and accurate directions to the school.

'Thanks for the lift,' she said, politely shaking hands as we stood beside the car.

'A pleasure.'

'And thanks . . .' she hesitated. 'Thanks anyway.'

I nodded, and she half-walked, half-ran to join a group of other girls going into the buildings. Looking briefly back she gave me a sketchy wave, which I acknowledged. Nice child, I thought, pointing the car homewards. Mixed up, as who wasn't at that age? Middling brains, not quite pretty, her future a clean stretch of sand waiting for footprints.

DECEMBER

It made the headlines in the *Sporting Life* (OLIVER
KNOWLES, KING OF THE SANDCASTLE) and turned up as
the lead story under less fanciful banners on the racing
pages of all the other dailies.

SANDCASTLE TO GO TO STUD, SANDCASTLE TO STAY IN
BRITAIN, SANDCASTLE SHARES NOT FOR SALE, SANDCASTLE
BOUGHT PRIVATELY FOR HUGE SUM. The story in every
case was short and simple. One of the year's top stallions had been acquired by the owner of a heretofore
moderately ranked stud farm. 'I am very happy,' Oliver
Knowles was universally reported as saying. 'Sandcastle
is a prize for British bloodstock.'

The buying price, all the papers said, was 'not
unadjacent to five million pounds,' and a few of them
added, 'the financing was private.'

'Well,' Henry said at lunch, tapping the *Sporting
Life*, 'not many of our loans make so much splash.'

'It's a belly-flop,' muttered the obstinate dissenter,
who on that day happened to be sitting at my elbow.

Henry didn't hear and was anyway in good spirits.

'If one of the foals runs in the Derby we'll take a party from the office. What do you say, Gordon? Fifty people on open-topped buses?'

Gordon agreed with the sort of smile which hoped he wouldn't actually be called upon to fulfil his promise.

'Forty mares,' Henry said musingly. 'Forty foals. Surely one of them might be Derby material.'

'Er,' I said, from new-found knowledge. 'Forty foals is stretching it. Thirty-five would be pretty good. Some mares won't "take", so to speak.'

Henry showed mild alarm. 'Does that mean that five or six fees will have to be returned? Doesn't that affect Knowles' programme of repayment?'

I shook my head. 'For a horse of Sandcastle's stature the fee is all up in front. Payable for services rendered, regardless of results. That's in Britain, of course, and Europe. In America they have the system of no foal, no fee, even for the top stallions. A live foal, that is. Alive, on its feet and suckling.'

Henry relaxed, leaning back in his chair and smiling. 'You've certainly learnt a lot, Tim, since this all started.'

'It's absorbing.'

He nodded. 'I know it isn't usual, but how do you feel about keeping an eye on the bank's money at close quarters? Would Knowles object to you dropping in from time to time?'

'I shouldn't think so. Not out of general interest.'

'Good. Do that, then. Bring us progress reports. I

must say I've never been as impressed with any horse as I was that day with Sandcastle.'

Henry's direct admiration of the colt had led in the end to Ekaterin's advancing three of the five million to Oliver Knowles, with private individuals subscribing the other two. The fertility tests had been excellent, the owner had been paid, and Sandcastle already stood in the stallion yard in Hertfordshire alongside Rotaboy, Diarist and Parakeet.

December was marching along towards Christmas, with trees twinkling all over London and sleet falling bleakly in the afternoons. On an impulse I sent a card embossed with tasteful robins to Calder Jackson, wishing him well, and almost by return of post received (in the office) a missive (Stubbs reproduction) thanking me sincerely and asking if I would be interested some time in looking round his place. If so, he finished, would I telephone – number supplied.

I telephoned. He was affable and far more spontaneous than usual. 'Do come,' he said, and we made a date for the following Sunday.

I told Gordon I was going. We were working on an interbank loan of nine and a half million for five days to a competitor, a matter of little more than a few telephone calls and a promise. My hair had almost ceased to rise at the size and speed of such deals, and with only verbal agreement from Val and Henry I had recently on my own lent seven million for forty-eight hours. The trick was never to lend for a longer time than we ourselves were able to borrow the necessary funds; if we did, we ran the risk of having to pay a higher rate of interest than we were receiving on the loan, a process which physically hurt Val Fisher. There had been a time in the past when owing to a client repaying late he had had to borrow several million for eighteen days at twenty-five per cent, and he'd never got over it.

Most of our dealings weren't on such a heavy scale, and next on my agenda was a request for us to lend fifty-five thousand pounds to a man who had invented a waste-paper basket for use in cars and needed funds for development. I read the letter out to Gordon, who made a fast thumbs-down gesture.

'Pity,' I said. 'It's a sorely needed object.'

'He's asking too little.' He put his left hand hard between his knees and clamped it there. 'And there are far better inventions dying the death.'

I agreed with him and wrote a brief note of regret. Gordon looked up from his pages shortly after and asked me what I'd be doing at Christmas.

'Nothing much,' I said.

'Not going to your mother in Jersey?'

'They're cruising in the Caribbean.'

'Judith and I wondered . . .' he cleared his throat, '. . . if you'd care to stay with us. Come on Christmas Eve, stay three or four days? Just as you like, of course. I daresay you wouldn't find us too exciting . . . but the offer's there, anyway.'

Was it wise, I wondered, to spend three or four days with Judith when three or four *hours* at Ascot had tempted acutely? Was it wise, when the sight of her aroused so many natural urges, to sleep so long – and so near – under her roof?

Most unwise.

'I'd like to,' I said, 'very much'; and I thought you're a bloody stupid fool, Tim Ekaterin, and if you ache it'll be your own ridiculous fault.

'Good,' Gordon said, looking as if he meant it. 'Judith will be pleased. She was afraid you might have younger friends to go to.'

'Nothing fixed.'

He nodded contentedly and went back to his work, and I thought about Judith wanting me to stay, because if she hadn't wanted it I wouldn't have been asked.

If I had any sense I wouldn't go; but I knew I would.

Calder Jackson's place at Newmarket, seen that next Sunday morning, was a gem of public relations, where everything had been done to please those visiting the sick. The yard itself, a three-sided quadrangle, had been cosmetically planted with central grass and a graceful tree, and brightly painted tubs, bare now of flowers, stood at frequent intervals outside the boxes. There were park-bench type seats here and there, and ornamental gates and railings in black iron scroll-work, and a welcoming archway labelled 'Comfort Room This Way.'

Outside the main yard, and to one side, stood a small separate building painted glossy white. There was a large prominent red cross on the door, with, underneath it, the single word 'Surgery'.

The yard and the surgery were what the visitor first saw; beyond and screened by trees stood Calder Jackson's own house, more private from prying eyes than his business. I parked beside several other cars on a stretch of asphalt, and walked over to ring the bell. The front door was opened to me by a manservant in a white coat. Butler or nurse?

'This way, sir,' he said deferentially, when I announced my name. 'Mr Jackson is expecting you.'

Butler.

Interesting to see the dramatic haircut in its home setting, which was olde-worlde cottage on a grand scale. I had an impression of a huge room, oak rafters, stone flagged floor, rugs, dark oak furniture, great brick fireplace with burning logs . . . and Calder advancing with a broad smile and outstretched arm.

'Tim!' he exclaimed, shaking hands vigorously. 'This is a pleasure, indeed it is.'

'Been looking forward to it,' I said.

'Come along to the fire. Come and warm yourself. How about a drink? And . . . oh . . . this is a friend of mine . . .' He waved towards a second man already standing by the fireplace, '. . . Ian Pargetter.'

The friend and I nodded to each other and made the usual strangers-meeting signals, and the name tumbled over in my mind as something I'd heard somewhere before but couldn't quite recall.

Calder Jackson clinked bottles and glasses and upon consultation gave me a Scotch of noble proportions.

'And for you, Ian,' he said, 'a further tincture?'

Oh yes, I thought. The vet. Ian Pargetter, the vet who didn't mind consorting with unlicensed practitioners.

Ian Pargetter hesitated but shrugged and held out his glass as one succumbing to pleasurable temptation.

'A small one, then, Calder,' he said. 'I must be off.'

He was about forty, I judged; large and reliable-looking, with sandy greying hair, a heavy moustache and an air of being completely in charge of his life. Calder explained that it was I who had deflected the knife aimed at him at Ascot, and Ian Pargetter made predictable responses about luck, fast reactions and who could have wanted to kill Calder?

'That was altogether a memorable day,' Calder said, and I agreed with him.

'We all won a packet on Sandcastle,' Calder said. 'Pity he's going to stud so soon.'

I smiled. 'Maybe we'll win on his sons.'

There was no particular secret, as far as I knew, about where the finance for Sandcastle had come from, but it was up to Oliver Knowles to reveal it, not me. I thought Calder would have been interested, but bankers' ethics as usual kept me quiet.

'A superb horse,' Calder said, with all the enthusiasm he'd shown in Dissdale's box. 'One of the greats.'

Ian Pargetter nodded agreement, then finished his drink at a gulp and said he'd be going. 'Let me know how that pony fares, Calder.'

'Yes, of course.' Calder moved with his departing guest towards the door and slapped him on the shoulder. 'Thanks for dropping in, Ian. Appreciate it.'

There were sounds of Pargetter leaving by the front door, and Calder returned rubbing his hands together and saying that although it was cold outside, I might care to look round before his other guests arrived for lunch. Accordingly we walked across to the open-sided quadrangle, where Calder moved from box to box giving me a brief résumé of the illness and prospects of each patient.

'This pony only came yesterday . . . it's a prize show pony supposedly, and look at it. Dull eyes, rough coat, altogether droopy. They say it's had diarrhoea on and off for weeks. I'm their last resort, they say.' He smiled philosophically. 'Can't think why they don't send me sick horses as a *first* resort. But there you are, they always try regular vets first. Can't blame them, I suppose.'

We moved along the line. 'This mare was coughing blood when she came three weeks ago. I was her owner's last resort.' He smiled again. 'She's doing fine now. The cough's almost gone. She's eating well, putting on condition.' The mare blinked at us lazily as we strolled away.

'This is a two-year-old filly,' Calder said, peering over a half-door. 'She'd had an infected ulcer on her withers for six weeks before she came here. Antibiotics had proved useless. Now the ulcer's dry and healing. Most satisfactory.'

We went on down the row.

'This is someone's favourite hunter, came all the way from Gloucestershire. I don't know what I can do for him, though of course I'll try. His trouble, truthfully, is just age.'

Further on: 'Here's a star three-day-eventer. Came to me with intermittent bleeding in the urine, intractable to antibiotics. He was clearly in great pain, and almost dangerous to deal with on account of it. But now he's fine. He'll be staying here for a while longer but I'm sure the trouble is cured.

'This is a three-year-old colt who won a race back in July but then started breaking blood vessels and went on doing it despite treatment. He's been here a fortnight. Last resort, of course!'

By the next box he said, 'Don't look at this one if you're squeamish. Poor wretched little filly, she's so weak she can't hold her head up and all her bones are sharp under the skin. Some sort of wasting sickness. Blood tests haven't shown what it is. I don't know if I can heal her. I've laid my hands on her twice so far, but there's been nothing. No . . . feeling. Sometimes it takes a long time. But I'm not giving up with her, and there's always hope.'

He turned his curly head and pointed to another box further ahead. 'There's a colt along there who's been here two months and is only just responding. His owners were in despair, and so was I, privately, but then just three days ago when I was in his box I could feel the force flowing down my arms and into him, and the next day he was mending.'

He spoke with a far more natural fluency on his home ground and less as if reciting from a script, but all the same I felt the same reservations about the healing touch as I had at Ascot. I was a doubter, I supposed. I would never in my life have put my trust in a seventh son of a seventh son, probably because the only direct knowledge I had of any human seeking out 'the touch' had been a close friend of mine at college who'd had hopeless cancer and had gone to a woman healer as a last resort, only to be told that he was dying because he wanted to. I could vividly remember his anger, and mine on his behalf; and standing in Calder's yard I wondered if that same woman would also think that *horses* got sick to death because they wanted to.

'Is there anything you can't treat?' I asked. 'Anything you turn away?'

'I'm afraid so, yes.' He smiled ruefully. 'There are some things like advanced laminitis, with which I feel hopeless, and as for coryne . . .' He shook his head, '. . . It's a killer.'

'You've lost me,' I said.

'So sorry. Well, laminitis is a condition of the feet where the bone eventually begins to crumble, and horses in the end can't bear the pain of standing up. They lie down, and horses can't live for more than a few days lying down.' He spoke with regret. 'And coryne,' he went on, 'is a frightful bacterial infection which is deadly to foals. It induces a sort of pneumonia with abscesses in the lungs. Terribly contagious. I know of one stud farm in America which lost seventy foals in one day.'

I listened in horror. 'Do we have it in England?' I asked.

'Sometimes, in pockets, but not widespread. It doesn't affect older horses. Foals of three months or over are safe.' He paused. 'Some very young foals do survive, of course, but they're likely to have scar tissue in the lungs which may impair their breathing for racing purposes.'

'Isn't there a vaccine?' I said.

He smiled indulgently. 'Very little research is done into equine diseases, chiefly because of the cost but also because horses are so large, and can't be kept in a laboratory for any controlled series of tests.'

I again had the impression that he had said all this many times before, but it was understandable and I was getting used to it. We proceeded on the hospital round (four-year-old with general debility, show-jumper with festering leg) and came at length to a box with an open door.

'We're giving this one sun treatment,' Calder said, indicating that I should look; and inside the box a thin youth was adjusting the angle of an ultra-violet lamp set on a head-high, wall-mounted bracket. It wasn't at the dappled grey that I looked, however, but at the lad, because in the first brief glimpse I thought he was the boy who had tried to attack Calder.

I opened my mouth . . . and shut it again.

He wasn't the boy. He was of the same height, same build, same litheness, same general colouring, but not with the same eyes or jawline or narrow nose.

Calder saw my reaction and smiled. 'For a split second, when I saw that boy move at Ascot, I thought it was Jason here. But it wasn't, of course.'

I shook my head. 'Alike but different.'

Calder nodded. 'And Jason wouldn't want to kill me, would you, Jason?' He spoke with a jocularity to which Jason didn't respond.

'No, sir,' he said stolidly.

'Jason is my right-hand man,' said Calder heartily. 'Indispensable.'

The right-hand man showed no satisfaction at the flattery and maintained an impassive countenance throughout. He touched the grey horse and told it to shift over a bit in the manner of one equal talking to another, and the horse obediently shifted.

439

'Mind your eyes with that lamp,' Calder said. 'Where are your glasses?'

Jason fished into the breast pocket of his shirt and produced some ultra-dark sun-shades. Calder nodded. 'Put them on,' he said, and Jason complied. Where before there had already been a lack of mobility of expression, there was now, with the obscured eyes, no way at all of guessing Jason's thoughts.

'I'll be finished with this one in ten minutes,' he said. 'Is there anything else after that, sir?'

Calder briefly pondered and shook his head. 'Just the evening rounds at four.'

'Your invalids get every care,' I said, complimenting them.

Jason's blacked-out eyes turned my way, but it was Calder who said, 'Hard work gets results.' And you've said that a thousand times, I thought.

We reached the last box in the yard, the first one which was empty.

'Emergency bed,' Calder said, jokingly, and I smiled and asked how much he charged for his patients.

He replied easily and without explanation or apology. 'Twice the training fees currently charged for horses in the top Newmarket stables. When their rates go up, so do mine.'

'*Twice* . . .?'

He nodded. 'I could charge more, you know. But if I charged less I'd be totally swamped by all those "last resort" people, and I simply haven't the room or the time or the spiritual resources to take more cases than I do.'

I wondered how one would ever get to the essence of the man behind the temperate, considerate public face, or indeed if the public face was not a façade at all but the essence itself. I looked at the physical strength of the shoulders below the helmet head and listened to the plain words describing a mystical force, considered the dominating voice and the mild manner, and still found him a man to admire rather than like.

'The surgery,' he said, gesturing towards it as we walked that way. 'My drug store!' He smiled at the joke (how often, I wondered, had he said it?) and produced a key to unlock the door. 'There's nothing dangerous or illegal in here, of course, but one has to protect against vandals. So sad, don't you think?'

The surgery, which had no windows, was basically a large brick-built hut. The internal walls, like the outer, were painted white, and the floor was tiled in red. There were antiseptic-looking glass-fronted cabinets along the two end walls and a wide bench with drawers underneath along the wall facing the door. On the bench, a delicate-looking set of scales, a pestle and mortar and a pair of fine rubber gloves: behind the glass of the cabinets, rows of bottles and boxes. Everything very businesslike and tidy; and along the wall which contained the door stood three kitchen appliances, refrigerator, cooker and sink.

Calder pointed vaguely towards the cabinets. 'In

there I keep the herbs in pill and powder form. Comfrey, myrrh, sarsaparilla, golden seal, fo-ti-tieng, things like that.'

'Er . . .' I said. 'What do they do?'

He ran through them obligingly. 'Comfrey knits bones, and heals wounds, myrrh is antiseptic and good for diarrhoea and rheumatism, sarsaparilla contains male hormones and increases physical strength, golden seal cures eczema, improves appetite and digestion, fo-ti-tieng is a revitalizing tonic second to none. Then there's liquorice for coughs and papaya enzymes for digesting proteins and passiflora to use as a general pacifier and tranquillizer.' He paused. 'There's ginseng also, of course, which is a marvellous rejuvenator and invigorator, but it's really too expensive in the quantities needed to do a horse significant good. It has to be taken continuously, for ever.' He sighed. 'Excellent for humans, though.'

The air in the windowless room was fresh and smelled very faintly fragrant, and as if to account for it Calder started showing me the contents of the drawers.

'I keep seeds in here,' he said. 'My patients eat them by the handful every day.' Three or four of the drawers contained large opaque plastic bags fastened by bull-dog clips. 'Sunflower seeds for vitamins, phosphorus and calcium, good for bones and teeth. Pumpkin seeds for vigour – they contain male hormones – and also for phosphorus and iron. Carrot seeds for calming nervous horses. Sesame seeds for general health.'

He walked along a yard or two and pulled open an extra-large deep drawer which contained larger bags; more like sacks. 'These are hops left after beer-making. They're packed full of all good things. A great tonic, and cheap enough to use in quantity. We have bagfuls of them over in the feed shed to grind up as chaff but I use these here as one ingredient of my special decoction, my concentrated tonic.'

'Do you make it . . . on the stove?' I asked.

He smiled. 'Like a chef.' He opened the refrigerator door. 'I store it in here. Want to see?'

I looked inside. Nearly the whole space was taken with gallon-sized plastic containers full of brownish liquid. 'We mix it in a bran mash, warmed of course, and the horses thrive.'

I knew nothing about the efficiency of his remedies, but I was definitely impressed.

'How do you get the horses to take pills?' I said.

'In an apple, usually. We scoop out half the core, put in the tablet or capsule, or indeed just powder, and replace the plug.'

So simple.

'And incidentally, I make most of my own pills and capsules. Some, like comfrey, are commercially available, but I prefer to buy the dried herbs in their pure form and make my own recipes.' He pulled open one of the lower drawers under the work-bench and lifted out a heavy wooden box. 'This,' he said, laying it on the work surface and opening the lid, 'contains the makings.'

I looked down at a whole array of brass dies, each a small square with a pill-sized cavity in its centre. The cavities varied from tiny to extra large, and from round to oblong.

'It's an antique,' he said with a touch of pride. 'Early Victorian. Dates from when pills were always made by hand – and it's still viable, of course. You put the required drug in powder form into whatever sized cavity you want, and compress it with the rod which exactly fits.' He lifted one of a series of short brass rods from its rack and fitted its end into one of the cavities, tamping it up and down; then picked the whole die out of the box and tipped it right over. 'Hey presto,' he said genially, catching the imaginary contents, 'a pill!'

'Neat,' I said, with positive pleasure.

He nodded. 'Capsules are quicker and more modern.' He pulled open another drawer and briefly showed me the empty tops and bottoms of a host of gelatin capsules, again of varying sizes, though mostly a little larger than those swallowed easily by humans. 'Veterinary size,' he explained.

He closed his gem of a pill-making box and returned it to its drawer, straightening up afterwards and casting a caring eye around the place to make sure everything was tidy. With a nod of private satisfaction he opened the door for us to return to the outside world, switching off the fluorescent lights and locking the door behind us.

A car was just rolling to a stop on the asphalt, and presently two recognized figures emerged from it: Dissdale Smith and his delectable Bettina.

'Hello, hello,' said Dissdale, striding across with ready hand. 'Calder said you were coming. Good to see you. Calder's been showing you all his treasures, eh? The conducted tour, eh, Calder?' I shook the hand. 'Calder's proud of his achievements here, aren't you, Calder?'

'With good reason,' I said civilly, and Calder gave me a swift glance and a genuine-looking smile.

Bettina drifted more slowly to join us, a delight in high-heeled boots and cuddling fur, a white silk scarf round her throat and smooth dark hair falling glossily to her shoulders. Her scent travelled sweetly across the quiet cold air and she laid a decorative hand on my arm in an intimate touch.

'Tim the saviour,' she said. 'Calder's hero.'

The over-packaged charm unaccountably brought the contrasting image of Ginnie sharply to my mind, and I briefly thought that the promise was more beckoning than the performance, that child more interesting than that woman.

Calder took us all soon into his maxi-cottage sitting room and distributed more drinks. Dissdale told me that Sandcastle had almost literally saved his business and metaphorically his life, and we all drank a toast to the wonder horse. Four further guests arrived – a married couple with their two twentyish daughters – and the occasion became an ordinarily enjoyable lunch party, undemanding, unmemorable, good food handed round by the manservant, cigars offered with the coffee.

Calder at some point said he was off to America in the New Year on a short lecture tour.

'Unfortunately,' he said, 'I'll be talking to health clubs, not horse people. American racehorse trainers aren't receptive to me. Or not yet. But then, it took a few years for Newmarket to decide I could make a contribution.'

Everyone smiled at the scepticism of America and Newmarket.

Calder said, 'January is often a quiet month here. We don't take any new admissions if I'm away, and of course my head lad just keeps the establishment routines going until I return. It works pretty well.' He smiled. 'If I'm lucky I'll get some skiing; and to be honest, I'm looking forward to the skiing much more than the talks.'

Everyone left soon after three, and I drove back to London through the short darkening afternoon wondering if the herbs of antiquity held secrets we'd almost wilfully lost.

'Caffeine,' Calder had been saying towards the end, 'is a get-up-and-go stimulant, tremendously useful. Found in coffee beans of course, and in tea and cocoa and in cola drinks. Good for asthma. Vigorous, marvellous tonic. A life-saver after shock. And now in America, I ask you, they're casting caffeine as a villain and are busy taking it out of everything it's naturally *in*. You might as well take the alcohol out of bread.'

'But Calder dear,' Bettina said, 'there's no alcohol in bread.'

He looked at her kindly as she sat on his right. 'Bread that is made with yeast definitely does contain alcohol before it's cooked. If you mix yeast with water and sugar you get alcohol and carbon dioxide, which is the gas which makes the dough rise. The air in a bakery smells of wine . . . simple chemistry, my dear girl, no magic in it. Bread is the staff of life and alcohol is good for you.'

There had been jokes and lifted glasses, and I could have listened to Calder for hours.

The Christmas party at Gordon Michael's home was in a way an echo, because Judith's apothecary friend Pen Warner was in attendance most of the time. I got to know her quite well and to like her very much, which Judith may or may not have intended. In any case, it was again the fairy-tale day at Ascot which had led on to friendly relations.

'Do you remember Burnt Marshmallow?' Pen said. 'I bought a painting with my winnings.'

'I spent mine on riotous living.'

'Oh yes?' She looked me up and down and shook her head. 'You haven't the air.'

'What do I have the air of?' I asked curiously, and she answered in amusement, 'Of intelligent laziness and boring virtue.'

'All wrong,' I said.

'Ho hum.'

She seemed to me to be slightly less physically solid than at Ascot, but it might have been only the change of clothes; there were still the sad eyes and the ingrained worthiness and the unexpected cast of humour. She had apparently spent twelve hours that day – it was Christmas Eve – doling out remedies to people whose illnesses showed no sense of timing, and proposed to go back at six in the morning. Meanwhile she appeared at the Michaels' house in a long festive caftan with mood to match, and during the evening the four of us ate quails with our fingers, and roasted chestnuts, and played a board game with childish gusto.

Judith wore rose pink and pearls and looked about twenty-five. Gordon in advance had instructed me 'Bring whatever you like as long as it's informal' and himself was resplendent in a plum velvet jacket and bow tie. My own newly bought cream wool shirt which in the shop had looked fairly theatrical seemed in the event to be right, so that on all levels the evening proved harmonious and fun, much more rounded and easy than I'd expected.

Judith's housekeeping throughout my stay proved a poem of invisibility. Food appeared from freezer and cupboard, remnants returned to dishwasher and dustbin. Jobs were distributed when essential but sitting and talking had priority; and nothing so smooth, I reflected, ever got done without hard work beforehand.

'Pen will be back soon after one tomorrow,' Judith said at midnight on that first evening. 'We'll have a drink then and open some presents, and have our Christmas feast at half past three. There will be break-fast in the morning, and Gordon and I will go to church.' She left an invitation lingering in the air, but I marginally shook my head. 'You can look after yourself, then, while we're gone.'

She kissed me goodnight, with affection and on the cheek. Gordon gave me a smile and a wave, and I went to bed across the hall from them and spent an hour before sleep deliberately not thinking at all about Judith in or out of her nightgown – or not much.

Breakfast was taken in dressing gowns. Judith's was red, quilted and unrevealing.

They changed and went to church. Pray for me, I said, and set out for a walk on the common.

There were brightly wrapped gifts waiting around the base of the silver-starred Christmas tree in the Michaels' drawing room, and a surreptitious inspection had revealed one from Pen addressed to me. I walked across the windy grass, shoulders hunched, hands in pockets, wondering what to do about one for her, and as quite often happens came by chance to a solution.

A small boy was out there with his father, flying a kite, and I stopped to watch.

'That's fun,' I said.

The boy took no notice but the father said, 'There's no satisfying the little bleeder. I give him this and he says he wants roller skates.'

The kite was a brilliant phosphorescent Chinese dragon with butterfly wings and a big frilly tail, soaring and circling like a joyful tethered spirit in the Christmas sky.

'Will you sell it to me?' I asked. 'Buy the roller skates instead?' I explained the problem, the need for an instant present.

Parent and child consulted and the deal was done. I wound up the string carefully and bore the trophy home, wondering what on earth the sober pharmacist would think of such a thing; but when she unwrapped it from gold paper (cadged from Judith for the purpose) she pronounced herself enchanted, and back we all went onto the common to watch her fly it.

The whole day was happy. I hadn't had so good a Christmas since I was a child. I told them so, and kissed Judith uninhibitedly under some mistletoe, which Gordon didn't seem to mind.

'You were born sunny,' Judith said, briefly stroking my cheek, and Gordon, nodding, said, 'A man without sorrows, unacquainted with grief.'

'Grief and sorrow come with time,' Pen said, but not as if she meant it imminently. 'They come to us all.'

*

On the morning after Christmas Day I drove Judith across London to Hampstead to put flowers on her mother's grave.

'I know you'll think me silly, but I always go. She died on Boxing Day when I was twelve. It's the only way I have of remembering her . . . of feeling I had a mother at all. I usually go by myself. Gordon thinks I'm sentimental and doesn't like coming.'

'Nothing wrong with sentiment,' I said.

Hampstead was where I lived in the upstairs half of a friend's house. I wasn't sure whether or not Judith knew it, and said nothing until she'd delivered the pink chrysanthemums to the square marble tablet let in flush with the grass and communed for a while with the memories floating there.

It was as we walked slowly back towards the iron gates that I neutrally said, 'My flat's only half a mile from here. This part of London is home ground.'

'Is it?'

'Mm.'

After a few steps she said, 'I knew you lived somewhere here. If you remember, you wouldn't let us drive you all the way home from Ascot. You said Hampstead was too far.'

'So it was.'

'Not for Sir Galahad that starry night.'

We reached the gates and paused for her to look back. I was infinitely conscious of her nearness and of my own stifled desire; and she looked abruptly into my eyes and said, 'Gordon knows you live here, also.'

'And does he know how I feel?' I asked.

'I don't know. He hasn't said.'

I wanted very much to go that last half-mile: that short distance on wheels, that far journey in commitment. My body tingled . . . rippled . . . from hunger, and I found myself physically clenching my back teeth.

'What are you thinking?' she said.

'For God's sake . . . you know damn well what I'm thinking . . . and we're going back to Clapham right this minute.'

She sighed. 'Yes. I suppose we must.'

'What do you mean . . . you suppose?'

'Well, I . . .' she paused. 'I mean, yes we must. I'm sorry . . . it was just that . . . for a moment . . . I was tempted.'

'As at Ascot?' I said.

She nodded. 'As at Ascot.'

'Only here and now,' I said, 'we have the place and the time and the opportunity to do something about it.'

'Yes.'

'And what we're going to do . . . is . . . nothing.' It came out as half a question, half a statement: wholly an impossibility.

'Why do we *care*?' she said explosively. 'Why don't we just get into your bed and have a happy time? Why is the whole thing so tangled up with bloody concepts like honour?'

We walked down the road to where I'd parked the car and I drove southwards with careful observance at every red light; stop signals making round eyes at me all the way to Clapham.

'I'd have liked it,' Judith said as we pulled up outside her house.

'So would I.'

We went indoors in a sort of deprived companionship, and I realized only when I saw Gordon's smiling unsuspicious face that I couldn't have returned there if it had been in any other way.

It was at lunch that day, when Pen had again resurfaced from her stint among the pills that I told them about my visit to Calder. Pen, predictably, was acutely interested and said she'd dearly like to know what was in the decoction in the refrigerator.

'What's a decoction?' Judith asked.

'A preparation boiled with water. If you dissolve things in alcohol, that's a tincture.'

'One lives and bloody well learns!'

Pen laughed. 'How about carminative, anodyne and vermifuge ... effects of drugs. They simply roll off the tongue with grandeur.'

'And what do they mean?' Gordon asked.

'Getting rid of gas, getting rid of pain, getting rid of worms.'

Gordon too was laughing. 'Have some anodyne

tincture of grape.' He poured wine into our glasses. 'Do you honestly believe, Tim, that Calder cures horses by touch?'

'I'm sure *he* believes it.' I reflected. 'I don't know if he will let anyone watch. And if he did, what would one see? I don't suppose with a horse it's a case of "take up your bed and walk."'

Judith said in surprise, 'You sound as if you'd like it to be true. You, that Gordon and Harry have trained to doubt!'

'Calder's impressive,' I admitted. 'So is his place. So are the fees he charges. He wouldn't be able to set his prices so high if he didn't get real results.'

'Do the herbs come extra?' Pen said.

'I didn't ask.'

'Would you expect them to?' Gordon said.

'Well . . .' Pen considered. 'Some of those that Tim mentioned are fairly exotic. Golden seal – that hydrastis – said in the past to cure practically anything you can mention, but mostly used nowadays in tiny amounts in eye-drops. Has to be imported from America. And fo-ti-tieng – which is *Hydrocotyle asiatica minor*, also called the source of the elixir of long life – that only grows as far as I know in the tropical jungles of the Far East. I mean, I would have thought that giving things like that to horses would be wildly expensive.'

If I'd been impressed with Calder I was probably more so with Pen. 'I didn't know pharmacists were so clued up on herbs,' I said.

'I was just interested so I learned their properties,' she explained. 'The age-old remedies are hardly even hinted at on the official pharmacy courses, though considering digitalis and penicillin one can't exactly see why. A lot of chemist's shops don't sell non-prescription herbal remedies, but I do, and honestly for a stack of people they seem to work.'

'And do you advocate garlic poultices for the feet of babies with whooping cough?' Gordon asked.

Pen didn't. There was more laughter. If one believed in Calder, Judith said firmly, one believed in him, garlic poultices and all.

The four of us spent a comfortable afternoon and evening together, and when Judith and Gordon went to bed I walked along with Pen to her house, where she'd been staying each night, filling my lungs with the fresh air off the common.

'You're going home tomorrow, aren't you?' she said, fishing out her key.

I nodded. 'In the morning.'

'It's been great fun.' She found the keys and fitted one in the lock. 'Would you like to come in?'

'No . . . I'll just walk for a bit.'

She opened the door and paused there. 'Thank you for the kite . . . it was brilliant. And goodbye for this time, though I guess if Judith can stand it I'll be seeing you again.'

'Stand what?' I asked.

She kissed me on the cheek. 'Goodnight,' she said.

'And believe it or not, the herb known as passion flower is good for insomnia.'

Her grin shone out like the Cheshire Cat's as she stepped inside her house and closed the door, and I stood hopelessly on her pathway wanting to call her back.

The Second Year

FEBRUARY

Ian Pargetter was murdered at about one in the morning on February the first.

I learned about his death from Calder when I telephoned that evening on impulse to thank him belatedly for the lunch party, invite him for a reciprocal dinner in London and hear whether or not he had enjoyed his American tour.

'Who?' he said vaguely when I announced myself. 'Who? Oh... Tim... Look, I can't talk now, I'm simply distracted, a friend of mine's been killed and I can't think of anything else.'

'I'm so sorry,' I said inadequately.

'Yes... Ian Pargetter... but I don't suppose you know...'

This time I remembered at once. The vet: big, reliable, sandy moustache.

'I met him,' I said, 'in your house.'

'Did you? Oh, yes. I'm so upset I can't concentrate. Look, Tim, ring some other time, will you?'

'Yes, of course.'

'It's not just that he's been a friend for years,' he said, 'but I don't know... I really don't know how my business will fare without him. He sent so many horses my way... such a good friend... I'm totally distraught... Look, ring me another time... Tim, so sorry.' He put his receiver down with the rattle of a shaking hand.

I thought at the time that he meant Ian Pargetter had been killed in some sort of accident, and it was only the next day when my eye was caught by a paragraph in a newspaper that I realized the difference.

Ian Pargetter, well-known, much respected New-market veterinary surgeon, was yesterday morning found dead in his home. Police suspect foul play. They state that Pargetter suffered head injuries and that certain supplies of drugs appear to be missing. Pargetter's body was discovered by Mrs Jane Halson, a daily cleaner. The vet is survived by his wife and three young daughters, all of whom were away from home at the time of the attack. Mrs Pargetter was reported last night to be very dis-tressed and under sedation.

A lot of succinct bad news, I thought, for a lot of sad bereft people. He was the first person I'd known who'd been murdered, and in spite of our very brief meeting I found his death most disturbing: and if I felt so unsettled about a near-stranger, how, I wondered, did anyone ever recover from the murder of someone one knew well and loved. How did one deal with the anger? Come to terms with the urge to revenge?

I'd of course read reports of husbands and wives who pronounced themselves 'not bitter' over the slaughter of a spouse, and I'd never understood it. I felt furious on Ian Pargetter's behalf that anyone should have the arrogance to wipe him out.

Because of Ascot and Sandcastle my long-dormant interest in racecourses seemed thoroughly to have reawakened, and on three or four Saturday afternoons that winter I'd trekked to Kempton or Sandown or Newbury to watch the jumpers. Ursula Young had become a familiar face, and it was from this brisk well-informed lady bloodstock agent that I learnt most about Ian Pargetter and his death.

'Drink?' I suggested at Kempton, pulling up my coat collar against a bitter wind.

She looked at her watch (I'd never seen her do anything without checking the time) and agreed on a quick one. Whisky-mac for her, coffee for me, as at Doncaster.

'Now tell me,' she said, hugging her glass and yelling in my ear over the general din of a bar packed with other cold customers seeking inner warmth, 'when you asked all those questions about stallion shares, was it for Sandcastle?'

I smiled without actually answering, shielding my coffee inadequately from adjacent nudging elbows.

'Thought so,' she said. 'Look – there's a table. Grab it.'

We sat down in a corner with the racket going on over our heads and the closed-circuit television playing re-runs of the last race fortissimo. Ursula bent her head towards mine. 'A wow-sized coup for Oliver Knowles.'

'You approve?' I asked.

She nodded. 'He'll be among the greats in one throw. Smart move. Clever man.'

'Do you know him?'

'Yes. Meet him often at the sales. He had a snooty wife who left him for some Canadian millionaire or other, and maybe that's why he's aiming for the big-time; just to show her.' She smiled fiendishly. 'She was a real pain and I hope he makes it.'

She drank half her whisky and I said it was a shame about Ian Pargetter, and that I'd met him once at Calder's house.

She grimaced with a stronger echo of the anger I had myself felt. 'He'd been out all evening saving the life of a classic-class colt with colic. It's so beastly. He went home well after midnight, and they reckon whoever killed him was already in the house stealing whatever he could lay his hands on. Ian's wife and family were away visiting her mother, you see, and the police think the killer thought the house would be empty for the night.' She swallowed. 'He was hit on the back of the head with a brass lamp off one of the tables in the sitting room. Just casual. Unpremeditated. Just . . . *stupid*.' She looked moved, as I guessed everyone must have been who had known him. 'Such a waste. He was a really nice man, a good vet, everyone liked him. And all for practically nothing . . . The police found a lot of silver and jewellery lying on a blanket ready to be carried away, but they think the thief just panicked and left it when Ian came home . . . all that anyone can think of that's missing is his case of instruments and a few drugs that he'd had with him that evening . . . nothing worth killing for . . . not even for an addict. Nothing in it like that.' She fell silent and looked down into her nearly empty glass, and I offered her a refill.

'No, thanks all the same, one's enough. I feel pretty maudlin as it is. I liked Ian. He was a good sort. I'd like to *throttle* the little beast who killed him.'

'I think Calder Jackson feels much as you do,' I said.

She glanced up, her good-looking fifty-ish face full of genuine concern. 'Calder will miss Ian terribly. There aren't that number of vets around who'd not only put up with a faith-healer on their doorstep but actually treat him as a colleague. Ian had no professional jealousy. Very rare. Very good man. Makes it all the worse.'

We went out again into the raw air and I lost five pounds on the afternoon, which would have sent Lorna Shipton swooning to Uncle Freddie, if she'd known.

*

Two weeks later with Oliver Knowles' warm approval I paid another visit to his farm in Hertfordshire, and although it was again a Sunday and still winter, the atmosphere of the place had fundamentally changed. Where there had been quiet sleepy near-hibernation there was now a wakeful bustle and eagerness, where a scattering of dams and foals across the paddocks, now a crowd of mares moving alone and slowly with big bellies.

The crop had come to the harvest. Life was ripening into the daylight, and into the darkness the new seed would be sown.

I had not been truly a country child (ten acres of wooded hill in Surrey) and to me the birth of animals still seemed a wonder and joy; to Oliver Knowles, he said, it meant constant worry and profit and loss. His grasp of essentials still rang out strong and clear, but there were lines on his forehead from the details.

'I suppose,' he said frankly, walking me into the first of the big yards, 'that the one thing I hadn't mentally prepared myself for was the value of the foals now being born here. I mean . . .' he gestured around at the atient heads looking over the rows of half-doors, '. . . these mares have been to the top stallions. They're carrying fabulous blood-lines. They're history.' His awe could be felt. 'I didn't realize, you know, what anxiety they would bring me. We've always done our best for the foals, of course we have, but if one died it wasn't a tragedy, but with this lot . . .' He smiled ruefully. 'It's not enough just owning Sandcastle. I have to make sure that our reputation for handling top broodmares is good and sound.'

We walked along beside one row of boxes with him telling me in detail the breeding of each mare we came to and of the foal she carried, and even to my ignorant ears it sounded as if every Derby and Oaks winner for the past half-century had had a hand in the coming generation.

'I had no trouble selling Sandcastle's nominations,' he said. 'Not even at forty thousand pounds a throw. I could even choose, to some extent, which mares to accept. It's been utterly amazing to be able to turn away mares that I considered wouldn't do him justice.'

'Is there a temptation,' I asked mildly, 'to sell more than forty places? To ... er ... accept an extra fee ... in untaxed cash ... on the quiet?'

He was more amused than offended. 'I wouldn't say it hasn't been done on every farm that ever existed. But I wouldn't do it with Sandcastle ... or at any rate not this year. He's still young. And untested, of course. Some stallions won't look at as many as forty mares ... though shy breeders do tend to run in families, and there's nothing in his pedigree to suggest he'll be anything but energetic and fertile. I wouldn't have embarked on all this if there had been any doubts.'

It seemed that he was trying to reassure himself as much as me; as if the size and responsibility of his undertaking had only just penetrated, and in penetrating, frightened.

I felt a faint tremor of dismay but stifled it with the reassurance that come hell or high water Sandcastle was worth his buying price and could be sold again even at this late date for not much less. The bank's money was safe on his hoof.

It was earlier in the day than my last visit – eleven in the morning – and more lads than before were to be seen mucking out the boxes and carrying feed and water.

'I've had to take on extra hands,' Oliver Knowles said matter-of-factly. 'Temporarily, for the season.'

'Has recruitment been difficult?' I asked.

'Not really. I do it every spring. I keep the good ones on for the whole year, if they'll stay, of course: these lads come and go as the whim takes them, the unmarried ones, that is. I keep the nucleus on and put them painting fences and such in the autumn and winter.'

We strolled into the second yard, where the burly figure of Nigel could be seen peering over a half-door into a box.

'You remember Nigel?' Oliver said. 'My stud manager?'

Nigel, I noted, had duly been promoted.

'And Ginnie,' I asked, as we walked over, 'is she home today?'

'Yes, she's somewhere about.' He looked around as

if expecting her to materialize at the sound of her name, but nothing happened.

'How's it going, Nigel?' he asked.

Nigel's hairy eyebrows withdrew from the box and aimed themselves in our direction. 'Floradora's eating again,' he said, indicating the inspected lady and sounding relieved. 'And Pattacake is still in labour. I'm just going back there.'

'We'll come,' Oliver said. 'If you'd like to?' he added, looking at me questioningly.

I nodded and walked on with them along the path into the third, smaller quadrangle, the foaling yard.

Here too, in this place that had been empty, there was purposeful life, and the box to which Nigel led us was larger than normal and thickly laid with straw.

'Foals usually drop at night,' Oliver said, and Nigel nodded. 'She started about midnight. She's just lazy, eh, girl?' He patted the brown rump. 'Very slow. Same thing every year.'

'She's not come for Sandcastle, then?' I said.

'No. She's one of mine,' Oliver said. 'The foal's by Diarist.'

We hovered for a few minutes but there was no change in Pattacake. Nigel, running delicately know-ledgeable hands over the shape under her ribs, said she'd be another hour, perhaps, and that he would stay with her for a while. Oliver and I walked onwards, past the still closed breeding shed and down the path between the two small paddocks towards the stallion yard. Everything, as before, was meticulously tidy.

There was one four-legged figure in one of the paddocks, head down and placid. 'Parakeet,' Oliver said. 'Getting more air than grass, actually. It isn't warm enough yet for the new grass to grow.'

We came finally to the last yard, and there he was, the gilt-edged Sandcastle, looking over his door like any other horse.

One couldn't tell, I thought. True there was a poise to the well-shaped head, and an interested eye and alertly pricked ears, but nothing to announce that this was the marvellous creature I'd seen at Ascot. No one ever again, I reflected, would see that arrow-like raking gallop, that sublime throat-catching valour; and it seemed a shame that he should be denied his ability in the hope that he would pass it on.

A lad, broom in hand, was sweeping scatterings of peat off the concrete apron in front of the six stallion boxes, watched by Sandcastle, Rotaboy and Diarist with the same depth of interest as a bus queue would extend to a busker.

'Lenny,' Oliver said, 'you can take Sandcastle down to the small paddock opposite to the one with Parakeet.' He looked up at the sky as if to sniff the coming weather. 'Put him back in his box when you return for evening stables.'

'Yes, sir.'

Lenny was well into middle age, small, leathery and

of obviously long experience. He propped the broom against one of the empty boxes and disappeared into a doorway to reappear presently carrying a length of rope.

'Lenny is one of my trusted helpers,' Oliver Knowles said. 'Been with me several years. He's good with stallions and much stronger than he looks. Stallions can be quite difficult to handle, but Lenny gets on with them better than with mares. Don't know why.'

Lenny clipped the rope onto the headcollar which Sandcastle, along with every other equine resident, wore at all times. Upon the headcollar was stapled a metal plate bearing the horse's name, an absolute essential for identification. Shuffle all those mares together without their headcollars, I thought, and no one would ever sort them. I suggested the problem mildly to Oliver, who positively blenched. 'God forbid! Don't suggest such things. We're very careful. Have to be. Otherwise, as you say, we could breed the wrong mare to the wrong stallion and never know it.'

I wondered, but privately, how often that in fact had happened, or whether indeed it was possible for two mares or two foals to be permanently swapped. The opportunities for mistakes, if not for outright fraud, put computer manipulation in the shade.

Nigel arrived in the yard, and with his scarcely necessary help Lenny opened Sandcastle's door and led the colt out; and one could see in all their strength the sleek muscles, the tugging sinews, the spring-like joints. The body that was worth its weight in gold pranced and scrunched on the hard apron, wheeling round impatiently and tossing its uncomprehending head.

'Full of himself,' Oliver explained. 'We have to feed him well and keep him fairly fit, but of course he doesn't get the exercise he used to.'

We stepped to one side with undignified haste to avoid Sandcastle's restless hindquarters. 'Has he ... er ... started work yet?' I asked.

'Not yet,' Oliver said. 'Only one of his mares has foaled so far. She's almost through her foal-heat, so when she comes into use in fifteen or sixteen days' time, she'll be his first. After that there will be a pause – give him time to think! – then he'll be busy until into June.'

'How often ...?' I murmured delicately.

Oliver fielded the question as if he, like Calder, had had to give the same answer countless times over.

'It depends on the stallion,' he said. 'Some can cover one mare in the morning and another in the afternoon and go on like that for days. Others haven't that much stamina or that much desire. Occasionally you get very shy and choosy stallions. Some of them won't go near some mares but will mate all right with others. Some will cover only one mare a fortnight, if that. Stallions aren't machines, you know, they're individuals like everyone else.'

With Nigel in attendance Lenny led Sandcastle out

of the yard, the long bay legs stalking in powerful strides beside the almost trotting little man.

'Sandcastle will be all right with mares,' Oliver said again firmly. 'Most stallions are.'

We stopped for Oliver to give two carrots and a pat each to Rotaboy and Diarist, so that we didn't ourselves see the calamity. We heard a distant clatter and a yell and the thud of fast hooves, and Oliver went white as he turned to run to the disaster.

I followed him, also sprinting.

Lenny lay against one of the white-painted posts of the small paddock's rails, dazedly trying to pull himself up. Sandcastle, loose and excited, had found his way into one of the paths between the larger paddocks and from his bolting speed must have taken the rails to be those of a racecourse.

Nigel stood by the open gate of the small paddock, his mouth wide as if arrested there by shock. He was still almost speechless when Oliver and I reached him, but had at least begun to unstick.

'For Christ's sake,' Oliver shouted. 'Get going. Get the Land Rover. He can get out onto the road that way through the Watcherleys'.' He ran off in the direction of his own house leaving a partially resurrected Nigel to stumble off towards the bungalow, half in sight beyond the stallion yard.

Lenny raised himself and began his excuses, but I didn't wait to listen. Unused to the problem and ignorant of how best to catch fleeing horses, I simply set off in Sandcastle's wake, following his path between the paddocks and seeing him disappear ahead of me behind a distant hedge.

I ran fast along the grassy path between the rails, past the groups of incurious mares in the paddocks, thinking that my brief January holiday skiing down the pistes at Gstaad might have its practical uses after all; there was currently a lot more muscle in my legs than was ever to be found by July.

Whereas on my last visit the hedge between Oliver Knowles' farm and the Watcherleys' run-down hospital for sick horses had been a thorny unbroken boundary, there were now two or three wide gaps, so that passing from one side to the other was easy. I pounded through the gap which lay straight ahead and noticed almost unconsciously that the Watcherleys' dilapidation had not only halted but partially reversed, with new fencing going up and repairs in hand on the roofs.

I ran towards the stable buildings across a thistly field in which there was no sign of Sandcastle, and through an as yet unmended gate which hung open on broken hinges on the far side. Beyond there between piles of rubble and rusting iron I reached the yard itself, to find Ginnie looking around her with unfocused anxiety and a man and a girl walking towards her enquiringly.

Ginnie saw me running, and her first instinctively cheerful greeting turned almost at once to alarm.

'What is it?' she said. 'Is one of the mares out?'

'Sandcastle.'

'Oh no . . .' It was a wail of despair. 'He can get on the road.' She turned away, already running, and I ran after her; out of the Watcherleys' yard, round their ramshackle house and down the short weedy gateless drive to the dangerous outside world where a car could kill a horse without even trying.

'We'll never catch him,' Ginnie said as we reached the road. 'It's no use running. We don't know which way he went.' She was in great distress: eyes flooding, tears on her cheeks. 'Where's Dad?'

'I should think he's out in his car, looking. And Nigel's in a Land Rover.'

'I heard a horse gallop through the Watcherleys',' she said. 'I was in one of the boxes with a foal. I never thought . . . I mean, I thought it might be a mare . . .'

A speeding car passed in front of us, followed closely by two others doing at least sixty miles an hour, one of them dicily passing a heavy articulated lorry which should have been home in its nest on a Sunday. The thought of Sandcastle loose in that battlefield was literally goose-pimpling and I began for the first time to believe in his imminent destruction. One of those charging monsters would be sure to hit him. He would waver across the road into their path, swerving, rudderless, hopelessly vulnerable . . . a five million-pound traffic accident in the making.

'Let's go this way,' I said, pointing to the left. A

motorcyclist roared from that direction, head down in a black visor, going too fast to stop.

Ginnie shook her head sharply. 'Dad and Nigel will be on the road. But there's a track over there . . .' She pointed slantwise across the road. 'He might just have found it. And there's a bit of a hill and even if he isn't up there at least we might see him from there . . . you can see the road in places . . . I often ride up there.' She was off again, running while she talked, and I fell in beside her. Her face was screwed up with the intensity of her feelings and I felt as much sympathy for her as dismay about the horse. Sandcastle was insured – I'd vetted the policy myself – but Oliver Knowles' prestige wasn't. The escape and death of the first great stallion in his care would hardly attract future business.

The track was muddy and rutted and slippery from recent rain. There were also a great many hoofprints, some looking new, some overtrodden and old. I pointed to them as we ran and asked Ginnie pantingly if she knew if any of those were Sandcastle's.

'Oh.' She stopped running suddenly. 'Yes. Of course. He hasn't got shoes on. The blacksmith came yesterday. Dad said . . .' She peered at the ground dubiously, '. . . he left Sandcastle without new shoes because he was going to make leather pads for under them . . . I wasn't really listening.' She pointed. 'I think that might be him. Those new marks . . . they could be, they really could.' She began running again up the track, impelled by hope now as well as horror, fit in her jeans and sweater and jodhpur boots after all that compulsory jogging.

I ran beside her thinking that mud anyway washed easily from shoes, socks and trouser legs. The ground began to rise sharply and to narrow between bare-branched scratchy bushes; and the jumble of hoof marks inexorably led on and on.

'Please be up here,' Ginnie was saying. 'Please, Sandcastle, please be up here.' Her urgency pumped in her legs and ran in misery down her cheeks. 'Oh please . . . *please* . . .'

The agony of adolescence, I thought. So real, so overpowering . . . so remembered.

The track curved through the bushes and opened suddenly into a wider place where grass grew in patches beside the rutted mud; and there stood Sandcastle, head high, nostrils twitching to the wind, a brown and black creature of power and beauty and majesty.

Ginnie stopped running in one stride and caught my arm fiercely.

'Don't move,' she said. 'I'll do it. You stay here. Keep still. Please keep still.'

I nodded obediently, respecting her experience. The colt looked ready to run again at the slightest untimely movement, his sides quivering, his legs stiff with tension, his tail sweeping up and down restlessly.

He's frightened, I thought suddenly. He's out here, lost, not knowing where to go. He's never been free before, but his instinct is still wild, still against being caught. Horses were never truly tamed, only accustomed to captivity.

Ginnie walked towards him making crooning noises and holding out her hand palm upwards, an offering hand with nothing to offer. 'Come on, boy,' she said. 'Come on boy, there's a good boy, it's all right, come on now.'

The horse watched her as if he'd never seen a human before, his alarm proclaimed in a general volatile trembling. The rope hung down from his headcollar, its free end curling on the ground; and I wondered whether Ginnie would be able to control the colt if she caught him, where Lenny with all his strength had let him go.

Ginnie came to within a foot of the horse's nose, offering her open left hand upwards and bringing her right hand up slowly under his chin, reaching for the headcollar itself, not the rope; her voice made soothing, murmuring sounds and my own tensed muscles began to relax.

At the last second Sandcastle would have none of it. He wheeled away with a squeal, knocking Ginnie to her knees; took two rocketing strides towards a dense patch of bushes, wheeled again, laid back his ears and accelerated in my direction. Past me lay the open track, downhill again to the slaughtering main road.

Ginnie, seen in peripheral vision, was struggling to her feet in desperation. Without thinking of anything much except perhaps what that horse meant to her family, I jumped not out of his way but at his flying head, my fingers curling for the headcollar and missing that and fastening round the rope.

He nearly tore my arms out of their sockets and all the skin off my palms. He yanked me off my feet, pulled me through the mud and trampled on my legs. I clung all the same with both hands to the rope and bumped against his shoulder and knee, and shortly more by weight than skill hauled him to the side of the track and into the bushes.

The bushes, indeed, acted as an anchor. He couldn't drag my heaviness through them, not if I kept hold of the rope; and I wound the rope clumsily round a stump of branch for leverage, and that was roughly that. Sandcastle stood the width of the bush away, crossly accepting the inevitable, tossing his head and quivering but no longer trying for full stampede.

Ginnie appeared round the curve in the track, running and if possible looking more than ever distraught. When she saw me she stumbled and half fell and came up to me uninhibitedly crying.

'Oh, I'm so glad, and you should never do that, you can be killed, you should never do it, and I'm so grateful, so glad . . . oh dear.' She leant against me weakly and like a child wiped her eyes and nose on my sleeve.

'Well,' I said pragmatically, 'what do we do with him now?'

What we decided, upon consideration, was that I and Sandcastle should stay where we were, and that

Ginnie should go and find Nigel or her father, neither she nor I being confident of leading our prize home without reinforcements.

While she was gone I made an inventory of damage, but so far as my clothes went there was nothing the cleaners couldn't see to, and as for the skin, it would grow again pretty soon. My legs though bruised were functioning, and there was nothing broken or frightful. I made a ball of my handkerchief in my right palm which was bleeding slightly and thought that one of these days a habit of launching oneself at things like fleeing stallions and boys with knives might prove to be unwise.

Oliver, Ginnie, Nigel and Lenny all appeared in the Land Rover, gears grinding and wheels spinning in the mud. Sandcastle, to their obvious relief, was upon inspection pronounced sound, and Oliver told me forcefully that *no one*, should *ever*, repeat *ever*, try to stop a bolting horse in that way.

'I'm sorry,' I said.

'You could have been killed.'

'So Ginnie said.'

'Didn't it occur to you?' He sounded almost angry; the aftermath of fright. 'Didn't you *think*?'

'No,' I said truthfully. 'I just did it.'

'Never do it again,' he said. 'And thanks.' He paused and swallowed and tried to make light of his own shattered state. 'Thanks for taking care of my investment.'

Lenny and Nigel had brought a different sort of

headcollar which involved a bit in the mouth and a fierce-looking curb chain, and with these in place the captive (if not chastened) fugitive was led away. There seemed to me to be a protest in the stalking hind-quarters, a statement of disgust at the injustices of life. I smiled at that fanciful thought: the pathetic fallacy, the ascribing to animals of emotions one felt only oneself.

Oliver drove Ginnie and me back in the Land Rover, travelling slowly behind the horse and telling how Nigel and Lenny had allowed him to go free.

'Sheer bloody carelessness,' he said forthrightly. 'Both of them should know better. They could see the horse was fresh and jumping out of his skin yet Lenny was apparently holding the rope with only one hand and stretching to swing the gate open with the other. He took his eyes off Sandcastle so he wasn't ready when Nigel made some sharp movement or other and the horse reared and ran backwards. I ask you! Lenny! Nigel! How can they be so bloody stupid after all these years?'

There seemed to be no answer to that so we just let him curse away, and he was still rumbling like distant thunder when the journey ended. Once home he hurried off to the stallion yard and Ginnie trenchantly said that if Nigel was as sloppy with discipline for animals as he was with the lads, it was no wonder any horse with any spirit would take advantage.

'Accidents happen,' I said mildly.

'Huh.' She was scornful. 'Dad's right. That accident

shouldn't have happened. It was an absolute miracle that Sandcastle came to no harm at all. Even if he hadn't got out on the road he could have tried to jump the paddock rails – horses often do – and broken his leg or something.' She sounded as angry as her father, and for the same reason: the flooding release after fear. I put my arm around her shoulders and gave her a quick hug, which seemed to disconcert her horribly. 'Oh dear, you must think me so silly . . . and crying like that . . . and everything.'

'I think you're a nice dear girl who's had a rotten morning,' I said. 'But all's well now, you know; it really is.'

I naturally believed what I said, but I was wrong.

APRIL

Calder Jackson finally came to dinner with me while he was staying in London to attend a world conference of herbalists. He would be glad, he said, to spend one of the evenings away from his colleagues, and I met him in a restaurant on the grounds that although my flat was civilized my cooking was not.

I sensed immediately a difference in him, though it was hard to define; rather as if he had become a figure still larger than life. Heads turned and voices whispered when we walked through the crowded place to our table, but because of television this would have happened anyway. Yet now, I thought, Calder really enjoyed it. There was still no overt arrogance, still a becoming modesty of manner, but something within him had intensified, crystallized, become a governing factor. He was now, I thought, even to himself, the Great Man.

I wondered what, if anything, had specifically altered him, and it turned out to be the one thing I would have least expected: Ian Pargetter's death.

Over a plateful of succulent smoked salmon Calder apologized for the abrupt way he'd brushed me off on the telephone on that disturbing night, and I said it was most understandable.

'Fact is,' Calder said, squeezing lemon juice, 'I was afraid my whole business would collapse. Ian's partners, you know, never approved of me. I was afraid they would influence everyone against me, once Ian had gone.'

'And it hasn't worked out that way?'

He shook his head, assembling a pink forkful. 'Remarkably not. Amazing.' He put the smoked salmon in his mouth and made appreciative noises, munching. I was aware, and I guessed he was, too, that the ears of the people at the tables on either side were almost visibly attuned to the distinctive voice, to the clear loud diction with its country edge. 'My yard's still full. People have faith, you know. I may not get quite so many racehorses, that's to be expected, but still a few.'

'And have you heard any more about Ian Pargetter's death? Did they ever find out who killed him?'

He looked regretful. 'I'm sure they haven't. I asked one of his partners the other day, and he said no one seemed to be asking questions any more. He was quite upset. And so am I. I suppose finding his murderer won't bring Ian back, but all the same one wants to *know*.'

'Tell me some of your recent successes,' I said, nodding, changing the subject and taking a slice of paper-thin brown bread and butter. 'I find your work tremendously interesting.' I also found it about the only thing else to talk about, as we seemed to have few other points of contact. Regret it as I might, there was still no drift towards an easy personal friendship.

Calder ate some more smoked salmon while he thought. 'I had a colt,' he said at last, 'a two-year-old in training. Ian had been treating him, and he'd seemed to be doing well. Then about three weeks after Ian died the colt started bleeding into his mouth and down his nose and went on and on doing it, and as Ian's partner couldn't find out the trouble the trainer persuaded the owner to send the horse to me.'

'And did you discover what was wrong?' I asked.

'Oh no.' He shook his head. 'It wasn't necessary. I laid my hands on him on three succeeding days, and the bleeding stopped immediately. I kept him at my place for two weeks altogether, and returned him on his way back to full good health.'

The adjacent tables were fascinated, as indeed I was myself.

'Did you give him herbs?' I asked.

'Certainly. Of course. And alfalfa in his hay. Excellent for many ills, alfalfa.'

I had only the haziest idea of what alfalfa looked like, beyond it being some sort of grass.

'The one thing you can't do with herbs,' he said confidently, 'is *harm*.'

I raised my eyebrows with my mouth full.

He gave the nearest thing to a grin. 'With ordinary medicines one has to be so careful because of their power and their side-effects, but if I'm not certain what's wrong with a horse I can give it all the herbal remedies I can think of all at once in the hope that one of them will hit the target, and it quite often does. It may be hopelessly unscientific, but if a trained vet can't tell exactly what's wrong with a horse, how can I?'

I smiled with undiluted pleasure. 'Have some wine,' I said.

He nodded the helmet of curls, and the movement I made towards the bottle in its ice-bucket was instantly forestalled by a watchful waiter who poured almost reverently into the healer's glass.

'How was the American trip,' I asked, 'way back in January?'

'Mm.' He sipped his wine. 'Interesting.' He frowned a little and went back to finishing the salmon, leaving me wondering whether that was his total answer. When he'd laid down his knife and fork, however, he sat back in his chair and told me that the most enjoyable part of his American journey had been, as he'd expected, his few days on the ski slopes; and we discussed skiing venues throughout the roast beef and burgundy which followed.

With the crêpes Suzette I asked after Dissdale and Bettina and heard that Dissdale had been to New York on a business trip and that Bettina had been acting a small part in a British movie, which Dissdale hadn't known whether to be pleased about or not. 'Too many gorgeous young studs around,' Calder said, smiling. 'Dissdale gets worried anyway, and he was away for ten days.'

I pondered briefly about Calder's own seemingly non-existent sex-life; but he'd never seen me with a girl either, and certainly there was no hint in him of the homosexual.

Over coffee, running out of subjects, I asked about his yard in general, and how was the right-hand man Jason in particular.

Calder shrugged. 'He's left. They come and go, you know. No loyalty these days.'

'And you don't fear ... well, that he'd take your knowledge with him?'

He looked amused. 'He didn't know much. I mean, I'd hand out a pill and tell Jason which horse to give it to. That sort of thing.'

We finished amiably enough with a glass of brandy for each and a cigar for him, and I tried not to wince over the bill.

'A very pleasant evening,' Calder said. 'You must come out to lunch again one day.'

'I'd like to.'

We sat for a final few minutes opposite each other in a pause of mutual appraisal: two people utterly different but bonded by one-tenth of a second on a pavement in Ascot. Saved and saver, inextricably interested each in the other; a continuing curiosity which would never quite lose touch. I smiled at him slowly and got a smile in return, but all surface, no depth, a mirror exactly of my own feelings.

In the office things were slowly changing. John had boasted too often of his sexual conquests and complained too often about my directorship, and Gordon's almost-equal had tired of such waste of time. I'd heard from Val Fisher in a perhaps edited version that at a small and special seniors meeting (held in my absence and without my knowledge) Gordon's almost-equal had said he would like to boot John vigorously over St Paul's. His opinion was respected. I heard from Alec one day merely that the mosquito which had stung me for so long had been squashed, and on going along the passage to investigate had found John's desk empty and his bull-like presence but a quiver in the past.

'He's gone to sell air-conditioning to Eskimos,' Alec said, and Gordon's almost-equal, smiling affably, corrected it more probably to a partnership with some brokers on the Stock Exchange.

Alec himself seemed restless, as if his own job no longer held him enthralled.

'It's all right for you,' he said once. 'You've the gift. You've the *sight*. I can't tell a gold-mine from a pomegranate at five paces, and it's taken me all these years to know it.'

'But you're a conjuror,' I said. 'You can rattle up outside money faster than anyone.'

'Gift of the old gab, you mean.' He looked uncharacteristically gloomy. 'Syrup with a chisel in it.' He waved his hand towards the desks of our new older colleagues, who had both gone out to lunch. 'I'll end up like them, still here, still smooth-talking, part of the furniture, coming up to *sixty*.' His voice held disbelief that such an age could be achieved. 'That isn't life, is it? That's not *all*?'

I said that I supposed it might be.

'Yes, but for you it's exciting,' he said. 'I mean, you love it. Your eyes *gleam*. You get your kicks right here in this room. But I'll never be made a director, let's face it, and I have this grotty feeling that time's slipping away, and soon it will be too late to start anything else.'

'Like what?'

'Like being an actor. Or a doctor. Or an acrobat.'

'It's been too late for that since you were six.'

'Yeah,' he said. 'Lousy, isn't it?' He put his heart and soul ten minutes later, however, into tracking down a source of a hundred thousand for several years and lending it to a businessman at a profitable rate, knitting together such loan packages all afternoon with diligence and success.

I hoped he would stay. He was the yeast of the office: my bubbles in the dough. As for myself, I had grown accustomed to being on the board and had slowly found I'd reached a new level of confidence. Gordon seemed to treat me unreservedly as an equal, though it was not until he had been doing it for some time that I looked back and realized.

Gordon's hitherto uniformly black hair had grown a streak or two of grey. His right hand now trembled also, and his handwriting had grown smaller through his efforts to control his fingers. I watched his valiant struggles to appear normal and respected his privacy by never making even a visual comment: it had become second nature to look anywhere but directly at his hands. In the brain department he remained energetic, but physically overall he was slowing down.

I had only seen Judith once since Christmas, and that had been in the office at a retirement party given for the head of Corporate Finance, a golden-handshake affair to which all managers' wives had been invited.

'How are you?' she said amid the throng, holding a glass of wine and an unidentifiable canapé and smelling of violets.

'Fine. And you?'

'Fine.'

She was wearing blue, with diamonds in her ears. I looked at her with absolute and unhappy love and saw the strain it put into her face.

'I'm sorry,' I said.

She shook her head and swallowed. 'I thought . . . it might be different . . . here in the bank.'

'No.'

She looked down at the canapé, which was squashy

and yellow. 'If I don't eat this damned thing soon it'll drop down my dress.'

I took it out of her fingers and deposited it in an ashtray. 'Invest in a salami cornet. They stay rock-hard for hours.'

'What's Tim telling you to invest in?' demanded Henry Shipton, turning to us a beaming face.

'Salami,' Judith said.

'Typical. He lent money to a seaweed processor last week. Judith, my darling, let me freshen your glass.'

He took the glass away to the bottles and left us again looking at each other with a hundred ears around.

'I was thinking,' I said, 'when it's warmer, could I take you and Gordon, and Pen if she'd like it, out somewhere one Sunday? Somewhere not ordinary. All day.'

She took longer than normal politeness allowed to answer, and I understood all the unspoken things, but finally, as Henry could be seen returning, she said, 'Yes. We'd all like it. I'd like it . . . very much.'

'Here you are,' Henry said. 'Tim, you go and fight for your own refill, and leave me to talk to this gorgeous girl.' He put his arm round her shoulders and swept her off, and although I was vividly aware all evening of her presence, we had no more moments alone.

From day to day when she wasn't around I didn't precisely suffer: her absence was more of a faint background ache. When I saw Gordon daily in the office I felt no constant envy, nor hated him, nor even thought

489

much of where he slept. I liked him for the good clever man he was, and our office relationship continued unruffled and secure. Loving Judith was both pleasure and pain, delight and deprivation, wishes withdrawn, dreams denied. It might have been easier and more sensible to have met and fallen heavily for some young glamorous unattached stranger, but the one thing love never did have was logic.

'Easter,' I said to Gordon one day in the office. 'Are you and Judith going away?'

'We had plans – they fell through.'

'Did Judith mention that I'd like to take you both somewhere – and Pen Warner – as a thank you for Christmas?'

'Yes, I believe she did.'

'Easter Monday, then?'

He seemed pleased at the idea and reported the next day that Judith had asked Pen, and everyone was poised. 'Pen's bringing her kite,' he said. 'Unless it's a day trip to Manchester.'

'I'll think of something,' I said, laughing. 'Tell her it won't be raining.'

What I did eventually think of seemed to please them all splendidly and also to be acceptable to others concerned, and I consequently collected Gordon and Judith and Pen (but not the kite) from Clapham at eight-thirty on Easter Bank Holiday morning. Judith and Pen were in fizzing high spirits, though Gordon seemed already tired. I suggested abandoning what was bound to be a fairly taxing day for him, but he wouldn't hear of it.

'I want to go,' he said. 'Been looking forward to it all week. But I'll just sit in the back of the car and rest and sleep some of the way.' So Judith sat beside me while I drove and touched my hand now and then, not talking much but contenting me deeply by just being there. The journey to Newmarket lasted two and a half hours and I would as soon it had gone on for ever.

I was taking them to Calder's yard, to the utter fascination of Pen. 'But don't tell him I'm a pharmacist,' she said. 'He might clam up if he knew he had an informed audience.'

'We won't tell,' Judith assured her. 'It would absolutely spoil the fun.'

Poor Calder, I thought: but I wouldn't tell him either.

He greeted us expansively (making me feel guilty) and gave us coffee in the huge oak-beamed sitting room where the memory of Ian Pargetter hovered peripherally by the fireplace.

'Delighted to see you again,' Calder said, peering at Gordon, Judith and Pen as if trying to conjure a memory to fit their faces. He knew of course who they were by name, but Ascot was ten months since, and although it had been an especially memorable day for him he had met a great many new people between then

491

and now. 'Ah *yes*,' he said with relief, his brow clearing. 'Yellow hat with roses.'

Judith laughed. 'Well done.'

'Can't forget anyone so pretty.'

She took it as it was meant, but indeed he hadn't forgotten: as one tended never to forget people whose vitality brought out the sun.

'I see Dissdale and Bettina quite often,' he said, making conversation, and Gordon agreed that he and Judith, also, sometimes saw Dissdale, though infrequently. As a topic it was hardly riveting, but served as an acceptable unwinding interval between the long car journey and the Grand Tour.

The patients in the boxes were all different but their ailments seemed the same; and I supposed surgeons could be excused their impersonal talk of 'the appendix in bed 14', when the occupants changed week by week but the operation didn't.

'This is a star three-day-eventer who came here five weeks ago with severe muscular weakness and no appetite. Wouldn't eat. Couldn't be ridden. He goes home tomorrow, strong and thriving. Looks well, eh?' Calder patted the glossy brown neck over the half-stable door. 'His owner thought he was dying, poor girl. She was weeping when she brought him here. It's really satisfying, you know, to be able to help.'

Gordon said civilly that it must be.

'This is a two-year-old not long in training. Came with an intractably infected wound on his fetlock. He's

been here a week, and he's healing. It was most grati-
fying that the trainer sent him without delay, since I'd
treated several of his horses in the past.'

'This mare,' Calder went on, moving us all along,
'came two or three days ago in great discomfort with
blood in her urine. She's responding well, I'm glad to
say.' He patted this one too, as he did them all.

'What was causing the bleeding?' Pen asked,
but with only an uninformed-member-of-the-public
intonation.

Calder shook his head. 'I don't know. His vet diagnosed a kidney infection complicated by crystalluria,
which means crystals in the urine, but he didn't know
the type of germ and every antibiotic he gave failed to
work. So the mare came here. Last resort.' He gave me
a wink. 'I'm thinking of simply re-naming this whole
place "Last Resort".'

'And you're treating her,' Gordon asked, 'with
herbs?'

'With everything I can think of,' Calder said. 'And
of course . . . with hands.'

'I suppose,' Judith said diffidently, 'that you'd never
let anyone watch . . .?'

'My dear lady, for you, anything,' Calder said. 'But
you'd see nothing. You might stand for half an hour,
and nothing would happen. It would be terribly boring.
And I might, perhaps, be *unable*, you know, if someone
was waiting and standing there.'

Judith smiled understandingly and the tour continued, ending as before in the surgery.

Pen stood looking about her with sociable blankness and then wandered over to the glass-fronted cabinets to peer myopically at the contents.

Calder, happily ignoring her in favour of Judith, was pulling out his antique tablet-maker and demonstrating it with pride.

'It's beautiful,' Judith said sincerely. 'Do you use it much?'

'All the time,' he said. 'Any herbalist worth the name makes his own pills and potions.'

'Tim said you had a universal magic potion in the fridge.'

Calder smiled and obligingly opened the refrigerator door, revealing the brown-filled plastic containers, as before.

'What's in it?' Judith asked.

'Trade secret,' he said smiling. 'Decoction of hops and other things.'

'Like beer?' Judith said.

'Yes, perhaps.'

'Horses do drink beer,' Gordon said. 'Or so I've heard.'

Pen bent down to pick up a small peach-coloured pill which was lying unobtrusively on the floor in the angle of one of the cupboards, and put it without comment on the bench.

'It's all so *absorbing*,' Judith said. 'So tremendously

kind of you to show us everything. I'll watch all your programmes with more fervour than ever.'

Calder responded to her warmly as all men did and asked us into the house again for a drink before we left. Gordon, however, was still showing signs of fatigue and now also hiding both hands in his pockets which meant he felt they were trembling badly, so the rest of us thanked Calder enthusiastically for his welcome and made admiring remarks about his hospital and climbed into the car, into the same places as before.

'Come back any time you like, Tim,' he said; and I said thank you and perhaps I would. We shook hands, and we smiled, caught in our odd relationship and unable to take it further. He waved, and I waved back as I drove away.

'Isn't he amazing?' Judith said. 'I must say, Tim, I do understand why you're impressed.'

Gordon grunted and said that theatrical surgeons weren't necessarily the best; but yes, Calder was impressive.

It was only Pen, after several miles, who expressed her reservations.

'I'm not saying he doesn't do a great deal of good for the horses. Of course he must do, to have amassed such a reputation. But I don't honestly think he does it all with herbs.'

'How do you mean?' Judith asked, twisting round so as to see her better.

Pen leaned forward. 'I found a pill on the floor. I don't suppose you noticed.'

'I did,' I said. 'You put it on the bench.'

'That's right. Well, that was no herb, it was plain straightforward warfarin.'

'It may be plain straightforward war-whatever to you,' Judith said. 'But not to me.'

Pen's voice was smiling. 'Warfarin is a drug used in humans, and I dare say in horses, after things like heart attacks. It's a coumarin – an anticoagulant. Makes the blood less likely to clot and block up the veins and arteries. Widely used all over the place.'

We digested the information in silence for a mile or two, and finally Gordon said, 'How did you know it was warfarin? I mean, how can you tell?'

'I handle it every day,' she said. 'I know the dosages, the sizes, the colours, the manufacturers' marks. You see all those things so often, you get to know them at a glance.'

'Do you mean,' I said interestedly, 'that if you saw fifty different pills laid out in a row you could identify the lot?'

'Probably. If they all came from major drug companies and weren't completely new, certainly, yes.'

'Like a wine-taster,' Judith said.

'Clever girl,' Gordon said, meaning Pen.

'It's just habit.' She thought. 'And something else in those cupboards wasn't strictly herbal, I suppose. He had one or two bags of potassium sulphate, bought from Goodison's Garden Centre, wherever that is.'

'Whatever for?' Judith asked. 'Isn't potassium sulphate a fertilizer?'

'Potassium's just as essential to animals as to plants,' Pen said. 'I wouldn't be surprised if it isn't one of the ingredients in that secret brew.'

'What else would you put in it, if you were making it?' I asked curiously.

'Oh heavens.' She pondered. 'Any sort of tonic. Perhaps liquorice root, which he once mentioned. Maybe caffeine. All sorts of vitamins. Just a pepping-up mish-mash.'

The hardest part of the day had been to find somewhere decent to have lunch, and the place I'd chosen via the various gourmet guides turned out, as so often happens, to have changed hands and chefs since the books were written. The resulting repast was slow to arrive and disappointing to eat, but the mood of my guests forgave all.

'You remember,' Gordon said thoughtfully over the coffee, 'that you told us on the way to Newmarket that Calder was worried about his business when that vet was killed?'

'Yes,' I said. 'He was, at the time.'

'Isn't it possible,' Gordon said, 'that the vet was letting Calder have regular official medicines, like warfarin, and Calder thought his supplies would dry up, when the vet died?'

'Gordon!' Judith said. 'How devious you are, darling.'

We all thought about it, however, and Pen nodded. 'He must have found another willing source, I should think.'

'But,' I protested, 'would vets really do that?'

'They're not particularly brilliantly paid,' Pen said. 'Not badly by my standards, but they're never *rich*.'

'But Ian Pargetter was very much liked,' I said.

'What's that got to do with it?' Pen said. 'Nothing to stop him passing on a few pills and advice to Calder in return for a fat untaxed fee.'

'To their mutual benefit,' Gordon murmured.

'The healer's feet of clay,' Judith said. 'What a shame.'

The supposition seemed slightly to deflate the remembered pleasure of the morning, but the after-noon's visit put the rest of the day up high.

We went this time to Oliver Knowles' stud farm and found the whole place flooded with foals and mares and activity.

'How *beautiful*,' Judith said, looking away over the stretches of white-railed paddocks with their colonies of mothers and babies. 'How speechlessly *great*.'

Oliver Knowles, introduced, was as welcoming as Calder and told Gordon several times that he would never, ever, be out of his debt of gratitude to Paul Ekaterin's, however soon he had paid off his loan.

The anxiety and misgivings to be seen in him on my

February visit had all disappeared: Oliver was again, and more so, the capable and decisive executive I had met first. The foals had done well, I gathered. Not one from the mares coming to Sandcastle had been lost, and none of those mares had had any infection, a triumph of care. He told me all this within the first ten minutes, and also that Sandcastle had proved thoroughly potent and fertile and was a dream of a stallion. 'He's tireless,' he said. 'Forty mares will be easy.'

'I'm so glad,' I said, and meant it from the bottom of my banking heart.

With his dog Squibs at his heels he showed us all again through the succession of yards, where since it was approximately four o'clock the evening ritual of mucking out and feeding was in full swing.

'A stud farm is not like a racing stable, of course,' Oliver was explaining to Gordon. 'One lad here can look after far more than three horses, because they don't have to be ridden. And here we have a more flexible system because the mares are sometimes in, sometimes out in the paddocks, and it would be impossible to assign particular mares to particular lads. So here a lad does a particular section of boxes, regardless of which animals are in them.'

Gordon nodded, genially interested.

'Why are some foals in the boxes and some out in the paddocks?' Judith asked, and Oliver without hesitation told her it was because the foals had to stay with their dams, and the mares with foals in the boxes were due to come into heat, or were already in heat, and would go from their boxes to visit the stallion. When their heat was over they would go out into the paddocks, with their foals.

'Oh,' Judith said, blinking slightly at this factory aspect. 'Yes, I see.'

In the foaling yard we came across Nigel and also Ginnie, who ran across to me when she saw me and gave me a great hug and a smacking kiss somewhere to the left of the mouth. Quite an advance in confidence, I thought, and hugged her back, lifting her off her feet and whirling her round in a circle. She was laughing when I put her down, and Oliver watched in some surprise.

'I've never known her so demonstrative,' he said.

Ginnie looked at him apprehensively and held onto my sleeve. 'You didn't mind, did you?' she asked me worriedly.

'I'm flattered,' I said, meaning it and also thinking that her father would kill off her spontaneity altogether if he wasn't careful.

Ginnie, reassured, tucked her arm into mine and said, 'Come and look at the newest foal. It was born only about twenty minutes ago. It's a colt. A darling.' She tugged me off, and I caught a fleeting glance of Judith's face which was showing a mixture of all sorts of unreadable thoughts.

'Oliver's daughter,' I said in explanation over my shoulder, and heard Oliver belatedly introducing Nigel.

They all came to look at the foal over the half-door; a glistening little creature half-lying, half-sitting on the thick straw, all long nose, huge eyes and folded legs, new life already making an effort to balance and stand up. The dam, on her feet, alternatively bent her head to the foal and looked up at us warily.

'It was an easy one,' Ginnie said. 'Nigel and I just watched.'

'Have you seen many foals born?' Pen asked her.

'Oh, hundreds. All my life. Most often at night.'

Pen looked at her as if she, as I did, felt the imagination stirred by such an unusual childhood: as if she, like myself, had never seen one single birth of any sort, let alone a whole procession by the age of fifteen.

'This mare has come to Sandcastle,' Oliver said.

'And will that foal win the Derby?' Gordon asked, smiling.

Oliver smiled in return. 'You never know. He has the breeding.' He breathed deeply, expanding his chest. 'I've never been able to say anything like that before this year. No foal born or conceived here has in the past won a classic, but now . . .' He gestured widely with his arm, '. . . one day, from these . . .' He paused. 'It's a whole new world. It's . . . tremendous.'

'As good as you hoped?' I asked.

'Better.'

He had a soul after all, I thought, under all that tidy martial efficiency. A vision of the peaks, which he was reaching in reality. And how soon, I wondered, before the glossy became commonplace, the classic winners a routine, the aristocrats the common herd. It would be what he'd aimed for; but in a way it would be blunting.

We left the foal and went on down the path past the breeding shed, where the main door was today wide open, showing the floor thickly covered with soft brown crumbly peat. Beyond succinctly explaining what went on there when it was inhabited, Oliver made no comment, and we all walked on without stopping to the heart of the place, to the stallions.

Lenny was there, walking one of the horses round the small yard and plodding with his head down as if he'd been doing it for some time. The horse was dripping with sweat, and from the position of the one open empty box I guessed he would be Rotaboy.

'He's just covered a mare,' Oliver said matter-of-factly. 'He's always like that afterwards.'

Judith and Gordon and Pen all looked as if the overt sex of the place was earthier than they'd expected, even without hearing, as I had at one moment, Oliver quietly discussing a vaginal disinfectant process with Nigel. They rallied valiantly, however, and gazed with proper awe at the head of Sandcastle which swam into view from the inside-box shadows.

He held himself almost imperiously, as if his new role had basically changed his character; and perhaps it had. I had myself seen during my renewed interest in racing how constant success endowed some horses with definite 'presence', and Sandcastle, even lost and frightened up on top of the hill, had perceptibly had it; but now, only two months later, there was a new quality one might almost call arrogance, a fresh certainty of his own supremacy.

'He's splendid,' Gordon exclaimed. 'What a treat to see him again after that great day at Ascot.'

Oliver gave Sandcastle the usual two carrots and a couple of pats, treating the King with familiarity. Neither Judith nor Pen, nor indeed Gordon or myself, tried even to touch the sensitive nose: afraid of getting our fingers bitten off at the wrist, no doubt. It was all right to admire, but distance had virtue.

Lenny put the calming-down Rotaboy back in his box and started mucking out Diarist next door.

'We have two lads looking after the stallions full time,' Oliver said. 'Lenny, here, and another much trusted man, Don. And Nigel feeds them.'

Pen caught the underlying thought behind his words and asked, 'Do you need much security?'

'Some,' he said, nodding. 'We have the yard wired for sound, so either Nigel or I, when we're in our houses, can hear if there are any irregular noises.'

'Like hooves taking a walk?' Judith suggested.

'Exactly.' He smiled at her. 'We also have smoke alarms and massive extinguishers.'

'And brick-built boxes and combination locks on these door bolts at night and lockable gates on all the ways out to the roads,' Ginnie said, chattily. 'Dad's really gone to town on security.'

'Glad to hear it,' Gordon said.

I smiled to myself at the classic example of bolting the stable door after the horse had done likewise, but indeed one could see that Oliver had learned a dire lesson and knew he'd been lucky to be given a second chance.

We began after a while to walk back towards the house, stopping again in the foaling yard to look at the new baby colt, who was now shakily on his feet and searching round for his supper.

Oliver drew me to one side and asked if I would like to see Sandcastle cover a mare, an event apparently scheduled for a short time hence.

'Yes, I would,' I said.

'I can't ask them all – there isn't room,' he said. 'I'll get Ginnie to show them the mares and foals in the paddocks and then take them indoors for tea.'

No one demurred at this suggested programme, especially as Oliver didn't mention where he and I were going: Judith, I was sure, would have preferred to join us. Ginnie took them and Squibs off, and I could hear her saying, 'Over there, next door, there's another yard. We could walk over that way if you like.'

Oliver, eyeing them amble along the path that Sand- castle had taken at a headlong gallop and I at a sprint, said, 'The Watcherleys look after any delicate foals or any mares with infections. It's all worked out most satisfactorily. I rent their place and they work for me, and their expertise with sick animals comes in very useful.'

'And you were mending their fences for them, I guess, when I came in February.'

'That's right.' He sighed ruefully. 'Another week and the gates would have been up in the hedge and across their driveway, and Sandcastle would never have got out.'

'No harm done,' I said.

'Thanks to you, no.'

We went slowly back towards the breeding shed. 'Have you seen a stallion at work before?' he asked.

'No, I haven't.'

After a pause he said, 'It may seem strong to you. Even violent. But it's normal to them. Remember that. And he'll probably bite her neck, but it's as much to keep himself in position as an expression of passion.'

'All right,' I said.

'This mare, the one we're breeding, is receptive, so there won't be any trouble. Some mares are shy, some are slow to arouse, some are irritable, just like humans.' He smiled faintly. 'This little lady is a born one-nighter.'

It was the first time I'd heard him make anything like a joke about his profession and I was almost startled. As if himself surprised at his own words he said more soberly, 'We put her to Sandcastle yesterday morning, and all went well.'

'The mares go more than once then, to the stallion?' I asked.

He nodded. 'It depends of course on the stud farm, but I'm very anxious as you can guess that all the mares here shall have the best possible chance of conceiving. I bring them all at least twice to the stallion during their heat, then we put them out in the paddocks and wait, and if they come into heat again it means they haven't conceived, so we repeat the breeding process.'

'And how long do you go on trying?'

'Until the end of July. That means the foal won't be born until well on in June, which is late in the year for racehorses. Puts them at a disadvantage as two-year-olds, racing against March and April foals which have had more growing time.' He smiled. 'With any luck Sandcastle won't have any late June foals. It's too early to be complacent, but none of the mares he covered three weeks or more ago has come back into use.'

We reached and entered the breeding shed where the mare already stood, held at the head in a loose twitch by one lad and being washed and attended to by another.

'She can't wait, sir,' that lad said, indicating her tail, which she was holding high, and Oliver replied rather repressively, 'Good.'

Nigel and Lenny came with Sandcastle, who looked eagerly aware of where he was and what for. Nigel closed the door to keep the ritual private; and the mating which followed was swift and sure and utterly primeval. A copulation of thrust and grandeur, of

vigour and pleasure, not without tenderness: remarkably touching.

'They're not all like that,' Oliver remarked prosaically, as Sandcastle slid out and backwards, and brought
his forelegs to earth with a jolt. 'You've seen a good
one.'

I thanked him for letting me be there, and in truth I
felt I understood more about horses then than I'd ever
imagined I would.

We walked back to the house with Oliver telling me
that with the four stallions there were currently six,
seven or eight matings a day in the breeding shed,
Sundays included. The mind stuttered a bit at the
thought of all that rampaging fertility, but that, after
all, was what the bank's five million pounds was all
about. Rarely, I thought, had anyone seen Ekaterin's
money so fundamentally at work.

We set off homewards fortified by tea, scones and
whisky, with Oliver and Gordon at the end competing
over who thanked whom most warmly. Ginnie gave me
another but more composed hug and begged me to
come again, and Judith kissed her and offered female
succour if ever needed.

'Nice child,' she said as we drove away. 'Growing up
fast.'

'Fifteen,' I said.

'Sixteen. She had a birthday last week.'

'You got on well with her,' I said.

'Yes.' She looked round at Pen and Gordon, who were again sitting in the back. 'She told us about your little escapade here two months ago.'

'She didn't!'

'She sure did,' Pen said, smiling. 'Why ever didn't you say?'

'I know why,' Gordon said drily. 'He didn't want it to be known in the office that the loan he'd recommended had very nearly fallen under a lorry.'

'Is that right?' Judith asked.

'Very much so,' I admitted wryly. 'Some of the board were against the whole thing anyway, and I'd have never heard the end of the horse getting out.'

'What a coward,' Pen said, chuckling.

We pottered slowly back to Clapham through the stop-go end-of-Bank Holiday traffic, and Judith and Pen voted it the best day they'd had since Ascot. Gordon dozed, I drove with relaxation and so finally reached the tall gates by the common.

I went in with them for supper as already arranged, but all of them, not only Gordon, were tired from the long day, and I didn't stay late. Judith came out to the car to see me off and to shut the gates after I'd gone.

We didn't really talk. I held her in my arms, her head on my shoulder, my head on hers, close in the dark night, as far apart as planets.

We stood away and I took her hand, lingering, not wanting all contact lost.

'A great day,' she said, and I said, 'Mm', and kissed her very briefly.

Got into the car and drove away.

OCTOBER

Summer had come, summer had gone, sodden, cold and unloved. It had been overcast and windy during Royal Ascot week and Gordon and I, clamped to our telephones and pondering our options, had looked at the sullen sky and hardly minded that this year Dissdale hadn't needed to sell half-shares in his box.

Only with the autumn, far too late, had days of sunshine returned, and it was on a bright golden Saturday that I took the race train to Newbury to see the mixed meeting of two jump races and four flat.

Ursula Young was there, standing near the weighing room when I walked in from the station and earnestly reading her racecard.

'Hello,' she said when I greeted her. 'Haven't seen you for ages. How's the money-lending?'

'Profitable,' I said.

She laughed. 'Are you here for anything special?'

'No. Just fresh air and a flutter.'

'I'm supposed to meet a client.' She looked at her

watch. 'Time for a quick sandwich, though. Are you on?'

I was on, and bought her and myself a thin pallid slice of tasteless white meat between two thick pallid tasteless slices of soggy-crusted bread, the whole wrapped up in cardboard and cellophane and costing a fortune.

Ursula ate it in disgust. 'They used to serve proper luscious sandwiches, thick, juicy handmade affairs which came in a whole stack. I can't stand all this repulsive hygiene.' The rubbish from the sandwiches indeed littered most of the tables around us . . . 'Every so-called advance is a retreat from excellence,' she said, dogmatic as ever.

I totally agreed with her and we chewed in joyless accord.

'How's trade with you?' I said.

She shrugged. 'Fair. The cream of the yearlings are going for huge prices. They've all got high reserves on them because they've cost so much to produce – stallion fees and the cost of keeping the mare and foal to start with, let alone vet's fees and all the incidentals. My sort of clients on the whole settle for a second, third or fourth rank, and many a good horse, mind you, has come from the bargain counter.'

I smiled at the automatic sales pitch. 'Talking of vets,' I said, 'is the Pargetter murder still unsolved?'

She nodded regretfully. 'I was talking to his poor wife in Newmarket last week. We met in the street.

511

She's only half the girl she was, poor thing, no life in her. She said she asked the police recently if they were still even trying, and they assured her they were, but she doesn't believe it. It's been so long, nine months, and if they hadn't any leads to start with, how can they possibly have any now? She's very depressed, it's dreadful.'

I made sympathetic murmurs, and Ursula went on, 'The only good thing you could say is that he'd taken out decent life insurance and paid off the mortgage on their house, so at least she and the children aren't penniless as well. She was telling me how he'd been very careful in those ways, and she burst into tears, poor girl.'

Ursula looked as if the encounter had distressed her also.

'Have another whisky-mac,' I suggested. 'To cheer you up.'

She looked at her watch. 'All right. You get it, but I'll pay. My turn.'

Over the second drink, in a voice of philosophical irritation, she told me about the client she was presently due to meet, a small-time trainer of steeplechasers. 'He's such a fool to himself,' she said. 'He makes hasty decisions, acts on impulse, and then when things go wrong he feels victimized and cheated and gets angry. Yet he can be perfectly nice when he likes.'

I wasn't especially interested in the touchy trainer, but when I went outside again with Ursula he spotted her from a short distance away and practically pounced on her arm.

'There you are,' he said, as if she'd had no right to be anywhere but at his side. 'I've been looking all over.'

'It's only just time,' she said mildly.

He brushed that aside, a short wiry intense man of about forty with a pork-pie hat above a weatherbeaten face.

'I wanted you to see him before he's saddled,' he said. 'Do come on, Ursula. Come and look at his conformation.'

She opened her mouth to say something to me but he almost forcefully dragged her off, holding her sleeve and talking rapidly into her ear. She gave me an apologetic look of long-suffering and departed in the direction of the pre-parade ring, where the horses for the first race were being led round by their lads before going off to the saddling boxes.

I didn't follow but climbed onto the steps of the main parade ring, round which walked several of the runners already saddled. The last of the field to appear some time later was accompanied by the pork-pie hat, and also Ursula, and for something to do I looked the horse up in the racecard.

Zoomalong, five-year-old gelding, trained by F. Barnet.

F. Barnet continued his dissertation into Ursula's ear, aiming his words from approximately six inches away, which I would have found irritating but which she bore without flinching. According to the flickering numbers on the Tote board Zoomalong had a medium chance in the opinion of the public, so for interest I put a medium stake on him to finish in the first three.

I didn't see Ursula or F. Barnet during the race, but Zoomalong zoomed along quite nicely to finish third, and I walked down from the stands towards the unsaddling enclosure to watch the patting-on-the-back post-race routine.

F. Barnet was there, still talking to Ursula and pointing out parts of his now sweating and stamping charge. Ursula nodded non-committally, her own eyes knowledgeably raking the gelding from stem to stern, a neat competent good-looking fifty in a rust-coloured coat and brown velvet beret.

Eventually the horses were led away and the whole cycle of excitement began slowly to regenerate towards the second race.

Without in the least meaning to I again found myself standing near Ursula, and this time she introduced me to the pork-pie hat, who had temporarily stopped talking.

'This is Fred Barnet,' she said. 'And his wife Susan.' A rounded motherly person in blue. 'And their son, Ricky.' A boy taller than his father, dark-haired, pleasant-faced.

I shook hands with all three, and it was while I was still touching the son that Ursula in her clear voice said my name, 'Tim Ekaterin.'

The boy's hand jumped in mine as if my flesh had burned him. I was astonished, and then I looked at his whitening skin, at the suddenly frightened dark eyes, at the stiffening of the body, at the rising panic: and I wouldn't have known him if he hadn't reacted in that way.

'What's the matter, Ricky?' his mother said, puzzled.

He said 'Nothing' hoarsely and looked around for escape, but all too clearly he knew I knew exactly who he was now and could always find him however far he ran.

'What do you think, then, Ursula?' Fred Barnet demanded, returning to the business in hand. 'Will you buy him? Can I count on you?'

Ursula said she would have to consult her client.

'But he was third,' Fred Barnet insisted. 'A good third ... In that company, a pretty good showing. And he'll win, I'm telling you. He'll win.'

'I'll tell my client all about him. I can't say fairer than that.'

'But you do like him, don't you? Look, Ursula, he's a good sort, easy to handle, just right for an amateur ...' He went on for a while in this vein while his wife listened with a sort of aimless beam meaning nothing at all.

To the son, under cover of his father's hard sell, I quietly said, 'I want to talk to you, and if you run away from me now I'll be telephoning the police.'

He gave me a sick look and stood still.

515

'We'll walk down the course together to watch the next race,' I said. 'We won't be interrupted there. And you can tell me *why*. And then we'll see.'

It was easy enough for him to drop back unnoticed from his parents, who were still concentrating on Ursula, and he came with me through the gate and out across the track itself to the centre of the racecourse, stumbling slightly as if not in command of his feet. We walked down towards the last fence, and he told me why he'd tried to kill Calder Jackson.

'It doesn't seem real, not now, it doesn't really,' he said first. A young voice, slightly sloppy accent, full of strain.

'How old are you?' I asked.

'Seventeen.'

I hadn't been so far out, I thought, fifteen months ago.

'I never thought I'd see you again,' he said explosively, sounding faintly aggrieved at the twist of fate. 'I mean, the papers said you worked in a bank.'

'So I do. And I go racing.' I paused. 'You remembered my name.'

'Yeah. Could hardly forget it, could I? All over the papers.'

We went a few yards in silence. 'Go on,' I said.

He made a convulsive gesture of frustrated despair. 'All right. But if I tell you, you won't tell *them*, will you, not Mum and Dad?'

I glanced at him, but from his troubled face it was

clear that he meant exactly what he'd said: it wasn't my telling the police he minded most, but my telling his parents.

'Just get on with it,' I said.

He sighed. 'Well, we had this horse. Dad did. He'd bought it as a yearling and ran it as a two-year-old and at three, but it was a jumper really, and it turned out to be good.' He paused. 'Indian Silk, that's what it was called.'

I frowned. 'But Indian Silk . . . didn't that win at Cheltenham this year, in March?'

He nodded. 'The Gold Cup. The very top. He's only seven now and he's bound to be brilliant for years.' The voice was bitter with a sort of resigned, stifled anger.

'But he doesn't any longer belong to your father?'

'No, he doesn't.' More bitterness, very sharp.

'Go on, then,' I said.

He swallowed and took his time, but eventually he said, 'Two years ago this month, when Indian Silk was five, like, he won the Hermitage 'Chase very easily here at Newbury, and everyone was tipping him for the Gold Cup *last* year, though Dad was saying he was still on the young side and to give him time. See, Dad was that proud of that horse. The best he'd ever trained, and it was his own, not someone else's. Don't know if you can understand that.'

'I do understand it,' I said.

He gave a split-second glance at my face. 'Well,

Indian Silk got sick,' he said. 'I mean, there was nothing you could put your finger on. He just lost his speed. He couldn't even gallop properly at home, couldn't beat the other horses in Dad's yard that he'd been running rings round all year. Dad couldn't run him in races. He could hardly train him. And the vet couldn't find out what was wrong with him. They took blood tests and all sorts, and they gave him antibiotics and purges, and they thought it might be worms or something, but it wasn't.'

We had reached the last fence, and stood there on the rough grass beside it while in twos and threes other enthusiasts straggled down from the grandstand towards us to watch the horses in action at close quarters.

'I was at school a lot of the time, see,' Ricky said. 'I was home every night of course but I was taking exams and had a lot of homework and I didn't really want to take much notice of Indian Silk getting so bad or anything. I mean, Dad does go on a bit, and I suppose I thought the horse just had the virus or something and would get better. But he just got slowly worse and one day Mum was crying.' He stopped suddenly, as if that part was the worst. 'I hadn't seen a grown-up cry before,' he said. 'Suppose you'll think it funny, but it upset me something awful.'

'I don't think it funny,' I said.

'Anyway,' he went on, seeming to gather confidence, 'it got so that Indian Silk was so weak he could barely walk down the road and he wasn't eating, and Dad was in real despair because there wasn't nothing anyone could do, and Mum couldn't bear the thought of him going to the knackers, and then some guy telephoned and offered to buy him.'

'To buy a sick horse?' I said, surprised.

'I don't think Dad was going to tell him just how bad he was. Well, I mean, at that point Indian Silk was worth just what the knackers would pay for his carcass, which wasn't much, and this man was offering nearly twice that. But the man said he knew Indian Silk couldn't race any more but he'd like to give him a good home in a nice field for as long as necessary, and it meant that Dad didn't have the expense of any more vets' bills and he and Mum didn't have to watch Indian Silk just getting worse and worse, and Mum wouldn't have to think of him going to the knackers for dog meat, so they let him go.'

The horses for the second race came out onto the course and galloped down past us, the jockeys' colours bright in the sun.

'And then what?' I said.

'Then nothing happened for weeks and we were getting over it, like, and then someone told Dad that Indian Silk was back in training and looking fine, and he couldn't believe it.'

'When was that?' I asked.

'It was last year, just before . . . before Ascot.'

A small crowd gathered on the landing side of the

fence, and I drew him away down the course a bit further, to where the horses would set themselves right to take off.

'Go on,' I said.

'My exams were coming up,' he said. 'And I mean, they were important, they were going to affect my whole life, see?'

I nodded.

'Then Dad found that the man who'd bought Indian Silk hadn't put him in any field, he'd sent him straight down the road to Calder Jackson.'

'Ah,' I said.

'And there was this man saying Calder Jackson had the gift of healing, some sort of magic, and had simply touched Indian Silk and made him well. I ask you . . . And Dad was in a frightful state because someone had suggested he should send the horse there, to Calder Jackson, while he was so bad, of course, and Dad had said don't be so ridiculous, it was all a lot of rubbish. And then Mum was saying he should have listened to her, because she'd said why not try it, it couldn't do any harm, and he wouldn't do it, and they were having rows, and she was crying . . .' He gulped for air, the story now pouring out faster almost than he could speak. 'And I wasn't getting any work done with it all going on, they weren't ever talking about anything else, and I took the first exam and just sat there and couldn't do it, and I knew I'd failed and I was going to fail them all because I couldn't concentrate . . . and then there was Calder Jackson one evening talking on television, saying he'd got a friend of his to buy a dying horse, because the people who owned it would just have let it die because they didn't believe in healers, like a lot of people, and he hoped the horse would be great again some day, like before, thanks to him, and I knew he was talking about Indian Silk. And he said he was going to Ascot on that Thursday . . . and there was Dad screaming that Calder Jackson had stolen the horse away, it was all a filthy swindle, which of course it wasn't, but at the time I believed him . . . and it all got so that I hated Calder Jackson so much that I couldn't think straight. I mean, I thought *he* was the reason Mum was crying and I was failing my exams and Dad had lost the only really top horse he'd have in his whole life, and I just wanted to *kill* him.'

The bedrock words were out, and the flood suddenly stopped, leaving the echo of them on the October air.

'And did you fail your exams?' I asked, after a moment.

'Yeah. Most of them. But I took them again at Christmas and got good passes.' He shook his head, speaking more slowly, more quietly. 'I was glad, even that night, that you'd stopped me stabbing him. I mean . . . I'd have thrown my whole life away, I could see it afterwards, and all for nothing, because Dad wasn't going to get the horse back whatever I did, because it was a legal sale, like.'

I thought over what he'd told me while in the

distance the horses lined up and set off on their three-mile steeplechase.

'I was sort of mad,' he said. 'I can't really understand it now. I mean, I wouldn't go around trying to kill people. I really wouldn't. It seems like I was a different person.'

Adolescence, I thought, and not for the first time, could be hell.

'I took Mum's knife out of the kitchen,' he said. 'She never could think where it had gone.'

I wondered if the police still had it; with Ricky's fingerprints on file.

'I didn't know there would be so many people at Ascot,' he said. 'And so many gates into the course. Much more than Newmarket. I was getting frantic because I thought I wouldn't find him. I meant to do it earlier, see, when he arrived. I was out on the road, running up and down the pavement, mad, you know, really, looking for him and feeling the knife kind of burning in my sleeve, like I was burning in my mind . . . and I saw his head, all those curls, crossing the road, and I ran, but I was too late, he'd gone inside, through the gate.'

'And then,' I suggested. 'You simply waited for him to come out?'

He nodded. 'There were lots of people around. No one took any notice. I reckoned he'd come up that path from the station, and that was the way he would go back. It didn't seem long, the waiting. Went in a flash.'

The horses came over the next fence down the course like a multi-coloured wave and thundered towards the one where we were standing. The ground trembled from the thud of the hooves, the air rang with the curses of jockeys, the half-ton equine bodies brushed through the birch, the sweat and the effort and the speed filled eyes and ears and mind with pounding wonder and then were gone, flying away, leaving the silence. I had walked down several times before to watch from the fences, both there and on other tracks, and the fierce fast excitement had never grown stale.

'Who is it who owns Indian Silk now?' I asked.

'A Mr Chacksworth, comes from Birmingham,' Ricky answered. 'You see him at the races sometimes, slobbering all over Indian Silk. But it wasn't him that bought him from Dad. He bought him later, when he was all right again. Paid a proper price for him, so we heard. Made it all the worse.'

A sad and miserable tale, all of it.

'Who bought the horse from your father?' I said.

'I never met him ... his name was Smith. Some funny first name. Can't remember.'

Smith. Friend of Calder's.

'Could it,' I asked, surprised, 'have been *Dissdale* Smith?'

'Yeah. That sounds like it. How do you know?'

'He was there that day at Ascot,' I said. 'There on the pavement, right beside Calder Jackson.'

'Was he?' Ricky looked disconcerted. 'He was a dead liar, you know, all that talk about nice fields.'

'Who tells the truth,' I said, 'when buying or selling horses?'

The runners were round again on the far side of the track, racing hard now on the second circuit.

'What are you going to do?' Ricky said. 'About me, like? You won't tell Mum and Dad. You won't, will you?'

I looked directly at the boy-man, seeing the continuing anxiety but no longer the first panic-stricken fear. He seemed to sense now that I would very likely not drag him into court, but he wasn't sure of much else.

'Perhaps they should know,' I said.

'No!' His agitation rose quickly. 'They've had so much trouble and I would have made it so much worse if you hadn't stopped me, and afterwards I used to wake up sweating at what it would have done to them; and the only good thing was that I did learn that you can't put things right by killing people, you can only make things terrible for your family.'

After a long pause I said, 'All right. I won't tell them.' And heaven help me, I thought, if he ever attacked anyone again because he thought he could always get away with it.

The relief seemed to affect him almost as much as the anxiety. He blinked several times and turned his head away to where the race was again coming round into the straight with this time an all-out effort to the winning post. There was again the rise and fall of the field over the distant fences but now the one wave had split into separate components, the runners coming home not in a bunch but a procession.

I watched again the fierce surprising speed of horse and jockey jumping at close quarters and wished with some regret that I could have ridden like that; but like Alec I was wishing too late, even strong and healthy and thirty-three.

The horses galloped off towards the cheers on the grandstand and Ricky and I began a slow walk in their wake. He seemed quiet and composed in the aftermath of confession, the soul's evacuation giving him ease.

'What do you feel nowadays about Calder Jackson?' I asked.

He produced a lop-sided smile. 'Nothing much. That's what's so crazy. I mean, it wasn't his fault Dad was so stubborn.'

I digested this. 'You mean,' I said, 'that you think your father should have sent him the horse himself?'

'Yes, I reckon he should've, like Mum wanted. But he said it was rubbish and too expensive, and you don't know my dad but when he makes his mind up he just gets fighting angry if anyone tries to argue, and he shouts at her, and it isn't fair.'

'If your father had sent the horse to Calder Jackson, I suppose he would still own it,' I said thoughtfully.

'Yes, he would, and don't think he doesn't know it,

of course he does, but it's as much as anyone's life's worth to say it.'

We trudged back over the thick grass, and I asked him how Calder or Dissdale had known that Indian Silk was ill.

He shrugged. 'It was in the papers. He'd been favourite for the King George VI on Boxing Day, but of course he didn't run, and the press found out why.'

We came again to the gate into the grandstand enclosure and went through it, and I asked where he lived.

'Exning,' he said.

'Where's that?'

'Near Newmarket. Just outside.' He looked at me with slightly renewed apprehension. 'You meant it, didn't you, about not telling?'

'I meant it,' I said. 'Only . . .' I frowned a little, thinking of the hot-house effect of his living with his parents.

'Only what?' he asked.

I tried a different tack. 'What are you doing now? Are you still at school?'

'No, I left once I'd passed those exams. I really needed them, like. You can't get a halfway decent job without those bits of paper these days.'

'You're not working for your father, then?'

He must have heard the faint relief in my voice because for the first time he fully smiled. 'No, I reckon it wouldn't be good for his temper, and anyway I don't want to be a trainer, one long worry, if you ask me.'

'What do you do, then?' I asked.

'I'm learning electrical engineering in a firm near Cambridge. An apprentice, like.' He smiled again. 'But not with horses, not me.' He shook his head ruefully and delivered his young-Solomon judgement of life. 'Break your heart, horses do.'

NOVEMBER

To my great delight the cartoonist came up trumps, his twenty animated films being shown on television every weeknight for a month in the best time-slot for that sort of humour, seven in the evening, when older children were still up and the parents home from work. The nation sat up and giggled, and the cartoonist telephoned breathlessly to ask for a bigger loan.

'I do need a proper studio, not this converted warehouse. And more animators, and designers, and recordists, and equipment.'

'All right,' I said into the first gap. 'Draw up your requirements and come and see me.'

'Do you *realize*,' he said, as if he himself had difficulty, 'that they'll take as many films as I can make? No limit. They said just go on making them for years and years . . . they said *please* go on making them.'

'I'm very glad,' I said sincerely.

'You gave me faith in myself,' he said. 'You'll never believe it, but you did. I'd been turned down so often, and I was getting depressed, but when you lent me the money to start it was like being uncorked. The ideas just rushed out.'

'And are they still rushing?'

'Oh sure. I've got the next twenty films roughed out in drawings already and we're working on those, and now I'm starting on the batch after that.'

'It's terrific,' I said.

'It sure is, brother, life's amazing.' He put down his receiver and left me smiling into space.

'The cartoonist?' Gordon said.

I nodded. 'Going up like a rocket.'

'Congratulations.' There was warmth and genuine pleasure in his voice. Such a generous man, I thought: so impossible to do him harm.

'He looks like turning into a major industry,' I said.

'Disney, Hanna Barbera, eat your hearts out,' Alec said from across the room.

'Good business for the bank.' Gordon beamed. 'Henry will be pleased.'

Pleasing Henry, indeed, was the aim of us all.

'You must admit, Tim,' Alec said, 'that you're a fairish rocket yourself . . . so what's the secret?'

'Light the blue paper and retire immediately,' I said good humouredly, and he balled a page of jottings to throw at me, and missed.

At mid-morning he went out as customary for the six copies of *What's Going On Where It Shouldn't* and having distributed five was presently sitting back in his chair reading our own with relish.

Ekaterin's had been thankfully absent from the probing columns ever since the five per cent business, but it appeared that some of our colleagues along the road weren't so fortunate.

'Did you know,' Alec said conversationally, 'that some of our investment manager chums down on the corner have set up a nice little fiddle on the side, accepting pay-offs from brokers in return for steering business their way?'

'How do you know?' Gordon asked, looking up from a ledger.

Alec lifted the paper. 'The gospel according to this dicky bird.'

'Gospel meaning good news,' I said.

'Don't be so damned erudite.' He grinned at me with mischief and went back to reading aloud, '*Contrary to popular belief the general run of so-called managers in merchant banks are not in the princely bracket.*' He looked up briefly. 'You can say that again.' He went on, '*We hear that four of the investment managers in this establishment have been cosily supplementing their middle-incomes by steering fund money to three stock-brokers in particular. Names will be revealed in our next issue. Watch this space.*'

'It's happened before,' Gordon said philosophically, 'and will happen again. The temptation is always there.' He frowned. 'All the same, I'm surprised their senior managers and the directors haven't spotted it.'

'They'll have spotted it *now*,' Alec said.

'So they will.'

'It would be pretty easy,' I said musingly, 'to set up a computer programme to do the spotting for Ekaterin's, in case we should ever find the pestilence cropping up here.'

'Would it?' Gordon asked.

'Mm. Just a central programme to record every deal in the Investment Department with each stockbroker, with running totals, easy to see. Anything hugely unexpected could be investigated.'

'But that's a vast job, surely,' Gordon said.

I shook my head. 'I doubt it. I could get our tame programmer to have a go, if you like.'

'We'll put it to the others. See what they say.'

'There will be screeches from Investment Management,' Alec said. 'Cries of outraged virtue.'

'Guards them against innuendo like this, though,' Gordon said, pointing to *What's Going On* . . .

The board agreed, and in consequence I spent another two days with the programmer, building dykes against future leaks.

Gordon these days seemed no worse, his illness not having progressed in any visible way. There was no means of knowing how he felt, as he never said and hated to be asked, but on the few times I'd seen Judith since the day at Easter, she had said he was as well as could be hoped for.

The best of those times had been a Sunday in July when Pen had given a lunch party in her house in

531

Clapham; it was supposed to have been a lunch-in-the-garden party, but like so much that summer was frustrated by chilly winds. Inside was to me much better, as Pen had written place-cards for her long refectory table and put me next to Judith, with Gordon on her right hand.

The other guests remained a blur, most of them being doctors of some sort or another, or pharmacists like herself. Judith and I made polite noises to the faces on either side of us but spent most of the time talking to each other, carrying on two conversations at once, one with voice, one with eyes; both satisfactory.

When the main party had broken up and gone, Gordon and Judith and I stayed to supper, first helping Pen clear up from what she described as 'repaying so many dinners at one go.'

It had been a day when natural opportunities for touching people abounded, when kisses and hugs of greeting had been appropriate and could be warm, when all the world could watch and see nothing between Judith and me but an enduring and peaceful friendship: a day when I longed to have her for myself worse than ever.

Since then I'd seen her only twice, and both times were when she'd come to the bank to collect Gordon before they went on to other events. On each of these times I'd managed at least five minutes with her, stiffly circumspect, Gordon's colleague being polite until Gordon himself was ready to leave.

It wasn't usual for wives to come to the bank: husbands normally joined them at wherever they were going. Judith said, the second time, 'I won't do this often. I just wanted to see you, if you were around.'

'Always here,' I said.

She nodded. She was looking as fresh and poised as ever, wearing a neat blue coat with pearls showing. The brown hair was glossy, the eyes bright, the soft mouth half smiling, the glamour born in her and unconscious.

'I get . . . well . . . thirsty, sometimes,' she said.

'Permanent state with me,' I said lightly.

She swallowed. 'Just for a moment or two . . .'

We were standing in the entrance hall, not touching, waiting for Gordon.

'Just to see you . . .' She seemed uncertain that I understood, but I did.

'It's the same for me,' I assured her. 'I sometimes think of going to Clapham and waiting around just to see you walk down the street to the bakers. Just to see you, even for seconds.'

'Do you really?'

'I don't go, though. You might send Gordon to buy the bread.'

She laughed a small laugh, a fitting size for the bank; and he came, hurrying, struggling into his overcoat. I sprang to help him and he said to her, 'Sorry, darling, got held up on the telephone, you know how it is.'

'I've been perfectly happy,' she said, kissing him, 'talking to Tim.'

'Splendid. Splendid. Are we ready then?'

They went off to their evening smiling and waving and leaving me to hunger futilely for this and that.

In the office one day in November Gordon said, 'How about you coming over to lunch on Sunday? Judith was saying it's ages since she saw you properly.'

'I'd love to.'

'Pen's coming, Judith said.'

Pen, my friend; my chaperone.

'Great,' I said positively. 'Lovely.'

Gordon nodded contentedly and said it was a shame we couldn't all have a repeat of last Christmans, he and Judith had enjoyed it so much. They were going this year to his son and daughter-in-law in Edinburgh, a visit long promised; to his son by his first long-dead wife, and his grandchildren, twin boys of seven.

'You'll have fun,' I said regretfully.

'They're noisy little brutes.'

His telephone rang, and mine also, and money-lending proceeded. I would be dutiful, I thought, and spend Christmas with my mother in Jersey, as she wanted, and we would laugh and play backgammon, and I would sadden her as usual by bringing no girl-friend, no prospective producer of little brutes.

'*Why*, my love,' she'd said to me once a few years earlier in near despair, 'do you take out these perfectly presentable girls and never marry them?'

'There's always something I don't want to spend my life with.'

'But you do *sleep* with them?'

'Yes, darling, I do.'

'You're too choosy.'

'I expect so,' I said.

'You haven't had a single one that's lasted,' she complained. 'Everyone else's sons manage to have live-in girlfriends, sometimes going on for years even if they don't marry, so why can't you?'

I'd smiled at the encouragement to what would once have been called sin, and kissed her, and told her I preferred living alone, but that one day I'd find the perfect girl to love for ever; and it hadn't even fleetingly occurred to me that when I found her she would be married to someone else.

Sunday came and I went to Clapham: bitter-sweet hours, as ever.

Over lunch I told them tentatively that I'd seen the boy who had tried to kill Calder, and they reacted as strongly as I'd expected, Gordon saying, 'You've told the police, of course,' and Judith adding, 'He's dangerous, Tim.'

I shook my head. 'No. I don't think so. I hope not.' I smiled wryly and told them all about Ricky Barnet and Indian Silk, and the pressure which had led to the try at stabbing. 'I don't think he'll do anything like that again. He's grown so far away from it already that he feels a different person.'

'I hope you're right,' Gordon said.

'Fancy it being Dissdale who bought Indian Silk,' Pen said. 'Isn't it amazing?'

'Especially as he was saying he was short of cash and wanting to sell box-space at Ascot,' Judith added.

'Mm,' I said. 'But after Calder had cured the horse Dissdale sold it again pretty soon, and made a handsome profit, by what I gather.'

'Typical Dissdale behaviour,' Gordon said without criticism. 'Face the risk, stake all you can afford, take the loot if you're lucky, and get out fast.' He smiled. 'By Ascot I guess he'd blown the Indian Silk profit and was back to basics. It doesn't take someone like Dissdale any longer to lose thousands than it does to make them.'

'He must have colossal faith in Calder,' Pen said musingly.

'Not colossal, Pen,' Gordon said. 'Just twice what a knacker would pay for a carcass.'

'Would *you* buy a sick-to-death horse?' Judith asked. 'I mean, if Calder said buy it and I'll cure him, would you believe it?'

Gordon looked at her fondly. 'I'm not Dissdale, darling, and I don't think I'd buy it.'

'And that is precisely,' I pointed out, 'why Fred Barnet lost Indian Silk. He thought Calder's powers were all rubbish and he wouldn't lash out good money to put them to the test. But Dissdale *did*. Bought the horse and presumably also paid Calder . . . who boasted about his success on television and nearly got himself killed for it.'

'Ironic, the whole thing,' Pen said, and we went on discussing it desultorily over coffee.

I stayed until six, when Pen went off to her shop for a Sunday-evening stint and Gordon began to look tired, and I drove back to Hampstead in the usual post-Judith state: half-fulfilled, half-starved.

Towards the end of November, and at Oliver Knowles' invitation, I travelled to another Sunday lunch, this time at the stud farm in Hertfordshire.

It turned out, not surprisingly, to be one of Ginnie's days home from school, and it was she, whistling to Squibs, who set off with me through the yards.

'Did you know we had a hundred and fifty-two mares here all at the same time, back in May?' she said.

'That's a lot,' I said, impressed.

'They had a hundred and fourteen foals between them, and only one of the mares and three of the foals died. That's a terrifically good record, you know.'

'Your father's very skilled.'

'So is Nigel,' she said grudgingly. 'You have to give him his due.'

I smiled at the expression.

'He isn't here just now,' she said. 'He went off to Miami yesterday to lie in the sun.'

'Nigel?'

She nodded. 'He goes about this time every year. Sets him up for the winter, he says.'

'Always Miami?'

'Yes, he likes it.'

The whole atmosphere of the place was back to where I'd known it first, to the slow chill months of gestation. Ginnie, snuggling inside her padded jacket, gave carrots from her pocket to some of the mares in the first yard and walked me without stopping through the empty places, the second yard, the foaling yard, and past the breeding shed.

We came finally as always to the stallion yard where the curiosity of the residents brought their heads out the moment they heard our footsteps. Ginnie distributed carrots and pats with the aplomb of her father, and Sandcastle graciously allowed her to stroke his nose.

'He's quiet now,' she said. 'He's on a much lower diet at this time of year.'

I listened to the bulk of knowledge behind the calm words and I said, 'What are you going to do when you leave school?'

'This, of course.' She patted Sandcastle's neck. 'Help Dad. Be his assistant.'

'Nothing else?'

She shook her head. 'I love the foals. Seeing them

born and watching them grow. I don't want to do anything else, ever.'

We left the stallions and walked between the paddocks with their foals and dams, along the path to the Watcherleys', Squibs trotting on ahead and marking his fence posts. The neighbouring place, whose ramshackle state I'd only glimpsed on my pursuit of the loose five million, proved now to be almost as neat as the parent spread, with much fresh paint in evidence and weeds markedly absent.

'Dad can't bear mess,' Ginnie said when I remarked on the spit-and-polish. 'The Watcherleys are pretty lucky, really, with Dad paying them rent *and* doing up their place *and* employing them to look after the animals in this yard. Bob may still gripe a bit at not being on his own, but Maggie was telling me just last week that she would be everlastingly thankful that Calder Jackson stole their business.'

'He hardly stole it,' I said mildly.

'Well, you know what I mean. Did better at it, if you want to be pedantic.' She grinned. 'Anyway, Maggie's bought some new clothes at last, and I'm glad for her.'

We opened and went into a few of the boxes where she handed out the last of the carrots and fondled the inmates, both mares and growing foals, talking to them, and all of them responded amiably to her touch, nuzzling her gently. She looked at peace and where she belonged, all growing pains suspended.

The Third Year

APRIL

Alec had bought a bunch of yellow tulips when he went out for *What's Going On...*, and they stood on his desk in a beer mug, catching a shaft of spring sunshine and standing straight like guardsmen.

Gordon was making notes in a handwriting growing even smaller, and the two older colleagues were counting the weeks to their retirement. Office life: an ordinary day.

My telephone rang, and with eyes still bent on a letter from a tomato grower asking for more time to repay his original loan because of needing a new green-house (half an acre) right this minute, I slowly picked up the receiver.

'Oliver Knowles,' the voice said. 'Is that you, Tim?'

'Hello,' I replied warmly. 'Everything going well?'

'No.' The word was sickeningly abrupt, and both mentally and physically I sat up straighter.

'What's the matter?'

'Can you come down here?' he asked, not directly answering. 'I'm rather worried. I want to talk to you.'

'Well . . . I could come on Sunday,' I said.

'Could you come today? Or tomorrow?'

I reviewed my workload and a few appointments. 'Tomorrow afternoon, if you like,' I said. 'If it's bank business.'

'Yes, it is.' The anxiety in his voice was quite plain, and communicated itself with much ease to me.

'Can't you tell me what's the trouble?' I asked. 'Is Sandcastle all right?'

'I don't know,' he said. 'I'll tell you when you come.'

'But Oliver . . .'

'Listen,' he said. 'Sandcastle is in good health and he hasn't escaped again or anything like that. It's too difficult to explain on the telephone. I want your advice, that's all.'

He wouldn't say any more and left me with the dead receiver in my hand and some horrid suspenseful question marks in my mind.

'Sandcastle?' Gordon asked.

'Oliver says he's in good health.'

'That horse is insured against everything – those enormous premiums – so don't worry too much,' Gordon said. 'It's probably something minor.'

It hadn't sounded like anything minor, and when I reached the stud farm the next day I found that it certainly wasn't. Oliver came out to meet me as I braked to a standstill by his front door, and there were new deep lines on his face that hadn't been there before.

'Come in,' he said, clasping my hand. 'I'm seriously worried. I don't know what to do.'

He led the way through the house to the office-sitting room and gestured me to a chair. 'Sit down and read this,' he said, and gave me a letter.

There had been no time for 'nice day' or 'how is Ginnie?' introductory noises, just this stark command. I sat down, and I read, as directed.

The letter, dated April 21st, said:

Dear Oliver,

I'm not complaining, because of course one pays one's fee and takes one's chances, but I'm sorry to tell you that the Sandcastle foal out of my mare Spiral Binding has been born with a half of one ear missing. It's a filly, by the way, and I dare say it won't affect her speed, but her looks are ruined.

So sad.

I expect I'll see you one day at the sales.

Yours,

Jane.

'Is that very bad?' I asked, frowning.

In reply he wordlessly handed me another letter. This one said:

Dear Mr Knowles,

You asked me to let you know how my mare Girandette, whom you liked so much, fared on

545

foaling. She gave birth safely to a nice colt foal, but unfortunately he died at six days. We had a post mortem, and it was found that he had malformed heart-valves, like hole-in-the-heart babies.

This is a great blow to me, financially as well as all else, but that's life I suppose.

Yours sincerely,
George Page.

'And now this,' Oliver said, and handed me a third.

The heading was that of a highly regarded and well-known stud farm, the letter briefly impersonal.

Dear Sir,
Filly foal born March 31st to Poppingcorn.
Sire: Sandcastle.
Deformed foot, near fore.
Put down.

I gave him back the letters and with growing misgiving asked, 'How common are these malformations?'

Oliver said intensely, 'They happen. They happen occasionally. But those letters aren't all. I've had two telephone calls – one last night. Two other foals have died of holes in the heart. Two more! That's five with something wrong with them.' He stared at me, his eyes like dark pits. 'That's far too many.' He swallowed. 'And what about the others, the other thirty-five? Suppose . . . suppose there are more . . .'

'If you haven't heard, they're surely all right.'

He shook his head hopelessly. 'The mares are scattered all over the place, dropping Sandcastle's foals where they are due to be bred next. There's no automatic reason for those stud managers to tell me when a foal's born, or what it's like. I mean, some do it out of courtesy but they just don't usually bother, and nor do I. I tell the owner of the mare, not the manager of the stallion.'

'Yes, I see.'

'So there may be other foals with deformities ... that I haven't heard about.'

There was a long fraught pause in which the enormity of the position sank coldly into my banking consciousness. Oliver developed sweat on his forehead and a tic beside his mouth, as if sharing his anxiety had doubled rather than halved it.

The telephone rang suddenly, making us both jump.

'You answer it,' he said. 'Please.'

I opened my mouth to protest that it would be only some routine call about anything else on earth, but then merely picked up the receiver.

'Is that Oliver Knowles?' a voice said.

'No ... I'm his assistant.'

'Oh. Then will you give him a message?'

'Yes, I will.'

'Tell him that Patrick O'Marr rang him from Limballow, Ireland. Have you got that?'

'Yes,' I said. 'Go ahead.'

'It's about a foal we had born here three or four weeks ago. I thought I'd better let Mr Knowles know that we've had to put it down, though I'm sorry to give him bad news. Are you listening?'

'Yes,' I said, feeling hollow.

'The poor little fellow was born with a sort of curled-in hoof. The vet said it might straighten out in a week or two, but it didn't, so we had it X-rayed, and the lower pastern bone and the coffin bone were fused and tiny. The vet said there was no chance of them developing properly, and the little colt would never be able to walk, let alone race. A beautiful little fella too, in all other ways. Anyway, I'm telling Mr Knowles because of course he'll be looking out for Sandcastle's first crop to win for him, and I'm explaining why this one won't be there. Pink Roses, that's the mare's name. Tell him, will you? Pink Roses. She's come here to be bred to Dallaton. Nice mare. She's fine herself, tell Mr Knowles.'

'Yes,' I said. 'I'm very sorry.'

'One of those things.' The cultured Irish accent sounded not too despairing. 'The owner of Pink Roses is cut up about it, of course, but I believe he'd insured against a dead or deformed foal, so it's a case of wait another year and better luck next time.'

'I'll tell Mr Knowles,' I said. 'And thank you for letting us know.'

'Sorry and all,' he said. 'But there it is.'

I put the receiver down slowly and Oliver said dully, 'Another one? Not another one.'

I nodded and told him what Patrick O'Marr had said.

'That's six,' Oliver said starkly. 'And Pink Roses . . . that's the mare you saw Sandcastle cover, this time last year.'

'Was it?' I thought back to that majestic mating, that moment of such promise. Poor little colt, conceived in splendour and born with a club foot.

'What am I going to do?' Oliver said.

'Get out Sandcastle's insurance policy.'

He looked blank. 'No, I mean, about the mares. We have all the mares here who've come this year to Sandcastle. They've all foaled except one and nearly all of them have already been covered. I mean . . . there's another crop already growing, and suppose those . . . suppose all of those . . .' He stopped as if he simply couldn't make his tongue say the words. 'I was awake all night,' he said.

'The first thing,' I said again, 'is to look at that policy.'

He went unerringly to a neat row of files in a cupboard and pulled out the needed document, a many-paged affair, partly printed, partly typed. I spread it open and said to Oliver, 'How about some coffee? This is going to take ages.'

'Oh. All right.' He looked around him vaguely. 'There'll be some put ready for me for dinner. I'll go and plug it in.' He paused. 'Percolator,' he explained.

I knew all the symptoms of a mouth saying one thing while the mind was locked on to another. 'Yes,' I said. 'That would be fine.' He nodded with the same un-meshed mental gears, and I guessed that when he got to the kitchen he'd have trouble remembering what for.

The insurance policy had been written for the trade and not the customer, a matter of jargon-ridden sentences full of words that made plain sense only to people who used them for a living. I read it very care-fully for that reason; slowly and thoroughly from start to finish.

There were many definitions of the word 'accident', with stipulations about the number of veterinary sur-geons who should be consulted and should give their signed opinions before Sandcastle (hereinafter called the horse) could be humanely destroyed for any reason whatsoever. There were stipulations about fractures, naming those bones which should commonly be held to be repairable, and about common muscle, nerve and tendon troubles which would not be considered grounds for destruction, unless of such severity that the horse couldn't actually stand up.

Aside from these restrictions the horse was to be considered to be insured against death from any natural causes whatsoever, to be insured against accidental death occurring while the horse was free (such a contin-gency to be guarded against with diligence, gross negligence being a disqualifying condition), to be insured against death by fire should the stable be consumed, and against death caused maliciously by human hand. He was insured fully against malicious or accidental castration and against such accidental damage being caused by veterinarians acting in good faith to treat the horse. He was insured against infertility on a sliding scale, his full worth being in question only if he proved one hundred per cent infertile (which laboratory tests had shown was not the case).

He was insured against accidental or malicious poisoning and against impotence resulting from non-fatal illness, and against incapacitating or fatal injuries inflicted upon him by any other horse.

He was insured against death caused by the weather (storm, flood, lightning, etc.) and also, surprisingly, against death or incapacity caused by war, riot or civil commotion, causes usually specifically excluded from insurance.

He was insured against objects dropped from the sky and against being driven into by mechanical objects on the ground and against trees falling on him and against hidden wells opening under his feet.

He was insured against every foreseeable disaster except one. He was not insured against being put out of business because of congenital abnormalities among his progeny.

Oliver came back carrying a tray on which sat two kitchen mugs containing tea, not coffee. He put the tray on the desk and looked at my face, which seemed only very slightly to deepen his despair.

'I'm not insured, am I,' he said, 'against possessing a healthy potent stallion to whom no one will send their mares?'

'I don't know.'

'Yes . . . I see you do.' He was shaking slightly. 'When the policy was drawn up about six people, including myself and two vets, besides the insurers themselves, tried to think of every possible contingency, and to guard against it. We threw in everything we could think of.' He swallowed. 'No one . . . no one thought of a whole crop of deformed foals.'

'No,' I said.

'I mean, breeders usually insure their own mares, if they want to, and the foal, to protect the stallion fee, but many don't because of the premiums being high. And I . . . I'm paying this enormous premium . . . and the one thing . . . the one thing that happens is something we never . . . no one ever imagined . . . could happen.'

The policy, I thought, had been too specific. They should have been content with something like 'any factor resulting in the horse not being considered fit for stud purposes'; but perhaps the insurers themselves couldn't find underwriters for anything so open to interpretation and opinion. In any case, the damage was done. All-risk policies all too often were not what they said; and insurance companies never paid out if they could avoid it.

My own skin felt clammy. Three million pounds of the bank's money and two million subscribed by private people were tied up in the horse, and if Oliver couldn't repay, it was we who would lose.

I had recommended the loan. Henry had wanted the adventure and Val and Gordon had been willing, but it was my own report which had carried the day. I couldn't have foreseen the consequences any more than Oliver, but I felt most horribly and personally responsible for the mess.

'What shall I do?' he said again.

'About the mares?'

'And everything else.'

I stared into space. The disaster that for the bank would mean a loss of face and a sharp dip in the profits and to the private subscribers just a painful financial setback meant in effect total ruin for Oliver Knowles.

If Sandcastle couldn't generate income, Oliver would be bankrupt. His business was not a limited company, which meant that he would lose his farm, his horses, his house; everything he possessed. To him too, as to my mother, the bailiffs would come, carrying off his furniture and his treasures and Ginnie's books and toys...

I shook myself mentally and physically and said, 'The first thing to do is nothing. Keep quiet and don't tell anyone what you've told me. Wait to hear if any

more of the foals are ... wrong. I will consult with the
other directors at Ekaterin's and see what can be done
in the way of providing time. I mean ... I'm not
promising ... but we might consider suspending repayments while we look into other possibilities.'

He looked bewildered. 'What possibilities?'

'Well ... of having Sandcastle tested. If the original
tests of his fertility weren't thorough enough, for
instance, it might be possible to show that his sperm
had always been defective in some way, and then the
insurance policy would protect you. Or at least it's a
very good chance.'

The insurers, I thought, might in that case sue the
laboratory that had originally given the fertility all-
clear, but that wasn't Oliver's problem, nor mine. What
did matter was that all of a sudden he looked a fraction
more cheerful, and drank his tea absentmindedly.

'And the mares?' he said.

I shook my head. 'In fairness to their owners you'll
have to say that Sandcastle's off colour.'

'And repay their fees,' he said gloomily.

'Mm.'

'He'll have covered two today,' he said. 'I haven't
mentioned any of this to Nigel. I mean, it's his job to
organize the breeding sessions. He has a great eye for
those mares, he knows when they are feeling receptive.
I leave it to his judgement a good deal, and he told me
this morning that two were ready for Sandcastle. I just
nodded. I felt sick. I didn't tell him.'

'So how many does that leave, er, uncovered?'

He consulted a list, fumbling slightly. 'The one that hasn't foaled, and . . . four others.'

Thirty-five more mares, I thought numbly, could be carrying that seed.

'The mare that hasn't yet foaled,' Oliver said flatly, 'was bred to Sandcastle last year.'

I stared. 'You mean . . . one of his foals will be born *here*?'

'Yes.' He rubbed his hand over his face. 'Any day.'

There were footsteps outside the door and Ginnie came in, saying on a rising, enquiring inflection, 'Dad?'

She saw me immediately and her face lit up. 'Hello! How lovely. I didn't know you were coming.'

I stood up to give her a customarily enthusiastic greeting, but she sensed at once that the action didn't match the climate. 'What's the matter?' She looked into my eyes and then at her father. 'What's happened?'

'Nothing,' he said.

'Dad, you're lying.' She turned again to me. 'Tell me. I can see something bad has happened. I'm not a child any more. I'm seventeen.'

'I thought you'd be at school,' I said.

'I've left. At the end of last term. There wasn't any point in me going back for the summer when all I'm interested in is here.'

She looked far more assured, as if the schooldays had been a chrysalis and she were now the imago, flying free. The beauty she had longed for hadn't quite arrived, but her face was full of character and far from plain, and she would be very much liked, I thought, throughout her life.

'What is it?' she said. 'What's happened?'

Oliver made a small gesture of despair and capitulation. 'You'll have to know sometime.' He swallowed. 'Some of Sandcastle's foals . . . aren't perfect.'

'How do you mean, not perfect?'

He told her about all six and showed her the letters, and she went slowly, swaying, pale. 'Oh Dad, no. No. It can't be. Not Sandcastle. Not that beautiful boy.'

'Sit down,' I said, but she turned to me instead, burying her face against my chest and holding on to me tightly. I put my arms round her and kissed her hair and comforted her for an age as best I could.

I went to the office on the following morning, Friday, and with a slight gritting of teeth told Gordon the outcome of my visit to Oliver.

He said 'My God,' several times, and Alec came over from his desk to listen also, his blue eyes for once solemn behind the gold-rimmed spectacles, the blond eyelashes blinking slowly and the laughing mouth grimly shut.

'What will you do?' he said finally, when I stopped.

'I don't really know.'

Gordon stirred, his hands trembling unnoticed on his blotter in his overriding concern. 'The first thing, I suppose,' he said, 'is to tell Val and Henry. Though what any of us can do is a puzzle. As you said, Tim, we'll have to wait to assess quite how irretrievable the situation is, but I can't imagine anyone with a top-class broodmare having the confidence to send her to Sandcastle in future. Can you, really, Tim? Would *you*?'

I shook my head. 'No.'

'Well, there you are,' Gordon said. 'No one would.'

Henry and Val received the news with undisguised dismay and told the rest of the directors at lunch. The man who had been against the project from the beginning reacted with genuine anger and gave me a furious dressing-down over the grilled sole.

'No one could foresee this,' Henry protested, defending me.

'Anyone could foresee,' said the dissenting director caustically, 'that such a scatterbrained scheme would blow up in our faces. Tim has been given too much power too soon, and it's his judgement that's at fault here, his alone. If he'd had the common nous to recognize the dangers, you would have listened to him and turned the proposal down. It's certainly because of his stupidity and immaturity that the bank is facing this loss, and I shall put my views on record at the next board meeting.'

There were a few uncomfortable murmurs round the table, and Henry with unruffled geniality said, 'We are all to blame, if blame there is, and it is unfair to call Tim stupid for not foreseeing something that escaped the imaginations of all the various experts who drew up the insurance policy.'

The dissenter however repeated his 'I told you so' remarks endlessly through the cheese and coffee, and I sat there depressedly enduring his digs because I wouldn't give him the satisfaction of seeing me leave before he did.

'What will you do next?' Henry asked me, when at long last everyone rather silently stood up to drift back to their desks. 'What do you propose?'

I was grateful that by implication he was leaving me in the position I'd reached and not taking the decisions out of my hands. 'I'm going down to the farm tomorrow,' I said, 'to go through the financial situation. Add up the figures. They're bound to be frightful.'

He nodded with regret. 'Such a marvellous horse. And no one, Tim, whatever anyone says, could have dreamt he'd have such a flaw.'

I sighed. 'Oliver has asked me to stay tomorrow night and Sunday night. I don't really want to, but they do need support.'

'They?'

'Ginnie, his daughter, is with him. She's only just seventeen. It's very hard on them both. Shattering, in fact.'

Henry patted my arm and walked with me to the lift. 'Do what you can,' he said. 'Let us know the full state of affairs on Monday.'

*

558

Before I left home that Saturday morning I had a telephone call from Judith.

'Gordon's told me about Sandcastle. Tim, it's so terrible. Those poor, poor people.'

'Wretched,' I said.

'Tim, tell Ginnie how sorry I am. Sorry . . . how hopeless words are, you say sorry if you bump someone in the supermarket. That dear child . . . she wrote to me a couple of times from school, just asking for feminine information, like I'd told her to.'

'Did she?'

'Yes. She's such a nice girl. So sensible. But this . . . this is too much. Gordon says they're in danger of losing *everything*.'

'I'm going down there today to see where he stands.'

'Gordon told me. Do please give them my love.'

'I will.' I paused fractionally. 'My love to you, too.'

'Tim . . .'

'I just wanted to tell you. It's still the same.'

'We haven't seen you for weeks. I mean . . . I haven't.'

'Is Gordon in the room with you?' I asked.

'Yes, that's right.'

I smiled twistedly. 'I do hear about you, you know,' I said. 'He mentions you quite often, and I ask after you . . . it makes you feel closer.'

'Yes,' she said in a perfectly neutral voice. 'I know exactly what you mean. I feel the same about it exactly.'

'Judith . . .' I took a breath and made my own voice

calm to match hers. 'Tell Gordon I'll telephone him at home, if he'd like, if there is anything that needs consultation before Monday.'

'I'll tell him. Hang on.' I heard her repeating the question and Gordon's distant rumble of an answer, and then she said, 'Yes, he says please do, we'll be at home this evening and most of tomorrow.'

'Perhaps you'll answer when the telephone rings.'

'Perhaps.'

After a brief silence I said, 'I'd better go.'

'Goodbye then, Tim,' she said. 'And do let us know. We'll both be thinking of you all day, I know we will.'

'I'll call,' I said. 'You can count on it.'

The afternoon was on the whole as miserable as I'd expected and in some respects worse. Oliver and Ginnie walked about like pale automatons making disconnected remarks and forgetting where they'd put things, and lunch, Ginnie version, had consisted of eggs boiled too hard and packets of potato crisps.

'We haven't told Nigel or the lads what's happening,' Oliver said. 'Fortunately there is a lull in Sandcastle's programme. He's been very busy because nearly all his mares foaled in mid-March, close together, except for four and the one who's still carrying.' He swallowed. 'And the other stallions, of course, their mares are all here too, and we have their foals to deliver and their

matings to be seen to. I mean . . . we have to go on.
We have to.'

Towards four o'clock they both went out into the
yards for evening stables, visibly squaring their
shoulders to face the stable hands in a normal manner,
and I began adding the columns of figures I'd drawn
up from Oliver's records.

The tally when I'd finished was appalling and meant
that Oliver could be an undischarged bankrupt for the
rest of his life. I put the results away in my briefcase
and tried to think of something more constructive; and
Oliver's telephone rang.

'Oliver?' a voice said, sounding vaguely familiar.

'He's out,' I said. 'Can I take a message?'

'Get him to ring me. Ursula Young. I'll give you the
number.'

'Ursula!' I said in surprise. 'This is Tim Ekaterin.'

'Really?' For her it was equally unexpected. 'What
are *you* doing there?'

'Just staying the weekend. Can I help?'

She hesitated slightly but then said, 'Yes, I suppose
you can. I'm afraid it's bad news for him, though. Disappointing, you might say.' She paused. 'I've a friend
who has a small stud farm, just one stallion, but quite
a good one, and she's been so excited this year because
one of the mares booked to him was in foal to Sandcastle. She was thrilled, you see, to be having a foal of
that calibre born on her place.'

'Yes,' I said.

'Well, she rang me this morning, and she was crying.'
Ursula herself gulped: she might appear tough but
other people's tears always moved her. 'She said the
mare had dropped the Sandcastle foal during the night
and she hadn't been there. She said the mare gave no
sign yesterday evening, and the birth must have been
quick and easy, and the mare was all right, but . . .'

'But what?' I said, scarcely breathing.

'She said the foal – a filly – was on her feet and
suckling when she went to the mare's box this morning,
and at first she was overjoyed, but then . . . but then . . .'

'Go on,' I said hopelessly.

'Then she saw. She says it's dreadful.'

'Ursula . . .'

'The foal has only one eye.'

Oh my God, I thought: dear *God*.

'She says there's nothing on the other side,' Ursula
said. 'No proper socket.' She gulped again. 'Will you
tell Oliver? I thought he'd better know. He'll be most
disappointed. I'm so sorry.'

'I'll tell him.'

'These things happen, I suppose,' she said. 'But it's
so upsetting when they happen to your friends.'

'You're very right.'

'Goodbye then, Tim. See you soon, I hope, at the
races.'

I put down the receiver and wondered how I would
ever tell them, and in fact I didn't tell Ginnie, only

Oliver, who sat with his head in his hands, despair in every line of his body.

'It's hopeless,' he said.

'Not yet,' I said encouragingly, though I wasn't as certain as I sounded. 'There are still the tests to be done on Sandcastle.'

He merely slumped lower. 'I'll get them done, but they won't help. The genes which are wrong will be minute. No one will see them, however powerful the microscope.'

'You can't tell. If they can see DNA, why not a horse's chromosomes?'

He raised his head slowly. 'Even then . . . it's such a long shot.' He sighed deeply. 'I think I'll ask the Equine Research Establishment at Newmarket to have him there, to see what they can find. I'll ring them on Monday.'

'I suppose,' I said tentatively. 'Well, I know it sounds silly, but I suppose it couldn't be anything as simple as something he'd *eaten*? Last year, of course.'

He shook his head. 'I thought of that. I've thought of bloody well everything, believe me. All the stallions had the same food, and none of the others' foals are affected . . . or at least we haven't heard of any. Nigel feeds the stallions himself out of the feed room in that yard, and we're always careful what we give them because of keeping them fit.'

'Carrots?' I said.

'I give carrots to every horse on the place. Everyone

here does. Carrots are good food. I buy them by the hundredweight and keep them in the first big yard where the main feed room is. I put handfuls in my pockets every day. You've seen me. Rotaboy, Diarist and Parakeet all had them. It can't possibly be anything to do with carrots.'

'Paint: something like that? Something new in the boxes, when you put in all the security? Something he could chew?'

He again shook his head. 'I've been over it and over it. We did all the boxes exactly the same as each other. There's nothing in Sandcastle's box that wasn't in the others. They're all exactly alike.' He moved restlessly. 'I've been down there to make sure there's nothing Sandcastle could reach to lick if he put his head right over the half-door as far as he could get. There's nothing, nothing at all.'

'Drinking pails?'

'No. They don't always have the same pails. I mean, when Lenny fills them he doesn't necessarily take them back to the particular boxes they come from. The pails don't have the stallions' names on, if that's what you mean.'

I didn't mean anything much: just grabbing at straws.

'Straw . . .' I said. 'How about an allergy? An allergy to something around him? Could an allergy have such an effect?'

'I've never heard of anything like that. I'll ask the Research people, though, on Monday.'

He got up to pour us both a drink. 'It's good to have you here,' he said. 'A sort of net over the bottomless pit.' He gave me the glass with a faint half-smile, and I had a definite impression that he would not in the end go to pieces.

I telephoned then to the Michaels' house and Gordon answered at the first ring as if he'd been passing near by. Nothing good to report, I said, except that Ginnie sent Judith her love. Gordon said Judith was in the garden picking parsley for supper, and he would tell her. 'Call tomorrow,' he said, 'if we can help.'

Our own supper, left ready in the refrigerator by Oliver's part-time housekeeper, filled the hollows left by lunch, and Ginnie went to bed straight afterwards, saying she would be up at two o'clock and out with Nigel in the foal yard.

'She goes most nights,' Oliver said. 'She and Nigel make a good team. He says she's a great help, particularly if three or four mares are foaling at the same time. I'm often out there myself, but with all the decisions and paperwork as well I get very tired if I do it too much. Fall asleep over meals, that sort of thing.'

We ourselves went to bed fairly early, and I awoke in the large high-ceilinged guest room while it was still blackly dark. It was one of those fast awakenings which mean that sleep won't come back easily, and I got out of bed and went to the window, which looked out over the yard.

I could see only roofs and security lights and a small

section of the first yard. There was no visible activity, and my watch showed four-thirty.

I wondered if Ginnie would mind if I joined her in the foaling yard; and got dressed and went.

They were all there, Nigel and Oliver as well as Ginnie, all in one open-doored box where a mare lay on her side on the straw. They all turned their heads as I approached but seemed unsurprised to see me and gave no particular greeting.

'This is Plus Factor,' Oliver said. 'In foal to Sandcastle.'

His voice was calm and so was Ginnie's manner, and I guessed that they still hadn't told Nigel about the deformities. There was hope, too, in their faces, as if they were sure that this one, after all, would be perfect.

'She's coming,' Nigel said quietly. 'Here we go.'

The mare gave a grunt and her swelling sides heaved. The rest of us stood silent, watching, taking no part. A glistening half-transparent membrane with a hoof showing within it appeared, followed by the long slim shape of the head, followed very rapidly by the whole foal, flopping out onto the straw, steaming, the membrane breaking open, the fresh air reaching the head, new life beginning with the first fluttering gasp of the lungs.

Amazing, I thought.

'Is he all right?' Oliver said, bending down, the anxiety raw, unstifled.

'Sure,' Nigel said. 'Fine little colt. Just his foreleg's doubled over . . .'

He knelt beside the foal who was already making the first feeble efforts to move his head, and he stretched out both hands gently to free the bent leg fully from the membrane, and to straighten it. He picked it up . . . and froze.

We could all see.

The leg wasn't bent. It ended in a stump at the knee. No cannon bone, no fetlock, no hoof.

Ginnie beside me gave a choking sob and turned abruptly towards the open door, towards the dark. She took one rocky pace and then another, and then was running: running nowhere, running away from the present, the future, the unimaginable. From the hopeless little creature on the straw.

I went after her, listening to her footsteps, hearing them on gravel and then losing them, guessing she had reached the grass. I went more slowly in her wake down the path to the breeding pen, not seeing her, but sure she was out somewhere in the paths round the paddocks. With eyes slowly acclimatizing I went that way and found her not far off, on her knees beside one of the posts, sobbing with the deep sound of a wholly adult desperation.

'Ginnie,' I said.

She stood up as if to turn to me was natural and clung to me fiercely, her body shaking from the sobs, her face pressed hard against my shoulder, my arms tightly round her. We stood like that until the paroxysm passed; until, dragging a handkerchief from her jeans, she could speak.

'It's one thing knowing it in theory,' she said, her voice full of tears and her body still shaking spasmodically from aftersobs. 'I read those letters. I did know. But *seeing* it . . . that's different.'

'Yes,' I said.

'And it means . . .' She took gulps of air, trying hard for control. 'It means, doesn't it, that we'll lose our farm. Lose everything?'

'I don't know yet. Too soon to say that.'

'Poor Dad.' The tears were sliding slowly down her cheeks, but like harmless rain after a hurricane. 'I don't see how we can bear it.'

'Don't despair yet. If there's a way to save you, we'll find it.'

'Do you mean . . . your bank?'

'I mean everybody.'

She wiped her eyes and blew her nose, and finally moved away a pace, out of my arms, strong enough to leave shelter. We went slowly back to the foaling yard and found nobody there except horses. I undid the closed top half of Plus Factor's box and looked inside; looked at the mare standing there patiently without her foal and wondered if she felt any fretting sense of loss.

'Dad and Nigel have taken him, haven't they?' Ginnie said.

'Yes.'

She nodded, accepting that bit easily. Death to her was part of life, as to every child brought up close to animals. I closed Plus Factor's door and Ginnie and I went back to the house while the sky lightened in the east to the new day, Sunday.

The work of the place went on.

Oliver telephoned to various owners of the mares who had come to the other three stallions, reporting the birth of foals alive and well and one dead before foaling, very sorry. His voice sounded strong, civilized, controlled, the competent captain at the helm, and one could almost see the steel creeping back, hour by hour, into his battered spirit. I admired him for it; and I would fight to give him time, I thought, to come to some compromise to avert permanent ruin.

Ginnie, showered, breakfasted, tidy in sweater and shirt, went off to spend the morning at the Watcherleys' and came back smiling; the resilience of youth.

'Both of those mares are better from their infections,' she reported, 'and Maggie says she's heard Calder Jackson's not doing so well lately, his yard's half empty. Cheers Maggie up no end, she says.'

For the Watcherleys too, I thought briefly, the fall of Oliver's business could mean a return to rust and weeds, but I said, 'Not enough sick horses just now, perhaps.'

'Not enough sick horses with rich owners, Maggie says.'

In the afternoon Ginnie slept on the sofa looking very childlike and peaceful, and only with the awakening did the night's pain roll back.

'Oh dear . . .' The slow tears came. 'I was dreaming it was all right. That that foal was a dream, only a dream . . .'

'You and your father,' I said, 'are brave people.'

She sniffed a little, pressing against her nose with the back of her hand. 'Do you mean,' she said slowly, 'that whatever happens, we mustn't be defeated?'

'Mm.'

She looked at me, and after a while nodded. 'If we have to, we'll start again. We'll work. He did it all before, you know.'

'You both have the skills,' I said.

'I'm glad you came.' She brushed the drying tears from her cheeks. 'God knows what it would have been like without you.'

I went with her out into the yards for evening stables, where the muck-carrying and feeding went on as always. Ginnie fetched the usual pocketful of carrots from the feed room and gave them here and there to the mares, talking cheerfully to the lads while they bent to their chores. No one, watching and listening, could ever have imagined that she feared the sky was falling.

'Evening, Chris, how's her hoof today?'

'Hi, Danny. Did you bring this one in this morning?'

'Hello, Pete. She looks as if she'll foal any day now.'

'Evening, Shane. How's she doing?'

'Hi, Sammy, is she eating now OK?'

The lads answered her much as they spoke to Oliver himself, straightforwardly and with respect, and in most cases without stopping what they were doing. I looked back as we left the first big yard for the second, and for a moment took one of the lads to be Ricky Barnet.

'Who's that?' I said to Ginnie.

She followed my gaze to where the lad walked across to the yard tap, swinging an empty bucket with one hand and eating an apple with the other.

'Shane. Why?'

'He reminded me of someone I knew.'

She shrugged. 'He's all right. They all are, when Nigel's looking, which he doesn't do often enough.'

'He works all night,' I said mildly.

'I suppose so.'

The mares in the second yard had mostly given birth already and Ginnie that evening had special eyes for the foals. The lads hadn't yet reached those boxes and Ginnie didn't go into any of them, warning me that mares with young foals could be protective and snappy.

'You never know if they'll bite or kick you. Dad doesn't like me going in with them alone.' She smiled. 'He still thinks I'm a baby.'

We went on to the foaling yard, where a lad greeted as Dave was installing a heavy slow-walking mare into one of the boxes.

'Nigel says she'll foal tonight,' he told Ginnie.

'He's usually right.'

We went on past the breeding pen and came to the stallions, where Larry and Ron were washing down Diarist (who appeared to have been working) in the centre of the yard, using a lot of water, energy and oaths.

'Mind his feet,' Larry said. 'He's in one of his moods.'

Ginnie gave carrots to Parakeet and Rotaboy, and we came finally to Sandcastle. He looked as great, as charismatic as ever, but Ginnie gave him his tit-bit with her own lips compressed.

'He can't help it all, I suppose,' she said sighing. 'But I do wish he'd never won any races.'

'Or that we'd let him die that day on the main road?'

'Oh no!' She was shocked. 'We couldn't have done that, even if we'd known . . .'

Dear girl, I thought; many people would personally have mown him down with a truck.

We went back to the house via the paddocks, where she fondled any heads that came to the railings and parted with the last of the crunchy orange goodies. 'I can't believe that this will all end,' she said, looking over the horse-dotted acres. 'I just *can't* believe it.'

I tentatively suggested to both her and Oliver that they might prefer it if I went home that evening, but they both declared themselves against.

'Not yet,' Ginnie said anxiously and Oliver nodded forcefully. 'Please do stay, Tim, if you can.'

I nodded, and rang the Michaels, and this time got Judith.

'Do let me speak to her,' Ginnie said, taking the receiver out of my hand. 'I do so want to.'

And I, I thought wryly, I too want so much to talk to her, to hear her voice, to renew my own soul through her: I'm no one's universal pillar of strength, I need my comfort too.

I had my crumbs, after Ginnie. Ordinary words, all else implied; as always.

'Take care of yourself,' she said finally.

'You, too,' I said.

'Yes.' The word was a sigh, faint and receding, as if she'd said it with the receiver already away from her mouth. There was the click of disconnection, and Oliver was announcing briskly that it was time for whisky, time for supper; time for anything perhaps but thinking.

Ginnie decided that she felt too restless after supper to go to bed early, and would go for a walk instead.

'Do you want me to come?' I said.

'No. I'm all right. I just thought I'd go out. Look at the stars.' She kissed her father's forehead, pulling on a thick cardigan for warmth. 'I won't go off the farm. You'll probably find me in the foal yard, if you want me.'

He nodded to her fondly but absentmindedly, and with a small wave to me she went away. Oliver asked me gloomily, as if he'd been waiting for us to be alone, how soon I thought the bank would decide on his fate, and we talked in snatches about his daunting prospects, an hour or two sliding by on possibilities.

Shortly before ten, when we had probably twice repeated all there was to say, there came a heavy hammering on the back door.

'Whoever's that?' Oliver frowned, rose to his feet and went to find out.

I didn't hear the opening words, but only the goose-pimpling urgency in the rising voice.

'She's where?' Oliver said loudly, plainly, in alarm. 'Where?'

I went quickly into the hallway. One of the lads stood in the open doorway, panting for breath, wide-eyed and looking very scared.

Oliver glanced at me over his shoulder, already on the move. 'He says Ginnie's lying on the ground unconscious.'

The lad turned and ran off, with Oliver following and myself close behind; and the lad's breathlessness, I soon found, was owing to Ginnie's being on the far side of the farm, away down beyond Nigel's bungalow and the lads' hostel, right down on the far drive, near the gate to the lower road.

We arrived there still running, the lad now doubling over in his fight for breath, and found Ginnie lying on her side on the hard asphalt surface with another of the lads on his knees beside her, dim figures in weak moonlight, blurred outlines of shadow.

Oliver and I too knelt there and Oliver was saying

to the lads, 'What happened, what happened? Did she fall?'

'We just found her,' the kneeling lad said. 'We were on our way back from the pub. She's coming round, though, sir, she's been saying things.'

Ginnie in fact moved slightly, and said, 'Dad.'

'Yes, Ginnie, I'm here.' He picked up her hand and patted it. 'We'll soon get you right.' There was relief in his voice, but short-lived.

'Dad,' Ginnie said, mumbling. 'Dad.'

'Yes, I'm here.'

'Dad . . .'

'She isn't hearing you,' I said worriedly.

He turned his head to me, his eyes liquid in the dark of his face. 'Get an ambulance. There's a telephone in Nigel's house. Tell him to get an ambulance here quickly. I don't think we'll move her . . . Get a blanket.'

I stood up to go on the errand but the breathless lad said, 'Nigel's out. I tried there. There's no one. It's all locked.'

'I'll go back to the house.'

I ran as fast on the way back and had to fight to control my own gulping breaths there to make my words intelligible. 'Tell them to take the lower road from the village . . . the smaller right fork . . . where the road divides. Nearly a mile from there . . . wide metal farm gate, on the left.'

'Understood,' a man said impersonally. 'They'll be on their way.'

I fetched the padded quilt off my bed and ran back across the farm and found everything much as I'd left it. 'They're coming,' I said. 'How is she?'

Oliver tucked the quilt round his daughter as best he could. 'She keeps saying things. Just sounds, not words.'

'Da—' Ginnie said.

Her eyelids trembled and slightly opened.

'Ginnie,' Oliver said urgently. 'This is Dad.'

Her lips moved in a mumbling unformed murmur. The eyes looked at nothing, unfocused, the gleam just reflected moonlight, not an awakening.

'Oh God,' Oliver said. 'What's happened to her? What can have happened?'

The two lads stood there, awkward and silent, not knowing the answer.

'Go and open the gate,' Oliver told them. 'Stand on the road. Signal to the ambulance when it comes.'

They went as if relieved; and the ambulance did come, lights flashing, with two brisk men in uniform who lifted Ginnie without much disturbing her onto a stretcher. Oliver asked them to wait while he fetched the Land Rover from Nigel's garage, and in a short time the ambulance set off to the hospital with Oliver and me following.

'Lucky you had the key,' I said, indicating it in the ignition. Just something to say: anything.

'We always keep it in that tin on the shelf.'

The tin said 'Blackcurrant Coughdrops. Take as Required'.

Oliver drove automatically, following the rear lights ahead. 'Why don't they go faster?' he said, though their speed was quite normal.

'Don't want to jolt her, perhaps.'

'Do you think it's a stroke?' he said.

'She's too young.'

'No. I had a cousin . . . an aneurysm burst when he was sixteen.'

I glanced at his face: lined, grim, intent on the road.

The journey seemed endless, but ended at a huge bright hospital in a sprawling town. The men in uniform opened the rear doors of the ambulance while Oliver parked the Land Rover and we followed them into the brightly lit emergency reception area, seeing them wheel Ginnie into a curtained cubicle, watching them come out again with their stretcher, thanking them as they left.

A nurse told us to sit on some nearby chairs while she fetched a doctor. The place was empty, quiet, all readiness but no bustle. Ten o'clock on Sunday night.

A doctor came in a white coat, stethoscope dangling. An Indian, young, black-haired, rubbing his eyes with forefinger and thumb. He went behind the curtains with the nurse and for about a minute Oliver clasped and unclasped his fingers, unable to contain his anxiety.

The doctor's voice reached us clearly, the Indian accent making no difference.

'They shouldn't have brought her here,' he said. 'She's dead.'

Oliver was on his feet, bounding across the shining floor, pulling back the curtains with a frantic sweep of the arm.

'She's not dead. She was talking. Moving. She's not dead.'

In dread I followed him. She couldn't be dead, not like that, not so fast, not without the hospital fighting long to save her. She *couldn't* be.

The doctor straightened up from bending over her, withdrawing his hand from under Ginnie's head, looking at us across the small space.

'She's my daughter,' Oliver said. 'She's not dead.'

A sort of weary compassion drooped in the doctor's shoulders. 'I am sorry,' he said. 'Very sorry. She is gone.'

'No!' The word burst out of Oliver in an agony. 'You're wrong. Get someone else.'

The nurse made a shocked gesture but the young doctor said gently, 'There is no pulse. No heartbeat. No contraction of the pupils. She has been gone for perhaps ten minutes, perhaps twenty. I could get someone else, but there is nothing to be done.'

'But *why*?' Oliver said. 'She was talking.'

The dark doctor looked down to where Ginnie was lying on her back, eyes closed, brown hair falling about her head, face very pale. Her jerseys had both been unbuttoned for the stethoscope, the white bra showing, and the nurse had also undone the waistband of the skirt, pulling it loose. Ginnie looked very young, very defenceless, lying there so quiet and still, and I stood numbly, not believing it, unable, like Oliver, to accept such a monstrous change.

'Her skull is fractured,' the doctor said. 'If she was talking, she died on the way here, in the ambulance. With head injuries it can be like that. I am sorry.'

There was a sound of an ambulance's siren wailing outside, and sudden noise and rushing people by the doors where we had come in, voices raised in a jumble of instructions.

'Traffic accident,' someone shouted, and the doctor's eyes moved beyond us to the new need, to the future, not the past.

'I must go,' he said, and the nurse, nodding, handed me a flat white plastic bottle which she had been holding.

'You may as well take this,' she said. 'It was tucked into the waistband of her skirt, against the stomach.'

She made as if to cover Ginnie with a sheet, but Oliver stopped her.

'I'll do it,' he said. 'I want to be with her.'

The young doctor nodded, and he and I and the nurse stepped outside the cubicle, drawing the curtains behind us. The doctor looked in a brief pause of stillness towards the three or four stretchers arriving at the entrance, taking a breath, seeming to summon up energy from deep reserves.

'I've been on duty for thirty hours,' he said to me. 'And now the pubs are out. Ten o'clock, Sundays. Drunk drivers, drunk pedestrians. Always the same.'

He walked away to his alive and bleeding patients and the nurse pinned a 'Do Not Enter' sign onto the curtains of Ginnie's cubicle, saying she would be taken care of later.

I sat drearily on a chair, waiting for Oliver. The white plastic bottle had a label stuck onto one side saying 'Shampoo'. I put it into my jacket pocket and wondered if it was just through overwork that the doctor hadn't asked how Ginnie's skull had been fractured, asked whether she'd fallen onto a rock or a kerb . . . or been hit.

The rest of the night and all the next day were in their own way worse, a truly awful series of questions, answers, forms and officialdom, with the police slowly taking over from the hospital and Oliver trying to fight against a haze of grief.

It seemed to me wicked that no one would leave him alone. To them he was just one more in a long line of bereaved persons, and although they treated him with perfunctory sympathy, it was for their own paperwork and not for his benefit that they wanted signature, information and guesses.

Large numbers of policemen descended on the farm early in the morning, and it gradually appeared that that area of the country was being plagued by a stalker of young girls who jumped out of bushes, knocked them unconscious and sexually assaulted them.

'Not Ginnie . . .' Oliver protested in deepening horror.

The most senior of the policemen shook his head. 'It would appear not. She was still wearing her clothing. We can't discount, though, that it was the same man, and that he was disturbed by your grooms. When young girls are knocked unconscious at night, it's most often a sexual attack.'

'But she was on my own land,' he said, disbelieving.

The policeman shrugged. 'It's been known in suburban front gardens.'

He was a fair-haired man with a manner that was not exactly brutal but spoke of long years of acclimatization to dreadful experiences. Detective Chief Inspector Wyfold, he'd said, introducing himself. Forty-fiveish, I guessed, sensing the hardness within him at sight and judging him through that day more dogged than intuitive, looking for results from procedure, not hunches.

He was certain in his own mind that the attack on Ginnie had been sexual in intent and he scarcely considered anything else, particularly since she'd been carrying no money and had expressly said she wouldn't leave the farm.

581

'She could have talked to someone over the gate,' he said, having himself spent some time on the lower drive. 'Someone walking along the road. And there are all your grooms that we'll need detailed statements from, though from their preliminary answers it seems they weren't in the hostel but down at the village, in the pubs.'

He came and went and reappeared again with more questions at intervals through the day and I lost track altogether of the hours. I tried, in his presence and out, and in Oliver's the same, not to think much about Ginnie herself. I thought I would probably have wept if I had, of no use to anyone. I thrust her away into a defensive compartment knowing that later, alone, I would let her out.

Some time in the morning one of the lads came to the house and asked what they should do about one of the mares who was having difficulty foaling, and Lenny also arrived wanting to know when he should take Rotaboy to the breeding pen. Each of them stood awkwardly, not knowing where to put their hands, saying they were so shocked, so sorry, about Ginnie.

'Where's Nigel?' Oliver said.

They hadn't seen him, they said. He hadn't been out in the yards that morning.

'Didn't you try his house?' Oliver was annoyed rather than alarmed: another burden on a breaking back.

'He isn't there. The door's locked and he didn't answer.'

Oliver frowned, picked up the telephone and pressed the buttons: listened; no reply.

He said to me, 'There's a key to his bungalow over there on the board, third hook from the left. Would you go and look . . . would you mind?'

'Sure.'

I walked down there with Lenny who told me repeatedly how broken up the lads were over what had happened, particularly Dave and Sammy, who'd found her. They'd all liked her, he said. All the lads who lived in the hostel were saying that perhaps if they'd come back sooner, she wouldn't have been attacked.

'You don't live in the hostel, then?' I said.

'No. Down in the village. Got a house. Only the ones who come just for the season, they're the ones in the hostel. It's shut up, see, all winter.'

We eventually reached Nigel's bungalow where I rang the doorbell and banged on the knocker without result. Shaking my head slightly I fitted the key in the lock, opened the door, went in.

Curtains were drawn across the windows, shutting out a good deal of daylight. I switched on a couple of lights and walked into the sitting room, where papers, clothes and dirty cups and plates were strewn haphazardly and the air smelled faintly of horse.

There was no sign of Nigel. I looked into the equally untidy kitchen and opened a door which proved to be

583

that of a bathroom and another which revealed a room with bare-mattressed twin beds. The last door in the small inner hall led into Nigel's own bedroom . . . and there he was, face down, fully clothed, lying across the counterpane.

Lenny, still behind me, took two paces back.

I went over to the bed and felt Nigel's neck behind the ear. Felt the pulse going like a steam-hammer. Heard the rasp of air in the throat. His breath would have an anaesthetized a crocodile, and on the floor beside him lay an empty bottle of gin. I shook his shoulder unsympathetically with a complete lack of result.

'He's drunk,' I said to Lenny. 'Just drunk.'

Lenny looked all the same as if he was about to vomit. 'I thought . . . I thought.'

'I know,' I said; and I'd feared it also, instinctively, the one because of the other.

'What will we do, then, out in the yard?' Lenny asked.

'I'll find out.'

We went back into the sitting room where I used Nigel's telephone to call Oliver and report.

'He's flat out,' I said. 'I can't wake him. Lenny wants instructions.'

After a brief silence Oliver said dully, 'Tell him to take Rotaboy to the breeding shed in half an hour. I'll see to things in the yards. And Tim?'

'Yes?'

'Can I ask you ... would you mind ... helping me here in the office?'

'Coming straight back.'

The disjointed, terrible day wore on. I telephoned to Gordon in the bank explaining my absence and to Judith also, at Gordon's suggestion, to pass on the heartbreak, and I took countless incoming messages as the news spread. Outside on the farm nearly two hundred horses got fed and watered, and birth and procreation went inexorably on.

Oliver came back stumbling from fatigue at about two o'clock, and we ate some eggs, not tasting them, in the kitchen. He looked repeatedly at his watch and said finally, 'What's eight hours back from now? I can't even *think*.'

'Six in the morning,' I said.

'Oh.' He rubbed a hand over his face. 'I suppose I should have told Ginnie's mother last night.' His face twisted. 'My wife ... in Canada ...' He swallowed. 'Never mind, let her sleep. In two hours I'll tell her.'

I left him alone to that wretched task and took myself upstairs to wash and shave and lie for a while on the bed. It was in taking my jacket off for those purposes that I came across the plastic bottle in my pocket, and I took it out and stood it on the shelf in the bathroom while I shaved.

An odd sort of thing, I thought, for Ginnie to have tucked into her waistband. A plastic bottle of shampoo; about six inches high, four across, one deep, with a screw cap on one of the narrow ends. The white label saying 'Shampoo' had been handwritten and stuck on top of the bottle's original dark brown, white-printed label, of which quite a bit still showed round the edges.

'*Instructions*,' part of the underneath label said. '*Shake well. Be careful not to get the shampoo in the dog's eyes. Rub well into the coat and leave for ten or fifteen minutes before rinsing.*'

At the bottom, below the stuck-on label, were the words, in much smaller print, '*Manufactured by Eagle Inc., Michigan, U.S.A. List number 29931.*'

When I'd finished shaving I unscrewed the cap and tilted the bottle gently over the basin.

A thick greenish liquid appeared, smelling powerfully of soap.

Shampoo: what else?

The bottle was to all intents full. I screwed on the cap again and put it on the shelf, and thought about it while I lay on the bed with my hands behind my head.

Shampoo for dogs.

After a while I got up and went down to the kitchen, and in a high cupboard found a small collection of empty, washed, screw-top glass jars, the sort of thing my mother had always saved for herbs and picnics. I took one which would hold perhaps a cupful of liquid and returned upstairs, and over the washbasin I shook the bottle well, unscrewed the cap and carefully poured more than half of the shampoo into the jar.

I screwed the caps onto both the bottle and the

jar, copied what could be seen on the original label into the small engagement diary I carried with me everywhere, and stowed the now half full, round glass container from Oliver's kitchen inside my own sponge-bag; and when I went downstairs again I took the plastic bottle with me.

'Ginnie had it?' Oliver said dully, picking it up and squinting at it. 'Whatever for?'

'The nurse at the hospital said it was tucked into the waistband of her skirt.'

A smile flickered. 'She always did that when she was little. Plimsolls, books, bits of string, anything. To keep her hands free, she said. They all used to slip down into her little knickers, and there would be a whole shower of things sometimes when we undressed her.' His face went hopelessly bleak at this memory. 'I can't believe it, you know,' he said. 'I keep thinking she'll walk through the door.' He paused. 'My wife is flying over. She says she'll be here tomorrow morning.' His voice gave no indication as to whether that was good news or bad. 'Stay tonight, will you?'

'If you want.'

'Yes.'

Chief Inspector Wyfold turned up again at that point and we gave him the shampoo bottle, Oliver explaining about Ginnie's habit of carrying things in her clothes.

'Why didn't you give this to me earlier?' he asked me.

'I forgot I had it. It seemed so paltry at the time, compared with Ginnie dying.'

The Chief Inspector picked up the bottle by its serrated cap and read what one could see of the label, and to Oliver he said, 'Do you have a dog?'

'Yes.'

'Would this be what you usually use, to wash him?'

'I really don't know. I don't wash him myself. One of the lads does.'

'The lads being the grooms?'

'That's right.'

'Which lad washed your dog?' Wyfold asked.

'Um . . . any. Whoever I ask.'

The Chief Inspector produced a thin white folded paper bag from one of his pockets and put the bottle inside it. 'Who to your knowledge has handled this, besides yourselves?' he asked.

'I suppose,' I said, 'the nurse at the hospital . . . and Ginnie.'

'And it spent from last night until now in your pocket?' He shrugged. 'Hopeless for prints, I should think, but we'll try.' He fastened the bag shut and wrote on a section of it with a ball pen. To Oliver, almost as an aside, he said, 'I came to ask you about your daughter's relationship with men.'

Oliver said wearily, 'She didn't have any. She's only just left school.'

Wyfold made small negative movements with head

and hands as if amazed at the naivety of fathers. 'No sexual relationship to your knowledge?'

Oliver was too exhausted for anger. 'No,' he said.

'And you sir?' He turned to me. 'What were your relations with Virginia Knowles?'

'Friendship.'

'Including sexual intercourse?'

'No.'

Wyfold looked at Oliver who said tiredly, 'Tim is a business friend of mine. A financial adviser, staying here for the weekend, that's all.'

The policeman frowned at me with disillusion as if he didn't believe it. I gave him no amplified answer because I simply couldn't be bothered, and what could I have said? That with much affection I'd watched a child grow into an attractive young woman and yet not wanted to sleep with her? His mind ran on carnal rails, all else discounted.

He went away in the end taking the shampoo with him, and Oliver with immense fortitude said he had better go out into the yards to catch the tail end of evening stables. 'Those mares,' he said. 'Those foals . . . they still need the best of care.'

'I wish I could help,' I said, feeling useless.

'You do.'

I went with him on his rounds, and when we reached the foaling yard, Nigel, resurrected, was there.

His stocky figure leaned against the doorpost of an open box as if without its support he would collapse, and the face he slowly turned towards us had aged ten years. The bushy eyebrows stood out starkly over charcoal shadowed eyes, puffiness in his skin swelling the eyelids and sagging in deep bags on his cheeks. He was also unshaven, unkempt and feeling ill.

'Sorry,' he said. 'Heard about Ginnie. Very sorry.' I wasn't sure whether he was sympathizing with Oliver or apologizing for the drunkenness. 'A big noise of a policeman came asking if I'd killed her. As if I would.' He put a shaky hand on his head, almost as if physically to support it on his shoulders. 'I feel rotten. My own fault. Deserve it. This mare's likely to foal tonight. That shit of a policeman wanted to know if I was sleeping with Ginnie. Thought I'd tell you . . . I wasn't.'

Wyfold, I reflected, would ask each of the lads individually the same question. A matter of time, perhaps, before he asked Oliver himself; though Oliver and I, he had had to concede, gave each other a rock-solid alibi.

We walked on towards the stallions and I asked Oliver if Nigel often got drunk, since Oliver hadn't shown much surprise.

'Very seldom,' Oliver said. 'He's once or twice turned out in that state but we've never lost a foal because of it. I don't like it, but he's so good with the mares.' He shrugged. 'I overlook it.'

He gave carrots to all four stallions but scarcely glanced at Sandcastle, as if he could no longer bear the sight.

'I'll try the Research people tomorrow,' he said. 'Forgot about it, today.'

From the stallions he went, unusually, in the direction of the lower gate, past Nigel's bungalow and the hostel, to stand for a while at the place where Ginnie had lain in the dark on the night before.

The asphalt driveway showed no mark. Oliver looked to where the closed gate sixty feet away led to the road and in a drained voice said, 'Do you think she could have talked to someone out there?'

'She might have, I suppose.'

'Yes.' He turned to go back. 'It's all so *senseless*. And unreal. Nothing feels real.'

Exhaustion of mind and body finally overtook him after dinner and he went grey-faced to bed, but I in the first quiet of the long day went out again for restoration: for a look at the stars, as Ginnie had said.

Thinking only of her I walked slowly along some of the paths between the paddocks, the way lit by a half-moon with small clouds drifting, and stopped eventually at the place where on the previous morning I'd held her tight in her racking distress. The birth of the deformed foal seemed so long ago, yet it was only yesterday: the morning of the last day of Ginnie's life.

I thought about that day, about the despair in its dawn and the resolution of its afternoon. I thought of her tears and her courage, and of the waste of so much goodness. The engulfing, stupefying sense of loss which had hovered all day swamped into my brain until my body felt inadequate, as if it wanted to burst, as if it couldn't hold in so much feeling.

When Ian Pargetter had been murdered I had been angry on his behalf and had supposed that the more one loved the dead person the greater one's fury against the killer. But now I understood that anger could simply be crowded out by something altogther more over-whelming. As for Oliver, he had displayed shock, daze, desolation and disbelief in endless quantities all day, but of anger, barely a flicker.

It was too soon to care who had killed her. The fact of her death was too much. Anger was irrelevant, and no vengeance could give her life.

I had loved her more than I'd known, but not as I loved Judith, not with desire and pain and longing. I'd loved Ginnie as a friend; as a brother. I'd loved her, I thought, right back from the day when I'd returned her to school and listened to her fears. I'd loved her up on the hill, trying to catch Sandcastle, and I'd loved her for her expertise and for her growing adult certainty that here, in these fields, was where her future lay.

I'd thought of her young life once as being a clear stretch of sand waiting for footprints, and now there would be none, now only a blank, chopping end to all she could have been and done, to all the bright love she had scattered around her.

'Oh . . . *Ginnie*,' I said aloud, calling to her hopelessly in tearing body-shaking grief. 'Ginnie ... little Ginnie ... come back.'

But she was gone from there. My voice fled away into darkness, and there was no answer.

MAY

On and off for the next two weeks I worked on Oliver's financial chaos at my desk in the bank, and at a special board meeting argued the case for giving him time before we foreclosed and made him sell all he had.

I asked for three months, which was considered scandalously out of the question, but got him two, Gordon chuckling over it quietly as we went down together afterwards in the lift.

'I suppose two months was what you wanted?' he said.

'Er ... yes.'

'I know you,' he said. 'They were talking of twenty-one days maximum before the meeting, and some wanted to bring in liquidators at once.'

I telephoned Oliver and told him. 'For two months you don't have to pay any interest or capital repayments, but this is only temporary, and it is a special, fairly unusual concession. I'm afraid, though, that if we can't find a solution to Sandcastle's problem or come up with a cast-iron reason for the insurance company to pay out, the prognosis is not good.'

'I understand,' he said, his voice sounding calm. 'I haven't much hope, but thank you, all the same, for the respite – I will at least be able to finish the programmes for the other stallions, and keep all the foals here until they're old enough to travel safely.'

'Have you heard anything about Sandcastle?'

'He's been at the Research Establishment for a week, but so far they can't find anything wrong with him. They don't hold out much hope, I'd better tell you, of being able to prove anything one way or another about his sperm, even though they're sending specimens to another laboratory, they say.'

'They'll do their best.'

'Yes, I know. But . . . I walk around here as if this place no longer belongs to me. As if it isn't mine. I know, inside, that I'm losing it. Don't feel too badly, Tim. When it comes, I'll be prepared.'

I put the receiver down not knowing whether such resignation was good because he would face whatever came without disintegration, or bad because he might be surrendering too soon. A great host of other troubles still lay ahead, mostly in the shape of breeders demanding the return of their stallion fees, and he needed energy to say that in most cases he couldn't return them. The money had already been lodged with us, and the whole situation would have to be sorted out by lawyers.

The news of Sandcastle's disgrace was so far only a

doubtful murmur here and there, but when it broke open with a screech it was, I suppose predictably, in *What's Going On Where It Shouldn't*.

The bank's six copies were read to rags before lunch on the day Alec fetched them, eyes lifting from the page with anything from fury to a wry smile.

Three short paragraphs headed 'House on Sand' said:

Build not your house on sand. Stake not your banking house on a Sandcastle.

The five million pounds advanced by a certain prestigious merchant bank for the purchase of the stallion Sandcastle now look like being washed away by the tide. Sadly, the investment has produced faulty stock, or in plain language, several deformed foals.

Speculation now abounds as to what the bank can do to minimize its losses, since Sandcastle himself must be considered as half a ton of highly priced dog-meat.

'That's done it,' Gordon said, and I nodded; and the dailies, who always read *What's Going On . . .* as a prime news source, came up in the racing columns the next day with a more cautious approach, asking 'Sandcastle's Progeny Flawed?' and saying things like 'rumours have reached us' and 'we are reliably informed.'

Since our own home-grown leaker for once hadn't mentioned the bank by name, none of the dailies did either, and for them of course the bank itself was unimportant compared with the implications of the news.

Oliver, in the next weekday issues, was reported as having been asked how many, precisely, of Sandcastle's foals were deformed, and as having answered that he didn't know. He had heard of some, certainly, yes. He had no further comment.

A day later still the papers began printing reports telephoned into them by the stud farms where Sandcastle's scattered progeny had been foaled, and the tally of disasters mounted. Oliver was reported this time as having said the horse was at the Equine Research Establishment at Newmarket, and everything possible was being done.

'It's a mess,' Henry said gloomily at lunch, and even the dissenting director had run out of insults, beyond saying four times that we were the laughing-stock of the City and it was all my fault.

'Have they found out who killed Knowles' daughter?' Val Fisher asked.

'No.' I shook my head. 'He says the police no longer come to the house.'

Val looked regretful. 'Such a sadness for him, on top of the other.'

There were murmurs of sympathy and I didn't think I'd spoil it by telling them what the police thought of Oliver's lads.

'That man Wyfold,' Oliver had said on the telephone during one of our almost daily conversations, 'he more or less said I was asking for trouble, having a young girl on the place with all those lads. What's more, it seems many of them were halfway drunk that night, and with three pubs in the village they weren't even all together and have no idea of who was where at what time, so one of Wyfold's theories is that one of them jumped her and Dave and Sammy interrupted him. Alternatively Nigel did it. Alternatively some stranger walking down the road did it. Wyfold's manner is downright abrasive but I'm past caring. He despises my discipline. He says I shouldn't let my lads get drunk – as if anyone could stop them. They're free men. It's their business, not mine, what they do with their money and time on Sunday nights. I can only take action if they don't turn up on Monday morning. And as for Nigel being paralytic!' Words momentarily failed him. 'How can Nigel possibly expect the lads to stay more or less sober if he gets like that? And he says he can't remember anything that happened the night Ginnie died. Nothing at all. Total, alcoholic black-out. He's been very subdued since.'

The directors, I felt, would not be any more impressed than the Detective Chief Inspector with the general level of insobriety, and I wondered whether Nigel's slackness with the lads in general had always stemmed from a knowledge of his own occasional weakness.

The police had found no weapon, Oliver said on
another day. Wyfold had told him that there was no way
of knowing what had been used to cause the depressed
fracture at the base of her brain. Her hair over the
fracture bore no traces of anything unexpected. The
forensic surgeon was of the opinion that there had been
a single very heavy blow. She would have been knocked
unconscious instantly. She wouldn't even have known.
The period of apparent semi-consciousness had been
illusory: parts of her brain would have functioned but
she would not have been aware of anything at all.

'I suppose it's a mercy,' Oliver said. 'With some girls
you hear of ... How do their parents bear it?'

His wife, he said, had gone back to Canada. Ginnie's
death seemed not to have brought mother and father
together, but to have made the separation complete.

'The dog shampoo?' Oliver repeated, when I asked.
'Wyfold says that's just what it was, they checked it.
He asked Nigel and all the lads if it was theirs, if they'd
used it for washing Squibs, but none of them had. He
seems to think Ginnie may have seen it lying in the
road and picked it up, or that she got into conversation
over the gate with a man who gave her the shampoo
for Squibs as a come-on and then killed her afterwards.'

'No,' I said.

'Why not?'

'Because he'd have taken the shampoo away again
with him.'

'Wyfold says not if he couldn't find it, because of its

being dark and her having hidden it to all intents and purposes under her skirt and two jumpers, and not if Dave and Sammy arrived at that point.'

'I suppose it's possible,' I said doubtfully.

'Wyfold says that particular shampoo isn't on sale at all in England, it's American, and there's absolutely no way at all of tracing how it got here. There weren't any fingerprints of any use; all a blur except a few of yours and mine.'

Another day he said, 'Wyfold told me the hardest murders to solve were single blows on the head. He said the case would remain open, but they are busy again with another girl who was killed walking home from a dance, and this time she definitely is one of that dreadful series, poor child... I was lucky, Tim, you know, that Dave and Sammy came back when they did.'

There came a fine May day in the office when Alec, deciding we needed some fresh air, opened one of the windows which looked down to the fountain. The fresh air duly entered but like a lion, not a lamb, and blew papers off all the desks.

'That's a hurricane,' I said. 'For God's sake shut it.'

Alec closed off the gale and turned round with a grin. 'Sorry and all that,' he said.

We all left our chairs and bent down like gleaners to retrieve our scattered work, and during my search for page 3 of a long assessment of a proposed sports complex I came across a severe and unwelcome shock in the shape of a small pale blue sheet off a memo pad.

There were words pencilled on it and crossed out with a wavy line, with other words underneath.

Build your castle not on Sand was crossed out, and so was *Sandcastle gone with the tide*, and underneath was written *Build not your house on Sand. Build not your banking house on a Sandcastle.*

'What's that?' Alec said quickly, seeing it in my hand and stretching out his own. 'Let's see.'

I shook my head and kept it in my own hand while I finished picking up the sportsdrome, and when order was restored throughout the office I said, 'Come along to the interview room.'

'Right now?'

'Right now.'

We went into the only room on our floor where any real privacy was possible and I said without shilly-shallying, 'This is your handwriting. Did you write the article in *What's Going On...?*'

He gave me a theatrical sigh and a tentative smile and a large shrug of the shoulders.

'That's just doodling,' he said. 'It means nothing.'

'It means, for a start,' I said, 'that you shouldn't have left it round the office.'

'Didn't know I had.'

'Did you write the article?'

601

The blue eyes unrepentantly gleamed at me from behind the gold rims. 'It's a fair cop, I suppose.'

'But *Alec* . . .' I protested.

'Yeah.'

'And the others,' I said, 'those other leaks, was that you?'

He sighed again, his mouth twisting.

'Was it?' I repeated, wanting above all things to hear him deny it.

'Look,' he said, 'what harm did it do? Yes, all right, the stories did come from me. I wrote them myself, actually, like that one.' He pointed to the memo paper in my hand. 'And don't give me any lectures on disloyalty because none of them did us any harm. Did us good, if anything.'

'Alec . . .'

'Yes,' he said, 'but just think, Tim, what did those pieces really do? They stirred everyone up, sure, and it was a laugh a minute to see all their faces, but what else? I've been thinking about it, I assure you. It wasn't why I did it in the first place, that was just wanting to stir things, I'll admit, but *because* of what I wrote we've now got much better security checks than we had before.'

I listened to him open-mouthed.

'All that work you did with the computer, making us safer against frauds, that was because of what I wrote. And the Corporate Finance boys, they now go around with their mouths zipped up like suitcases so as not to spill the beans to the investment managers. I did *good*, do you see, not harm.'

I stood and looked at him, at the tight tow-coloured curls, the cream-coloured freckled skin, the eyes that had laughed with me for eight years. I don't want to lose you, I thought: I wish you hadn't done it.

'And what about this piece about Sandcastle? What good has that done?' I said.

He half grinned. 'Too soon to say.'

I looked at the damaging scrap in my hands and almost automatically shook my head.

'You're going to say,' Alec said, 'that I'll have to leave.'

I looked up. His face was wholly calm.

'I knew I'd have to leave if any of you ever found out.'

'But don't you *care*?' I said frustratedly.

He smiled. 'I don't know. I'll miss *you*, and that's a fact. But as for the job . . . well, I told you, it's not my whole life, like it is yours. I loved it, I grant you, when I came here. All I wanted was to be a merchant banker, it sounded great. But to be honest it was the glamour I suppose I wanted, and glamour never lasts once you've got used to something. I'm not a dedicated money-man at heart . . . and there's honesty for you, I never thought I'd admit that, even to myself.'

'But you do it well.'

'Up to a point. We discussed all that.'

'I'm sorry,' I said helplessly.

'Yeah, well, so am I in a way, and in a way I'm not. I've been dithering for ages, and now that it isn't my choice I'm as much relieved as anything.'

'But . . . what will you do?'

He gave a full cherubic smile. 'I don't suppose you'll approve.'

'What, then?'

'*What's Going On . . .*,' he said, 'have offered me a whole-time job.' He looked at my shattered expression. 'I've written quite a bit for them, actually. About other things, of course, not us. But in most editions there's something of mine, a paragraph or two or a whole column. They've asked me several times to go, so now I will.'

I thought back to all those days when Alec had bounded out for the six copies and spent his next hour chuckling. Alec, the gatherer of news, who knew all the gossip.

'They get masses of information in,' Alec said, 'but they need someone to evaluate it all properly, and there aren't so many merchant bankers looking for that sort of job.'

'No,' I said drily. 'I can imagine. For a start, won't your salary be much less?'

'A bit,' he admitted, cheerfully. 'But my iconoclastic spirit will survive.'

I moved restlessly, wishing things had been different.

'I'll resign from here,' he said. 'Make it easier.'

Rather gloomily I nodded. 'And will you say why?'

He looked at me thoughtfully. 'If you really want me to, yes,' he said finally. 'Otherwise not. You can tell them yourself, though, after I've gone, if you want to.'

'You're a damned fool,' I said explosively, feeling the loss of him acutely. 'The office will be bloody dull without you.'

He grinned, my long-time colleague, and pointed to the piece of memo paper. 'I'll send you pin-pricks now and then. You won't forget me. Not a chance.'

Gordon, three days later, said to me in surprise, 'Alec's leaving, did you know?'

'I knew he was thinking of it.'

'But why? He's good at his job, and he always seemed happy here.'

I explained that Alec had been unsettled for some time and felt he needed to change direction.

'Amazing,' Gordon said. 'I tried to dissuade him, but he's adamant. He's going in four weeks.'

Alec, indeed, addressed his normal work with the bounce and zealousness of one about to be liberated, and for the rest of his stay in the office was better company than ever. Chains visibly dropped from his spirits, and I caught him several times scribbling speculatively on his memo pad with an anything but angelic grin.

Oliver had sent me at my request a list of all the breeders who had sent their mares to Sandcastle the previous year, and I spent two or three evenings on the telephone asking after those foals we didn't know about. Oliver himself, when I'd asked him, said he frankly couldn't face the task, and I didn't in the least blame him: my enquiries brought forth an ear-burning amount of blasphemy.

The final count came to:

Five foals born outwardly perfect but dead within two weeks because of internal abnormalities.
One foal born with one eye. (Put down.)
Five foals born with deformed legs, deformation varying from a malformed hoof to the absent half-leg of Plus Factor's colt. (All put down.)
Three foals born with part of one or both ears missing. (All still living.)
One foal born with no tail. (Still living.)
Two foals born with malformed mouths, the equivalent of human hare lip. (Both put down.)
One foal born with a grossly deformed head. (Foaled with heart-beat but couldn't breathe; died at once.)

Apart from this horrifying tally, four mares who had been sent home as in foal had subsequently 'slipped' and were barren; one mare had failed to conceive at all; three mares had not yet foaled (breeders' comments incendiary); and fourteen mares had produced live healthy foals with no defects of any sort.

I showed the list to Gordon and Henry, who went

shockedly silent for a while as if in mourning for the superb racer they had so admired.

'There may be more to come,' I said, not liking it. 'Oliver says thirty mares covered by Sandcastle this year are definitely in foal. Some of those will be all right . . . and some may not.'

'Isn't there a test you can do to see if a baby is abnormal?' Henry said. 'Can't they do that with the mares, and abort the deformed foals now, before they grow?'

I shook my head. 'I asked Oliver that. He says amniocentesis – that's what that process is called – isn't possible with mares. Something to do with not being able to reach the target with a sterile needle because of all the intestines in the way.'

Henry listened with the distaste of the non-medical to these clinical realities. 'What it means, I suppose,' he said, 'is that the owners of all of those thirty-one mares will have the foals aborted and demand their money back.'

'I'd think so, yes.'

He shook his head regretfully. 'So sad, isn't it? Such a shame. Quite apart from the financial loss, a tragedy in racing terms.'

Oliver said on the telephone one morning, 'Tim, I need to talk to you. Something's happened.'

'What?' I said, with misgivings.

'Someone has offered to buy Sandcastle.'

I sat in a mild state of shock, looking at Alec across the room sucking his pencil while he wrote his future.

'Are you there?' Oliver said.

'Yes. What for and for how much?'

'Well, he says to put back into training. I suppose it's possible. Sandcastle's only five. I suppose he could be got fit to race by August or September, and he might still win next year at six.'

'Good heavens.'

'He's offering twenty-five thousand pounds.'

'Um,' I said. 'Is that good or bad?'

'Realistically, it's as much as he's worth.'

'I'll consult with my seniors here,' I said. 'It's too soon, this minute, to say yes or no.'

'I did tell him that my bankers would have to agree, but he wants an answer fairly soon, because the longer the delay the less time there is for training and racing this season.'

'Yes,' I said, understanding. 'Where is he? Sandcastle, I mean.'

'Still in Newmarket. But it's pointless him staying there any longer. They haven't found any answers. They say they just don't know what's wrong with him, and I think they want me to take him away.'

'Well,' I pondered briefly. 'You may as well fetch him, I should think.'

'I'll arrange it,' he said.

608

'Before we go any further,' I said. 'Are you sure it's a bona fide offer and not just some crank?'

'I had a letter from him and I've talked to him on the telephone, and to me he sounds genuine,' Oliver answered. 'Would you like to meet him?'

'Perhaps, yes.'

We fixed a provisional date for the following Saturday morning, and almost as an afterthought I asked the potential buyer's name.

'Smith,' Oliver said. 'A Mr Dissdale Smith.'

I went to Hertfordshire on that Saturday with a whole host of question marks raising their eyebrows in my mind, but it was Dissdale, as it so happened, who had the deeper astonishment.

He drove up while I was still outside Oliver's house, still clasping hands in greeting and talking of Ginnie. Dissdale had come without Bettina, and the first thing he said, emerging from his car, was, 'Hello, Tim, what a surprise, didn't know you knew Oliver Knowles.'

He walked across, announced himself, shook hands with Oliver, and patted me chubbily on the shoulder. 'How's things, then? How are you doing, Tim?'

'Fine,' I said mildly.

Oliver looked from one of us to the other. 'You know each other already?'

Dissdale said, 'How do you mean, already?'

'Tim's my banker,' Oliver said in puzzlement. 'It

was his bank, Ekaterin's, which put up the money for Sandcastle.'

Dissdale stared at me in stunned amazement and looked bereft of speech.

'Didn't you know?' Oliver said. 'Didn't I mention it?'

Dissdale blankly shook his head and finally found his voice. 'You just said your banker was coming . . . I never for a moment thought . . .'

'It doesn't make much odds,' Oliver said. 'If you know each other it may simply save some time. Let's go indoors. There's some coffee ready.' He led the way through his immaculate house to the sitting room office, where a tray stood on the desk with coffee hot in a pot.

Oliver himself had had four weeks by then in that house without Ginnie, but to me, on my first visit back, she seemed still most sharply alive. It was I, this time, who kept expecting her to walk into the room; to give me a hug, to say hello with her eyes crinkling with welcome. I felt her presence vividly, to an extent that to start with I listened to Dissdale with only surface attention.

'It might be better to geld him,' he was saying. 'There are some good prizes, particularly overseas, for geldings.'

Oliver's instinctive response of horror subsided droopingly to defeat.

'It's too soon,' I said, 'to talk of that.'

'Tim, face facts,' Dissdale said expansively. 'At this moment in time that horse is a walking bomb. I'm making an offer for him because I'm a bit of a gambler, you know that, and I've a soft spot for him, whatever his faults, because of him winning so much for me that day the year before last, when we were all in my box at Ascot. You remember that, don't you?'

'I do indeed.'

'He saved my life, Sandcastle did.'

'It was partly because of that day,' I said, nodding, 'that Ekaterin's lent the money for him. When the request came in from Oliver, it was because Henry Shipton – our chairman, if you remember – and Gordon and I had all seen the horse in action that we seriously considered the proposition.'

Dissdale nodded his comprehension. 'A great surprise, though,' he said. 'I'm sorry it's you and Gordon. Sorry it's your bank, I mean, that's been hit so hard. I read about the deformed foals in the papers, of course, and that's what gave me the idea of buying Sandcastle in the first place, but it didn't say which bank . . .'

I wondered fleetingly if Alec could claim that omission as a virtue along with everything else.

Oliver offered Dissdale more coffee which he accepted with cream and sugar, drinking almost absent-mindedly while he worked through the possible alterations he would need in approach now he'd found he was dealing with semi-friends. Having had time myself over several days to do it, I could guess at the speed he was needing for reassessment.

'Dissdale,' I said neutrally, deciding to disrupt him, 'did the idea of buying Sandcastle come from your profitable caper with Indian Silk?'

His rounded features fell again into shock. 'How . . . er . . . did you know about that?'

I said vaguely, 'Heard it on the racecourse, I suppose. But didn't you buy Indian Silk for a pittance because he seemed to be dying, and then send him to Calder?'

'Well . . .'

'And didn't Calder cure him? And then you sold him again, but well this time, no doubt needing the money as don't we all, since when Indian Silk's won the Cheltenham Gold Cup? Isn't that right?'

Dissdale raised a plump hand palm upwards in a gesture of mock defeat. 'Don't know where you heard it, but yes, there's no secret, that's what happened.'

'Mm.' I smiled at him benignly. 'Calder said on television, didn't he, that buying Indian Silk was his idea originally, so I wondered . . . I'm wondering if this is his idea too. I mean, did he by any chance suggest a repeat of the gamble that came off so happily last time?'

Dissdale looked at me doubtfully.

'There's nothing wrong in it,' I said. 'Is it Calder's idea?'

'Well, yes,' he said, deciding to confide. 'But it's my money, of course.'

'And, um, if you do buy Sandcastle, will you send him too along to Calder, like Indian Silk?'

Dissdale seemed not to know whether to answer or not, but appearing to be reasssured by my friendly interest said finally, 'Calder said he could give him a quick pepping-up to get him fit quickly for racing, yes.'

Oliver, having listened restlessly up to this point, said, 'Calder Jackson can't do anything for Sandcastle that I can't.'

Both Dissdale and I looked at Oliver in the same way, hearing the orthodox view ringing out with conviction and knowing that it was very likely untrue.

'I've been thinking these past few days,' I said to Dissdale, 'first about Indian Silk. Didn't you tell Fred Barnet, when you offered him a rock-bottom price, that all you were doing was providing a dying horse with a nice quiet end in some gentle field?'

'Well, Tim,' he said knowingly. 'You know how it is. You buy for the best price you can. Fred Barnet, I know he goes round grousing that I cheated him, but I didn't, he could have sent his horse to Calder the same as I did.'

I nodded. 'So now, be honest, Dissdale, are you planning again to buy for the best price you can? I mean, does twenty-five thousand pounds for Sandcastle represent the same sort of bargain?'

'Tim,' Dissdale said, half affronted, half in sorrow, 'what a naughty suspicious mind. That's not friendly, not at all.'

I smiled. 'I don't think I'd be wise, though, do you, to recommend to my board of directors that we should accept your offer without thinking it over very carefully?'

For the first time there was a shade of dismay in the chubby face. 'Tim, it's a fair offer, anyone will tell you.'

'I think my board may invite other bids,' I said. 'If Sandcastle is to be sold, we must recoup the most we can.'

The dismay faded: man-of-the-world returned. 'That's fair,' he said. 'As long as you'll come back to me, if anyone tops me.'

'Sure,' I said. 'An auction, by telephone. When we're ready, I'll let you know.'

With a touch of anxiety he said, 'Don't wait too long. Time's money, you know.'

'I'll put your offer to the board tomorrow.'

He made a show of bluff contentment, but the anxiety was still there underneath. Oliver took the empty coffee cup which Dissdale still held and asked if he would like to see the horse he wanted to buy.

'But isn't he in Newmarket?' Dissdale said, again looking disconcerted.

'No, he's here. Came back yesterday.'

'Oh. Then yes, of course, yes, I'd like to see him.'

He's out of his depth, I thought abruptly: for some reason Dissdale is very very unsettled.

We went on the old familiar walk through the yards, with Oliver explaining the layout to the new visitor. To me there was now a visible thinning out of numbers, and Oliver, with hardly a quiver in his voice, said that he was sending the mares home with their foals in an orderly progression as usual, with in consequence lower feed bills, fewer lads to pay wages to, smaller expenses all round: he would play fair with the bank, he said, matter-of-factly, making sure to charge what he could and also to conserve what he could towards his debt. Dissdale gave him a glance of amused incredulity as if such a sense of honour belonged to a bygone age, and we came in the end to the stallion yard, where the four heads appeared in curiosity.

The stay in Newmarket hadn't done Sandcastle much good, I thought. He looked tired and dull, barely arching his neck to lift his nose over the half-door, and it was he, of the four, who turned away first and retreated into the gloom of his box.

'Is that Sandcastle?' Dissdale said, sounding disappointed. 'I expected something more, somehow.'

'He's had a taxing three weeks,' Oliver said. 'All he needs is some good food and fresh air.'

'And Calder's touch,' Dissdale said with conviction. 'That magic touch most of all.'

When Dissdale had driven away Oliver asked me what I thought, and I said, 'If Dissdale's offering twenty-five thousand he's certainly reckoning to make much more than that. He's right, he is a gambler, and I'll bet he has some scheme in mind. What we need to do is guess what the scheme is, and decide what we'll do on that basis, such as doubling or trebling the ante.'

Oliver was perplexed. 'How can we possibly guess?'

'Hm,' I said. 'Did you know about Indian Silk?'

'Not before today.'

'Well, suppose Dissdale acts to a pattern, which people so often do. He told Fred Barnet he was putting Indian Silk out to grass, which was diametrically untrue; he intended to send him to Calder and with luck put him back in training. He told *you* he was planning to put Sandcastle back into training, so suppose that's just what he *doesn't* plan to do. And he suggested gelding, didn't he?'

Oliver nodded.

'Then I'd expect gelding to be furthest from his mind,' I said. 'He just wants us to believe that's his intention.' I reflected 'Do you know what I might do if I wanted to have a real gamble with Sandcastle?'

'What?'

'It sounds pretty crazy,' I said. 'But with Calder's reputation it might just work.'

'What are you talking about?' Oliver said in some bewilderment. 'What gamble?'

'Suppose,' I said, 'that you could buy for a pittance a stallion whose perfect foals would be likely to win races.'

'But no one would risk . . .'

'Suppose,' I interrupted. 'There was nearly a fifty per cent chance, going on this year's figures, that you'd get a perfect foal. Suppose Dissdale offered Sandcastle as a sire at say a thousand pounds, the fee only payable if the foal was born perfect and lived a month.'

Oliver simply stared.

'Say Sandcastle's perfect progeny do win, as indeed they should. There are fourteen of them so far this year, don't forget. Say that in the passage of time his good foals proved to be worth the fifty per cent risk. Say Sandcastle stands in Calder's yard, with Calder's skill on the line. Isn't there a chance that over the years Dissdale's twenty-five thousand-pound investment would provide a nice steady return for them both?'

'It's impossible,' he said weakly.

'No, not impossible. A gamble.' I paused. 'You wouldn't get people sending the top mares, of course, but you might get enough dreamers among the breeders who'd chance it.'

'Tim . . .'

'Just think of it,' I said. 'A perfect foal by Sandcastle for peanuts. And if you got a malformed foal, well, some years your mare might slip or be barren anyway.'

He looked at his feet for a while, and then into the iddle distance, and then he said, 'Come with me. I've something to show you. Something you'd better know.'

He set off towards the Watcherleys', and would say nothing more on the way. I walked beside him down the familiar paths and thought about Ginnie because I couldn't help it, and we arrived in the next-door yard that was now of a neatness to be compared with all the others.

'Over here,' Oliver said, going across to one of the boxes. 'Look at that.'

I looked where directed: at a mare with a colt foal suckling, not unexpected in that place.

'He was born three days ago,' Oliver said. 'I do so wish Ginnie had seen him.'

'Why that one, especially?'

'The mare is one of my own,' he said. 'And that foal is Sandcastle's.'

It was my turn to stare. I looked from Oliver to the foal and back again. 'There's nothing wrong with him,' I said.

'No.'

'But . . .'

Oliver smiled twistedly. 'I was going to breed her to Diarist. She was along here at the Watcherleys' because the foal she had then was always ailing, but she herself was all right. I was along here looking at her one day when she'd been in season a while, and on impulse I led her along to the breeding pen and told Nigel to fetch Sandcastle, and we mated them there and then. That foal's the result.' He shook his head regretfully. 'He'll be sold, of course, with everything else. I wish I could have kept him, but there it is.'

'He should be worth quite a bit,' I said.

'I don't think so,' Oliver said. 'And that's the flaw in your gamble. It's not just the racing potential that raises prices at auction, it's the chance of breeding. And no one could be sure, breeding from Sandcastle's stock, that the genetic trouble wouldn't crop up for evermore. It's not on, I'm afraid. No serious breeder would send him mares, however great the bargain.'

We stood for a while in silence.

'It was a good idea,' I said, 'while it lasted.'

'My dear Tim . . . we're clutching at straws.'

'Yes.' I looked at his calm strong face; the captain whose ship was sinking. 'I'd try anything, you know, to save you,' I said.

'And to save the bank's money?'

'That too.'

He smiled faintly. 'I wish you could, but time's running out.'

The date for bringing in the receivers had been set, the insurance company had finally ducked, the lawyers were closing in and the respite I'd gained for him was trickling away with no tender plant of hope growing in the ruins.

We walked back towards the house, Oliver patting the mares as usual as they came to the fences.

'I suppose this may all be here next year,' he said, 'looking much the same. Someone will buy it . . . it's just I who'll be gone.'

He lifted his head, looking away over his white-painted rails to the long line of the roofs of his yards. The enormity of the loss of his life's work settled like a weight on his shoulders and there was a haggard set to his jaw.

'I try not to mind,' he said levelly. 'But I don't quite know how to bear it.'

When I reached home that evening my telephone was ringing. I went across the sitting room expecting it to stop the moment I reached it, but the summons continued, and on the other end was Judith.

'I just came in,' I said.

'We knew you were out. We've tried once or twice.'

'I went to see Oliver.'

'The poor, poor man.' Judith had been very distressed over Ginnie and still felt that Oliver needed more sympathy because of his daughter than because of his bankruptcy, which I wasn't sure was any longer the case. 'Anyway,' she said, 'Pen asked me to call you as she's tied up in her shop all day and you were out when she tried ... She says she's had the reply from America about the shampoo and are you still interested?'

'Yes, certainly.'

'Then ... if you're not doing anything else ... Gordon and I wondered if you'd care to come here for the day tomorrow, and Pen will bring the letter to show you.'

'I'll be there,' I said fervently, and she laughed.

'Good, then. See you.'

I was at Clapham with alacrity before noon, and Pen, over coffee, produced the letter from the drug company.

'I sent them a sample of what you gave me in that little glass jar,' she said. 'And, as you asked, I had some of the rest of it analysed here, but honestly, Tim, don't hope too much from it for finding out who killed Ginnie, it's just shampoo, as it says.'

I took the official-looking letter which was of two pages clipped together, with impressive headings.

Dear Madam,

We have received the enquiry from your pharmacy and also the sample you sent us, and we now reply with this report, which is a copy of that which we recently sent to the Hertfordshire police force on the same subject.

The shampoo in question is our 'Bannitch' which is formulated especially for dogs suffering from various skin troubles, including eczema. It is distributed to shops selling goods to dog owners and offering cosmetic canine services, but would not normally be used except on the advice of a veterinarian.

We enclose the list of active ingredients and excipients, as requested.

'What are excipients?' I asked, looking up.

'The things you put in with the active drug for

various reasons,' she said. 'Like for instance chalk for bulk in pills.'

I turned the top page over and read the list on the second.

BANNITCH

EXCIPIENTS

Bentonite

Ethylene glycol monostearate

Citric acid

Sodium phosphate

Glyceryl monoricinoleate

Perfume

ACTIVE INGREDIENTS

Captan

Amphoteric

Selenium

'Terrific,' I said blankly. 'What do they all mean?'

Pen, sitting beside me on the sofa, explained. 'From the top ... Bentonite is a thickening agent so that everything stays together and doesn't separate out. Ethylene glycol monostearate is a sort of wax, probably there to add bulk. Citric acid is to make the whole mixture acid, not alkaline, and the next one, sodium phosphate, is to keep the acidity level more or less constant. Glyceryl monoricinoleate is a soap, to make lather, and perfume is there so that the dog smells nice to the owner when she's washing him.'

'How do you know so much?' Gordon asked, marvelling.

'I looked some of them up,' said Pen frankly, with a smile. She turned back to me and pointed to the short lower column of active ingredients. 'Captan and amphoteric are both drugs for killing fungi on the skin, and selenium is also anti-fungal and is used in shampoos to cure dandruff.' She stopped and looked at me doubtfully. 'I did tell you not to hope too much. There's nothing there of any consequence.'

'And nothing in the sample that isn't on the manufacturer's list?'

She shook her head. 'The analysis from the British lab came yesterday, and the shampoo in Ginnie's bottle contained exactly what it should.'

'What did you expect, Tim?' Gordon asked.

'It wasn't so much expect, as hope,' I said regretfully. 'Hardly hope, really. Just a faint outside chance.'

'Of what?'

'Well . . . the police thought – think – that the purpose of killing Ginnie was sexual assault, because of those other poor girls in the neighbourhood.'

They all nodded.

'But it doesn't *feel* right, does it? Not when you know she wasn't walking home from anywhere, like the others, and not when she wasn't actually, well, interfered with. And then she had the shampoo . . . and the farm was in such trouble, and it seemed to me possible, just slightly possible, that she had somehow discovered that something in that bottle was significant...' I paused, and then said slowly to Pen, 'I suppose what I was looking for was something that could have been put into Sandcastle's food or water that affected his reproductive organs. I don't know if that's possible. I don't know anything about drugs... I just *wondered*.'

They sat in silence with round eyes, and then Gordon, stirring, said with an inflection of hope, 'Is that possible, Pen? Could it be something like that?'

'Could it *possibly*?' Judith said.

'My loves,' Pen said. 'I don't know.' She looked also as if whatever she said would disappoint us. 'I've never heard of anything like that, I simply haven't.'

'That's why I took the shampoo and gave it to you,' I said. 'I know it's a wild and horrible idea, but I told Oliver I'd try everything, however unlikely.'

'What you're suggesting,' Judith said plainly, 'is that someone might *deliberately* have given something to Sandcastle to make him produce deformed foals, and that Ginnie found out... and was killed for it.'

There was silence.

'I'll go and get a book or two,' Pen said. 'We'll look up the ingredients, just in case. But honestly, don't *hope*.'

She went home leaving the three of us feeling subdued. For me this had been the last possibility, although since I'd heard from Oliver that the police check had revealed only the expected shampoo in the bottle, it had become more and more remote.

Pen came back in half an hour with a thick tome, a piece of paper, and worried creases across her forehead. 'I've been reading,' she said. 'Sorry to be so long. I've been checking up on sperm deformities, and it seems the most likely cause is radiation.'

I said instantly, 'Let's ring Oliver.'

They nodded and I got through to him with Pen's suggestion.

'Tim!' he said. 'I'll see if I can get anyone in Newmarket . . . even though it's Sunday . . . I'll ring you back.'

'Though how a stallion could get anywhere near a radioactive source,' Pen said while we were waiting, 'would be a first-class mystery in itself.' She looked down at the paper she carried. 'This is the analysis report from the British lab, bill attached, I'm afraid. Same ingredients, though written in the opposite order, practically, with selenium put at the top, which means that that's the predominant drug, I should think.'

Oliver telephoned again in a remarkably short time. 'I got the chief researcher at home. He says they did think of radiation but discounted it because it would be more likely to result in total sterility, and there's also the improbability of a horse being near any radioactive isotopes.' He sighed. 'Sandcastle has never even been X-rayed.'

'See if you can check,' I said. 'If he ever was irradiated in any way it would come into the category of accidental or even malicious damage, and we'd be back into the insurance policy.'

'All right,' he said. 'I'll try.'

I put down the receiver to find Pen turning the pages of her large pharmacological book with concentration.

'What's that?' Judith asked, pointing.

'Toxicity of minerals,' Pen answered absentmindedly. 'Ethylene glycol . . .' She turned pages, searching. 'Here we are.' She read down the column, shaking her head. 'Not that, anyway.' She again consulted the index, read the columns, shook her head. 'Selenium . . . selenium . . .' She turned the pages, read the columns, pursed her lips. 'It says that selenium is poisonous if taken internally, though it can be beneficial on the skin.' She read some more. 'It says that if animals eat plants which grow in soil which has much selenium in it, they can die.'

'What is selenium?' Judith asked.

'It's an element,' Pen said. 'Like potassium and sodium.' She read on, 'It says here that it is mostly found in rocks of the Cretaceous Age – such useful information – and that it's among the most poisonous of elements but also an essential nutrient in trace quantities for both animals and plants.' She looked up. 'It says it's useful for flower-growers because it kills insects, and that it accumulates mostly in plants which flourish where there's a low annual rainfall.'

'Is that all?' Gordon asked, sounding disappointed.

'No, there's pages of it. I'm just translating the gist into understandable English.'

She read on for a while, and then it seemed to me that she totally stopped breathing. She raised her head and looked at me, her eyes wide and dark.

'What is it?' I said.

'Read it.' She gave me the heavy book, pointing to the open page.

I read:

Selenium is absorbed easily from the intestines and affects every part of the body, more lodging in the liver, spleen, and kidneys than in brain and muscle. Selenium is teratogenic.

'What does teratogenic mean?' I asked.

'It means,' Pen said, 'that it produces deformed offspring.'

'*What*?' I exclaimed. 'You don't mean . . .'

Pen was shaking her head. 'It couldn't affect Sandcastle. It's impossible. It would simply poison his system. Teratogens have nothing to do with males.'

'Then what . . .?'

'They act on the developing embryo,' she said. Her face crumpled almost as if the knowledge was too much and would make her cry. 'You could get deformed foals if you fed selenium *to the mares*.'

*

627

I went on the following morning to see Detective Chief Inspector Wyfold, both Gordon and Harry concurring that the errand warranted time off from the bank. The forceful policeman shook my hand, gestured me to a chair and said briskly that he could give me fifteen minutes at the outside, as did I know that yet another young girl had been murdered and sexually assaulted the evening before, which was now a total of six, and that his superiors, the press and the whole flaming country were baying for an arrest? 'And we are no nearer now,' he added with anger, 'than we were five months ago, when it started.'

He listened all the same to what I said about selenium, but in conclusion shook his head.

'We looked it up ourselves. Did you know it's the main ingredient in an anti-dandruff shampoo sold off open shelves all over America in the drug stores? It used to be on sale here too, or something like it, but it's been discontinued. There's no mystery about it. It's not rare, nor illegal. Just ordinary.'

'But the deformities . . .'

'Look,' he said restively, 'I'll bear it in mind. But it's a big jump to decide from one bottle of ordinary dog shampoo that *that*'s what's the matter with those foals. I mean, is there any way of proving it?'

With regret I said, 'No, there isn't.' No animal, Pen's book had implied, would retain selenium in its system for longer than a day or two if it was eaten only once or twice and in non-fatal amounts.

'And how, anyway,' Wyfold said, 'would you get a whole lot of horses to drink anything as nasty as shampoo?' He shook his head. 'I know you're very anxious to catch Virginia Knowles' killer, and don't think we don't appreciate your coming here, but we've been into the shampoo question thoroughly, I assure you.'

His telephone buzzed and he picked up the receiver, his eyes still turned in my direction, but his mind already elsewhere. 'What?' he said. 'Yes, all right. Straightaway.' He put down the receiver. 'I'll have to go.'

'Listen,' I said, 'isn't it possible that one of the lads was giving selenium to the mares this year also, and that Ginnie somehow found out . . .'

He interrupted. 'We tried to fit that killing onto one of those lads, don't think we didn't, but there was no evidence, absolutely none at all.' He stood up and came round from behind his desk, already leaving me in mind as well as body. 'If you think of anything else Mr Ekaterin, by all means let us know. But for now – I'm sorry, but there's a bestial man out there we've got to catch – and I'm still of the opinion he tried for Virginia Knowles too, and was interrupted.'

He gave me a dismissing but not impatient nod, holding open the door and waiting for me to leave his office ahead of him. I obliged him by going, knowing that realistically he couldn't be expected to listen to any further unsubstantiated theories from me while another victim lay more horribly and recently dead.

Before I went back to him, I thought, I had better dig further and come up with connected, believable facts, and also a basis, at least, for proof.

Henry and Gordon heard with gloom in the bank before lunch that at present we were 'insufficient data' in a Wyfold pigeonhole.

'But you still believe, do you, Tim . . .?' Henry said enquiringly.

'We have to,' I answered. 'And yes, I do.'

'Hm.' He pondered. 'If you need more time off from the office, you'd better take it. If there's the slightest chance that there's nothing wrong with Sandcastle after all, we must do our absolute best not only to prove it to our own satisfaction but also to the world in general. Confidence would have to be restored to breeders, otherwise they wouldn't send their mares. It's a tall order altogether.'

'Yes,' I said. 'Well . . . I'll do all I can'; and after lunch and some thought I telephoned Oliver, whose hopes no one had so far raised.

'Sit down,' I said.

'What's the matter?' He sounded immediately anxious. 'What's happened?'

'Do you know what teratogenic means?' I said.

'Yes, of course. With mares one always has to be careful.'

'Mm . . . Well, there was a teratogenic drug in the bottle of dog shampoo that Ginnie had.'

'*What*?' His voice rose an octave on the word, vibrating with instinctive unthinking anger.

'Yes,' I said. 'Now calm down. The police say it proves nothing either way, but Gordon and Henry, our chairman, agree that it's the only hope we have left.'

'But Tim . . .' The realization hit him. 'That would mean . . . that would mean . . .'

'Yes,' I said. 'It would mean that Sandcastle was always breeding good and true and could return to gold-mine status.'

I could hear Oliver's heavily disturbed breathing and could only guess at his pulse rate.

'No,' he said. 'No. If shampoo had got into a batch of feed, all the mares who ate it would have been affected, not just those covered by Sandcastle.'

'If the shampoo got into the feed accidentally, yes. If it was given deliberately, no.'

'I can't . . . I can't . . .'

'I did tell you to sit down,' I said reasonably.

'Yes, so you did.' There was a pause. 'I'm sitting,' he said.

'It's at least possible,' I said, 'that the Equine Research people could find nothing wrong with Sandcastle because there actually *isn't* anything wrong with him.'

'Yes,' he agreed faintly.

'It is possible to give teratogenic substances to mares?'

'Yes.'

'But horses wouldn't drink shampoo.'

'No, thoroughbreds especially are very choosy.'

'So how would you give them shampoo, and when?'

After a pause he said, still breathlessly, 'I don't know how. They'd spit it out. But when it's easier, and that could probably be no more than three or four days after conception, is when the body tube is forming in the embryo ... that's when a small amount of teratogenic substance could do a lot of damage.'

'Do you mean,' I said, 'that giving a mare selenium just *once* would ensure a deformed foal?'

'Giving a mare what?'

'Sorry. Selenium. A drug for treating dandruff.'

'Good ... heavens.' He rallied towards his normal self. 'I suppose it would depend on the strength of the dose, and its timing. Perhaps three or four doses ... No one could really *know* because no one would have tried ... I mean, there wouldn't have been any research.'

'No,' I agreed. 'But supposing that in this instance someone got the dosage and the timing right, and also found a way of making the shampoo palatable, then *who was it*?'

There was a long quietness during which even his breathing abated.

'I don't know,' he said finally. 'Theoretically it could

have been me, Ginnie, Nigel, the Watcherleys or any of the lads who were here last year. No one else was on the place often enough.'

'Really no one? How about the vet or the blacksmith or just a visiting friend?'

'But there were *eighteen* deformed foals,' he said. 'I would think it would have to have been someone who could come and go here all the time.'

'And someone who knew which mares to pick,' I said. 'Would that knowledge be easy to come by?'

'Easy!' he said explosively. 'It is positively thrust at everyone on the place. There are lists in all the feed rooms and in the breeding pen itself saying which mares are to be bred to which stallion. Nigel has one, there's one in my office, one at the Watcherleys' – all over. Everyone is supposed to double-check the lists all the time, so that mistakes aren't made.'

'And all the horses,' I said slowly, 'wear headcollars with their names on.'

'Yes, that's right. An essential precaution.'

All made easy, I thought, for someone intending mischief towards particular mares and not to any others.

'Your own Sandcastle foal,' I said, 'he's perfect . . . and it may be because on the lists your mare was down for Diarist.'

'Tim!'

'Look after him,' I said. 'And look after Sandcastle.'

'I will,' he said fervently.

'And Oliver . . . is the lad called Shane still with you?'

'No, he's gone. So have Dave and Sammy, who found Ginnie.'

'Then could you send me at the bank a list of the names and addresses of all the people who were working for you last year, and also this year? And I mean *everyone*, even your housekeeper and anyone working for Nigel or cleaning the lads' hostel, things like that.'

'Even my part-time secretary girl?'

'Even her.'

'She only comes three mornings a week.'

'That might be enough.'

'All right,' he said. 'I'll do it straight away.'

'I went to see Chief Inspector Wyfold this morning,' I said. 'But he thinks it's just a coincidence that Ginnie had shampoo with a foal-deforming drug in it. We'll have to come up with a whole lot more, to convince him. So anything you can think of . . .'

'I'll think of nothing else.'

'If Dissdale Smith should telephone you, pressing for an answer,' I said, 'just say the bank are deliberating and keeping you waiting. Don't tell him anything about this new possibility. It might be best to keep it to ourselves until we can prove whether or not it's true.'

'Dear God,' he said fearfully, 'I hope it is.'

*

In the evening I talked to Pen, asking her if she knew of any way of getting the selenium out of the shampoo.

'The trouble seems to be,' I said, 'that you simply couldn't get the stuff into a horse as it is.'

'I'll work on it,' she said. 'But of course the manufacturer's chemists will have gone to a good deal of trouble to make sure the selenium stays suspended throughout the mixture and doesn't all fall to the bottom.'

'It did say "Shake Well" on the bottle.'

'Mm, but that might be for the soap content, not for the selenium.'

I thought. 'Well, could you get the soap out, then? It must be the soap the horses wouldn't like.'

'I'll try my hardest,' she promised. 'I'll ask a few friends.' She paused. 'There isn't much of the shampoo left. Only what I kept after sending the samples off to America and the British lab.'

'How much?' I said anxiously.

'Half an egg-cupful. Maybe less.'

'Is that enough?'

'If we work in test tubes . . . perhaps.'

'And Pen . . . Could you or your friends make a guess, as well, as to how much shampoo you'd need to provide enough selenium to give a teratogenic dose to a mare?'

'You sure do come up with some difficult questions, dearest Tim, but we'll certainly try.'

Three days later she sent a message with Gordon, saying that by that evening she might have some answers, if I would care to go down to her house after work.

I cared and went, and with a smiling face she opened her front door to let me in.

'Like a drink?' she said.

'Well, yes, but . . .'

'First things first.' She poured whisky carefully for me and Cinzano for herself. 'Hungry?'

'Pen . . .'

'It's only rolls with ham and lettuce in. I never cook much, as you know.' She disappeared to her seldom-used kitchen and returned with the offerings, which turned out to be nicely squelchy and much what I would have made for myself.

'All right,' she said finally, pushing away the empty plates. 'Now I'll tell you what we've managed.'

'At last.'

She grinned. 'Yes. Well then, we started from the premise that if someone had to use shampoo as the source of selenium then that someone didn't have direct or easy access to poisonous chemicals, which being so he also wouldn't have sophisticated machinery available for separating one ingredient from another – a centrifuge, for instance. OK so far?'

I nodded.

'So what we needed, as we saw it, was a *simple* method that involved only everyday equipment. Something anyone could do anywhere. So the first thing we did was to let the shampoo drip through a paper filter, and we think you could use almost anything for that purpose, like a paper towel, a folded tissue or thin blotting paper. We actually got the best and fastest results from a coffee filter, which is after all specially designed to retain very fine solids while letting liquids through easily.'

'Yes,' I said. 'Highly logical.'

Pen smiled. 'So there we were with some filter-papers in which, we hoped, the microscopic particles of selenium were trapped. The filters were stained bright green by the shampoo. I brought one here to show you . . . I'll get it.' She whisked off to the kitchen taking the empty supper plates with her, and returned carrying a small tray with two glasses on it.

One glass contained cut pieces of green-stained coffee filter lying in what looked like oil, and the second glass contained only an upright test tube, closed at the top with a cork and showing a dark half-inch of solution at the bottom.

'One of my friends in the lab knows a lot about horses,' Pen said, 'and he reckoned that all racehorses are used to the taste of linseed oil, which is given them in their feed quite often as a laxative. So we got some linseed oil and cut up the filter and soaked it.' She pointed to the glass. 'The selenium particles floated out of the paper into the oil.'

'Neat,' I said.

'Yes. So then we poured the result into the test tube and just waited twenty-four hours or so, and the selenium particles slowly gravitated through the oil to the bottom.' She looked at my face to make sure I understood. 'We transferred the selenium from the wax-soap base in which it would remain suspended into an oil base, in which it *wouldn't* remain suspended.'

'I do understand,' I assured her.

'So here in the test tube,' she said with a conjuror's flourish, 'we have concentrated selenium with the surplus oil poured off.' She picked the tube out of the glass, keeping it upright, and showed me the brownish shadowy liquid lying there, darkest at the bottom, almost clear amber at the top. 'We had such a small sample to start with that this is all we managed to collect. But that dark stuff is definitely selenium sulphide. We checked it on a sort of scanner called a gas chromatograph.' She grinned. 'No point in not using the sophisticated apparatus when it's there right beside you – and we were in a research lab of a teaching hospital, incidentally.'

'You're marvellous.'

'Quite brilliant,' she agreed with comic modesty. 'We also calculated that that particular shampoo was almost ten per cent selenium, which is a very much higher proportion than you'd find in shampoos for humans. We all agree that this much, in the test tube, is enough to cause deformity in a foal – or in any other species, for that matter. We found many more references in

638

other books – lambs born with deformed feet, for instance, where the sheep had browsed off plants growing on selenium-rich soil. We all agree that it's the *time* when the mare ingests the selenium that's most crucial, and we think that to be sure of getting the desired result you'd have to give selenium every day for three or four days, starting two or three days after conception.'

I slowly nodded. 'That's the same sort of time-scale that Oliver said.'

'And if you gave too much,' she said, 'too large a dose, you'd be more likely to get abortions than really gross deformities. The embryo would only go on growing at all, that is, if the damage done to it by the selenium was relatively minor.'

'There were a lot of *different* deformities,' I said.

'Oh sure. It could have affected any developing cell, regardless.'

I picked up the test tube and peered closely at its murky contents. 'I suppose all you'd have to do would be stir this into a cupful of oats.'

'That's right.'

'Or . . . could you enclose it in a capsule?'

'Yes, if you had the makings. We could have done it quite easily in the lab. You'd need to get rid of as much oil as possible, of course, in that case, and just scrape concentrated selenium into the capsules.'

'Mm. Calder could do it, I suppose?'

'Calder Jackson? Why yes, I guess he could if you

wanted him to. He had everything there that you'd need.' She lifted her head, remembering something. 'He's on the television tomorrow night, incidentally.'

'Is he?'

'Yes. They were advertising it tonight just after the news, before you came. He's going to be a guest on that chat show . . . Micky Bonwith's show . . . Do you ever see it?'

'Sometimes,' I said, thoughtfully. 'It's transmitted live, isn't it?'

'Yes, that's right.' She looked at me with slight puzzlement. 'What's going on in that computer brain?'

'A slight calculation of risk,' I said slowly, 'and of grasping unrepeatable opportunities. And tell me, dearest Pen, if I found myself again in Calder's surgery, what should I look for, to bring out?'

She stared at me literally with her mouth open. Then, recovering, she said, 'You can't mean . . . *Calder*?'

'Well,' I said soberly. 'What I'd really like to do is to make sure one way or another. Because it does seem to me, sad though it is to admit it, that if you tie in Dissdale's offer for Sandcastle with someone deliberately poisoning the mares, and then add Calder's expertise with herbs – in which selenium-soaked plants might be included – you do at least get a *question mark*. You do want to know for sure, don't you think, whether or not Calder and Dissdale set out deliberately to debase Sandcastle's worth so that they could buy him for peanuts . . . So that Calder could perform a well-publicized "miracle cure" of some sort on Sandcastle, who would thereafter always sire perfect foals, and gradually climb back into favour. Whose fees might never return to forty thousand pounds, but would over the years add up to a fortune.'

'But they couldn't,' Pen said, aghast. 'I mean . . . Calder and Dissdale . . . we *know* them.'

'And you in your trade, as I in mine, must have met presentable, confidence-inspiring crooks.'

She fell silent, staring at me in a troubled way, until finally I said, 'There's one other thing. Again nothing I could swear to – but the first time I went to Calder's place he had a lad there who reminded me sharply of the boy with the knife at Ascot.'

'Ricky Barnet,' Pen said, nodding.

'Yes. I can't remember Calder's lad's name, and I wouldn't identify him at all now after all this time, but at Oliver's I saw another lad, called Shane, who *also* reminded me of Ricky Barnet. I've no idea whether Shane and Calder's lad are one and the same person, though maybe not, because I don't think Calder's lad was called Shane, or I *would* have remembered, if you see what I mean.'

'Got you,' she said.

'But *if* – and it's a big if – if Shane did once work for Calder, he might *still* be working for him . . . feeding selenium to mares.'

Pen took her time with gravity in the experienced

eyes, and at last said, '*Someone* would have had to be there on the spot to do the feeding, and it certainly couldn't have been Calder or Dissdale. But couldn't it have been that manager, Nigel? It would have been easy for him. Suppose Dissdale and Calder paid him . . .? Suppose they promised to employ him, or even give him a share in Sandcastle, once they'd got hold of the horse.'

I shook my head. 'I did wonder. I did think of Nigel. There's one good reason why it probably isn't him, though, and that's because he and only he besides Oliver knew that one of the mares down for Diarist was covered by Sandcastle.' I explained about Oliver's impulse mating. 'The foal is perfect, but might very likely not have been if it was Nigel who was doing the feeding.'

'Not conclusive,' Pen said, slowly.

'No.'

She stirred. 'Did you tell the police all this?'

'I meant to,' I said, 'but when I was there with Wyfold on Monday it seemed impossible. It was all so insubstantial. Such a lot of guesses. Maybe wrong conclusions. Dissdale's offer could be genuine. And a lad I'd seen for half a minute eighteen months ago . . . it's difficult to remember a strange face for half an hour, let alone all that time. I have only an impression of blankness and of sunglasses . . . and I don't have the same impression of Oliver's lad Shane. Wyfold isn't the sort of man to be vague to. I thought I'd better come up with something more definite before I went back to him.'

She bit her thumb. 'Can't you take another good look at this Shane?'

I shook my head. 'Oliver's gradually letting lads go, as he does every year at this time, and Shane is one who has already left. Oliver doesn't know where he went and has no other address for him, which he doesn't think very unusual. It seems that lads can drift from stable to stable for ever with their papers always showing only the address of their last or current employer. But I think we *might* find Shane, if we're lucky.'

'How?'

'By photographing Ricky Barnet, side view, and asking around on racetracks.'

She smiled. 'It might work. It just might.'

'Worth a try.'

My mind drifted back to something else worth a try, and it seemed that hers followed.

'You don't really mean to break into Calder's surgery, do you?' she said.

'Pick the lock,' I said. 'Yes.'

'But . . .'

'Time's running out, and Oliver's future and the bank's money with it, and yes, sure, I'll do what I can.'

She curiously looked into my face. 'You have no real conception of danger, do you?'

'How do you mean?'

'I mean . . . I saw you, that day at Ascot, simply hurl yourself at that boy, at that knife. You could have been badly stabbed, very easily. And Ginnie told us that you frightened her to tears jumping at Sandcastle the way you did, to catch him. She said it was suicidal . . . and yet you yourself seemed to think nothing of it. And at Ascot, that evening, I remembered you being *bored* with the police questions, not stirred up high by a brush with death . . .'

Her words petered away. I considered them and found in myself a reason and an answer.

'Nothing that has happened so far in my life,' I said seriously, 'has made me fear I might die. I think . . . I know it sounds silly . . . I am unconvinced of my own mortality.'

JUNE

On the following day, Friday, June 1st, I took up a long-offered invitation and went to lunch with the board of a security firm to whom we had lent money for launching a new burglar alarm on the market. Not greatly to their surprise I was there to ask a favour, and after a repast of five times the calories of Ekaterin's they gave me with some amusement three keys which would unlock almost anything but the crown jewels, and also a concentrated course on how to use them.

'Those pickers are strictly for opening doors in emergencies,' the locksmiths said, smiling. 'If you end up in jail, we don't know you.'

'If I end up in jail, send me another set in a fruit cake.'

I thanked them and left, and practised discreetly on the office doors in the bank, with remarkable results. Going home I let myself in through my own front door with them, and locked and unlocked every cupboard and drawer which had a keyhole. Then I put on a dark roll-neck jersey over my shirt and tie and with scant trepidation drove to Newmarket.

I left my car at the side of the road some distance from Calder's house and finished the journey on foot, walking quietly into his yard in the last of the lingering summer dusk, checking against my watch that it was almost ten o'clock, the hour when Micky Bonwith led his guests to peacock chairs and dug publicly into their psyches.

Calder would give a great performance, I thought; and the regrets I felt about my suspicions of him redoubled as I looked at the outline of his house against the sky and remembered his uncomplicated hospitality.

The reserve which had always at bottom lain between us I now acknowledged as my own instinctive and stifled doubt. Wanting to see worth, I had seen it; and the process of now trying to prove myself wrong gave me more sadness than satisfaction.

His yard was dark and peaceful, all lads long gone. Within the hall of the house a single light burned, a dim point of yellow glimpsed through the bushes fluttering in a gentle breeze. Behind the closed doors of the boxes the patients would be snoozing, those patients with festering sores and bleeding guts and all manner of woes awaiting the touch.

Sandcastle, if I was right, had been destined to stand there, while Calder performed his 'miracle' without having to explain how he'd done it. He never had explained: he'd always broadcast publicly that he didn't know *how* his power worked, he just knew it did. Thousands, perhaps millions, believed in his power. Perhaps even breeders, those dreamers of dreams, would have believed, in the end.

I came to the surgery, a greyish block in the advancing night, and fitted one of the lock-pickers into the keyhole. The internal tumblers turned without protest, much oiled and used, and I pushed the door open and went in.

There were no windows to worry about. I closed the door behind me and switched on the light, and immediately began the search for which I'd come: to find selenium in home-made capsules, or in a filtering device, or in bottles of shampoo.

Pen had had doubts that anyone would have risked giving selenium a second year if the first year's work had proved so effective, but I'd reminded her that Sandcastle had already covered many new mares that year before the deformed foals had been reported.

'Whoever did it couldn't have known at that point that he'd been successful. So to make sure, I'd guess he'd go on, and maybe with an increased dose . . . and if no selenium was being given this year, *why did Ginnie have it?*'

Pen had reluctantly given in. 'I suppose I'm just trying to find reasons for you not to go to Calder's.'

'If I find anything, Chief Inspector Wyfold can go there later with a search warrant. Don't worry so.'

'No,' she'd said, and gone straight on looking anxious.

The locked cabinets at both ends of Calder's surgery proved a doddle for the picks, but the contents were a puzzle, as so few of the jars and boxes were properly labelled. Some indeed had come from commercial suppliers, but these seemed mostly to be the herbs Calder had talked of: hydrastis, comfrey, fo-ti-tieng, myrrh, sarsaparilla, liquorice, passiflora, papaya, garlic; a good quantity of each.

Nothing was obligingly labelled selenium.

I had taken with me a thickish polythene bag which had a zip across one end and had formerly enclosed a silk tie and handkerchief, a present from my mother at Christmas. Into that I systematically put two or three capsules from each bottle, and two or three pills of each ort, and small sachets of herbs; and Pen, I thought, was going to have a fine old time sorting them all out.

With the bag almost half full of samples I carefully locked the cabinets again and turned to the refrigerator, which was of an ordinary domestic make with only a magnetic door fastening.

Inside there were no bottles of shampoo. No coffee filters. No linseed oil. There were simply the large plastic containers of Calder's cure-all tonic.

I thought I might as well take some to satisfy Pen's curiosity, and rooted around for a small container, finding some empty medicine bottles in a cupboard below the work-bench. Over the sink I poured some of the tonic into a medicine bottle, screwed on the cap, and returned the plastic container carefully to its place in the fridge. I stood the medicine bottle on the work-bench ready to take away, and turned finally to the drawers where Calder kept things like hops and also his antique pill-making equipment.

Everything was clean and tidy, as before. If he had made capsules containing selenium there, I could see no trace.

With mounting disappointment I went briefly through every drawer. Bags of seeds: sesame, pumpkin, sunflower. Bags of dried herbs, raspberry leaves, alfalfa. Boxes of the empty halves of gelatine capsules, waiting for contents. Empty unused pill bottles. All as before: nothing I hadn't already seen.

The largest bottom drawer still contained the plastic sacks of hops. I pulled open the neck of one of them and found only the expected strong-smelling crop; closed the neck again, moving the bag slightly to settle it back into its place, and saw that under the bags of hops lay a brown leather briefcase, ordinary size, six inches deep.

With a feeling of wasting time I hauled it out onto the working surface on top of the drawers, and tried to open it.

Both catches were locked. I fished for the keys in my trouser pocket and with the smallest of the picks delicately twisted until the mechanisms clicked.

Opened the lid. Found no bottles of dog shampoo,

but other things that turned me slowly to a state of stone.

The contents looked at first sight as if the case belonged to a doctor: stethoscope, pen torch, metal instruments, all in fitted compartments. A cardboard box without its lid held four or five small tubes of antibiotic ointment. A large bottle contained only a few small white pills, the bottle labelled with a long name I could scarcely read, let alone remember, with 'diuretic' in brackets underneath. A pad of prescription forms, blank, ready for use.

It was the name and address rubber-stamped onto the prescription forms and the initials heavily embossed in gold into the leather beneath the case's handle which stunned me totally.

I.A.P. on the case.

Ian A. Pargetter on the prescriptions.

Ian Pargetter, veterinary surgeon, address in Newmarket.

His case had vanished the night he died.

This case . . .

With fingers beginning to shake I took one of the tubes of antibiotics and some of the diuretic pills and three of the prescription forms and added them to my other spoils, and then with a heart at least beating at about twice normal speed checked that everything was in its place before closing the case.

I felt as much as heard the surgery door open, the current of air reaching me at the same instant as the night sounds. I turned thinking that one of Calder's lads had come on some late hospital rounds and wondering how I could ever explain my presence; and I saw that no explanation at all would do.

It was Calder himself crossing the threshold. Calder with the light on his curly halo, Calder who should have been a hundred miles away talking to the nation on the tube.

His first expression of surprise turned immediately to grim assessment, his gaze travelling from the medicine bottle of tonic mixture on the work-bench to the veterinary case lying open. Shock, disbelief and fury rose in an instantly violent reaction, and he acted with such speed that even if I'd guessed what he would do I could hardly have dodged.

His right arm swung in an arc, coming down against the wall beside the door and pulling from the bracket which held it a slim scarlet fire extinguisher. The swing seemed to me continuous. The red bulbous end of the fire extinguisher in a split second filled my vision and connected with a crash against my forehead, and consciousness ceased within a blink.

The world came back with the same sort of on–off switch: one second I was unaware, the next, awake. No grey area of daze, no shooting stars, simply on–off, off–on.

I was lying on my back on some smelly straw in an

electrically lit horse box with a brown horse peering at me suspiciously from six feet above.

I couldn't remember for a minute how I'd got there; it seemed such an improbable position to be in. Then I had a recollection of a red ball crashing above my eyes, and then, in a snap, total recall of the evening.

Calder.

I was in a box in Calder's yard. I was there because, presumably, Calder had put me there.

Pending? I wondered.

Pending what?

With no reassuring thoughts I made the moves to stand up, but found that though consciousness was total, recovery was not. A whirling dizziness set the walls tilting, the grey concrete blocks seeming to want to lean in and fall on me. Cursing slightly I tried again more slowly and made it to one elbow with eyes balancing precariously in their sockets.

The top half of the stable door abruptly opened with the sound of an unlatching bolt. Calder's head appeared in the doorway, his face showing shock and dismay as he saw me awake.

'I thought,' he said, 'that you'd be unconscious . . . that you wouldn't know. I hit you so hard . . . you're supposed to be out.' His voice saying these bizarre words sounded nothing but normal.

'Calder . . .' I said.

He was looking at me no longer with anger but

almost with apology. 'I'm sorry, Tim,' he said. 'I'm sorry you came.'

The walls seemed to be slowing down.

'Ian Pargetter . . .' I said. 'Did *you* . . . kill him? Not you?'

Calder produced an apple and fed it almost absent-mindedly to the horse. 'I'm sorry, Tim. He was so stubborn. He refused . . .' He patted the horse's neck. 'He wouldn't do what I wanted. Said it was over, he'd had enough. Said he'd stop me, you know.' He looked for a moment at the horse and then down to me. 'Why did you come? I've liked you. I wish you hadn't.'

I tried again to stand up and the whirling returned as before. Calder took a step backwards, but only one, stopping when he saw my inability to arise and charge.

'Ginnie,' I said. 'Not Ginnie . . . Say it wasn't you who hit Ginnie . . .'

He simply looked at me, and didn't say it. In the end he said merely, and with clear regret, 'I wish I'd hit you harder . . . but it seemed . . . enough.' He moved another step backwards so that I could see only the helmet of curls under the light and dark shadows where his eyes were; and then while I was still struggling to my knees he closed the half-door and bolted it, and from outside switched off the light.

Night-blindness made it even harder to stand up but at least I couldn't *see* the walls whirl, only feel they were spinning. I found myself leaning against one of them and ended more or less upright, spine supported, brain at last settling into equilibrium.

The grey oblong of window gradually detached itself from the blackness, and when my equine companion moved his head I saw the liquid reflection of an eye.

Window . . . way out.

I slithered round the walls to the window and found it barred on the inside, not so much to keep horses in, I supposed, but to prevent them breaking the glass. Five strong bars, in any case, were set in concrete top and bottom, as secure as any prison cell, and I shook them impotently with two hands in proving them immovable.

Through the dusty window panes I had a sideways view across the yard towards the surgery, and while I stood there and held onto the bars and watched, Calder went busily in and out of the open lighted doorway, carrying things from the surgery to his car. I saw what I was sure was Ian Pargetter's case go into the boot, and remembered with discomfiture that I'd left the bunch of picks in one of its locks. I saw him carry also an armful of the jars which contained unlabelled capsules and several boxes of unguessable contents, stowing them in the boot carefully and closing them in.

Calder was busy obliterating his tracks.

I yelled at him, calling his name, but he didn't even hear or turn his head. The only result was startled movement in the horse behind me, a stamping of hooves and a restless swinging round the box.

'All right,' I said soothingly. 'Steady down. All right. Don't be frightened.'

The big animal's alarm abated, and through the window I watched Calder switch off the surgery light, lock the door, get into his car and drive away.

He drove away out of his driveway, towards the main road, not towards his house. The lights of his car passed briefly over the trees as he turned out through the gates, and then were gone: and I seemed suddenly very alone, imprisoned in that dingy place for heaven knew how long.

Vision slowly expanded so that from the dim light of the sky I could see again the outlines within the box: walls, manger . . . horse. The big dark creature didn't like me being there and wouldn't settle, but I could think of no way to relieve him of my presence.

The ceiling was solid, not as in some stables open through the rafters to the roof. In many it would have been possible for an agile man to climb the partition from one box to the next, but not here; and in any case there was no promise of being better off next door. One would be in a different box but probably just as simply and securely bolted in.

There was nothing in my trouser pockets but a handkerchief. Penknife, money and house keys were all in my jacket in the boot of my own unlocked car out on the road. The dark jersey which had seemed good for speed, quiet and concealment had left me without even a coin for a screwdriver.

I thought concentratedly of what a man could do with his fingers that a horse couldn't do with superior strength, but found nothing in the darkness of the door to unwind or unhinge; nothing anywhere to pick loose. It looked most annoyingly as if that was where I was going to stay until Calder came back.

And then . . . what?

If he'd intended to kill me, why hadn't he already made sure of it? Another swipe or two with the fire extinguisher would have done . . . and I would have known nothing about it.

I thought of Ginnie, positive now that that was how it had been for her, that in one instant she had been thinking, and in the next . . . not.

Thought of Ian Pargetter, dead from one blow of his own brass lamp. Thought of Calder's shock and grief at the event, probably none the less real despite his having killed the man he mourned. Calder shattered over the loss of a business friend . . . the friend he had himself struck down.

He must have killed him, I thought, on a moment's ungovernable impulse, for not . . . what had he said? . . . for not wanting to go on, for wanting to stop Calder doing . . . what Calder planned.

Calder had struck at me with the same sort of speed: without pause for consideration, without time to think of consequences. And he had lashed at me as a friend too, without hesitation, while saying shortly after that he liked me.

Calder, swinging the fire extinguisher, had ruthlessly aimed at killing the man who had saved his life.

Saved Calder's life . . . Oh God, I thought, why ever did I do it?

The man in whom I had wanted to see only goodness had after that day killed Ian Pargetter, killed Ginnie; and if I hadn't saved him they would both have lived.

The despair of that thought filled me utterly, swelling with enormity, making me feel, as the simpler grief for Ginnie had done, that one's body couldn't hold so much emotion. Remorse and guilt could rise like dragons' teeth from good intentions, and there were in truth unexpected paths to hell.

I thought back to that distant moment that had affected so many lives: to that instinctive reflex, faster than thought, which had launched me at Ricky's knife. If I could have called it back I would have been looking away, not seeing, letting Calder die . . . letting Ricky take his chances, letting him blast his young life to fragments, destroy his caring parents.

One couldn't help what came after.

A fireman or a lifeboatman or a surgeon might fight to the utmost stretch of skill to save a baby and find he had let loose a Hitler, a Nero, Jack the Ripper. It couldn't always be Beethoven or Pasteur whose life one extended. All one asked was an ordinary, moderately sinful, normally well-intentioned, fairly harmless human. And if he cured horses . . . all the better.

Before that day at Ascot Calder couldn't even have

thought of owning Sandcastle, because Sandcastle at that moment was in mid-career with his stud value uncertain. But Calder had seen, as we all had, the majesty of that horse, and I had myself listened to the admiration in his voice.

At some time after that he must have thought of selenium, and from there the wickedness had grown to encompass us all: the wickedness which would have been extinguished before birth if I'd been looking another way.

I knew logically that I couldn't have not done what I did; but in heart and spirit that didn't matter. It didn't stop the engulfing misery or allow me any ease.

Grief and sorrow came to us all, Pen had said: and she was right.

The horse became more restive and began to paw the ground.

I looked at my watch, the digital figures bright in the darkness: twenty minutes or thereabouts since Calder had left. Twenty minutes that already seemed like twenty hours.

The horse swung round suddenly in the gloom with unwelcome vigour, bumping against me with his rump.

'Calm down now, boy,' I said soothingly. 'We're stuck with each other. Go to sleep.'

The horse's reply was the equivalent of unprintable: the crash of a steel-clad hoof against a wall.

Perhaps he didn't like me talking, I thought, or indeed even moving about. His head swung round towards the window, his bulk stamping restlessly from one side of the box to the other, and I saw that he, unlike Oliver's horses, wore no headcollar: nothing with which to hold him, while I calmed him, patting his neck.

His head reared up suddenly, tossing violently, and with a foreleg he lashed forward at the wall.

Not funny, I thought. Horrific to have been in the firing-line of that slashing hoof. For heaven's sake, I said to him mentally, I'll do you no harm. Just stay quiet. Go to sleep.

I was standing at that time with my back to the door, so that to the horse I must have been totally in shadow; but he would know I was there. He could smell my presence, hear my breathing. If he could see me as well, would it be better?

I took a tentative step towards the dim oblong of window, and had a clear, sharp, and swiftly terrifying view of one of his eyes.

No peace. No sleep. No prospect of anything like that. The horse's eye was stretched wide with white showing all round the usual darkness, staring not at me but as if blind, glaring wildly at nothing at all.

The black nostrils looked huge. The lips as I watched were drawing back from the teeth. The ears had gone flat to the head and there was froth forming in the mouth. It was the face, I thought incredulously, not of unrest or alarm . . . but of madness.

The horse backed suddenly away, crashing his hind-quarters into the rear wall and rocking again forwards, but this time advancing with both forelegs off the ground, the gleams from thrashing hooves curving in silvery streaks in the gloom, the feet hitting the wall below the window with sickening intent.

I pressed in undoubted panic into the corner made by wall and door, but it gave no real protection. The box was roughly ten feet square by eight feet high, a space even at the best of times half filled by horse. For that horse at that moment it was a straitjacket confinement out of which he seemed intent on physically smashing his way.

The manger, I thought. Get in the manger.

The manger was built at about waist height diagonally across one of the box's rear corners; a smallish metal trough set into a sturdy wooden support. As a shelter it was pathetic, but at least I would be off the ground . . .

The horse turned and stood on his forelegs and let fly backwards with an almighty double kick that thudded into the concrete wall six inches from my head, and it was then, at that moment, that I began to fear that the crazed animal might not just hurt but kill me.

He wasn't purposely trying to attack; most of his kicks were in other directions. He wasn't trying to bite, though his now open mouth looked savage. He was uncontrollably wild, but not with me ... though that, in so small a space, made little difference.

He seemed in the next very few seconds to go utterly berserk. With speeds I could only guess at in the scurrying shadows he whirled and kicked and hurled his bulk against the walls, and I, still attempting to jump through the tempest into the manger, was finally knocked over by one of his flailing feet.

I didn't realize at that point that he'd actually broken one of my arms because the whole thing felt numb. I made it to the manger, tried to scramble up, got my foot in ... sat on the edge ... tried to raise my other, now dangling foot ... and couldn't do it fast enough. Another direct hit crunched on my ankle and I knew, that time, that there was damage.

The air about my head seemed to hiss with hooves and the horse was beginning a high bubbling whinny. Surely someone, I thought desperately, someone would hear the crashing and banging and come ...

I could see him in flashes against the window, a rearing, bucking, kicking, rocketing nightmare. He came wheeling round, half-seen, walking on his hind legs, head hard against the ceiling, the forelegs thrashing as if trying to climb invisible walls ... and he knocked me off my precarious perch with a swiping punch in the chest that had half a ton of weight behind it and no particular aim.

I fell twisting onto the straw and tried to curl my head away from those lethal feet, to save instinctively one's face and gut . . . and leave backbone and kidney to their fate. Another crushing thud landed on the back of my shoulder and jarred like a hammer through every bone, and I could feel a scream forming somewhere inside me, a wrenching cry for mercy, for escape, for an end to battering, for release from terror.

His mania if anything grew worse, and it was he who was finally screaming, not me. The noise filled my ears, bounced off the walls, stunning, mind-blowing, the roaring of furies.

He somehow got one hoof inside my rolled body and tumbled me fast over, and I could see him arching above me, the tendons like strings, the torment in him too, the rage of the gods bursting from his stretched throat, his forelegs so high that he was hitting the ceiling.

This is death, I thought. This is dreadful, pulverizing extinction. Only for this second would I see and feel . . . and one of his feet would land on my head and I'd go . . . I'd go . . .

Before I'd even finished the thought his forelegs came crashing down with a hoof so close it brushed my hair; and then again, as if driven beyond endurance, he reared dementedly on his hind legs, the head going up like a reverse thunderbolt towards the sky, the skull meeting the ceiling with the force of a ram. The whole building shook with the impact, and the horse, his voice cut off, fell in a huge collapsing mass across my legs, spasms shuddering through his body, muscles jerking in stiff kicks, the air still ringing with the echoes of extremity.

He was dying in stages, unconscious, reluctant, the brain finished, the nerve messages still passing to convulsing muscles, turmoil churning without direction in stomach and gut, the head already inert on the straw.

An age passed before it was done. Then the heavy body fell flaccid, all systems spent, and lay in perpetual astonishing silence, pinning me beneath.

The relief of finding him dead and myself alive lasted quite a long time, but then, as always happens with the human race, simple gratitude for existence progressed to discontent that things weren't better.

He had fallen with his spine towards me, his bulk lying across my legs from my knees down; and getting out from under him was proving an impossibility.

The left ankle, which felt broken, protested screechingly at any attempted movement. I couldn't lift my arm for the same reason. There was acute soreness in my chest, making breathing itself painful and coughing frightful; and the only good thing I could think of was that I was lying on my back and not face down in the straw.

A very long time passed very slowly. The crushing weight of the horse slowly numbed my legs altogether and transferred the chief area of agony to the whole of my left arm, which I might have thought totally mangled if I hadn't been able to see it dimly lying there looking the same as usual, covered in blue sweater, white cuff slightly showing, hand with clean nails, gold watch on wrist.

Physical discomfort for a while shut out much in the way of thought, but eventually I began to add up memories and ask questions, and the biggest, most immediate question was what would Calder do when he came back and found me alive?

He wouldn't expect it. No one could really expect anyone to survive being locked in with a mad horse, and the fact that I had was a trick of fate.

I remembered him giving the horse an apple while I'd struggled within the spinning walls to stand up. Giving his apple so routinely, and patting the horse's neck.

I remembered Calder saying on my first visit that he gave his remedies to horses in hollowed-out apples. But this time it had been no remedy, this time something opposite, this time a drug to make crazy, to turn a normal steel-shod horse into a killing machine.

What had he said when he'd first found me conscious? Those bizarre words ... 'I thought you'd be out. I thought you wouldn't know ...' And something else ... 'I wish I'd hit you harder, but it seemed enough.'

He had said also that he was sorry, that he wished I hadn't come ... He hadn't meant, I thought, that I should be aware of it when the horse killed me. At the very least, he hadn't meant me to see and hear and suffer that death. But also, when he found me awake, it hadn't prevented him from *then* giving the apple, although he knew that I *would* see, *would* hear, would . . . suffer.

The horse hadn't completed the task. When Calder returned, he would make good the deficit. It was certain.

I tried, on that thought, again to slide my legs out, though how much it would have helped if I had succeeded was debatable. It was as excruciating as before, since the numbness proved temporary. I concluded somewhat sadly that dragging a broken ankle from beneath a dead horse was no jolly entertainment, and in fact, given the state of the rest of me, couldn't be done.

I had never broken any bones before, not even skiing. I'd never been injured beyond the transient bumps of childhood. Never been to hospital, never troubled a surgeon, never slept from anaesthetic. For thirty-four years I'd been thoroughly healthy and, apart from chicken-pox and such, never ill. I even had good teeth.

I was unprepared in any way for the onslaught of so much pain all at once, and also not quite sure how to deal with it. All I knew was that when I tried to pull out my ankle the protests throughout my body brought actual tears into my eyes and no amount of theoretical resolution could give me the power to continue. I wondered if what I felt was cowardice. I didn't much care if it was. I lay with everything stiffening and getting cold and worse, and I'd have given a good deal to be as oblivious as the horse.

The oblong of window at length began to lighten towards the new day: Saturday, June 2nd, Calder would come back and finish the job, and no reasonable pathologist would swear the last blow had been delivered hours after the first. Calder would say in bewilderment, 'But I had no idea Tim was coming to see me . . . I was in London for the television . . . I have no idea how he came to shut himself into one of the boxes . . . because it's just possible to do that, you know, if you're not careful . . . I've no idea why the horse should have kicked him, because he's a placid old boy, as you can see . . . the whole thing's a terrible accident, and I'm shattered . . . most distressed . . .', and anyone would look at the horse from whose bloodstream the crazing drug would have departed and conclude that I'd been pretty unintelligent and also unlucky, and too bad.

Ian Pargetter's veterinary case had gone to a securer hiding place or to destruction, and there would be only a slight chance left of proving Calder a murderer. Whichever way one considered it, the outlook was discouraging.

I couldn't be bothered to roll my wrist over to see the time. The sun rose and shone slantingly through the bars with the pale brilliance of dawn. It had to be five o'clock, or after.

Time drifted. The sun moved away. The horse and I lay in intimate silence, dead and half dead; waiting.

A car drove up fast outside and doors slammed.

It will be now, I thought. Now. Very soon.

There were voices in the distance, calling to each other. Female and male. *Strangers.*

Not Calder's distinctive, loud, edgy, public voice. Not his at all.

Hope thumped back with a tremendous surge and I called out myself, saying, 'Here . . . Come here,' but it was at best a croak, inaudible beyond the door.

Suppose they were looking for Calder, and when they didn't find him, drove away . . . I took all possible breath into my lungs and yelled, 'Help . . . Come here.'

Nothing happened. My voice ricocheted off the walls and mocked me, and I dragged in another grinding lungful and shouted again . . . and again . . . and again.

The top half of the door swung outward and let in a dazzle of light, and a voice yelled incredulously, 'He's *here.* He's in here . . .'

The bolt on the lower half-door clattered and the daylight grew to an oblong, and against the light three figures appeared, coming forward, concerned, speaking with anxiety and joy and bringing life.

Judith and Gordon and Pen.

Judith was gulping and so I think was I.

'Thank God,' Gordon said. 'Thank God.'

'You didn't go home,' Pen said. 'We were worried.'

'Are you all right?' Judith said.

'Not really . . . but everything's relative. I've never been happier, so who cares.'

'If we put our arms under your shoulders,' Gordon said, surveying the problem, 'we should be able to pull you out.'

'Don't do that,' I said.

'Why not?'

'One shoulder feels broken. Get a knacker.'

'My dear Tim,' he said, puzzled.

'They'll come with a lorry . . . and a winch. Their job is dead horses.'

'Yes, I see.'

'And an ambulance,' Pen said. 'I should think.'

I smiled at them with much love, my fairly incompetent saviours. They asked how I'd got where I was, and to their horror I briefly told them; and I in turn asked why they'd come, and they explained that they'd been worried because Calder's television programme had been cancelled.

'Micky Bonwith was taken ill,' Pen said. 'They just announced it during the evening. There would be no live Micky Bonwith show, just an old recording, very sorry, expect Calder Jackson at a later date.'

'Pen telephoned and told us where you were going, and why,' Judith said.

'And we were worried,' Gordon added.

'You didn't go home . . . didn't telephone,' Pen said.

'We've been awake all night,' Gordon said. 'The girls were growing more and more anxious . . . so we came.'

They'd come a hundred miles. You couldn't ask for better friends.

Gordon drove away to find a public telephone and Pen asked if I'd found what I'd come for.

'I don't know,' I said. 'Half the things had no labels.'

'Don't talk any more,' Judith said. 'Enough is enough.'

'I might as well.'

'Take your mind off it,' Pen nodded, understanding.

'What time is it?' I asked.

Judith looked at her watch. 'Ten to eight.'

'Calder will come back...' And the lads too, I thought. He'd come when the lads turned up for work. About that time. He'd need witnesses to the way he'd found me.

'Tim,' Pen said with decision, 'if he's coming... Did you take any samples? Did you get a chance?'

I nodded weakly.

'I suppose you can't remember what they were...'

'I hid them.'

'Wouldn't he have found them?' She was gentle and prepared to be disappointed; careful not to blame.

I smiled at her. 'He didn't find them. They're here.'

She looked blankly round the box and then at my face. 'Didn't he search you?' she said in surprise. 'Pockets... of course, he would.'

'I don't know... but he didn't find the pills.'

'Then where *are* they?'

'I learned from Ginnie about keeping your hands free,' I said. 'They're in a plastic bag... below my waistband... inside my pants.'

They stared incredulously, and then they laughed, and Judith with tears in her eyes said, 'Do you mean . . . all the time . . .?'

'All the time,' I agreed. 'And go easy getting them out.'

Some things would be best forgotten but are impossible to forget, and I reckon one could put the next half-hour into that category: at the end of it I lay on a table-like stretcher in the open air, and my dead-weight pal was half up the ramp of the knacker's van that Gordon with exceptional persuasiveness had conjured out at that hour of the morning.

The three lads who had at length arrived for work stood around looking helpless, and the two ambulance men, who were not paramedics, were farcically trying to get an answer on a radio with transmission troubles as to where they were supposed to take me.

Gordon was telling the knacker's men that I said it was essential to remove a blood sample from the horse and that the carcass was not to be disposed of until that was done. Judith and Pen both looked tired, and were yawning. I wearily watched some birds wheeling high in the fair blue sky and wished I were up there with them, as light as air; and into this riveting tableau drove Calder.

Impossible to know what he thought when he saw

all the activity, but as he came striding from his car his mouth formed an oval of apprehension and shock.

He seemed first to fasten his attention on Gordon, and then on the knacker's man who was saying loudly, 'If you want a blood sample you'll have to give us a written authorization, because of calling in a vet and paying him.'

Calder looked from him to the dead horse still halfway up the ramp, and from there towards the horse's normal box, where the door stood wide open.

From there he turned with bewilderment to Judith, and then with horror saw the bag Pen held tightly, the transparent plastic bag with the capsules, pills and other assorted treasures showing clearly inside.

Pen remarkably found her voice and in words that must have sounded like doom to Calder said, 'I didn't tell you before . . . I'm a pharmacist.'

'Where did you get that?' Calder said, staring at the bag as if his eyes would burn it. 'Where . . .'

'Tim had it.'

Her gaze went to me and Calder seemed finally to realize that my undoubted stillness was not that of death. He took two paces towards the stretcher and looked down at my face and saw me alive, awake, aware.

Neither of us spoke. His eyes seemed to retreat in the sockets and the shape of the upper jaw stood out starkly. He saw in me I dare say the ravages of the night and I saw in him the realization become certainty that my survival meant his ruin.

I thought: you certainly should have hit harder; and maybe he thought it too. He looked at me with a searing intensity that defied analysis and then turned abruptly away and walked with jerky steps back to his car.

Gordon took two or three hesitant steps towards perhaps stopping him, but Calder without looking back started his engine, put his foot on the accelerator and with protesting tyres made a tight semicircular turn and headed for the gate.

'We should get the police,' Gordon said, watching him go.

Judith and Pen showed scant enthusiasm and I none at all. I supposed we would have to bring in the police in the end, but the longer the boring rituals could be postponed, from my point of view, the better. Britain was a small island, and Calder too well known to go far.

Pen looked down at the plastic storehouse in her hands and then without actual comment opened her handbag and put the whole thing inside. She glanced briefly at me and smiled faintly, and I nodded with relief that she and her friends would have the unravelling of the capsules to themselves.

On that same Saturday, at about two-thirty in the afternoon, a family of picnickers came across a car which had been parked out of sight of any road behind some clumps of gorse bushes. The engine of the car was running and the children of the family, peering through the windows, saw a man slumped on the back seat with a tube in his mouth.

They knew him because of his curly hair, and his beard.

The children were reported to be in a state of hysterical shock and the parents were angry, as if some authority, somewhere or other, should prevent suicides spoiling the countryside.

Tributes to Calder's miracle-working appeared on television that evening, and I thought it ironic that the master who had known so much about drugs should have chosen to gas his way out.

He had driven barely thirty miles from his yard. He had left no note. The people who had been working with him on the postponed Micky Bonwith show said they couldn't understand it, and Dissdale telephoned Oliver to say that in view of Calder's tragic death he would have to withdraw his offer for Sandcastle.

I, by the time I heard all this, was half covered in infinitely irritating plaster of Paris, there being more grating edges of bone inside me than I cared to hear about, and horseshoe-shaped crimson bruises besides.

I had been given rather grudgingly a room to myself, privacy in illness being considered a sinful luxury in the National Health Service, and on Monday evening

Pen came all the way from London again to report on the laboratory findings.

She frowned after she'd kissed me. 'You look exhausted,' she said.

'Tiring place, hospital.'

'I suppose it must be. I'd never thought . . .'

She put a bunch of roses in my drinking-water jug and said they were from Gordon and Judith's garden.

'They send their love,' she said chattily, 'and their garden's looking lovely.'

'Pen . . .'

'Yes. Well.' She pulled the visitor's chair closer to the bed upon which I half sat, half lay in my plaster and borrowed dressing gown on top of the blankets. 'You have really, as they say, hit the jackpot.'

'Do you mean it?' I exclaimed.

She grinned cheerfully. 'It's no wonder that Calder killed himself, not after seeing you alive and hearing you were going to get the dead horse tested, and knowing that after all you had taken all those things from his surgery. It was either that or years in jail and total disgrace.'

'A lot of people would prefer disgrace.'

'Not Calder, though.'

'No.'

She opened a slim black briefcase on her knees and produced several typewritten pages.

'We worked all yesterday and this morning,' she said. 'But first I'll tell you that Gordon got the dead horse's

674

blood test done immediately at the Equine Research Establishment, and they told him on the telephone this morning that the horse had been given ethyl isobutrazine, which was contrary to normal veterinary practice.'

'You don't say.'

Her eyes gleamed. 'The Research people told Gordon that any horse given ethyl isobutrazine would go utterly berserk and literally try to climb the walls.'

'That's just what he did,' I said soberly.

'It's a drug which is used all the time as a tranquillizer to stop dogs barking or getting car-sick, but it has an absolutely manic effect on horses. One of its brand names is Diquel, in case you're interested. All the veterinary books warn against giving it to horses.'

'But normally . . . in a horse . . . it would wear off?'

'Yes, in six hours or so, with no trace.'

Six hours, I thought bleakly. *Six hours* . . .

'In your bag of goodies,' Pen said, 'guess what we found? Three tablets of Diquel.'

'Really?'

She nodded. 'Really. And now pin back your ears, dearest Tim, because when we found what Calder had been doing, words simply failed us.'

They seemed indeed to fail her again, for she sat looking at the pages with a faraway expression.

'You remember,' she said at last, 'when we went to Calder's yard that time at Easter, we saw a horse that had been bleeding in its urine . . . crystalluria was what he called it ... that antibiotics hadn't been able to cure?'

'Yes,' I said. 'Other times too, he cured horses with that.'

'Mm. And those patients had been previously treated by Ian Pargetter before he died, hadn't they?'

I thought back. 'Some of them, certainly.'

'Well ... you know you told me before they carted you off in the ambulance on Saturday that some of the jars of capsules in the cupboards were labelled only with letters like a+w, b+w, and c+s?'

I nodded.

'Three capsules each with one transparent and one blue end, *did* contain c and s. Vitamin C, and sulpha-nilamide.' She looked at me for a possible reaction, but vitamin C and sulphanilamide sounded quite harmless, and I said so.

'Yes,' she said, 'separately they do nothing but good, but *together they can cause crystalluria.*'

I stared at her.

'Calder had made those capsules expressly to *cause the horse's illness* in the first place, so that he could "cure" it afterwards. And then the only miracle he'd have to work would be to stop giving the capsules.'

'My God,' I said.

She nodded. 'We could hardly believe it. It meant, you see, that Ian Pargetter almost certainly *knew*. Because it was he, you see, who could have given the horse's trainer or owner or lad or whatever a bottle of capsules labelled "antibiotic" to dole out every day. And those capsules were precisely what was making the horse ill.'

'*Pen!*'

'I'd better explain just a little, if you can bear it,' she said. 'If you give sulpha drugs to anyone – horse or person – who doesn't need them, you won't do much harm because urine is normally slightly alkaline or only slightly acid and you'll get rid of the sulpha safely. But vitamin C is ascorbic acid and makes the urine *more* acid, and the acid works with sulpha drugs to form crystals, and the crystals cause pain and bleeding ... like powdered glass.'

There was a fairly long silence, and then I said, 'It's diabolical.'

She nodded. 'Once Calder had the horse in his yard he could speed up the cure by giving him bicarbonate of soda, which will make the urine alkaline again and also dissolve the crystals, and with plenty of water to drink the horse would be well in no time. Miraculously fast, in fact.' She paused and smiled, and went on, 'We tested a few more things which were perfectly harmless herbal remedies and then we came to three more home-made capsules, with pale green ends this time, and we reckon that they were your a+w.'

'Go on, then,' I said. 'What's a, and what's w?'

'A is antibiotic, and w is warfarin. And before you ask, warfarin is a drug used in humans for reducing the clotting ability of the blood.'

'That pink pill you found on the surgery floor,' I said. 'That's what you said.'

'Oh yes.' She looked surprised. 'So I did. I'd forgotten. Well ... if you give certain antibiotics *with* warfarin you increase the effect of the warfarin to the extent that blood will hardly clot at all ... and you get severe bleeding from the stomach, from the mouth, from anywhere where a small blood vessel breaks ... when normally it would clot and mend at once.'

I let out a held breath. 'Every time I went, there was a bleeder.'

She nodded. 'Warfarin acts by drastically reducing the effect of vitamin K, which is needed for normal clotting, so all Calder had to do to reverse things was feed lots of vitamin K ... which is found in large quantities in alfalfa.'

'And b+w?' I asked numbly.

'Barbiturate and warfarin. Different mechanism, but if you used them together and then stopped just the barbiturate, you could cause a sort of delayed bleeding about three weeks later.' She paused. 'We've all been looking up our pharmacology textbooks, and there are warnings there, plain to see if you're looking for them, about prescribing antibiotics or barbiturates or indeed phenylbutazone or anabolic steroids for people on warfarin without carefully adjusting the warfarin dosage. And you see,' she went on, 'putting two drugs together in one capsule was really brilliant, because no one would think they were giving a horse two drugs, but just one . . . and we reckon Ian Pargetter could have put Calder's capsules into any regular bottle, and the horse's owner would think that he was giving the horse what it said on the label.'

I blinked. 'It's incredible.'

'It's easy,' she said. 'And it gets easier as it goes on.'

'There's more?'

'Sure there's more.' She grinned. 'How about all those poor animals with extreme debility who were so weak they could hardly walk?'

I swallowed. 'How about them?'

'You said you found a large bottle in Ian Pargetter's case with only a few pills in it? A bottle labelled "diuretic", or in other words, pills designed to increase the passing of urine?'

I nodded.

'Well, we identified the ones you took, and if you simply gave those particular thiazide diuretic pills over a long period to a horse you would cause *exactly* the sort of general progressive debility shown by those horses.'

I was past speech.

'And to cure the debility,' she said, 'you just stop the diuretics and provide good food and water. And hey presto!' She smiled blissfully. 'Chemically, it's so elegant. The debility is caused by constant excessive excretion of potassium which the body needs for strength, and the cure is to restore potassium as fast as safely possible . . . with potassium salts, which you can buy anywhere.'

I gazed at her with awe.

She was enjoying her revelations. 'We come now to the horses with non-healing ulcers and sores.'

Always those, too, in the yard, I thought.

'Ulcers and sores are usually cleared up fairly quickly by applications of antibiotic cream. Well . . . by this time we were absolutely bristling with suspicions, so last of all we took that little tube of antibiotic cream you found in Ian Pargetter's case, and we tested it. And lo and behold, it didn't contain antibiotic cream at all.'

'What then?'

'Cortisone cream.'

She looked at my non-comprehension and smiled. 'Cortisone cream is fine for eczema and allergies, but *not* for general healing. In fact, if you scratched a horse and smeared some dirt into the wound to infect it and then religiously applied cortisone cream twice a day you would get a nice little ulcer which would never heal. Until, of course, you sent your horse to Calder, who would lay his hands upon your precious . . . and apply antibiotics at once, to let normal healing begin.'

'Dear God in heaven.'

'Never put cortisone cream on a cut,' she said. 'A lot of people do. It's stupid.'

'I never will,' I said fervently.

Pen grinned. 'They always fill toothpaste from the

blunt end. We looked very closely and found that the end of the tube had been unwound and then re-sealed. Very neat.'

She seemed to have stopped, so I asked, 'Is that the lot?'

'That's the lot.'

We sat for a while and pondered.

'It does answer an awful lot of questions,' I said finally.

'Such as?'

'Such as why Calder killed Ian Pargetter,' I said. 'Ian Pargetter wanted to stop something . . . which must have been this illness caper. Said he'd had enough. Said also that he would stop Calder too, which must have been his death warrant.'

Pen said, 'Is that what Calder actually told you?'

'Yes, that's what he said, but at the time I didn't understand what he meant.'

'I wonder,' Pen said, 'why Ian Pargetter wanted to stop altogether? They must have had a nice steady income going between the two of them. Calder must have recruited him years ago.'

'Selenium,' I said.

'What?'

'Selenium was different. Making horses ill in order to cure them wasn't risking much permanent damage, if any at all. But selenium would be for ever. The foals would be deformed. I'd guess when Calder suggested it the idea sickened Ian Pargetter. Revolted him, probably, because he was after all a vet.'

'And Calder wanted to go on with it all . . . enough to kill.'

I nodded. 'Calder would have had his sights on a fortune as well as an income. And but for Ginnie somehow getting hold of that shampoo, he would very likely have achieved it.'

'I wonder how she did,' Pen said.

'Mm.' I shifted uncomfortably on the bed. 'I've remembered the name of the lad Calder had who looked like Ricky Barnet. It was Jason. I remembered it the other night . . . in that yard . . . funny the way the mind works.'

'What about him?' Pen said sympathetically.

'I remembered Calder saying he gave the pills to Jason for Jason to give to the horses. The herb pills, he meant. But with Ian Pargetter gone, Calder would have needed someone else to give those double-edged capsules to horses . . . because he still had horses in his yard with those same troubles long after Ian Pargetter was dead.'

'So he did,' she said blankly. 'Except . . .'

'Except what?'

'Only that when we got to the yard last Saturday, before I heard you calling, we looked into several other boxes, and there weren't many horses there. The place wasn't full, like it had been.'

'I should think,' I said slowly, 'that it was because

Jason had been busy working for three months or more at Oliver's farm, feeding selenium apples.'

A visual memory flashed in my brain. *Apples* . . . Shane, the stable lad, walking across the yard, swinging a bucket and eating an apple. Shane, Jason: one and the same.

'What is it?' Pen said.

'Photos of Ricky Barnet.'

'Oh yes.'

'They say I can leave here tomorrow,' I said, 'if I insist.'

She looked at me with mock despair. 'What exactly did you break?'

'They said this top lot was scapula, clavicle, humerus, sternum and ribs. Down there,' I pointed, 'they lost me. I didn't know there *were* so many bones in one ankle.'

'Did they pin it?'

'God knows.'

'How will you look after yourself?'

'In my usual clumsy fashion.'

'Don't be silly,' she said. 'Stay until it stops hurting.'

'That might be weeks . . . there's some problem with ligaments or tendons or something.'

'What problem?'

'I didn't really listen.'

'*Tim*.' She was exasperated.

'Well . . . it's so boring,' I said.

She gave an eyes-to-heaven laugh. 'I brought you a

present from my shop.' She dug into her handbag. 'Here you are, with my love.'

I took the small white box she offered, and looked at the label on its side.

Comfrey, it said.

She grinned. 'You might as well try it,' she said. 'Comfrey does contain allantoin, which helps to knit bones. And you never know ... Calder really was an absolute expert with all sorts of drugs.'

On Tuesday, June 5th, Oliver Knowles collected me from the hospital to drive me on some errands and then take me to his home, not primarily as an act of compassion but mostly to talk business. I had expected him to accept my temporary disabilities in a straightforward and unemotional manner, and so he did, although he did say drily when he saw me that when I had invited myself over the telephone I had referred to a 'crack or two' and not to half an acre of plaster with clothes strung on in patches.

'Never mind,' I said. 'I can hop and I can sit and my right arm is fine.'

'Yes. So I see.'

The nurse who had wheeled me in a chair to his car said, however, 'He can't hop, it jars him,' and handed Oliver a slip of paper. 'There's a place along that road ...' She pointed, '... where you can hire wheelchairs.' To me she said, 'Get a comfortable one. And one which lets your leg lie straight out, like this one. You'll ache less. All right?'

'All right,' I said.

'Hm. Well . . . take care.'

She helped me into the car with friendly competence and went away with the hospital transport, and Oliver and I did as she advised, storing the resulting cushioned and chromium comfort into the boot of his car.

'Right,' I said. 'Then the next thing to do is buy a good instant camera and a stack of films.'

Oliver found a shop and bought the camera while I sat in the front passenger seat as patiently as possible.

'Where next?' he said, coming back with parcels.

'Cambridge. An engineering works. Here's the address.' I handed him the piece of paper on which I'd written Ricky Barnet's personal directions. 'We're meeting him when he comes out of work.'

'Who?' Oliver said. 'Who are we meeting?'

'You'll see.'

We parked across the road from the firm's gate and waited, and at four-thirty on the dot the exodus occurred.

Ricky Barnet came out and looked this way and that in searching for us, and beside me I heard Oliver stir and say, 'But that's Shane,' in surprise, and then relax and add doubtfully, 'No it isn't.'

'No, it isn't.' I leaned out of the open window and called to him, 'Ricky . . . over here.'

He crossed the road and stopped beside the car.

'Hop in,' I said.

'You been in an accident?' he said disbelievingly.

'Sort of.'

He climbed into the back of the car. He hadn't been too keen to have his photograph taken for the purpose I'd outlined, but he was in no great position to refuse; and I'd made my blackmailing pressure sound like honey, which I wasn't too bad at, in my way. He still wasn't pleased, however, which had its own virtues, as the last thing I wanted was forty prints of him grinning.

Oliver drove off and stopped where I asked at a suitably neutral background – a grey-painted factory wall – and he said he would take the photographs if I explained what I wanted.

'Ricky looks like Shane,' I said. 'So take pictures of Ricky in the way he *most* looks like Shane. Get him to turn his head slowly like he did when he came out of work, and tell him to hold it where it's best.'

'All right.'

Ricky got out of the car and stood in front of the wall, with Oliver focusing at head-and-shoulder distance. He took the first picture and we waited for it to develop.

Oliver looked at it, grunted, adjusted the light meter, and tried again.

'This one's all right,' he said, watching the colours emerge. 'Looks like Shane. Quite amazing.'

With a faint shade of sullenness Ricky held his pose

for as long as it took to shoot four boxes of film. Oliver passed each print to me as it came out of the camera, and I laid them in rows along the seat beside me while they developed.

'That's fine,' I said, when the films were finished. 'Thank you, Ricky.'

He came over to the car window and I asked him without any great emphasis, 'Do you remember, when Indian Silk got so ill with debility, which vet was treating him?'

'Yeah, sure, that fellow that was murdered. Him and his partners. The best, Dad said.'

I nodded non-committally. 'Do you want a ride to Newmarket?'

'Got my motorbike, thanks.'

We took him back to his engineering works where I finally cheered him up with payment for his time and trouble, and watched while he roared off with a flourish of self-conscious bravado.

'What's now?' Oliver said. 'Did you say Newmarket?'

I nodded. 'I've arranged to meet Ursula Young.'

He gave me a glance of bewilderment and drove without protest, pulling duly into the mid-town car park where Ursula had said to come.

We arrived there first, the photography not having taken as long as I'd expected, and Oliver finally gave voice to a long-restrained question.

'Just what,' he said, 'are the photographs *for*?'

687

'For finding Shane.'

'But why?'

'Don't explode.'

'No.'

'Because I think he gave the selenium to your mares.'

Oliver sat very still. 'You asked about him before,' he said. 'I did wonder . . . if you thought . . . he killed Ginnie.'

It was my own turn for quiet.

'I don't know if he did,' I said at last. 'I don't know.'

Ursula arrived in her car with a rush, checking her watch and apologizing all the same, although she was on time. She, like Oliver and Ricky, looked taken aback at my unorthodox attire, but rallied in her usual no-nonsense fashion and shuffled into the back seat of Oliver's car, leaning forward to bring her face on a level with ours.

I passed her thirty of the forty pictures of Ricky Barnet who, of course, she knew immediately.

'Yes, but,' I explained, 'Ricky looks like a lad who worked for Oliver, and it's *that* lad we want to find.'

'Well, all right. How important is it?'

Oliver answered her before I could. 'Ursula, if you find him, we might be able to prove there's nothing wrong with Sandcastle. And don't ask me how, just believe it.'

Her mouth had opened.

'And Ursula,' Oliver said, 'if you find him – Shane,

that lad – I'll put business your way for the rest of my life.'

I could see that to her, a middle-rank bloodstock agent, it was no mean promise.

'All right,' she said briskly. 'You're on. I'll start spreading the pictures about at once, tonight, and call you with results.'

'Ursula,' I said. 'If you find where he is now, make sure he isn't frightened off. We don't want to lose him.'

She looked at me shrewdly. 'This is roughly police work?'

I nodded. 'Also, if you find anyone who employed him in the past, ask if by any chance a horse he looked after fell ill. Or any horse in the yard, for that matter. And don't give him a name . . . he isn't always called Shane.'

'Is he dangerous?' she said straightly.

'We don't want him challenged,' I said. 'Just found.'

'All right. I trust you both, so I'll do my best. And I suppose one day you'll explain what it's all about?'

'If he's done what we think,' I said, 'we'll make sure the whole world knows. You can count on it.'

She smiled briefly and patted my unplastered shoulder. 'You look grey,' she said, and to Oliver, 'Tim told me a horse kicked him and broke his arm. Is that right?'

'He told me that, too.'

'And what else?' she asked me astringently. 'How did you get in this state?'

689

'The horse didn't know its own strength.' I smiled at her. 'Clumsy brute.'

She knew I was dodging in some way, but she lived in a world where the danger of horse kicks was ever present and always to be avoided, and she made no more demur. Stowing the photographs in her capacious handbag she wriggled her way out of the car, and with assurances of action drove off in her own.

'What now?' Oliver said.

'A bottle of Scotch.'

He gave me an austere look which then swept over my general state and softened to understanding.

'Can you wait until we get home?' he said.

That evening, bit by bit, I told Oliver about Pen's analysis of the treasures from Calder's surgery and of Calder's patients' drug-induced illnesses. I told him that Calder had killed Ian Pargetter, and why, and I explained again how the idea of first discrediting, then buying and rebuilding Sandcastle had followed the pattern of Indian Silk.

'There may be others besides Indian Silk that we haven't heard of,' I said thoughtfully. 'Show jumpers, eventers, even prize ponies. You never know. Dissdale might have gone along more than twice with his offer to buy the no-hoper.'

'He withdrew his offer for Sandcastle the same night Calder died.'

'What exactly did he say?' I asked.

'He was very upset. Said he'd lost his closest friend, and that without Calder to work his miracles there was no point in buying Sandcastle.'

I frowned. 'Do you think it was genuine?'

'His distress? Yes, certainly.'

'And the belief in miracles?'

'He did *sound* as if he believed.'

I wondered if it was in the least possible that Dissdale was an innocent and duped accomplice and hadn't known that his bargains had been first made ill. His pride in knowing the Great Man had been obvious at Ascot, and perhaps he had been flattered and foolish but not wicked after all.

Oliver asked in the end how I'd found out about the drug-induced illnesses and Ian Pargetter's murder, and I told him that too, as flatly as possible.

He sat staring at me, his gaze on the plaster.

'You're very lucky to be in a wheelchair, and not a coffin,' he said. 'Damn lucky.'

'Yes.'

He poured more of the brandy we had progressed to after dinner. Anaesthesia was coming along nicely.

'I'm almost beginning to believe,' he said, 'that somehow or other I'll still be here next year, even if I do have to sell Sandcastle and whatever else is necessary.'

I drank from my replenished glass. 'Tomorrow we'll make a plan contingent upon Sandcastle's being reinstated in the eyes of the world. Look out the figures, see what the final damage is likely to be, draw up a time-scale for recovery. I can't promise because it isn't my final say-so, but if the bank gets all its money in the end, it'll most likely be flexible about when.'

'Good of you,' Oliver said, hiding emotion behind his clipped martial manner.

'Frankly,' I said, 'you're more use to us salvaged than bust.'

He smiled wryly. 'A banker to the last drop of blood.'

Because of stairs being difficult I slept on the sofa where Ginnie had dozed on her last afternoon, and I dreamed of her walking up a path towards me looking happy. Not a significant dream, but an awakening of fresh regret. I spent a good deal of the following day thinking of her instead of concentrating on profit and loss.

In the evening Ursula telephoned with triumph in her strong voice and also a continual undercurrent of amazement.

'You won't believe it,' she said, 'but I've already found three racing stables in Newmarket where he worked last summer and autumn, and in *every case* one of the horses in the yard fell sick!'

I hadn't any trouble at all with belief and asked what sort of sickness.

'They all had crystalluria. That's crystals . . .'

'I know what it is,' I said.

'And . . . it's absolutely incredible but all three were in stables which had in the past sent horses to Calder Jackson, and these were sent as well, and he cured them straight away. Two of the trainers said they would swear by Calder, he had cured horses for them for years.'

'Was the lad called Shane?' I asked.

'No. Bret. Bret Williams. The same in all three places.'

She dictated the addresses of the stables, the names of the trainers, and the dates (approximate) when Shane – Jason – Bret had been in their yards.

'These lads just come and go,' she said. 'He didn't work for any of them for as long as a month. Just didn't turn up one morning. It happens all the time.'

'You're marvellous,' I said.

'I have a feeling,' she said with less excitement, 'that what I'm telling you is what you expected to hear.'

'Hoped.'

'The implications are unbelievable.'

'Believe them.'

'But *Calder*,' she protested. 'He couldn't . . .'

'Shane worked for Calder,' I said. 'All the time. Permanently. Wherever he went, it was to manufacture patients for Calder.'

She was silent so long that in the end I said, 'Ursula?'

'I'm here,' she said. 'Do you want me to go on with the photos?'

'Yes, if you would. To find him.'

'Hanging's too good for him,' she said grimly. 'I'll do what I can.'

She disconnected, and I told Oliver what she'd said.

'Bret Williams? He was Shane Williams here.'

'How did you come to employ him?' I asked.

Oliver frowned, looking back. 'Good lads aren't that easy to find, you know. You can advertise until you're blue in the face and only get third- or fourth-rate applicants. But Nigel said Shane impressed him at the interview and that we should give him a month's trial, and of course after that we kept him on, and took him back gladly this year when he telephoned asking, because he was quick and competent and knew the job backwards, and was polite and a good time-keeper . . .'

'A paragon,' I said drily.

'As lads go, yes.'

I nodded. He would have to have been good; to have taken pride in his deception, with the devotion of all traitors. I considered those fancy names and thought that he must have seen himself as a sort of macho hero, the great foreign agent playing out his fantasies in the day to day tasks, feeling superior to his employers while he tricked them with contempt.

He could have filled the hollowed cores of apples with capsules, and taken a bite or two round the outside to convince, and fed what looked like remainders to his victims. No one would ever have suspected, because suspicion was impossible.

I slept again on the sofa and the following morning

Oliver telephoned to Detective Chief Inspector Wyfold and asked him to come to the farm. Wyfold needed persuading; reluctantly agreed; and nearly walked out in a U-turn when he saw me waiting in Oliver's office.

'No. Look,' he protested, 'Mr Ekaterin's already approached me with his ideas and I simply haven't time . . .'

Oliver interrupted. 'We have a great deal more now. Please do listen. We quite understand that you are busy with all those other poor girls, but at the very least we can take Ginnie off that list for you.'

Wyfold finally consented to sit down and accept some coffee and listen to what we had to say: and as we told him in turns and in detail what had been happening his air of impatience dissipated and his natural sharpness took over.

We gave him copies of Pen's analyses, the names of 'Bret's' recent employers and the last ten photographs of Ricky. He glanced at them briefly and said, 'We interviewed this groom, but . . .'

'No, you didn't,' Oliver said. 'The photo is of a boy who looks like him if you don't know either of them well.'

Wyfold pursed his lips, but nodded. 'Fair enough.'

'We do think he may have killed Ginnie, even if you couldn't prove it,' Oliver said.

Wyfold began putting together the papers we'd given him. 'We will certainly redirect our enquiries,' he said, and giving me a dour look added, 'If you had left it to the police to search Calder's surgery, sir, Calder Jackson would not have had the opportunity of disposing of Ian Pargetter's case and any other material evidence. These things are always mishandled by amateurs.' He looked pointedly at my plaster jacket. 'Better have left it to the professionals.'

I gave him an amused look but Oliver was gasping. 'Left to you,' he said, 'there would have been no search at all . . . or certainly not in time to save my business.'

Wyfold's expression said plainly that saving people's businesses wasn't his prime concern, but beyond mentioning that picking locks and stealing medicinal substances constituted a breach of the law he kept any further disapproval to himself.

He was on his feet ready to go when Ursula rang again, and he could almost hear every word she said because of her enthusiasm.

'I'm in Gloucestershire,' she shouted. 'I thought I'd work from the other end, if you see what I mean. I remembered Calder had miraculously cured Binty Rockingham's utterly brilliant three-day-eventer who was so weak he could hardly totter, so I came here to her house to ask her, and guess what?'

'What?' I asked obligingly.

'That lad worked for her!' The triumph exploded. 'A good lad, she says, would you believe it? He called himself Clint. She can't remember his last name, it was more than two years ago and he was only here a few weeks.'

'Ask her if it was Williams,' I said.

There was some murmuring at the other end and then Ursula's voice back again, 'She thinks so, yes.'

'You're a dear, Ursula,' I said.

She gave an embarrassed laugh. 'Do you want me to go on down the road to Rube Golby's place? He had a show pony Calder cured a fair time ago of a weeping wound that wouldn't heal.'

'Just one more, then, Ursula. It's pretty conclusive already, I'd say.'

'Best to be sure,' she said cheerfully. 'And I'm enjoying myself, actually, now I'm over the shock.'

I wrote down the details she gave me and when she'd gone off the line I handed the new information to Wyfold.

'Clint,' he said with disillusion. 'Elvis next, I shouldn't wonder.'

I shook my head. 'A man of action, our Shane.'

Perhaps through needing to solve at least one murder while reviled for not catching his rapist, Wyfold put his best muscle into the search. It took him two weeks only to find Shane, who was arrested on leaving a pub in the racing village of Malton, Yorkshire, where he had been heard boasting several times about secret exploits of undisclosed daring.

Wyfold told Oliver, who telephoned me in the office,

to which I'd returned via a newly installed wheelchair ramp up the front steps.

'He called himself Dean,' Oliver said. 'Dean Williams. It seems the police are transferring him from Yorkshire back here to Hertfordshire, and Wyfold wants you to come to his police headquarters to identify Shane as the man called Jason at Calder's yard.'

I said I would.

I didn't say that with honesty I couldn't.

'Tomorrow,' Oliver added. 'They're in a hurry because of holding him without a good enough change, or something.'

'I'll be there.'

I went in a chauffeur-driven hired car, a luxury I seemed to have spent half my salary on since leaving Oliver's house.

I was living nearer the office than usual with a friend whose flat was in a block with a lift, not up stairs like my own. The pains in my immobile joints refused obstinately to depart, but owing to a further gift from Pen (via Gordon) were forgettable most of the time. A new pattern of 'normal' life had evolved, and all I dearly wanted was a bath.

I arrived at Wyfold's police station at the same time as Oliver, and together we were shown into an office, Oliver pushing me as if born to it. Two months minimum, they'd warned me to expect of life on wheels. Even if my shoulder would be mended before then, it wouldn't stand my weight on crutches. Patience, I'd been told. Be patient. My ankle had been in bits and they'd restored it like a jigsaw puzzle and I couldn't expect miracles, they'd said.

Wyfold arrived, shook hands briskly (an advance) and said that this was not a normal identity parade, as of course Oliver knew Shane very well, and I obviously knew him also, because of Ricky Barnet.

'Just call him Jason,' Wyfold told me. 'If you are sure he's the same man you saw at Calder Jackson's.'

We left the office and went along a fiercely lit institutional corridor to a large interview room which contained a table, three chairs, a uniformed policeman standing . . . and Shane, sitting down.

He looked cocky, not cowed.

When he saw Oliver he tilted his head almost jauntily, showing not shame but pride, not apology but a sneer. On me he looked with only a flickering glance, neither knowing me from our two very brief meetings nor reckoning on trouble from my direction.

Wyfold raised his eyebrows at me to indicate the need for action.

'Hello, Jason,' I said.

His head snapped round immediately and this time he gave me a full stare.

'I met you at Calder Jackson's yard,' I said.

'You never did.'

Although I hadn't expected it, I remembered him clearly. 'You were giving sunlamp treatment to a horse and Calder Jackson told you to put on your sunglasses.'

He made no more effort to deny it. 'What of it, then?' he said.

'Conclusive evidence of your link with the place, I should think,' I said.

Oliver, seeming as much outraged by Shane's lack of contrition as by his sins, turned with force to Wyfold and in half-controlled bitterness said, 'Now prove he killed my daughter.'

'*What!*'

Shane had risen in panic to his feet, knocking his chair over behind him and losing in an instant the smart-alec assurance. 'I never did,' he said.

We all watched him with interest, and his gaze travelled fast from one face to another, seeing only assessment and disbelief and nowhere admiration.

'I didn't kill her,' he said, his voice hoarse and rising. 'I didn't. Straight up, I didn't. It was him. He did it.'

'Who?' I said.

'Calder. Mr Jackson. He did it. It was him, not me.' He looked across at us all again with desperation. 'Look, I'm telling you the truth, straight up I am. I never killed her, it was him.'

Wyfold began telling him in a flat voice that he had a right to remain silent and that anything he said might be written down and used in evidence, but Shane wasn't clever and fright had too firm a hold. His fantasy world had vanished in the face of unimaginable reality, and I found myself believing every word he said.

'We didn't know she was there, see. She heard us talking, but we didn't know. And when I carried the stuff back to the hostel he saw her moving so he hit her. I didn't see him do it, I didn't, but when I went back there he was with Ginnie on the ground and I said she was the boss's daughter, which he didn't even know, see, but he said all the worse if she was the boss's daughter because she would have gone straight off and told everybody.'

The words, explanations, excuses came tumbling out in self-righteous urgency and Wyfold thankfully showed no signs of regulating the flow into the careful officialese of a formal statement. The uniformed policeman, now sitting behind Shane, was writing at speed in a notebook, recording, I imagined, the gist.

'I don't believe you,' Wyfold said impatiently. 'What did he hit her with?'

Shane redoubled his efforts to convince, and from then on I admired Wyfold's slyly effective interrogatory technique.

'With a fire extinguisher,' Shane said. 'He kept it in his car, see, and he had it in his hand. He was real fussy about fire always. Would never let anyone smoke anywhere near the stables. That Nigel . . .' The sneer came back temporarily, '. . . the lads all smoked in the feed room, I ask you, behind his back. He'd no idea what went on.'

'Fire extinguisher . . .' Wyfold spoke doubtfully, shaking his head.

'Yeah, it was. It was. One of them red things about this long.' Shane anxiously held up his hands about fifteen inches apart. 'With the nozzle, sort of, at the top. He was holding it by that, sort of swinging it. Ginnie was lying flat on the ground, face down, like, and I said, "What have you gone and done?" and he said she'd been listening.'

Wyfold sniffed.

'It was like that, straight up,' Shane said urgently.

'Listening to what?'

'We were talking about the stuff, see.'

'The shampoo . . .'

'Yeah.' He seemed only briefly to feel the slightest alarm at the mention of it. 'I told him, see, that the stuff had really worked because there'd been a foal born that morning with half a leg, that Nigel had tried to hush it up but by afternoon he was half cut and told one of the lads so we all knew. So I told Mr Jackson and he said great, because it was time we'd heard, and there hadn't been a murmur in the papers and he was getting worried he hadn't got the dose right, or something. So anyway when I told him about the foal with half a leg he laughed, see, he was so pleased, and he said this was probably the last lot I'd have to do, just do the six bottles he'd brought and then scarper.'

Oliver looked very pale, with sweat along his hairline and whitely clenched fists. His mouth was rigidly closed with the effort of self-control, and he listened throughout without once interrupting or cursing.

'I took the six bottles off to the hostel but when I got there I'd only got five, so I went back to look for the one I'd dropped, but I forgot it, see, when I saw him standing there over Ginnie and him saying she'd heard us talking, and then he said for me to come with him down to the village in his car and he'd drop me at a pub where the other lads were, so as I couldn't have been back home killing the boss's daughter, see? I remembered about the bottle I'd dropped when we were on our way to the village but I didn't think he'd be best pleased and anyway I reckoned I'd find it all right when I went back, but I never did. I didn't think it would matter much, because no one would know what it was for, it was just dog shampoo, and anyway I reckoned I'd skip using the new bottles after all because of the fuss there would be over Ginnie. But if it hadn't been for that bottle I wouldn't have gone out again at all, see, and I wouldn't know it was him that killed her, and it wasn't me, it *wasn't*.'

He came to what appeared in his own mind to be a halt, but as far as Wyfold, Oliver and myself were concerned he had stopped short of enough.

'Are you saying,' Wyfold said, 'that you walked back from the village with the other grooms, knowing what you would find?'

'Well, yeah. Only Dave and Sammy, see, they'd got back first, and when I got back there was an ambulance there and such, and I just kept in the background.'

'What did you do with the other five bottles of

shampoo?' Wyfold asked. 'We searched all the rooms in the hostel. We didn't find any shampoo.'

The first overwhelming promptings of fear were beginning to die down in Shane, but he answered with only minimal hesitation, 'I took them down the road a ways and threw them in a ditch. That was after they'd all gone off to the hospital.' He nodded in the general direction of Oliver and myself. 'Panicked me a bit, it did, when Dave said she was talking, like. But I was glad I'd got rid of the stuff afterwards, when she was dead after all, with everyone snooping around.'

'You could show me which ditch?' Wyfold said.

'Yeah, I could.'

'Good.'

'You mean,' Shane said, with relief, 'you believe what I told you . . .'

'No, I don't mean that,' Wyfold said repressively. 'I'll need to know what you ordinarily did with the shampoo.'

'What?'

'How you prepared it and gave it to the mares.'

'Oh.' An echo of the cocky cleverness came back: a swagger to the shoulders, a curl to the lip. 'It was dead easy, see. Mr Jackson showed me how. I just had to put a coffee filter in a wash basin and pour the shampoo through it, so's the shampoo all ran down the drain and there was that stuff left on the paper, then I just turned the coffee filter inside out and soaked it in a little jar with some linseed oil from the feed shed, and then I'd stir a quarter of it into the feed if it was for a mare I was looking after anyway, or let the stuff fall to the bottom and scrape up a teaspoonful and put it in an apple for the others. Mr Jackson showed me how. Dead easy, the whole thing.'

'How many mares did you give it to?'

'Don't rightly know. Dozens, counting last year. Some I missed. Mr Jackson said better to miss some than be found out. He liked me to do the oil best. Said too many apples would be noticed.' A certain amount of anxiety returned. 'Look, now I've told you all this, you know I didn't kill her, don't you?'

Wyfold said impasssively, 'How often did Mr Jackson bring you bottles of shampoo?'

'He didn't. I mean, I had a case of it under my bed. Brought it with me when I moved in, see, same as last year. But this year I ran out, like, so I rang him up from the village one night for some more. So he said he'd meet me at the back gate at nine on Sunday when all the lads would be down in the pub.'

'That was a risk he wouldn't take,' Wyfold said sceptically.

'Well, he did.'

Wyfold shook his head.

Shane's panic resurfaced completely. 'He was there,' he almost shouted. 'He was. He *was*.'

Wyfold still looked studiedly unconvinced and told Shane that it would be best if he now made a formal statement, which the sergeant would write down for

him to sign when he, Shane, was satisfied that it represented what he had already told us; and Shane in slight
bewilderment agreed.

Wyfold nodded to the sergeant, opened the door of
the room, and gestured to Oliver and me to leave.
Oliver in undiluted grimness silently pushed me out.
Wyfold, with a satisfied air, said in his plain un-
cushioning way, 'There you are then, Mr Knowles,
that's how your daughter died, and you're luckier than
some. That little sod's telling the truth. Proud of
himself, like a lot of crooks. Wants the world to know.'
He shook hands perfunctorily with Oliver and nodded
briefly to me, and walked away to his unsolved horrors
where the papers called for his blood and other fathers
choked on their tears.

Oliver pushed me back to the outside world but not
directly to where my temporary chauffeur had said he
would wait. I found myself making an unscheduled turn
into a small public garden, where Oliver abruptly left
me beside the first seat we came to and walked jerkily
away.

I watched his back, ramrod stiff, disappearing behind
bushes and trees. In grief, as in all else, he would be
tidy.

A boy came along the path on roller skates and
wheeled round to a stop in front of me.

'You want pushing?' he said.

'No. But thanks all the same.'

706

He looked at me judiciously. 'Can you make that chair go straight, using just one arm?'

'No. I go round in a circle and end where I started.'

'Thought so.' He considered me gravely. 'Just like the earth,' he said.

He pushed off with one foot and sailed away straight on the other and presently, walking firmly, Oliver came back.

He sat on the bench beside me, his eyelids slightly reddened, his manner calm.

'Sorry,' he said, after a while.

'She died happy,' I said. 'It's better than nothing.'

'How do you mean?'

'She heard what they were doing. She picked up the shampoo Shane dropped. She was coming to tell you that everything was all right, there was nothing wrong with Sandcastle and you wouldn't lose the farm. At the moment she died she must have been full of joy.'

Oliver raised his face to the pale summer sky.

'Do you think so?'

'Yes, I do.'

'Then I'll believe it,' he said.

OCTOBER

Gordon was coming up to sixty, the age at which everyone retired from Ekaterin's, like it or not. The bustle of young brains, the founder Paul had said, was what kept money moving, and his concept still ruled in the house.

Gordon had his regrets but they were balanced, it seemed to me, by a sense of relief. He had battled for three years now against his palsy and had finished the allotted work span honourably in the face of the enemy within. He began saying he was looking forward to his leisure, and that he and Judith would go on a celebratory journey as soon as possible. Before that, however, he was to be away for a day of medical tests in hospital.

'Such a bore,' he said, 'but they want to make these checks and set me up before we travel.'

'Very sensible,' I said. 'Where will you go?'

He smiled with enthusiasm. 'I've always wanted to see Australia. Never been there, you know.'

'Nor have I.'

He nodded and we continued with our normal work in the accord we had felt together for so many years. I would miss him badly for his own sake, I thought, and even more because through him I would no longer have constant news and contact with Judith. The days seemed to gallop towards his birthday and my spirits grew heavy as his lightened.

Oliver's problems were no longer the day-to-day communiqués at lunch. The dissenting director had conceded that even blue-chip certainties weren't always proof against well-planned malice and no longer grumbled about my part in things, particularly since the day that Henry in his mild-steel voice made observations about defending the bank's money beyond the call of duty.

'And beyond the call of common sense,' Val murmured in my ear. 'Thank goodness.'

Oliver's plight had been extensively aired by Alec in *What's Going On Where It Shouldn't*, thanks to comprehensive leaks from one of Ekaterin's directors; to wit, me.

Some of the regular newspapers had danced round the subject, since with Shane still awaiting trial the business of poisoning mares was supposed to be sub judice. Alec's paper with its usual disrespect for secrecy had managed to let everyone in the bloodstock industry know that Sandcastle himself was a rock-solid investment, and that any foals already born perfect would not be carrying any damaging genes.

As for the mares covered this year, [the paper continued] there is a lottery as to whether they will produce deformed foals or not. Breeders are advised to let their mares go to term, because there is a roughly fifty per cent chance that the foal will be perfect. Breeders of mares who produce deformed or imperfect foals will, we understand, have their stallion fees refunded and expenses reimbursed.

The bloodstock industry is drawing up its own special guidelines to deal with this exceptional case.

Meanwhile, fear not. Sandcastle is potent, fertile and fully reinstated. Apply without delay for a place in next year's programme.

Alec himself telephoned me in the office two days after the column appeared.

'How do you like it?' he said.

'Absolutely great.'

'The editor says the newsagents in Newmarket have been ringing up like mad for extra copies.'

'Hm,' I said. 'I think perhaps I'll get a list of all breeders and bloodstock agents and personally – I mean anonymously – send each of them a copy of your column, if your editor would agree.'

'Do it without asking him,' Alec said. 'He would probably prefer it. We won't sue you for infringement of copyright, I'll promise you.'

'Thanks a lot,' I said. 'You've been really great.'

'Wait till you get an eyeful of the next issue. I'm

working on it now. *Do-it-yourself Miracles*, that's the heading. How does it grab you?'

'Fine.'

'The dead can't sue,' he said cheerfully. 'I just hope I spell the drugs right.'

'I sent you the list,' I protested.

'The typesetters,' he said, 'can scramble eggs, let alone sulphanilamide.'

'See you someday,' I said, smiling.

'Yeah. Pie and beer. We'll fix it.'

His miracle-working column in the next issue demolished Calder's reputation entirely and made further progress towards restoring Sandcastle's and after a third bang on the Sandcastle-is-tops gong in the issue after that, Oliver thankfully reported that confidence both in his stallion and his stud farm was creeping back. Two-thirds of the nominations were filled already, and enquiries were arriving for the rest.

'One of the breeders whose mare is in foal now is threatening to sue me for negligence, but the blood-stock associations are trying to dissuade him. He can't do anything, anyway, until after Shane's trial and after the foal is born, and I just hope to God it's one that's perfect.'

From the bank's point of view his affairs were no longer in turmoil. The board had agreed to extend the period of the loan for three extra years, and Val, Gordon and I had worked out the rates at which Oliver could repay without crippling himself. All finally rested on Sandcastle, but if his progeny should prove to have inherited his speed, Oliver should in the end reach the prosperity and prestige for which he had aimed.

'But let's not,' Henry said, smiling one day over roast lamb, 'let's not make a habit of going to the races.'

Gordon came to the office one Monday saying he had met Dissdale the day before at lunch in a restaurant which they both liked.

'He was most embarrassed to see me,' Gordon said. 'But I had quite a talk with him. He really didn't know, you know, that Calder was a fake. He says he can hardly believe, even now, that the cures weren't cures, or that Calder actually killed two people. Very subdued, he was, for Dissdale.'

'I suppose,' I said diffidently, 'you didn't ask him if he and Calder had ever bought, cured and sold sick animals before Indian Silk.'

'Yes, I did, actually, because of your thoughts. But he said they hadn't. Indian Silk was the first, and Dissdale rather despondently said he supposed Calder and Ian Pargetter couldn't bear to see all their time and trouble go to waste, so when Ian Pargetter couldn't persuade Fred Barnet to try Calder, Calder sent Dissdale to buy the horse outright.'

'And it worked a treat.'

Gordon nodded. 'Another thing Dissdale said was that Calder was as stunned as he was himself to find it was Ekaterin's who had lent the money for Sandcastle. There had been no mention of it in the papers. Dissdale asked me to tell you that when he told Calder who it was who had actually put up the money, Calder said "My God" several times and walked up and down all evening and drank far more than usual. Dissdale didn't know why, and Calder wouldn't tell him, but Dissdale says he thinks now it was because Calder was feeling remorse at hammering Ekaterin's after an Ekaterin had saved his life.'

'Dissdale,' I said drily, 'is still trying to find excuses for his hero.'

'And for his own admiration of him,' Gordon agreed. 'But perhaps it's true. Dissdale said Calder had liked you very much.'

Liked me, and apologized, and tried to kill me: that too.

Movement had slowly returned to my shoulder and arm once the body-restricting plaster had come off, and via electrical treatment, exercise and massage normal strength had returned.

In the ankle department things weren't quite so good: I still after more than four months wore a brace, though now of removable aluminium, and strapping, not plaster. No one would promise I'd be able to ski on the final outcome and meanwhile all but the shortest journeys required sticks. I had tired of hopping up and down my Hampstead stairs on my return there to the extent of renting a flat of my own with a lift to take me aloft and a garage in the basement, and I reckoned life had basically become reasonable again on the day

I drove out of there in my car: automatic gear change, no work for the left foot, perfect.

A day or two before he was due to go into hospital for his check-up Gordon mentioned in passing that Judith was coming to collect him from the bank after work to go with him to the hospital, where he would be spending the night so as to be rested for the whole day of tests on Friday.

She would collect him again on Friday evening and they would go home together, and he would have the weekend to rest in before he returned to the office on Monday.

'I'll be glad when it's over,' he said frankly. 'I hate all the needles and the pulling and pushing about.'

'When Judith has settled you in, would she like me to give her some dinner before she goes home?' I said.

He looked across with interest, the idea taking root. 'I should think she would love it. I'll ask her.'

He returned the next day saying Judith was pleased, and we arranged between us that when she left him in the hospital she would come to join me in a convenient restaurant that we all knew well; and on the following day, Thursday, the plan was duly carried out.

She came with a glowing face, eyes sparkling, white teeth gleaming; wearing a blue full-skirted dress and shoes with high heels.

'Gordon is fine, apart from grumbling about

tomorrow,' she reported, 'and they gave him almost no supper, to his disgust. He says to think of him during our fillet steaks.'

I doubt if we did. I don't remember what we ate. The feast was there before me on the other side of the small table, Judith looking beautiful and telling me nonsensical things like what happens to a blasé refrigerator when you pull its plug out.

'What, then?'

'It loses its cool.'

I laughed at the stupidity of it and brimmed over with the intoxication of having her there to myself, and I wished she was my own wife so fiercely that my muscles ached.

'You'll be going to Australia . . .' I said.

'Australia?' She hesitated. 'We leave in three weeks.'

'It's so soon.'

'Gordon's sixty the week after next,' she said. 'You know he is. There's the party.'

Henry, Val and I had clubbed together to give Gordon a small sending-off in the office after his last day's work, an affair to which most of the banking managers and their wives had been invited.

'I hate him going,' I said.

'To Australia?'

'From the bank.'

We drank wine and coffee and told each other much without saying a word. Not until we were nearly leaving did she say tentatively, 'We'll be away for months, you know.'

My feelings must have shown. 'Months ... How many?'

'We don't know. We're going to all the places Gordon or I have wanted to see that couldn't be fitted into an ordinary holiday. We're going to potter. Bits of Europe, bits of the Middle East. India, Singapore, Bali, then Australia, New Zealand, Tahiti, Fiji, Hawaii, America.' She fell silent, her eyes not laughing now but full of sadness.

I swallowed. 'Gordon will find it exhausting.'

'He says not. He passionately wants to go, and I know he's always yearned to have the time to see things ... and we're going slowly, with lots of rests.'

The restaurant had emptied around us and the waiters hovered with polite faces willing us to go. Judith put on her blue coat and we went outside onto the cold pavement.

'How do you plan to go home now?' I asked.

'Underground.'

'I'll drive you,' I said.

She gave me a small smile and nodded, and we walked slowly across the road to where I'd left the car. She sat in beside me and I did all the automatic things like switching on the lights and letting off the hand-brake, and I drove all the way to Clapham without consciously seeing the road.

Gordon's house behind the big gates lay quiet and

dark. Judith looked up at its bulk and then at me, and I leaned across in the car and put my arms round her and kissed her. She came close to me, kissing me back with a feeling and a need that seemed as intense as my own, and for a while we stayed in that way, floating in passion, dreaming in deep unaccustomed touch.

As if of one mind we each at the same time drew back and slowly relaxed against the seat. She put her hand on mine and threaded her fingers through, holding tight.

I looked ahead through the windscreen, seeing trees against the stars; seeing nothing.

A long time passed.

'We can't,' I said eventually.

'No.'

'Especially not,' I said, 'in his own house.'

'No.'

After another long minute she let go of my hand and opened the door beside her, and I too opened mine.

'Don't get out,' she said, 'because of your ankle.'

I stood up, however, on the driveway and she walked round the car towards me. We hugged each other but without kissing, a long hungry minute of body against body; commitment and farewell.

'I'll see you,' she said, 'at the party'; and we both knew how it would be, with Lorna Shipton talking about watching Henry's weight and Henry flirting roguishly with Judith whenever he could, and everyone talking loudly and clapping Gordon on the back.

She walked over to the front door and unlocked it, and looked back, briefly, once, and then went in, putting the walls between us in final, mutual, painful decision.

DECEMBER

I felt alone and also lonely, which I'd never been before, and I telephoned Pen one Sunday in December and suggested taking her out to lunch. She said to come early as she had to open her shop at four, and I arrived at eleven-thirty to find coffee percolating richly and Pen trying to unravel the string of the Christmas kite.

'I found it when I was looking for some books,' she said. 'It's so pretty. When we've had coffee, let's go out and fly it.'

We took it onto the common, and let the string out gradually until the dragon was high on the wind, circling and darting and fluttering its frilly tail. It took us slowly after it across the grass, Pen delightedly intent and I simply pleased to be back there in that place.

She glanced at me over her shoulder. 'Are we going too far for your ankle? Or too fast?'

'No and no,' I said.

'Still taking the comfrey?'

'Religiously.'

The bones and other tissues round my shoulder had

mended fast, I'd been told, and although the ankle still lagged I was prepared to give comfrey the benefit of the doubt. Anything which would restore decent mobility attracted my enthusiasm: life with brace and walking stick, still boringly necessary, made even buying groceries a pest.

We had reached a spot on a level with Gordon and Judith's house when a gust of wind took the kite suddenly higher, setting it weaving and diving in bright-coloured arcs and stretching its land-line to tautness. Before anything could be done the string snapped and the dazzling butterfly wings soared away free, rising in a spiral, disappearing to a shape, to a black dot, to nothing.

'What a pity,' Pen said, turning to me with disappointment and then pausing, seeing where my own gaze had travelled downwards to the tall cream gates, firmly shut.

'Let her go,' Pen said soberly, 'like the kite.'

'She'll come back.'

'Take out some other girl,' she urged.

I smiled lop-sidedly. 'I'm out of practice.'

'But you can't spend your whole life ...' She stopped momentarily, and then said, 'Parkinson's disease isn't fatal. Gordon could live to be eighty or more.'

'I wouldn't want him dead,' I protested. 'How could you think it?'

'Then what?'

'Just to go on, I suppose, as we are.'

She took my arm and turned me away from the gates to return to her house.

'Give it time,' she said. 'You've got months. You both have.'

I glanced at her. 'Both?'

'Gordon and I don't go around with our eyes shut.'

'He's never said anything . . .'

She smiled. 'Gordon likes you better than you like him, if possible. Trusts you, too.' She paused. 'Let her go, Tim, for your own sake.'

We went silently back to her house and I thought of all that had happened since the day Gordon stood in the fountain, and of all I had learned and felt and loved and lost. Thought of Ginnie and Oliver and Calder, and of all the gateways I'd gone through to grief and pain and the knowledge of death. So much – too much – compressed into so small a span.

'You're a child of the light,' Pen said contentedly. 'Both you and Judith. You always take sunshine with you. I don't suppose you know it, but everything brightens when people like you walk in.' She glanced down at my slow foot. 'Sorry. When you limp in. So carry the sunlight to a new young girl who isn't married to Gordon and doesn't break your heart.' She paused. 'That's good pharmacological advice, so take it.'

'Yes, doctor,' I said; and knew I couldn't.

*

On Christmas Eve when I had packed to go to Jersey and was checking around the flat before leaving, the telephone rang.

'Hello,' I said.

There was a series of clicks and hums and I was about to put the receiver down when a breathless voice said, 'Tim . . .'

'Judith?' I said incredulously.

'Yes.'

'Where are you?'

'Listen, just listen. I don't know who else to ask, not at Christmas . . . Gordon's ill and I'm alone and I don't know, I don't know . . .'

'Where are you?'

'India . . . He's in hospital. They're very good, very kind, but he's so ill . . . unconscious . . . they say cerebral haemorrhage . . . I'm so afraid . . . I do so love him . . .' She was suddenly crying, and trying not to, the words coming out at intervals when control was possible. 'It's so much to ask . . . but I need . . . help.'

'Tell me where,' I said. 'I'll come at once.'

'Oh . . .'

She told me where. I was packed and ready to go, and I went.

Because of the date and the off-track destination there were delays and it took me forty hours to get there. Gordon died before I reached her, on the day after Christmas, like her mother.

PROOF

My thanks to
MARGARET GILES
of
PANGBOURNE WINES
who taught me her business

and to
BARRY MACKANESS
and
my brother-in-law
DICK YORKE,
wineshippers

and to
LEN LIVINGSTONE-LEARMONTH
long-time friend.

CHAPTER ONE

Agony is socially unacceptable. One is not supposed to weep. Particularly one is not supposed to weep when one is moderately presentable and thirty-two. When one's wife has been dead for six months and everyone else has done grieving.

Ah well, they say: he'll get over it. There's always another pretty lady. Time's a great healer, they say. He'll marry again one day, they say.

No doubt they're right.

But oh dear God . . . the emptiness in my house. The devastating, weary, ultimate loneliness. The silence where there used to be laughter, the cold hearth that used to leap with fire for my return, the permanent blank in my bed.

Six months into unremitting ache I felt that my own immediate death would be no great disaster. Half of myself had gone; the fulfilled joyful investment of six years' loving, gone into darkness. What was left simply suffered . . . and looked normal.

Habit kept me checking both ways when I crossed the road; and meanwhile I tended my shop and sold my wines, and smiled and smiled and smiled at the customers.

CHAPTER TWO

Customers came in all possible shapes, from the school children who bought crisps and cola because I was near the bus stop, to the sergeants' mess of the local barracks: from pensioners saving for apologetic half bottles of gin to the knowledgeably lavish laying down port. Customers came once a year and daily, with ignorance and expertise, for happiness and comfort, in gloom and insobriety. Customers ranged from syrup to bitters, like their drinks.

My foremost customer, one Sunday morning that cold October, was a racehorse trainer splashing unstinted fizz over a hundred or so guests in his more or less annual celebration of the Flat races his stable had won during the passing season. Each autumn as his name came high on the winners' list he gave thanks by inviting his owners, his jockeys, his ramifications of friends to share his satisfaction for joys past and to look forward and make plans for starting all over again the following spring.

729

Each September he would telephone in his perpetual state of rush. 'Tony? Three weeks on Sunday, right? Just the usual, in the tent. You'll do the glasses? And sale or return, of course, right?'

'Right,' I would say, and he'd be gone before I could draw breath. It would be his wife Flora who later came to the shop smilingly with details.

Accordingly on that Sunday I drove to his place at ten o'clock and parked as close as I could to the large once-white marquee rising tautly from his back lawn. He came bustling out of his house the moment I stopped, as if he'd been looking out for me, which perhaps he had: Jack Hawthorn, maybe sixty, short, plump and shrewd.

'Tony. Well done.' He patted me lightly on the shoulder, his usual greeting, as he habitually avoided the social custom of shaking hands. Not, as I had originally guessed, because he feared to catch other people's contagious germs but because, as an acid racing lady had enlightened me, he had 'a grip like a defrosting jellyfish' and hated to see people rub their palms on their clothes after touching him.

'A good day for it,' I said.

He glanced briefly at the clear sky. 'We need rain. The ground's like concrete.' Racehorse trainers, like farmers, were never satisfied with the weather. 'Did you bring any soft drinks? The Sheik's coming, with his whole teetotal entourage. Forgot to tell you.'

I nodded. 'Champagne, soft drinks and a box of oddments.'

'Good. Right. I'll leave you to it. The waitresses will be here at eleven, guests at twelve. And you'll stay yourself, of course? My guest, naturally. I take it for granted.'

'Your secretary sent me an invitation.'

'Did he? Good heavens. How efficient. Right then. Anything you want, come and find me.'

I nodded and he hurried away, taking his life as usual at a trot. Notwithstanding the secretary, a somewhat languid man with a supercilious nose and an indefatigable capacity for accurate detailed work, Jack never quite caught up with what he wanted to do. Flora, his placid wife, had told me, 'It's Jimmy (the secretary) who enters the horses for the races, Jimmy who sends out the bills, Jimmy who runs all the paperwork singlehanded, and Jack never so much as has to pick up a postage stamp. It's habit, all this rushing. Just habit.' But she'd spoken fondly, as everyone did, more or less, of Jack Hawthorn: and maybe it was actually the staccato energy of the man which communicated to his horses and set them winning.

He always invited me to his celebrations, either formally or not, partly no doubt so that I should be on the spot to solve any booze-flow problems immediately, but also because I had myself been born into a section of the racing world and was still considered part of it, despite my inexplicable defection into retail liquor.

'Not his father's son,' was how the uncharitable put it. Or more plainly, 'Lacks the family guts.'

731

My father, a soldier, had won both the Distinguished Service Order and the Military Gold Cup, dashing as valiantly into steeplechase fences as he had into enemy territory. His bravery on all battlefields had been awe-inspiring, and he died from a broken neck on Sandown Park racecourse when I was eleven, and watching.

He had been forty-seven at the time and remained, of course, at that age in the racing world's memory, a tall, straight, laughing, reckless man, untouched, it still seemed to me, by the world's woes. No matter that he was not an ideal shape for jockeyship, he had resolutely followed in the wake of his own father, my grandfather, a distant Titan who had finished second one year in the Grand National before covering himself with military glory in the First World War. My grandfather's Victoria Cross lay beside my father's DSO in the display case I had inherited. It was their dash, their flair, their dare-devilment that they had not passed on.

'Are you going to grow up like your father, then?' had been said to me in friendly, expectant fashion countless times through my childhood, and it had only slowly dawned on everyone, as on me, that no, I wasn't. I learned to ride, but without distinction. I went to Wellington, the school for soldiers' sons, but not in turn to Sandhurst to put on uniform myself. My mother too often said, 'Never mind, dear,' suffering many disappointments nobly; and I developed deep powerful feelings of inferiority, which still lingered, defying common sense.

Only with Emma had they retreated to insignificance, but now that she had gone, faint but persistent, they were back. A discarded habit of mind insidiously creeping into unguarded corners. Miserable.

Jimmy, the secretary, never helped. He sauntered out of the house, hands in pockets, and watched as I lugged three galvanized wash tubs from the rear of my van.

'What are those for?' he said. He couldn't help looking down that nose, I supposed, as he topped six feet four. It was just that his tone of voice matched.

'Ice,' I said.

He said, 'Oh,' or rather 'Ah-oh,' as a diphthong.

I carried the tubs into the tent, which contained a row of trestle tables with tablecloths near one end and clusters of potted chrysanthemums round the bases of the two main supporting poles. The living grass of the lawn had been covered with serviceable fawn matting, and bunches of red and gold ribbons decorated the streaky greyish canvas walls at regular intervals. In one far corner stood a blower-heater, unlit. The day was marginally not cold enough. The tent was almost festive. Almost. Jack and Flora, and who could blame them, never wasted good cash on unnecessaries.

There was no tremble in the air. No shudder. No premonition at all of the horror soon to happen there. All was quiet and peaceful; expectant certainly, but benign. I remembered it particularly, after.

Jimmy continued to watch while I carted in a case of champagne and unpacked the bottles, standing them

733

upright in one of the tubs on the floor by the tent wall behind the tables. I didn't actually have to do this part of the job, but for Jack Hawthorn, somehow, it was easy to give service beyond contract.

I was working in shirtsleeves, warmed by a pale blue V-necked sleeveless pullover (typical racing world clothes) with my jacket waiting in the van for the metamorphosis to guest. Jimmy was understatedly resplendent in thin fawn polo-necked sweater under a navy blue blazer; plain brass buttons, no crests, no pretensions. That was the trouble. If he'd had any pretensions I could perhaps have despised him instead of suspecting it was the other way round.

I fetched a second box of champagne and began unpacking it. Jimmy bent from his great height and picked up one of the bottles, staring at the foil and the label as if he'd never seen such things before.

'What's this muck?' he said. 'Never heard of it.'

'It's the real thing,' I said mildly. 'It comes from Epernay.'

'So I see.'

'Flora's choice,' I said.

He said 'Ah-oh' in complete understanding and put the bottle back. I fetched ice cubes in large black plastic bags and poured them over and round the standing bottles.

'Did you bring any Scotch?' he asked.

'Front seat of the van.'

He strolled off on the search and came back with an unopened bottle.

'Glass?' he enquired.

For reply I went out to the van and fetched a box containing sixty.

'Help yourself.'

Without comment he opened the box, which I'd set on a table, and removed one of the all-purpose goblets.

'Is this ice drinkable?' he said dubiously.

'Pure tap water.'

He put ice and whisky in the glass and sipped the result.

'Very prickly this morning, aren't you?' he said.

I glanced at him, surprised. 'Sorry.'

'Someone knocked off a whole load of this stuff in Scotland yesterday, did you know?'

'Champagne?'

'No. Scotch.'

I shrugged. 'Well . . . it happens.'

I fetched a third case and unpacked the bottles. Jimmy watched, clinking his ice.

'How much do you know about whisky, Tony?' he said.

'Well . . . some.'

'Would you know one from another?'

'I'm better at wine.' I straightened from filling the second tub. 'Why?'

'Would you know for certain,' he said with a bad stab at casualness, 'if you asked for a malt and got sold an ordinary standard, like this?' He raised his glass, nodding to it.

'They taste quite different.'

He relaxed slightly, betraying an inner tension I hadn't until then been aware of. 'Could you tell one malt from another?'

I looked at him assessingly. 'What's all this about?'

'Could you?' He was insistent.

'No,' I said. 'Not this morning. Not to name them. I'd have to practise. Maybe then. Maybe not.'

'But . . . if you learned one particular taste, could you pick it out again from a row of samples? Or say if it wasn't there?'

'Perhaps,' I said. I looked at him, waiting, but he was taking his own troubled time, consulting some inner opinion. Shrugging, I went to fetch more ice, pouring it into the second tub, and then carried in and ripped open the fourth case of champagne.

'It's very awkward,' he said suddenly.

'What is?'

'I wish you'd stop fiddling with those bottles and listen to me.'

His voice was a mixture of petulance and anxiety, and I slowly straightened from putting bottles into the third tub and took notice.

'Tell me, then,' I said.

He was older than me by a few years, and our acquaintanceship had mostly been limited to my visits to the Hawthorn house, both as drinks supplier and as occasional guest. His usual manner to me had been fairly civil but without warmth, as no doubt mine to him. He was the third son of the fourth son of a racehorse-owning earl, which gave him an aristocratic name but no fortune, and his job with Jack Hawthorn resulted directly, it was said, from lack of enough brain to excel in the City. It was a judgement I would have been content to accept were it not for Flora's admiration of him, but I hadn't cared enough one way or the other to give it much thought.

'One of Jack's owners has a restaurant,' he said. 'The Silver Moondance, near Reading. Not aimed at top class. Dinner dances. A singer sometimes. Mass market.' His voice was fastidious but without scorn: stating a fact, not an attitude.

I waited non-committally.

'He invited Jack and Flora and myself to dinner there last week.'

'Decent of him,' I said.

'Yes.' Jimmy looked at me down the nose. 'Quite.' He paused slightly. 'The food was all right, but the drinks . . . Look, Tony, Larry Trent is one of Jack's good owners. He has five horses here. Pays his bills on the nail. I don't want to upset him . . . but what it says on the label of at least one of the bottles in his restaurant is not what they pour out of it.'

He spoke with pained disgust, at which I almost smiled.

'That's not actually unusual,' I said.

'But it's illegal.' He was indignant.

'Sure it's illegal. Are you certain?'

'Yes. Well yes, I think so. But I wondered if perhaps, before I said anything to Larry Trent, you could taste their stuff? I mean, suppose his staff are ripping him off? I mean, er ... he could be prosecuted, couldn't he?'

I said, 'Why didn't you mention it to him that evening, while you were there?'

Jimmy looked startled. 'But we were his guests! It would have been terribly bad form. Surely you can see that.'

'Hm,' I said dryly. 'Then why don't you just tell him now, and privately, what you thought about his drinks? He might be grateful. He would certainly be warned. Anyway, I can't see him whisking his five horses away in a huff.'

Jimmy made a pained noise and drank some Scotch. 'I mentioned this to Jack. He said I must be mistaken. But I'm not, you know. I'm pretty sure I'm not.'

I considered him.

'Why does it bother you so much?' I asked.

'What?' He was surprised. 'Well, I say, a fraud's a fraud, isn't it? It annoys one.'

'Yes.' I sighed. 'What were these drinks supposed to be?'

'I thought the wine wasn't much, considering its label, but you know how it is, you don't suspect anything ... but there was the Laphroaig.'

738

I frowned. 'The malt from Islay?'

'That's right,' Jimmy said. 'Heavy malt whisky. My grandfather liked it. He used to give me sips when I was small, much to my mother's fury. Funny how you never forget tastes you learn as a child . . . and of course I've had it since . . . so there it was, on the trolley of drinks they rolled round with the coffee, and I thought I would have some . . . Nostalgia, and all that.'

'And it wasn't Laphroaig?'

'No.'

'What was it?'

He looked uncertain. 'I thought that you, actually, might know. If you drank some, I mean.'

I shook my head. 'You'd need a proper expert.'

He looked unhappy. 'I thought myself, you see, that it was just an ordinary blend, just ordinary, not even pure malt.'

'You'd better tell Mr Trent,' I said. 'Let him deal with it himself.'

He said doubtfully, 'He'll be here this morning.'

'Easy,' I said.

'I don't suppose . . . er . . . that you yourself . . . er . . . could have a word with him?'

'No, I certainly couldn't,' I said positively. 'From you it could be a friendly warning, from me it would be a deadly insult. Sorry, Jimmy, but honestly, no.'

With resignation he said, 'I thought you wouldn't. But worth a try.' He poured himself more Scotch and again put ice into it, and I thought in passing that true whisky aficionados thought ice an abomination, and wondered about the trustworthiness of his perception of Laphroaig.

Flora, rotund and happy in cherry red wool, came in her light-stepped way into the tent, looking around and nodding in satisfaction.

'Looks quite bright, doesn't it, Tony dear?'

'Splendid,' I said.

'When it's filled with guests . . .'

'Yes,' I agreed.

She was conventional, well-intentioned and cosy, the mother of three children (not Jack's) who telephoned her regularly. She liked to talk about them on her occasional visits to my shop and tended to place larger orders when the news of them was good. Jack was her second husband, mellowing still under her wing but reportedly jealous of her offspring. Amazing the things people told their wine merchants. I knew a great deal about a lot of people's lives.

Flora peered into the tubs. 'Four cases on ice?'

I nodded. 'More in the van, if you need it.'

'Let's hope not.' She smiled sweetly. 'But my dear, I wouldn't bet on it. Jimmy love, you don't need to drink whisky. Open some champagne. I'd like a quick glass before everyone swamps us.'

Jimmy obliged with languid grace, easing out the cork without explosion, containing the force in his hand. Flora smilingly watched the plume of released gas float from the bottle and tilted a glass forward to catch the first bubbles. At her insistence both Jimmy and I drank also, but from Jimmy's expression it didn't go well with his Scotch.

'Lovely!' Flora said appreciatively, sipping; and I thought the wine as usual a bit too thin and fizzy, but sensible enough for those quantities. I sold a great deal of it for weddings.

Flora took her glass and wandered down the marquee to the entrance through which the guests would come, the entrance which faced away from the house, towards the field where the cars would be parked. Jack Hawthorn's house and stableyard were built in a hollow high on the eastern end of the Berkshire Downs, in a place surrounded by hills, invisible until one was close. Most people would arrive by the main road over the hill which faced the rear of the house, parking in the field, and continuing the downward journey on foot through a gate in the low-growing rose hedge, and onto the lawn. After several such parties, Flora had brought crowd control to a fine art: and besides, this way, no one upset the horses.

Flora suddenly exclaimed loudly and came hurrying back.

'It's really too bad of him. The Sheik is here already. His car's coming over the hill. Jimmy, run and meet him. Jack's still changing. Take the Sheik round the yard. Anything. Really, it's too bad. Tell Jack he's here.'

Jimmy nodded, put down his glass without haste and ambled off to intercept the oil-rich prince and

741

his retinue. Flora hovered indecisively, not following,
talking crossly with maximum indiscretion.

'I don't like that particular Sheik. I can't help it.
He's fat and horrible and he behaves as if he owns the
place, which he doesn't. And I don't like the way he
looks at me with those half-shut eyes, as if I were of
no account ... and Tony, dear, I haven't said any
of those things, you understand? I don't like the way
Arabs treat women.'

'And his horses win races,' I said.

'Yes,' Flora sighed. 'It's not all sweetness and light
being a trainer's wife. Some of the owners make me
sick.' She gave me a brief half-smile and went away to
the house, and I finished the unloading with things like
orange juice and cola.

Up on the hill the uniformed chauffeur parked the
elongated black-windowed Mercedes, which was so
identifiably the Sheik's, with its nose pointing to the
marquee, and gradually more cars arrived to swell
the row there, bringing waitresses and other helpers,
and finally, in a steady stream, the hundred-and-
something guests.

They came by Rolls, by Range Rover, by Mini and
by Ford. One couple arrived in a horsebox, another by
motorcycle. Some brought children, some brought dogs,
most of which were left with the cars. In cashmere
and cords, in checked shirts and tweeds, in elegance and
pearls they walked chatteringly down the grassy slope,
through the gate in the rose hedge, across a few steps

of lawn, into the beckoning tent. A promising Sunday morning jollification ahead, most troubles left behind.

As always with racing-world parties, everyone there knew somebody else. The decibel count rose rapidly to ear-aching levels and only round the very walls could one talk without shouting. The Sheik, dressed in full Arab robes and flanked by his wary-eyed entourage, was one, I noticed, who stood resolutely with his back to the canvas, holding his orange juice before him and surveying the crush with his half-shut eyes. Jimmy was doing his noble best to amuse, rewarded by unsmiling nods, and gradually and separately other guests stopped to talk to the solid figure in the banded white headgear, but none of them with complete naturalness, and none of them women.

Jimmy after a while detached himself and I found him at my elbow.

'Sticky going, the Sheik?' I said.

'He's not such a bad fellow,' Jimmy said loyally. 'No social graces in western gatherings and absolutely paranoid about being assassinated . . . never even sits in the dentist's chair, I'm told, without all those body-guards being right there in the surgery . . . but he does know about horses. Loves them. You should have seen him just now, going round the yard, those bored eyes came right to life.' He looked round the gathering and suddenly exclaimed, 'See that man talking to Flora? That's Larry Trent.'

'Of the absent Laphroaig?'

743

Jimmy nodded, wrinkled his brow in indecision and moved off in another direction altogether, and I for a few moments watched the man with Flora, a middle-aged, dark-haired man with a moustache, one of the few people wearing a suit, in his case a navy pinstripe with the coat buttoned, a line of silk handkerchief showing in the top pocket. The crowd shifted and I lost sight of him, and I talked, as one does, to a succession of familiar half-known people, seen once a year or less, with whom one took on as one had left off, as if time hadn't existed in between. It was one of those, with best intentions, who said inevitably, 'And how's Emma? How's your pretty wife?'

I thought I would never get used to it, that jab like a spike thrust into a jumpy nerve, that positively physical pain. Emma . . . dear God.

'She's dead,' I said, shaking my head slightly, breaking it to him gently, absolving him from embarrassment. I'd had to say it like that often: far too often. I knew how to do it now without causing discomfort. Bitter, extraordinary skill of the widowed, taking the distress away from others, hiding one's own.

'I'm so sorry,' he said, meaning it intensely for the moment, as they do. 'I'd no idea. None at all. Er . . . when . . .?'

'Six months ago,' I said.

'Oh.' He adjusted his sympathy level suitably. 'I'm really very sorry.'

I nodded. He sighed. The world went on. Transaction

over, until next time. Always a next time. And at least he hadn't asked 'How . . .?', and I hadn't had to tell him, hadn't had to think of the pain and the coma and the child who had died with her, unborn.

A fair few of Jack's guests were also my customers, so that even in that racing gathering I found myself talking as much about wine as horses, and it was while an earnest elderly lady was soliciting my views on Côtes du Rhône versus Côte de Nuits that I saw Jimmy finally talking to Larry Trent. He spotted me too and waved for me to come over, but the earnest lady would buy the better wine by the caseful if convinced, and I tele-graphed 'later' gestures to Jimmy, to which he flipped a forgiving hand.

Waitresses wove through the throng carrying dishes of canapés and sausages on sticks, and I reckoned that many more than a hundred throats had turned up and that at the present rate of enthusiasm the forty-eight original bottles would be emptied at any minute. I had already begun to make my way to the tent's service entrance near the house when Jack himself pounced at me, clutching my sleeve.

'We'll need more champagne and the waitresses say your van is locked.' His voice was hurried. 'The party's going well, wouldn't you say?'

'Yes, very.'

'Great. Good. I'll leave it to you, then.' He turned away, patting shoulders in greeting, enjoying his role as host.

I checked the tubs, now empty but for two standing bottles in a sea of melting ice, and went onwards out to the van, fishing in my pocket for the keys. For a moment I glanced up the hill to where all the cars waited, to the Range Rover, the horsebox, the Sheik's Mercedes. No gaps in the line: no one had yet gone home. There was a child up there, playing with a dog.

I unlocked the rear door of my van and leaned in to pull forward the three spare cases which were roughly cooling under more black bags of ice. I threw one of the bags out onto the grass, and I picked up one of the cases.

Movement on the edge of my vision made me turn my head, and in a flash of a second that ordinary day became a nightmare.

The horsebox was rolling forwards down the hill.

Pointing straight at the marquee, gathering speed.

It was already only feet from the rose hedge. It smashed its way through the fragile plants, flattening the last pink flowers of autumn. It advanced inexorably onto the grass.

I leapt to the doorway of the tent screaming a warning which nobody heard above the din and which was anyway far too late.

For a frozen infinitesimal moment I saw the party still intact, a packed throng of people smiling, drinking, living and unaware.

Then the horsebox ploughed into the canvas, and changed many things for ever.

CHAPTER THREE

Total communal disbelief lasted through about five seconds of silence, then someone screamed and went on screaming, a high commentary of hysteria on so much horror.

The horsebox had steam-rollered on over the canvas side-wall, burying people beneath; and it had plunged forward into one of the main supporting poles, which had snapped under the weight. The whole of the end of the tent nearest me had collapsed inwards so that I stood on the edge of it with the ruin at my feet.

Where I had seen the guests, I now in absolute shock saw expanses of heavy grey canvas with countless bulges heaving desperately beneath.

The horsebox itself stood there obscenely in the middle, huge, dark green, unharmed, impersonal and frightful. There seemed to be no one behind the driving wheel; and to reach the cab one would have had to walk over the shrouded lumps of the living and the dead.

Beyond the horsebox, at the far end of the tent, in

the still erect section, people were fighting their way out through the remains of the entrance and rips in the walls, emerging one by one, staggering and falling like figures in a frieze.

I noticed vaguely that I was still holding the case of champagne. I put it down where I stood, and turned and ran urgently to the telephone in the house.

So quiet in there. So utterly normal. My hands were shaking as I held the receiver.

Police and ambulances to Jack Hawthorn's stables. A doctor. And lifting gear. Coming, they said. All coming. At once.

I went back outside, meeting others with stretched eyes intent on the same errand.

'They're coming,' I said. 'Coming.'

Everyone was trembling, not just myself.

The screaming had stopped, but many were shouting, husbands trying to find their wives, wives their husbands, a mother her son. All the faces were white, all the mouths open, all breaths coming in gasps. People had begun making slits in the canvas with penknives to free those trapped underneath. A woman with small scissors was methodically cutting the lacings of a section of side-wall, tears streaming down her face. The efforts all looked puny, the task so immense.

Flora and Jack and Jimmy, I knew, had all been in the part of the tent which had collapsed.

A horse was whinnying nearby and kicking wood, and it was with fresh shock that I realized that the noise was coming from the horsebox itself. There was a horse in there. Inside.

With stiff legs I went along to the standing section of tent, going in through a gap where other people had come out. The second pole stood upright, the potted chrysanthemums bright round its foot. There were many scattered and broken glasses, and a few people trying to lift up the folds of the heavily fallen roof, to let the trapped crawl from under.

'We might make a tunnel,' I said to one man, and he nodded in understanding, and by lifting one section only, but together, and advancing, he and I and several others made a wide head-high passage forward into the collapsed half, through which about thirty struggling people, dazedly getting to their feet, made their way out upright. Many of their faces and hands were bleeding from glass cuts. Few of them knew what had happened. Two of them were children.

One of the furthest figures we reached that way was Flora. I saw the red wool of her dress on the ground under a flap of canvas and bent down to help her: and she was half unconscious with her face to the matting, suffocating.

I pulled her out and carried her down to the free end, and from there gave her to someone outside, and went back.

The tunnel idea gradually extended until there was a ring of humans instead of tent poles holding up a fair section of roof, one or two helpers exploring continuously into the edges until as far as we could tell all the people not near the horsebox itself were outside, walking and alive.

The horsebox . . .

Into that area no one wanted to go, but my original tunneller and I looked at each other for a long moment and told everyone to leave if they wanted to. Some did, but three or four of us made a new, shorter and lower tunnel, working towards the side of the horsebox facing the standing section of the tent, lifting tautly stretched canvas to free people still pinned underneath.

Almost the first person we came to was one of the Arabs who was fiercely vigorous and at any other time would have seemed comic, because as soon as he was released and mobile he began shouting unintelligibly, producing a repeating rifle from his robes and waving it menacingly about.

All we wanted, I thought: a spray of terrified bullets.

The Sheik, I thought. . . . Standing against the side wall, so that his back should be safe.

We found two more people alive on that side, both women, both beyond speech, both white-faced, in torn clothes, bleeding from glass cuts, one with a broken arm. We passed them back into comfort, and went on.

Crawling forward I came then to a pair of feet, toes upwards, then to trouser legs, unmoving. Through the canvas-filtered daylight they were easily recognizable; pinstripe cloth, navy blue.

I lifted more space over him until I could see along

to the buttoned jacket and the silk handkerchief and a hand flung sideways holding a glass in fragments. And beyond, where a weight pressed down where his neck should have been, there was a line of crimson pulp.

I let the canvas fall back, feeling sick.

'No good,' I said to the man behind me. 'I think his head's under the front wheel. He's dead.'

He gave me a look as shattered as my own, and we moved slowly sideways towards the horsebox's rear, making our tunnel with difficulty on hands and knees.

Above us, inside the box, the horse kicked frantically and squealed, restless, excited and alarmed no doubt by the smell; horses were always upset by blood. I could see no prospect all the same of anyone lowering the ramps to let him out.

We found another Arab, alive, flat on his back, an arm bleeding, praying to Allah. We pulled him out and afterwards found his rifle lying blackly where he'd been.

'They're mad,' said my companion.

'It didn't save their master,' I said.

On our knees we both looked in silence at what we could see of the Sheik, which was his head, still in its white headdress with its gold cords. A fold of reddened canvas lay over the rest of him, and my companion, gripping my wrist, said, 'Leave it. Don't look. What's the point.'

I thought fleetingly of the policemen and the ambulancemen who would soon be forced to look, but I did as he asked. We made our way silently back to the standing section and began a new tunnel round to the other side of the horsebox.

It was there that we came to Jack and also Jimmy, both with pulses, though both were unconscious and pinned to the ground by the thick tent pole, which lay across Jack's legs and Jimmy's chest. We scarcely touched the pole ourselves, but the tremor of our movements brought Jack up to semi-consciousness and to groaning pain.

My companion said 'Hell' through his teeth, and I said, 'I'll stay here if you go and get something to keep the canvas off them,' and he nodded and disappeared, the heavy material falling behind, closing me in.

Jimmy looked dreadful; eyes shut above the long nose, a thread of blood trickling from his mouth.

Jack went on groaning. I held up a bit of tent on my shoulders like Atlas, and presently my fellow tunneller returned, bringing two further helpers and a trestle table for a makeshift roof.

'What do we do?' the first tunneller said, irresolutely.

'Lift the pole,' I said. 'It may hurt Jack . . . but it may be killing Jimmy.'

Everyone agreed. We slowly, carefully, took the weight off the two injured men and laid the pole on the ground. Jack lapsed into silence. Jimmy lay still like a log. But they were both shallowly breathing: I felt their wrists again, one after the other, with relief.

We stood the trestle table over them and gingerly crawled on, and came to a girl lying on her back with one arm up over her face. Her skirt had been ripped away, and the flesh on the outer side of her thigh had been torn open and was sagging away from the bone from hip to knee. I lifted the canvas away from her face and saw that she was to some extent conscious.

'Hello,' I said inadequately.

She looked at me vaguely. 'What's happening?' she said.

'There was an accident.'

'Oh?' She seemed sleepy, but when I touched her cheek it was icy.

'We'll get another table,' the first tunneller said.

'And a rug, if you can,' I said. 'She's far too cold.'

He nodded and said 'Shock,' and they all went away as it needed the three of them to drag the tables through.

I looked at the girl's leg. She was fairly plump, and inside the long widely-gaping wound one could easily identify the cream-coloured bubbly fat tissue and the dense red muscle, open like a jagged book to inspection. I'd never seen anything like it: and extraordinarily she wasn't bleeding a great deal, certainly not as much as one would have expected.

The body shutting down, I thought. The effects of trauma, as deadly as injury itself.

There was little I could do for her, but I did have a penknife in my pocket incorporating a tiny pair of scissors. With a sigh I pulled up my jersey and cut and tore one side from my shirt, stopping a few inches below the collar and cutting across so that from in front it looked as if I had a whole shirt under my sweater; and I thought that my doing that was ridiculous, but all the same I did it.

Torn into two wide strips the shirt front made reasonable bandages. I slid both pieces under her leg and pulled the flesh back into position, tying her leg together round the bone like trussing a joint of meat. I looked anxiously several times at the girl's face, but if she felt what I was doing it must have been remotely. She lay with her eyes open, her elbow bent over her head, and all she said at one point was, 'Where is this?' and later, 'I don't understand.'

'It's all right,' I said.

'Oh . . . Is it . . . Good.'

The tunnellers returned with a table and a travelling rug and also a towel.

'I thought we might wrap that wound together, with this,' said the first tunneller, 'but I see you've done it.'

We put the towel round her leg anyway for extra protection, and then wrapped her in the rug and left her under her table roof and crawled apprehensively on; but we found no one else we could help. We found one of the waitresses, dead, lying over her tray of canapés, her smooth young face frosty-white, and we found the protruding legs of a different Arab: and somewhere underneath the horsebox there were dreadful red shapes we couldn't reach even if we'd wanted to.

In accord the four of us retreated, hearing as we emerged into the blessed fresh air the bells and sirens of the official rescuers as they poured over the hill.

I walked along to where Flora was sitting on a kitchen chair that someone had brought out for her: there were women beside her trying to comfort, but her eyes were dark and staring into far spaces, and she was shivering.

'Jack's all right,' I said. 'The pole knocked him out. One leg is maybe broken . . . but he's all right.'

She looked at me blindly. I took my jacket off and wrapped it round her. 'Flora . . . Jack's alive.'

'All those people . . . all our guests . . .' Her voice was faint. 'Are you sure . . . about Jack?'

There was no real consolation. I said yes and hugged her, rocking her in my arms like a baby, and she put her head silently on my shoulder, still too stunned for tears.

Things ran after that into a blur, time passing at an enormous rate but not seeming to.

The police had brought a good deal of equipment and after a while had cut away the marquee from an area round the horsebox, and had set up a head-high ring of screens to hide the shambles there.

Jack, fully conscious, lay on a stretcher with a pain-killer taking the worst off, protesting weakly that he couldn't go to hospital, he couldn't leave his guests, he couldn't leave his horses, he couldn't leave his wife to cope with everything on her own. Still objecting he was lifted into an ambulance and, beside a still unconscious Jimmy, slowly driven away.

The guests drifted into the house or sat in their cars and wanted to go home: but there was an enormous fuss going on somewhere over telephone wires because of the death of the Sheik, and the uniformed police had been instructed not to let anyone leave until other investigators had arrived.

The fuss was nonsense, really, I thought. No one could possibly have told where the Sheik would stand in that tent. No one could possibly have aimed the horsebox deliberately. The brakes had given way and it had rolled down the hill . . . as selective in its victims as an earthquake.

The distraught young couple who had come in it and parked it were both in tears, and I heard the man saying helplessly, 'But I left it in gear, with the brakes on . . . I know I did . . . I'm always careful . . . how could it have happened, how could it?' A uniformed police-man was questioning them, his manner less than sympathetic.

I wandered back to my van, to where I'd dumped the case of champagne. It had gone. So had the sixth and seventh cases from inside. So had the back-up gin and whisky from the front seat.

Disgusting, I thought; and shrugged. After carnage, thieves. Human grade-ten sour age-old behaviour. It didn't seem to matter, except that I would rather have given it away than that.

Flora was indoors, lying down. Someone brought my coat back. It had blood on the sleeves, I noticed. Blood on my shirt cuffs, blood on my pale blue sweater. Blood, dry, on my hands.

A large crane on caterpillar tracks came grinding slowly over the hill and was manoeuvred into position near the horsebox; and in time, with chains, the heavy green vehicle was lifted a few inches into the air, and, after a pause, lifted higher and swung away onto a stretch of cleared grass.

The horse, still intermittently kicking, was finally released down a ramp and led away by one of Jack's lads, and, closing the box again, two policemen took up stances to deter the inquisitive.

There was a small dreadful group of people waiting, unmoving, staring silently at the merciful screens. They knew, they had to know, that those they sought were dead, yet they stood with dry eyes, their faces haggard with persisting hope. Five tons of metal had smashed into a close-packed crowd . . . yet they hoped.

One of them turned his head and saw me, and walked unsteadily towards me as if his feet were obeying different orders from his legs. He was dressed in jeans and a dirty T-shirt, and he neither looked nor sounded like one of the guests. More like one of Jack's lads on his Sunday off.

'You went in there, didn't you?' he said. 'You're the guy who brings the drinks, aren't you? Someone said you went in . . .' He gestured vaguely towards the remains of the tent. 'Did you see my wife? Was she in there? Is she?'

'I don't know.' I shook my head.

'She was carrying things round. Drinks and such. She likes doing that . . . seeing people.'

One of the waitresses. He saw the movement in my face, and interpreted it unerringly.

'She's there . . . isn't she?' I didn't answer for a moment, and he said with pride and despair inextricably mixed. 'She's pretty, you know. So pretty.'

I nodded and swallowed. 'She's pretty.'

'Oh no . . .' He let the grief out in a tearing wail. 'Oh no . . .'

I said helplessly, 'My own wife died . . . not long ago. I do know . . . I'm so . . . so appallingly sorry.'

He looked at me blankly and went back to the others to stare at the screens, and I felt useless and inadequate and swamped with pity.

The horsebox had hit at shortly before one-thirty: it was after five before the new investigators would let anyone leave. Messages were eventually passed that all could go, but that each car would have to stop at the gate for the passengers to give their names.

Tired, hungry, dishevelled, many with bandaged cuts, the guests who had trooped so expectantly down the hill climbed slowly, silently up. Like refugees, I thought. An exodus. One could hear the engines starting in a chorus, and see the first movement of wheels.

A man touched my arm: the fellow tunneller. A tall man, going grey, with intelligent eyes.

'What's your name?' he asked.

'Tony Beach.'

'Mine's McGregor. Gerard McGregor.' He pronounced the G of Gerard soft, like a J, in a voice that was remotely but detectably Scots, 'Glad to know you,' he said. He held out his hand, which I shook.

We smiled slightly at each other, acknowledging our shared experience; then he turned away and put his arm round the shoulders of a good-looking woman at his side, and I watched them thread their way across to the gate through the roses. Pleasant man, I thought; and that was all.

I went into the house to see if there was anything I could do for Flora before I left, and found a shambles of a different sort. Every downstairs room, now empty, looked as if a full-scale army had camped there, which in a way it had. Every cup and saucer in the place must have been pressed into service, and every glass. The bottles on the drinks tray were all empty, open-necked. Ashtrays overflowed. Crumbs of food lay on plates. Cushions were squashed flat.

In the kitchen, locust-like, the lunchless guests had eaten everything to hand. Empty soup tins littered the worktops, egg shells lay in the sink, a chicken carcass, picked clean, jostled gutted packets of biscuits and crackers. Everything edible had gone from the refrigerator and saucepans lay dirty on the stove.

759

There was a faint exclamation from the doorway, and I turned to see Flora there, her face heavy and grey above the creased red dress. I made a frustrated gesture at the mess, but she looked at it all without emotion.

'They had to eat,' she said. 'It's all right.'

'I'll straighten it.'

'No. Leave it. Tomorrow will do.' She came into the room and sat wearily on one of the wooden chairs. 'It simply doesn't matter. I told them to help themselves.'

'They might have cleaned up afterwards,' I said.

'You should know the racing world better.'

'Is there anything I can do, then?'

'No, nothing.' She sighed deeply. 'Do you know how many of them are dead?' Her voice itself was lifeless, drained by too much horror.

I shook my head. 'The Sheik and one of his men. Larry Trent. And one of the waitresses, married, I think, to one of your lads. Some others. I don't know who.'

'Not Janey,' Flora said, distressed.

'I don't know.'

'Young and pretty. Married Tom Wickens in the summer. Not her.'

'I think so.'

'Oh dear.' Flora grew if anything paler. 'I don't care about the Sheik. It's a wicked thing to say, and we'll lose those horses, but I've known about him for hours and I simply don't care. But Janey . . .'

'I think you would help Tom Wickens,' I said.

She stared at me for a moment, then rose to her feet and walked out into the garden, and through the window I saw her go over to the man in the T-shirt and put her arms round him. He turned and hugged her desperately in return, and I wondered fleetingly which of them felt the most released.

I chucked all the worst of the litter into the dustbin, but left the rest of it, as she'd said. Then I went out to the van to go home, and found a very young constable by my side as I opened the door.

'Excuse me, sir,' he said, holding pen and notebook ready.

'Yes?'

'Name, sir?'

I gave it, and my address, which he wrote down.

'Where were you in the marquee, sir, when the incident occurred?'

The *incident* . . . ye gods.

'I wasn't in the marquee,' I said. 'I was here, by the van.'

'Oh!' His eyes widened slightly. 'Then would you wait here, sir?' He hurried away and returned presently with a man out of uniform who walked slowly, with hunched shoulders.

'Mr . . . er . . . Beach?' the newcomer said. A shortish man, not young. No aggression.

I nodded. 'Yes.'

761

'You were outside, here, is that right, when this happened?'

'Yes.'

'And did you . . . by any chance . . . see the horsebox on its way down the hill?' He had a quiet voice and pronounced every syllable carefully, like talking to a lip-reader.

I nodded again. He said 'Ah,' with deep satisfaction, as if that were the answer he had long been seeking, and he smiled on me with favour and suggested we go into the house (where it would be warmer), accompanied by the constable, to take notes.

Among the litter in the drawing room we sat while I answered his questions.

His name was Wilson, he said. He was disappointed that I hadn't seen the horsebox start down the hill, and he was disappointed that I hadn't seen anyone in or near it before it rolled.

'I'll tell you one thing for certain, though,' I said. 'It was not parked in any prearranged place. I watched quite a few of the cars arrive. I could see them coming over the hill, the horsebox among them. They parked in a row just as they arrived, in the same order.' I paused, then said, 'The Sheik came to the stables a good hour before the other guests, which is why his Mercedes is first in the row. When he arrived he went to look round the yard, to see his horses. Then when several other guests came, he joined them in the marquee. No one manoeuvred him into any particular place. I was in there when he came. He was walking with Jack Hawthorn and Jimmy – Jack's secretary. It was just chance he stood where he did. And he didn't of course stand totally still all the time. He must have moved several yards during the hour he was there.'

I stopped. There was a small silence.

'Did you get all that, constable?' Wilson asked.

'Yes, sir.'

'According to your van, you are a wine merchant, Mr Beach? And you supplied the drinks for the party?'

'Yes,' I agreed.

'And you are observant.' His voice was dry, on the edge of dubious.

'Well . . .'

'Could you describe the position of any other of the guests so accurately? For a whole hour, Mr Beach?'

'Yes, some. But one tends to notice a Sheik. And I do notice where people are when I'm anywhere on business. The hosts, and so on, in case they want me.'

He watched my face without comment, and presently asked, 'What did the Sheik drink?'

'Orange juice with ice and mineral water.'

'And his followers?'

'One had fizzy lemonade, the other two, Coca-Cola.'

'Did you get that, constable?'

'Yes, sir.'

Wilson stared for a while at his toecaps, then took a deep breath as if reaching a decision.

'If I described some clothes to you, Mr Beach,' he said, 'could you tell me who was wearing them?'

'Uh . . . if I knew them.'

'Navy pinstripe suit . . .'

I listened to the familiar description. 'A man called Larry Trent,' I said. 'One of Jack Hawthorn's owners. He has . . . had . . . a restaurant; the Silver Moondance, near Reading.'

'Got that, constable?'

'Yes, sir.'

'And also, Mr Beach, a blue tweed skirt and jacket with a light blue woollen shirt, pearls round the neck, and pearl earrings?'

I concentrated, trying to remember, and he said, 'Greenish, slightly hairy trousers, olive-coloured sweater over a mustard shirt. Brown tie with mustard stripes.'

'Oh . . .'

'You know him?'

'Both of them. Colonel and Mrs Fulham. I was talking to them. I sell them wine.'

'Sold, Mr Beach,' Wilson said regretfully. 'That's all, then. I'm afraid all the others have been identified, poor people.'

I swallowed. 'How many . . .?'

'Altogether? Eight dead, I'm afraid. It could have been worse. Much worse.' He rose to his feet and perfunctorily shook my hand. 'There may be political repercussions. I can't tell whether you may be needed for more answers. I will put in my report. Good day, Mr Beach.'

He went out in his slow hunched way, followed by the constable, and I walked after them into the garden.

It was growing dark, with lights coming on in places.

The square of screens had been taken down, and two ambulances were preparing to back through the gap the horsebox had made in the hedge. A row of seven totally covered stretchers lay blackly on the horribly bloodstained matting, with the eighth set apart. In that, I supposed, lay the Sheik, as two living Arabs stood there, one at the head, one at the foot, still tenaciously guarding their prince.

In the dusk the small haggard group of people, all hope gone now, watched silently, with Flora among them, as ambulancemen lifted the seven quiet burdens one by one to bear them away; and I went slowly to my van and sat in it until they had done. Until only the Sheik remained, aloof in death as in life, awaiting a nobler hearse.

I switched on lights and engine and followed the two ambulances over the hill, and in depression drove down to the valley, to my house.

Dark house. Empty house.

I let myself in and went upstairs to change my clothes, but when I reached the bedroom I just went and lay on the bed without switching on the lamps; and from exhaustion, from shock, from pity, from loneliness and from grief . . . I wept.

CHAPTER FOUR

Monday mornings I always spent in the shop restocking the shelves after the weekend's sales and drawing up lists of what I would need as replacements. Monday afternoons I drove the van to the wholesalers for spirits, soft drinks, cigarettes, sweets and crisps, putting some directly into the shop on my return, and the reserves into the storeroom.

Mondays also I took stock of the cases of wines stacked floor to shoulder level in the storeroom and telephoned shippers for more. Mondays the storeroom got tidied by five p.m., checked and ready for the week ahead. Mondays were always hard work.

That particular Monday morning, heavy with the dead feeling of aftermath, I went drearily to work sliding Gordon's gin into neat green rows and slotting Liebfraumilch into its rack; tidying the Teacher's, counting the Bell's, noticing we were out of Moulin à Vent. All of it automatic, my mind still with the Hawthorns, wondering how Jack was, and Jimmy, and how soon I should telephone to find out.

When I first had the shop I had just met Emma, and we had run it together with a sense of adventure that had never quite left us. Nowadays I had more prosaic help in the shape of a Mrs Palissey and also her nephew, Brian, who had willing enough muscles but couldn't read.

Mrs Palissey, generous both as to bosom and gossip, arrived punctually at nine-thirty and told me wide-eyed that she'd seen on the morning television news about the Sheik being killed at the party.

'You were there, Mr Beach, weren't you?' She was agog for gory details and waited expectantly, and with an inward sigh I satisfied at least some of her curiosity. Brian loomed over her, six feet tall, listening intently with his mouth open. Brian did most things with his mouth open, outward sign of inward retardation. Brian worked for me because his aunt had begged me piteously. 'It's giving my sister a nervous breakdown having him mooning round the house all day every day, and he could lift things here for me when you're out, and he'll be no trouble, I'll see to that.'

At first I feared I had simply transferred the imminent breakdown from the sister to myself, but when one got used to Brian's heavy breathing and permanent state of anxiety, one could count on the plus side that he would shift heavy cases of bottles all day without complaining, and didn't talk much.

'All those poor people!' exclaimed Mrs Palissey,

enjoying the drama. 'That poor Mrs Hawthorn. Such a nice lady, I always think.'

'Yes,' I said, agreeing: and life did, I supposed, have to go on. Automatic, pointless life, like asking Brian to go into the storeroom and fetch another case of White Satin.

He nodded without closing the mouth and went off on the errand, returning unerringly with the right thing. He might not be able to read, but I had found he could recognize the general appearance of a bottle and label if I told him three or four times what it was, and he now knew all the regular items by sight. Mrs Palissey said at least once a week that she was ever so proud of him, considering.

Mrs Palissey and I remained by common consent on formal terms of Mrs and Mr: more dignified, she said. By nature she liked to please and was in consequence a good saleswoman, making genuinely helpful suggestions to irresolute customers. 'Don't know their own minds, do they, Mr Beach?' she would say when they'd gone and I would agree truthfully that no, they often didn't. Mrs Palissey and I tended to have the same conversations over and over and slightly too often.

She was honest in all major ways and unscrupulous in minor. She would never cheat me through the till, but Brian ate his way through a lot more crisps and Mars bars than I gave him myself, and spare light bulbs and half-full jars of Nescafé tended to go home with Mrs P. if she was short. Mrs Palissey considered such things 'perks' but would have regarded taking a bottle of sherry as stealing. I respected the distinction and was grateful for it, and paid her a little over the norm.

Whenever we were both there together, Mrs Palissey served the shop customers while I sat in the tiny office within earshot taking orders over the telephone and doing the paperwork, ready to help her if necessary. Some customers, particularly men, came for the wine chat as much as the product, and her true knowledge there was sweet, dry, cheap, expensive, popular.

It was a man's voice I could hear saying, 'Is Mr Beach himself in?' and Mrs Palissey's helpfully answering, 'Yes, sir, he'll be right with you,' and I rose and took the few steps into his sight.

The man there, dressed in a belted fawn raincoat, was perhaps a shade older than myself and had a noticeably authoritative manner. Without enormous surprise I watched him reach into an inner pocket for a badge of office and introduce himself as Detective Sergeant Ridger, Thames Valley police. He hoped I might be able to help him with his inquiries.

My mind did one of those quick half-guilty canters round everything possible I might have done wrong before I came to the more sensible conclusion that his presence must have something to do with the accident. And so it had, in a way, but not how I could have expected.

'Do you know a Mr d'Alban, sir?' He consulted his memory. 'The Honourable James d'Alban, sir?'

'Yes I do,' I said. 'He was injured yesterday at the Hawthorn party. He's not . . . dying?' I shied at the last minute away from 'dead'.

'No, sir, he's not. As far as I know he's in Battle Hospital with broken ribs, a pierced lung, and concussion.'

Enough to be going on with, I thought ironically. Poor Jimmy.

Ridger had a short over-neat haircut, watchful brown eyes, a calculator-wristwatch bristling with knobs and no gift for public relations. He said impersonally, 'Mr d'Alban woke up to some extent in the ambulance taking him to hospital and began talking disjointedly but repeatedly about a man called Larry Trent and some unpronounceable whisky that wasn't what it ought to be, and you, sir, who would know for certain if you tasted it.'

I just waited.

Ridger went on, 'There was a uniformed policeman in the ambulance with Mr d'Alban, and the constable reported the substance of those remarks to us, as he was aware we had reason to be interested in them. Mr d'Alban, he said, was totally unable to answer any questions yesterday and indeed appeared not to know he was being addressed.'

I wished vaguely that Ridger would talk more naturally, not as if reading from a notebook. Mrs Palissey was listening hard though pretending not to, with Brian frowning uncomprehendingly beside her. Ridger glanced at them a shade uneasily and asked if we could talk somewhere in private.

I took him into the miniscule office, large enough only for a desk, two chairs and a heater: about five feet square, approximately. He sat in the visitors' chair without waste of time and said, 'We've tried to interview Mr d'Alban this morning but he is in Intensive Care and the doctor refused us entry.' He shrugged. 'They say to try tomorrow, but for our purposes tomorrow may be too late.'

'And your purposes are . . . what?' I asked.

For the first time he seemed to look at me as a person, not just as an aid to inquiries; but I wasn't sure I liked the change because in his warming interest there was also a hint of manipulation. I had dealt in my time with dozens of salesmen seeking business, and Ridger's was the same sort of approach. He needed something from me that called for persuasion.

'Do you verify, sir, that Mr d'Alban did talk to you about this whisky?'

'Yes, he did, yesterday morning.'

Ridger looked almost smug with satisfaction.

'You may not know, sir,' he said, 'that Mr Larry Trent died in yesterday's accident.'

'Yes, I did know.'

'Well, sir . . .' he discreetly cleared his throat, lowering his voice for the sales pitch, softening the natural bossiness in his face. 'To be frank, we've had other complaints about the Silver Moondance. On two former occasions investigations have been carried out there, both times by the Office of Weights and Measures, and by Customs and Excise. On neither occasion was any infringement found.'

He paused.

'But this time?' I prompted obligingly.

'This time we think that in view of Mr Trent's death, it might be possible to make another inspection this morning.'

'Ah.'

I wasn't sure that he liked the dry understanding in my voice, but he soldiered on. 'We have reason to believe that in the past someone at the Silver Moondance, possibly Mr Trent himself, has been tipped off in advance that the investigations were in hand. So this time my superiors in the CID would like to make some preliminary inquiries of our own, assisted, if you are agreeable, by yourself, as an impartial expert.'

'Um,' I said, doubtfully. 'This morning, did you say?'

'Now, sir, if you would be so good.'

'This very minute?'

'We think, sir, the quicker the better.'

'You must surely have your own experts?' I said.

It appeared ... er ... that there was no official expert available at such short notice, and that as time was all important ... would I go?

I could see no real reason why not to, so I said briefly, 'All right', and told Mrs Palissey I'd be back as soon as I could. Ridger drove us in his car, and I wondered on the way just how much of an expert the delirious Jimmy had made me out to be, and whether I would be of any use at all, when it came to the point.

The Silver Moondance, along the valley from the small Thames-side town where I had my shop, had originally been a sprawlingly ugly house built on the highest part of a field sloping up from the river. It had over the years metamorphosed successively into school, nursing home, and general boarding house, adding inappropriate wings at every change. Its most recent transformation had been also the most radical, so that little could now be seen of the original shiny yellow-grey bricks for glossier expanses of plate glass. At night from the river the place looked like Blackpool fully illuminated, and even by day, from the road, one could see 'Silver Moondance' blinking on and off in white letters over the doorway.

'Do they know you here, sir?' Ridger belatedly asked as we turned into the drive.

I shook my head. 'Shouldn't think so. The last time I came here it was the Riverland Guest Home, full of old retired people. I used to deliver their drinks.'

Dears, they had been, I remembered nostalgically, and great topers, on the whole, taking joy in their liquid pleasures.

Ridger grunted without much interest and parked on an acre or two of unpopulated tarmac. 'They should just be open,' he said with satisfaction, locking the car doors. 'Ready, sir?'

'Yes,' I said. 'And Sergeant . . . um . . . let me do the talking.'

'But . . .'

'Best not to alarm them,' I said, persuasively, 'if you don't want them pouring the Laphroaig down the sink.'

'The what?'

'What we're looking for.'

'Oh.' He thought. 'Very well.'

I said, 'Fine,' without emphasis and we walked through the flashing portal into the ritzy plush of the entrance hall.

There were lights on everywhere, but no one in sight. A reception desk; unattended. A flat air of nothing happening and nothing expected.

Ridger and I walked toward a wrought iron and driftwood sign announcing 'Silver Moondance Saloon', and pushed through Western-style swing doors into the room beyond. It was red, black and silver, very large and uninhabited. There were many tables, each with four bentwood chairs set neatly round, and an orthodox bar at one end, open for business.

No bartender.

Ridger walked purposefully across and rapped on the counter, I following him more slowly.

No one came. Ridger rapped again, louder and longer, and was presently rewarded by a youngish fair-haired man coming through another swinging door at the back of the bar area, sweating visibly and struggling into a white jacket.

'Give us a chance,' he said crossly. 'We've only been open five minutes.' He wiped his damp forehead with his fingers and buttoned his coat. 'What can I get you?'

'Is the restaurant open?' I said.

'What? Not yet. They don't start serving before twelve.'

'And the wine waiter, would he be here?'

The barman looked at the clock and shook his head. 'What do you want him for? Whatever drinks you want, I'll get them.'

'The wine list,' I said humbly. 'Could I see it?'

He shrugged, reached under the bar, and produced a padded crimson folder. 'Help yourself,' he said, handing it across.

He was not actively rude, I thought, just thrown off the rails by the boss's demise. Practised, a touch effeminate, with unfortunate pimples and a silver identification bracelet inscribed with 'Tom'. I could feel Ridger beginning to bristle beside me, so I said mildly, 'Could I have a Scotch, please?'

The barman gave a half-exasperated glance at the wine list in my hand but turned away and thrust a regulation glass against the optic measure on a standard-sized bottle of Bell's.

'Something for you?' I said to Ridger.

'Tomato juice. Without Worcester sauce.'

The barman put my whisky on the counter. 'Anything in yours?' he asked.

'No, thanks.'

I paid for the two drinks and we went to sit at one of the tables furthest away from the bar.

'This isn't what we came for,' Ridger said pro-testingly.

'First things first,' I said, smelling the whisky. 'Start at the bottom and work up. Good wine-tasting tactics.'

'But . . .' He thought better of it, and shrugged. 'All right, then. Your way. But don't take too long.'

I sucked a very small amount of whisky into my mouth and let it wander back over my tongue. One can't judge whisky with the taste buds at the tip, up by the front teeth, but only along the sides of the tongue and at the back, and I let everything that was there in the way of flavour develop to the full before I swallowed, and then waited a while for the aftertaste.

'Well?' said Ridger. 'What now?'

'For a start,' I said, 'this isn't Bell's.'

Ridger looked unexpectedly startled. 'Are you sure?'

'Do you know anything about whisky?' I asked.

'No. I'm a beer man, myself. Drink the odd whisky and ginger now and then, that's all.'

'Do you want to know?' I flicked a finger at the glass. 'I mean, shall I explain?'

'Will it take long?'

'No.'

'Go on, then.'

'Scotch whisky is made of barley,' I said. 'You can malt barley, like is done for beer. You let the grains start to grow, to form shoots about an inch or two long.

Then for whisky you smoke the shoots, which are called malts, over burning peat, until they pick up the peat and smoke flavours and are crisp. Then you make a mash of the malts with water and let it ferment, then you distil it and put the distillation in wooden casks to age for several years, and that's pure malt whisky, full of overtones of various tastes.'

'Right,' Ridger said, nodding, his crisp hair-cut clearly concentrating.

'It's much cheaper,' I said, 'to make the barley into a mash without going through the malting and smoking stages, and much quicker because the ageing process is years shorter, and that sort of whisky is called grain whisky and is a great deal plainer on the tongue.'

'OK,' he said. 'Go on.'

'Good standard scotches like Bell's are a mixture of malt and grain whiskies. The more malt, the more varied and subtle the flavour. This in this glass has very little or no malt, which doesn't matter at all if you want to mix it with ginger, because you'd kill the malt flavour anyway.'

Ridger looked round the empty room. 'With this place full, with smoke and perfume and ginger ale, who's to know the difference?'

'It would take a brave man,' I said, smiling.

'What next, then?'

'We might hide the Scotch in your tomato juice,' I poured the one into the other, to his horror. 'I can't

777

drink it,' I explained. 'Do you want a drunk expert? No good at all.'

'I suppose not,' he said, weakly for him, and I went over to the bar and asked the barman if he had any malts.

'Sure,' he said, waving a hand along a row of bottles. 'Glenfiddich, down at the other end there.'

'Mm,' I said doubtfully. 'Do you have any Laphroaig?'

'La-what?'

'Laphroaig. A friend of mine had some here. He said it was great. He said as I liked malts I should definitely try it.'

The barman looked at his stock, but shook his head.

'Perhaps it's in the restaurant,' I said. 'I think he did mention drinking it after dinner. Perhaps it's on the drinks trolley.' I pulled out my wallet and opened it expectantly, and with a considering glance at the notes in sight the barman decided to go on the errand. He returned quite soon with a genuine Laphroaig bottle and charged me outrageously for a nip, which I paid without demur, giving him a tip on top.

I carried the glass to the far table to join Ridger.

'What do you do now?' I asked. 'Pray?'

'Taste it,' he said tersely.

I smelled it first, however, and tasted it slowly as before, Ridger sitting forward tensely in his chair.

'Well?' he demanded.

'It's not Laphroaig.'

'Are you certain?'

'Absolutely positive. Laphroaig is as smoky as you can get. Pure malt. There's almost no malt at all in what I've just tasted. It's the same whisky as before.'

'Thanks very much, Mr Beach,' he said with deep satisfaction. 'That's great.'

He stood up, walked over to the bar and asked to see the bottle from which his friend had just drunk. The bartender obligingly pushed it across the counter, and Ridger picked it up. Then with his other hand he pulled out his identification, and the barman, angry, started shouting.

Ridger proved to have a radio inside his jacket. He spoke to some unseen headquarters, received a tinny reply, and told the bartender the police would be prohibiting the sale of all alcohol at the Silver Moondance for that day at least, while tests were made on the stock.

'You're barmy,' the bartender yelled, and to me, viciously, 'Creep.'

His loud voice brought colleagues in the shape of a worried man in a dark suit who looked junior and ineffective, and a girl in a short pert waitress uniform, long fawn legs below a scarlet tunic, scarlet headband over her hair.

Ridger took stock of the opposition and found himself very much in charge. The ineffective junior announced himself to be the assistant manager, which drew looks of scorn and amazement from the waitress

779

and the barman. Assistant to the assistant, I rather gathered. Ridger explained forcibly again that no liquor was to be sold pending investigations, and all three of them said they knew nothing about anything, and we would have to talk to ... er ... talk to ...

'The management?' I suggested.

They nodded dumbly.

'Let's do that,' I said. 'Where's the manager?'

The assistant to the assistant manager finally said that the manager was on holiday and the assistant manager was ill. Head office was sending someone to take over as soon as possible.

'Head office?' I said. 'Didn't Larry Trent own the place?'

'Er ...' said the assistant unhappily. 'I really don't know. Mr Trent never said he didn't, I mean, I thought he did. But when I got here this morning the telephone was ringing, and it was head office. That's what he said, anyway. He wanted to speak to the manager, and when I explained he said he would send someone along straight away.'

'Who ran things last night?' Ridger demanded.

'What? Oh ... we're closed, Sunday nights.'

'And yesterday lunchtime?'

'The assistant manager was here, but he'd got flu. He went home to bed as soon as we closed. And of course Mr Trent had been here until opening time, seeing that everything was all right before he went to Mr Hawthorn's party.'

All three looked demoralized but at the same time slightly defiant, seeing the policeman as their natural enemy. Relations scarcely improved when Ridger's reinforcements rolled up: two uniformed constables bringing tape and labels for sealing all the bottles.

I diffidently suggested to Ridger that he should extend his suspicions to the wines.

'Wines?' he frowned. 'Yes, if you like, but we've got enough with the spirits.'

'All the same,' I murmured, and Ridger told the assistant to show me where they kept the wine, and to help me and one of his constables bring any bottles I wanted into the bar. The assistant, deciding that help-fulness would establish his driven-snow innocence, put no obstacles in my way, and in due course, and after consulting the wine list, the assistant, the constable and I returned to the bar carrying two large baskets full of bottles.

The spirits bottles all having been sealed, there was at our return a lull of activity in the Silver Moondance Saloon. I unloaded the bottles onto two tables, six white wine on one, six red on another, and from my jacket pocket produced my favourite corkscrew.

'Hey,' the barman protested. 'You can't do that.'

'Every bottle I open will be paid for,' I said, matter-of-factly. 'And what's it to you?'

The barman shrugged. 'Give me twelve glasses,' I said, 'and one of those pewter tankards,' and he did. I opened the six bottles of varying white wines and under the interested gaze of six pairs of eyes poured a little of the first into a glass. Niersteiner, it said on the label: and Niersteiner it was. I spat the tasted mouthful into the pewter tankard, to disgusted reaction from the audience.

'Do you want him to get drunk?' Ridger demanded, belatedly understanding. 'The evidence of a drunk taster wouldn't be acceptable.'

I tasted the second white. Chablis, as it should have been.

The third was similarly OK, a Pouilly Fuissé.

By the time I'd finished the sixth, a Sauternes, the barman had greatly relaxed.

'Nothing wrong with them?' Ridger asked, not worried.

'Nothing,' I agreed, stuffing the corks back. 'I'll try the reds.'

The reds were a St Emilion, a St Estèphe, a Mâcon, a Valpolicella, a Volnay and a Nuits St Georges, all dated 1979. I smelled and tasted each one carefully, spitting and waiting a few moments in between sips so that each wine should be fresh on the tongue, and by the time I'd finished everyone else was restive.

'Well,' Ridger demanded, 'are they all right?'

'They're quite pleasant,' I said, 'but they're all the same.'

'What do you mean?'

'I mean,' I said, 'that notwithstanding all those pretty labels, the wine in all of these bottles is none of them.

It's a blend. Mostly Italian, I would say, mixed with some French and possibly some Yugoslav, but it could be anything.'

'You don't know what you're talking about,' the barman said impatiently. 'We have people every day saying how good the wines are.'

'Mm,' I said neutrally. 'Perhaps you do.'

'Are you positive?' Ridger asked me. 'They're all the same?'

'Yes.'

He nodded as if that settled it and instructed the constables to seal and label the six reds with the date, time and place of confiscation. Then he told the barman to find two boxes to hold all the labelled bottles, which brought a toss of the head, a mulish petulance and a slow and grudging compliance.

I kept my word and paid for all the wine, the only action of mine which pleased the barman from first to last. I got him to itemize every bottle on a Silver Moondance billhead and sign it 'received in full', and then I paid him by credit card, tucking away the receipts.

Ridger seemed to think paying was unnecessary, but then shrugged, and he and the constable began putting the wine into one of the boxes and the whiskies into the other; and into this sullenly orderly scene erupted the man from head office.

CHAPTER FIVE

The man from head office was not at first sight intimidating. Short, fortyish, dark-haired, of medium build and wearing glasses, he walked enquiringly into the saloon in a grey worsted business suit as if not sure of the way.

Ridger, taking him, as I did, for a customer, raised his voice and said, 'The bar is closed, sir.'

The man took no notice but advanced more purposefully until he stood near enough to see the bottles in the boxes. He frowned at them and glanced at the policeman, and I could see in him a distinct change of mental gear. A tightening of muscles; a sharpening of attention: cruise to overdrive in three seconds.

'I'm a police officer,' said Ridger firmly, producing his authorization. 'The bar is closed until further notice.'

'Is it indeed?' said the newcomer ominously. 'Be so good as to explain why.' The first impression was wrong, I thought. This man could intimidate quite easily.

Ridger blinked. 'It's a police matter,' he said. 'It's no concern of yours.'

'Every concern,' said the man shortly. 'I've come from head office to take over. So just what exactly is going on?' His voice had the edge of one not simply used to command but used to instant action when he spoke. His accent, so far as he had one, was straightforward business-English, devoid both of regional vowels and swallowed consonants, but also without timbre. Good plain grain, I thought; not malt.

'Your name, sir?' asked Ridger stolidly, ignoring the sharp tone as if he hadn't heard it, which I was sure he had.

The man from head office looked him up and down, assessing the altogether statement of brushed hair, belted raincoat, polished shoes. Ridger reacted to that aggressively, his spine stiffening, the desire to be the dominator growing unmistakably in the set of his jaw. Interesting, I thought.

The man from head office allowed the pause to lengthen until it was clear to everyone that he was giving his name as a result of thought, not out of obedience to Ridger.

'My name is Paul Young,' he said finally, with weight. 'I represent the company of which this restaurant is a subsidiary. And now, what exactly is going on here?'

Ridger's manner remained combative as he began announcing in his notebook terminology that the Silver Moondance would be prosecuted for contraventions of the Sale of Goods Act.

Paul Young from head office interrupted brusquely. 'Cut the jargon and be precise.'

Ridger glared at him. Paul Young grew impatient. Neither would visibly defer to the other, but Ridger did in the end explain what he was removing in the boxes.

Paul Young listened with fast growing anger, but this time not aiming it at Ridger himself. He turned his glare instead on the barman (who did his best to shelter behind his pimples), and thunderously demanded to know who was responsible for selling substitutions. From the barman, the waitress and the assistant assistant in turn he got weak disclaiming shakes of the head and none of the defiance that they had shown to Ridger.

'And who are you?' he enquired rudely, giving me the up and down inspection. 'Another policeman?'

'A customer,' I said mildly.

Seeing nothing in me to detain him he returned his forceful attention to Ridger, assuring him authoritatively that head office had had no knowledge of the substitutions and that the fraud must have originated right here in this building. The police could be assured that head office would discover the guilty person and prosecute him themselves, ensuring that nothing of this sort could happen again.

It was perfectly clear to Ridger as to everyone else present that Paul Young was in fact badly jolted and surprised by the existence of fraud, but Ridger with smothered satisfaction said that the outcome would be for the police and the courts to decide, and that meanwhile Mr Young could give him the address and telephone number of head office, for future reference.

I watched Paul Young while he wrote the required information onto another billhead provided by the barman and wondered vaguely why he didn't carry business cards to save himself that sort of bother. He had large hands, I noticed, full fleshed, with pale skin, and as he bent his head over the paper I saw the discreet pink hearing aid tucked behind his right ear, below the frame of his glasses. One could get hearing aids built-in with the earpieces of eyeglass frames, I thought, and wondered why he didn't.

What a mess, I thought, for a parent company to walk into unawares. And who, I wondered, had been on the fiddle – the manager, the wine waiter, or Larry Trent himself? Not that I wondered at all deeply. The culprit's identity was to me less interesting than the crime, and the crime itself was hardly unique.

The six corks from the bottles of red were lying where I'd left them on the small table, the constables having sealed the open necks with wide wrappings of sticky tape instead of trying to ram back the original plugs, and I picked the corks up almost absentmindedly and put them in my pocket, tidy-minded out of habit.

Paul Young straightened from his writing and handed the sheet of paper to the assistant assistant, who handed it to me, who passed it on to Ridger, who glanced at it, folded it, and tucked it into some inner pocket below the raincoat.

'And now, sir,' he said, 'close the bar.'

The barman looked to Paul Young for instructions and got a shrug and an unwilling nod, and presently an ornamental grille unrolled from ceiling to bar-top, imprisoning the barman in his cage. He clicked a few locks into place and went out through the rear door, not returning to the saloon.

Ridger and Paul Young argued for a while about how soon the Silver Moondance could resume full business, each still covertly manoeuvring for domination. I reckoned it came out about quits because they finally backed off from each other inconclusively, both still in aggressive postures, more snarl than teeth.

Ridger removed his constables, the boxes and myself to the car park leaving Paul Young to deal with his helpless helpers, and the last I saw of the man from head office, in a backward glance as I went through the western swing doors, was the businesslike glasses turning to survey his large empty-tabled discontinued asset in black and scarlet, the colours of roulette.

Ridger muttered under his breath several times as he drove me back to my shop and broke out into plain exasperation when I asked him for a receipt for the case of wines, which he was transporting in the boot.

'Those twelve bottles do belong to me,' I pointed

out. 'I paid for them, and I want them back. You said yourself that you'd got enough with the whisky to prosecute. The wines were my own idea.'

He grudgingly admitted it and gave me a receipt.

'Where do I find you?' I asked.

He told me the address of his station and without the least gratitude for the help he had solicited, drove brusquely away. Between him and Paul Young I thought, definitely not much to choose.

In the shop Mrs Palissey had had a veritable barrage of customers as sometimes happened on Monday mornings, and was showing signs of wear.

'Go to lunch,' I said, although it was early, and with gratitude she put on her coat, took Brian in tow, and departed to the local café for pie and chips and a gossip with her constant friend, the traffic warden.

The customers kept coming and I served them with automatic ease, smiling, always smiling, giving pleasure to the pleasure-seekers. For years, with Emma, I had positively enjoyed the selling, finding my own satisfaction in giving it to others. Without her the warmth I had felt had grown shallow, so that now I dispensed only a surface sympathy, nodding and smiling and hardly listening, hearing only sometimes, not always, the unsaid things in the shopping voices. The power I'd once had had drained away, and I didn't really care.

During a short lull I wrote the list for the wholesaler, planning to go as soon as Mrs Palissey returned, and noticed that Brian, unasked by me, had swept and straightened the store room. The telephone rang three times with good substantial orders and the till, when consulted, showed a healthy profit margin on the morning's trading. Ironic, the whole thing.

Two customers came in together, and I served the woman first, a middle-aged frightened lady who called every day for a bottle of the cheapest gin, tucking it away secretively in a large handbag while taking furtive glances out of the window for passing neighbours. Why didn't she buy it by the case, I'd once long ago asked her teasingly, as it was cheaper by the case, but she'd been alarmed and said no, she enjoyed the walk; and the loneliness had looked out of her eyes along with the fear of being called an alcoholic, which she wasn't quite, and I'd felt remorse for being heartless, because I'd known perfectly well why she bought one private bottle at a time.

'Nice day, Mr Beach,' she said breathlessly, her glance darting to the street.

'Not too bad, Mrs Chance.'

She gave me the exact money, coins warmed by her palm, notes carefully counted, watching nervously while I wrapped her comfort in tissue.

'Thank you, Mrs Chance.'

She nodded dumbly, gave me a half smile, pushed the bottle into her handbag and departed, pausing at the door to reconnoitre. I put the money in the till and looked enquiringly at the man waiting patiently to be served next, and found myself face to face with no customer but the investigator Wilson from the day before.

'Mr Beach,' he said.

'Mr Wilson.'

Externally he wore exactly the same clothes, as if he had never been to bed or to shave, which he had. He looked rested and clean, and moved comfortably in his slow hunchbacked fashion with the knowing eyes and the non-communicating face.

'Do you always know what your customers want without asking them?' he said.

'Quite often,' I nodded, 'but usually I wait for them to say.'

'More polite?'

'Infinitely.'

He paused. 'I came to ask you one or two questions. Is there anywhere we can talk?'

'Just talk,' I said apologetically. 'Would you like a chair?'

'Are you alone here?'

'Yes.'

I fetched the spare chair for him from the office and put it by the counter, and had no sooner done so than three people came in for Cinzano, beer and sherry. Wilson waited through the sales without doing much more than blink, and when the door closed for the third time he stirred without impatience and said, 'Yesterday, during the party, were you at any time talking to the Sheik?'

I smiled involuntarily. 'No, I wasn't.'

'Why does the idea amuse you?'

'Well . . . the Sheik considers all this . . .' I waved a hand around the bottle-lined walls, ' . . . as being positively sinful. Forbidden. Pernicious. Much as we regard cocaine. To him I'm a pusher. In his own country I'd be in jail, or worse. I wouldn't have introduced myself to him. Not unless I wanted to invite contempt.'

'I see,' he said, almost nodding, contemplating the Islamic view. Then he slightly pursed his lips approaching, I guessed, the question he had really come to ask.

'Think back,' he said, 'to when you were outside the tent, when the horsebox rolled.'

'Yes.'

'Why were you out there?'

I told him about fetching more champagne.

'And when you went out, the horsebox was already rolling?'

'No,' I said. 'When I went out I glanced up at the cars and everything was all right. I remember noting that no one had yet left . . . and hoped I'd taken enough champagne to last out.'

'Was there anyone near the horsebox?'

'No.'

'You're certain?'

'Yes. No one that I could see.'

'You've consulted your memory . . . before this moment?'

I half smiled. 'Yes. You might say so.'

He sighed. 'Did you see anyone at all anywhere near any of the cars?'

'No. Except . . . only a child with a dog.'

'Child?'

'They weren't near the horsebox. Nearer the Sheik's Mercedes, really.'

'Can you describe the child?'

'Well . . .' I frowned. 'A boy.'

'Clothes?'

I looked away from him, gazing vacantly at the racks of wine, thinking back. 'Dark trousers . . . perhaps jeans . . . and a dark blue sweater.'

'Hair?'

'Um . . . light brown, I suppose. Not blond, not black.'

'Age?'

I pondered, looking again at the patient questioner. 'Young. Small. Four, I should think.'

'Why are you so definite?'

'I'm not . . . his head was still big in proportion to his body.'

Wilson's eyes glimmered deeply. 'What sort of dog?' he said.

I stared vaguely once more into the distance, seeing the child on the hill. 'A whippet,' I said.

'On a leash?'

'No . . . running and turning back towards the boy.'

'What sort of shoes did the boy have?'

'For God's sake,' I said, 'I only saw him for a couple of seconds.'

His mouth twitched. He looked down at his hands and then up again. 'No one else?'

'No.'

'How about the Sheik's chauffeur?'

I shook my head. 'He might have been sitting in the car, but one couldn't tell. It had tinted windows, as you saw.'

He stirred and said thank you and began to get to his feet.

'Incidentally,' I said, 'someone stole three cases of champagne and some other bottles out of my van some-time after the accident. I need to report the theft to the police before I claim insurance . . . May I report it to you?'

He gave me a smile. 'I will note that you have reported it.'

'Thanks.'

He held his hand out to me over the counter and I shook it. 'It's I who thank you, Mr Beach,' he said.

'I haven't been much help.'

He smiled his small uncommunicative smile, nodded benignly, and went away.

Good grief, I thought inconsequentially, watching his hunched departing back, one hundred and fifty goblets were lying in splinters in the Hawthorns' back garden, and it was all very well talking of insurance, I was due to supply those very glasses to the Thames Ladies

Christmas Charities fund-raising wine and cheese party on the following day, Tuesday, which I had forgotten clean about.

Tentatively I rang the Hawthorns' number, not wanting to overload Flora but to ask all the same how many glasses if any remained intact, and I got not Flora but an answering machine with Jimmy's voice, loud, healthy and languid, inviting me to leave my name, number, and message.

I complied, wondering how Jimmy was doing in intensive care, and when Mrs Palissey came back I took Brian with me to the wholesalers, where he helped me shift umpteen cases from the stores onto trolleys, and from those trolleys to other trolleys at the pay desk, for rolling out to the van, and from the second trolleys into the van, and, back at the shop, from the van into the storeroom. My own muscles, after roughly twelve years of such exercise, would have rivalled a fork-lift truck, and Brian's, too, were coming along nicely. He grinned while he worked. He enjoyed lifting the cases. Two-at-a-time he had begun to scorn; he liked me to pile him with three.

Brian never talked much, which I appreciated. He sat placidly beside me in the van on the way back, lips apart as usual, and I wondered what went on in that big vacant head, and how much one could teach him if one tried. He'd learned quite a lot in the three or so months he'd been with me, I reflected. He was brilliantly useful compared with day one.

He unloaded the van by himself when we returned and put everything in the right places in the storeroom, which I had arranged with much more method since his arrival. Mrs Palissey had taken two more orders on the telephone, and I spent some time making up those and the ones from earlier in the day, collecting all the various items together into boxes for Brian to carry out to the van. Being a wine merchant, I often thought, was not a gentle artistic occupation, but thoroughly backbreakingly physical.

The telephone rang yet again while I was sitting in the office writing the bills to go out with the orders and I stretched out one hand for the receiver with my eyes on my work.

'Tony?' a woman's voice said tentatively. 'It's Flora.'

'Dear Flora,' I said. 'How are you? How's Jack? How's everything?'

'Oh . . .' She seemed tired beyond bearing. 'Everything's so awful. I know I shouldn't say that . . . but . . . oh dear.'

'I'll come and fetch the glasses,' I said, hearing the appeal she hadn't uttered. 'I'll come practically at once.'

'There . . . there aren't many left whole . . . but yes, do come.'

'Half an hour,' I said.

She said, 'Thank you,' faintly and disconnected.

I looked at my watch. Four-thirty. Most often at about that time on Mondays Mrs Palissey and Brian set off in the van to do any deliveries which lay roughly on their way home, finishing the round the following morning. Mrs Palissey's ability to drive had been the chief reason I'd originally hired her, and she on her part had been pleased to be given the use of the shop's second string, an elderly capacious Rover estate. We swopped the two vehicles around as required, so I said I would do the deliveries that day, if she would stay until five to close the shop, and go home again in the car.

'By all means, Mr Beach.' She was graciously obliging. 'And I'll be here at nine-thirty, then, in the morning.'

I nodded my thanks and took the bills, the orders, van and myself off up the hill to Jack Hawthorn's stables, where not a great deal had changed since the day before.

I saw, as I came over the hill, that the great green horsebox still stood on the lawn, with, beyond it, the heaped canvas remains of the marquee. The Sheik had gone, and his body-guards. The mute bloodstained expanse of fawn matting was scattered with trestle tables and sections of tent pole, and glittering here and there in the rays of late afternoon sunshine lay a million pieces of glass.

I parked as before outside the kitchen entrance and locked the van with a sigh. Flora came slowly out of the house to greet me, dressed in a grey skirt and a green cardigan, dark smudges under exhausted eyes.

I gave her a small hug and a kiss on the cheek. We

had never before been on those sort of terms, but disasters could work wonders in that area.

'How's Jack?' I said.

'They've just now set his leg . . . pinned it, they say. He's still unconscious . . . but I saw him this morning . . . before.' Her voice was quavery, as it had been on the telephone. 'He was very down. So depressed. It made me so miserable.' The last word came out in a gasp as her face crumpled into tears. 'Oh dear . . . Oh dear . . .'

I put my arm round her shaking shoulders. 'Don't worry,' I said. 'He'll be all right. Truly.'

She nodded mutely, sniffing and fumbling in a pocket for a handkerchief, and after a while, through gulps, said, 'He's alive, and I should be grateful for that, and they say he'll be home quite soon. It's just . . . everything . . . everything . . .'

I nodded. 'Just too much.'

She nodded also and dried her eyes with a re-emergence of spirit, and I asked whether any of her children might not come to help her through this patch.

'They're all so busy . . . I told them not to. And Jack, you know, he's jealous of them really, he wouldn't want them here when he's away, though I shouldn't say that, only I do seem to tell you things, Tony dear, and I don't know why.'

'Like telling the wallpaper,' I said.

She smiled very faintly, a considerable advance.

'How's Jimmy?' I asked.

'I didn't see him. He's conscious, they say, and no

worse. I don't know what we'll do if he isn't well soon ... he runs everything, you know ... and without them both ... I feel so lost. I can't help it.'

'Anything I can do?' I said.

'Oh yes,' she said instantly. 'I was so hoping ... I mean, when you said you'd come ... Have you got time?'

'For what?' I asked.

'Um ... Tony dear, I don't know how much I can ask of you, but would you ... could you possibly ... walk round the yard with me?'

'Well, of course,' I said, surprised. 'If you want.'

'It's evening stables,' she explained in a rush. 'Jack was so insistent I walked round. He wants me to tell him how everything is, because we've a new head lad, he came only last week, and Jack says he's not sure of him in spite of his references, and he made me promise I'd walk round. And he knows, he really does, that I don't know enough about horses, but he wanted me to promise ... and he was so depressed, that I did.'

'No problem at all,' I said. 'We'll walk round together, and we'll both listen, and afterwards we'll make notes for you to relay to Jack.'

She sighed with relief and looked at her watch. 'It's time now, I should think.'

'OK,' I said, and we walked round the house to the stables and to the sixty or so equine inmates.

In Jack's yard there were two big old quadrangles, built of wood mostly, with a preponderance of white

799

paint. Some of the many doors stood wide open with lads carrying sacks and buckets in and out, and some were half closed with horses' heads looking interestedly over the tops.

'We'd better do the colts' yard first,' Flora said, 'and the fillies' yard after, like Jack does, don't you think?'

'Absolutely,' I agreed.

I knew about horses to the extent that I'd been brought up with them, as much after my father's death as before. My mother, wholly dedicated, seldom talked of much else. She had in her time ridden in point-to-point races and also adored to go hunting, which filled her life whenever my father was away on duty, and his as well when he was at home and not that minute racing. I had seen day after day the glowing enjoyment in their faces and had tried hard to feel it myself, but whatever enthusiasm I'd shown had been counterfeit, for their sakes. Galloping after hounds across muddy November fields I had thought chiefly of how soon one could decently go home, and the only part of the ritual I had actually enjoyed had been the cleaning and feeding of the horses afterwards. Those great creatures, tired and dirty, were so uncritical. They never told one to keep one's heels down, one's elbows in, one's head up, one's spine straight. They didn't expect one to be impossibly brave and leap the largest fences. They didn't mind if one sneaked through gates instead. Closed into a box with a horse, humming while I brushed off dried mud and sweat, I'd felt a sort of dumb complete communion, and been happy.

After my father died my mother had hunted on with unfaltering zeal and had for the past ten years been joint master of the local hounds, to her everlasting fulfilment. It had been a relief to her, I often thought, when I had finally left home.

Jack Hawthorn's lads were halfway through the late afternoon programme of mucking out, feeding and watering, a process known throughout the racing world as 'evening stables'. It was the custom for the trainer to walk round, usually with the head lad, stopping at every box to inspect the racer within, feeling its legs for heat (bad sign) and looking for a bright eye (good).

Jack's new head lad had greeted Flora's appearance with an exaggerated obsequiousness which I found distasteful and which seemed also to make Flora even less sure of herself. She introduced him as Howard, and told him Mr Beach would be accompanying her on the rounds.

Howard extending the Uriah Heep manner to myself, we set off on what was clearly the normal pattern, and I listened attentively for Flora's sake to every Howard opinion.

Very little, it seemed to me, could have been different from the morning before, when Jack himself had been there. One horse had trodden on a stone out at exercise and was slightly footsore. Another had eaten only half of his midday feed. A third had rubbed skin off a hock, which would need watching.

Flora said 'I see,' and I'll tell Mr Hawthorn,' at regular intervals and Howard ingratiatingly said that Flora could safely leave everything to him, Howard, until Mr Hawthorn's return.

We came in turn to the Sheik's horses, still in residence, and also to Larry Trent's, bursting with health. They had been prolific winners all year, it seemed. Both the Sheik and Larry Trent had been excellent judges of potential, and were lucky as well.

'We'll be losing all of these horses, I suppose,' Flora sighed. 'Jack says it will be a heavy financial loss for us.'

'What will happen to them?' I asked.

'Oh . . . I expect the Sheik's will be sold. I don't know. I don't know if he has any family. And Larry Trent's five, of course, will go back to their owners.'

I raised my eyebrows slightly but because of Howard's unctuous presence said no more, and it wasn't until Flora and I were at length walking back towards my van that I asked her what she meant.

'Larry Trent's horses?' she repeated. 'They weren't his own property. He leased them.'

'Paid rent for them?'

'My dear, no. A lease is only an agreement. Say someone owns a horse but can't really afford the training fees, and someone else wants to have a horse racing in his name and can afford the training fees but not the cost of the horse itself, then those two people make an agreement, all signed and registered, of course. The usual terms are that when the horse earns any prize-money it's divided fifty-fifty between the two parties. It's done quite often, you know.'

'No, I didn't know,' I said humbly.

'Oh yes. Larry Trent always did it. He was pretty shrewd at it. He would lease a horse for a year, say, and if it turned out all right he might lease it for another year, but if it won nothing, he'd try another. You can lease a horse for as long as you like, as long as you both agree, for a year or a season or three months . . . whatever you want.'

I found it interesting and asked, 'How are the leases fixed up?'

'Jack has the forms.'

'No, I meant, how does anyone know who has a horse they will lease but not sell?'

'Word of mouth,' she said vaguely. 'People just say. Sometimes they advertise. And sometimes one of our owners will ask Jack to find someone to lease their horse so they don't have to pay the training bills. Very often they do it with mares, so that they can have their horse back for breeding afterwards.'

'Neat,' I said.

Flora nodded. 'Larry Trent always liked it because it meant he could run five horses instead of owning only one outright. He was a great gambler, that man.'

'Gambler?'

803

'A thousand on this, a thousand on that ... I used to get tired of hearing about it.'

I gave her an amused glance. 'Didn't you like him?'

'I suppose he was all right,' she said dubiously. 'He was always friendly. A good owner, Jack always said. Paid regularly and understood that horses aren't machines. Hardly ever blamed the jockey if he lost. But secretive, somehow. I don't really know why I think that, but that's how he seemed to me. Generous, though. He took us to dinner only last week at that place of his, the Silver Moondance. There was a band playing ... so noisy.' She sighed. 'But of course you know about us going there ... Jimmy said he told you about that whisky. I told him to forget it ... Jack didn't want Jimmy stirring up trouble.'

'Mm,' I said. 'The trouble got stirred, all the same, not that it matters.'

'What do you mean?'

I told her of Jimmy's semi-conscious wanderings and my visit with Detective Sergeant Ridger to the Silver Moondance Saloon, and she said 'Good heavens' faintly, with round eyes.

'Someone in that place had a great fiddle going,' I said. 'Whether Larry Trent knew or not.'

She didn't answer directly, but after a long pause said, 'You know, he did something once that I didn't understand. I happened to be at Doncaster sales last year with some friends I was staying with. Jack wasn't there, he was too busy at home. Larry Trent was there . . . He didn't see me, but I saw him across the sale ring, and he was bidding for a horse . . . it was called Ramekin.' She paused, then went on. 'The horse was knocked down to him and I thought good, Jack will be getting it to train. But it never came. Larry Trent never said a word. I told Jack of course, but he said I must have been mistaken, Larry Trent never bought horses, and he wouldn't even ask him about it.'

'So who did train Ramekin afterwards?' I asked.

'No one.' She looked at me anxiously. 'I'm not crazy, you know. I looked it up in the sale prices in the *Sporting Life* and it was sold for more than thirty thousand pounds. They didn't say who had bought it, but I'm absolutely certain it was Larry Trent because the auctioneer's man went right up to him to ask him his name when it had been knocked down to him, but after that . . . nothing happened.'

'Well . . . someone must have him,' I said reasonably.

'I suppose so. But he's not down in any trainer's list of horses-in-training. I checked, you know, because it would have been so annoying if Larry had sent the horse to someone else after all the races Jack's won for him, but Ramekin wasn't down anywhere, and he hasn't raced the whole season, I've been looking for him. Ramekin just . . . really . . . vanished.'

CHAPTER SIX

Flora took me into the kitchen to collect the glasses which were left whole: precisely nineteen.

'I'm sorry,' she said.

I shrugged. 'It's a wonder there are as many as that, considering. And don't worry, I'm insured.'

She helped me slot the survivors into the box I'd brought, her kind round face looking worried.

'Insurance!' she said. 'I've been hearing that word all morning. But who, I ask you, insures against such a tragedy? Of course we didn't have any insurance, not special insurance for the party. And those poor young things who own the horsebox . . . I had Sally . . . that's the wife . . . on the telephone at lunch time telling me over and over hysterically that Peter never never never left the handbrake off and always always always left the horsebox in gear, and that they're going to be ruined if the insurance companies can prove negligence. Poor things. Poor things.' She glanced at me. 'He didn't lock the doors, you know. I asked her. I'm afraid I made her angry. She said you don't lock the doors when you're at a friend's house.'

I thought sourly of my stolen champagne and kept quiet.

'She said they came in the horsebox only because they'd been to fetch a new hunter they'd just bought and were on their way home. The hunter's still here, you know, in one of our spare boxes round the back. Sally says she never wants to see it again. She was totally, absolutely, distraught. It's all so awful.'

Flora came with me as I carried the box of empty glasses out to the van, reluctant to let me go. 'We didn't make that list for Jack,' she said; so we returned to the kitchen and made it.

'If you still feel shaky tomorrow I'll come again for evening stables,' I said. 'I enjoyed it, to be honest.'

'You're a dear, Tony,' she said. 'I'd love you to,' and again she came out to the van to say goodbye.

'The police were here all morning swarming around the horsebox,' she said, looking over to the silent green monster. 'Blowing dust all over it and shaking their heads.'

'Looking for fingerprints, I suppose.'

'I suppose so. Whatever it was they found, they didn't like it. But you know how they are, they didn't tell me a thing.'

'Did you take a look, when they'd gone?' I asked.

She shook her head as if it hadn't occurred to her, but immediately set off towards the horsebox across the grass. I followed, and together we made a rectangular tour, looking at a great deal of pinkish-greyish dust with smudges all over it.

'Hundreds of people must have touched it,' Flora said resignedly.

Including the people with the crane, I thought, and the people who'd released the horse, and any number of people before that.

On impulse I opened the passenger door, which was still not locked, and climbed into the cab.

'Do you think you ought to, dear?' Flora asked anxiously.

'They didn't tell you to stay away, did they?'

'No . . . not today.'

'Don't worry, then.'

I looked around. There was a great deal more of the dust inside the cab, and also a great many fingerprints, but those inside were less smudged. I looked at them curiously but without expectation: it was just that I'd never actually seen the real thing, only dozens of representations in films.

Something about many of the prints struck me suddenly with a distinct mental jolt.

They were *tiny*.

Tiny fingerprints all over the vinyl surfaces of both front seats. Tiny fingerprints all over the steering-wheel and on the gear lever and on the brake. Tiny . . .

I climbed down from the cab and told Flora, and I

told her also about the investigator Wilson's interest when I'd mentioned a little boy and a dog.

'Do you mean,' she said, very distressed, ' . . . it was a *child* who caused such horror?'

'Yes. I'd think so. You know how they play. They love cars. They're always climbing into my van when I deliver things. Little wretches, if you don't watch them. I'd guess that that child released the brake and gear. Then when he'd run off with the dog the weight of the van would eventually make it roll if it was on even the slightest incline.'

'Oh dear.' She looked increasingly upset. 'Whose child?'

I described the boy as best I could but she said she didn't know everyone's children by sight, they changed so fast as they grew.

'Never mind,' I said. 'Wilson has addresses for all your guests. He'll find out. And dearest Flora, be grateful. If it was someone else's child who let off the brakes, your friends Peter and Sally won't be ruined.'

'It wasn't their child . . . they haven't any. But that poor little boy!'

'If everyone's got any sense,' I said, 'which you can be sure they haven't, no one will tell him he killed eight people until he's long grown up.'

On my way home from Flora's I got no further than the second delivery because my customer, a retired solicitor, was delighted (he said) that I had brought his order myself, and I must come in straight away and share a bottle of Château Palmer 1970 which he had just decanted.

I liked the man, who was deeply experienced after countless holidays spent touring vineyards, and we passed a contented evening talking about the small parcels of miraculous fields in Pauillac and Margaux and about the universal virtues of the great grape Cabernet Sauvignon which would grow with distinction almost anywhere on earth. Given poor soil, of course, and sun.

The solicitor's wife, it transpired, was away visiting relatives. The solicitor suggested cold underdone beef with the claret, to which I easily agreed, thinking of my own empty house, and he insisted also on opening a bottle of Clos St Jacques 1982 to drink later.

'It's so seldom,' he said to my protestations, 'that I have anyone here with whom I can truly share my enthusiasm. My dear wife puts up with me, you know, but even after all these years she would as soon drink ordinary everyday Beaujolais or an undemanding Mosel. Tonight, and please don't argue, my dear chap, tonight is a treat.'

It was for me also. I drank my share of the Château Palmer and of the Clos St Jacques, which I had originally tasted when I sold it to him a year earlier; and I greatly enjoyed discovering how that particular wine was satisfactorily changing colour from purplish youth to a smooth deep burgundy red as it matured in excellence and power. It might well improve, I thought, and he said he would put it away for maybe a year. 'But I'm getting old, my dear chap. I want to drink all my treasures, you know, before it's too late.'

What with one thing and another it was nearly midnight before I left. Alcohol decays in the blood at a rate of one glass of wine an hour, I thought driving home, so with luck, after six glasses in five hours, I should be legitimately sober. It wasn't that I was unduly moral; just that to survive in business I needed a driving licence.

Perhaps because of the wine, perhaps because of the tossing and turning I'd done the previous night, I slept long and soundly without bad dreams, and in the morning rose feeling better than usual about facing a new day. The mornings were in any case always better than the nights. Setting out wasn't so bad; it was going home that was hell.

My mother had advised me on the telephone to sell and live somewhere else.

'You'll never be happy there,' she said. 'It never works.'

'You didn't move when Dad died,' I protested.

'But this house was mine to begin with,' she said, surprised. 'Inherited from my family. Quite different, Tony darling.'

I wasn't quite sure where the difference lay, but I didn't argue. I thought she might possibly be right that

I should move, but I didn't. All my memories of Emma were alive there in the old renovated cottage over-looking the Thames, and to leave it seemed to be an abandonment of her: an ultimate unfaithfulness. I thought that if I sold the place I would feel guilty, not released, so I stayed there and sweated for her at nights and paid the mortgage and could find no ease.

The morning deliveries were widely scattered which meant a fair amount of zigzagging, but free home delivering brought me so much extra business that I never minded.

Bad news travels as fast as the thud of jungle drums, and it was at only ten-fifteen, at my last port of call, that I heard about the Silver Moondance.

'Frightful, isn't it?' said a cheerful woman opening her back door to me on the outskirts of Reading. 'Someone broke in there last night and stole every bottle in the place.'

'Did they?' I said.

She nodded happily, enjoying the bad news. 'The milkman just told me, five minutes ago. The Silver Moondance is just along the road from here, you know. He went in there as usual with the milk and found the police standing around scratching their heads. Well, that's what the milkman said. He's not overkeen on the police, I don't think.'

I carried her boxes into the kitchen and waited while she wrote a cheque.

'Did you know the owner of the Silver Moondance

was killed in that accident on Sunday, the one with the horsebox?' she asked.

I said that I'd heard.

'Frightful, isn't it, people going in and looting his place as soon as he's dead?'

'Frightful,' I agreed.

'Goodbye, Mr Beach,' she said blithely. 'Wouldn't it be boring if everyone was good?'

The plundered Silver Moondance, so close to her house, lay on my own direct route back to the shop, and I slowed as I approached it, unashamedly curious. There was indeed a police car standing much where Ridger had parked the day before, and on impulse I turned straight into the driveway and pulled up alongside.

There was no one about outside, nor, when I went in, in the entrance hall. There were fewer lights on than before and even less air of anything happening. I pushed through the swinging western doors to the saloon, but the black and scarlet expanse lay dark and empty, gathering dust.

I tried the restaurant on the opposite side of the entrance hall, but that too was deserted. That left the cellars, and I made my way as on the previous day along a passage to a door marked 'Private' and into the staff area beyond. The cellars were not actually in a basement but consisted of two cool interconnecting windowless storerooms off a lobby between the dining room and what had been Larry Trent's office. The lobby opened onto a back yard through a door laden with locks and bolts which now stood wide open, shedding a good deal of physical light onto the hovering figure of Sergeant Ridger, if no enlightenment.

The belted raincoat had been exchanged for an overcoat buttoned with equal military precision, and every hair was still rigidly in place. His brusque manner, too, was unchanged. 'What are you doing here?' he demanded, stiffly, as soon as he saw me.

'Just passing.'

He gave me a dour look but didn't tell me to leave, so I stayed.

'What was in here yesterday?' he asked, pointing to the open doors of the cellars. 'The assistant manager is useless. But you saw what was here. You came here for that wine, didn't you, so what do you remember of the contents?' No 'sir', I noticed, today. I'd progressed in his mind to 'police expert', perhaps.

'Quite a lot,' I said reflectively. 'But what about the wine list? Everything was itemized on that.'

'We can't find any wine lists. They seem to have gone with the wine.'

I was astonished. 'Are you sure?'

'We can't find any,' he said again. 'So I'm asking you to make a list.'

I agreed that I would try. He took me into Larry Trent's office, which was plushly comfortable rather than functional with a busily patterned carpet, several armchairs and many framed photographs on the walls.

The photographs, I saw, were nearly all of the finishes of races, the winning post figuring prominently. Larry Trent had been a good picker, Flora had said, and a good gambler . . . whose luck had finally run out.

I sat in his own chair behind his mahogany desk and wrote on a piece of paper from Ridger's official notebook. Ridger himself remained standing as if the original occupant were still there to disturb him, and I thought fleetingly that I too felt like a trespasser on Larry Trent's privacy.

His desk was almost too neat to be believable as the hub of a business the size of the Silver Moondance. Not an invoice, not a letter, not a billhead showing. No government forms, no cash book, no filing cabinets, no typewriter and no readily available calculator. Not a working room, I thought: more a sanctuary.

I wrote what I could remember of bins and quantities of wines and then said I could perhaps add to the list if I went into the cellars and visualised what I'd seen before. We transferred therefore into the first of the rooms, where the bulk of the wines had been kept, and I looked at the empty racks and partitioned shelving and added a couple more names to my list.

From there we went through the sliding inner door into the second cellar, which had contained stocks of spirits, liqueurs, canned beer and mixers. The beer and mixers remained: brandy, gin, vodka, whisky, rum and liqueurs were absent.

'They did a thorough job,' I remarked, writing.

Ridger grunted. 'They cleared the trolley in the dining room besides.'

'And the bar?'

'That too.'

'Highly methodical,' I said. 'Head office must be fuming. What did your friend Paul Young have to say?'

Ridger looked at me broodingly and then glanced at the list which I still held. 'As a matter of fact,' he said unwillingly, 'the telephone number he gave me is unobtainable. I'm having it checked.'

I blinked. 'He wrote it down himself,' I said.

'Yes, I know that.' He slightly pursed his lips. 'People sometimes make mistakes.'

Whatever comment I might have made was forestalled by the arrival at the open door of the lobby of a young man in an afghan jacket who turned out to be a detective constable in plain(ish) clothes. He reported briefly that he'd finished peering into outhouses with the assistant manager, and that there seemed to be nothing missing from those. The assistant manager, he added, would be in the manager's office, if required.

'Where's that?' Ridger asked.

'Near to the front door. Behind the door marked "Staff only" in the entrance hall, so the assistant manager said.'

'Did you search in there?' Ridger asked.

'No, Sergeant, not yet.'

816

'Get on with it, then,' Ridger said brusquely, and without expression the constable turned and went away.

The radio inside Ridger's coat crackled to life, and Ridger pulled it out and extended its aerial. The metallic voice which came from it reached me clearly in the quiet cellar. It said, 'Further to your inquiry timed ten-fourteen, the telephone number as given does not exist and never has existed. Furthermore the address as given does not exist. There is no such street. This message timed ten forty-eight. Please acknowledge. Over.'

'Acknowledged,' Ridger said grimly. 'Out.' He pushed the aerial down and said, 'I suppose you heard that?'

'Yes.'

'Shit,' he said forcefully.

'Quite so,' I agreed sympathetically, for which I received an absentminded glare. I handed him the completed list of what had all at once become not just the simple tally of an opportunist break-in but the evidence of a more thorough and purposeful operation. His job, however, not mine. 'I'll be in my shop if you want me again,' I said. 'I'll be glad to help.'

'Very good, sir,' he said vaguely, and then with more attention, 'Right, then. Thanks.'

I nodded and went back through the 'Private' door into the entrance hall, glancing across at the inconspicuous 'Staff only' door which merged chameleon-like with the decor of the walls: and it was while I was supposing that the manager preferred not to be tracked down by grievance-bearing diners that the door itself opened and the assistant assistant manager reeled out backwards through the gap, staring at some sight cut off by the door swinging shut behind him.

The weakly inefficient man of the day before was now in a complete state of non-function, gasping and looking faint. I fairly sprinted across the entrance hall carpet and caught him as he sagged.

'What is it?' I said.

He moaned slightly, his eyes rolling upwards, his weight growing heavier. I let him slide all the way to the carpet until he lay flat and spent a second or two pulling his tie loose. Then with a raised pulse and some shortening of my own breath I opened the door of the manager's office and went in.

It was here, I saw immediately, that the real business was done. Here in this office, very functional indeed, were all the forms, files and untidy heaps of paperwork in progress so conspicuously missing from Larry Trent's. Here there was a metal desk, old and scratched, with a plastic chair behind it and pots of pens among the clutter on its top.

There were stacks of miscellaneous stores in boldly labelled boxes all around: light bulbs, ashtrays, toilet rolls, tablets of soap. There was a floor-to-ceiling cupboard, open, spilling out stationery. There was a view through the single window to the sweep of drive outside, my van and Ridger's car in plain view. There was a sturdy safe the size of a tea-chest, its door wide, its interior bare: and there was the plain clothes constable sitting on the linoleum, his back against a wall, his head down between his knees.

Nothing in that place looked likely at first sight to cause mass unconsciousness. Nothing until one walked round to the chair behind the desk, and looked at the floor; and then I felt my own mouth go dry and my own heart beat suffocatingly against my ribs. There was no blood; but it was worse, much more disturbing than the accidental carnage in the tent.

On the floor, on his back, lay a man in grey trousers with a royal blue padded jacket above. Its zip was fully fastened up the front, I noted, concentrating desperately on details, and there was an embroidered crest sewn on one sleeve, and he was wearing brown shoes with grey socks. His neck was pinkish red above the jacket, the tendons showing tautly, and his arms and hands, neatly arranged, were crossed at the wrists over his chest, in the classic position of corpses.

He was dead. He had to be dead. For a head, above the bare stretched neck, he had a large white featureless globe like a giant puffball, and it was only when one fought down nausea and looked closely that one could see that from the throat up he had been entirely, smoothly and thickly encased in plaster of Paris.

CHAPTER SEVEN

Retreating shakily I walked out of the office with every sympathy for the constable and the assistant assistant and leaned my back against the wall outside with trembling legs.

How could anyone be so barbaric, I wondered numbly. How could anyone do that, how could anyone think of it?

Sergeant Ridger emerged into the hall from the passage and came towards me, looking with more irritation than concern at the still prostrate assistant.

'What's the matter with him?' he said in his usual forceful way.

I didn't answer. He looked sharply at my face and said with more interest, 'What's the matter?'

'A dead man,' I said. 'In the office.'

He gave me a pitying look of superiority and walked purposefully through the door. When he came out he was three shades paler but still admirably in command and behaving every inch like a detective sergeant.

'Did you touch anything in there?' he asked me

820

sharply. 'Any surface? Would your fingerprints be on anything?'

'No,' I said.

'Certain?'

'Certain.'

'Right.' He pulled out his radio, extended the aerial and said he needed top priority technical teams in connection with the death in suspicious circumstances of a so far unidentified male.

The disembodied voice in reply said that his message was timed at ten fifty-seven and would be acted upon. Ridger collapsed the aerial, put his head through the office door and crisply told his constable to come out of there, refrain from touching things and go outside for fresh air.

As much to himself as to me Ridger said, 'It won't be my case from now on.'

'Won't it?'

'Murder cases go to chief inspectors or superintendents.'

I couldn't tell from his voice whether he was pleased or sorry and concluded he simply accepted the hierarchy without resentment. I said reflectively, 'Is a man called Wilson anything to do with your force?'

'There are about four Wilsons. Which one do you mean?'

I described the hunch-shouldered quiet-mannered investigator and Ridger nodded immediately. 'That's Detective Chief Superintendent Wilson. He's not at our station, of course. He's head of the whole district. Near retirement, they say.'

I said that I'd met him at the Hawthorn accident, and Ridger guessed that Wilson had gone there himself because of the importance of the Sheik. 'Not his job, normally, traffic incidents.'

'Will he be coming here?' I asked.

'Shouldn't think so. He's too senior.'

I wondered in passing why a man of such seniority should come to my shop to ask questions instead of sending a constable, but didn't get to mentioning it to Ridger because at that point the assistant to the assistant manager began to return to life.

He was disorientated after his long faint, sitting up groggily and looking blankly at Ridger and me.

'What happened?' he said; and then without us telling him, he remembered. 'Oh my God...' He looked on the point of passing out again but instead pressed his hands over his eyes as if that would shut sight out of memory. 'I saw ... I saw ...'

'We know what you saw, sir,' said Ridger without sympathy. 'Can you identify that man? Is he the manager?'

The assistant assistant shook his head and spoke in a muffled voice through his hands. 'The manager's fat.'

'Go on,' Ridger prompted.

'It's Zarac, said the assistant assistant. 'It's his jacket ...'

'Who's Zarac?' Ridger said.

'The wine waiter.' The assistant assistant rose unsteadily to his feet and transferred his hands to his mouth before departing with heaving stomach towards the door marked 'Guys'.

'The wine waiter,' Ridger repeated flatly. 'Might have guessed.'

I pushed myself off the wall. 'You don't actually need me here, do you? I should go back to my shop.'

He thought it over briefly and agreed, saying he supposed he could find me easily if I were wanted. I left him standing virtual guard over the office door and went outside to my van, passing the constable who had relieved himself of his breakfast onto the drive.

'Cripes,' he said weakly in an endearing local accent, 'I've never seen anything like that.'

'Not an everyday sight,' I agreed, taking refuge in flippancy: and I thought that I too had seen enough horrors since Sunday to last a lifetime.

I bought more glasses at Tuesday lunchtime and ferried them and the wines to the Thames Ladies for their fund-raising; and little else of note happened for the next three days.

The news media reported briefly on the man with the plaster topping, but no words, I thought, conveyed anything like the shock of actually seeing that football-head lying there blank and inhuman, attached to a human neck.

Cutting off the plaster at the autopsy had confirmed the identity of the victim: Feydor Zaracievesa, British born of Polish descent, succinctly known as Zarac. He had been employed as wine waiter for eighteen months at the Silver Moondance, which had itself been open for business for almost three years. An inquest would shortly be held, it was said, and meanwhile the police were pursuing their inquiries.

Good luck to them, I thought. Pursue away.

On Tuesday, Wednesday and Thursday Mrs Palissey and Brian set off with the deliveries at four o'clock and at approximately four-thirty I stuck a notice on the shop door saying 'Open 6–9 pm' and scooted up the hill to go round the yard with Flora.

Shop hours as far as I was concerned were flexible, and I'd found it didn't much matter what one did as long as one said what one was doing. The pattern of when most customers came and when they stayed away was on the whole constant: a stream in the mornings, predominantly women, a trickle of either sex in the afternoons, a healthy flow, mostly men, in the evenings.

When Emma had been alive we had opened the shop on Friday and Saturday evenings only, but since I'd been alone I'd added Tuesday, Wednesday and Thursday, not simply for the extra trade, but for the company. I enjoyed the evenings. Most of the evening people came for wine, which I liked best to sell: a bottle to go with dinner, champagne for a job promotion, a present on the way to a party.

It was life on a small scale, I dared say. Nothing that would change history or the record books. A passage through time of ordinary mortal dimensions: but with Emma alongside it had contented.

I had never had much ambition, a sadness to my mother and a source of active irritation to my Wellington schoolmasters, one of whom on my last term's report had written acidly, 'Beach's conspicuous intelligence would take him far if only he would stir himself to choose a direction.' My inability to decide what I wanted to be (except not a soldier) had resulted in my doing nothing much at all. I passed such exams as were thrust my way but hadn't been drawn to university. French, my best subject, was scarcely in itself a career. I didn't feel like a stockbroker or anything tidy in the City. I wasn't artistic. Had no ear for music. Couldn't face life behind a desk and couldn't ride boldly enough for racing. My only real ability throughout my teens had been a party trick of telling all makes of chocolate blindfold, which had hardly at that time seemed a promising foundation for gainful employment.

Six months after I left school I thought I might go to France for a while, ostensibly to learn the language better, but unhappily admitting to myself that it was to avoid being seen all too clearly as a disappointing failure at home. I could stand being a failure much better on my own.

By total chance, because of friends of friends of my despairing mother's, I was despatched to live as a paying guest with a family in Bordeaux, and it had meant nothing to me at first that my unknown host was a wine shipper. It was Monsieur Henri Tavel himself who had discovered that I could tell one wine from another, once I'd tasted them. He was the only adult I'd ever met who was impressed by my trick with the chocolate. He had laughed loudly and begun to set me tests with wine each evening, and I'd grown more confident the more I got them right.

It had still seemed a game, however, and at the end of the planned three months I'd returned home with still no idea of what to do next. My mother applauded my French accent but said it was hardly to be considered a lifetime's achievement, and I spent my days sneaking out of her sight as much as possible.

She had had to come looking for me the day the letter came, about a month after my return. She held it out in front of her, frowning at it as if it were incomprehensible.

'Monsieur Tavel suggests you go back,' she said. 'He is offering to train you. Train you in what, Tony darling?'

'Wine,' I said, feeling the first pricking of interest for many a long day.

'You?' She was puzzled more than amazed.

'To learn the trade, I expect,' I said.

'Good heavens.'

'Can I go?' I asked.

'Do you want to?' she said, astonished. 'I mean, have you actually found something you'd like to do?'

'I don't seem to be able to do anything else.'

'No,' she agreed prosaically: and she paid my fare again and my board and lodging with the family and a substantial fee to Monsieur Tavel for tuition.

Monsieur Tavel gave me a year's intensive instruction, taking me everywhere himself, showing me every stage of wine-making and shipping, teaching me rapidly what he'd spent a long lifetime learning, expecting me never to need telling twice.

I grew to feel at home in the Quai des Chatrons, where many doors into the warehouses were too narrow for modern lorries as a legacy from an ancient tax and where no wine could still be stored within a hundred yards of the street because it had been thought the vibration from horses' hooves on the quayside would upset it. In the de Luze warehouse, stretching nearly half a mile back, the staff went from end to end by bicycle.

In the city long buses had concertina central sections for turning sharp corners into narrow streets and in the country mimosa trees bloomed fluffily yellow in March, and everywhere, every day, all day, there was the talk and the smell of wine. By the time I left it, Bordeaux was my spiritual home. Henri Tavel hugged me with moist eyes and told me he could place me with de Luze or one of the other top *négociants* if I would stay: and sometimes since then I'd wondered why I hadn't.

On my return to England, armed with a too-flattering Tavel reference, I'd got a job with a wine shipper, but I was too junior for much besides paper-work and after the intensities of Bordeaux grew quickly bored. Impulsively one day I'd walked into a wine shop which said 'Help wanted' and offered my services, and in a short time began a brilliant non-stop career of lugging cases of booze from place to place.

'Tony works in a shop,' my mother would say bravely. My mother was nothing if not courageous. Large fences had to be met squarely. She also, in due course, made me an interest-free loan for basic stock for a shop of my own and had refused to accept repayments once I could afford to start them. As mothers went, in fact, mine wasn't at all bad.

Flora, in essence a more motherly lady, grew day by day less exhausted and depressed. Jack's leg was doing well and Jimmy was tentatively out of danger, although with pierced lungs, it seemed, one couldn't be sure for a fortnight.

Jimmy, Flora said, couldn't remember anything at all of the party. He couldn't remember escorting the Sheik round the yard. The last thing he could remember was talking to me about the Laphroaig; and he had been very shocked to learn that Larry Trent was dead.

'And Jack's spirits?' I asked. 'How are those?'

'Well, you know him, Tony dear, he hates to sit still,

and he's growing more bad-tempered by the minute, which I suppose I shouldn't say, but you know how he is. He'll be home by the weekend, he says, and he won't sit in a wheelchair, he wants crutches, and he's quite a weight, you know, to support on his arms, and not as young as he was.'

The daily reports, faithfully written by Flora and me, had not unduly cheered Jack, it appeared, because he thought we were keeping disasters from him; but as if in a burst of good luck after bad there had been fewer than usual sprains, knocks and skin eruptions among the string.

By Thursday the horsebox had gone, also the remains of the tent and the matting, only the churned lawn and the gap in the rose hedge remaining.

'We'll never be able to walk on the grass without shoes,' Flora said. 'Not that we ever do, come to that. But everywhere you look there are splinters of glass.'

She'd heard of course about the robbery and murder at the Silver Moondance and listened wide-eyed when I told her I'd been there again on the Tuesday morning. 'How awful,' she said, and 'Poor Larry . . .' and then with confusion, 'Oh dear, I'd forgotten for a minute . . . it's all so dreadful, so dreadful.'

On Wednesday she told me that Sally and Peter now knew who had let off the brakes of their horsebox. Sally had been again on the telephone, almost equally upset, telling Flora that the parents of the little boy were blaming Peter for leaving the doors unlocked and saying it was all Peter's fault, not their son's. They had denied at first that their child could have caused the accident and were very bitter about the fingerprints. Sally was saying they shouldn't have let their beastly brat run around unsupervised and should have taught it never to touch other people's property and especially never to get into strange cars or horseboxes and meddle.

'And who's right?' Flora asked rhetorically, sighing. 'They used to be friends and now they're all so miserable – it's awful.' She shook her head sadly. 'I wish we'd never had that party. We'll never have another, I don't suppose.'

By Thursday afternoon she was almost back to her old cosy self, handling the smarmy Howard on the stable round with sweet-natured assurance, and I said that unless she felt panic-stricken I wouldn't come the next day, Friday.

'Dear Tony, you've been such a rock, I can't tell you . . .' and she gave me a warm kiss on the cheek when I left and said she would see me again soon, very soon.

Friday proceeded up to a point in the way of most Fridays: morning extra-busy with customers and early afternoon spent making up the big load of orders for weekend delivery. Brian carried countless customers' goods for them personally to their parked cars and received their tips, beaming. Mrs Palissey gave him six Mars bars when she thought I wasn't looking and told me brightly that we were running out of Coca-Cola.

Mrs Chance came for her surreptitious gin. A wine shipper telephoned that he'd reserved me fifty cases of Beaujolais Nouveau for November 15th, and did I want more? (November 15th was to the drinks trade what August 12th was to the food: the race to be first with the new wine, as first with the grouse, was intense. I never waited for the Nouveau to be delivered but fetched it myself from the shipper very early on November 15th so as to be able to open my doors at practically dawn with it already displayed in the window. At least, I had done that for six years. Whether I would bother without Emma I wasn't sure. The fun had all gone. Wait and see.) Fifty cases would be fine, I said, considering Nouveau's short life: it was at its best sold and drunk before Christmas.

Mrs Palissey set off with Brian soon after three on the extra-long delivery round and someone rang up in a great fuss because I'd sent half the amount of beer ordered.

'Do you need it tonight?' I asked, apologizing.

'No, Sunday, for after the village football match.'

'I'll bring it myself,' I said. 'Tomorrow morning at nine.'

In order not to forget I carried the beer immediately out of the back door to the Rover estate, and found on my return that I had a visitor in the shop in the quiet shape of Detective Chief Superintendent Wilson.

'Mr Beach,' he said as before, extending his hand.

'Mr Wilson,' I said, trying to smother my surprise and no doubt not succeeding.

'A bottle of wine,' he said with a small smile. 'For dinner. What do you suggest?'

He liked full-bodied red, he said, and I offered him a Rioja of distinction.

'Spanish?' he murmured dubiously, reading the label.

'Very well made,' I said. 'It's excellent.'

He said he would take my word for it and punctiliously paid. I rolled the bottle in tissue and stood it on the counter, but he was not, it appeared, in a hurry to pick it up and depart.

'Your chair ...' he murmured. 'Would it be available?'

I fetched it at once from the office and he sat gratefully as before.

'A question or two, Mr Beach ...' His gaze unhurriedly rested on my face and then wandered as if vaguely round the shop. 'I heard that you called in at the Silver Moondance last Tuesday morning, Mr Beach.'

'Yes,' I said.

'And wrote a list of the stolen goods.'

'As much as I could remember, yes.'

'And on Monday last you went there with Detective

832

Sergeant Ridger and tasted various whiskies and wines?'

'Yes,' I said again.

'And you saw a certain Paul Young there?'

'Yes.'

His slow gaze finished its wandering and came to rest tranquilly on my face. 'Can you describe him, Mr Beach?'

That's why he's here, I thought. For that.

'Sergeant Ridger . . .' I began.

'Sergeant Ridger made a full description,' he said, nodding. 'But two sets of eyes . . . Mr Beach?'

I thought back and told him what I could remember of the man from the head office that didn't exist.

'A businessman,' I said. 'About fifty. Thickset, rather short, dark haired, pale skin. Big fleshy hands. No rings. He wore glasses with black frames, but narrow frames, not heavy. He had . . . um . . . the beginnings of a double chin . . . and a hearing aid behind his right ear.'

Wilson received the description benignly without giving me any indication of whether or not it was a carbon copy of Ridger's. 'His voice, Mr Beach?'

'No special accent,' I said. 'Plain English. I doubt if he'd been deaf from birth . . . he didn't sound toneless. He spoke ordinarily and heard everything anyone said. One wouldn't have known he was deaf without seeing the hearing aid.'

'And his manner, Mr Beach?'

'A bull,' I said without hesitation. 'Used to having

people jump when he said so.' I thought back. 'He didn't seem like that at first sight, though. I mean, if he came in here now, he wouldn't seem aggressive . . . but he developed aggression very fast. He didn't like Sergeant Ridger's authority . . . he wanted to diminish him somehow.' I smiled faintly. 'Sergeant Ridger was pretty much a match for him.'

Wilson lowered his eyes briefly as if to avoid showing whatever comment lay there and then with a few blinks raised them again. 'Other impressions, Mr Beach?'

I pondered. 'Paul Young was definitely shocked to find so many bottles containing the wrong liquids.'

'Shocked that they did, or shocked that anyone had discovered it?'

'Well . . . at the time I thought it was the first, but now . . . I don't know. He was surprised and angry, that's for sure.'

Wilson rubbed his nose absentmindedly. 'Anything else, Mr Beach? Any insignificant little thing?'

'I don't know . . .'

A customer came in for several items at that point and wanted a detailed receipted bill, which I wrote for her: and the act of writing jogged a few dormant brain cells.

'Paul Young,' I said when she'd gone, 'had a gold coloured ball point with two wide black bands inset near the top. He wrote with his right hand, but with the pen between his first and second fingers and with the fingers curled round so that the pen was above what he was writing, not below. It looked very awkward. It looked how left-handed people sometimes write . . . but I'm sure he was right-handed. He wrote with the hand the same side as his hearing aid, and I was wondering why he didn't have the hearing aid incorporated into the frame of his glasses.'

Wilson incuriously studied the tissue wrapping his waiting bottle.

'Did Paul Young seem genuine to you, Mr Beach?'

'Oh, yes,' I said. 'He behaved very definitely as if the Silver Moondance belonged to an organization of which he was an executive of the highest rank. He seemed at first only to have come himself to deal with the crisis of Larry Trent's death because the manager was away and the assistant manager had flu. The third in line, the assistant to the assistant, was so hopeless that it seemed perfectly natural that head office should appear in person.'

'Quite a long string of command, wouldn't you say?' murmured Wilson. 'Trent himself, a manager, an assistant, an assistant to the assistant?'

'I don't know,' I said, moderately disagreeing. 'A place like that, open long hours, half the night sometimes, they'd need that number. And the assistant assistant struck me as just a general dogsbody in togs above his station . . . poor chap.'

Wilson communed vaguely for a while with the South African sherries and then said, 'Would you know

Paul Young again, Mr Beach? Could you pick him out in a roomful of people?'

'Yes,' I said positively. 'As long as I saw him again within a year. After that . . . I don't know. Maybe.'

'And in a photograph?'

'Um . . . it would depend.'

He nodded noncommittally and shifted on his chair.

'I've read Sergeant Ridger's reports. You've been most helpful all along, Mr Beach.'

'Sergeant Ridger did tell me,' I said mildly, 'who you are. I asked him if he knew of you, and he told me. And I've been surprised, you know, that you've come here yourself both times.'

He smiled patiently. 'I like to keep my hand in, Mr Beach, now and again. When I'm passing, you might say, for a bottle of wine.'

He stood up slowly, preparing to go, and I asked him the thing that had been on my mind since Tuesday.

'Was Zarac . . . the wine waiter . . . dead . . . before . . .?'

I stopped in mid-sentence and he finished it for me. 'Dead before the plaster was applied? Since you ask, Mr Beach, no, he wasn't. Zarac died of suffocation.'

'Oh,' I said numbly.

'It is possible,' Wilson said unemotionally, 'that he had been knocked unconscious first. You may find that thought more bearable perhaps.'

'Is it true?'

'It's not for me to say before the coroner has decided.'

There was a bleakness, I saw, behind his undemanding face. He had been out there for a long time in the undergrowth and found it easy to believe in all manner of horrors.

'I don't think,' I said, 'that I would like your job.'

'Whereas yours, Mr Beach,' he said, his gaze again roving the bottles, 'yours I would like very much.'

He gave me the small smile and the unemphatic handshake and went on his way: and I thought of people bandaging all over a live man's head and then soaking the bandage with water to turn it to rock.

CHAPTER EIGHT

Flora sent Gerard McGregor down to see me: or so he said, that Friday evening, when he came into the shop.

He looked just as he had on Sunday when tunnelling away and hauling trestle tables through under the canvas for roofs. Tall, in his fifties, going grey. Ultra-civilized, with experienced eyes. Gerard with a soft J.

We shook hands again, smiling.

'My wife and I took Flora home to dinner with us yesterday evening,' he said. 'We insisted. She said it was chiefly thanks to you that she was feeling better.'

'No,' I said.

'She talked about you for hours.'

'How utterly boring. She can't have done.'

'You know how Flora talks.' His voice was affectionate. 'We heard all about you and Larry Trent and the goings-on at the Silver Moondance.'

'I'm sorry,' I said.

'Whatever for? Fascinating stuff.'

Not for Zarac, I thought.

Gerard McGregor was looking around him with interest.

'We don't live so far from Flora,' he said. 'Five miles or so, but we shop in the opposite direction, not in this town. I've never been here before.' He began to walk down the row of wine racks, looking at labels. 'From what Flora said of the size of the trade you do, I somehow thought your shop would be bigger.' His faintly Scottish voice was without offence, merely full of interest.

'It doesn't need to be bigger,' I explained. 'In fact large brightly-lit expanses tend to put real wine-lovers off, if anything. This is just right, to my mind. There's room to show examples of everything I normally sell. I don't keep more than a dozen of many things out here. The rest's in the storeroom. And everything moves in and out pretty fast.'

The shop itself was about twenty-five feet by thir-teen, or eight by four if one counted in metres. Down the whole of one long side there were wine racks in vertical columns, each column capable of holding twelve bottles (one case), the top bottle resting at a slant for display. Opposite the wine racks was the counter with, behind it, the shelves for spirits and liqueurs.

More wine racks took up the furthest wall except for the door through to the office and storeroom, and on every other inch of wall-space there were shelves

for sherries, beers, mixers and coke and all the oddments that people asked for.

At the end of the counter, standing at a slight angle
into the main floorspace, was a medium-sized table
covered to the ground with a pretty swagged tablecloth
that Emma had made. A sheet of plate glass protected
the top, and on it there stood a small forest of liqueur
and aperitif and wine bottles, all opened, all available
for customers to taste before buying. Coyly out of sight
below the tablecloth stood open cartons of the same
wines, ready to hand. We'd always sold a great deal
because of the table: impulse buys leading to more and
more repeat orders. Gerard fingered the bottles with
interest, as so many did.

'Would you like to see behind the scenes?' I said,
and he answered, 'Very much.'

I showed him my tiny office and also the tiny washroom, and the not-so-tiny storeroom beyond. 'That
door,' I said, pointing, 'opens outward to the yard
where we park the cars and load and unload deliveries.
I usually keep it bolted. Through here is the storeroom.' I switched on the lights as the store had no
window, and he looked with interest at the columns of
cases ranged all round the walls and in a double row
down the centre.

'I didn't always have as much stock as this,' I said.
'It was a terrible struggle to begin with. The storeroom
was almost empty. Some weeks I'd buy things one afternoon, sell them the next morning and buy more with

the same money again in the afternoon, and so on, round and round. Hair-raising.'

'But not now, I see.'

'Well, no. But it took us a while to get known, because this wasn't a wine shop before. We had to start from utter scratch.'

'We?' he said.

'My wife.'

'Oh yes . . . Flora said . . .'

'Yes,' I said flatly. 'She died.'

He made sympathetic motions with his hands, and we went back to the shop.

'When do you close?' he said, and suggested we might have dinner together.

'Is nine o'clock too late?'

Nine o'clock would do quite well, he said, and he returned at that time and drove me to a restaurant far outside my own catchment area. It seemed a long way to go, but he had reserved a table there, saying the food would be worth it.

We talked on the way about the accident and our excursions in the tent, and over dinner about Flora and Jack, and after that about the Silver Moondance and Larry Trent. We ate trout mousse followed by wild duck and he asked me to choose the wine. It was a pleasant enough evening and seemed purposeless; but it wasn't.

'What would you say,' he said casually over coffee, 'to a consultant's fee?'

'For what?'

'For what you're good at. Distinguishing one whisky from another.'

'I wouldn't mind the fee,' I said frankly. 'But I'm not an expert.'

'You've other qualities.' His eyes, it seemed to me, were all at once concentrating on my face as if he could read every hidden response I might have. 'Observation, resource and leadership.'

I laughed. 'Not me. Wrong guy.'

'I'd like to hire your services,' he said soberly, 'for one particular job.'

I said in puzzlement, 'What sort of job?'

For answer he felt in an inner pocket and drew out a sheet of paper which he unfolded and spread on the tablecloth for me to read: and it was a photostat copy, I saw in some bewilderment, of a page from the Yellow Pages telephone directory.

DETECTIVE AGENCIES, it said in capital letters at the top. Underneath were several boldly outlined box advertisements and a column of small firms. The word 'investigation' figured prominently throughout.

'I am one of the management team of that concern,' McGregor said, pointing to one of the bigger boxes.

'A private detective?' I asked, astounded. 'About the last thing I'd have guessed.'

'Mm.' McGregor's tone was dry. 'We prefer to be known as investigative consultants. Read the advertisement.'

I did as he asked.

'Deglet Ltd', it announced. 'Comprehensive service offered in complete confidence to commercial clients. Experienced consultants in the fields of industrial counter-espionage, fraud detection, electronic security, personnel screening. Business investigations of all sorts. International links.'

At the bottom there was a London box number and telex and telephone numbers, but no plain address. Confidential to the bone, I thought.

'No divorce?' I asked lightly.

'No divorce,' McGregor agreed easily. 'No debt collecting and no private clients. Commercial enquiries only.'

Any image one might have of mean streets didn't fit with McGregor. Boardrooms and country weekends, yes. Fist fights and sleazy night-life, no.

'Do you yourself personally . . .' I flicked a finger at the page, 'go rootling around in factories?'

'Not exactly.' He was quietly amused. 'When we're approached by a prospective client I go along to size up what's happening and what's needed, and then either alone or with colleagues, according to the size of the problem, I plan how to get results.'

There was a pause while I thought over what he had and hadn't so far told me. I evaded all the head-on questions and in the end said only, 'Don't you have any better business cards than photostats of the phone book?'

Unruffled, he said, 'We don't advertise anywhere else. We have no pamphlets or brochures and carry only personal cards ourselves. I brought the photostat to show you that we exist, and what we do.'

'And all your business comes from the Yellow Pages?' I asked.

He nodded. 'And from word of mouth. Also, of course, once-satisfied clients call upon us again when-ever they need us, which believe me the larger corporations do constantly.'

'You enjoy your job?'

'Very much,' he said. I listened to the quiet assurance in his depths and thought that I wasn't a hunter and never would be. Not I, who ducked through gates to avoid jumping fences, even if the fox escaped.

'Occasionally,' he said conversationally, 'we're asked to investigate in areas for which none of our regular people are ideal.'

I looked at my coffee.

'We need someone now who knows whisky. Someone who can tell malt whisky from grain whisky, as Flora says you can.'

'Someone who knows a grain from the great grey green greasy Limpopo River?' I said. 'The Limpopo River, don't forget, was full of crocodiles.'

'I'm not asking you to do anything dangerous,' he said reasonably.

'No.' I sighed. 'Go on, then.'

'What are you doing on Sunday?' he said.

'Opening the shop from twelve to two. Washing the car. Doing the crossword.' Damn all, I thought.

'Will you give me the rest of your day from two o'clock on?' he asked.

It sounded harmless, and in any case I still felt considerable camaraderie with him because of our labours in the tent, and Sundays after all were depressing, even without horseboxes.

'OK,' I said. 'Two o'clock onwards. What do you want me to do?'

He was in no great hurry, it seemed, to tell me. Instead he said, 'Does all grain whisky taste the same?'

'That's why you need a real expert,' I said. 'The answer is no it doesn't quite, but the differences are small. It depends on the grain used and the water, and how long the spirit's been aged.'

'Aged?'

'Newly distilled Scotch,' I said, 'burns your throat and scrubs your tongue like fire. It has to be stored in wooden casks for at least three years to become drinkable.'

'Always in wood?'

'Yes. Wood breathes. In wooden casks all spirit grows blander but if you put it in metal or glass containers instead it stays the same for ever. You could keep newly distilled spirits a thousand years in glass and when you opened it it would be as raw as the day it was bottled.'

'One lives and learns,' he said.

'Anyway,' I added after a pause. 'Practically no one sells pure grain whisky. Even the cheapest bulk whisky is a blend of grain and malt, though the amount of malt in some of them is like a pinch of salt in a swimming pool.'

'Flora said you told her some of the scotch at the Silver Moondance was like that,' McGregor said.

'Yes, it was. They were selling it in the bar out of a Bell's bottle, and in the restaurant as Laphroaig.'

McGregor called for the bill. 'This wasn't my case to begin with,' he said almost absentmindedly as he sorted out a credit card. 'One of my colleagues passed it on to me because it seemed to be developing so close to my own doorstep.'

'Do you mean,' I asked, surprised, 'that your firm were already interested in the Silver Moodance?'

'That's right.'

'But how? I mean, in what connection?'

'In connection with some stolen Scotch that we were looking for. And it seems, my dear Tony, that you have found it.'

'Good grief,' I said blankly. 'And lost it again.'

'I'm afraid so. We're very much back where we started. But that's hardly your fault, of course. If Jack's secretary had been less fond of Laphroaig . . . if Larry Trent hadn't invited him to dinner . . . One can go back and back saying "if", and it's profitless. We were treading delicately towards the Silver Moondance when the horsebox plunged into the marquee; and it's ironic in the extreme that I didn't know that the Arthur Lawrence Trent who owned that place had horses in training with Jack, and I didn't know he was at the party. I didn't know him by sight . . . and I didn't know that he was one of the men we found dead. If I'd known he was going to be at the party I'd have got Jack or Flora to introduce me.' He shrugged, 'If and if.'

'But you were . . . um . . . investigating him?' I asked.

'No,' McGregor said pleasantly. 'The person we suspected was an employee of his. A man called Zarac.'

I'm sure my mouth physically dropped open. Gerard McGregor placidly finished paying the bill, glancing with dry understanding at my face.

'Yes, he's dead,' he said. 'We really are totally back at the beginning.'

'I don't consider,' I said intensely, 'that Zarac is a matter of no crocodiles.'

I spent most of Saturday with my fingers hovering over the telephone, almost deciding at every minute to ring Flora and ask her for Gerard McGregor's number so that I could cancel my agreement for Sunday. If I did nothing he would turn up at two o'clock and whisk me off heaven knew where to meet his client, the one whose Scotch had turned up on my tongue. (Probably.)

In the end I did ring Flora but even after she'd answered I was still shilly-shallying.

'How's Jack?' I said.

'In a vile temper, I'm afraid, Tony dear. The doctors won't let him come home for several more days. They put a rod right down inside his bone, through the marrow, it seems, and they want to make sure it's all settled before they let him loose on crutches.'

'And are you all right?'

'Yes, much better every day.'

'A friend of yours,' I said slowly, 'came to see me. Er . . . Gerard McGregor.'

'Oh yes,' Flora said warmly. 'Such a nice man. And his wife's such a dear. He said you and he together had helped a good few people last Sunday. He asked who you were, and I'm afraid, Tony dear, that I told him quite a lot about you and then about everything that happened at the Silver Moondance, and he seemed frightfully interested though it seems to me now that I did go on and on a bit.'

'I don't think he minded,' I said soothingly. 'Um . . . what does he do, do you know?

'Some sort of business consultant, I believe. All those jobs are so frightfully vague, don't you think? He's always travelling all over the place, anyway, and Tina . . . that's his wife . . . never seems to know when he'll be home.'

'Have you known them long?' I asked.

'We met them at other people's parties several times before we really got to know them, which would be about a year ago.'

'I mean . . . has he always lived near here?'

848

'Only about five years, I think. They were saying the other evening how much they preferred it to London even though Gerard has to travel more. He's such a clever man, Tony dear, it just oozes out of his pores. I told him he should buy some wine from you, so perhaps he will.'

'Perhaps,' I said. 'Er . . . do you have his telephone number?'

'Of course,' Flora said happily, and found it for me. I wrote it down and we disconnected, and I was still looking at it indeterminately at nine o'clock when I closed the shop.

'I half expected you to cry off,' he said, when he picked me up at two the next day.

'I half did.'

'But?'

'Curiosity, I suppose.'

He smiled. Neither of us pointed out that it was curiosity that got the Elephant's Child into deep trouble with the crocodiles in the Limpopo River, though it was quite definitely in my mind, and Gerard, as he had told me to call him, was of the generation that would have had the *Just So Stories* fed to him as a matter of course.

He was dressed that afternoon in a wool checked shirt, knitted tie and tweed jacket, much like myself, and he told me we were going to Watford.

849

I sensed a change in him immediately I'd committed myself and was too far literally along the road to ask him to turn back. A good deal of surface social manner disappeared and in its place came a tough professional attitude which I felt would shrivel irrelevant comment in the utterer's throat. I listened therefore in silence, and he spoke throughout with his eyes straight ahead, not glancing to my face for reactions.

'Our client is a man called Kenneth Charter,' he said. 'Managing director and founder of Charter Carriers, a company whose business is transporting bulk liquids by road in tankers. The company will transport any liquid within reason, the sole limiting factor being that it must be possible to clean the tanker thoroughly afterwards, ready for a change of contents. Today's hydrochloric acid, for instance, must not contaminate next week's crop-sprayer.'

He drove steadily, not fast, but with easy judgement of available space. A Mercedes, fairly new, with velvety upholstery and a walnut dash, automatic gears changing on a purr.

'More than half of their business,' he went on, 'is the transport of various types of inflammable spirit, and in this category they include whisky.' He paused. 'It's of course in their interest if they can arrange to pick up one load near to where they deliver another, the limiting factor again being the cleaning. They have steam cleaning facilities and chemical scrubbing agents at their Watford headquarters, but these are not readily available everywhere. In any case, one of their regular runs has been to take bulk gin to Scotland, wash out the tanker with water, and bring Scotch back.'

He stopped talking to navigate through a town of small streets, and then said, 'While the Scotch is in the tanker it is considered to be still in a warehouse. That is to say, it is still in bond. Duty has not been paid.'

I nodded. I knew that.

'As Charter's tankers carry six thousand imperial gallons,' Gerard said neutrally, 'the amount of duty involved in each load is a good deal more than a hundred thousand pounds. The whisky itself, as you know, is of relatively minor worth.'

I nodded slightly again. Customs and Excise duty, value added tax and income tax paid by the shopkeeper meant that three-quarters of the selling price of every standard bottle of whisky went in one way or another to the inland revenue. One quarter paid for manufacture, bottles, shipping, advertising, and all the labour force needed between the sowing of the barley and the wrapping in a shop. The liquid itself, in that context, cost practically nothing.

'Three times this year,' Gerard said, 'a tanker of Charter's hasn't reached its destination. It wouldn't be accurate to say the tanker was stolen, because on each occasion it turned up. But the contents of course had vanished. The contents each time were bulk Scotch. The Customs and Excise immediately demanded duty since the Scotch was no longer in the tanker. Charter Carriers have twice had to pay up.'

He paused as if to let me catch up with what he was saying.

'Charter Carriers are of course insured, or have been, and that's where they've run into serious trouble. The insurers, notwithstanding that they rocketed their premiums on each past occasion, now say that enough is enough, they are not satisfied and are withholding payment. They also say no further cover will be extended. Charter's face having to raise the cash themselves, which would be crippling, but more seriously they can't operate without insurance. On top of that the Customs and Excise are threatening to take away their licence to carry goods in bond, which would in itself destroy a large part of their business.' He paused again for appreciable seconds. 'The Excise people are investigating the latest theft, but chiefly because they want the duty, and the police also, but routinely. Charter's feel that this isn't enough because it in no way guarantees the continuation of their licence or the reinstatement of their insurance. They're extremely worried indeed, and they applied to us for help.'

We were speeding by this time along the M40. Another silence lengthened until Gerard eventually said, 'Any questions?'

'Well . . . dozens, I suppose.'

'Such as?'

'Such as why was it always the Scotch that was stolen

and not the gin? Such as was it always the same driver and was it always the same tanker? Such as what happened to the driver, did he say? Such as where did the tankers turn up? Such as how did you connect it all with Zarac?'

He positively grinned, his teeth showing in what looked like delight.

'Anything else?' he asked.

'Such as where did the Scotch start from and where was it supposed to be going and how many crooks have you turned up at each place, and such as does Kenneth Charter trust his own office staff and why wasn't his security invincible third time around?'

I stopped and he said without sarcasm, 'Those'll do to be going on with. The answers I can give you are that no it wasn't always the same driver but yes it was always the same tanker. The tanker turned up every time abandoned in Scotland in transport café car parks, but always with so many extra miles on the clock that it could have been driven as far as London or Cardiff and back.'

Another pause, then he said, 'The drivers don't remember what happened to them.'

I blinked. 'Don't remember?'

'No. They remember setting off. They remember driving as far as the English border, where they all stopped at a motorway service station for a pee. They stopped at two different service stations. None of them remembers anything else except waking up in a ditch.

Never the same ditch.' He smiled. 'After the second theft Kenneth Charter made it a rule that on that run no one was to eat or drink in cafés. The drivers had to take what they wanted with them in the cab. All the same they still had to stop for nature. The police say the thieves must have been following the tanker each time, waiting for that. Then when the driver was out of the cab, they put in an open canister of gas . . . perhaps nitrous oxide, which has no smell and acts fast . . . it's what dentists use . . . and when the driver climbed back in he'd be unconscious before he could drive off.'

'How regular was that run?' I asked.

'Normally twice a week.'

'Always the same tanker?'

'No,' he said contentedly. 'Charter's keep four tankers exclusively for drinkable liquids. One of those. The other three made the run just as often, but weren't touched. It may be coincidence, maybe not.'

'How long ago was the last load stolen?' I asked.

'Three weeks last Wednesday.'

'And before that?'

'One in April, one in June.'

'That's three in six months,' I said, surprised.

'Yes, exactly.'

'No wonder the insurers are kicking up a fuss.'

'Mm.' He drove quietly for a while and then said, 'Every time the Scotch was destined for the same place, a bottling plant at Watford, north of London. The

Scotch didn't however always come from the same distillery, or the same warehouse. The stolen loads came from three different places. The last lot came from a warehouse near Helensburgh in Dunbartonshire, but it set off from there in the normal way and we don't think that's where the trouble is.'

'In the bottling plant?' I asked.

'We don't know, for sure, but we don't think so. The lead to the Silver Moondance looked so conclusive that it was decided we should start from there.'

'What was the lead?' I said.

He didn't answer immediately but in the end said, 'I think Kenneth Charter had better tell you himself.'

'OK.'

'I should explain,' he said presently, 'that when firms call us in it's often because there are things they don't necessarily want to tell the police. Companies very often like to deal privately, for instance, with frauds. By no means do they always want to prosecute, they just want the fraud stopped. Public admission that a fraud was going on under their noses can be embarrassing.'

'I see,' I said.

'Kenneth Charter told me certain things in confidence which he didn't tell the police or the Customs and Excise. He wants his transport firm to survive, but not at any price. Not if the price in personal terms is too high. He agreed I should bring you in as a consultant, but I'll leave it to him to decide how much he wants you to know.'

'All right,' I said peacefully.

We left the motorway and Gerard began threading his way across the semi-suburban sprawl to the north of London where one town ran into another without noticeable difference.

'You're an understanding sort of man,' Gerard observed after a while.

'What should I demand?'

'How much a consultancy fee is, perhaps. Conditions, maybe. Assurances.'

'Life's like the weather,' I said wryly. 'What comes, comes. Even with a sunny forecast you can get wet.'

'A fatalist.'

'It rains. You can't stop it.'

He glanced at my face for almost the first time on the journey, but I doubt if he read much there. I'd spoken not bitterly but with a sort of tiredness, result of failing to come to terms with my own private deluge. I was in truth quite interested in the stolen Scotch and the tankers, but it was on an upper and minor level, not down where it mattered.

As if sensing it he said, 'You'll do your best for me?'

'Such as it is,' I assured him. 'Yes.'

He nodded as if a doubt had been temporarily stilled and turned off the road into an industrial area where small factories had sprung like recent mushrooms in a concrete field. The fourth on the right bore the words

'Charter Carriers Ltd' in large red letters on a white board attached to the front, while down the side, like piglets to a sow, stretched a long row of silver tankers side by side, engines inwards, sterns out.

CHAPTER NINE

Kenneth Charter wasn't in the least what I expected, which was, I suppose, a burly North Londoner with a truculent manner. The man who came into the entrance hall to greet us as we pushed through the glass front door was tall, thin, reddish-haired and humorous with an accent distinctly more Scottish than Gerard's faint Highland.

'Is this the consultant?' he said with a lilt. He found my youth more a matter of laughter than concern, it seemed. 'No greybeard, are you?' He shook my hand firmly. 'Come away in, then. And how are you today, Mr McGregor?'

He led the way into a square uninspiring cream-walled office and waved us to two upright armless chairs facing a large unfussy modern desk. There was a brown floor-covering of utilitarian matting, a row of grey filing cabinets, a large framed map of the British Isles and a settled chill in the air which might or might not have been because it was Sunday. Kenneth Charter seemed not to notice it and offered no comment. He had the Scots habit, I suspected, of finding sin in comfort and virtue in thrift and believing morality grew exclusively in a cold climate.

Gerard and I sat in the offered chairs. Kenneth Charter took his place behind his desk in a swivelling chair which he tilted recklessly backward.

'How much have you told this bonny expert?' he said, and listened without visible anxiety to Gerard's recapitulation.

'Well, now,' he said to me cheerfully at the end. 'You'll want to know what liquid you're looking for. Or could you guess, laddie, could you guess?' His very blue eyes were quizzically challenging, and I did a quick flip and a turnover through past occasional nips in customers' houses and sought for a check against the memory from the bar of the Silver Moondance and said on an instinctive, unreasoned impulse, 'Rannoch.'

Charter looked cynical and said to Gerard, 'You told him, then.'

Gerard shook his head. 'I didn't.' He himself was looking smug. His consultant, it seemed, had come up trumps at the first attempt.

'I guessed,' I said mildly. 'I sell that make. I've tasted it quite a few times. There aren't so many whiskies that would be shipped in bulk and bottled in England. Rannoch . . . just fitted.'

'Very well, then.' He opened a drawer in his desk and produced from it a full bottle of Rannoch whisky, the familiar label adorned with an imposing male kilted figure in red and yellow tartan. The seal, I noticed, was unbroken, and Charter showed no signs of altering that.

'A Christmas gift from the bottling company,' he said.

'Last Christmas?' I asked.

'Of course last Christmas. We'll not be getting one this year, now will we?'

'I guess not,' I said meekly. 'I meant . . . it's a long time for the bottle to be full.'

He chuckled. 'I don't drink alcohol, laddie. Addles your brains, rots your gut. What's more, I can't stand the taste. We need someone like you because I wouldn't recognize that stolen load of firewater if it turned up in the pond in my garden.'

The goldfish would tell him, I thought. They'd die.

'Did you have a profile of that load?' I asked.

'A what?'

'Um . . . its composition. What it was blended from. You could get a detailed list from the distiller, I should think. The profile is a sort of chemical analysis in the form of a graph . . . it looks something like the skyline of New York. Each different blend shows a different skyline. The profile is important to some people . . . the Japanese import scotch by profile alone, though actually a perfect-looking profile can taste rotten. Anyway, profiles are minutely accurate. Sort of like human tissue typing . . . a lot more advanced than just a blood test.'

'All I can tell you is it was fifty-eight per cent alcohol by volume,' Charter said. 'The same strength as always with Rannoch. It's here on the manifest.' He produced from a drawer a copy of the Customs and Excise declaration and pushed it across for me to see. 'I don't ask what's in the stuff, I just ferry it.'

'We'll get on to the profile straight away,' Gerard murmured.

'The Customs people probably have already,' I said. 'They'll have the equipment. A gas chromatograph.'

I had an uncomfortable feeling that Gerard was thinking I should have told him about profiles on the way, but it hadn't crossed my mind.

'I mean,' I said, 'if they took a sample from the distillers and matched it with the sample the police took from the Silver Moondance, they would know for sure one way or another.'

There was a silence. Finally Gerard cleared his throat and said, 'Perhaps you might tell Tony how we were led to the Silver Moondance. Because at this moment,' he looked straight at me, 'there is no reason for the Customs to connect that place to the stolen tanker or to compare the samples. They aren't aware of any link.'

I said 'Oh' fairly vaguely and Kenneth Charter consulted the ceiling, tipping his chair back to where it should surely have overbalanced. He finally let his weight fall forward with a thud and gave me the full blast from the blue eyes.

'Promise of silence, laddie,' he said.

I looked at Gerard, who nodded off-handedly as if

such demands were an everyday business fact, which I supposed to him they were.

'Promise of silence,' I said.

Kenneth Charter nodded his long head sharply as if taking it for granted that promises would be kept; then he pulled a bunch of keys from his pocket and unlocked the centre drawer of his desk. The object within needed no searching for. He pulled out a small slim black notebook and laid it on the desk before him, the naturally humorous cast of his face straightening to something like grimness.

'You can trust this laddie?' he said to Gerard.

'I'd believe so.'

Charter sighed, committed, turned to the page that fell open immediately in a way that spoke of constant usage.

'Read that,' he said, turning the notebook round for me to see but retaining it under the pressure of his thumb. 'That' was a long telephone number beginning 0735, which was the code for the Reading area, with underneath it two lines of writing.

'*Tell Z UNP 786 Y picks up B's Gin Mon 10 a.m. approx.*'

'I've read it,' I said, not knowing what exactly was expected.

'Mean anything?'

'I suppose it's the Silver Moondance number, and Z is Zarac?'

'Right. And UNP 786 Y is the registration number of my tanker.' His voice was cold and unemotional.

'I see,' I said.

'Berger's Gin is where it set out from at 10.15 a.m. a month ago tomorrow. It went to Scotland, discharged the gin, was sluiced through in Glasgow and picked up the bulk Scotch at Fairley's warehouse near Helensburgh, in Dunbartonshire. Wednesday morning it set off from there. Wednesday evening it didn't arrive at the bottling plant. By Thursday morning we know it was parked outside a drivers' café on the outskirts of Edinburgh, but it wasn't identified until Friday as its registration plates had been changed. The Customs and Excise have impounded it, and we haven't got it back.'

I looked at Gerard and then again at Kenneth Charter.

'And you know,' I said slowly. 'You know who wrote the message.'

'Yes, I do,' he said. 'My son.'

Highly complicating, as Gerard had hinted.

'Um . . .' I said, trying to make my question as non-committal as Charter's own voice. 'What does your son say? Does he know where the bulk in the tanker vanished to? Because . . . er . . . six thousand gallons of Scotch can't be hidden all that easily, and the Silver Moondance wouldn't use three times that much in six years, let alone six months . . . if you see.'

The blue eyes if anything grew more intense. 'I haven't spoken to my son. He went to Australia two weeks ago for a holiday and I don't expect him back for three months.'

There was an element of good riddance in that statement, I thought. He wasn't so much grieving over his offspring's treason as finding it thoroughly awkward. I smiled at him faintly without thinking and to my surprise he grinned suddenly and broadly back.

'You're right,' he said. 'The little bugger can stay there, as far as I'm concerned. I'm certainly not trying to fetch him home. I don't want him charged and tried and maybe flung in jail. I don't, I definitely don't want any son of mine behind bars embarrassing the whole family. Making his mother cry, spoiling his sister's wedding next spring, messing up his brother's chances of a degree in law. If I have to sell up here, well, I will. There'll be enough left for me to start something else. And that's the end of the damage that sod will do. I won't have him casting a worse blight on the family.'

'No,' I said slowly. 'When was it, did you say, that he went to Australia?'

'Two weeks ago yesterday, laddie. I took him to Heathrow myself. When I got home I found this notebook on the floor of the car, fallen out of his pocket. I guess he's sweating now, hoping like hell he dropped it anywhere but at my very feet. I opened it to make sure it was his.' Charter shrugged, locking it back into the desk drawer. 'It was his, all right. His writing. Nothing much in it, just a few telephone numbers and lists of things to do. He always made lists of things to do, right from when he was small.'

Something like regret touched Kenneth Charter's mouth. Any son, I supposed, was loved when small, before he grew up a disappointment.

'The tanker's number sort of shouted at me,' he said. 'I felt sick, I'll tell you. My own son! There were the police and the Customs and Excise chasing all over the place looking for the crook who tipped off the thieves, and he'd been right there in my own house.' He shook his head in disgust. 'So then I took advice from a business I knew who'd had their troubles sorted out for them quietly, and I got on to Deglet's, and finally Mr McGregor, here. And there you have it, laddie.'

Kenneth Charter's son, I was thinking, had gone to Australia ten days after the Scotch had been stolen and a week before the horsebox had rolled into the marquee. If he was truly in Australia, he'd had nothing to do with the disappearance of the Silver Moondance's liquid assets or the murder of Zarac. For such small crumbs his father could be grateful.

'Would it be easy for your son to find out when exactly the tanker would be going to fetch whisky?' I asked diffidently.

'Back in April, yes, easy. In June, not so easy. Last month, damned difficult. But there you are, I didn't know I had to defend myself so close to home.' Kenneth Charter got to his feet, his tall body seeming to rise for ever. He grasped the frame of the map of the British Isles and gave it a tug, and the map opened away from the wall like a door, showing a second chart beneath.

The revealed chart was an appointments calendar with registration numbers in a long column down the left-hand side, and dates across the top.

'Tankers,' Charter said succinctly, pointing to the registration numbers. 'Thirty-four of them. There's UNP 786 Y, sixth from the top.'

All the spaces across from that number had a line drawn through: tanker out of commission. For many of the others some of the spaces across were filled with stuck-on labels of many colours; blue, green, red, yellow, grey, purple, orange, each label bearing a hand-written message.

'We use the labels to save time,' Charter said. 'Purple for instance is always hydrochloric acid. We can see at a glance which tanker is carrying it. On the label it says where from, where to. Grey is gin, yellow is whisky. Red is wine. Blue is sulphuric acid. Green is any of several disinfectants. And so on. My secretary, whom I trust absolutely, she's been with me twenty years, writes the labels and keeps the chart. We don't as a company tell the drivers where they're going or what they're carrying until the moment they set out. They change tankers regularly. We often switch drivers at the last minute. Some of the loads could be dangerous, see, if they fell into the wrong hands. We have an absolute rule that all the tanker doors have to be locked if the drivers so much as set foot out of the cabs, and in all three stolen loads the drivers swore they did that, and found nothing to alarm them when they returned. We've been careful and until this year we've been fortunate.' His voice was suddenly full of suppressed fury. 'It took my own son . . . my own son . . . to crack our system.'

'He could come in here, I suppose,' I said.

'Not often, he didn't. I told him if he wouldn't work in the company, he could stay away. He must have sneaked in here somehow, but I don't know when. He knew about the chart, of course. But since the first two thefts I've not allowed the whisky labels to be written up, just in case the leak was in our own company. Yellow labels, see? All blank. So if he saw the yellow label for that tanker for the Wednesday, it wouldn't say where it was picking up. Grey for gin, on the Monday, that was written up, but only for the pick up, not the destination. If someone wanted to steal the return load of Scotch they'd have to follow the tanker all the way from Berger's Gin distillery to find out where it was going.'

I frowned, thinking the theory excessive, but Gerard was nodding as if such dedication to the art of theft was commonplace.

'Undoubtedly what happened,' Gerard said. 'But the question remains, to whom did Zarac pass on that message? He didn't take part in the event himself. He wasn't away from the Silver Moondance long enough, and was definitely at his post both the Tuesday and Wednesday lunchtimes and also in the evenings until after midnight. We checked.'

My mind wandered from the problem I didn't consider very closely my own (and in any case unanswerable) and I found my attention fastening on the few red labels on the chart. All the information on them had been heavily crossed out, as indeed it had on the grey labels as well. Kenneth Charter followed my gaze, his hairy Scots eyebrows rising.

'The wine,' I said, almost apologetically. 'Didn't you say red for wine?'

'Aye, I did. All those shipments have had to be cancelled. Normally we fetch it from France and take it direct to the shippers near here, who bottle it themselves. We used to carry a lot more wine once, but they bottle more of it in France now. Half the bottling plants over here have been scratching round for new business. Hard times, laddie. Closures. Not their fault. The world moves on and changes. Always happening. Spend your life learning to make longbows, and someone invents guns.'

He closed the chart into its secrecy behind the map and dusted his hands on his trousers as if wiping off his son's perfidy.

'There's life in tankers yet,' he observed. 'D'you want to see them?'

I said yes, please, as they were clearly his pride, and we left his office with him carefully locking the door behind us. He led the way not to the outside but down a passage lined on either side by office doors and through a heavier door, also locked, at the far end. That door led directly into a large expanse given to the maintenance and cleaning of the silver fleet. There was all the paraphernalia of a commercial garage: inspection pit, heavy-duty jacks, benches with vices, welding equipment, a rack of huge new tyres. Also, slung from the ceiling, chains and machinery for lifting. Two tankers stood in this space, receiving attention from men in brown overalls who from their manner already knew Charter was around on Sunday afternoon and gave Gerard and myself cursory incurious glances.

'Over there,' Charter said, pointing, 'down that side, inside that walled section, we clean the tanks, pumps, valves and hoses. The exteriors go through a carwash outside.' He began walking down the garage, expecting us to follow. The mechanics called him Ken and told him there was trouble with an axle, and I looked with interest at the nearest tanker, which seemed huge to me, indoors.

The tank part was oval in section, resting solidly on its chassis with what I guessed was a low centre of gravity, to make overturning a minor hazard. There was a short ladder bolted on at the back so that one could climb onto the top, where there were the shapes of hatches and loading gear. The silver metal was unpainted and carried no information as to its ownership, only the words 'Flammable Liquid' in small red capitals towards the rear.

The paintwork of the cab, a dark brownish red, was also devoid of name, address and telephone number. The tanker was anonymous, as the whole fleet was, I later saw. Kenneth Charter's security arrangements had kept them safe for years from every predator except the traitor within.

'Why did he do it?' Charter said from over my shoulder, and I shook my head, not knowing.

'He was always jealous as a little boy, but we thought he'd grow out of it.' He sighed. 'The older he got the more bad tempered he was, and sullen, and dead lazy. I tried to speak kindly to him but he'd be bloody rude back and I've have to go out of the room so as not to hit him sometimes.' He paused, seeking no doubt for the thousandth time for guilt in himself, where there was none. 'He wouldn't work. He seemed to think the world owed him a living. He'd go out and refuse to say where he'd been, and he wouldn't lift a finger to help his mother in the house. He sneered all the time at his brother and sister, who are bonny kids. I offered him his fare to Australia and some money to spend there, and he said he'd go. I hoped, you know, that they'd knock some sense into him over there.' His tall body moved in a sort of shudder. 'I'd no idea he'd done anything criminal. He was a pain in the arse . . . Didn't he know he would ruin me in this business? Did he care? Did he mean to?'

The son sounded irredeemable to me and for the sake of the rest of the Charter family I hoped he'd never come home, but life was seldom so tidy.

'Mr McGregor may save your business,' I said, and he laughed aloud in one of his mercurial changes of mood and clapped me on the shoulder. 'A politician, Mr McGregor, that's what you've brought me here. Aye, laddie, so he may, so he may for the healthy fee I'm paying him.'

Gerard smiled indulgently and we walked on through the length of the maintenance area and out to the door at the far end. Outside, as Charter had said, there was a tall commercial-sized car wash, but he turned away from that and led us round to the side of the building to where the fleet of tankers nestled in line.

'We've some out on the road,' Charter said. 'And I'm having to arrange huge insurance for every one separately, which is wiping out our profit. I've drivers sitting at home watching television and customers going elsewhere. We can't carry alcohol, the Customs won't let us. It's illegal for this company to operate if it can't pay its workforce and other debts; and I reckon we can keep running on reserves for perhaps two weeks from now, if we're lucky. We could be shut down in five minutes then if the bank foreclosed on the tankers, which they will. Half of these tankers at any one time are being bought on loans, and if we can't service the loans, we're out.' He smoothed a loving hand over one

871

of the gleaming monsters. 'I'll be bloody sorry, and that's a fact.'

The three of us walked soberly along the imposing row until we were back at the entrance, and Gerard's car.

'Two weeks, Mr McGregor,' Kenneth Charter said. He shook our hands vigorously. 'Hardly a sporting chance, would you say?'

'We'll try for results,' Gerard assured him in a stock-broker voice, and we climbed into his car and drove away.

'Any thoughts?' he asked me immediately, before we'd even left the industrial estate.

'Chiefly,' I said, 'why you need me at all.'

'For your knowledge, as I told you. And because people talk to you.'

'How do you mean?'

'Kenneth Charter told you far more about his son than he told me. Flora says she talks to you because you listen. She says you hear things that aren't said. I was most struck by that. It's a most useful ability in a detective.'

'I'm not . . .'

'No. Any other thoughts?'

'Well . . .' I said. 'Did you see the rest of the son's notebook, when you were there before?'

'Yes, I did. Charter didn't want me to take it for some reason, so I used his photocopier to reproduce every page that was written on. As he said, there were just some telephone numbers and a few memos about things to do. We've checked on all the telephone numbers these last few days but they seem to be harmless. Friends' houses, a local cinema, a snooker club and a barber. No lead to how the son knew Zarac, if that's what you're thinking.'

'Yes,' I said.

'Mm. I'll show you the photostats presently. See if you can suggest anything we've missed.'

Unlikely, I thought.

'Is he actually in Australia?' I asked.

'The son? Yes, he is. He stayed in a motel in Sydney the night he arrived. His father made the reservation, and the son did stay there. We checked. Beyond that, we've lost him, except that we know he hasn't used his return ticket. Quite possibly he doesn't know Zarac's dead. If he does know, he's likely to drop even further out of sight. In any case, Kenneth Charter's instructed us not to look for him, and we'll comply with that. We're having to work from the Silver Moondance end, and frankly, since Zarac's murder, that's far from easy.'

I reflected for a while and then said, 'Can you pick the police brains at all?'

'Sometimes. It depends.'

'They'll be looking for Paul Young,' I said.

'Who?'

'Did Flora mention him? A man who came to the Silver Moondance from what he said was head office.

He arrived while I was there with Detective Sergeant Ridger, who took me there to taste the Laphroaig.'

Gerard frowned as he drove. 'Flora said one of the managers had come in when you were tasting the whisky and wine, and was furious.'

I shook my head. 'Not a manager.' I told Gerard in detail about Paul Young's visit, and he drove more and more slowly as he listened.

'That makes a difference,' he said almost absently when I'd finished. 'What else do you know that Flora didn't tell me?'

'The barman's homosexual,' I said flippantly. Gerard didn't smile. 'Well,' I sighed, 'Larry Trent bought a horse for thirty thousand pounds, did she tell you that?'

'No . . . Is that important?'

I related the saga of the disappearing Ramekin. 'Maybe the Silver Moondance made that sort of money, but I doubt it,' I said. 'Larry Trent kept five horses in training which takes some financing, and he gambled in thousands. Gamblers don't win, bookmakers do.'

'When did Larry Trent buy this horse?' Gerard asked.

'At Doncaster Sales a year ago.'

'Before the whisky thefts,' he said regretfully.

'Before those particular whisky thefts. Not necessarily before all the red wines in his cellar began to taste the same.'

'Do you want a full-time job?' he said.

'No thanks.'

'What happened to Ramekin, do you think?'

'I would think,' I said, 'that at a guess he was shipped abroad and sold.'

CHAPTER TEN

At the rear of the row where my shop was located there was a service road with several small yards opening from it, leading to back doors, so that goods could be loaded and unloaded without one having to carry everything in and out through the front. It was into one of these yards that the bolted door next to my storeroom led, and it was in that yard that we commonly parked the van and the car.

Mrs Palissey, that Sunday, had the van. The Rover estate was standing in the yard where I'd left it when Gerard picked me up. Despite my protestations, when we returned at six he insisted on turning into the service road to save me walking the scant hundred yards from the end.

'Don't bother,' I said.

'No trouble.'

He drove along slowly, saying he'd be in touch with me the following day as we still had things to discuss, turning into the third yard on the left, at my direction.

Besides my car there was a medium-sized van in the

yard, its rear doors wide open. I looked at it in vague surprise, as the two other shops who shared the yard with me were my immediate neighbour, a hairdresser, and next to that a dress shop, both of them firmly closed all day on Sundays.

My other immediate neighbour, served by the next yard, was a Chinese takeaway, open always; the van, I thought in explanation, must have driven into my yard in mistake for his.

Gerard slowed his car to a halt ... and a man carrying a case of wine elbowed his way sideways out of the back door of my shop: the door I had left firmly bolted at two o'clock. I exclaimed furiously, opening the passenger door to scramble out.

'Get back in,' Gerard was saying urgently, but I hardly listened. 'I'll find a telephone for the police.'

'Next yard,' I said over my shoulder. 'Sung Li. Ask him.' I slammed the door behind me and fairly ran across to the intruding van, so angry that I didn't give my own safety the slightest thought. Extremely foolish, as everyone pointed out to me continually during the next week, a view with which in retrospect I had to agree.

The man who had walked from my shop hadn't seen me and had his head in the van, transferring the weight of the case from his arms to the floor, a posture whose mechanics I knew well.

I shoved him hard at the base of the spine to push him off balance forwards and slammed both of the van's doors into his buttocks. He yelled out, swearing with shock and outrage, his voice muffled to all ears but mine. He couldn't do much to free himself: I'd got him pinned into the van by the doors, his legs protruding beneath, and I thought with fierce satisfaction that I could easily hold him there until Gerard returned.

I'd overlooked, unfortunately, that robbers could work in pairs. There was a colossal crunch against the small of my back which by thrusting me into the van doors did more damage still, I should imagine, to the man half in the van, and as I struggled to turn I saw a second, very similar man, carrying another case of wine with which he was trying to bore a hole straight through me, or so it felt.

The man half in half out of the van was practically screaming. The urgency of his message seemed to get through to his pal who suddenly removed the pressure from my back and dropped the case of wine at my feet. I had a flurried view of fuzzy black hair, a heavy black moustache and eyes that boded no good for anybody. His fist slammed into my jaw and shook bits I never knew could rattle, and I kicked him hard on the shin.

No one had ever taught me how to fight because I hadn't wanted to learn. Fighting involved all the scary things like people trying to hurt you, where I considered the avoidance of being hurt a top priority. Fighting led to stamping about with guns, to people shooting at you round corners, to having to kill someone yourself. Fighting led to the Victoria Cross and the Distinguished Service Order, or so it had seemed to my child mind, and the bravery of my father and my grandfather had seemed not only unattainable but alien, as if they belonged to a different race.

The inexpert way I fought that Sunday afternoon had nothing to do with bravery but everything to do with rage. They had no bloody right, I thought breathlessly, to steal my property and they damned well shouldn't, if I could stop them.

They had more to lose than I, I suppose. Liberty, for a start. Also I had undoubtedly damaged the first one rather severely around the pelvis, and as far as he was able he was looking for revenge.

It wasn't so much a matter of straight hitting with fists: more of clutching and kicking and ramming against hard surfaces and using knees as blunt instruments. At about the instant I ran out of enthusiasm the second man succeeded finally in what I'd been half aware he was trying to do, and reached in through the driver's door of the van, momentarily leaning forward in that same risky posture which I would have taken advantage of if I hadn't had my hands full with robber number one. Too late I kicked free of him and went to go forward.

Number two straightened out of the front of the van, and the fight stopped right there. He was panting a little but triumphantly holding a short-barrelled shotgun which he nastily aimed at my chest.

'Back off,' he said to me grimly.

I backed.

All my feelings about guns returned in a rush. It was suddenly crystal clear that a few cases of wine weren't worth dying for. I walked one step backwards and then another and then a third, which brought me up against the wall beside my rear door. The door tended to close if not propped open, and was at that point shut but on the latch. If I could go through it, I thought dimly, I'd be safe, and I also thought that if I tried to escape through it, I'd be shot.

At the very second it crossed my mind that the man with the gun didn't know whether to shoot me or not, Gerard drove his car back into my yard. The man with the gun swung round towards him and loosed off one of the barrels and I yanked open my door and leaped to go through it. I knew the gun was turning back my way: I could see it in the side of my frantic vision. I knew also that having shot once he'd shoot again, that the moment of inhibition was past. At five paces he was so close that the full discharge would have blown a hole in an ox. I suppose I moved faster in that second than ever before in my life, and I was jumping sideways through the doorway like a streak when he pulled the trigger.

I fell over inside but not entirely from the impact of pellets: mainly because the passage was strewn with more cases of wine. The bits of shot that had actually landed felt like sharp stings in my arm: like hot stabs.

The door swung shut behind me. If I bolted it, I thought, I would be safe. I also thought of Gerard outside in his car, and along with these two thoughts I noticed blood running down my right hand. Oh well . . . I wasn't dead, was I? I struggled to my feet and opened the door enough to see what I'd be walking out to, and found that it wouldn't be very much, as the two black-headed robbers were scrambling into their van with clear intentions of driving away.

I didn't try to stop them. They rocketed past Gerard's car and swerved into the service road, disappearing with the rear doors swinging open and three or four cases of wine showing within.

The windscreen of Gerard's car was shattered. I went over there with rising dread and found him lying across both front seats, the top of one shoulder reddening and his teeth clenched with pain.

I opened the door beside the steering wheel. One says really such inadequate things at terrible times. I said, 'I'm so sorry . . .' knowing he'd come back to help me, knowing I shouldn't have gone in there, shouldn't have needed help.

Sung Li from next door came tearing round the corner on his feet, his broad face wide with anxiety.

'Shots,' he said. 'I heard shots.'

Gerard said tautly, 'I ducked. Saw the gun. I guess not totally fast enough,' and he struggled into a sitting position, holding on to the wheel and shedding crazed crumbs of windscreen like snow. 'The police are coming and you yourself are alive, I observe. It could fractionally have been worse.'

Sung Li, who spoke competent English, looked at Gerard as if he couldn't believe his ears, and I laughed, transferring his bewilderment to myself.

'Mr Tony,' he said anxiously as if fearing for my reason, 'do you know you are bleeding also?'

'Yes,' I said.

Sung Li's face mutely said that all English were mad, and Gerard didn't help by asking him to whistle up an ambulance, dear chap, if he wouldn't mind.

Sung Li went away looking dazed and Gerard gave me what could only be called a polite social smile.

'Bloody Sundays,' he said, 'are becoming a habit.' He blinked a few times. 'Did you get the number of that van?'

'Mm,' I nodded. 'Did you?'

'Yes. Gave it to the police. Description of men?'

'They were wearing wigs,' I said. 'Fuzzy black wigs, both the same. Also heavy black moustaches, identical. Clip-ons, I should think. Also surgical rubber gloves. If you're asking would I know them again without those additions, then unfortunately I don't think so.'

'Your arm's bleeding,' he said. 'Dripping from your hand.'

'They were stealing my wine.'

After a pause he said, 'Which wine, do you think?'

'A bloody good question. I'll go and look,' I said. 'Will you be all right?'

'Yes.'

I went off across the yard to my back door, aware of the warm stickiness of my right arm, feeling the stinging soreness from shoulder to wrist, but extraordinarily not worried. Elbow and fingers still moved per instructions, though after the first exploratory twitches I decided to leave them immobile for the time being. Only the outer scatterings of the shot had caught me, and compared with what might have happened it did truthfully at that moment seem minor.

I noticed at that point how the thieves had got in: the barred washroom window had been comprehensively smashed inward, frame, bars and all, leaving a hole big enough for a man. I went into the washroom, scrunching on broken glass, and picked up the cloth with which I usually dried the glasses after customers had tasted wines, wrapping it a few times round my wrist to mop up the crimson trickles before going out to see what I'd lost.

For a start I hadn't lost my small stock of really superb wines in wooden boxes at the back of the storeroom. The prizes, the appreciating Margaux and Lafite, were still there.

I hadn't lost, either, ten cases of champagne or six very special bottles of old cognac, or even a readily handy case of vodka. The boxes I'd fallen over in the passage were all open at the tops, the necks of the bottles showing, and when one went into the shop one could see why.

The robbers had been stealing the bottles from the racks. More peculiarly they had taken all the half-drunk wine bottles standing re-corked on the tasting table, and all the opened cases from beneath the tablecloth.

The wines on and below the table had come from St Emilion, Volnay, Côtes de Roussillon and Graves, all red. The wines missing from the shop's racks were of those and some from St Estèphe, Nuits St Georges, Mâcon and Valpolicella; also all red.

I went back out into the yard and stooped to look at the contents of the case robber number two had jabbed me with and then dropped. It contained some of the bottles from the tasting table, four of them broken.

Straightening I continued over to Gerard's car and was relieved to see him looking no worse.

'Well?' he said.

'They weren't ordinary thieves,' I said.

'Go on, then.'

'They were stealing only the sorts of wines I tasted at the Silver Moondance. The wines which weren't what the labels said.'

He looked at me, the effort of concentration showing.

I said, 'I bought those wines, the actual ones, at the Silver Moondance. Paid for them. Got a receipt from the barman. He must have thought I took them away with me . . . but in fact the police have them. Sergeant Ridger. He too gave me a receipt.'

'You are saying,' Gerard said slowly, 'that if you'd

brought those wines here to your shop, today they would have vanished.'

'Yeah.'

'Given another half-hour . . .'

I nodded.

'They must be of extraordinary importance.'

'Mm,' I said. 'Be nice to know why.'

'Why did you buy them?'

We were both talking, I saw, so as to give a semblance of normality to the abnormal reality of two ordinary Englishmen quietly bleeding from shotgun wounds in a small town on a Sunday afternoon. I thought 'This is bloody ridiculous' and I answered him civilly, 'I bought them for the labels . . . to see if the labels themselves were forgeries. As a curio. Like collecting stamps.'

'Ah,' he said placidly.

'Gerard . . .'

'Yes?'

'I'm very sorry.'

'So you should be. Stupid behaviour.'

'Yes.'

We waited for a while longer until a police car rolled into the yard without haste, two policemen emerging enquiringly, saying they could see no evidence of any break-in at the wine shop, and did we know who had called them out.

Gerard closed his eyes. I said, 'This is the back of the wine shop. The thieves broke in the back, not the front. If you look closely you'll see they broke the wash-room window, climbed in over the loo and unbolted the back door from the inside.'

One of them said 'Oh,' and went to look. The other took out his notebook. I said mildly, 'The thieves had a shotgun and . . . er . . . shot us. They are driving away in a grey Bedford van, brown lines along the sides, licence number MMO 229Y, containing about four cases of red wine . . . and they'll have gone ten miles by now, I shouldn't wonder.'

'Name, sir?' he said blandly.

I wanted to giggle. I told him my name, however, and to do him justice he wasted no time once he realized that red wasn't in the original weave of Gerard's jacket. Gerard and I in due course found ourselves in the casualty department of the local major hospital where he was whisked off to regions unseen and I sat with my bare newly-washed arm on a small table while a middle-aged nursing sister expertly and unemotionally picked pellets out with a glittering instrument reminiscent of tweezers.

'You look as if you've done this before,' I observed.

'Every year during the shooting season.' She paused. 'Can you feel this?'

'No, not really.'

'Good. Some of them have gone deep. If the local anaesthetic isn't enough, tell me.'

'I sure will,' I said fervently.

She dug around for a while until there were eleven

886

little black balls like peppercorns rattling redly in the dish, each of them big enough to kill a pheasant; and to my morbid amusement she said I could take them with me if I liked, many people did.

Carrying my jacket and with a thing like a knitted tube over antiseptic patches replacing the shredded sleeve of my shirt I went to find Gerard, discovering him in a cubicle, sitting in a wheelchair, wearing a hospital-issue fawn dressing gown over his trousers and looking abysmally bored. He had stopped bleeding both inside and out, it appeared, but several pellets were inaccessible to tweezers and he would have to stay overnight until the theatre staff returned in force in the morning. Life-and-death alone got seen to on Sundays, not small spheres of lead lodged behind collar bones.

He said he had telephoned to Tina, his wife, who was bringing his pyjamas. Tina also would retrieve his car and get the windscreen fixed; and I wondered whether he had told Tina that the velvety upholstery that was where his head would have been if he hadn't thrown himself sideways was ripped widely apart with the stuffing coming out.

I went back to my shop in a taxi and checked that the police had, as they had promised, sent someone to board up the absent washroom window. I let myself in through the front door, switching on a light, assessing the extent of the mess, seeing it not now with anger but as a practical problem of repair.

For all that it wouldn't be permanently damaged I had an arm not currently of much use. Lifting cases of wine could wait a day or two. Likewise sweeping up broken glass. Thank goodness for Brian, I thought tiredly, and checked that the bolts were once again in position over the door and the sheet of plywood nailed securely in the washroom.

I left everything as it was, switched off the lights and went out again by the front door. Sung Li was emerging reluctantly from his restaurant, his forehead lined with worry.

'Oh, it is you, Mr Tony,' he said with relief. 'No more burglars.'

'No.'

'You want some food?'

I hesitated. I'd eaten nothing all day but felt no hunger.

'It's best to eat,' he said. 'Lemon chicken, your favourite. I made it fresh.' He gave me a brief bow. I bowed courteously in return and went in with him: between us there was the same sort of formality as between myself and Mrs Palissey, and Sung Li, also, seemed to prefer it. I ate the lemon chicken seated at a table in the small restaurant section and after that fried shrimp and felt a good deal less lightheaded. I hadn't known I was lightheaded until then, rather like not knowing how ill one had been until after one felt well again, but, looking back, I imagined I hadn't been entirely ground-based since I'd looked into the business end of a shotgun and found my legs didn't reliably belong to my body. The euphoria of escape, I now saw, accounted for Gerard's and my unconcerned conversation in the yard and for my methodical checking of my losses. It was really odd how the mind strove to pretend things were normal . . . and there were good chemical reasons why that happened after injury. I'd read an article about it, somewhere.

I stood up, making a stiff attempt to pick my wallet out of my pocket, and Sung Li was at my side instantly, telling me to pay him in the morning. I asked if I could go out to my car in the yard through his kitchen door instead of walking all the way round and he was too polite to tell me I wasn't fit to drive. We bowed to each other again outside in the darkness, and I'd managed to grasp my keys pretty firmly by the time I reached the Rover.

I drove home. I hit nothing. The anaesthetic wore off my arm and the whole thing started burning. I swore aloud, most obscenely, half surprised that I should say such things, even alone. Half surprised I could think them.

I let myself into the cottage. The second Sunday in a row, I thought, that I had gone back there with blood on my clothes and my mind full of horrors.

Emma, I thought, for God's sake help me. I walked through the empty rooms, not really looking for her, knowing perfectly well she wasn't there, but desperately in need all the same of someone to talk to, someone to hold me and love me as she had done.

With the lights all brightly shining I swallowed some aspirin and sat in my accustomed chair in the sitting room and told myself to shut up and be sensible. I'd been robbed ... so what? Fought ... and lost ... so what? Been shot in the arm ... so what? So Emma ... my darling love ... help me.

Get a bloody grip on things, I told myself.

Switch off the lights. Go to bed. Go to sleep.

My arm throbbed unmercifully all night.

The new day, Monday, crept into the world at about the level of my perception of it: dull, overcast, lifeless. Stiffly I dressed and shaved and made coffee, averting my mind from the temptation to go back to bed and abdicate. Mondays were hard at the best of times. The shambles ahead beckoned with all the appeal of a cold swamp.

I put the aspirin bottle in my pocket. The eleven separate punctures, announcing themselves as unready to be overlooked, seemed to be competing against each other for my attention, and various bruises were developing gingerly almost everywhere else. Bugger the lot of you, I thought: to little avail.

I drove to the shop and parked in the yard. Gerard's car stood exactly in the same place where he'd stalled it askew, stamping on the footbrake when he caught sight of the gun swinging round to his face. The keys weren't in the ignition and I couldn't remember who had them. One more problem to shelve indefinitely.

There was a police car already outside my door when I walked round to the front. Inside it, Detective Sergeant Ridger. He emerged from the driver's side at my approach, every button and hair regimentally aligned as before. He stood waiting for me and I stopped when I reached him.

'How are you?' he said. He cleared his throat. 'I'm . . . er . . . sorry.'

I smiled at least a fraction. Sergeant Ridger was becoming quite human. I unlocked the door, let us in and locked it again; then I sat in the tiny office slowly opening the mail while he walked round the place with a notebook, writing painstakingly.

He came to a halt finally and said, 'You weren't trying to be funny, were you, with the list of missing property you dictated to the constable yesterday evening before you went off to the hospital?'

'No.'

'You do realize it was almost identical with the red wines stolen from the Silver Moondance.'

'I do indeed,' I said. 'And I hope you've got my Silver Moondance bottles tucked away safely in your police station. Twelve bottles of wine, all opened. My own property.'

'I haven't forgotten,' he said with a touch of starch. 'You'll get them back in due course.'

'I'd like one of them now,' I said reflectively.

'Which one?'

'The St Estèphe.'

'Why that one particularly?' He wasn't exactly suspicious; just naturally vigilant.

'Not that one particularly. It was the first that came to mind. Any would do.'

'What do you want it for?'

'Just to look at it again. Smell it . . . taste it again. You never know . . . it might just be helpful. To you, I mean.'

He shrugged, slightly puzzled but not antagonistic. 'All right. I'll get you one if I can, but I might not be able to. They're evidence.' He looked around the tiny office. 'Did they touch anything in here?'

I shook my head, grateful for that at least. 'They were definitely looking for the wine from the Silver Moondance. The bottles they loaded first and succeeded in taking away with them in the van were all opened and re-corked.' I explained about the bottles missing from on and beneath the tasting table, and he went to have a further look.

'Anything you can add to the description you gave of the thieves?' he asked, coming back.

I shook my head.

'Could one of them have been the barman from the Silver Moondance?'

'No,' I said definitely. 'Not his sort at all.'

'You said they wore wigs,' Ridger said. 'So how can you be sure?'

'The barman has acne. The robbers didn't.'

Ridger wrote it down in his notebook.

'The barman knew exactly what you bought,' he observed. 'He spelled them out item by item on your receipt.'

'Have you asked him about it?' I said neutrally.

Ridger gave me another of the uncertain looks which showed him undecided still about my status: member of the not-to-be-informed public or helpful-consultant-expert.

'We haven't been able to find him,' he said eventually.

I refrained from impolite surprise. I said, 'Since when?'

'Since . . .' he cleared his throat. 'Not actually since you yourself last saw him leaving the bar last Monday after he'd locked the grille. Apparently he drove off immediately in his car, packed his clothes, and left the district entirely.'

'Where did he live?'

'With . . . um . . . a friend.'

'Male friend?'

Ridger nodded. 'Temporary arrangement. No roots. At the first sign of trouble, he was off. We'll look out for him, of course, but he'd gone by early afternoon that Monday.'

'Not suspected of killing Zarac,' I suggested.

'That's right.'

'The assistant assistant and the waitress both knew what I bought,' I said thoughtfully. 'But . . .'

'Too wet,' Ridger said.

'Mm. Which leaves Paul Young.'

'I suppose he wasn't one of the thieves.' Hardly a question, more a statement.

'No,' I said. 'They were both younger and taller, for a start.'

'You would obviously have said.'

'Yes. Have you . . . er . . . found him? Paul Young?'

'We're proceeding with our inquiries.' He spoke without irony: the notebook jargon came naturally to his tongue. He wasn't much older than myself; maybe four or five years. I wondered what he'd be like off duty, if such a structured and self-disciplined person were ever entirely off duty. Probably always as watchful, as careful, as ready to prickle into suspicion. I was probably seeing, I thought, the real man.

I looked at my watch. Nine-twenty. Mrs Palissey and Brian should be arriving in ten minutes.

I said, 'I suppose it's OK with you if I get all this mess cleared up? Replace the window, and so on?'

He nodded. 'I'll just take a look round outside, though, before I go. Come and tell me what's different from before the break-in.'

I got slowly to my feet. We went out into the littered passage and without comment Ridger himself unbolted the heavy door and opened it.

'My car was parked all day yesterday just about where it is now,' I said. 'Gerard McGregor's car wasn't there, of course.'

Ridger looked back through his notebook, found an entry, nodded, and flipped forward again. The door swung shut in its slow way. Ridger pushed it open and went out, looking over his shoulder for me to follow. I stepped after him into the raw cold air and watched him pacing about, measuring distances.

'The thieves' van was here?' he asked, standing still.

'A bit to your right.'

'Where was the man with the shotgun standing when he fired at you?'

'About where you are now.'

He nodded matter-of-factly, swung round towards Gerard's car and raised his arm straight before him. 'He fired at the car,' he said.

'Yes.'

'Then . . .' he turned his body with the arm still outstretched until it was pointing at me. 'He fired again.'

'I wasn't actually standing here by that time.'

Ridger permitted a smile. 'Too close for comfort, I'd say.' He walked the five steps separating us and ran his hand over the outside of the door. 'Want to see what nearly hit you?'

The toughly-grained wood was dark with creosote, the preservative recently applied against the coming winter. I looked more closely to where he pointed, to an area just below the latch, a few inches in from the edge of the door. Wholly embedded in the wood as if they were part of it were dozens and dozens of little black pellets, most of them in a thick cluster, with others making marks like woodworm holes in a wider area all around.

'There are three hundred of those in a normal cartridge,' Ridger observed calmly. 'The report we got from the hospital said they dug eleven of them out of your right arm.'

I looked at the deadly grouping of the little black shots and remembered the frenzied panic of my leap through the door. I'd left my elbow too far out for a split second too long.

The main cluster in the wood was roughly at the height of my heart.

CHAPTER ELEVEN

Mrs Palissey and Brian arrived on time and fell into various attitudes of horror, which couldn't be helped. I asked her to open the shop for business and asked Brian to start clearing up, and I stayed out in the yard myself knowing it was mostly to postpone answering their eagerly probing questions.

Ridger was still pacing about, estimating and making notes, fetching up finally at a dark red stain on the dirty concrete.

He said, frowning, 'Is this blood?'

'No. It's red wine. The thieves dropped a case of bottles there. Some of them smashed in the case and seeped through onto the ground.'

He looked around. 'Where's the case now?'

'In the sink in the washroom. Your policemen carried it there yesterday evening.'

He made a note.

'Sergeant . . .?'

'Yes?' He looked up with his eyes only, his head still bent over the notebook.

'Let me know, would you, how things are going?'

'What things, for instance?'

'Whether you find that van . . . Whether you find a lead to Paul Young.'

He looked up fully and soberly, not refusing at once. I could almost feel his hesitation and certainly see it; and his answer when it came was typically ambivalent.

'We could perhaps warn you that you might be needed at some future date for identification purposes.'

'Thank you,' I said.

'Not promising, mind.' He was retreating into the notebook.

'No.'

He finished eventually and went away, and Mrs Palissey enjoyed her ooh/ahh sensations. Mrs Palissey wasn't given to weeping and wailing and needing smelling salts. Mrs Palissey's eyes were shining happily at the news value of the break-in and at the good isn't-it-awful gossip she'd have at lunchtime with the traffic warden.

Brian with little change to his normal anxious expression swept and tidied and asked me what to do about the case in the sink.

'Take out the whole bottles and put them on the draining board,' I said, and presently he came to tell me he'd done that. I went into the washroom to see, and there they were, eight bottles of St Emilion from under the tablecloth.

Brian was holding a piece of paper as if not knowing where to put it.

'What's that?' I said.

'Don't know. It was down in the case.' He held it out to me and I took it: a page from a notepad, folded across the centre, much handled, and damp and stained all down one side with wine from the broken bottles. I read it at first with puzzlement and then with rising amazement.

In a plain strong angular handwriting it read:

FIRST

All opened bottles of wine.

SECOND

All bottles with these names:

St Emilion.

St Estèphe.

Volnay.

Nuits St Georges.

Valpolicella.

Mâcon.

IF TIME

Spirits, etc. Anything to hand.

DARKNESS 6.30. DO NOT USE LIGHTS

'Shall I throw that away, Mr Beach?' Brian asked helpfully.

'You can have six Mars Bars,' I said.

He produced his version of a large smile, a sort of

sideways leer, and followed me into the shop for his reward.

Mrs Palissey, enjoyably worried, said she was sure she could cope if I wanted to step out for ten minutes, in spite of customers coming and almost nothing on the shelves, seeing as it was Monday. I assured her I valued her highly and went out along the road to the office of a solicitor of about my age who bought my wine pretty often in the evenings.

Certainly I could borrow his photocopier, he said. Any time.

I made three clear copies of the thieves' shopping list and returned to my own small lair, wondering whether to call Sergeant Ridger immediately and in the end not doing so.

Brian humped cases of whisky, gin and various sherries from storeroom to shop, telling me each time as he passed what he was carrying, and each time getting it right. There was pride on his big face from the accomplishment; job satisfaction at its most pure. Mrs Palissey restocked the shelves, chattering away interminably, and five people telephoned with orders.

Holding a pen was unexpectedly painful, arm muscles stiffly protesting. I realized I'd been doing almost everything left-handedly, including eating Sung Li's chicken, but writing that way was beyond me. I took down the orders right-handedly with many an inward curse, and when it came to the long list for the wholesalers, picked it out left-handed on the typewriter.

No one had told me how long the punctures might take to heal. No time was fast enough.

We got through the morning somehow, and Mrs Palissey, pleasantly martyred, agreed to do the wholesalers run with Brian in the afternoon.

When they'd gone I wandered round my battered domain thinking that I should dredge up some energy to telephone for replacement wines, replacement window . . . replacement self-respect. It was my own silly fault I'd been shot. No getting away from it. It hadn't seemed natural, all the same, to tiptoe off and let the robbery continue. Wiser, of course. Easy in retrospect to see it. But at the time . . .

I thought about it in a jumbled way, without clarity, not understanding the compulsive and utterly irrational urge that had sent me running towards danger when every scared and skin-preserving instinct in my life had been to shy away from it.

Not that I'd been proud of that, either. Nor ashamed of it. I'd accepted that that was the way I was: not brave in the least. Disappointing.

I supposed I had better make a list of the missing wines for the insurance company, who would be getting as fed up with my repeated claims as Kenneth Charter's insurers were with his. I supposed I should, but I didn't do it. Appetite for chores, one might have said, was at an extremely low ebb.

I took some aspirin.

A customer came in for six bottles of port and

901

relentlessly brought me up to date on the family's inexhaustible and usually disgusting woes. (Father-in-law had something wrong with his bladder.)

Sung Li appeared, bowing, with a gift of spring rolls. He wouldn't be paid for my previous evening's dinner, he said. I was an honoured and frequent customer. When I was in need, he was my friend. I would honour him by not offering payment for yesterday. We bowed to each other, and I accepted.

He had never seen China, but his parents had been born there and had taught him their ways. He was a most punctilious neighbour and because of his roaringly successful but unlicensed take-away I sold much wine in the evenings. Whenever I could without offending him I gave him cigars, which he smoked on sunny afternoons sitting on a wooden chair outside his kitchen door.

At three Sergeant Ridger returned carrying a paper bag from which he produced a bottle, setting it on the counter.

St Estèphe: just as I'd asked. Uncorked and sealed with sticky tape, untouched since its departure from the Silver Moondance.

'Can I keep it?' I said.

He gave one brief sharp nod. 'For now. I said you'd been helpful, that it would be helpful for you to have this. I obtained permission from the Chief Inspector in charge of the Silver Moondance murder investigations.'

He dug into a pocket and produced a piece of paper, holding it out. 'Please sign this chit. It makes it official.'

I signed the paper and returned it to him.

'I've something for you, as well,' I said, and fetched for him the thieves' shopping list. The original.

His body seemed to swell physically when he understood what it was, and he looked up from it with sharply bright eyes.

'Where did you find it?'

I explained about Brian clearing up.

'This is of great significance,' he said with satisfaction.

I agreed. I said, 'It would be particularly interesting if this is Paul Young's handwriting.'

His staring gaze intensified, if anything.

'When he wrote his name and address,' I said, 'do you remember, he held his pen so awkwardly? He wrote in short sharp downward strokes. It just seemed to me that this list looked similar . . . though I only saw his name and address very briefly, of course.'

Sergeant Ridger, who had looked at them long and carefully, stared now at the thieves' list, making the comparison in his mind. Almost breathlessly he said, 'I think you're right. I think they're the same. The Chief Inspector will be very pleased.'

'A blank wall, otherwise?' I suggested. 'You can't find him?'

His hesitation was small. 'There are difficulties, certainly,' he said.

903

No trace at all, I diagnosed.

'How about his car?' I suggested.

'What car?'

'Yes . . . well . . . he didn't come to the Silver Moondance that day on foot, would you think? It's miles from anywhere. But when we went out with the boxes of drinks, there wasn't an extra car in the car park. So . . . um . . . he must have parked round at the back where the cars of the staff were. Round by that door into the lobby where Larry Trent's office is, and the wine cellars. So Paul Young must have been to the Silver Moondance some other time . . . or he would have parked out front. If you see what I mean.'

Detective Sergeant Ridger looked at me long and slowly. 'How do you know the staff parked round at the back?'

'I saw cars through the lobby window when I went to fetch the bottles of wine. It seemed common sense to assume those were the staff's cars . . . barman, assistant assistant, waitress, kitchen staff and so on. They all had to get to work somehow, and the front car park was empty.'

He nodded, remembering.

'Paul Young stayed there after we left,' I said. 'So maybe the assistant or the waitress . . . or somebody . . . remembers what car he drove away in. Pretty long shot, I suppose.'

Ridger carefully put the folded shopping list into the back of his notebook and then wrote a sentence or two on a fresh page. 'I'm not of course in charge of that investigation,' he said eventually, 'and I would expect this line of questioning has already been thoroughly explored, but . . . I'll find out.'

I didn't ask again if he would tell me the results, nor did he even hint that he might. When he left, however, it was without finality: not so much goodbye as see you later. He would be interested, he said, in anything further I could think of in connection with the bottle of wine he had brought. If I came to any new conclusions, no doubt I would pass them on.

'Yes, of course,' I said.

He nodded, shut the notebook, tucked it into his pocket and collectedly departed, and I took the bottle of St Estèphe carefully into the office, putting it back into the bag in which Ridger had brought it so that it should be out of plain sight.

I sat down at the desk, lethargy deepening. Still a load of orders to make up to go out on the van; couldn't be bothered even to start on them. Everyone would get their delivery a day late. Goblets and champagne needed for a coming-of-age on Thursday... by Thursday I mightn't feel so bone weary and comprehensively sore.

Women's voices in the shop. I stood up slowly and went out there, trying to raise a smile. Found the smile came quite easily when I saw who it was.

Flora stood there, short, plump and concerned, her kind eyes searching my face. Beside her, tall and elegant, was the woman I'd seen fleetingly with Gerard after the horsebox accident: his wife, Tina.

'Tony, dear,' Flora exclaimed, coming down the shop to meet me, 'are you sure you should be here? You don't look well, dear. They really should have kept you in hospital, it's too bad they sent you home.'

I kissed her cheek. 'I wouldn't have wanted to stay.' I glanced at Mrs McGregor. 'How's Gerard?'

'Oh dear,' Flora said. 'I should introduce . . . Tina, this is Tony Beach . . .'

Tina McGregor smiled, which was noble considering that her husband's predicament was my fault, and in answer to my enquiry said Gerard had had the pellets removed that morning, but would be staying one more night for recovery.

'He wants to see you,' she said. 'This evening, if you can.'

I nodded. 'I'll go.'

'And Tony, dear,' Flora said, 'I was so wanting to ask you . . . but now I see how dreadfully pale you look I don't suppose . . . It would be too much, I'm sure.'

'What would be too much?' I said.

'You were so frightfully kind coming round the stables with me, and Jack's still in hospital, they still won't let him come home, and every day he gets crosser . . .'

'You want me to visit Jack too, after Gerard?' I guessed.

'Oh no!' She was surprised. 'Though he would love

906

it, of course. No . . . I wondered . . . silly of me, really . . . if you would come with me to the races?' She said the final words in a rush and looked of all things slightly ashamed of herself.

'To the races . . .'

'Yes, I know it's a lot to ask . . . but tomorrow . . . we've a horse running which has a very awkward owner and Jack insists I must be there and honestly that owner makes me feel so flummoxed and stupid, I know it's silly, but you were so good with that horrible Howard and I just thought you might enjoy a day at the races and I would ask you . . . only that was before Tina rang me and told me about last night . . . and now I can see it wouldn't be a pleasure for you after all.'

A day at the races . . . well, why not? Maybe I'd feel better for a day off. No worse, at any rate.

'Which races?' I said.

'Martineau.'

Martineau Park, slightly north-east of Oxford, large, popular and not too far away. If ever I went to the races it was either to Martineau Park or to Newbury, because I could reach either track inside forty minutes and combine the trip with shop hours, Mrs Palissey graciously permitting.

'Yes, I'll come,' I said.

'But Tony dear . . . are you sure?'

'Yes, sure. I'd like to.'

She looked greatly relieved and arranged to pick me up at one o'clock the next day, promising faithfully to

907

return me by six. Their runner, she explained, was in the big race of the day at three-thirty, and the owner always expected to talk for hours afterwards, analysing every step and consequence.

'As if I can tell him anything,' Flora said despairingly. 'I do so wish the horse would win, but Jack's afraid he won't, which is why I've got to be there . . . Oh dear, oh dear.'

The Flat racing season was due to end in two or three weeks and none too soon, I judged, from Jack Hawthorn's point of view. No stable could long survive the absence of both its main driving forces, left as it was in the hands of a kind unbusinesslike woman with too little knowledge.

'Listen to the owner with respect and agree with everything he says and he'll think you're wonderful,' I said.

'How very naughty, Tony dear,' she said, but looked more confident all the same.

I took them out to the yard, as Flora had chiefly brought Tina to retrieve Gerard's car. It appeared that Tina herself had the ignition key: Gerard had given it to her the previous evening. Tina gazed without comment for a while at the shattered windscreen and the exploded upholstery and then turned towards me, very tall and erect, all emotions carefully straitjacketed.

'This is the third time,' she said, 'that he's been shot.'

*

I went to see him in the evening and found him propped against pillows in a room with three other beds but no inmates. Blue curtains, hospital smell, large modern spaces, shiny floors, few people about.

'Utterly boring,' Gerard said. 'Utterly impersonal. A waiting room to limbo. People keep coming to read my notes to see why I'm here, and going away again, never to return.'

His arm was in a sling. He looked freshly shaved, hair brushed, very collected and in control. Hung on the foot of the bed was the clipboard of notes to which he'd referred, so I picked them off and read them also.

'Your temperature's ninety-nine, your pulse seventy-five, you're recovering from birdshot pellets, extracted. No complications. Discharge tomorrow.'

'None too soon.'

'How do you feel?'

'Sore,' he said. 'Like you, no doubt.'

I nodded, put the notes back and sat on a chair.

'Tina said this was the third time for you,' I said.

'Huh.' He smiled lopsidedly. 'She's never totally approved of my job. An embezzler took a pot at me once. Very unusual, that, they're normally such mild people. I suppose it was true to form that he wasn't altogether successful even at murder. He used too small a pistol and shot me in the thigh. Couldn't hold the thing steady . . . I'd swear he shut his eyes just before he fired.'

'He didn't fire again?'

'Ah. Well I was rushing him, you know. He dropped the pistol and started crying. Pathetic, the whole thing.'

I eyed Gerard respectfully. Rushing someone intent on killing you wasn't my idea of pathos.

'And the other time?' I asked.

He grimaced. 'Mm. Much closer to home. Touch and go, that time. Tina wanted me to promise to do office work only after that, but one can't, you know. If you're hunting out criminals of any sort there's always the outside chance they'll turn on you, even the industrial spies I'm normally concerned with.' He smiled again, ironically. 'It wasn't anyway the disloyal little chemist who sold his company's secrets to their chief rival who shot me, it was his father. Extraordinary. Father wouldn't believe his precious son guilty. He telephoned about six times, shouting I'd sent the most brilliant man of a generation to jail out of spite and ruined his career to cover up for someone else . . . he was obsessed, you know. Mentally disturbed. Anyway, he was waiting for me one day outside the office. Just walked across the pavement and shot me in the chest.' He sighed. 'I'll never forget his face. Evil triumph . . . quite mad.'

'What happened to them?' I asked, riveted.

'The father's in and out of padded cells. Don't know what's happened to the son, though he'll have been out of jail long ago. Sad, you know. Such a clever young man. His father's pride and joy.'

I was interested. 'Do you ever try to find out what becomes of the people you catch . . . afterwards?'

'No, not often. On the whole they are vain, greedy, heartless and cunning. I don't care for them. One can feel sorry for them, but it's with their victims my sympathies normally lie.'

'Not like the old joke,' I said.

'What old joke?'

'About the man who fell among thieves, who beat him and robbed him and left him bleeding and unconscious in the gutter. And along came two sociologists who looked down upon him lying there and said, the one to the other, "The man who did this needs our help".'

Gerard chuckled and made a face, putting his free hand to his shoulder.

'You mustn't think,' he said, 'that my record is normal. I've been unlucky. Only one other man in our firm has ever been wounded. And most policemen, don't forget, go through their entire careers uninjured.'

Some didn't, I thought.

'Your bad luck this time,' I apologized, 'was my stupidity.'

He shook his head stiffly, with care. 'Don't blame yourself. I drove back into the yard of my own accord. Let's leave it at that, eh?'

I thought gratefully that he was generous but I felt nonetheless still guilty. Absolution, it had always seemed to me, was a fake. To err was human, to be easily forgiven was to be sentimentally set free to err again. To be repeatedly forgiven destroyed the soul.

With luck, I thought, I wouldn't do anything else to incur Gerard's forgiveness.

The word that best described Gerard, I thought, was decent. As a detective he wasn't 'colourful' as understood in fiction: that's to say a womanizer, unshaven and drunk. Goodness, easy enough to perceive, was as quicksilver to define, but that most difficult of virtues lived in the strong lines of his face. Serious, rational, calm, he seemed to be without the mental twitches which afflicted many: the bullying pleasure in petty power, the self-regarding pomposity, the devouring anxiety of the insecure, all the qualities I saw at work daily not only among customers but in people to whom others had to go in trust, officials and professional people of all sorts. One never knew for certain: Gerard might indulge secret sins galore, locking his Hyde in a closet; but what I saw, I liked.

I told him about Brian finding the thieves' shopping list and gave him one of the photostats out of my pocket, explaining about it being very likely in Paul Young's own handwriting.

'Great God,' he said, reading it. 'He might as well have signed a confession.'

'Mm.'

'But you can see why the robbers needed a written list,' he said. 'All those French names. They needed a visible check actually in their hand. They'd never have been sure to take the right things without.'

'Not unless they knew the right labels intimately.'

Gerard looked up from the list. 'You mean, the men who broke in are therefore not the designers of the swindle.'

'If they were they wouldn't have needed the list.'

'Right.' He smiled slightly. 'How would they grab you as the murderers of Zarac?'

I opened my mouth and shut it again: then when the small shock had passed, I slowly and undecidedly shook my head.

'I don't know,' I said. 'They were rough . . . but there was a moment, when the bigger one picked the gun out of the van, that he pointed it at me and visibly hesitated. If he'd already helped to kill Zarac . . . wouldn't he have killed me then?'

Gerard considered it. 'We can't tell. Zarac died out of earshot of a Chinese takeaway. The hesitation may have been because of the more public nature of the yard. But people who take shotguns to robberies have at least thought of killing, never forget.'

I wouldn't forget, I thought.

'What made you become a detective?' I asked curiously.

'Don't say detective. Tina doesn't like it.'

'Investigating consultant, then.'

'I was baby-snatched from college while detection still seemed a glamorous idea to my immature mind.' Again the lopsided self-mocking smile. 'I'd done an accountancy course and was at business school but not much looking forward to living what it taught. Rather

913

dismayed, actually, by my prospects. I mentioned to an uncle of mine one day that I thought I'd like to join the police only the family would have mass heart attacks, and a friend of his who was there said why didn't I join the business police ... I didn't know what he meant, of course, but he steered me to an agency and I think spoke in their ear. They offered me a trial year and started to teach me how to search ... It was a different agency, not Deglet's. Deglet's took us over, and I was part of the furniture and fittings.'

'And you've never regretted it?'

He said thoughtfully, 'It's fashionable to explain away all crime as the result of environment and upbringing, always putting the blame on someone else, never the actual culprit. No one's born bad, all that sort of thing. If it weren't for poor housing, violent father, unemployment, capitalism, et cetera, et cetera ... You'll have heard it all, over and over. Then you get a villain from a good home with normal parents who's in a job and can't keep his fingers out of the till. I've seen far far more of those. They're the ones I investigate. Sometimes there's a particular set of circumstances you can point to as the instigation of their thieving or spying or betraying of confidence, but so many of them, I find, simply have an urge to be dishonest. Often not out of dire need, but because that's how they get their kicks. And whichever way you look at them, as poor little victims of society or as marauding invaders, they damage everyone in their path.' He shifted against his pillows. 'I was brought up to respect that most old-fashioned concept, fair play. Even the present weary world tends not to think all's fair in war . . . I seek to restore fair play. I only achieve a bit here and there and the next trickster with a computer is being born every minute . . . What did you ask me?'

'You've answered it,' I said.

He ran his tongue round his lips as if they were dry. 'Pass me that water, will you?' he said.

I gave him the glass and put it down when he'd drunk.

Be grateful for villainy, I thought. The jobs of millions depended on it, Gerard's included. Police, lawyers, tax inspectors, prison warders, court officials, security guards, locksmiths and people making burglar alarms . . . Where would they be the world over but for the multiple faces of Cain.

'Gerard,' I said.

'Mm?'

'Where does my consultancy start and end?'

'How do you mean?'

'Well . . . there wasn't a tankerful of Scotch at the Silver Moondance. That Rannoch Scotch is still about somewhere . . . masquerading perhaps as Laphroaig but more likely as Bell's.'

Gerard saw the smile twisting the corners of my mouth and gave another painful chuckle.

'You mean you might find it,' he said, 'if you drank at every hostelry from here to John o'Groats?'

'Just Berkshire and Oxfordshire and all the way to Watford. Say fifty thousand places, for starters . . . A spot of syncopation. Syncopation, as you know, is an uneven movement from bar to bar.'

'Please be quiet,' he said. 'Laughing hurts.'

'Mm,' I said. 'Cirrhosis, I love you.'

'All the same . . .'

'I was only joking.'

'I know. But . . . as you said.'

'Yeah. Well, I'll drink Scotch at every opportunity, if not every bar. But I won't find it.'

'You never know. Some dark little pub in a Reading backstreet . . .'

I shook my head. 'Somewhere like the Silver Moondance with smoke and noise and dancing and a huge turnover.'

His glance grew thoughtful. 'It depends how much Kenneth Charter wants to spend. As you say, it's an incredibly long shot . . . but I'll put it to him. Incredibly long shots sometimes pay off, and I've known them happen at worse than fifty thousand to one.'

I hadn't expected him to take me seriously and it made what I had chiefly been going to say sound unimportant. I said, all the same, 'I persuaded Sergeant Ridger to let me have one of the Silver Moondance wine bottles. The label might be informative. I know it's nothing on the face of it to do with Kenneth Charter's tankers, but . . . er, if you found out more about the wine it might lead you back to the Scotch.'

He looked at the photostat lying on the sheet. 'To Paul Young, do you mean?'

'I suppose so . . . yes.'

He said calmly, 'Information about wine labels very definitely comes under the heading of consultancy. Getting too close to Paul Young does not.'

CHAPTER TWELVE

Henri Tavel in his robust French asked me to give his felicitations to my dear mother.

I said I would.

He said he was delighted to hear my voice after so many months and he again regretted infinitely the death of my so dear Emma.

I thanked him.

He said I would have enjoyed the harvest, it had been an abundant crop of small excellent grapes full of flavour: everyone in Bordeaux was talking of equalling 1970.

I offered congratulations.

He asked if I could spare time to visit. All his family and my many friends would welcome it, he said.

I regretted that my shop prevented an absence at present.

He understood. *C'est la vie.* He hoped to be of help to me in some way, as I had telephoned.

Thus invited and with gratitude I explained about the substitute wine and the existence of various labels.

'Alas,' he said. 'This is unfortunately too common. A matter of great annoyance.'

'If I describe one of the labels, could you find out for me if it's genuine?' I asked.

'Certainly,' he agreed. 'Tomorrow, my dear Tony.'

I was telephoning from the office in the shop with the St Estèphe bottle in front of me.

I said, 'The label is of a château in the region of St Estèphe, a village you know so well.'

'The home of my grandparents. There is no one there of whom I cannot enquire.'

'Yes ... Well, this label purports to come from Château Caillot.' I spelled it out for him. 'Do you know of it?'

'No, I don't but don't forget there must be two hundred small châteaux in that part of Haut Médoc. I don't know them all. I will find out.'

'Great,' I said. 'The rest of the label reads: "Mis en bouteille par W. Thiery et Fils, négociants à Bordeaux."'

Henri Tavel's suspicions came clearly down the line. 'I know of no W. Thiery et Fils,' he said. Monsieur Tavel, *négociant à Bordeaux* himself, was more likely to be aware of a fellow wineshipper than of a château seventy kilometres to the north. 'I'll find out,' he said.

'Also the label bears the year of vintage,' I said.

'Which year?'

'1979.'

He grunted. 'Plentiful and quite good.'

'It's an attractive label altogether,' I said. 'Cream background with black and gold lettering, and a line drawing of an elegant château. The château reminds me of somewhere . . . I wish you could see it, you might recognize it.'

'Soak it off, my dear Tony, and send it.'

'Yes, I might.'

'And the wine under the label?' he asked. 'What of the wine?'

'At a guess, mostly Italian. Blended with maybe Yugoslav, blended again with anything handy. Impossible, I would think, to distinguish its origins, even for a master of wine. It's light. Not much body. No finish. But pleasant enough. Palatable. No one would think it undrinkable. Wherever it came from it wasn't abused too much before it was bottled.'

'Bordeaux bottled . . .' he said thoughtfully.

'If the château doesn't exist, the wine could have been bottled anywhere,' I said. 'I kept the cork. It looks pretty new and there is no lettering on it.'

The row of six corks stood before me on the desk, all identical. When châteaux bottled their own wine in their own cellars they stamped the corks with their name and the year of vintage. Anyone ordering a château-bottled wine would expect to see the cork, consequently a swindler would be less likely to present his work as château-bottled: too great a risk of a clued-up customer knowing what he wasn't being given.

Whoever had chosen the Silver Moondance labels

had chosen well: all familiar-sounding respected names, all saleable at a substantial price. At a guess the wine itself, part of the great European wine lake, might have cost the bottler one-fiftieth of what Larry Trent's diners had been charged.

I asked Henri Tavel when I could telephone again.

'Tomorrow night, again at this time. I will enquire at once in the morning.'

I thanked him several times and we disconnected, and I pictured him as I'd so often seen him, sitting roundly at his big dining table with its lace cloth, drinking armagnac alone after the evening meal and refusing to watch television with his wife.

Flora collected me from the shop at one the following day as arranged and drove me in Jack's opulent car to Martineau Park races. She talked most of the way there out of what seemed a compulsive nervousness, warning me mostly about what not to say to Orkney Swayle, the owner she felt cowed by.

Flora, I thought, had no need to be cowed by anybody. She had status in the racing world, she was pleasant to look at in a motherly middle-aged way and she was dressed for action in tailored suit and plainly expensive shoes. Self-confidence had to come from within, however, and within Flora one could discern a paralysed jelly.

921

'Don't ask him why he's called Orkney,' she said. 'He was conceived there.'

I laughed.

'Yes, but he doesn't like it. He likes the name itself because it has grandeur which he's always looking for, and Tony dear, if you can be a bit grand like Jimmy it will do very well with Orkney. Put on your most upper-class voice like you do sometimes when you aren't thinking, because I know you damp it down a bit in the shop so as not to be intimidating to a lot of people, if you see what I mean.'

I was amused and also rueful at her perception. I'd learned on my first day of sweeping and carrying as general wine shop dogsbody that my voice didn't fit the circumstances, and had altered my ways accordingly. It had been mostly a matter, I'd found, of speaking not far back in the throat but up behind the teeth, a reversal of the way I'd just painstakingly learned to speak French like a Frenchman.

'I'll do my best Jimmy imitation,' I promised. 'And how is he, by the way?'

'Much better, dear, thank goodness.'

I said I was glad.

'Orkney thinks he owns Jack, you know,' she said, reverting to what was more immediately on her mind. 'He hates Jack talking to other owners.' She slowed for a roundabout and sighed. 'Some owners are dreadfully jealous, though I suppose I shouldn't say so, but Orkney gets quite miffed if Jack has another runner in Orkney's race.'

She was driving well and automatically, her mind far from the road. She told me she usually drove Jack to meetings: he liked to read and think on the way there and sleep on the way back. 'About the only time he sits still, dear, so it has to be good for him.'

'How old is this Orkney?' I asked.

'Getting on for fifty, I should think. He manufactures some frantically unmentionable undergarments, but he'll never say exactly what. He doesn't like one to talk about it, dear.' She almost giggled. 'Directoire knickers, do you think?'

'I'll be careful not to ask,' I said ironically. 'Directoire knickers! Do even great-grannies wear them any more?'

'You see them in those little advertisements on Saturdays in the newspapers,' Flora said, 'along with things to hold your shoulders back if you're round-shouldered and sonic buzzers that don't actually say what they're for, and all sorts of amazing things. Haven't you noticed?'

'No,' I said, smiling.

'I think sometimes of all the people who buy all those things,' she said. 'How different everyone's lives are.'

I glanced at her benign and rounded face, at the tidy greying hair and the pearl earstuds, and reflected not for the first time that the content of what she said was a lot more acute than her manner of saying it.

'I did tell you, dear, didn't I, that Orkney has a box at the races? So we'll be going up there when we get there and of course after the race for ages and ages; he does go on so. He'll probably have a woman there . . . I'm just telling you dear, because she's not his wife and he doesn't like people to ask about that either, dear, so don't ask either of them if they're married, will you dear?'

'There's an awful lot he doesn't like talking about,' I said.

'Oh yes, dear, he's very awkward, but if you stick to horses it will be all right, that's all he likes to talk about and he'll do that all night, and of course that's just what I can't do, as you know.'

'Any other bricks I might drop?' I asked. 'Religion, politics, medical history?'

'Yes, well, Tony dear, you're teasing me . . .' She turned into the entrance of Martineau Park, where the gateman waved her through with welcoming recognition. 'Don't forget his horse is called Breezy Palm and it's a two-year-old colt, and it's run nine times this season and won twice, and once it smashed its way out of the stalls and nearly slaughtered the assistant starter so maybe you'd better not mention that too much either.'

She parked the car but didn't get out immediately,

instead pulling on a becoming hat and adjusting the angle in the driving mirror.

'I haven't asked you how your arm is, dear,' she said, 'because it's perfectly obvious it's hurting you.'

'Is it?' I said, slightly dismayed.

'When you move it, dear, you wince.'

'Oh.'

'Wouldn't it be better in a sling, dear?'

'Better to use it, I should think.'

The kind eyes looked my way. 'You know, Tony dear, I think we should go first of all to the first aid room and borrow one of those narrow black wrist-supporting slings that the jumping jockeys use when they've broken things, and then you won't have to shake hands with people, which I noticed you avoided doing with Tina yesterday, and other people won't bang into you if they see they shouldn't.'

She left me speechless. We went to the first aid room, where by a mixture of charm and bullying she got what she wanted, and I emerged feeling both grateful and slightly silly.

'That's better, dear,' she said, nodding. 'Now we can go up to Orkney's box . . .' All her decisiveness in the first aid room vanished. 'Oh dear . . . he makes me feel so stupid and clumsy and as if I'd never stepped out of the schoolroom.'

'You look,' I said truthfully, 'poised, well-dressed and anybody's match. Stifle all doubts.'

Her eyes however were full of them and her

nervousness shortened her breath in the lift going up to the fourth floor.

The Martineau Park grandstands were among the best in the country, the whole lot having been designed and built at one time, not piecemeal in modernization programmes as at many other courses. The old stands having decayed to dangerous levels around 1950, it had been decided to raze the lot and start again, and although one could find fault about wind tunnels (result of schools of architecture being apparently ignorant of elementary physics), the cost-cutting disasters of some other places had been avoided. One could nearly everywhere, for instance, if one wanted to, watch the races from under cover and sitting down, and could celebrate afterwards in bars large enough for the crush. There was a warmed (or cooled) glass-walled gallery overlooking the parade ring and a roof above the unsaddling enclosures (as at Aintree) to keep all the back-slapping dry.

The two long tiers of high-up boxes were reached by enclosed hallways along which, when we came out of the lift, waitresses were pushing trolleys of food: a far cry from Ascot where they tottered with trays along open galleries, eclairs flying in the wind. Martineau Park, in fact, was almost too comfortable to be British.

Flora said, 'This way,' and went ahead of me with foreboding. Orkney Swale, I thought, simply couldn't be as intimidating as she made out.

The door of his box stood open. Flora and I reached

it together and looked in. A sideboard scarcely groaning with food and drink stood against the wall. Three small tables with attendant chairs filled the rest of the floor space, with glass doors to the viewing balcony beyond. To the right of the entrance door, a small serving pantry, clean and uncluttered. Orkney's, unlike some of the boxes we'd passed, wasn't offering lunch.

A man sat alone at one of the tables, head bent over a racing newspaper and form book, pen at the ready for making notes.

Flora cleared her throat, said 'Orkney?' waveringly and took three tentative steps into the box. The man at the table turned his head without haste, an enquiring expression raising his eyebrows. Even when he saw Flora and clearly knew her he was in no rush to stand up. He finally made it, but as if the politeness were something he'd belatedly thought of, not an instinctive act of greeting.

He was tall, sandy haired, wore glasses over pale blue eyes, smiled with reluctance.

'This is Tony Beach, Orkney,' Flora said.

Orkney looked me calmly up and down, gaze pausing briefly on the sling. 'Jack's assistant?' he asked.

'No, no,' Flora said, 'a friend.'

'How do you do?' I said in my best Jimmy manner, and got a nod for it, which seemed to relieve Flora, although she still tended to shift from foot to foot.

'Jack asked me to tell you he'd had good reports

about Breezy Palm from the head lad,' she said valiantly.

'I talked to Jack myself,' Orkney said. After a noticeable pause he added, 'Would you care for a drink?'

I could sense Flora about to refuse so I said 'Yes, why not?' in a Jimmy drawl, because a stiffener might be just what Flora needed.

Orkney looked vaguely at the sideboard upon which stood a bottle of gin, a bottle of Scotch, an assortment of mixers and several glases. He picked up an empty glass which had been near him on the small table, transferred it to the sideboard and stretched out his hand to a Seagram's bottle.

'Gin and tonic, Flora?' he offered.

'That would be nice, Orkney.'

Flora bought gin from me to give to visiting owners, saying she didn't much care for it herself. She watched apprehensively as Orkney poured two fingersworth and barely doubled it with tonic.

'Ice? Lemon?' he asked, and added them without waiting for an answer. He handed her the glass while looking at me. 'And you . . . er . . . same for you?'

'Scotch,' I said. 'Most kind.'

It was Teacher's whisky, standard premium. He poured the two fingers and hovered a hand between ginger ale and soda, eyebrows elevated.

'Just as it comes,' I said. 'No ice.'

The eyebrows rose higher. He gave me the glass, recapped the whisky and returned to the gin for himself. Two and a half fingers. Very little tonic. Two chunks of ice.

'To luck,' I said, taking a sip. 'To . . . ah . . . Breezy Palm.'

'Oh yes,' Flora said. 'Breezy Palm.'

The blended flavours trickled back over my tongue, announcing their separate presences, grain, malt and oakwood, familiar and vivid, fading slowly to aftertaste. I maybe couldn't have picked Teacher's reliably from a row of similar blends, but one thing was certain: what I was drinking wasn't Rannoch.

'Hurt your arm?' Orkney asked.

'Er . . .' I said. 'Had an accident with a door.'

Flora's eyes widened but to my relief she refrained from rushing in with details. Orkney merely nodded, acknowledging life's incidental perils. 'Too bad,' he said.

A waitress appeared at the doorway, pushing a trolley. A quick glance at Flora's face showed me one couldn't expect too much from this, and the reality turned out to be three moderately large plates bearing respectively crustless sandwiches, cheese with biscuits and strawberry tartlets, all tautly wrapped in transparent cling-film. The waitress asked if she could liberate the modest feast but Orkney said no, he would do it later, and there it all sat, mouthwateringly out of reach.

'In the good old days,' Flora told me later, 'one used to be able to take one's own food and drink to one's box, but now the caterers have an absolute stranglehold and everyone has to buy everything from them, and for some things they are frightfully expensive, absolutely exorbitant my dear, and Orkney resents it so much that he buys the absolute minimum. He's not really so mean as he looks today, it's just his way ... he told us once that the caterers charge bar prices in the boxes, whatever that means, and that it made him very angry.'

'Bar prices?' I said. 'Are you sure?'

'Is that so bad, dear?'

'Judging from race meeting bar prices, about a hundred and fifty per cent profit on a bottle of Scotch.'

Flora worked it out. 'So Orkney has to pay in his box more than double what the same bottle costs in your shop?'

'Yes, a good deal more than double.'

'My dear,' she said, 'I'd no idea drinks in the boxes cost so much.'

'A pound barely wets the glass.'

'You're teasing me.'

'Not entirely,' I said.

'No wonder Orkney resents having to pay that much when he used to take his own.'

'Mm,' I said reflectively. 'The caterers do have big overheads, of course, but to charge by the tot in the boxes ...'

'By the tot, dear?'

'Thirty-two tots to a bottle. That's the single measure

for spirits in all bars, racing or not. Two centilitres. One large mouthful or two small.'

Flora hardly believed me. 'I suppose I don't often buy drinks in bars, dear,' she said sighing. 'Jack does it, you see.'

In hindsight Orkney Swayle's hand on the bottles had been lavish: generosity well disguised by a cold demeanour. And the external manners, I came to see during the afternoon, were not intentionally rude, but a thoughtless habit, the sort of behaviour one could inherit in ultra-reserved families. He appeared not to be aware of the effect he had on others and would perhaps have been astonished to know he reduced Flora to quivers.

Orkney made inroads in his gin with his eyes impassively on my face.

'Are you knowledgeable about horses?' he asked.

I began to say 'marginally' but Flora didn't want any sort of modest disclaimers on my part, she wanted Orkney to be impressed. 'Yes of course he is, Orkney, his mother is a master of hounds and his father was a colonel and the greatest amateur rider of his generation and his grandfather was also a colonel and nearly won the Grand National . . .'

The faintest of gleams entered and left Orkney's eyes and I thought with surprise that somewhere deep down he might have after all a sense of humour.

'Yes, Flora,' he said. 'Those references are impeccable.'

'Oh.' She fell silent, not knowing if he were mocking her, and went pink round the nose, looking unhappily down at her drink.

'Breezy Palm,' Orkney said, oblivious, 'is by Desert Palm out of Breezy City, by Draughty City, which was a half-brother to Goldenburgh whose sire won the Arc de Triomphe, of course.'

He paused as if expecting comment so I obligingly said, 'What interesting breeding,' which seemed to cover most eventualities, including my own absolute ignorance of all the horses involved.

He nodded judiciously. 'American blood, of course. Draughty City was by Chicago Lake out of a dam by Michigan. Good strong hard horses. I never saw Draughty City of course, but I've talked to people who saw him race. You can't do better than mixed American and British blood, I always say.'

'I'm sure you're right,' I said.

Orkney discoursed for several further minutes on Breezy Palm's antecedents with me making appropriate comments here and there and Flora, on the edge of my vision, slowly beginning to relax.

Such progress as she had made was however ruined at that point by the arrival from the powder room of the lady to whom Orkney wasn't married, and it was clear that however much Orkney himself made Flora feel clumsy, his lady did it double.

Compared with Flora she was six inches taller, six inches slimmer and approximately six years younger.

She also had strikingly large grey eyes, a long thin neck and luminous make-up, and was wearing almost the same clothes but with distinctly more chic: tailored suit, good shoes, neat felt hat at a becoming angle. An elegant, mature, sophisticated knock-out.

To the eye it was no contest. Flora looked dumpy beside her, and knew it. I put my arm round her shoulders and hugged her and thought for one dreadful second that I'd reduced her to tears.

'Flora,' Orkney said, 'of course you and Isabella know each other . . . Isabella, my dear, this is Flora's walker . . . er . . . what did you say your name was?'

I told him. He told Isabella. Isabella and I exchanged medium hello smiles and Orkney returned to the subject of American forebears.

The races came and went: first, second, third. Everyone went down each time to inspect the horses as they walked round the parade ring, returning to the box to watch the race. Orkney gambled seriously, taking his custom to the bookmakers on the rails. Isabella flourished fistfuls of Tote tickets. Flora said she couldn't be bothered to bet but would rather check to make sure everything was all right with Breezy Palm.

I went with her to find Jack's travelling head lad (not the unctuous Howard but a little dynamo of a man with sharp restless eyes) who said cryptically that the horse was as right as he would ever be and that Mrs Hawthorn wasn't to worry, everything was in order.

Mrs Hawthorn naturally took no need of his good advice and went on worrying regardless.

'Why didn't you tell Orkney what really happened to your arm, dear?' she asked.

'I'm not proud of it,' I said prosaically. 'Don't want to talk about it. Just like Orkney.'

Flora the constant chatterer deeply sighed. 'So odd, dear. It's nothing to be ashamed of.'

We returned in the lift to the box where Flora wistfully eyed the still-wrapped food and asked if I'd had any lunch.

'No,' I said. 'Did you?'

'I should have remembered,' she sighed, 'but I didn't,' and she told me then about Orkney's hate reaction to the caterers.

Orkney had invited no other guests. He appeared to expect Flora and myself to return to the box for each race but didn't actually say so. An unsettling host, to say the least.

It was out on the balcony when we were waiting for the runners in the third race to canter down to the start that he asked Flora if Jack had found anyone else to lease his mare: he had forgotten to ask him on the hospital telephone.

'He'll do it as soon as he's home, I'm sure,' Flora said placatingly, and to me she added, 'Orkney owns one of the horses that Larry Trent leased.'

Orkney said austerely. 'My good filly by Fringe. A

three-year-old, good deep heart room, gets that from her dam, of course.'

I thought back. 'I must have seen her in Jack's yard,' I said. Four evenings in a row, to be precise.

'Really?' Orkney showed interest. 'Liver chestnut, white blaze, kind eye.'

'I remember,' I said. 'Good bone. Nice straight hocks. And she has some cleanly healed scars on her near shoulder. Looked like barbed wire.'

Orkney looked both gratified and annoyed. 'She got loose one day as a two-year-old. The only bit of barbed wire in Berkshire and she had to crash into it. Horses have no sense.'

'They panic easily,' I agreed.

Orkney's manner to me softened perceptibly at that point, which Flora noted and glowed over.

'Your filly did well for Larry Trent,' I said.

'Not bad. Won a nice handicap at Newbury and another at Kempton. Both Larry and I made a profit through the books, but I was hoping for black print, of course.'

I caught Flora starting to look anxious. 'Of course,' I said confidently; and she subsided. 'Black print' had come back just in time as an echo from childhood. Races of prestige and high prizes were printed in heavy black type in auction catalogues: black print earned by a broodmare upped the price of her foals by thousands.

'Will you keep her in training next year?' I asked.

'If I can get someone else to lease her.' He paused

slightly. 'I prefer to run two-year-olds myself, of course. I've had four in training with Jack this year. I sell them on if they're any good, or lease them, especially fillies, if they're well bred, so that I can either breed from them later or sell them as brood-mares. Larry often took one of my fillies as three- or four-year-olds. Good eye for a horse, Larry had, poor fellow.'

'Yes, so I hear.'

'Did you know him?'

'No.' I shook my head. 'I saw him at the party . . . but that was all.' In my mind's eye I saw him alive and also lifeless, the man whose death had started so many worms crawling.

'I didn't go to the party,' Orkney said calmly. 'Too bad he was killed.'

'You knew him well?' I asked.

'Pretty well. We weren't close friends, of course. Just had the mutual interest in horses.'

Orkney's voice clearly announced what his lips hadn't said: Larry Trent hadn't been, in Orkney's estimation, Orkney's social equal.

'So . . . er . . .' I said, 'you didn't go to his place . . . the Silver Moondance?'

The faintest spasm crossed Orkney's undemonstrative face. 'I met him there, once, yes, in his office, to discuss business. We dined afterwards. A dinner dance, Larry said. Very loud music . . .' He left the sentence hanging, criticism implied but not uttered.

'What did you think of the wine?' I asked.

'Wine?' He was surprised.

'I'm a wine merchant,' I said.

'Oh, really?' Wine merchants, it seemed, were in Orkney's world provisionally OK. 'Interesting. Well, as far as I remember it was perfectly adequate. For a dinner dance, of course.'

Perfectly adequate for a dinner dance brilliantly summed up the superior plonk in all those suspect bottles. There wasn't any point, I thought, in asking Orkney about the Scotch; he was a gin man himself.

The horses for the third race emerged onto the track and cantered past the stands. Orkney raised a massive pair of binoculars and studied his fancy, a flashy looking bay with a bounding impatient stride like an impala and sweat already on his neck.

'Fighting his jockey,' Orkney muttered. 'Losing the race on the way down.' He lowered the raceglasses and scowled.

'Larry Trent sometimes bought horses at the sales,' I said casually, watching the runners. 'Not for you?'

'No, no. For his brother.' Orkney's eyes and attention were anywhere but on me. 'Horses in training. Three-year-olds, or four or five. Shipped them abroad, that sort of thing. No, no, I buy yearlings . . . on bloodstock agents' advice, of course.'

Flora, listening, wore an expression that changed rapidly from surprise to comprehension. The disappearing Ramekin had been explained in the most mundane unmysterious way. She wasn't exactly disappointed but in the comprehension there was definite anticlimax.

'Look at that!' Orkney exclaimed crossly. 'The damn thing's bolting.'

His fancy had won the battle with his jockey and was departing into the distance at a flat gallop. Orkney raised his binoculars and folded his mouth into a grim and almost spiteful line as if he would have wrung the jockey's neck if he could have caught him.

'Did you know Larry Trent's brother?' I asked.

'What? No. No, never met him. Larry just said . . . Look at that! Bloody fool ought to be fined. I saw Larry buying a good horse for around fifty thousand at the sales. I said if he had that sort of money, why did he prefer leasing? It was his brother's cash, he said. Out of his league. But he could pick horses, he said, and his brother couldn't. The one thing his brother couldn't do, he said. Sounded envious to me. But there you are, that's people. Look at that bloody boy! Gone past the start. It's too bad! It's disgraceful!' Ungovernable irritation rose in his voice. 'Now they'll be late off, and we'll be rushed for Breezy Palm.'

CHAPTER THIRTEEN

He was right. They were late off. Orkney's fancy finished dead tired and second to last and we were indeed rushed for Breezy Palm.

Orkney was seriously displeased. Orkney became coldly and selfishly unpleasant.

I dutifully walked Flora down to the saddling boxes, though more slowly than our angry host had propelled his lady. ('You didn't mind him calling you my walker, did you, dear?' Flora asked anxiously. 'Not at all. Delighted to walk you anywhere, any time.' 'You're such a comfort, Tony dear.') We reached the saddling boxes as the tiny saddle itself went on over the number cloth, elastic girths dangling.

Breezy Palm, a chestnut with three white socks, looked as if he had a certain amount of growing still to do, particularly in front. Horses, like children, grew at intervals with rests in between: Breezy Palm's forelegs hadn't yet caught up with the last spurt in the hind.

'Good strong rump,' I said, in best Jimmy fashion.

The brisk travelling head lad, busy with girth

buckles, glanced at me hopefully but Orkney was in no mood for flattery. 'He's coming to hand again at last,' he said sourly. 'He won twice back in July, but since then there have been several infuriating disappointments. Not Jack's fault, of course . . .' His voice all the same was loaded with criticism. ' . . . jockeys' mistakes, entered at the wrong courses, frightened in the starting gate, needed the race, always something.'

Neither the head lad nor Flora looked happy, but nor were they surprised. Orkney's pre-race nerves, I supposed, were part of the job.

'Couldn't you have saddled up sooner?' Orkney said crossly. 'You must have known the last race was delayed.'

'You usually like to see your horses saddled, sir.'

'Yes, yes, but use some common sense.'

'Sorry, sir.'

'Can't you hurry that up?' Orkney said with increasing brusqueness as the head lad began sponging the horse's nose and mouth. 'We're damned late already.'

'Just coming, sir.' The head lad's glance fell on the horse's rug, still to be buckled on over the saddle for warming muscles on the October day. There was a pot of oil also for brushing gloss onto the hooves . . . and a prize to the lad, it said in the racecard, for the best turned-out horse.

'It's too bad,' Orkney said impatiently. 'We should be in the parade ring already.' He turned away sharply and stalked off in that direction, leaving Isabella, Flora and me to follow as we would.

Isabella looked stoically unaffected. Flora began to scurry after Orkney but I caught her abruptly by the arm, knowing he'd think less of her for hurrying, not more.

'Slow down, slow down, the jockeys aren't out yet.'

'Oh. All right, then.' She looked guilty as much as flustered, and walked with small jerky steps between the long-legged Isabella and myself as we joined Orkney in the parade ring, no later than any other owner-trainer group.

Orkney was still in the grip of his outburst of bad temper, which failed to abate when Breezy Palm finally appeared in the ring looking polished. The jockey, approaching it seemed to me unsmilingly out of past experience, was sarcastically told not to leave his winning run as bloody late as last time and not to go to sleep in the stalls, if he didn't mind.

The featherweight jockey listened expressionlessly, his gaze on the ground, his body relaxed. He's heard it all before, I thought, and he simply doesn't care. I wondered, if I'd been a jockey, whether I would have ridden my heart out for owners who spoke in that way, and concluded that possibly not. Breezy Palm's uncertain prospects developed a certainty for me at that moment: and I wondered what Orkney would be like in defeat when he was so obnoxious in hope.

The bell rang for the jockeys to mount. Breezy

Palm's jockey nodded to Orkney and went away with Orkney still telling him that if he used his whip too much he'd have him up in front of the stewards.

Flora was standing so close to me she was virtually clinging on. When Orkney turned away and strode out of the parade ring without waiting for Isabella or to see his horse mounted she said to me shakily, 'Jack manages him, but I can't. Jack stops him being so rude to the jockeys. One of them refused to ride his horses . . . can you imagine?'

'Mm,' I said. 'Do we have to go up to the box to watch the race?'

'Oh, my goodness, yes,' she said emphatically. 'At least . . . I mean . . . you don't have to . . . I could go alone.'

'Don't be silly.'

I looked around for the decorative Isabella, but she too had disappeared.

'They've both gone to bet,' Flora said, sighing. 'Jack said the opposition was stiff . . . I'm so afraid Breezy Palm won't win.'

We went up in the lift to the empty box. The sandwiches and tartlets were still wrapped, but the gin level had dropped considerably since we had arrived. Gin itself, I reflected, was a notorious inducer, in some people, of catty ill-humour.

Flora and I went onto the balcony to see the runners go down to the start, and Orkney arrived breathlessly, moving in front of us without apology, raising his binoculars to see what sins his jockey might already be committing. Isabella collectedly arrived with her clutched tickets and I glanced at the flickering light of the Tote board to see Breezy Palm's odds. Seven to one; by no means favourite but fairly well backed.

There were eighteen runners, several of them past winners. Breezy Palm, well drawn, went into the stalls quietly and showed no signs of re-assaulting the assistant starter. Orkney's slightly frantic agitation stilled suddenly to concentration and in the six-furlong distance the dark green starting gates opened in unison and spilled out their brilliant accelerating rainbow cargo.

Flora raised her own small raceglasses but I doubted if she could see much for trembling. Three-quarter-mile straight races were in any case difficult to read in the early stages as the runners were so far away and coming straight towards one, and it took me a fair time myself to sort out Orkney's jockey in red and grey. The commentator, rattling off names, hadn't mentioned Breezy Palm at all by the time they reached halfway but I could see him there, bobbing along in the pack, making no move either forward or backward, proving merely at that stage that he was no better and no worse than his opponents.

Flora gave up the struggle with her raceglasses, lowered them, and watched the last two furlongs simply with anxiety. The bunch of runners which had seemed to be moving slowly was suddenly perceived to be flying, the tiny foreshortened distances from first to last stretching before one's eyes to gaps of a length, to definite possibles and positive losers. The young colts stuck out their necks and strove to be first as they would have done in a wild herd on an unrailed plain, the primaeval instinct flashing there undiluted on the civilized track. The very essence of racing, I thought. The untamed force that made it all possible. Exciting, moving . . . beautiful.

Breezy Palm had the ancient instinct in full measure. Whether urged to the full by his jockey or not he was straining ahead with passion, legs angular beneath the immature body, stride hurried and scratchy, the compulsion to be first all there but the technical ability still underdeveloped.

The trick of race-riding, my father had once said, was to awaken a horse's natural panic fear and then control it. My father, of course, had had no doubt at all that he could do both. It was I, his son, who couldn't do either. Pity . . .

Breezy Palm's natural panic, jockey controlling it to the extent of letting it have its head and keeping it running straight, was still lustily aiming a shade beyond his ability. Orkney watched in concentrated silence. Flora seemed to be holding her breath. Isabella behind me was saying 'Come on, you bugger, come on, you bugger,' continuously under her breath, her most human reaction to date. Breezy Palm, oblivious, had his eyes fixed on the three horses still in front of him and over the last hundred yards ran as if the great god Pan were at his very heels.

Horses can only do their best. Breezy Palm's best on that day couldn't overhaul the winner, who went ahead by a length, or the second, who left clear space behind him, but he flashed over the line so close to the third of the leaders that from the angle of Orkney's box it was impossible to tell the exact placings. The judge, announced the tannoy, was calling for a photograph.

Orkney, still silent, lowered his glasses and stared up the track to where his hepped-up colt was being hauled back into the twentieth century. Then still saying nothing he turned and hurried away, again leaving his companions to fare for themselves.

'Come on, dear,' Flora said, tugging my sleeve. 'We must go down too. Jack said to be sure to. Oh dear . . .'

The three of us consequently made the downward journey as fast as possible and arrived to find Breezy Palm stamping around in the place allotted to the horse that finished fourth, the jockey unbuckling the girths and Orkney scowling.

'Oh dear . . .' Flora said again. 'The jockeys always know . . . He must have been beaten for third after all.'

The result of the photograph, soon announced, confirmed it: Breezy Palm had finished fourth. Distances: length, two lengths, short head.

Flora, Isabella and I stood beside Orkney, looking at the sweating, tossing, skittering two-year-old and making consoling and congratulatory remarks, none of which seemed to please.

'Ran extremely well in a strong field,' I said.

'The wrong race for him,' Orkney said brusquely. 'I've no idea why Jack persists in entering him in this class. Perfectly obvious they were too good for him.'

'Only just,' Isabella said reasonably.

'My dear woman, you know nothing about it.'

Isabella merely smiled; fortitude of an exceptional nature.

It struck me that she herself was totally uncowed by Orkney. He treated her rudely: she ignored it, neither embarrassed nor upset. Subtly, somewhere in their relationship, she was his equal... and both of them knew it.

Flora said bravely, 'I thought the horse ran splendidly,' and received a pityingly glance from on high.

'He fought to the end,' I said admiringly. 'Definitely not a quitter.'

'Fourth,' Orkney said repressively, as if fourth in itself bespoke a lack of character, and I wondered if he cared in the least how graceless he sounded.

The signal was given for the horses to be led away and Orkney made impatient movements which everyone interpreted as his own type of invitation to return to the box. There at last he busied himself with removing the wrappings from the overdue sandwiches, but without much method, finally pushing the plates towards Isabella for her to do it. Orkney himself

poured fresh drinks as unstintingly as before and indicated that we might all sit down round one of the
tables, if we so wished. All of us sat. All of us ate
politely, hiding our hunger.

As a post-race jollification it would have done a
funeral proud, but gradually the worst of Orkney's
sulks wore off and he began to make comments that
proved he had at least understood what he'd seen, even
if he took no joy in it.

'He's lost his action,' he said. 'Back in July, when he
won, he had a better stride. Much more fluent. That's
the only trouble with two-year-olds. You think you've
got a world beater and then they start developing
unevenly.'

'He might be better next year,' I suggested. 'Won't
you keep him? He could be worth it.'

Orkney shook his head. 'He's going to the sales next
week. I wanted a win today to put his price up. Jack
knew that.' The echo of grudge was still strong. 'Larry
Trent might have leased him. He thought, as you seem
to, that his action might come back once he'd finished
growing, but I'm not risking it. Sell, and buy yearlings,
that's my preference. Different runners every year . . .
more interesting.'

'You don't have time to grow fond of them,' I said
neutrally.

'Quite right,' he nodded. 'Once you get sentimental
you throw good money down the drain.'

I remembered the friendships my father had had

with his steeplechasers, treating each with camaraderie over many years, getting to interpret their every twitch and particularly loving the one that had killed him. Money down the drain, sure, but a bottomless pleasure in return such as Orkney would never get to feel.

'That damned jockey left his run too late,' Orkney said, but without undue viciousness. 'Breezy Palm was still making up ground at the end. You saw that. If he'd got at him sooner . . .'

'Difficult to tell,' I said, drawling.

'I told him not to leave it too late. I told him.'

'You told him not to hit the horse,' Isabella said calmly. 'You can't have it both ways, Orkney.'

Orkney could, however. Throughout the sandwiches, the cheese and the strawberry tartlets he dissected and discussed the race stride by stride, mostly with disapproval. My contention that his colt had shown great racing spirit was accepted. Flora's defence of the jockey wasn't. I grew soundly tired of the whole circus and wondered how soon we could leave.

The waitress appeared again in the doorway asking if Orkney needed anything else, and Orkney said yes, another bottle of gin.

'And make sure it's Seagram's,' he said. The waitress nodded and went away, and he said to me, 'I order Seagram's just because the caterers have to get it in specially. They serve their own brand if you don't ask. They charge disgraceful prices . . . I'm not going to make life easy for them if I can help it.'

Flora's and Isabella's expressions, I saw, were identical in pained resignation. Orkney had mounted his hobby horse and would complain about the caterers for another ten minutes. The arrival of the fresh bottle didn't check him, but at the end he seemed to remember my own job and said with apparently newly-reached decision, 'It's local people like you who should be providing the drinks, not this huge conglomerate. If enough people complain to the Clerk of the Course, I don't see why we couldn't get the system put back to the old ways. Do you?'

'Worth a try,' I said non-committally.

'What you want to do,' he insisted, 'is propose yourself as an alternative. Give these damn monopolists a jolt.'

'Something to think about,' I murmured, not meaning to in the least, and he lectured me at tiresome length on what I ought to do personally for the box-renters of Martineau Park, not to mention for all the other racecourses where the same caterers presided, and what I should do about the other firms of caterers who carved up the whole country's racecourses between them.

'Er ... Orkney,' Flora said uncertainly, when the tirade had died down, 'I do believe, you know, that at a few courses they really have finished with the conglomerates and called in local caterers, so perhaps ... you never know.'

Orkney looked at her with an astonishment which

949

seemed to be based less on what she'd said than on the fact of her knowing it. 'Are you sure, Flora?'

'Yes . . . I'm sure.'

'There you are then,' he said to me. 'What are you waiting for?'

'I wouldn't mind shuttling the drinks along,' I said. 'But what about the food? This food is good, you'd have to admit. That's where these caterers excel.'

'Food. Yes, their food's all right,' he said grudgingly.

We'd finished every crumb and I could have eaten the whole lot again. Orkney returned to the subject of Breezy Palm and two drinks later had exhausted even Isabella's long-suffering patience.

'If you want me to drive you home, Orkney, the time is now,' she said. 'You may not have noticed that they ran the last race ten minutes ago.'

'Really?' He looked at his watch and surprisingly took immediate action, standing up and collecting his papers. 'Very well then. Flora, I'll be talking to Jack on the telephone . . . and er . . .' he made an effort to remember my name as the rest of us stood up also. 'Good to have met you . . . er . . . Tony.' He nodded twice in lieu of shaking hands. 'Any time you're here with Flora . . . glad to have you.'

'Thank you, Orkney,' I said.

Isabella bent to give Flora a kiss in the air an inch off her cheek and looked vaguely at my sling, finding like Orkney that hands unavailable for shaking left goodbyes half unsaid.

'Er . . .' she said, 'so nice . . .'

They went away down the hallway and Flora sat down again abruptly.

'Thank goodness that's over,' she said fervently. 'I'd never have got through it without you. Thank goodness he liked you.'

'Liked?' I was sceptical.

'Oh yes, dear, he asked you back, that's practically unheard of.'

'How did Isabella,' I asked, 'get him to go home?'

Flora smiled the first carefree smile of the day, her eyes crinkling with fun. 'My dear, they will certainly have come in her car, and if he didn't go when she says she would drive off and leave him. She did it once . . . there was a terrible fuss and Jack and I had to put him on a train. Because, as you've noticed dear, he likes his gin and a few months ago he was breathalysed on the way home and lost his licence . . . but he doesn't like one to talk about that either.'

After the races, during the evening shift in the shop, I telephoned again to Henri Tavel in Bordeaux and listened without much surprise to his news.

'Mon cher Tony, there is no Château Caillot in St Estèphe. There is no Château Caillot in Haut Médoc. There is no Château Caillot in the whole region of Bordeaux.'

'One thought there might not be,' I said.

'As for the *négociant* Thiery et Fils ...' the heavy Gallic shrug travelled almost visibly along the wires, ' ... there is no person called Thiery who is *négociant* in Bordeaux. As you know, some people call themselves *négociants* who work only in paper and never see the wine they sell, but even among these there is no Thiery.'

'You've been most thorough, Henri.'

'To forge wine labels is a serious matter.'

His voice, vibrating deeply, reflected an outrage no less genuine for being unsurprised. To Henri Tavel, as to all the château owners and wineshippers of Bordeaux, wine transcended religion. Conscious and proud of producing the best in the world they worked to stiff bureaucratic criteria which had been laid down in Médoc in 1855 and only fractionally changed since.

They still spoke of 1816, a year of undrinkable quality, as if it were fresh in their memory. They knew the day the grape harvest had started every year back beyond 1795 (September 24th). They knew that wine had been made uninterruptedly in their same vineyards for at least two thousand years.

Every single bottle of the five hundred and fifty million sent out from the region each year had to be certified and accounted for; had to be worthy of the name it bore; had to be able to uphold the reputation for the whole of its life. And the life of a Bordeaux red wine could be amazing ... With Henri Tavel I had myself tasted one ninety years old which still shone with colour and sang on the palate.

To forge a Bordeaux château label and stick it on an amorphous product of the European wine lake was a heresy of burning-at-the-stake proportions. Henri Tavel wanted assurances that the forgers of Caillot would feel the flames. I could offer only weak-sounding promises that everyone would do their best.

'It is important,' he insisted.

'Yes, I know it is. Truly, Henri, I do know.'

'Give my regards,' he said, 'to your dear mother.'

Life continued normally on the next day, Wednesday, if a disgruntledly itching arm could be considered normal. I was due to take it back to the hospital for inspection the following afternoon and meanwhile went on using the sling much of the time, finding it comfortable and a good excuse for not lifting the cases. Brian had become anxiously solicitous at the sight of it and carefully took even single bottles out of my grasp. Mrs Palissey was writing down the telephone orders to save me the wincing. I felt cossetted and amused.

She and Brian left early with the deliveries because there were so many: some postponed and some in advance, including the glasses and champagne for the next day's coming-of-age. I kept shop, smiling, ever smiling as usual, and thinking, when I could.

Shortly after eight in the evening Gerard walked in looking grey and tired and asking if I could shut the damned place and come out and eat. Somewhere quiet. He wanted to talk.

I looked at the fatigued lines in his face and the droop of his normally erect body. I was twenty years younger than he and I hadn't had a general anaesthetic, and if in spite of taking things fairly easy I still felt battered and weak, then he must feel worse. And maybe the cause wasn't simply the profusion of little burning stab wounds but the residue also from the horsebox . . . the *frissons* of nearness to death.

'We could take Sung Li's food home to my house,' I suggested diffidently, 'if you'd like.'

He would like, he said. He would also buy the food while I fiddled with the till and locked up, and how soon would that be?

'Half an hour,' I said. 'Have some wine.'

He sighed with resignation, sat on the chair I brought from the office and ruefully smiled at our two slings.

'Snap' he said.

'Flora's idea, mine.'

'Sensible lady.'

'I'll get the wine.'

In the office I poured some genuine wine from St Estèphe and some of the Silver Moondance version into two glasses and carried them out to the counter.

'Taste them both,' I said. 'Say what you think.'

'What are they?'

'Tell you later.'

'I'm no expert,' he protested. He sipped the first,

however, rolling it round his gums and grimacing as if he'd sucked a lemon.

'Very dry,' he said.

'Try the other.'

The second seemed at first to please him better, but after a while he eyed it thoughtfully and put the glass down carefully on the counter.

'Well?' I asked.

He smiled. 'The first is demanding. The second is pleasant ... but light. You're going to tell me that the first is more expensive.'

'Pretty good. The second one, the pleasant but light one, came from the Silver Moondance. The first is near enough what it should have tasted like, according to the label.'

He savoured the various significances. 'Many might prefer the fake. People who didn't know what to expect.'

'Yes. A good drink. Nothing wrong with it.'

He sipped the genuine article again. 'But once you know this one, you grow to appreciate it.'

'If I had any just now I'd give you one of the great St Estèphes ... Cos d'Estournel, Montrose, Calon-Ségur ... but this is a good cru bourgeois ... lots of body and force.'

'Take your word for it,' he said amiably. 'I've often wished I knew more about wine.'

'Stick around.'

I tasted both the wines again myself, meeting them

as old friends. The Silver Moondance wine had stood up pretty well to being opened and refastened, but now that I'd poured the second sample out of the bottle what was left would begin to deteriorate. For wine to remain perfect it had to be in contact with the cork. The more air in the bottle the more damage it did.

I fetched and showed him both of the bottles, real and fake, and told him what Henri Tavel had had to say about forgeries.

He listened attentively, thought for a while, and then said, 'What is it about the fake wine that seems more significant to you than the fake whisky? Because it does, doesn't it?'

'Just as much. Equally.'

'Why, then?'

'Because . . .' I began, and was immediately interrupted by a row of customers wanting to know what to drink inexpensively with Sung Li's crispy duck and Peking prawn and beef in oyster sauce. Gerard listened with interest and watched them go one by one with their bottles of Bergerac and Soave and Côtes du Ventoux.

He said, 'You sell knowledge, don't you, as much as wine?'

'Yeah. And pleasure. And human contact. Anything you can't get from a supermarket.'

A large man with eyes awash shouldered his way unsteadily into the shop demanding beer loudly, and I sold him what he wanted without demur. He paid clumsily, belched, went on his weaving way: and Gerard frowned at his departing back.

'He was drunk,' he said.

'Sure.'

'Don't you care?'

'Not as long as they're not sick in the shop,'

'That's immoral.'

I grinned faintly. 'I sell escape also.'

'Temporary,' he objected disapprovingly, sounding austerely Scots.

'Temporary is better than nothing,' I said. 'Have an aspirin.'

He made a noise between a cough and a chuckle. 'I suppose you've lived on them since Sunday.'

'Yes, quite right.' I swallowed two more with some St Estèphe, in itself a minor heresy. 'I'm all for escape.'

He gave me a dry look which I didn't at first understand, and only belatedly remembered my rush down the yard.

'Well . . . as long as I'm not being robbed.'

He nodded sardonically and waited through two more sales and a discussion about whether Sauternes would go with lamb chops, which it wouldn't; they would each taste dreadful.

'What goes with Sauternes then? I like Sauternes.'

'Anything sweet,' I said. 'Also perhaps curry. Or ham. Also blue cheese.'

'Good heavens,' said Gerard when he'd gone. 'Blue cheese with sweet wine . . . how odd.'

'Wine and cheese parties thrive on it.'

He looked round the shop as if at a new world. 'Is there anything you can't drink wine with?' he said.

'As far as I'm concerned . . . grapefruit.'

He made a face.

'And that's from one,' I said, 'who drinks wine with baked beans . . . who practically scrubs his teeth in it.'

'You really love it?'

I nodded. 'Nature's magical accident.'

'What?'

'That the fungus on grapes turns the sugar in grape juice to alcohol. That the result is delicious.'

'For heaven's sake . . .'

'No one could have invented it,' I said. 'It's just there. A gift to the planet. Elegant.'

'But there are all sorts of different wines.'

'Oh, sure, because there are different sorts of grapes. But a lot of champagne is made from black-skinned grapes . . . things may not be as they seem, which should please you as a detective.'

'Hm,' he said dryly. His glance roved over the racks of bottles. 'As a detective what pleases me is proof . . . so what's proof?'

'If you mix a liquid with gunpowder and ignite it, and it burns with a steady blue flame, that's proof.'

He looked faintly bemused. 'Proof of what?'

'Proof that the liquid is at least fifty per cent alcohol. That's how they proved a liquid was alcohol three centuries ago when they first put a tax on distilled spirits.

Fifty per cent alcohol, one hundred per cent proved. They measure the percentage now with hydrometers, not gunpowder and fire. Less risky, I dare say.'

'Gunpowder,' he said, 'is something you and I have had too much of recently.' He stood up stiffly. 'Your half-hour is up. I'll get the food.'

CHAPTER FOURTEEN

Gerard followed me home in his mended Mercedes and came into the house bearing Sung Li's fragrant parcels.

'You call this a cottage?' he said sceptically, looking at perspectives. 'More like a palace.'

'It was a cottage beside a barn, both of them falling to pieces. The barn was bigger than the cottage . . . hence the space.'

We had joyfully planned that house, Emma and I, shaping the rooms to fit what we'd expected to be our lives, making provision for children. A big kitchen for family meals; a sitting room, future playroom; a dining room for friends; many bedrooms; a large quiet drawing room, splendid for parties. The conversion, done in three stages as we could afford it, had taken nearly five years. Emma had contentedly waited, wanting the nest to be ready for the chicks, and almost the moment it was done she had become pregnant.

Gerard and I had come into the house through the kitchen, but I seldom ate there any more. When the food was re-heated and in dishes we transferred it to the sitting room, putting it on a coffee table between two comfortable chairs and eating with our plates balanced on our knees.

It was in that warm-looking room with its bookshelves, soft lamplight, television, photographs and rugs that I mostly lived, when I was there at all. It was there that I now kept a wine rack and glasses lazily to hand and averted my mind from chores like gardening. It was there, I dare say, that my energy was chronically at its lowest ebb, yet it was to there also that I instinctively returned.

Gerard looked better for the food, settling deep into his chair when he'd finished with a sigh of relaxation. He put his arm back in its sling and accepted coffee and a second glass of Californian wine, a 1978 Napa Cabernet Sauvignon I'd been recently selling and liked very much myself.

'It's come a long way,' Gerard observed, reading the label.

'And going further,' I said. 'California's growing grapes like crazy, and their best wine is world class.'

He drank a little and shook his head. 'It's pleasant enough but I honestly couldn't tell it from any old plonk. A terrible admission, but there you are.'

'Just what the Silver Moondance ordered . . . customers like you.'

He smiled. 'And I'd guess I'm in the majority.'

'It doesn't matter. Liking wine at all is the main thing.'

He said, 'You were going to tell me why the substitute wines were equally as important as the substitute scotch at the Silver Moondance.'

I glanced at him, hearing the hardening tone in the sub-Scottish voice and seeing the same change in him as there had been in the car the previous Sunday: the shedding of the social shell, the emergence of the investigator. His eyes were steady and intent, his face concentrated, the mouth unsmiling: and I answered this second man with recognition and relief, dealing in facts and guesses dispassionately.

'People who steal Scotch whisky,' I said, 'usually go for a shipment of bottles in cases. The proceeds are ready to sell . . . the receiver's probably already lined up. There's no difficulty. It's all profit. But if you steal a tankerful of the liquid in bulk you have the trouble and expense of bottling it. Cost of bottles, cost of labour, all sorts of incidentals.'

'Right,' he said nodding.

'There were six thousand gallons of Scotch at roughly fifty-eight per cent alcohol content in each of Kenneth Charter's three lost loads.'

'Right.'

'Each load was of a higher concentration than is ever sold for drinking. When they received the tanker-load the Rannoch people would have added water to bring the Scotch down to retail strength, around forty per cent alcohol by volume.'

Gerard listened and nodded.

'At that point they'd have enough Scotch to fill approximately fifty thousand bottles of standard size.'

Gerard's mouth opened slightly with surprise. 'Kenneth Charter never said that.'

'He shifts the stuff, he doesn't bottle it. He maybe never did the arithmetic. Anyway, with three tankersful we're talking about one hundred and fifty thousand bottles in six months, and that's not something you can mess about with in the back yard.'

He was silent for a while thinking about it, and then said merely, 'Go on.'

'On each occasion the whole load was pumped out of the tanker pretty fast, as the tanker was found empty on the following day.'

'Right.'

'So unless the point of the operation was simply to ruin Kenneth Charter, in which case it's conceivable the loads were dumped in ditches like the drivers, the Scotch was pumped from the tanker into some sort of storage.'

'Yes, of course.'

'So the logical place for the tanker to be unloaded was at a bottling plant.'

'Yes, but it never reached there.'

'It never reached Rannoch's bottling plant. There's a difference.'

'All right.' His eyes smiled. 'Go on.'

'Fifty thousand bottles three times over isn't going to keep any reasonable plant in operation for anything like six months. Small châteaux bottle that much themselves in a few weeks without blinking. So ... um ... what if in between times the whisky bottling changed over to wine ... to Silver Moondance wine, to be precise?'

'Ah.' It was a deep note, an acknowledgement that we'd arrived at the centre of things. 'Carry on.'

'Well ... with a bottling plant it would be easy to fill any shape of bottle from a single source of wine ... and the shapes of the bottles at the Silver Moondance fitted the labels: claret bottles for claret labels, burgundy bottles for burgundy labels and so on. The very fact that there were both Scotch and wine under false labels at the Silver Moondance ... well, for the simplest explanation I'd bet you a pea to a case of Krug they were bottled in the same place.'

Gerard drank some of his wine absentmindedly.

'Where?' he said succinctly.

'Mm ... that's the rub.'

'Any ideas?'

'It did occur to me that it might be in one of those plants that Kenneth Charter described, that got into difficulties or went bust when the French started bottling more of their own wines. I mean ... suppose someone came to you if you were on the verge of bankruptcy and offered you work. Even if you knew it was crooked you might do it and keep quiet. Or suppose a bottling plant was for sale or lease at a ridiculous price, which they're bound to have been . . . if the game looked worth it . . . if it was going to go on maybe for years . . .'

'Yes,' Gerard said. 'It's possible.' He gave it about five seconds' thought. 'So provisionally we're looking for a bottling plant. Now let's shelve that for a moment.' He paused again, considering, and then said, 'In Deglet's we often work in pairs, discussing a case, bouncing ideas off each other, coming up sometimes with things neither of us had considered on our own. It's a way that I'm used to, that I like . . . but my usual partner's in London, and frankly I'm too tired to go there . . . and you're here on the doorstep loaded to the hairline with specialist knowledge . . . so do you mind letting me talk my ideas to you? And be sure to speak out if I start something in your thoughts. That's where the value of these sessions lies. Bouncing ideas back. Do you mind?'

'No, of course not. But I . . .'

'Just listen,' he said. 'Stop me if you've a comment. That's all there is to it.'

'All right.'

'And honestly . . . do you have any brandy?'

I smiled. 'Yes, I do. What would you like?'

'Anything.'

I gave him some Hine Antique, which he sighed over as if putting on friendly old shoes. I poured some for myself also on the grounds that people who said it had medicinal qualities weren't joking. If queasy, drink brandy, if tired, drink brandy, if suffering from green shivers and cold shakes . . . drink brandy.

'All right then,' he said, cradling his glass in the palm of one hand. 'First, review the status quo. Under that heading we have the prime and never-to-be-forgotten fact that our number one aim is to save Kenneth Charter's business without landing his son in jail. That's what we're being paid for. Justice and other considerations are secondary.'

He sipped his drink.

'Fact number two,' he went on, 'Kenneth Charter's son . . . whose name is also Kenneth, to be awkward, so we'll call him Kenneth Junior . . . Kenneth Charter Junior made the theft of the Scotch possible by telling Zarac of the Silver Moondance where to find the tanker.' He paused. 'We still have the unanswered question.'

'How did Kenneth Junior know Zarac?'

'Yes. Anyway, I've brought the photostats of the pages of Kenneth Junior's notebook.' He pulled a well-filled business-sized envelope from an inner pocket and laid it on the table. 'I'll leave these with you . . . see if you make anything from them that we haven't.'

He saw the doubt in my face. 'You'll try?' he said almost severely, and I without apology said, 'Yes.'

'Right, then. Fact three: Zarac passed on the message and wasn't present when the tanker was stolen.

Fact four: Scotch was being sold under the wrong labels at the Silver Moondance, which Zarac as head waiter must have known. Supposition arising: the substitute Scotch was part of an earlier load stolen from Charter's tankers. Any comment?'

I shook my head.

'Second supposition arising: Larry Trent knew his whisky and wines were cheating the customers.'

He stopped, waiting for an opinion. I said, 'I agree with that, yes. I'd say it was definite.'

'Supposition three: Larry Trent organized the theft of the tankers.'

I frowned.

'You don't think so?'

'I don't know,' I said. 'I never talked to him . . . can't make a first-hand guess. He certainly did have in his hands a great deal more cash than he would have made out of the Silver Moondance, but he said it was his brother's.' I told Gerard precisely what Orkney Swayle had told me at Martineau Park. 'Larry Trent was buying horses and shipping them abroad to be sold. As sweet a way as one can imagine of turning illegal money pure white.'

Gerard drank some brandy.

'Did you believe in the brother?' he asked.

'You mean, was it a case of the hypothetical friend? My friend has a problem, give me advice?'

He nodded.

'I would have thought so,' I said, 'except for one

967

thing which rang humanly true. Orkney said that Larry Trent said he, Larry, was buying the horses for his brother because his brother couldn't tell good from bad. About the only thing his brother couldn't do, he said. Orkney Swayle said Larry was envious. That sort of grudge sounds like a real brother to me. Or at any rate a real person. Partner, maybe.'

A small silence. We both thought about the partner who might or might not be a brother, and finally Gerard gave him his name. The name, anyway, that we knew him by.

'Paul Young.'

I agreed.

'Supposition four,' Gerard said. 'When Larry Trent was killed, Paul Young came to the Silver Moondance to take over, unaware that the police were investigating the drinks and unaware that Charter's tanker thefts had been linked with Zarac.'

'Those are certainties, not suppositions. I saw him arrive myself . . . he had no idea he was walking into trouble.'

'Right. And I'll add in a few certainties of my own at this point. I've spent all day interviewing people from the Silver Moondance, especially the waitress and the wet little assistant who were both there with you in the bar. They say that soon after you left, Paul Young told them to go home, the waitress until told to return and the assistant until the following day. Paul Young said he would discuss with the police about a re-opening date, and run the place himself until the manager returned from holiday. After that, Head Office would appoint a replacement for poor Mr Trent. None of the staff saw anything odd in his manner or proposals. Very sensible, they thought him, considering how angry he was about the drinks. He then sent the kitchen staff home, telling them also to return when told. The waitress said Zarac arrived for work just as she was leaving, and Paul Young told him to go into Larry Trent's office and wait for him.'

I was fascinated. 'Did she remember exactly what they said to each other?'

Gerard smiled thinly. 'She's used to remembering orders. An excellent ear. She said they knew each other . . . Paul Young called him Zarac without being told.'

'And the other way round?'

'She said Paul Young said "I'm Paul Young" which she thought silly because Zarac looked as if he knew him perfectly well.'

'Telling Zarac his alias.'

'Exactly. The waitress said Paul Young looked very angry with Zarac, which she thought natural, and she thought Zarac was going to get a right ticking off, which she was sorry about because Zarac was all right with the waitresses and kept his hands to himself, unlike some others she could mention.'

I appreciated the verbatim reporting. 'And who were those?'

'The manager, mostly.'

'Not Larry Trent?'

'No. Always the perfect gent, she said,' He paused. 'She said the police sergeant had been round before me, asking the same questions. She said he asked her about Paul Young's car.'

I was amused. 'What else did she say?'

'She said it was a Rolls.'

'Really?'

'Her exact words were "a black Roller with them tinted windows." She said it had to be Paul Young's because it was in the staff car park and it didn't belong to the regular staff, and it hadn't been there when she came to work an hour earlier.'

'Observant girl.'

Gerard nodded. 'I went to the wet assistant's home after I left the waitress and asked him mostly the same questions. He said he didn't know what car Paul Young had come in. He couldn't even describe Paul Young. Useless.'

'And the barman hoofed it.' I relayed Ridger's half-hearted search. 'I guess he knew he wasn't selling the right stuff, but you wouldn't get him to admit it, even if you found him.'

'No,' he agreed. 'So now we come to supposition . . . where are we? five? . . . supposition five: that Paul Young and Zarac spent the afternoon deciding what to do and organizing the removal of all the wines and spirits to look like burglary.'

'It would have taken them hours if they did it them-selves.'

'And they would have needed a van.'

'Large,' I said, nodding. 'There were dozens of cases.'

He put his head on one side. 'They had all day and all night, I suppose.'

'Do we know when Zarac actually died?' I asked.

Gerard shook his head. 'There was an opening inquest last Friday, adjourned for a week. The police aren't giving out much publicity on Zarac, but I've found a friend behind the forensic scenes and I'll hear everything the police know about times and so on by this Friday.'

'He suffocated . . .' I said with revulsion.

'It bothers you?'

'Like bricking up someone alive.'

'Much quicker,' he said prosaically. 'Supposition six: Paul Young and Zarac weren't the greatest of buddy-buddies.'

'A fair conclusion,' I said dryly.

'Supposition seven: Zarac was in some way a terrible threat to Paul Young.'

'Who solved the problem permanently.'

'Mm,' he reflected. 'So far, that seems reasonable. Any questions?'

'Yes . . . How did Paul Young happen to have plaster of Paris bandage with him on what he expected to be simply an organizational outing?'

'You mean it might be significant?'

971

'Something to add to what we know of him, anyway.'

'And why use it? Why not smash in his head?'

'Well, why?' I said.

'A warning to others, perhaps. Or genuine psychosis. Very nasty, in any case.' He drank some brandy. A brain alive above a flagging body. 'Our Mr Young is a middle-aged businessmen with a hearing aid, a black Rolls and a reason for carrying plaster of Paris. Pity we can't, as they say, run that lot through the computer.'

'Any self-respecting computer would come up with a consultant surgeon, ear, nose and throat.'

Gerard was startled. 'You don't suppose . . .? No, most unlikely.'

'Computers only spit out what you feed in.'

'Whereas you can feed countless facts into a human being and get no connections at all.' He sighed resignedly. 'All right, then. Work arising. Find out if Larry Trent had a brother. Search further to know how Kenneth Junior knew Zarac. Sort out bottling plants. And Rannoch, by the way, have posted to us profile analyses of the loads they sent in Charter's tankers. If you can wheedle a sample from the Silver Moondance out of your pal Ridger, I can get the comparisons made. For proof rather than speculation.' He paused. 'Anything else?'

'Well . . .' I hesitated.

'Go on.'

'Ramekin, then. The horse Flora saw Larry Trent buy at Doncaster Sales a year ago. If Ramekin was shipped abroad, someone shipped it. There aren't so very many shippers. They'd have Ramekin in their records ... racehorses have passports, like people. Masses of export documents, besides. If we could find the shipper we'd know the destination. Larry Trent might always have used the same shipper and sold all the horses through one agent at the same destination ... If you've set up a line, so to speak, you carry on using it. The agent at the far end might know ... just might know ... whose cash had bought the horses. The real owner, for whom Larry Trent was acting.'

He listened intently, but he said, 'That's stretching it.'

'I suppose so.'

'I'll see how much is involved.'

'Do you want me to do it?'

He shook his head. 'We'll do it in the office, if at all. We have country-wide phone books and our staff are used to that sort of routine. They make it sound enormously official and get the most surprising results. They'll do the bottling plant sales and leases first; a long job but more promising.'

'I suppose it would be too simple ...' I began diffidently.

'What would?'

'I mean ... you could try them first ... there's nothing to lose ...'

'Do get on,' he said.

I felt foolish. I said, 'The plants to which Kenneth Charter took red wine in his tankers.'

Gerard looked at me levelly for a while with unblinking eyes. 'Right,' he said eventually, without inflection. 'We'll start with those. As you say, nothing to lose.' He looked at his watch and took the second-to-last mouthful of his brandy. 'Tina will be locking me out.'

'Come any time,' I said.

I didn't mean to sound lonely, but maybe that's what he heard. He looked at the photograph of Emma and myself on our wedding day which stood on a table near him in a silver frame. We were laughing in a shower of bubbles from a shaken-up champagne bottle in the hands of my best man, and Emma had liked the picture for its informality. 'Most brides and grooms look like waxworks,' she'd said. 'At least you can tell we were alive.'

'You were a good-looking couple,' Gerard said neutrally. 'And happy.'

'Yes.'

'How did she die?'

He asked it straightforwardly, without emotion, and after a moment I answered him similarly, as I had learned to do, as if it had happened to someone else.

'She had a sub-arachnoid haemorrhage. Something called Berry's Aneurism. In effect a blood vessel split in her brain.'

'But . . .' His gaze slid to the photograph, ' . . . how old was she?'

'Twenty-seven.'

'So young.'

'Apparently it can happen at any age.'

'I'm so sorry.'

'She was pregnant,' I said, and surprised myself. I normally didn't say that. Normally I said the absolute minimum. But to Gerard, after months of silence, I found myself slowly telling it all, wanting to and not wanting to, trying to keep my voice steady and not cry . . . for God's sake don't cry.

'She'd been having headaches on and off for ages. Then she had backaches. Nothing specific. Just aches in her spine. Everyone put it down to her being pregnant. And it passed off . . . until next time. Every week or so, for a day or two. One Sunday when she was nearly six months pregnant she woke up with one of those headaches, a fairly bad one. She took some aspirins but they never did much good. It got worse during the morning and when I went to do the midday stint in the shop she said she would go to bed and sleep it off. But when I got back she was crying . . . moaning . . . with pain. I tried to get a doctor . . . but it took ages . . . it was Sunday afternoon . . . Sunday . . . An ambulance finally came for her but by then she was begging me . . . begging me somehow to knock her out . . . but how could I? I couldn't. We were both terrified . . . more than frightened . . . it was so implacable . . . she was in awful agony in the ambulance . . . hitting her head with her fists . . . nothing I could do . . . I couldn't even hold her . . . she was yelling, rolling, jerking with pain. At the end of the journey she went slowly unconscious, and I was glad for her, even though by then I feared . . . well, I feared.'

'My dear man.'

I sat for a while looking back to the past, and then swallowed and told him the rest of it coldly.

'She was in a coma for four days, going deeper . . . I stayed with her. They let me stay. They said they couldn't save the baby, it was too soon. In another month, perhaps . . . They told me the blood vessel must have been leaking for ages . . . it was the blood leaking into her brain and down her spinal nerves that had given her the headaches and backaches . . . but even if they'd diagnosed the trouble earlier they couldn't have done much . . . it would have split open more one day, as it did . . . so perhaps it was better we didn't know.'

I stopped. No tears. All I couldn't have borne at that point was sympathy, and Gerard didn't offer it.

'Life's most unfair,' he said calmly.

'Yes.'

He didn't say I would get over it, or that time was a great healer. He didn't say I would find another girl. Marry again . . . I approved of Gerard more and more.

'Thank you for telling me,' he said.

'I don't usually,' I said apologetically.

'No. Flora told me. You clam up, she said, if anyone asks.'

'Flora chatters.'

'Chattering does good, sometimes.'

I was silent. What I felt, having told him about Emma, was a sort of release. Chattering helped. Sometimes.

He finished his brandy and stood up to go. 'If you have any more thoughts, telephone.'

'OK.'

He walked towards the door and stopped by a side table upon which stood three or four more photo frames among Emma's collection of shells.

'Your mother?' he asked, picking up the lady on horseback with hounds. 'Most handsome.'

'Mother,' I nodded.

He put her down. Picked up another. 'Father?'

'Father.'

He looked at the strong amused face above the colonel's uniform with its double row of medal ribbons, at the light in the eyes and the tilt of the chin, at the firm half-smiling mouth.

'You're like him,' Gerard said.

'Only in looks.' I turned away. 'I loved him when I was small. Adored him. He died when I was eleven.'

He put the picture down and peered at the others. 'No brothers or sisters?'

'No.' I grinned faintly. 'My birth interfered with a whole season's hunting. Once was enough, my mother said.'

Gerard glanced at me. 'You don't mind?'

'No, I never did. I never minded being alone until I

got used to something else.' I shrugged abruptly. 'I'm basically all right alone. I will be again, in the end.'

Gerard merely nodded and moved on out into the hall and from there to the kitchen and beyond to the rear door, where neither of us shook hands because of the slings.

'A most productive and interesting evening,' he said.

'I enjoy your company.'

He seemed almost surprised. 'Do you? Why?'

'You don't expect too much.'

'Like what?'

'Like ... er ... Chinese takeaway on your knees.' It wasn't what I truly meant, but it would do.

He made an untranslatable noise low in his throat, hearing the evasion and not agreeing with it. 'I expect more than you think. You underestimate yourself.' He smiled sardonically. 'Good night.'

'Good night.'

He drove away and I locked the doors and went back through the house to fetch the supper dishes, to stack them in the dishwasher. I thought of what I'd said to him about being all right alone, hearing in memory in the accumulated voices of years of customers the sighs and sadnesses of the bereaved. They talked of the common experience that was freshly awful for each individual. Two years, they said, was what it took. Two years before the sun shone. After two years the lost person became a memory, the loss itself bearable. I'd listened to them long before I thought of needing their wisdom, and I believed them still. Grief couldn't be escaped, but it would pass.

I finished tidying downstairs and went up to bed, to the room where Emma and I had made love.

I still slept there. She often seemed extraordinarily near. I woke sometimes in the early hours and stretched out for her, forgetting. I heard the memory of her giggle in the dark.

We had been lucky in love; passionate and well matched, equal in satisfaction. I remembered chiefly her stomach flat, her breasts unswollen, remembered the years of utter fun, her gleeful orgasms, the sharp incredible ecstasy of ejaculation. It was better to remember that.

The room was quiet now. No unseen presence. No restless spirit hovering.

If I lived with ghosts, they were within me: Emma, my father and the titanic figure of my grandfather, impossibly brave. They lived in me not condemning but unconsoling. I struggled forever to come to terms with them, for if I didn't I was sunk, but all three of their shadows fell long.

Pregnancy might recently have raised Emma's blood pressure, they'd said. It was quite common. Higher blood pressure would have put too much strain on the slow leak, opening it wider . . . too wide.

Pregnancy itself, they'd said, had tipped the scales towards death. Although we had both wanted children, the seed that I'd planted had killed her.

CHAPTER FIFTEEN

I let myself into the shop the next morning wondering what I could trade with Sergeant Ridger for a sample of the Silver Moondance Scotch, and he solved the problem himself by appearing almost immediately at my door as if transported by telekinesis.

'Morning,' he said, as I let him in. Raincoat belted, shoes polished, hair brushed. Hadn't he heard, I wondered, that plain-clothes policemen these days were supposed to dress in grubby jeans and look unemployed?

'Good morning,' I replied, shutting the door behind him. 'Can I sell you something?'

'Information.' He was serious, as always, coming into the centre of the shop and standing solidly there with his feet apart.

'Ah. Yes, well fire away.'

'Is your arm worse? You didn't have a sling last time I came.'

'No worse.' I shook my head. 'More comfortable.'

He looked not exactly relieved but reassured. 'Good.

Then . . . I'm making an official request to you to aid us in our inquiries.'

'What aid? What inquiries?'

'This is a direct suggestion from Detective Chief Superintendent Wilson.'

'Is it?' I was interested. 'To me personally?'

'He suggested you himself, yes.' Ridger cleared his throat. 'It is in connection with our inquiries into complaints received about goods supplied by licensed premises other than the Silver Moondance.'

'Er . . .' I said. 'Sergeant, would you drop the jargon?'

Ridger looked surprised. What he'd said had been obviously of crystal clarity to his notebook mind. He said, 'In the course of our investigations into the murder of Zarac it was suggested that we should follow up certain other complaints of malpractice throughout the whole area. There was a top level regional conference yesterday, part of which I attended as the officer first on the spot in the drinks fraud, and Chief Superintendent Wilson requested me directly to enlist your help as before. He said if we could find another place passing off one whisky as another, and if such whisky were similar or identical to that in the Silver Moondance, we might also find a lead to Zarac's supplier and murderer. It was worth a try, he said, as there were so few other lines of inquiry. So, er, here I am.'

I gazed at him in awe. 'You're asking me to go on a pub crawl?'

'Er . . . if you must put it like that, yes.'

Beautiful, I thought. Stunning. Fifty thousand bars between home and Watford . . . with the known bad apples offered on the platter of a police list.

'Would you be driving me, like last time?' I asked.

'I've been assigned to that duty.' He showed no feelings either for or against. 'Can I take it you will be available?'

'You can,' I said. 'When?'

He consulted his bristling wristwatch. 'Ten-fifteen.'

'This morning?'

'Of course. I'll go back now and report and return for you later.'

'All right,' I said. 'And Sergeant, when you return, would you bring with you the Bell's whisky bottle from the Silver Moondance bar?'

He looked concentratedly doubtful.

'I'd like to taste its contents again,' I explained. 'It's ten days since that morning in the Silver Moondance. If more of that Scotch is what you're looking for in these inquiries, I'll have to learn it well enough to know it anywhere.'

He saw the logic. 'I'll request it.'

'Mm . . . say it's a requirement. I can't do what you're asking without it.'

'Very well.' He pulled out the notebook and wrote in it, rolling his wrist for another time check and adding nine-fourteen punctiliously.

'How many places are we going to?' I asked.

'It's quite a long list.' He spoke matter-of-factly. 'It's a big area, of course. My Chief Inspector's hoping we can complete the inquiry within two weeks.'

'Two weeks!'

'Working from ten-thirty to two o'clock daily in licensing hours.'

'Is this an official appointment with pay?'

He checked internally before he answered. 'It was being discussed.'

'And?'

'They used to have an available consultant expert, but he's just retired to live in Spain. He was paid. Sure to have been.'

'How often was he . . . consulted?'

'Don't rightly know. I only saw him once or twice. He could tell things by taste like you. The Customs and Excise people use instruments, same as the Weights and Measures. They're concerned with alcohol content, not flavour.'

'Did they check any of the places on your list?'

He said, 'All of them,' disapprovingly, and I remembered what he'd said before about someone in one of those two departments tipping off the Silver Moondance that investigators were on their way.

'With no luck?' I asked.

'No prosecutions have resulted.'

Quite so. 'All right, Sergeant. You drive, I'll drink, and I've got to be sober and back here by three to get my arm checked at the hospital.'

He went away looking smug and at nine-thirty to the half-minute Mrs Palissey arrived with Brian. I explained that I would be away every midday for a while and said I would get her some help by tomorrow if she could possibly manage that morning on her own.

'Help?' She was affronted. 'I don't need help.'

'But your lunch-hour . . .'

'I'll bring our lunch and we'll eat in the back,' she said. 'I don't want strangers in here meddling. Brian and I will see to things. You go off and enjoy yourself, you're still looking peaky.'

I was about to say that I wasn't doing police work to enjoy myself but then it occurred to me that I probably was. I'd had no hesitation at all in accepting Ridger's – or Wilson's – invitation. I was flattered to be thought an expert. Deplorable vanity. Laugh at yourself, Tony. Stay human.

For an hour the three of us restocked the shop, made lists, took telephone orders, served customers, swept and dusted. I looked back when I left with Ridger: to a clean, cosy, welcoming place with Mrs Palissey smiling behind the counter and Brian arranging wine boxes with anxious care. I wasn't an empire builder, I thought. I would never start a chain. That one prosperous place was enough.

Prosperous, I knew, against the odds. A great many small businesses like mine had died of trying to compete with chains and supermarkets, those giants engaged in such fierce undercutting price wars that they bled their own profits to death. I'd started that way and began losing money, and, against everything believed and advised in the trade, had restored my position by going back to fair, not suicidal prices. The losses had stopped, my customers had multiplied, not deserted, and I'd begun to enjoy life instead of waking up at night sweating.

Ridger had brought the Bell's bottle with him in his car; it sat upright on the back seat in the same box in which it had left the Silver Moondance, two-thirds full, as before.

'Before we go,' I said, 'I'll take that whisky into the shop and taste it there.'

'Why not here?'

'The car smells of petrol.' A gift, I thought.

'I've just filled up. What does it matter?'

'Petrol smells block out Scotch.'

'Oh. All right.' He got out of his car, removed the box and methodically locked his doors although the car was right outside the shop and perfectly visible through the window: then he carried the box in and set it on the counter.

Casually I slipped my wrist out of the sling, picked up the Bell's bottle, took it back to the office, and with a clink or two poured a good measure through a funnel into a clean small bottle I'd put ready, and then a very little into a goblet. The small bottle had a screw-on cap which I caught against the thread in my haste, but it was closed and hidden with the funnel behind box-files in an instant, and I walked unhurriedly back into the shop sipping thoughtfully at the glass, right wrist again supported.

Ridger was coming towards me. 'I'm not supposed to let that bottle out of my sight,' he said.

'Sorry.' I gestured with the glass. 'It's just on the desk in the office. Perfectly safe.'

He peered into the recess to make sure and turned back nodding. 'How long will you be?'

'Not long.'

The liquid in my mouth was definitely Rannoch, I thought. Straightforward Rannoch. Except that . . .

'What's the matter?' Ridger demanded; and I realized I'd been frowning.

'Nothing,' I said, looking happier. 'If you want to know if I'll recognize it again, then yes, I will.'

'You're sure?'

'Yes.'

'Why are you smiling?'

'Sergeant,' I said with exasperation, 'this is a collaboration not an inquisition. Let's take the bottle and get the show on the road.'

I wondered if Sergeant Ridger ever achieved friendship; if his suspicious nature ever gave him a rest. Certainly after all our meetings I found his porcupine reflexes as sensitive as at the beginning, and I made no attempt to placate him, as any such attempt would in itself be seen as suspicious.

He drove away from the kerb saying that he would

visit the nearest places first, with which I could find no quarrel, and I discovered that by nearest he meant nearest to the Silver Moondance. He turned off the main road about a mile before we reached it, and stopped in a village outside a country pub.

As an inn it had been old when Queen Anne died, when coaches had paused there to change horses. The building of the twentieth-century highway had left the pub in a backwater, the old coaching road a dead end now, an artery reduced to an appendix. Emma and I had drunk a few times there, liking the old bulging building with the windows leaning sideways and the Stuart brickwork still in the fireplaces.

'Not here!' I said, surprised, as we stopped.

'Do you know it?'

'I've been here, but not for a year.'

Ridger consulted a clipboard. 'Complaints of whisky being watered, gin ditto. Complaints investigated, found to be unfounded. Investigations dated August 23rd and September 18th last.'

'The landlord's a retired cricketer,' I said. 'Generous. Loves to talk. Lazy. The place needs a facelift.'

'Landlord: Noel George Darnley.'

I turned my head, squinting down at the page. 'Different man.'

'Right.' Ridger climbed out of the car and carefully locked it. 'I'll have a tomato juice.'

'Who's paying?'

Ridger looked blank. 'I haven't much money . . .'

'No instructions?' I asked. 'No police float?'

He cleared his throat. 'We must keep an account,' he said.

'OK,' I said. 'I'll pay. We'll write down at each place what I spend and you'll initial it.'

He agreed to that. Whether the police would reimburse me or not I didn't know, but Kenneth Charter very likely would, if not. If neither did, no great matter.

'And what if we find a match?' I asked.

He was on surer ground. 'We impound the bottle, sealing it, labelling it, and giving a receipt.'

'Right.'

We walked into the pub as customers, Ridger as relaxed as guitar strings.

The facelift, I saw at once, had occurred, but I found I preferred the old wrinkles. True, the worn Indian rugs with threadbare patches had needed renewing, but not with orange and brown stripes. The underpolished knobbly oak benches had vanished in favour of smooth leather-look vinyl, and there were shiny modern brass ornaments on the mantel instead of antique pewter platters.

The new landlord's new broom had resulted, however, in a much cleaner-looking bar, and the landlord himself, appearing from the rear, wasn't fat, sloppily dressed and beaming, but neat, thin and characterless. In the old days the pub had been full: I wondered how many of the regulars still came.

'A Bell's whisky, please,' I said. I looked at his row

of bottles. 'And a second Bell's whisky from that bottle over there, and a tomato juice, please.'

He filled the order without conversation. We carried the glasses to a small table and I began on the unlikely task with a judicious trial of the first tot of Bell's.

'Well?' Ridger asked, after fidgeting a full minute. 'What have we got?'

I shook my head. 'It's Bell's all right. Not like the Silver Moondance.'

Ridger had left his clipboard in the car, otherwise I was sure he would have crossed off mine host there and then.

I tried the second Bell's. No luck there either.

As far as I could tell, neither bottle had been watered: both samples seemed full strength. I told Ridger so while he was making inroads into the tomato juice, which he genuinely seemed to enjoy.

I left both whiskies on the table and wandered to the bar.

'You're new here?' I said.

'Fairly.' He seemed cautious, not friendly.

'Settling in well with the locals?' I asked.

'Are you here to make trouble?'

'No.' I was surprised at the resentment he hadn't bothered to hide. 'What do you mean?'

'Sorry, then. It was you ordering two whiskies from different bottles and tasting them carefully, as you did. Someone round here made trouble with the Weights and Measures, saying I gave short measures and watered the spirits. Some of them round here don't like me smartening the place up. But I ask you, trying to get me fined or lose my licence . . . too much.'

'Yes,' I agreed. 'Malicious.'

He turned away, still not sure of me, which was fair enough, considering. I collected Ridger who was wiping red stains from his mouth and we went outside leaving the unfinished whiskies on the table, which probably hardened the landlord's suspicions into certainty, poor man.

Ridger ticked off the pub on the clipboard and read out the notes of our next destination, which proved to be a huge soulless place built of brick in the thirties and run for a brewery by a prim-looking tenant with a passion for fresh air. Even Ridger in his raincoat shivered before the thrown-open windows of the bar and muttered that the place looked dull. We were the first customers, it was true, but on a greyly chilly morning there were no electric lights to warm and welcome thirsty strangers.

'Tomato juice, please,' I said. 'And a Bell's whisky.'

The puritan landlord provided them, stating the price in a tight-lipped way.

'And could we have the windows closed, please?'

The landlord looked at his watch, shrugged, and went round closing October out with ill grace. I wouldn't sell much in my shop, I reflected, with that scowl: everyone sought to buy more than the product they asked for and it was the intangible extra that repelled or attracted a return. The whisky in that place might be fine, but I'd never go back out of choice.

'Well?' Ridger said, initialling the cost on our list. 'What is it?'

'Bell's.'

Ridger nodded, drinking this time barely a mouthful from his glass. 'Shall we go, then?'

'Glad to.'

We left the landlord bitterly reopening his windows and Ridger consulted his clipboard in the car.

'The next place is a hotel, the Peverill Arms, on the Reading to Henley road. Several complaints of thin or tasteless whisky. Complaints investigated, September 12th. Whisky found to be full strength in random samples.'

His voice told something more than the usual dry information: a reservation, almost an alarm.

'You know the place?' I asked.

'I've been there. Disturbances.' He fell silent with determination and started the car, driving with dis-approval quivering in the stiffness of his neck. I thought from these signs that we might be on the way to a rowdy rendezvous with Hell's Angels, but found to my amusement on arrival that Ridger's devil was a woman.

A woman moreover of statuesque proportions, rising six feet tall with the voluptuous shape of Venus de Milo, who had forty-two-inch hips.

'Mrs Alexis,' Ridger muttered. 'She may not remember me.'

Mrs Alexis indeed gave our arrival scarcely a glance. Mrs Alexis was supervising the lighting of logs in the vast fireplace in the entrance lounge, an enterprise presently producing acrid smoke in plenty but few actual flames.

Apart from the heavyside layer floating in a haze below the ceiling the hall gave a lift to the entering spirit: clusters of chintz-covered armchairs, warm colours, gleaming copper jugs, an indefinable aura of success. Across the far end an extensive bar stood open but untended, and from the fireplace protruded the trousered behind of the luckless firelighter, to the interest and entertainment of scattered armchaired guests.

'For God's sake, Wilfred, fetch the bloody bellows,' Mrs Alexis said distinctly. 'You look idiotic with your arse in the air puffing like a beetroot.'

She was well over fifty, I judged, with the crisp assurance of a natural commander. Handsome, expensively dressed, gustily uninhibited. I found myself smiling in the same instant that the corners of Ridger's mouth turned down.

The unfortunate Wilfred removed his beetroot-red face from the task and went off obediently, and Mrs Alexis with bright eyes asked what we wanted.

'Drinks,' I said vaguely.

'Come along then.' She led the way, going towards the bar. 'It's our first fire this winter. Always smokes like hell until we get it going.' She frowned upwards at the drifting cloud. 'Worse than usual, this year.'

'The chimney needs sweeping,' Ridger said.

Mrs Alexis gave him a birdlike look from an eye as sharp and yellow as a hawk's. 'It's swept every year in the spring. And aren't you that policeman who told me if I served the local rugger team when they'd won I should expect them to swing from the chandeliers and put beer into my piano?'

Ridger cleared his throat. I swallowed a laugh with difficulty and received the full beam from the hawk eyes.

'Are you a policeman too?' she asked with good humour. 'Come to cadge for your bloody ball?'

'No,' I said. I could feel the smothered laugh escaping through my eyes. 'We came for a drink.'

She believed the simple answer as much as a declaration of innocence from a red-handed thief, but went around behind her bar and waited expectantly.

'A Bell's whisky and a tomato juice, please.'

She pushed a glass against the Bell's bottle and waited for the full measure to descend. 'Anything else?'

I said no thank you and she steered the whisky my way and the tomato juice towards Ridger, accepting my money and giving change. We removed ourselves to a pair of armchairs near a small table, where Ridger again initialled our itemized account.

'What happened with the rugger club?' I asked interestedly.

993

His face showed profound disapproval. 'She knew there'd be trouble. They're a rowdy lot. They pulled the chandeliers clean out of the ceiling with a lot of plaster besides and she had them lined up against the wall at gunpoint by the time we got here.'

'Gunpoint?' I said, astonished.

'It wasn't loaded, but the rugger club weren't taking chances. They knew her reputation against pheasants.'

'A shotgun?'

'That's right. She keeps it there behind the bar. We can't stop her, though I'd like to, personally, but she's got a licence for it. She keeps it there to repel villains, she says, though there isn't a local villain who'd face her.'

'Did she send to you for help with the rugger club?'

'Not her. Some of the other customers. She wasn't much pleased when we turned up. She said there wasn't a man born she couldn't deal with.' Ridger looked as if he believed it. 'She wouldn't bring charges for all the damage, but I heard they paid up pretty meekly.'

It would be a brave man, I reflected, who told Mrs Alexis that her Bell's whisky was Rannoch: but in fact it wasn't. Bell's it was: unadulterated.

'Pity,' Ridger said, at the news.

I said thoughtfully, 'She has some Laphroaig up there on the top shelf.'

'Has she?' Ridger's hopes were raised. 'Are you going to try it?'

I nodded and returned to the bar, but Mrs Alexis had departed again towards the fireplace where Wilfred with the bellows was merely adding to the smog.

'The chimney seems to be blocked,' he said anxiously, exonerating himself.

'Blocked?' Mrs Alexis demanded. 'How could it be?' She thought for barely two seconds. 'Unless some bloody bird has built a nest in it, same as three years ago.'

'We'd better wait until it's swept again,' Wilfred suggested.

'Wait? Certainly not.' She strode towards the bar. 'I'll be with you in a moment,' she said, seeing me waiting there. 'Bird's nest. Birds building their bloody nests in my chimney. They did it once before. I'll shift the little buggers. Give them the shock of their lives.'

I didn't bother to point out that nests in October were bound to be uninhabited. She was certain to know. She was also smiling with reckless mischief and reappeared from behind the bar carrying the fabled shotgun and feeding a cartridge into the breech. My own feelings at the sight seemed to be shared by most of the people present as she walked towards the fireplace, but no one thought of stopping her.

Ridger's mouth opened in disbelief.

Mrs Alexis thrust the whole gun up inside the vast chimney and at arm's length unceremoniously pulled the trigger. There was a muffled bang inside the brickwork and a clatter as she dropped the gun on the recoil onto the logs. The eyes of everyone else in the place were popping out but Mrs Alexis calmly picked up her fallen property and returned to the bar.

'Another Bell's?' she asked, stowing the shotgun lengthways under the counter. 'Another tomato juice?'

'Er . . .' I said.

She was laughing. 'Fastest way to clear a chimney. Didn't you know?'

'No.'

'It's an old gun . . . the barrel's not straight. I wouldn't treat a good gun like that.' She looked towards the fireplace. 'The damn smoke's clearing, anyway.'

It appeared that she was right. Wilfred, again on his knees with the bellows, was producing smoke which rose upwards, not out into the room. The eyes of the onlookers retreated to their accustomed sockets and the mouths slowly closed: even Ridger's.

'Laphroaig,' I said. 'Please. And could I look at your wine list?'

'Anything you like.' She stretched for the Laphroaig bottle and poured a fair measure. 'You and the policeman . . . what are you in here for?' The bright eyes searched my face. 'That policeman wouldn't come here just for a drink. Not him. Not tomato juice. Not early.'

I paid for the Laphroaig and took the wine list that she held out. 'We're looking for some scotch that turned up in a Bell's bottle at the Silver Moondance,' I said. 'More of the same, that is.'

The sharp gaze intensified. 'You won't find any here.'

'No, I don't suppose so.'

'Is this because of those complaints last month?'

'We're here because of them, yes.'

'You've shown me no authority.' No antagonism, I thought: therefore no guilt.

'I haven't any. I'm a wine merchant.'

'A wine . . .?' She considered it. 'What's your name?'

I told her, also the name of my shop.

'Never heard of you,' she said cheerfully. 'Would you know this Scotch if you tasted it?'

'That's the general idea. Yes.'

'Then good luck to you.' She gave me an amused and shining glance and turned away to another customer, and I carried my glass across to Ridger expecting the Laphroaig to be Laphroaig and nothing else.

'She's disgraceful,' Ridger said. 'I should arrest her.'

'On what charge?'

'Discharging a firearm in a public place.'

'The inside of a chimney is hardly a public place.'

'It's no laughing matter,' he said severely.

'The smoke's clearing,' I said. 'The shot worked.'

'I would have thought you'd had enough shooting for one lifetime.'

'Well, yes.'

I drank the Laphroaig: smoky, peaty, oak-aged historic Laphroaig, the genuine thing.

Ridger bit on his disappointment, complained about the price and fidgeted unhelpfully while I read the wine list, which was handwritten and extensive. All the familiar Silver Moondance names were there along with dozens of others, but when I pointed this out to him he said stiffly that his brief was for whisky only.

I took the wine list thoughtfully back to the bar and asked Mrs Alexis for a bottle of St Estèphe.

She smiled. 'By all means. Do you want it decanted?'

'Not yet.' I went through the rest of the list with her, picking out St Emilion, Mâcon, Valpolicella, Volnay and Nuits St Georges.

'Sure,' she said easily. 'Do you want all of them?'

'Yes, please.'

She disappeared briefly and came back with a partitioned basket containing the six asked for wines. I picked each bottle up in turn to read the labels: all the right names but none from the right year.

'We've sold all we had of 1979,' she explained patiently when I pointed it out. 'We constantly update the wine list, which is why we don't have it printed. We're writing another at the moment. These present wines are better. Do you want them, then, or not?'

'Sorry,' I said. 'Not.'

She put the basket of bottles without comment on the floor near her feet and smiled at me blandly.

'Do you know the Silver Moondance?' I asked.

'Heard of it. Who hasn't, round here? Never been there. Not my style. I'm told it's a tube job, anyway.'

'A tube . . .?'

'Down the tubes,' she said patiently. 'The bank's

foreclosing on the mortgage. As of this morning the staff have been sacked. I had one of the chefs telephoning to ask for a job.' She spoke with amusement as if the closure were comic, but she'd worn the same expression all the time we'd been there, her cheek muscles seeming to be permanently set in tolerant mockery.

'At the Silver Moondance,' I said mildly, 'they were selling one single wine under six different labels.'

Her expression didn't change but she glanced down at her feet.

'Yes, those,' I said. 'Or rather, not those.'

'Are you insulting me?'

'No, just telling you.'

The brilliant eyes watched me steadily. 'And you're looking for that wine as well as the Scotch?'

'Yes.'

'Sorry I can't help you.'

'Perhaps it's as well,' I said.

'Why?'

'Well . . . I don't think its too utterly safe to know much about that wine. The head waiter of the Silver Moondance undoubtedly knew what he was selling . . . and he's dead.'

Nothing altered in her face. 'I'm in no danger,' she said. 'I can promise you that. Do you want anything else?'

I shook my head. 'We'll be on our way.'

Her gaze slid past me to rest on Ridger and still

without any change of expression she said, 'Give me a man who'll swing from a chandelier. Give me a goddamn man.' Her glance came back to my face, the mockery bold and strong. 'The world's a bloody bore.'

Her abundant hair was a dark reddish brown gleaming with good health and hair dye, and her nails were hard and long like talons. A woman of vibrating appetite who reminded me forcibly of all the species where the female crunched her husband for breakfast.

Wilfred (currently on the menu?) was still on his knees to the fire god when Ridger and I eventually made our way to the door. As Ridger went out ahead of me there was a sort of soft thudding *flump* from the direction of the chimney and a cloud of dislodged shot-up soot descended in a sticky billowing mass onto logs, flames and man beneath.

Transfixed, the armchair audience watched Wilfred rise balefully to his feet like a fuzzily inefficient demon king, scattering black rain and blinking great eyes slowly like a surprised owl on a dark night.

'I'll sue that bloody sweep,' Mrs Alexis said.

CHAPTER SIXTEEN

We went to four more pubs on that first day and I grew tired of the perpetual taste of neat Bell's whisky. Ridger methodically annotated his clipboard and showed not the slightest disappointment as glass after glass proved genuine. The pub crawl was a job to him like any other, it seemed, and he would phlegmatically continue until instructed otherwise.

He was a man without rebellion, I thought, never questioning an order nor the order of things; living at the opposite end of the spectrum from that mean kicker-over-of-traces, Kenneth Charter's son. Somewhere between the two lay the rest of us, grousing, lobbying, enduring and philosophical, making what best we could of our imperfect evolution.

Towards the end I asked him if they'd found any trace of the Bedford van used in the robbery at my shop, and perhaps because by that time he had provisionally accepted me as a full colleague he answered without his usual reservations.

1001

'No, we haven't found it,' he said. 'And we don't expect to.'

'How do you mean?' I asked.

'It belonged to a firm called Quality House Provisions who hadn't noticed it was missing until one of our PCs went there early Monday asking about it. Dozy lot. They'd got several vans, they said. It's now on the stolen vehicle list marked urgent because of its tie-in with Zarac's murder, but a hot van like that's sure to be dumped somewhere already, probably in a scrap yard miles away with the number plates off. No one will find it except by luck, I shouldn't think.'

'Cheerful.'

'Fact of life.'

He drove me back towards the shop, saying he would return in the morning with tomorrow's list of suspicious premises.

'Can't you bring the whole list instead of in bits?' I asked.

'It's still being compiled. We started today with our own patch, but we may have to wait for information from others.'

'Mm – Do you have a first name, Sergeant?'

He looked faintly surprised. 'John,' he said.

'In the pubs tomorrow, do you mind if I use it? I damn nearly called you Sergeant twice in front of barmen today.'

He considered it. 'Yes. All right. Do you want me to call you Tony?'

'It would make more sense.'

'All right.'

'What do you do off duty?' I asked.

'Garden,' he said. 'Grow vegetables, mostly.'

'Married?'

'Yes, been married fourteen years. Two daughters, proper little madams.' An indulgence in his face belied the sharpness in his voice. 'Your wife died, they say.'

'Yes.'

'Sorry about that.'

'Thank you, Sergeant.'

He nodded. John was for business, a temporary intimacy that wouldn't commit him to friendship. I could sense his approval, almost his relief, at my avoidance of John in private.

He left me outside my door and drove tidily away, indicator blinking, carefully efficient to the last. Mrs Palissey had been rushed off her feet, she was glad to say, and was I sure I was fit to drive myself to the hospital because to be honest, Mr Beach, I did smell a wee bit of drink.

I reflected that I'd ordered, paid for and swallowed a good deal of a dozen neat whiskies and if I still felt sober it was an illusion. I went to the hospital by taxi and received disgusted sniffs from the nursing sister (the same one), who stripped off the tube bandage to see what was cooking underneath.

'People who drink heal more slowly,' she said severely.

'Do they?'

'Yes.'

With her head not far from mine she one by one unstuck the antiseptic patches she'd applied the previous Sunday, and I tried to breathe shallowly through my nose in the opposite direction. Without much success, it seemed, judging from the offended twitch of her nostrils.

'Most of these are healing better than you deserve,' she said finally. 'Three are inflamed and another looks troublesome . . . Do they hurt?'

'Well . . . sort of.'

She nodded. 'One should expect it. Several were more than an inch deep.' She began sticking on new patches. 'I'll put a stitch in this bad one up here on your biceps, to hold it together. And keep off alcohol. There are much better pain killers.'

'Yes, ma'am,' I said dryly, and thought of the boozy tomorrow and of fifty thousand pubs to Watford.

Back in the shop I saw Mrs Palissey and Brian off with the deliveries and dealt with some paperwork, and in the lull between late afternoon customers eventually got dutifully around to looking at the photostats of Kenneth Junior's notebook.

Gerard's firm had made a good job of their deciphering and checking and my respect for his organization consolidated from vague expectation into recognition that Deglet's were experienced experts in a way I hadn't appreciated.

Gerard's fat envelope contained an explanatory note and about fifteen sheets of typing paper. The centre of each sheet bore the stat of one page of the small notebook, and from each entry in the notebook a fine straight line led to an explanation in the margin.

Gerard's note was typewritten:

Tony,

All the enquiries were done by telephone, not in person. Answers were given freely by Kenneth Charter himself, also by his wife and daughter and elder son, although with them as with friends and shops our questions had to be cautious, as Kenneth Charter forbade us to represent Kenneth Junior in a criminal light.

The sheets are numbered in the order in which the pages occurred in the notebook. Kenneth Charter dates the first page as having been written at the beginning of August as it refers to Mrs Charter's birthday on August 8th. One may assume that the entries were written consecutively after that, but it is not certain, and there are no other positive dates, as you will see.

Please write down immediately any thoughts which cross your mind as you read. Don't leave such thoughts until afterwards as they are apt to evaporate.

G

I turned to the first of the notebook pages and found that the first entry of all read:

Buy card for Mum's birthday next week.
A fine straight line led to the marginal note: *August 8th.*

Kenneth Junior's handwriting was inclined to shoot off at both forward and backward sloping angles in the same word, but was otherwise distinctly formed and easy to read. The Deglet's annotator had written in neat fine black script, utterly different but equally legible. I could hardly complain that Gerard had set me a technically difficult task.

The second entry on the first page read:

Go to D.N.'s for w.g.

The marginal note said: *D.N. is David Naylor, Kenneth Junior's only close friend. It is thought the letters w.g. stand for war games, as they are David Naylor's hobby.*
The first page also read:

Collect trousers from cleaners.
Ask Dad for cash.
Tell B.T. to fuck off.

The line from the last entry led to: *B.T. is probably*

Betty Townsend, a girl Kenneth Junior had been seeing.
Mrs Charter says she was a nice girl but clinging.

Poor Betty Townsend.

I turned to page two and found a list of telephone numbers, each with an identification in the margin, along with an address.

Odeon cinema (local)
Diamond snooker club (local)
David Naylor (Friend. Unemployed)
Clipjoint (Barber's shop, local)
Lisa Smithson (Occasional girlfriend. Unemployed)
Ronald Haleby (Friend. Works as doorman at local disco)

The next many pages contained entries which were only understandable because of the telephone numbers and spoke eloquently of a drifting purposeless life. Kenneth Junior's lists were almost a diary, embracing such revelations as '*Snort with R.H. Sunday, take cash*' and '*Get abortion number for L.S.*' but were mainly on the more mundane level of '*Tell Mum to buy toothbrush*', '*Play snooker at Diamond's*' and '*Rewire plug on stereo*'.

One later page read:

Haircut.
Go to Halifax.
Buy tank for w.g., Phone D.N.

Get keys of N.T. for duplicates.
Meet R.H. in Diamond's.
Pay L.S. for abortion.

Deglet's annotations were:

(1) Clipjoint say Kenneth Junior went there at about ten day intervals for shampoo and styling. He bought expensive products and tipped lavishly.

(2) Kenneth Junior is most unlikely to have been to the town of Halifax. Suggest this reference means Halifax Building Society, though his parents don't know if he had an account there. Kenneth Charter thought that apart from unemployment benefit his son had no money except what he himself gave him, but this cannot be right as Charter did not give him enough extra for cocaine and abortions.

(3) Tank must be toy tank for war games.

(4) Not traced.

I frowned for a while over the letters N.T. but could make no more of them than Deglet's had. What did one need keys for? House, car, suitcase, drawer, locker, desk, mail box, deposit box . . . infinitum. N.T. was perhaps a person. Person unknown.

On the next page there was a single entry, the one which had started the bushfire.

The Reading telephone number followed by:

Tell Z UNP 786Y picks up B's Gin Mon 10 a.m. approx.

I made a wry face over the bald and still disturbing treachery and turned over to what was left: three more pages very much like the others, with only a few new themes.

Go with D.N. for w.g. with S.N! bore the Deglet explanation: *S.N. is Stewart Naylor, David Naylor's father. Stewart Naylor lives apart after divorce. David Naylor visits his father occasionally. Stewart Naylor is noted for skill in war games, which probably accounts for the exclamation mark.*

On the last page of all it said:

Get visa for Australia.
Ask R.H. about pushers in Sydney.
Pay L.S. That's her lot.
Go to Halifax.
Remember to ask Dad for cash.
Collect keys from Simpers and send them off.

There was a final Deglet explanation: *Simpers is a hardware shop which duplicates keys. They have no record of work done for Kenneth Junior or anyone else in the family. They normally cut keys immediately, while you wait, but not if they don't keep the blanks in stock and have to send away for them. In that case they ask for an address and a deposit. If Kenneth Junior obtained keys in that way from Simpers he gave a name and address not his own.*

I shuffled the pages together and put them back in

the envelope, looking dubiously at the very few thoughts and comments I'd jotted down for Gerard; and half an hour later, when he telephoned, I offered them reluctantly and apologetically.

'Just say what occurred to you,' he said a touch impatiently. 'Anything at all may be useful.'

'Well . . . those keys.'

'What about them?'

'Well . . . what sort of keys do the tankers have?'

There was utter silence from Gerard.

'Are you still there?' I asked.

'Yes, I am.' Another pause. 'Go on talking.'

'Um . . . I wondered at the beginning about it always being the same tanker which was stolen, and I thought it might be because of something dead simple, like that one being the only tanker the thieves had the keys for. Because they would have needed the keys to unlock the cab door when the driver was in the service stations, in order to put the gas in there, and lock the door again so the driver found nothing suspicious when he got back.'

'Hm,' Gerard said. 'The police assumed the thieves used lock-pickers.'

'The right key would be quicker.'

'I agree.'

'Kenneth Junior had easy access to Charter's office and everywhere else in the place before the first theft. You might ask Charter Senior where the tanker keys are kept.'

'Yes, I will.'

'It struck me that maybe it was keys to a second tanker that Kenneth Junior was having cut. I mean, N.T. might stand for Next Tanker or New Tanker or something. Anyway, it might be worth taking some tanker keys to Simpers and seeing if they keep those blanks in stock or if they'd need to send away for them. And it might be as well to warn Kenneth Charter that someone, somewhere, might have the keys to another of his tankers . . . if any of this is right, of course.'

'Right or wrong, I'll warn him.'

'I'm afraid that's all,' I said. 'I didn't think of much else. Except . . .'

'Except?'

'Except that to himself Kenneth Junior didn't seem so bad. He sold information for presumably spot cash and he banked it in something ultra-conservative like a building society. He might have enjoyed his snort with the disco doorman but he wasn't addicted. He paid for the girl's abortion. That's none of it heavy villainy.'

'No. A moderately stable personality. I thought so too. Staying at home, buying a birthday card for his mother, being impressed by his friend's father . . . but totally without loyalty to his own.'

'Teenage rebellion gone a step too far.'

'Right,' Gerard said. 'Untrustworthy little bugger. But there you are, he's earning us money. Life's full of such ironies.'

I said with a smile in my voice, 'Want another? We're now looking for that Scotch courtesy of the police.'

I told him about my day's journeyings with Ridger and raised a chuckle on account of Mrs Alexis.

'I wasn't sure about Mrs Alexis,' I said. 'She did have all those wines on her list. She says she's sold them all. She wears such a knowing expression the whole time that you can't tell if she knows anything specific. Maybe I'll go back.'

'She sounds an utter dragon.'

'Very good value,' I said. 'She likes men who swing from chandeliers.'

'But you don't. You're not the type.'

'No . . . I should be safe.'

He laughed. 'How was your arm? I have to go myself tomorrow.'

'Not bad. And good luck.'

Ridger returned punctually in the morning and we set off to cover a territory in and around Henley-on-Thames, where in July each year the rowing regatta brought the sleepy town to bulging expensive life. In late October, in a cold drizzle, it was quiet. Ducks swam silently on the grey river and shoppers huddled head-down under umbrellas. Ridger and I went into bar after bar brushing off raindrops and I lost count after a while of the Bell's.

All of the Bell's rang true. Not a cracked note among them.

One of the barmen gave us short change, slapping down coins in a handful while sloshing water onto the counter top, so that I should snatch them up without checking, but Ridger said that that didn't rate a clip-board entry. He produced his badge, however, and warned the barman, who scowled. As the high spot of the morning it didn't rate much, but one couldn't expect a Mrs Alexis every day of the week.

Some of the pubs had two bars. One had three. My friend John insisted on making sure of every Bell's bottle in sight.

Awash with tomato juice he returned me to my shop at two-thirty and I sat heavy-headed in my office regretting the whole enterprise. I would simply have to take something to spit into, I thought, even if spitting alerted the barman and disgusted the other customers. Getting half cut every lunch-time was no joke.

Mrs Palissey drove Brian away with a big load of deliveries and between each sporadic afternoon cus-tomer I sat down and felt thick with sleep. When the door buzzer roused me for the fifth time I went into the shop yawning.

'That's no way to greet manna from heaven,' my customer said.

Mrs Alexis stood there, larger than life, bringing out her own sun on a wet afternoon. I shut my mouth slowly, readjusted it to a smile, and said, 'I was coming to see you again at the first opportunity.'

'Were you now?' she said, mockery in full swing. 'So this is where our little wine merchant dwells.' She peered about her good-humouredly, oblivious to the fact that her 'little' wine merchant stood a fraction under six feet himself and could at least look her levelly in the eyes. Nearly all men, I guessed, were 'little' to her.

'I was passing,' she said.

I nodded. Amazing, the number of people who said that.

'No, I bloody well wasn't,' she amended explosively. 'I came here on purpose.' She lifted her chin almost defiantly. 'Does that surprise you?'

'Yes,' I said truthfully.

'I liked the look of you.'

'That surprises me too.'

'Bloody cool, aren't you?'

I was still half drunk, I thought. Almost a third of a bottle of Scotch on an empty stomach, whichever way you looked at it. Ulcer land.

'How's the chimney?' I asked.

She grinned, showing teeth like a shark.

'Bloody Wilfred hasn't forgiven me.'

'And the fire?'

'Burning like Rome.' She eyed me assessingly. 'You're young enough to be my bloody son.'

'Just about.'

'And do you want to know about those bloody wines or don't you?'

'Yes, I do indeed.'

'I wasn't going to tell that police sergeant. Wouldn't give him the satisfaction. Pompous little killjoy.'

I said 'Mm' non-committally.

'I bought them, all right,' she said. 'But I damn soon sent them back.'

I breathed in deeply, trying to do nothing to distract her.

'I ran short of Bell's,' she said. 'So I phoned across to the pub opposite to borrow some. Nothing odd in that, we always help each other out. So he brings a whole unopened bloody case over, saying it came from a new supplier who offered good discounts, especially on wine, which was more my sort of thing than his. He gave me a phone number and told me to ask for Vernon.'

I looked at her.

'Should have known better, shouldn't I?' she said cheerfully. 'Should have suspected it had all fallen off the back of a bloody lorry.'

'But you telephoned?'

'That's right. Very good wines, just under normal price. So I said right, shunt along a case of each, I'd put them on the wine list and see if anyone liked them.'

'And did they?'

'Sure.' She gave me the shark smile. 'Shows how much some of these so-called buffs really know.'

'And then what?'

'Then I got someone in the bar one day kicking up a fuss and saying he'd been given the wrong whisky. I'd given it to him myself out of a Bell's bottle, one I'd got from my neighbour. I tasted it but I don't like the stuff, can't tell one from another. Anyway I gave him some Glenlivet free to placate him and apologized and when he'd gone I rang up my neighbour pretty damn quick, but he said he was certain it was OK, Vernon worked for a big firm.'

'Which big firm?'

'How the hell do I know? I didn't ask. But I'll tell you, I wasn't taking any risks so I poured the rest of the case of Bell's down the drain and chalked it up to experience. Damn good thing I did, because the next bloody day I got the Weights and Measures people round with their little measuring instruments following a strong complaint from a customer. And that damned man drank my Glenlivet, too, and still reported me.'

'And I don't suppose he's been back,' I said, smiling.

'I'd've strangled him.'

'If it hadn't been him, it would have been someone else.'

'You don't have to be so bloody right. Anyway, after that I asked a man I know who buys for a wine society to come out straight away and taste those splendid wines, and when he told me they were all the same I rang up that bloody Vernon and told him to collect what was left and repay me for the whole lot or I'd give his bloody phone number to the police.'

'And what happened?' I asked, fascinated.

'The same man who delivered them came back with my cash and took his wines away, what wasn't already drunk. He said he wasn't Vernon, just a friend of his, but I'll bet it was Vernon himself. He said Vernon hoped I'd keep my word about the phone number because if not something very nasty would happen to me.' She grinned, superbly unconcerned. 'I told him if Vernon tried anything with me, I'd eat him.'

I laughed. 'And that was that?'

'That was bloody that. Until you came round yesterday snooping.'

'Well,' I said, 'do you still have the phone number?'

Her brilliant eyes shone yellowly. 'Yes, I do. How much is it worth to you? A case of Krug? Case of Pol Roger? Dom Pérignon?'

I reflected. 'Case of Bell's?' I suggested.

'Done.' She picked a piece of paper without ceremony out of her handbag and gave it to me.

'If you carry it,' I said.

She glanced at the sling I still wore. 'Hurt your arm?'

'Shotgun pellets . . . I wouldn't tell anyone, if I were you, that you'd been here to see me. I got shot at because of that wine. Vernon might not be pleased to know you'd given me his phone number.'

Her eyes opened wide and the mockery for once died right out of her face.

'I came here,' she said flatly, 'because of the head waiter at the Silver Moondance. Murder's going too far. But you didn't say . . .'

I shook my head. 'I'm sorry. There seemed no need. I had no idea you would come here. And I'm sure you'll be OK if you just keep quiet. After all, others must have Vernon's number. Your neighbour, for one.'

'Yes.' She thought it over. 'You're damn right.' Her face lightened back into its accustomed lines. 'Any time you're passing, my little wine merchant, call in for dinner.'

She came with me into the storeroom to collect her trophy which she bore easily away under her arm, diving out into the drizzle with the teeth and eyes gleaming against the grey sky.

Gerard said, 'That's great,' and promised to ring back as soon as his firm had traced the number.

'It's somewhere near Oxford,' I said.

'Yes,' he agreed. 'Oxford code.'

His voice for all his enthusiasm sounded tired and when I asked after his shoulder he merely grunted without comment, which I took to mean no good news.

'I'll call you back,' he said, and within half an hour did so, but not to say he had located Vernon's number.

'Thought you'd like to know . . . the office has checked with the Doncaster auctioneers. Ramekin was

1018

bought for actual cash. Banknotes. They've no record of who bought it. The office did a quick check also on transporters and sure enough, as you said, Ramekin was in their books. He was shipped to California to a well-known bloodstock agent. The agent is away travelling in Japan and no one in his office will release information in his absence. He's expected home next Thursday night. Ramekin's shipment costs were paid in cash by a Mr A.L. Trent, who has sent several other horses to California via the same shipper to the same agent. So there we are. The laundered cash is in California, either banked or still on the hoof.'

'Banked, I'd bet a million.'

'Yes, I'd think so. But a dead end until Friday.'

'Pity.'

'We're making progress,' he said. 'And you might also like to know about the tanker keys.'

'What about them?'

'I talked to Kenneth Charter. He says there's nothing exceptional about the keys to the cab or the ignition keys but he has special keys for the valves into the segments in his tankers. Part of his security arrangements. There are nine separate segments in those big tankers. He says it's so the tanker can carry several different liquids in small loads on the same journey, if necessary. Anyway, each segment has its own particular key, to avoid mistakes with unloading, so the Scotch tankers each have a bunch of nine valve keys. With goods in bond Charter has always posted a set of keys in advance to both shipper and destination so that they are never carried on the tanker itself, for security.'

'Most prudent,' I said.

'Yes. So Kenneth Charter went to the Simpers shop himself this afternoon, and sure enough they said they'd twice made a set of nine keys like that, and both times they'd had to send away for the blanks. The young man who'd ordered them had given his name as Harrison each time. Kenneth Charter is spitting mad as of course the shop has no record of the shapes they cut into the blanks, and he doesn't know which of his tankers is now at risk.'

'Awkward.'

'He says if he loses the whole business it won't matter a damn. What upset him most was Kenneth Junior going to such lengths.'

'Does he know how Kenneth Junior got hold of the keys?' I asked.

'He says they're usually kept in his office, but when the tankers' valves are being steam cleaned the keys are out in the workshop. He reckons Kenneth Junior took them from there.'

'Cunning little beast.'

'Absolutely. Incidentally, both Kenneth Charter and Deglet's have now received from Rannoch the profile analysis of all three of the stolen loads of Scotch. Apparently they are all slightly different because they were blends from more than one distillery. Too

technical for me. Anyway, they're in our office ready,
if we find anything to match.'

'Mm. I wonder if Mrs Alexis's neighbour still has
any.'

'What a thought! Get onto her pronto.'

'Pity she poured hers down the drain.'

Gerard and I disconnected and I got through to Mrs
Alexis who sounded breezily unaffected and said she
would find out at once; but she called back within ten
minutes to say her neighbour had sold the lot some
time ago and couldn't get any more at that price
because Vernon had discontinued the discount, but she
thought Vernon must have got the wind up after his
brush with her and had closed down altogether in her
area.

Damn, I thought, and told Gerard.

'Whenever we get near that stuff it seems to recede
from us like a phantom,' he said wearily.

'Maybe I'll find it tomorrow.'

He sighed. 'It's a very big haystack.'

CHAPTER SEVENTEEN

Flora came breathlessly into the shop soon after I'd opened it on the Saturday morning, saying she was on her way to fetch Jack home and wanted to thank me again for my help with Howard and Orkney Swayle.

'There's no need. I enjoyed it.'

'All the same, Tony dear, I want you to have this.' She put a gift-wrapped parcel on the counter, and when I opened my mouth to protest said, 'Now don't argue, Tony dear, it's for you and it's not enough, it's very small and I expect you have one already, but I'll have my hands full when Jack's home so I thought I'd bring it for you now.'

She patted my hand in motherly fashion and I bent to kiss her cheek.

'You're very naughty,' I said. 'But thank you.'

'That's right dear. Where's your sling?'

'I forgot it this morning. It's at home.'

'Don't tire yourself, dear, will you? And we'll need some more drinks whenever you've time.' She fished in her handbag and produced a list. 'After Jack's home the owners will start coming again and some of them drink like fish, though I shouldn't say it, and Jack says he's going to add it on their bills as medicine for the horses, which you can't blame him for, can you, dear?'

'Er . . . no.'

She put the list on the counter beside the present, and, saying she had a thousand things to see to on her way to the hospital, went lightfootedly away.

I unwrapped the parcel curiously and found that although it was small in size it couldn't have been in price. The box inside the glazed white paper had come from a jeweller in Reading, and it contained, in a nest of red velvet, a silver penknife.

Not one that would necessarily gladden the hearts of Boy Scouts. Not knobbly with thirteen blades and a hook for taking stones out of horses' hooves, like the one which had been the pride of my childhood. A slim elegantly tooled affair with a sharp steel cutting blade tucked into one side and a second blade on the other which turned out to be a screwdriver. I liked both the look and the feel, and although it was true I already had a knife, it was old and blunt. I took the old knife out of my pocket and replaced it with the new, and thought friendly thoughts of Flora all morning.

Ridger added to my pleasure by telephoning to say there would be no more pub crawls for a few days as he had been assigned to other duties, but we would resume on Wednesday and he would be along for me then at ten-fifteen.

I suppose I should have told him about Mrs Alexis and the mysterious Vernon with his telephone number, but I didn't. It seemed odd to me to find that my allegiance was to Gerard rather than to the police. I had caught from him quite thoroughly, it seemed, the belief that the paying client's interests came first, with public justice second.

I did actually half jokingly ask Ridger who I should tell if I came across the suspect Scotch when I wasn't in his own company, and he answered seriously, after earnest thought, that I'd probably better tell Chief Superintendent Wilson straight away, as Ridger himself along with many of the county's police was having to go up north to help deal with some ugly picketing, which made a change, and he couldn't tell who'd be on duty while he was away.

'How would I reach the Chief Superintendent?' I asked.

He told me to wait a moment and came back with a number which would reach the Zarac investigation room direct. Night or day, he said. Priority.

'Would the Silver Moondance Scotch be priority?'

'Of course,' he said. 'Anything would.'

'OK, Sergeant. See you on Wednesday.'

He said he hoped so, and goodbye.

Relieved at being let off the drinking I sold a lot of wine to a flood of customers, with Mrs Palissey busily beaming and Brian carrying the loads out to the cars, and it seemed as if it would be for once a normal day until Tina McGregor telephoned at eleven.

'Gerard's gone up to the office,' she said. 'I wish he wouldn't on Saturdays and particularly as he's not right yet from last Sunday, but it's like arguing with a bulldozer . . . Anyway, he asked me to tell you they've traced the number you gave him yesterday and it doesn't look too promising. It's the number of the big caterers at Martineau Park racecourse. He says if you'd care to go along there you might ask them if Vernon – is that right? – still works for them. He says if you should see Vernon yourself he'll leave it up to you to decide whether or not to ask him where he got the Scotch and wines from. Is that all right?'

'Yes, fine,' I said. 'How's his shoulder?'

'He's being utterly tight-lipped about it and they've put him on antibiotics.'

'It's infected?' I asked, alarmed.

'He didn't say. I just wish he'd slow down.'

She sounded neither anxious nor angry, but one could never tell Tina's reactions from her voice. I said weakly, 'I'm sorry,' and she answered, 'No need to be,' in the same calm tone, and said Gerard would like me to telephone him at his home later to let him know how I got on at Martineau Park.

It was odd, I reflected, putting down the receiver, to think that I had been at Martineau Park races so long on Tuesday afternoon totally oblivious of the existence of Vernon among the caterers Orkney Swayle so much detested. Life, as Gerard said, was full of ironies.

Mrs Palissey, geared to my planned absence with Ridger, took my substitute trip to Martineau Park in her stride. 'Of course, Mr Beach. No trouble at all.'

Grudge-and-spite might be the prevailing social climate but Mrs Palissey rose gloriously above it. Mrs Palissey was a non-interfering do-gooder, heaven reward her. I said I would make it up to her later, and she said, 'Yes, Yes,' as if it didn't matter one way or the other.

I drove to Martineau Park wondering if in fact there would be anyone there. It wasn't a race day. There would be no crowds. I hadn't before been to a racecourse on a non-racing day and didn't know what level of activity to expect in the way of managers, maintenance, groundsmen or cleaners. The whole catering department would very likely be locked. I would quite likely be turning round to drive straight back.

The gates into the members' car park at least stood open, unguarded. I drove through them and across the unpopulated expanses of cindery grass, leaving the Rover at the end of a short row of cars near the entrance to the paddock. That gate too was open and unattended, where on race days watchful officials checked the admittance badges of the throng streaming through.

It was eerie, I thought, to see the place so deserted. Without people the bulky line of buildings seemed huge. Bustling human life somehow reduced their proportions, filled their spaces, made them friendlier, brought them to comfortable size. I hadn't realized how big the place was in all the days I'd been there.

There was no one about around the weighing room area, though the doors there too were open. I went curiously inside, looking at the holies from where racegoers were normally barred, peering with interest at the scales themselves and at the flat pieces of lead used for packing weight-cloths. I went on into the jockeys' changing rooms and looked at the rows of empty pegs, empty benches, empty racks for saddles: all echoingly bare with no scrap of personal life remaining. When the racing circus moved on, it took all with it but the dust.

Gerard might consider the detour a waste of time, but I would probably never get such an opportunity again. I peered for good measure into a room marked 'Stewards' which contained merely a table, six undistinguished chairs and two pictures ditto. No mementos, no records of the make-or-break enquiries held there.

Returning to fresh air and the allotted task I came to a door marked 'Clerk of the Course' which stood slightly ajar. I pushed it open tentatively and found a man sitting at a desk, writing. He raised a smooth head and bushy eyebrows and said in a civilized voice, 'Can I help you?'

'I'm looking for the caterers,' I said.

'Delivery entrance?'

'Er . . . yes.'

'You'll want to go along the back of the stands to the far end. You'll find the Tote building facing you. Turn right. You'll see the Celebration Bar there alongside the Tote, but the door you want is to your right again before you get there. A green door. Not conspicuous. There are some empty beer crates just outside, unless they've moved them as I asked.'

'Thank you.'

He nodded civilly and bent to his writing, and I walked to the far end of the stands and found the green door and the beer crates, as he'd said.

I found also that deliveries were at that moment taking place. A large dark van had been drawn up outside the closed front of the Celebration Bar, a van with its rear doors opened wide and two workmen in brown overalls unloading a shipment of gin from it onto a pallet on a fork-lift truck.

The green door itself stood open, propped that way by a crate. I walked through it behind the two men in overalls as they trundled inwards the make of gin which Orkney had refused to have in his box.

The door, I saw, represented the outward end of a very dimly-lit passage about six feet wide which stretched away into the distance as far as one could see, and I realized that it must run under the whole length of the main bank of stands, an inner spinal thoroughfare, the gut life of the building, unseen from outside.

The gin-handlers walked onwards past three closed green painted doors marked Stores A, Stores B, and Stores C, and past an open one, Stores D, which revealed only a half dozen of the sort of deep trays used by bakers.

A few paces beyond that the gin turned abruptly to the left, and I, turning after it, found myself in a wider side passage aiming for an open but heavy and purposeful-looking door. Beyond the door were brighter lights and more people in what was clearly a larger area and I went in there wondering whether Vernon was a first name or surname, and whether there was the slightest chance of his being at work on a Saturday.

Immediately through the heavy door there was a large storeroom stacked head high with dense-packed beer crates like those outside, only these were full. To the left was a partitioned section, walls of wood to waist height, glass above, containing a desk, files, calendar, paperwork. To the right an inner door led into a still larger storeroom, a mini-warehouse where the ranks of cases of drink rose nearly to the ceiling and advanced into the central space in deep blocks. Martineau Park, I reflected, was due to hold its Autumn Carnival jump-racing meeting near the beginning of November and was stocking up accordingly. At the Cheltenham Festival in March, one wine merchant had told me, the jump-racing crowd had in three days, apart from beer by the lakeful, despatched six thousand bottles of champagne in addition to nine thousand bottles of other wines and four thousand bottles of spirits. At Martineau, by the look of things, at least double that was expected.

The gin went through into the inner warehouse to be added to a huge stack already growing there, and I again followed. One large man with a clipboard was checking off quantities and another with a black felt pen put a mark on each box as it was unloaded.

No one paid me any attention. I stood there as if invisible to all of them, and it slowly struck me that each set thought I belonged to the other. The two delivery men disengaged the fork-lift from the pallet they'd brought in, picked up an empty one from a low stack and began wheeling it back to the door. The man with the pen heaved the cases into their new positions, putting his mark on each, and the man with the clipboard watched and counted.

I thought I'd better wait until they'd finished before I interrupted, and looking back it seems possible that that brief hesitation saved my life.

The telephone rang in the office section, raucously loud.

'Go and answer that, Mervyn,' the man with the clipboard said, and his henchman with the marker went off to obey. Then the clipboard man frowned as if remembering something, looked sharply at his watch, and called out, 'Mervyn, I'll answer it. You go and shift those beer cases like the man says. Put them in store D. Wait outside until I tell you to come back. And tell those men not to bring in the next load until I'm off the phone, right?' His gaze flicked over me, scarcely reaching my face. 'Your job, of course,' he said. 'You tell them.'

He strode away fast in the direction of the office leaving me flat-footed in his wake, and presently I could hear his voice answering the telephone and could see a portion of his backview through the glass.

'Yes, speaking. Yes, yes. Go on.'

Before I'd consciously decided whether to retire or eavesdrop another and different voice spoke loudly from the passage outside, a voice accompanied by firm approaching footsteps.

'Vernon? Are you there?'

He came straight through the doorway and veered immediately to his left towards the office: and to my startled eyes he was unmistakable.

Paul Young.

'Vernon!'

'Yes, look, I'll be with you . . .' Vernon of the clip-board put the palm of his hand over the telephone and began to turn towards the newcomer, and while neither of them was looking my way I stepped backwards out of their line of sight.

Paul Young.

My mind seemed stuck; my body of lead.

To reach the outside world I would have to go past the office section and with all that glass around Paul Young would be sure to see me. He might not have taken particular note of me on that Monday morning in the Silver Moondance Saloon but he'd certainly thought of me a good deal since. The assistant assistant would have told him who I was. He'd sent the thieves to my shop with his list. He must know how that sortie had ended. He must also know it hadn't achieved its main purpose. I thought that if he saw me now he would know me, and the idea of that filled me with numbing, muscle-paralysing fright.

Neither Vernon nor Paul Young at that exact moment seemed to be moving, but impelled no doubt by the atavistic burrowing instincts of the hunted and trapped I sought in that brightly-lit warehouse for a dark place to hide.

There were no soft nooks or crannies, just solid blocks and columns of cases of drink. There were narrow spaces between some of the blocks into which I could squeeze . . . and where anyone glancing in as they walked past would easily see me. Down the far end, I thought in panicky fashion. They might not go right down there.

But I'd have to get there, and at any second, any second . . . It was too far. Something else . . . something fast . . .

I climbed.

I climbed the highest and most extensive stack, which happened to be of non-vintage champagne. I lay flat on my stomach along the top of it, at the back against the wall. The ceiling was eighteen inches above my head. The cases stretched beyond my feet at one end and beyond my head at the other. I could see nothing but cardboard. No floor. No people. My heart bounced around like a rubber ball and I wanted to shut my eyes on the ostrich principle that if I didn't look I wouldn't be seen.

Consultancy did not include getting too close to Paul Young.

What a hollow bloody laugh.

If he found me on top of the champagne it would be a crocodile job for sure. Did he take plaster of Paris with him always in his Rolls?

Why hadn't I run for it? If I'd run, he might not have caught me. I ought simply to have sprinted. It would have been better. There were people around . . . I'd have been safe. And now here I was, marooned eight feet up on a liquid mountain and feeling more frightened than I'd ever been in my life.

They left the office and came into the main store-room. I clenched my teeth and sweated.

If they searched for me . . . if they knew I was there . . . they would certainly find me.

'I'm not satisfied. I want to see for myself.'

It was Paul Young's own hard voice, full of aggressive determination and so close that he might have been speaking to me directly. I tried not to tremble . . . not to rustle against the cardboard . . . not to breathe.

'But I've told you . . .' the clipboard man said.

'I don't give a sod what you've told me. You're a

1033

twisty bastard, Vernon. You'd lie as soon as spit. I've warned you twice and I don't trust you. By my reckoning you should still have twenty-four cases of Scotch left here and I've written down on this list how much you should have under each label. And I'm telling you, Vernon, you'd better show me just that much because if I find you've been selling any more on your own account and pocketing the proceeds, you're out.'

Vernon said sullenly, 'Your list won't be up to date. I sold a lot to that wine bar in Oxford.'

'How many labels?' Paul Young asked sharply.

'Two.'

'That'd better be right. You can show me the invoices.'

Vernon said combatively, 'You make selling them too difficult, not letting more than two go to each place. No one ever says they're the same. How many complaints have we had, tell me that? Your brother's been selling all six for years and no one's ever said they aren't what's on the labels.'

Paul Young said heavily, 'Someone must have complained, otherwise why - was that snooping wine-merchant there tasting everything and telling the police? I'm not risking all six together any more, not for anyone. If you want to stay in business, Vernon, you'll do what I tell you and don't you forget it. Now let's check on the stocks, and you'd better not have been cheating me, Vernon, you'd better not.'

'It's all down the far end,' Vernon said glumly, and

their voices faded and became less distinct as they moved away down the long room.

At the far end . . . and I'd have gone down there to hide, if I'd had time. Great God Almighty . . .

I wondered if they would see my feet. I thought of escape but knew my first movement would alert them. I thought that if the worst came to the worst I could defend myself by throwing champagne bottles. Champagne bottles were reinforced because if they broke they were like mini-grenades exploding with gas into cutting knives of glass. Flying glass was lethal, which people tended to forget because of actors crashing out harmlessly through windows in television sagas: but that fictional glass was made of sugar to safeguard the stuntmen . . . and little children had been killed by dropping fizzy-drink bottles . . . and I'd fight with champagne if I had to.

They were down at the far end for several minutes, their voices still muffled. When they came back, nothing between them had improved.

'You had all the Silver Moondance Scotch back here,' Paul Young said furiously. 'I brought it myself. What have you done with it?'

Silence from Vernon.

'I put a red circle on every box from there when Zarac and I loaded it. You didn't notice that, I suppose? I didn't trust you, Vernon. I was sodding right not to trust you. You've been useful to me, I'm not saying different. But you're not the only stores manager who

can shuffle a bit of paper. You're greedy and you're
not safe. The party's over, Vernon. You're short a total
of twenty-eight cases by my reckoning and I won't have
people steal from me. You've had a fair cut. Very fair.
But enough's enough. We're through. I'll remove the
rest of my stock tomorrow afternoon in one of the vans,
and you'll be here with the keys of this place to see
to it.'

With defensive anger and no caution at all Vernon
said explosively, 'If you break with me I'll see you
regret it.'

There was a small intense silence, then in a deadly
voice Paul Young said, 'The last person who threatened
me in that way was Zarac.'

Vernon made no reply. I felt my own hairs rising,
my breath stifling, my skin chilling to cold.

I had heard too much.

If I'd been at risk before, it was now redoubled. And
it wasn't just the threat of death that terrified, but the
manner of it . . . the nightmare of a soft white bandage
over one's nose and mouth, turning to rock, choking
off breath . . . coming my way if Paul Young knew what
I'd heard . . . or so it seemed to me, lying in fear, trying
to prevent tremor or twitch from creaking through the
unstable columns of boxes.

Vernon must have known what had become of
Zarac. He made no reply at all, nor did Paul Young find
it necessary to spell out his meaning at more length. I
heard his strong gritty footsteps move away towards

the doorway to the office, and after them, hesitant, shuffling, the footfall of Vernon.

I heard Vernon's voice saying loudly, angrily, 'What are you doing? I told you not to bring that lot in until I was ready,' and with the sublime disrespect for orders shown by a certain type of British workman the two men in brown overalls pushed their fork-lift truck resolutely past him into the warehouse.

I couldn't see them, but I heard them plainly. One of them said truculently, 'Time and a half or no time and a half, we knock off at twelve-thirty, and if this isn't unloaded by then we'll take it back with us. We can't ponce about waiting for your private phone calls.'

Vernon was flustered. I heard him outside calling, 'Mervyn, Mervyn, get back here'; and when Mervyn returned it was with news that made my precarious position much worse.

'Did you know Bakerton's van's here? They've brought fifty more cases of Pol Roger White Foil.'

Pol Roger White Foil was what I was lying on.

If they were busy with Pol Roger someone would be bound to see me. They could hardly avoid it. Delivery men wouldn't exactly ignore a man lying on top of their boxes . . . they would for instance remark on it . . . who wouldn't?

Vernon said disorganizedly, 'Well if they've brought it . . . Go out and count what they unload, they left us short two cases last time . . . And you there with the gin, stack that lot separately, it's not checked . . .'

Paul Young's decisive voice cut through the hurrying orders. 'Tomorrow afternoon, Vernon. Two o'clock sharp.'

Vernon's reply was drowned as far as I was concerned by the gin handlers heating up an argument about football six paces from my toes. I could no longer hear Paul Young either. I heard too much about a questionable foul and the eyesight of the ref.

Staying on top of the champagne was hopeless, though the temptation to remain invisible was almost overwhelming. Discovery on my stomach, discovery on my feet . . . one or the other was inevitable.

There must be a safety of sorts, I thought, in the presence of all those delivery men.

On my feet, then.

I slithered backwards and dropped down into the narrow gap between the bulk of the Pol Roger and the smaller block of Krug beyond.

I was trembling. It wouldn't do. I stepped from the champagne shelter numb with fright and went down to the men with the gin.

One of them broke off his denunciation of a deliberate kick at a knee cap and said, 'Blimey, where did you come from?'

'Just checking,' I said vaguely. 'Have you finished?'

'Near enough.' They expertly off-loaded the last few cases. 'That's the lot. You want to sign our chit?'

One of them picked a yellow folded paper from his top overall pocket and held it out.

'Er . . .' I said, fishing for a pen. 'Yes.'

I opened the yellow paper, leaned it against a case of gin, signed it illegibly in the space provided and gave it back to them.

'Right. We'll be off.'

They left the fork-lift truck where it was in the middle of the wide central aisle, and set off for the door. Almost without thought I grasped the truck's handle and pushed it along in their wake, and it was in that way that I came face to face with Vernon.

There was sweat on his forehead. He looked harassed, small eyes anxious above a flourishing moustache, mouth open, breath hurried and heavy.

He gave me the smallest frown. He was accompanying an incoming load of white boxes. I let go of the truck I was pushing and walked past Vernon and the Pol Roger and was out into the passage with no sign of Paul Young, no shouts, no scalding pursuit.

I followed the brown-overalled gin men round the turn into the main passage with only a short way to go to the free open air . . . and there he was, Paul Young, outside the green entrance, lit by daylight, standing as if waiting, solid, shortish, unremarkable, a man without pity.

I glanced back the way I'd come. Vernon had peeled off from the champagne and was advancing after me, appearing undecided, enquiring, on the verge of suspicious.

'You, there,' he said. 'I didn't see you come in.'

'Maintenance,' I said briskly. 'Just checking.'

Vernon's frown deepened. Paul Young remained at the outer door motionless and in plain sight, watching something outside.

I turned towards the only alternative, the long passage leading deep under the stands. Vernon glanced to where I'd been looking and saw Paul Young, and his mouth tightened. I gave him no more time to crystallize his suspicions of me but set off down the long passage as if every step of the way was familiar. When I looked back after about fifteen paces Vernon was still there, still staring after me. I gave him a wave. Beyond him Paul Young still filled the way out. I continued to walk onwards, trying to control a terrible urge to run. At all costs, I told myself, don't look back again. Vernon would begin to follow.

Don't look back.

Don't actually run.

I went faster and deeper to I didn't know where.

CHAPTER EIGHTEEN

The passage ended in kitchens: vast cavernous halls with stainless steel growing everywhere in monstrous mixing bowls and sink-like trays.

Empty, cold, clean, greyly gleaming: a deserted science-fiction landscape which on Tuesday must have been alive with warmth and smells and food and bustle. There were a few lights on, inadequate for the area, but no sign that anyone was working. I glanced back against all my good intentions as I turned away from the passage and saw that Vernon had indeed followed; that he was almost half way along.

I waved again as I stepped out of his sight, a brief and I hoped reassuring signal.

Vernon was not apparently reassured. I heard his voice shouting loudly from the distance, 'Hey!'

He didn't know who I was, but he was alarmed that I could have overheard what I had. His unease sprang from guilt and his persistence in following me from a wholly accurate instinct. If he thought I was a danger to him, he was right.

1041

Damn him, I thought. He was a better prospect than Paul Young, but not much. I might be able to talk myself free of him with something like saying I was checking electric wiring ... or I might not. Better by far to vanish as inexplicably as I'd appeared.

The ovens were big enough to crawl into ... but they had glass doors ... and gas jets inside ... Where else?

Another way out ... There had to be a way out for food. They wouldn't push it along that passage out into possible rain. There would be a way into bars, into dining rooms. Exit doors, somewhere.

I sped round two corners. More stainless steel monsters. Sinks like bathtubs for dishwashing. Floor to ceiling stacks of trays. No doors out.

Nowhere to hide.

'Are you there?' Vernon's voice shouted. 'Hey you. Where are you?' He was much nearer. He sounded determined now, and more belligerent. 'Come out of there. Show yourself.'

I went desperately round the furthest possible corner into a small space which looked at first like a short blank corridor leading nowhere. I began to turn to go back the way I'd come, feverishly trying to remember electricians' terms to flourish around like interrupted resistance and circuit overload and other such nonsense when I saw that one wall of the blank corridor wasn't blank.

One wall contained a row of four small lifts, each

about a yard high, a yard wide, a yard deep. Constructed without fronts, they were of the sort especially designed for transporting food upwards from downstairs cooks. Dumb waiters the Victorians had called them. Beside each lift, selector buttons: 1, 2, 3.

I scrambled into the nearest lift, pressed button 3, not by choice but because my unsteady fingers hit it first, and wondered what on earth I would say now if Vernon at that moment appeared.

He didn't. I heard him still round a corner or two, calling angrily, 'Hey, you. Answer me.' And the food lift rose smoothly, quietly, taking me far upwards like a sandwich.

When it stopped I spilled hurriedly out, finding myself in a serving area high up in the stands. There was daylight from large windows and a row of food trolleys parked end to end along a wall.

No one about. No sound from below . . . but Vernon might have heard the lift's electric hum and be on his way . . . he knew every cranny . . . he belonged there. Out of a muddled thought that if the lift returned to the kitchens before he saw it had gone he might not think I'd used it, I pressed the down button and saw it disappear as fast as I'd come up.

Then I scorched out of the serving area and at any other time might have laughed, because I was up on the level of Orkney Swayle's box. Up where the waitresses had ferried the food whose origins I hadn't imagined.

I ran at last: softly but with terrible fear still at my heels. Ran past the big passenger lifts that might go down from there to the ground floor, but would go slowly with flashing lights announcing their progress and which might deliver me to Vernon waiting in anticipation at the doors . . . Ran past them to Orkney's box, because I knew it. Prayed the door wouldn't be locked.

None of the boxes was locked.

Marvellous.

Orkney's was ten or more along the glassed-in gallery, and I reached it at an Olympic sprint. I went in there and stood in the corner that couldn't be seen from the passage because of the out-jutting serving section just inside the door, and I made my breathing shallow and almost silent, and couldn't stop the noisy thump of my heart.

Nothing happened for a long long time.

Nothing at all.

There was no more voice shouting, 'Hey . . .'

No Vernon appeared like Nemesis in the doorway.

I couldn't bring myself to believe he'd given up. I thought that if I took a step into the gallery he would pounce on me. That somewhere, round a turning, he would be lying in wait. As in a childhood game I strained deep into a hiding place cringing from the heartstopping moment of capture . . . but this time for real, with a penalty beyond facing.

I wasn't good at this sort of thing, I thought

miserably. I felt sick. Why couldn't I have courage like my father?

I stood in my corner while time stretched agonizingly and silently out . . . and I'd almost got to the point of thinking it would perhaps be safe to move, when I saw him. He was down below in front of the stands out on the far edge of the tarmac where the bookmakers raised their tempting racket on racedays. He had his back to the racecourse rails. He was scanning the length of stands, searching for movement . . . searching for a sight of me.

Beside him, looking upward, was Paul Young.

If I could see them they could see me . . . but to them I must be in darkness . . . I could see them through glass, through the glass of the doors leading from the box to the steps on the balcony.

I stood frozen, afraid almost to blink. It was movement they would see, not a stock-still shadow in the angle of two walls.

Why ever, I thought hopelessly, had I dived into such a small dead end so close to the lifts, so easy to track down and find? Why hadn't I searched for a staircase and run downwards? Going upwards was fatal . . . one could run out of up. I'd always thought it stupid for fugitives in films to start climbing, and now I'd done it myself. Escape always lay downwards. I thought it and knew it, and couldn't bring myself to move even though if I ran fast enough and if I could find the way, I might escape down the stairs and be away through some exit before they came in from the tarmac . . .

Very slowly I turned my head to look along to where my car was parked by the paddock entrance. I could see it all right, elderly and serviceable, ready to go. I could see also a car parked next to it, where no car had stood when I arrived.

My eyes ached with looking at the newly arrived car with its noble unmistakable lines and its darkened glass and sable paint.

Black Rolls-Royce . . . 'a black Roller with them tinted windows' . . . next to my way out.

Reason told me that Paul Young didn't know the car next to his was mine. Reason said he didn't know it was I he was looking for, and that the urgency of his search must be relative. Reason had very little to do with lurching intestines.

The two men gave up their raking inspection and walked towards the stands, going out of my line of sight below the outer edge of the balcony. If I'd been rushing downstairs I could have run straight into them . . . If they started searching methodically, and I didn't move, they would find me. Yet I didn't move. I couldn't.

For a whole hour I saw nothing, heard nothing.

They were waiting for me, I thought.

Listening for my footfall on a stairway, for the whine of a lift, for a door stealthily opening. The tension in my body went screaming along like a roller-coaster, winding up as soon as it began to die down, kept going only by my own wretched thoughts.

Cat and mouse . . .

This mouse would stay a long time in his hole.

Orkney's box, I thought; where the tartlets had waited so long in their wrapping and Flora had flushed uncomplainingly for Jack's sake. The sideboard was emptier than ever. Orkney's bad temper rested sourly in the memory. Breezy Palm had run in panic and lost. Dear heavens . . .

When I'd been in Orkney's box for two hours, Paul Young returned to his Rolls and drove it out of the car park.

I should have been reassured that it no longer stood next to my Rover, but I wasn't. I feared that he'd driven out, round and back through a service entrance from the main road, where the delivery vans must come in and out. I feared that he was still down there below me, claws ready.

When I moved in the end it was out of a sort of shame. I couldn't stand there quivering forever. If the cat was waiting right outside Orkney's door . . . then all the same I'd have to risk it.

I looked most delicately out . . . and there was no one in sight. Breathing shallowly with a racing pulse I stepped slowly into the gallery and looked down from the windows there into the wide tarmacked area behind the stands along which I'd walked to find the green door.

The green door itself was round a corner out of sight, and from my angle I couldn't see any delivery vans . . . or any Rolls-Royce.

No one was out in the rear area looking up to the gallery, but I crabbed along it with my back against the walls of the boxes, sliding past their open doors nervously, ready at any moment to stop, to dive into any shelter, to freeze.

No sound. I reached the place where the gallery opened into a wider concourse, and in the last yard of window and with my last glance downwards I saw Vernon walk into sight.

He was still looking around him. Still looking upward. Still unsatisfied, still worried, still persistent.

I watched him breathlessly until he began to walk back towards the buildings, then I ran through the concourse because at least he couldn't see me at that point, and at the far end with trepidation approached the stairs to the next lower level; and I went down them in a blue funk and from there out to the huge viewing balcony where tiered rows of seats stretched away on each side, turning their blank tipped-up bottoms to the empty track.

I walked along behind the top row of seats in the direction of the winning post and saw no one, and at the end hopped over a railing into a similar enclosure labelled firmly 'Owners and Trainers Only'. Not an owner or trainer in sight. Nor Vernon, nor Paul Young.

From the 'Owners and Trainers' a small staircase led

downwards into the main bulk of the stands, and down there I went, heart thudding, trying to make myself believe that the smaller the place I was in, the less likely it was that I would be spotted from a distance.

The Owners' and Trainers' staircase led into the Owners and Trainers' bar. There were rattan armchairs, small glass-topped tables, sporting murals, not a bottle or glass in sight: and at the far end, a wide tier of steps allowed one to see through a wall of glass to the parade ring. Outside and to the left, before one reached the parade ring, lay the weighing room and the office of the Clerk of the Course. Beyond the parade ring lay the gate to the car park and to freedom.

I was there. Nearly there. A door at the bottom of the Owners and Trainers' enclosed viewing steps led straight out to the area in front of the weighing room, and if only that door like every one else in the building were unlocked, I'd be out.

I approached the steps thinking only of that, and along from behind the stands, barely twenty paces away from me, marched Vernon.

If he had walked up to the glass and looked through he would have seen me clearly. I could see even the brown and white checks of his shirt collar over his zipped jacket. I stood stock still in shuddering dismay and watched him walk along to the Clerk of the Course's office and knock on the door.

The man who had been writing there came outside. I watched them talking. Watched them both look across to the stands. The man from the office pointed to the way he'd told me to go to find the caterers. Vernon seemed to be asking urgent questions but the office man shook his head and after a while went back indoors; and with clearly evident frustration Vernon began to hurry back the way he'd come.

The door at the bottom of the Owners and Trainers' Bar steps proved to be bolted on the inside, top and bottom. I undid the bolts, fumbling. The door itself . . . the knob turned under my hand and the door opened inward towards me when I pulled, and I stepped out feeling that if Vernon or Paul Young jumped on me at that moment I would scream, literally scream with hysterics.

They weren't there. I shut the door behind me and started walking with unsteady knees, and the man from the office came out of his door and said, 'I say, do you know the caterer's store manager is looking for you?'

'Yes,' I said. It came out as a croak. I cleared my throat and said again, 'Yes. I just met him along there.' I pointed to the way Vernon had gone . . . and I feared he would come back.

'Did you? Righto.' He frowned at me, puzzled. 'He wanted to know your name. Most odd, what? I said I didn't know, but mentioned that it was hours since you'd asked the way to his door. I'd have thought he would have known.'

'Most odd,' I agreed. 'Anyway, he knows now. I told him. Er . . . Peter Cash. Insurance.'

'Ah.'

'Not a bad day,' I said, looking at the sky, 'after yesterday.'

'We needed the rain.'

'Yes. Well . . . good day.'

He nodded benignly over the civility and returned to his lair, and I went shakily onwards past the parade ring, down the path, through the still open entrance gate and out to the Rover; and no one yelled behind me, no one ran to pounce and clutch and drag me back at the last moment. No one came.

The keys went tremblingly into the locks. The engine started. There were no flat tyres. I pushed the old gear lever through the ancient gears, reverse and forward, and drove away over the cindery grass and through the main gates and away from Martineau Park with Pan at my shoulder fading slowly into the shadows on the journey.

When I went into the shop it was still only twenty-one minutes to four, although I felt as if I had lived several lifetimes. I headed straight through to the wash-room and was sick in the washbasin and spent a long time wretchedly on the loo and felt my skin still clammy with shivers.

I splashed water on my face and dried it, and when I eventually emerged it was to worried enquiries from Mrs Palissey and open-mouthed concern from Brian.

'Something I ate,' I said weakly, and took a brandy miniature from the shelves, and despatched it.

Mrs Palissey and Brian had been too busy with customers to make even a start on the telephone orders. I looked at the pile of numbered lists carefully written in Mrs Palissey's handwriting and felt absolutely incapable of the task of collecting each customer's requirements into cartons for delivery.

'Are any of these urgent?' I asked helplessly.

'Don't you worry,' Mrs Palissey said comfortingly. 'Only one . . . and Brian and I will see to it.'

'I'll make it up to you.'

'Yes, yes,' she said, nodding. 'I know that. I do really.'

I went and sat in the office and dialled Gerard's number.

Tina answered. Gerard had left his office to go home but would still be on his way to the train. He would telephone, she said, when he came in; and could it wait until after a shower and a drink?

'Preferably not.'

'All right. I'll tell him. He'll be tired.' It was more a warning than a plea, I thought.

'I'll be brief,' I said, and she said, 'Good,' and put her receiver down decisively.

Mrs Palissey and Brian left at four-thirty and I locked the shop door behind them, retreating out of sight to my desk while I returned physically to normal and mentally to the accustomed morass of no self-respect.

Gerard, when he telephoned, sounded very tired indeed.

'How did you get on?' he said, stifling a yawn. 'Tina said it wouldn't wait.'

I told him what I'd heard of the conversation between Vernon and Paul Young and where I'd been when I heard it: everything in detail to that point but very little after.

'Paul Young?' he said aghast.

'Yes.'

'Good grief. Look, I'm sorry.'

'Whatever for?'

'I shouldn't have sent you there.'

'You couldn't have known,' I said, 'but I'm afraid we're no nearer discovering who Paul Young is or where he came from. Vernon didn't call him by name from start to finish.'

'We now know for sure he's Larry Trent's brother,' Gerard pointed out. 'And that's not much help. Someone in our office traced Larry Trent's birth certificate yesterday afternoon. He was illegitimate. His mother was a Jane Trent. Father unknown.'

'What are you going to do?' I asked. 'Do you want me to tell the police?'

'No, not yet. Let me think it over and call you back. Will you be in your shop all evening?'

'Until nine, yes.'

'Right.'

I opened my doors again at six, trying and failing to raise genuine interest in the customers' needs. I felt limp and unsteady as if after illness and wondered how Gerard had survived a working lifetime of chasing villains with every nerve coolly intact.

He didn't telephone again until almost closing time, and by then he sounded exhausted.

'Look . . . Tony . . . can you meet me in the morning at nine at Martineau Park?'

'Er . . .' I said feebly. 'Well . . . yes.' Going back there, I thought, was so low on my priority list as to have dropped off the bottom.

'Good,' Gerard said, oblivious. 'I've had a good deal of trouble running to ground the proprietor of the caterers at Martineau. Why does everyone go away at weekends? Anyway, he's meeting us there tomorrow morning. We both agree it's best to find out just what's been going on there in the stores before we say anything to the police. I said I'd bring you because you'd know the Scotch and the wine if you tasted them, and he agreed you were essential. He himself is no expert, he says.'

Gerard made the expedition sound perfectly regular. I said, 'You won't forget Paul Young's going there tomorrow afternoon, will you?'

'No. That's why we must go early, before he removes anything.'

'I meant . . . the police could arrest him and find out who he is.'

'Once we're sure the whisky is at Martineau, we'll alert them.' He spoke patiently but there were reservations in his voice. He would do the police's work only when his own was completed.

'Can I count on you?' he said, after a pause.

'Not to tell them anyway?'

'Yes.'

'I won't,' I said.

'Good.' He yawned. 'Goodnight, then. See you in twelve hours.'

He was waiting in his Mercedes outside the main gates when I arrived, and sleep had clearly done a poor job on restoration. Grey shadows lay in his lean cheeks, with puffed bags under his eyes and lines of strain everywhere, ageing him by years.

'Don't say it,' he said as I approached. 'Antibiotics make me feel lousy.' He was still wearing his sling, I saw, for everything except actual driving. He yawned. 'How do we get into this place?'

We went in the way I'd gone the day before, all the gates again standing open, and walked as far as the Clerk of the Course's office before being challenged. At that point the same man as on the previous day came out with bushy eyebrows rising and asked civilly if he could help us.

'We've come to meet Mr Quigley . . . the caterer.'

'Ah.'

'I'm Gerard McGregor,' Gerard said. 'This is Tony Beach.'

The busy eyebrows frowned. 'I thought you said Cash,' he said to me. 'Peter Cash.'

I shook my head. 'Beach.'

'Oh.' He was puzzled, but shrugged. 'Well, you know the way.'

We smiled, nodded, walked on.

'Who's Peter Cash?' Gerard asked.

'No one.' I explained about Vernon still searching for me the day before. 'I didn't want him to know it was Tony Beach who was there. Peter Cash was the first name which came into my head.'

'Do you mean,' he said, alarmed, 'that this Vernon chased you all over the stands?'

'Hardly chased.'

'It must have felt like it to you.'

'Mm.'

We reached the green door, which on this occasion was firmly locked. Gerard looked at his watch, and almost immediately a proprietor-sized car appeared from behind the far end of the Tote building, pulled up near us outside the Celebration Bar, and disgorged a proprietor-shaped occupant.

He had black hair, a moustache and a paunch. First impressions also included an air of importance, a touch of irritability and a liking for white silk scarves worn cravat-style under nautical blazers.

'Miles Quigley,' he announced briefly. 'Gerard McGregor?'

Gerard nodded.

'Tony Beach,' I said.

'Right.' He looked us over without cordiality. 'Let's see what all this is about, shall we? Although I'll tell you again as I told you last night, I'm certain you're wrong. Vernon has worked for our family for years.'

I could almost feel Gerard thinking of a hundred clients who had said and believed much the same.

'Vernon who?' he said.

'What? No, Vernon's his last name. He's always called Vernon.'

The keyhole in the green door was round and uninformative. The key Miles Quigley produced was six inches long. The one inside the other turned with a good deal of pressure and the multiple click of a heavy mortice lock.

'That's the first locked door I've seen on this race-course,' I said.

'Really?' Miles Quigley raised his eyebrows. 'They do tend to open everything for easy maintenance between meetings in the daytime but I assure you everything's locked at night. A security guard comes on duty after dark. We're very security conscious of course because of all the alcohol stored here.'

The green door opened outwards like that by my

own storeroom: more difficult to break in. Miles Quigley pulled it wide and we went into the passage, where he importantly turned on the lights by slapping a double row of switches with his palm. Yesterday's all too familiar scene sprang to life, the long corridor stretching away dimly to the bowels of the kitchens.

In the wider passage leading to the drinks store Quigley opened a small cupboard marked First Aid and applied to the contents a second key, not as large as the first but equally intricate.

'Security alarm,' he explained with superiority. 'A heat-sensitive system. If anyone goes into the store when the system is on, an alarm rings in the security office here on the racecourse and also in the main police station in Oxford. We test the system regularly. I assure you it works.'

'Who has keys?' Gerard asked, and Quigley's irritated look was its own reply.

'I'd trust Vernon with my life,' he said.

Not me, I thought. I wouldn't.

'Only Vernon and yourself have keys?' Gerard persisted.

'Yes, that's right. Keys to the alarm and the store, that is. The racecourse has a key to the outer door, the green one.'

Gerard nodded non-committally. Quigley turned his back on the problem and produced a third and a fourth key to undo the heavy door into the actual store, each key having to be turned twice, alternately: and considering the value of the liquor stacked inside, I supposed the vault-like precautions weren't unjustified.

'Can your keys be duplicated?' Gerard asked.

'What? No, they can't. They can be obtained only from the firm who installed the system, and they wouldn't issue duplicates without my say-so.'

Quigley was younger than I first thought. Not mid-forties, I judged, standing near him in the brighter storeroom lights: more like mid-thirties aping the manner of fifty.

'A family firm, did you say?' I asked.

'Basically, yes. My father's retired.'

Gerard gave him a dry look. 'He's still chairman, I believe, your father?'

'Presides over board meetings, yes,' Quigley said patronizingly. 'Makes him feel wanted. Old people need that, you know. But I run things. Have done for three years. This is a big firm, you know. We don't cater only for this racecourse, but for many other sporting events and also for weddings and dances. Very big, and growing.'

'Do you keep everything here?' I asked. 'Your linen, tableware, glasses, things like that?'

He shook his head. 'Only the liquor here, because of the high security of this place. Everything else is at our central depot two miles away. Equipment, food stores and offices. We ship everything from there by van daily as required. It's a very big operation, as I said.'

He sounded vastly self-satisfied. 'I have streamlined the whole business considerably.'

'Were spirits by the tot in the private boxes here your own idea?' I asked.

'What?' His eyebrows rose. 'Yes, of course. Got to fall in line with other racecourse caterers. Much more profitable. Got to answer to shareholders, you know. Shareholders are always with us.'

'Mm,' I said.

He heard doubt in my tone. He said sharply, 'Don't forget it's to the box-holder's advantage. When only a little has been used, we don't insist on them buying the whole bottle.'

'True,' I said neutrally. A Quigley-Swayle face-to-face could draw blood: diverting prospect. 'Your strawberry tartlets are excellent.'

He looked at me uncertainly and explained to Gerard that all the paperwork to do with wines, beer and spirits passed through the small office to our left. Vernon, he said without happiness, was wholly in charge.

'He chooses and orders?' Gerard said.

'Yes. He's done it for years.'

'And pays the bills?'

'No. We have a computerized system. The checked invoices go from here to the office two miles away to be paid through the computer. Saves time. I installed it, of course.'

Gerard nodded, ignoring the smugness.

'We keep beer in here, as you see,' Quigley said. 'This is just back-up. Normally we get suppliers to deliver on the day of need.'

Gerard nodded.

'Outside in the passage . . . we've just passed it . . . is the one passenger lift which comes down here . . . in this part of the stands the ground floor as far as the public is concerned is above our heads. We transfer from here to the bars and the boxes using that lift: to the bars on all floors. Early on racedays we are extremely busy.'

Gerard said he was sure.

'Through here are the wines and spirits,' Quigley said, leading the way into the main storeroom. 'As you see.'

Gerard saw. Quigley walked a few steps ahead of us and Gerard said quietly, 'Where were you yesterday?'

'Lying up here . . . on the Pol Roger.'

He looked at me with curiosity. 'What's the matter?'

'What do you mean?'

'You look . . . it can't be right . . . you look of all things ashamed.'

I swallowed. 'When I was up there . . . I was frightened sick.'

He looked round the storeroom; at the possibilities and limitations of concealment; and he said judiciously, 'You'd have been a fool not to be scared stiff. I don't think there's much doubt Paul Young would have killed you if he'd found you. Killing the second time is easier,

I'm told. Fear in a fearful situation is normal. Absence of fear is not. Keeping one's nerve in spite of fear is courage.'

He had a way, I thought, of speaking without sympathy while giving incredible comfort. I didn't thank him, but profoundly in my heart I was grateful.

'Shall we start?' he said as we rejoined Quigley. 'Tony, you said the suspect cases are somewhere at the far end?'

'Yes.'

We all moved through the central canyon between the piled-high city blocks of cartons until we reached the end wall.

'Where now?' Quigley demanded. 'I see nothing wrong. This all looks exactly the same as usual.'

'Always Bell's whisky at the end here?'

'Of course.'

The size of the Bell's block would have shamed the wholesalers I regularly bought from. Even Gerard looked daunted at the possibility of having to open the whole lot to find the bad apples, which was nothing to the vision of paralytic drunkenness crossing my own imagination.

'Er . . .' I said. 'There may be marks of some sort on the boxes. Someone was putting black felt tip squiggles on the gin when it was being checked in.'

'Mervyn, probably,' Quigley said.

'Yes, that's right.'

I walked back to the gin and looked at Mervyn's

handiwork: a hasty curling cross with two diagonals almost joined in a circle on the right side. The only problem was that it appeared also on every Bell's case in sight. No other distinguishing mark seemed to be on any that we could see without dismantling the whole mountain.

'Vernon must have been able to tell one from another, easily,' Gerard said. 'He wouldn't risk not knowing his stuff at a glance.'

'I don't believe all this,' Quigley announced irritably. 'Vernon's a most efficient manager.'

'I don't doubt it,' Gerard murmured.

'Perhaps we could find the wine,' I suggested. 'It might be less difficult.'

Wine was stacked in narrower blocks on the opposite wall from the spirits, the quantity in each stack less but the variety more: and I found St Estèphe and St Emilion six deep behind a fronting wall of unimpeachable Mouton Cadet.

Quigley consented to the opening of a case of St Estèphe, which laid bare the familiar false label in all its duplicity.

'This is it,' I said. 'Shall we taste it to make sure?'

Quigley frowned. 'You can't be right. It's come from a respectable supplier. Vintners Incorporated. There's their name stamped on the box.'

'Taste the wine,' Gerard said.

I produced my corkscrew, opened a bottle and went back to the office section to search for a glass. All I could find were throwaway expanded polystyrene beakers which would have given Henri Travel a fit: but even in the featherweight plastic the bottle's contents were unmistakable.

'Not St Estèphe,' I said positively. 'Shall I try the St Emilion?'

Quigley shrugged. I opened a case and a bottle, and tasted.

'It's the same,' I said. 'Shall we look for the other four?'

They were all there, all hidden behind respectable façades of the same sort of wine: the Mâcon behind Mâcon, and so on. The contents of all were identical, as at the Silver Moondance: and all six wines had been supplied, according to the cases, by Vintners Incorporated.

'Um,' Gerard said thoughtfully, 'do Vintners Incorporated supply Bell's whisky also?'

'But they're a well-known firm,' Quigley protested.

'Anyone,' Gerard pointed out, 'can cut a stencil and slap the name Vintners Incorporated onto anything.'

Quigley opened his mouth and then slowly closed it. We returned to the Bell's and immediately found a section at the back of the block with Vintners Incorporated emblazoned obviously on the side.

'I can't believe it,' Quigley said. Then, 'Oh, very well. Taste it.'

I tasted it. Waited. Let aftertaste develop. Beyond that let nuances linger in mouth, throat and nose.

'He can't tell,' Quigley said impatiently to Gerard. 'There's nothing wrong with it. I told you.'

'Have you ever had complaints?' I asked eventually.

'Of course we have,' he said. 'What caterer hasn't? But none of them has been justified.'

I wondered if Martineau Park would turn up on Ridger's lists. No hope of finding out until he came back on Wednesday.

'This isn't Bell's,' I said. 'Too much grain, hardly any malt.'

'Sure?' Gerard said.

'It's what we're looking for,' I said, nodding.

'What do you mean?' Quigley asked, and then without waiting for an answer said aggrievedly, 'How could Vernon possibly be so disloyal?'

His reply came through the doorway in the shape of the man himself: Vernon in his leather jacket, large, angry and alarmed.

'What the bloody hell is going on here?' he shouted, advancing fast down the storeroom. 'What the hell do you think you're doing?'

He stopped dead when Gerard moved slightly, disclosing the presence of Quigley.

He said, 'Oh ... Miles ... I didn't expect ...'

He sensed something ominous in our stillness. His gaze shifted warily from Quigley to Gerard and finally to me: and I was a shock to him of cataclysmic proportions.

CHAPTER NINETEEN

'Let's straighten this out,' Gerard said matter of factly in the office section, to which we had all moved. 'The fraud as I see it is as follows.'

His voice was as unhurried and unemotional as an accountant summing up an unexciting audit and was having a positively calming effect on Quigley if not on Vernon.

'It appears to me from a preliminary inspection of the invoices at present to hand in this office that the following sequence of events has been taking place. And perhaps I should explain to you,' he said directly to Vernon, 'that the unravelling of commercial fraud is my normal and constant occupation.'

Vernon's small intense eyes stared at him blankly and under the large drooping moustache the mouth moved in twitches, tightening and loosening with tension. He half stood, half sat, his bulk supported by the desk on which he had done his constructive paperwork, and he had folded his arms across his chest as if not accepting in the least the accusations now coming his way. The fine dew, however, stood again on his forehead, and I guessed that all he could be grateful for was that this present inquisitor was not his dangerous friend Paul Young.

'A supplier proposed to you the following scheme,' Gerard said. 'You as liquor manager here would order extensively from him and in return receive a sizeable commission. A kick-back. You were to sell what he provided as if it were part of your firm's regular stock. However, what he provided was not as described on the invoice. Your firm was paying for Bell's whisky and fine wines and receiving liquor of lower quality. You certainly knew this. It considerably increased your pay-off.'

Quigley, standing by the doorway, rocked slowly on his heels as if disassociating himself from the proceedings. Gerard, seated on the only chair, dominated the moment absolutely.

'Your provider,' he said, 'chose the name of a respectable supplier with whom you didn't already do business and sent you everything stencilled "Vintners Incorporated". You received normal-looking invoices from your supplier with that heading and your treasurer's department sent cheques normally in return. They were perhaps negligent in not checking that the address printed on the invoice heading was truly that of Vintners Incorporated, as you have just heard me doing on the telephone, but no doubt Mr Quigley's firm as a whole deals with dozens of different suppliers and has no habit of checking each one.' He broke off and turned his head towards Quigley. 'I always advise firms to check and keep checking. Such a simple matter. When an address has been entered once into a computerized system such as yours, it's seldom ever checked. The computer goes on sending payments without question. Invoices may indeed be routinely paid without the goods ever being delivered.' He turned back to Vernon. 'On how many occasions did that happen?'

'Rubbish,' Vernon said.

'Vernon,' Quigley said, and it was a shattered word of disillusion, not of disbelief. 'Vernon, how could you? You've been with the family for years.'

Vernon gave him a look in which contempt was clearly a component. Vernon might have remained loyal to the father, I thought, but had been a pushover under the son.

'Who is this provider?' Quigley said.

I saw Gerard wince internally: it wasn't a question he would have asked except obliquely, trying to squeeze out a name by finesse.

Vernon said, 'No one.'

'He's coming here this afternoon,' I said.

Vernon stood up compulsively and unfolded his arms.

'You bloody spy,' he said intensely.

'And you're afraid of him,' I said. 'You don't want to follow Zarac to the cemetery.'

He glared at me. 'You're not Peter Cash,' he said suddenly. 'I know who you are. You're that interfering bloody wine merchant, that's who you are. Beach, bloody Beach.'

No one denied it. No one asked him, either, how he knew anything about any bloody interfering wine merchant called Beach. He could only have known if Paul Young had told him.

'Who's Peter Cash?' Quigley asked, lost.

'He told the racecourse people his name was Peter Cash,' Vernon said violently. 'Insurance.' He nearly spat. 'He didn't want us knowing who he was.'

'Us?' Gerard asked.

Vernon shut his mouth tight under the curtain of moustache.

'I'd guess,' I said slowly, 'that you turned up this early today because you intended to take all the "Vintners Incorporated" cases out of here and be long gone before your provider arrived at two.'

Vernon said, 'Rot,' but without conviction, and Quigley shook his head despairingly.

'It's possible,' Gerard said with authority, 'that Mr Quigley wouldn't himself press charges against you, Vernon, if you cared to answer some questions.'

Quigley stiffened. I murmured 'Shareholders?' at his elbow and felt his opposition falter and evaporate. With the faintest twitch of humour to his mouth Gerard said, 'For instance, Vernon, how close were your ties with Zarac at the Silver Moondance?'

Silence. The dew on Vernon's forehead coagulated into visible drops and he brushed the back of one hand over the moustache in evident nervousness. The struggle within him continued for a lengthening time until his doubts forced a way out.

'How can I know?' he said. 'How can I be sure he wouldn't get the force here the minute I said anything?' He, it appeared, was Miles Quigley. 'Keep the trap shut and stay out of trouble, that's what I say,' Vernon said.

'Wise advice, if we were the police,' Gerard said. 'But we're not. Whatever you say here won't be taken down and used in evidence. Mr Quigley can give you an assurance and you can believe it.'

Mr Quigley looked as if he were well on the way from injured sorrow to vengeful fury at Vernon's defection, but still had enough of an eye to the annual general meeting to see that swallowing the unpalatable now could save him corporate indigestion later on.

'Very well,' he said rigidly. 'No prosecutions.'

'On condition,' Gerard added, 'that we consider your answers to be frank.'

Vernon said nothing. Gerard neutrally repeated his question about Zarac, and waited.

'I knew him,' Vernon said at length, grudgingly. 'He used to come here for wine if they ran out at the Silver Moondance.'

'Your provider's wine?' Gerard said. 'The "Vintners Incorporated" labels?'

'Yes, of course.'

'Why of course?'

Vernon hesitated. Gerard knew the answer: testing him, I thought.

Vernon said jerkily, 'Larry Trent was his brother.'

'Zarac's brother?'

'No, of course not. My ... well ... provider's.'

'His name?'

'Paul Young.' Vernon had less trouble with that answer, not more. He sounded glib, I thought. He was lying.

Gerard didn't press it. He said merely, 'Paul Young was Larry Trent's brother, is that it?'

'Half-brother.'

'Did you know Zarac before this Paul Young persuaded you to join his scheme?'

'Yes, I did. He came here for regular wine like restaurants do sometimes and said he knew of a good fiddle, no risks, for someone in my position. If I was interested, he would let me in.'

Gerard pondered. 'Did the Silver Moondance normally get its wine straight from, er, Paul Young?'

'Yes, it did.'

'Did you know Larry Trent?'

'I met him.' Vernon's voice was unimpressed. 'All he cared about was horses. His brother was bloody good to him, letting him strut about pretending to own that place, giving him money by the fistful for his training fees and gambling. Too bloody good to him by half, Zarac said.'

1071

I heard in memory Orkney Swayle saying Larry Trent was jealous of his brother; the brother who gave him so much. Sad world; ironic.

'What was the relationship between Larry Trent and Zarac?'

'They both worked for his brother. For Paul Young.' Again the unfamiliarity over the name. Gerard again let it go.

'Equal footing?'

'Not in public, I don't suppose.'

'Why did Paul Young kill Zarac?'

'I don't know,' Vernon said, indistinctly, very disturbed. 'I don't know.'

'But you knew he did kill him?'

'Jesus . . .'

'Yes,' Gerard went on. 'Go on. You do know, and you can tell us.'

Vernon spoke suddenly as if compelled. 'He said Zarac wanted the Silver Moondance. Wanted it given to him on a plate. Given to him or else. Sort of blackmail.'

Vernon was a sweating mixture of fear, indignation, sympathy and candour and had begun to experience the cathartic release of confession.

I watched in fascination. Gerard said smoothly, 'He justified the killing to you?'

'Explained it,' Vernon said. 'He came here with the Silver Moondance liquor piled up in his Rolls. He said he was loading it with Zarac's help. He made three trips. There was so much. The third time he came he was different. He was flushed ... excited ... very strong. He said I would hear Zarac was dead, and to keep my mouth shut. He said Zarac had wanted power over him, and he couldn't have that ... and then I heard later how he'd killed him ... made me vomit ... Zarac wasn't a bad guy ... Jesus, I never meant to get mixed up in murder. I didn't. It was supposed to be just an easy fiddle for good money ...'

'And for how long,' Gerard said flatly, 'has the fiddle been in progress?'

'About fifteen months.'

'Wine and whisky all the time?'

'No. Just wine to start with. Whisky these past six months.'

'Always Bell's?'

'Yes.'

'Where did the fake Bell's whisky go from here?'

'Where?' Vernon took a moment to understand. 'Oh. We sold it in the bars here all the time. Sometimes in the boxes too. Also it went to the other sports fixtures Quigley's cater for, and weddings and dances in halls everywhere. All over.'

Quigley's face went stiff and blank with almost comical shock.

'Anywhere you thought no one would notice the difference?' Gerard asked.

'I suppose so. Most people can't. Not in a crowded place, they can't. There's too many other smells. Zarac told me that, and he was right.'

1073

Wine waiters, I knew, were cynics. I also thought that but for Orkney's anti-caterer obsession and his refusal to accept what they routinely offered, I might even have found the Rannoch/Bell's in his box.

'Do you know what precise whisky you were selling in Bell's bottles?' Gerard asked.

Vernon looked as if he hadn't considered it closely. 'It was Scotch.'

'And have you heard of a young man called Kenneth Charter?'

'Who?' Vernon said, bewildered.

'Return to Paul Young,' Gerard said without visible disappointment. 'Did he plan with you the robbery at Mr Beach's shop?'

Vernon wasn't so penitent as not to be able to afford me a venomous glance. 'No, not really. He just borrowed one of our vans. I lent him the keys.'

'What?' Quigley exclaimed. 'The van that was stolen?'

Quigley . . . Quality House Provisions. I picked up one of the printed catering pricelists from the desk beside Gerard and belatedly read the heading: Crisp, Duval and Quigley Ltd, incorporating Quality House Provisions. Quigley's own van outside my back door.

'They meant to bring it back,' Vernon said defensively. 'They didn't expect that bloody man to turn up on a Sunday teatime.' He glared at me balefully. 'They said he might have seen the number plate and they'd keep the van for a while but we'd get it back eventually.

When the heat died down they'd dump it somewhere. They told me to report it missing, but I didn't get a chance, the police were round at the office before you could sneeze.'

'They,' Gerard said calmly. 'Who are they?'

'They work for . . . Paul Young.'

'Names?'

'Don't know.'

'Try again.'

'Denny. That's all I know. One's called Denny. I was just told Denny would pick up the van. They were going to bring the wines here from the shop for me to sort through but they didn't come although I waited until nine. Then I heard *he* turned up,' Vernon jerked his head in my direction, 'and something happened to put them off so they never came here. I heard later they got the wrong stuff anyway, so it was all a bloody muddle for nothing.'

'Did anyone tell you what it was that happened to put them off?' Gerard asked casually.

'No, except they panicked or something because something happened they didn't expect, but I didn't hear what.'

Both Gerard and I believed him. He couldn't have stood there so unconcernedly disclaiming knowledge in front of us if he'd known that the something that had happened was our being shot.

'How well do you know them?' Gerard asked.

'I don't. Denny drives the delivery van which brings

the stuff here. The other comes sometimes. They never talk much.'

'How often do they deliver?'

'About once a week. Depends.'

'On how much you've sold?'

'Yes.'

'Why didn't they use that van to rob Mr Beach's shop?'

'It's big . . . it's got Vintners Incorporated on the door . . . it was in for repairs, or something.'

'And can you describe Denny and his mate?'

Vernon shrugged. 'They're young.'

'Hair style?'

'Nothing special.'

'Not frizzy black Afro?'

'No.' Vernon was positive and slightly puzzled. 'Just ordinary.'

'Where do they come from? Where do they bring the wine from?'

'I don't know,' Vernon said. 'I never asked. They wouldn't have said. They're not friendly. They work for Paul Young . . . that's all I know.'

He said Paul Young this time far more easily. Getting accustomed, I thought.

'When did you first meet Paul Young?'

'Right when I started. When I told Zarac I was interested. He said the boss would come to check me out and explain what he wanted, and he came. He said we'd get on well together, which we did mostly.'

Until Vernon started in business on the side, stealing from his master: but he wasn't confessing that, I noticed.

'And what is Paul Young's real name?' Gerard asked.

The open doors of the confessional slammed rapidly shut.

Vernon said tightly, 'His name is Paul Young.'

Gerard shook his head.

'Paul Young,' Vernon insisted. 'That's what his name is.'

'No,' Gerard said.

Vernon's sweat ran from his forehead across his temple and down to his jaw. 'He told me the police had seen him in the Silver Moondance when he went there unawares after his brother died, and that was the name he gave them because he didn't want to be investigated because of the drinks, and he said they'd be looking for him now because of Zarac, they'd be looking for Paul Young who didn't exist, he just said the first name that came into his head . . . He said if ever, if ever anyone came here asking, which he said he was certain they wouldn't, but if ever . . . I was to call him Paul Young. And my God, my God, that's what I'm calling him and I'm not telling you his real name, he'd kill me somehow . . . and I'm not joking, I know it. I'll go to jail . . . but I'm not telling you.'

He'd spoken with total conviction and in understandable fear, but all the same I was slightly surprised when Gerard didn't press him, didn't lean on him further.

He said merely, 'All right.' And after a pause, 'That's all, then.'

Vernon for a wild moment seemed to think he had been let off all hooks, straightening up with a returning echo of burly authority.

Quigley instantly deflated him, saying in pompous outrage, 'Give me your keys, Vernon. At once.' He held out his hand peremptorily. 'At once.'

Vernon silently brought a ring of keys from his pocket and handed them over.

'Tomorrow you can look for another job,' Quigley said. 'I'll stick to my agreement. I won't prosecute. But you'll get no reference. I'm disappointed in you, Vernon, I don't understand you. But you'll have to go, and that's it.'

Vernon said blankly, 'I'm forty-eight.'

'And you had a good job here for life,' Gerard said, nodding. 'You blew it. Your own fault.'

As if for the first time Vernon seemed to be looking realistically at his doubtful future. New lines of worry deepened round his eyes.

'Do you have a family?' Gerard said.

Vernon said faintly, 'Yes.'

'Unemployment is preferable to imprisonment,' Gerard said austerely, as no doubt he had said to many a detected cheat: and Quigley as well as Vernon and myself heard the iron in his voice. Actions had to be

accounted for and responsibility accepted. Consequences had to be faced. Constant forgiveness
destroyed the soul . . .

Vernon shivered.

With Quigley's permission, after Vernon had gone,
Gerard and I loaded into his Mercedes (driven round
to the green door) a case of 'Vintners Incorporated'
Bell's and a case each of the 'Vintners Incorporated'
wines. In effect Gerard and Quigley watched while
I shifted the cases. Back to my normal occupation, I
thought with a sigh, and let the fork-lift truck take most
of the strain off my mending muscles.

'What do I do with the rest?' Quigley said helplessly.
'And how are we going to cope with the Autumn Carnival without Vernon? No one else knows the routine.
He's been here so long. He *is* the routine . . . he
developed it.'

Neither Gerard nor I offered solutions. Quigley
gloomily set about double-double-locking his treasure
house and switching on the alarm, and we made the
final reverse trip to the outer world.

'What should I do?' Quigley asked, fastening the
green door. 'I mean . . . about that murder?'

Gerard said, 'Vernon told you his version of what
Paul Young told him, which was itself no doubt only a
version of the facts. That's a long way from first-hand
knowledge.'

'You mean . . . I could do nothing?'

'Act as your judgement dictates,' Gerard said pleasantly and unhelpfully, and for once in his life I guessed Quigley was searching his self-importance and finding only doubt and irresolution.

Gerard said, 'Tony and I will tell the police that Paul Young may arrive here at any time from now on. After that, it's up to them.'

'He said he was coming at two o'clock,' Quigley corrected.

'Mm. But he might suspect Vernon would do what Vernon did mean to do, in other words clear off with the loot before Paul Young got here. Paul Young could be here at any minute.' Gerard seemed unconcerned but he was alone in that. Quigley made his mind up to leave us as soon as possible and I felt very much like following.

'He won't be able to get in as I have all the keys,' Quigley said. 'I suppose I must thank you, Mr McGregor. I don't like any of this. I can only hope that with Vernon gone we'll have no more trouble.'

'Certainly hope not,' Gerard said blandly, and we both watched Quigley drive away with hope already straightening the shoulders and throwing forward the chin. 'He might be lucky, he might not,' Gerard said.

'I don't want to be here when Paul Young gets here,' I said.

He half smiled. 'More prudent not. Get in my car

and we'll fetch your car first and then find a telephone box.'

We both drove for five miles and stopped in a small village where he made the call from the public telephone outside the post office. I gave him the priority number Ridger had told me, and I listened to his brief message.

'It's possible,' he said to the police, 'that the man known as Paul Young may arrive at the caterers' entrance in the grandstands of Martineau Park racecourse at any time today from now onwards.' He listened to a reply and said, 'No. No names. Goodbye.'

Smiling, he replaced the receiver. 'OK,' he said. 'Duty done.'

'To some extent,' I said.

'Everything's relative.' He was cheerful although still looking far from well. 'We know where Kenneth Charter's Scotch is.'

'Some of it,' I said.

'Enough.'

'But not where it went between the tanker and the Vintners Incorporated deliveries.'

'To a bottling plant, as you said.'

He was leaning against his car, arm in sling, looking frail, a recuperating English gentleman out for a harmless Sunday morning drive in the country. There was also a glimmer of humour about him and the steel core looking out of the eyes, and I said abruptly, 'You know something you haven't told me.'

'Do you think so? What about?'

'You've found the bottling plant!'

'Found *a* bottling plant, yes. Somewhere to start from anyway. I thought I'd go and take a look this afternoon. Preliminary recce.'

'But it's Sunday. There'll be no one there.'

'That's sometimes an advantage.'

'You don't mean . . . break in?'

'We'll see,' he said. 'It depends. Sometimes there's a caretaker. I'm good at government inspectors, even on Sundays.'

Slightly aghast I said, 'Well . . . where is it?'

'Roughly twenty-five miles this side of Kenneth Charter's headquarters.' He smiled slightly. 'By Friday afternoon we had concluded in the office that your idea of looking first at the plants to which Charter's tankers took wine had been good but wrong. There were five of them. We screened them all first, and all of them were rock-solid businesses. Then some time during last night . . . you know how things float into your head while you're half asleep . . . I remembered that one of them had had two links with Charter, not just one, and that maybe, just maybe, that second link is more important than we thought.'

'Tell me,' I said.

'Mm. I don't want to be too positive.'

'For heaven's sake . . .'

'All right then. We established right at the beginning of our bottle-plant inquiries that one of the plants is owned by a man called Stewart Naylor. It was at the top of the list that Charter gave us, and the first we checked.'

'Stewart Naylor?' I thought. 'He's . . . he's . . . um . . . isn't he mentioned in Kenneth Junior's notebook? Oh yes . . . the father who plays war games . . . David Naylor's father.'

'Top of the class. Stewart Naylor owns Bernard Naylor Bottling. Started by his grandfather. Old respectable firm. I woke up with that word Naylor fizzing like a sparkler in my head. I telephoned Kenneth Charter himself early this morning and asked him about his son's friendship with David Naylor. He says he's known the father, Stewart Naylor, for years: they're not close friends but they know each other quite well because of their business connection and because their sons like each other's company. Kenneth Charter says David Naylor is the only good thing in Kenneth Junior's lazy life, he keeps Kenneth Junior off the streets. War games, Kenneth Charter thinks, are a waste of time, but better than glue-sniffing.'

'His words?' I asked amused.

'Aye, laddie.'

'Do you really think . . .'

'Kenneth Charter doesn't. Grasping at straws, he thinks it. He says Bernard Naylor Bottling is twenty-four carat. But we've found no other leads at all, and we've been checking bottling plants up and down the country until the entire staff are sick at the sound of the words. Three days' concentrated work, fruitless. A lot of them have gone out of business. One's a library now. Another's a boot and shoe warehouse.'

'Mm,' I said. 'Could Stewart Naylor have an illegitimate half-brother?'

'Anyone can have an illegitimate half-brother. It happens to the best.'

'I mean . . .'

'I know what you mean. Kenneth Charter didn't know of one.' He shrugged. 'Naylor's plant's a long shot. Either a bullseye or a case for apology. I'll go and find out.'

'Right now?'

'Absolutely right now. If Stewart Naylor is by any chance also Paul Young, he should be going to or from Martineau Park this afternoon, not stalking about among his bottles.'

'Did you ask Kenneth Charter what he looked like?'

'Yes . . . ordinary, he said.'

All these ordinary men . . . 'Is he deaf?' I asked.

Gerard blinked. 'I forgot about that.'

'Ask him,' I said. 'Telephone now, before you go.'

'And if Stewart Naylor is deaf . . . don't go?'

'Quite right. Don't go.'

Gerard shook his head. 'All the more reason to go.'

'It's flinging oneself into the Limpopo,' I said.

'Perhaps. Only perhaps. Nothing's certain.' He returned to the telephone, however, and dialled

Kenneth Charter's house and then his office, and to neither attempt was there a reply.

'That's it, then,' he said calmly. 'I'll be off.'

'Have you ever been in a bottling plant?' I said despairingly. 'I mean . . . do you know what to look for?'

'No.'

I stared at him. He stared right back. In the end I said, 'I spent a year in and out of bottling plants in Bordeaux.'

'Did you?'

'Yes.'

'Tell me, then, what to look for.'

I thought of pumps and machinery. I thought of vats and what might be in them. I said hopelessly, 'You need me with you, don't you?'

'I'd like it,' he said. 'But I won't ask. It's on the very edge of consultancy . . . and maybe beyond.'

'You wouldn't know the wine if you fell into it, would you?' I said. 'Nor the Scotch?'

'Not a chance,' he agreed placidly.

'Bloody sodding hell,' I said. 'You're a bugger.'

He smiled. 'I thought you'd come, really, if I told you.'

CHAPTER TWENTY

I put a notice on my shop door saying, 'Closed. Very sorry. Staff illness. Open Monday 9.30 a.m.'

I'm mad, I thought. Crazy.

If I didn't go, he would go on his own.

My thoughts stopped there. I couldn't let him go on his own when it was I who had the knowledge he needed. When he felt tired and ill and I was well and almost as strong as ever.

I sat at my desk and wrote a note to Sergeant John Ridger saying I'd been told to look in the Bernard Naylor bottling plant for the Silver Moondance Scotch, and I was going there with Gerard McGregor (I gave his address) to check. I sealed the note in an envelope and wrote on it an instruction to Mrs Palissey: Take this to the police station if you haven't heard from me by ten this morning and tell them to open it.

I wedged the envelope on the till where she couldn't miss it and hoped she would never read it. Then with a last look round I locked my door and drove away, and tried not to wonder if I would ever come back.

Half the time I thought Kenneth Charter must know his man. Stewart Naylor was true blue. Half the time I trusted Gerard's fizzler in the night. Intuition existed. Solutions came in sleep.

It would probably turn out to be an anticlimax of a journey not worth melodramatic notes to policemen or all this soul-searching. We would drive to the bottling plant, we would not break in, there would be plentiful evidence of legal prosperity and we would drive sedately home. It would not be another day of Sunday bloody horrors.

Gerard met me in a car park we had agreed on, he having meanwhile been home to leave the Martineau Park spoils in his garage. From there we went towards London in his Mercedes, but with me driving this time.

'Suppose you were Stewart Naylor,' Gerard said. 'Suppose you'd spent your entire working life learning to run the family bottling business and then because of the French changing their regulations found the wine flood drying to a trickle.'

'Longbows,' I said nodding.

'What? Oh yes. Kenneth Charter was wrong, you know, in point of fact. It was the crossbow which put paid to the longbow ... well, never mind. Crossbows, guns, whatever, from no fault of your own you're going out of business. Kenneth Charter confirmed this morning that he hardly takes a fifth of what he used to to the Naylor plant, but it's still quite a lot. More

1087

than to anywhere else. He says that's how he knows that Naylor's is healthy while others struggle.'

'Huh.'

'Yes, indeed. Suppose you are Stewart Naylor and you look anxiously around for other things to bottle . . . tomato sauce, cleaning fluid, whatever . . . and you find everyone else in your line of business is in the same boat and doing the same. Ruin raises its ugly head and gives you a good long threatening glare.' He paused as I passed a lorry, then went on, 'We supposed earlier that at that point a convenient crook came along offering salvation in return for dishonesty and that our belea-guered bottler accepted. But suppose it wasn't like that. Suppose Stewart Naylor needed no seducing but without help thought up his own crooked scheme?'

'Which was,' I said, 'to buy wine himself instead of bottling for others. To bottle it and label it as better than it was, and then sell it.' I frowned. 'And at that point you get discovered and prosecuted.'

'Not if you have a half-brother who likes horses. You set him up . . . on bank money . . . in a Silver Moon-dance, and you take him your wine to sell. It sells well and for about twenty times more than it costs you, even including the bottles. Money starts flowing in, not out . . . and that's when the greed complex hits you.'

'The greed complex?' I asked.

'Addiction,' Gerard said. 'The first step is the huge one. The decision. To snort cocaine or not to. To borrow the Christmas Club's money, just once. To sell the first secret. To design a label for a non-existent château and stick it on a bottle of wine-lake. The first step's huge, the second half the size, by the sixth step it's a habit. Suppose our Stewart Naylor begins to think that if he could arrange other outlets he could double and redouble his receipts?'

'OK,' I said. 'Suppose.'

'At this point we have to suppose a henchman called Zarac, whom one conveniently instals as head waiter at the Silver Moondance. One of his duties is to cast about for possibilities of expansion and in due course he arrives on Vernon's doorstep at Martineau Park. He reports back to Paul Young . . . er . . . Paul Young query Stewart Naylor . . . who goes to see Vernon and hey presto, the fake wine business takes a deep breath and swells to double size. Money now rolls in to the extent that concealing it is a problem. Never mind. Half-brother Larry is a whizz at horses. Pass Larry the embarrassing cash, magic-wand it into horseflesh, ship it to California, convert it again at a profit if possible and bank it . . . intending, I dare say, to collect it one day and live in the sun. In my experience the last chapter seldom happens. The addiction to the crime becomes so integral to the criminal that he can't give it up. I've caught several industrial spies because they couldn't kick their taste for creeping about with cameras.'

'Clean up and clear out,' I suggested.

'Absolutely. Almost never done. They come back for

a second bite, and a third, and just once more . . . and whammo, one too much.'

'So Stewart Naylor turned his ideas to Scotch?'

'Ah,' Gerard said. 'Suppose when your son visits his divorced father one day he brings his friend Kenneth Junior with him? Or suppose he's often brought him? Stewart Naylor knows Kenneth Junior's father quite well . . . Kenneth Charter's tankers have brought wine to Naylor's plant for many years. Suppose our crime-addicted Stewart casts an idle eye on Kenneth Junior and reflects that Charter's tankers carry Scotch and gin as well as wine, and that whereas the wine profits are healthy, from stolen Scotch they would be astro-nomical.'

'But he couldn't ask Kenneth Junior outright to sell his dad's tankers' routes and destinations and time-tables. Kenneth Junior might have gone all righteous and buzzed home to spill the beans . . .'

'But he does think Kenneth Junior is ripe for a spot of treason as he's probably heard him bellyaching about his life with father . . .'

'So he sends Zarac to recruit him,' I said. 'Sends Zarac perhaps to the Diamond snooker hall? Or the disco? Somewhere like that? And Zarac says here's a lot of money, kid. Get me a tanker's keys, get me a tanker's route, and I'll give you some more cash. And three months later he pays again. And again. And then says get me another tanker's keys, kid, the first one's too hot . . .'

'Don't see why not, do you?'

'No,' I said. 'I don't.'

'Zarac,' Gerard said thoughtfully, 'held a very strong hand anyway when it came to blackmail.'

I nodded. 'Too strong for his own good.'

We came to the end of the motorway and turned off into narrower streets to thread our way to Ealing.

'Do you know how to find this plant?' I said. 'Or do we ask a policeman?'

'Map,' Gerard said succinctly, producing one from the glove compartment. 'It shows the roads. When we reach the road, drive slowly, keep your eyes skinned.'

'Fair enough.'

'And drive straight past,' he said. 'When we see what's what, we'll decide what to do.'

'All right.'

'If you turn left a mile ahead we'll be about five miles from target. I'll steer you.'

'Right.'

We turned left at a major intersection onto a dual carriageway through sleepy suburbs where in countless ovens Sunday roasts spluttered to lunchtime.

'We'll get a profile done tomorrow of that Scotch we took from Martineau,' Gerard said.

'And of the sample I took from the Silver Moon-dance bottle.'

'They should be the same.'

'They will be.'

'You're exceedingly positive.'

I grinned. 'Yes.'

'Go on, then. What's the joke?'

'Well . . . you know that the tankerful set off from Scotland every time at fifty-eight per cent alcohol? And that at Rannoch's own bottling plant they would have added water to dilute it to forty?'

'Yes,' he nodded.

'Have you any idea how much water that entails?'

'No, of course not. How much?'

'About two thousand seven hundred gallons. More than ten tons by weight.'

'Good grief!'

'Well,' I said, 'Rannoch's would be careful about that water. They'd use pure spring water of some sort, even if it hadn't actually come from a Scottish loch. But I'll swear that Charter's stolen loads have been diluted from an ordinary tap.'

'Is that bad?'

I laughed. 'It sure is. Any Scottish distiller would have a fit. They say that Scotch whisky is only the way it is because of the softness and purity of loch water. When I tasted the Silver Moondance Scotch again in my shop I could sort of smell chemicals very faintly in the aftertaste. A lot of tap water isn't too bad, but some is awful. Makes disgusting tea. Ask the residents around here.'

'Here?' he exclaimed.

'Western parts of London. Notorious.'

'Good grief.'

'It will turn up in the profile, too.'

'Water?'

'Mm. Purifying chemicals. There shouldn't be any in neat scotch.'

'But won't tap water spoil the Scotch profile? I mean . . . will we still be able to prove our samples are identical with the original sent off from Scotland?'

'Yes, don't worry. Tap water won't affect the whisky profile, it'll just show up as extra components.'

'Will it matter that the Scotch is diluted?'

'No,' I said. 'The gas chromatograph just shows up the presence of things, not their quantity.'

He seemed relieved. 'Turn right at the next traffic lights. Could the gas chromatograph tell where any particular sample of tap water came from?'

'I don't know.'

'Amazing.'

'What is?'

'There's something you don't know.'

'Yeah . . . Well, I don't know the dynasties of China or how to say no thanks in fifteen languages or the way to this bottling plant.' And I'd like to turn straight round and go home, I thought. The nearer we got to Naylor's the more my nervousness increased . . . and I thought of my father, brave as brave, setting off into battlefields, inspiring his men . . . and why couldn't I be like him instead of feeling my mouth go dry and my breath shorten before we were even in the heartland of deepest Ealing.

'Turn left here,' Gerard said. 'Then the third on the right. That's our road.'

He was totally calm. No strain or anxiety in voice or face. I consciously unclenched my fingers from their grip on the steering wheel and tried without noticeable success to relax to Gerard's level.

Hopeless. Even my teeth were tightly together when we turned into the third on the right and went slowly along.

'There it is,' Gerard said matter-of-factly. 'See?'

I glanced to where he indicated and saw a pair of very tall entrance gates, shut, set in a length of very tall brick wall. On the gates in faded white lettering were the words 'Bernard Naylor Bottling', with below them a padlock the size of a saucer.

We wouldn't be able to get in, I thought. Thank goodness for that.

'Turn left at the end,' Gerard said. 'Park there if you can.'

It was one of those suburbs built before zoning where light industries sat among dwelling houses as an integral part of the community. When I'd parked the Mercedes at a kerbside among a row of residents' wheels we walked past lace curtains and shrubby front gardens to get back to the high wall. Eating their roast beef, I thought, and the Yorkshire puddings and the gravy ... ten minutes past lunchtime and my stomach fluttering with enough butterflies to stock a Brazilian rain forest.

We walked slowly as if out for a stroll and in the short street there was only one other pedestrian, an elderly man waiting patiently for his dog at lamp-posts.

When we reached the gates, eight feet high, dark green sun-faded paint, Gerard stopped and faced them, head back as if reading the big white letters spreading across.

'There's broken glass embedded in the top of those walls,' I said. 'Barbed wire along the top of the gates. Don't tell me you can pick that half-ton padlock.'

'No need,' Gerard said placidly. 'Open your eyes. In many massive gates conspicuously bolted there's a smaller door inset, wide enough for one person only. There's one right ahead of us in the left-hand gate with quite an ordinary looking spring lock, and if I can't let us in through there I've been wasting the best years of my life.'

He stopped his apparent reading of the legend on the gates and resumed his stroll, glancing as if casually at the small gate cut in the large.

'Do you smoke?' he said.

'No,' I said in surprise.

'Tie a shoelace.'

'Sure,' I said, understanding, and bent down obligingly to pretend to tie bows on my laceless slip-ons.

'A doddle,' Gerard said, above my head.

'What?'

'Step in.'

I saw to my astonishment that the narrow door

was already swinging open. He'd been so fast. He was tucking a piece of clear plastic into his top pocket and glancing down to where the dog was again detaining his master.

Gerard stepped through the gate as if belonging there and with a rapid acceleration of heartbeats I went after him. He pushed the gate shut behind me and the spring lock fell into place with a click. He smiled faintly, and I saw with incredulity that beneath the tiredness and the malaise he was quietly enjoying himself.

'There may be people in here,' I said.

'If there are ... we found the gate open. Curiosity.'

We both looked at the insides of the very large gates. The padlock outside had been at least partly for show: on the inside there were thick bolts into the ground and a bar let into sockets waist high so that no amount of direct pressure from outside could force the gates open.

'Factories often cut that hole in their defences,' Gerard said, waving at the way we had come in. 'Especially old ones like this, built in the age of innocence.'

We were in a big concreted yard with a high brick building running the whole length of it on our right: small square barred windows pierced the walls in two long rows, one up, one down. At the far end of the yard, facing us, was a one-storey modern office building of panel-like construction, and on our immediate left was a gatehouse which on busy days would have contained a man to check people and vehicles in and out.

No gatekeeper. His door was shut. Gerard twisted the knob, but to no avail.

Alongside the door was a window reminiscent of a ticket office, and I supposed that on working days that was where the gatehouse keeper actually stood. Gerard peered through it for some time at all angles, and then readdressed himself to the door.

'Mortice lock,' he said, inspecting a keyhole. 'Pity.'

'Does it matter?' I said. 'I mean, there wouldn't be much of interest in a gatehouse.'

Gerard glanced at me forgivingly. 'In old factories like this it's quite common to find the keys to all the buildings hanging on a board in the gatehouse. The gatekeeper issues keys as needed when employees arrive.'

Silenced, I watched with a parched mouth while he put a steel probe into the keyhole and concentrated on feeling his way through the tumblers, his eyes unfocused and unseeing, all the consciousness in his fingers.

The place was deserted. No one came running across the yard demanding impossible explanations. There was a heavy click from the gatehouse door and Gerard with a sigh of satisfaction put his steel probe away and again twisted the doorknob.

'That's better,' he said calmly, as the door opened without protest. 'Now let's see.'

We stepped into a wooden-floored room which contained a chair, a time-punch clock with barely six cards in a slot-holder designed for a hundred, a new-looking fire extinguisher, a poster announcing Factory Act regulations and a shallow unlocked wall-cupboard. Gerard opened the cupboard and it was just as he'd said: inside there were four rows of labelled hooks, and upon all the hooks, labelled keys.

'All there,' Gerard said with immense satisfaction. 'There really is no one here. We have the place to ourselves.' He looked along the labels, reading. 'We'll start with the offices. I know more about those. Then . . . what?'

I read the labels also. 'Main plant. Bottle store. Label room. Vats. Dispatch. How long have we got?'

'If Stewart Naylor is Paul Young and does what he said, he'll be on his way now to Martineau Park. If the police detain him there we've at least two or three hours.'

'It doesn't feel like that,' I said.

'No. Always scary, the first few times.'

He left me again speechless. He took the keys he wanted from the hooks and indicated that I should do the same. Then we left the gatehouse, closing the door (unnecessarily, I thought) behind us and walked on into the main part of the yard.

Another large brick building was revealed to the left; and any residual hopes I might have had of our establishing Stewart Naylor's innocence and retreating in prudence were cancelled at that point. Tucked into the left-hand corner of the yard stood a grey Bedford van, brown lines down the sides, devoid of number plates. I went across and looked through its windows but it held nothing: no wine, no fuzzy wigs, no shotgun.

'God in heaven,' Gerard said. 'That's the very one, isn't it?'

'Identical, if not.'

He sighed deeply and glanced round the yard. 'There's no big delivery van here marked Vintners Incorporated. It's probably on its way to Martineau. Let's take the offices, then, and ... er ... try not to leave any trace of our having been here.'

'No,' I said weakly.

We walked across the concrete, our shoes scrunching it seemed to me with alarming noise, and Gerard unlocked the door of the office building as if he were the manager arriving in pinstripes.

As revealed by the time-punch cards, the plant for its size was almost unstaffed. There were six small offices in the office block, four of them empty but for desk and chair, two of them showing slight paperwork activity: beyond those a locked suite of rooms marked 'Managing Director' on the outer door and in smaller letters underneath, 'Knock and Enter'.

We entered without knocking, using the appropriate key from the gatehouse. Inside, first of all, was a pleasant-looking office, walls lined with calendars, charts, and posters of wine districts in France. There were two desks, one managerial, one secretarial, both clearly in everyday use. In-trays bore letters, receipts were spiked, an African violet bloomed next to a pot of pens.

I left Gerard reading invoices with concentration and went through into the next room which was furnished with an expensive leather-topped desk, green leather armchairs, carpet, brass pot with six-foot-high evergreen, cocktail cabinet, framed drawings of Bernard Naylor and his bottling plant fifty years earlier and a door into a luxurious washroom.

On the far side of the plushy office another door led into what had probably been designed as a boardroom, but in there, with daylight pouring through the skylights, the whole centre space was taken up by a table larger than a billiard table upon which someone appeared to have been modelling a miniature terrain of hills, valleys, plains and plateaux, all of it green and brown like the earth, with a winding ribbon of pale blue stuck on in a valley as a river.

I looked at it in awe. Gerard poked his head round the door, glanced at the table, frowned and said 'What's that?'

'War games,' I said.

'Really?' He came closer for a look. 'A battlefield. So it is. Where are the soldiers?'

We found the soldiers in a cupboard against one wall, tidily stacked in trays, hundreds of them in different uniforms, many hand-painted. There were also ranks of miniature tanks and gun carriages of all historical ages and fierce-looking missiles in pits. There were troop-carrying helicopters and First World War biplanes, baby rolls of barbed wire, ambulances and small buildings of all sorts, some of them bombed-looking, some painted red as if on fire.

'Incredible,' Gerard said. 'Just as well wars aren't fought on the throw of dice. I've thrown a six, I'll wipe out your bridgehead.'

We closed the cupboard and in giving the table a last interested look I brushed my hand lightly over the contours of the nearest range of mountains.

They moved.

Slightly horrified I picked them up to put them back into place and stood looking at the hollowed out interior in absolute surprise. I picked up another hill or two. Same thing.

'What is it?' Gerard said.

'The mountains are white inside.'

'What of it?'

'See what they're made of?'

I held the mountains hollow side up so that he could see the hard white interior. 'Its plaster of Paris,' I said. 'Look at the edges . . . like bandage. I should think he's modelled that whole countryside in it.'

'Good grief.'

'Not an ear, nose and throat surgeon. A war games fanatic. Simple material . . . easily moulded, easily coloured, sets hard as rock.'

I put the hills and the mountains carefully back in position. 'There must be a fair few rolls of the stuff on this table. And if you don't mind . . . let's get out of here.'

'Yes,' Gerard agreed. 'I suppose he'd just bought some more, the day he went to the Silver Moondance. Just happened to have it in his Rolls.'

People didn't just happen to wrap people's heads in it. To do that, people had to have seriously vengeful thoughts and psychotic malice. Paul Young had gone a long way from where Stewart Naylor set out.

We closed the war games room door, crossed the green leather office, returned to the business sector.

'There's just enough legitimate trade going on to give an appearance of tottering a fraction this side of bankruptcy,' Gerard said. 'I can't find anything out of place. There were deliveries via Charter Carriers up to a month ago. Nothing since. No invoices as from Vintners Incorporated, no delivery notes, nothing. This office is for accountants and inspectors. Depressingly clean except for many samples of the Young-Naylor handwriting. Let's try the plant itself.'

He locked our way out of the office block and raised his eyebrows for a decision from me.

'Let's try over there,' I said, pointing to the building by the Bedford van. 'See what's in there first.'

'Right.'

There were two sets of double doors set into the long blank wall, and having tried 'bottle store' and 'vats' I found the key marked 'dispatch' opened one of them.

The hinges creaked as I pulled the door open. My body had almost given up on separate nervous reactions: how could one sweat in some places while one's mouth was in drought? We went into the building and found it was the store for goods already bottled and boxed ready for sending out.

There was a great deal more space than merchandise. There were three lonely pallets laden with cases marked 'House Wine – Red', addressed to a restaurant in Surrey and four other pallets for the same place marked 'House Wine – White': and that was all.

'The paperwork for that lot is in the office,' Gerard said. 'The restaurant bought and shipped the wine, Naylor bottled it. Regular consignments, it looked like.'

We went back into the yard and locked the dispatch doors.

'Main plant,' I said, looking at the high building opposite. 'Well . . . let's see what it's like.'

The key duly let us in. The building was old, it was clear at once, built by grandfather Naylor sturdily to last for generations. Internal walls were extensively tiled in white to shoulder height, cream-painted (long ago) above. From the central entrance some stairs on the left wound upwards, and Gerard chose to go that way first as his paper-oriented mind looked instinctively for most enlightenment aloft: so we went upstairs and to a great extent he was right.

1103

Upstairs, among much unused and dusty space, we found a locked door to further reaches, a door that opened like Sesame to the 'label room' key.

'Great heavens,' Gerard said. 'Is all this usual?'

We stood looking at an expanse of floor covered with heaps of bundles of labels, thousand upon thousand of them altogether, in an apparent muddle but no doubt in some sort of order.

'Quite usual,' I said. 'No one ever tries to order exactly the right number of labels needed for any particular job. You always have to have more, for contingencies. The unused ones just tend to be dumped, and they pile up.'

'So they do.'

'Labels in constant use are probably in those small drawers over there. The ones looking like safe deposit boxes. Some of those drawers have labels on the front . . . they'll have those labels in the drawers.'

'What we want are St Estèphe and all the rest, and Bell's.'

'Mm.'

We both set to, but none of the fake labels turned up, very much to our dismay.

'We need something,' Gerard said. 'We need proof.'

We didn't find it in the label room.

At the back of the label room a closed door led presumably to another room beyond, and I suggested taking a look through there, on the off chance.

'All right,' Gerard said, shrugging.

The door was locked and the 'label room' key didn't fit. Gerard diagnosed another mortice job and took what seemed to be an age with his probe turning the mechanism, but eventually that door too yielded to him, and we went through.

Inside that room there was a printing press. A clean, oiled, sleek modern machine capable of turning out impeccable labels.

Some of the press's recent work was still in uncut sheets: rows and rows of Bell's upon Bell's, brilliant in colour, indistinguishable from the real thing.

Neither Gerard nor I said a word. We turned instead to the cupboards and boxes stacked around the walls, and we found them all, the neatly printed oblongs saying St Estèphe, St Emilion, Valpolicella, Mâcon, Volnay and Nuits St Georges.

'It's the Château de Chenonceaux,' I said suddenly.

'What is?'

'On this St Estèphe label. I knew I'd seen it somewhere. It's the Château de Chenonceaux on the Loire, without its bridge.'

'I'm glad you know what you're talking about.'

He was taking one each of all the fake labels and stowing them tenderly in his wallet, tucking them away in his jacket. We left everything else as it was, but on the way out to my relief he didn't stop to relock the door. We went down again to the hall and from there to a door on the left which unlocked to 'vats'.

One could immediately smell the wine; a warm rosy

air-filling aroma like a lungful of earthy fruit. Gerard lifted his head in surprise and to me it felt like coming home.

'I'd no idea,' he said.

A small lobby opened into two long halls, the larger, on the left, containing a row of ten huge round vats down each side. Each vat, painted dark red, was eight feet high, six feet in diameter, and sat eighteen inches above ground level on thick brick pillars. Each vat, on its front, had large valves for loading and unloading, a small valve for testing, a quantity gauge, and a holder into which one could slot a card identifying the present contents.

'They're vast,' Gerard said.

'Kenneth Charter's tanker would fill four of these. That size vat holds fifteen hundred gallons. You can get them bigger.'

'Thanks.'

I smiled. 'Let's see what's in them.'

We read the contents cards. Most of them said 'EMPTY', the quantity gauges reading zero. The three nearest the entrance on the left side bore 'Keely house wine, shipped October 1st', and another further along, 'Dinzag private cuve, shipped Sept. 24th'. Two together on the opposite side said 'Linakket, shipped Sept. 10th'; and all of the occupied vats were only three-quarters full.

'They're all in the office paperwork,' Gerard said regretfully.

'Let's try the empties, then,' I said. 'Quantity gauges can be disconnected.'

I started at the far end under the premise that if Paul Young stacked his loot as far from the entrance as possible at Martineau Park then he might have done so on his own territory: and he had. The very first trickle which came out onto my fingers as I turned the small testing valve bore the raw volatile smell of Scotch.

'Bloody bingo,' I said. 'I'll find a bottle and we'll take a sample, if you like.'

'Later. Try the others.'

'All of them?'

'Yes.'

I loosed the small valves on all the 'EMPTY' monsters, and we found Scotch in five of them and wine in three. There was no way of telling how many gallons were in each, but to neither of us did that seem to matter. The wine, as far as I could tell from sucking it from my palm, was similar to our old friend 'St Estèphe', and the Scotch was Rannoch already mixed with tap water. Gerard looked like a cat in cream as I straightened from testing the last 'EMPTY' (which was in fact empty) and said we'd seen everything now except the actual bottling department, and where would that be?

'Follow the hoses,' I said.

He looked at the three or four hoses which were lying on the ground, fat lightweight grey ridged plastic hoses like giant earthworms as thick as a wrist, some in coils, some straightened out and running the length of the room between the vats.

I said, 'Those connectors at the end of the hoses lock into the valves on the vats. One of them is connected to one of the so-called "empty" vats we found the wine in, see? The wine is pumped from the vats to the bottling plant . . . so to find the plant, follow the hoses.'

The hoses snaked round a corner into another wide hall which this time contained only two vats, both painted a silvery white, taller, slimmer, and with several upright pipes attached from top to bottom of their sides.

'White wine?' Gerard said flippantly.

'Not really. They're refrigeration vats.'

'Go on then, what are they for?'

I went over to the nearest, but it was switched off, and so was the other, as far as I could see. 'They use them to clear cloudy particles out of spirits and white wine. If you drop the temperature, the bits and pieces fall to the bottom, and you run off the cleared liquid from higher up.'

The hoses ran straight past the refrigeration vats and through another wide doorway, and through there were found what Gerard was looking for, the long light and airy hall, two storeys high, where the liquids were fed into the bottles and stoppered by corks, where the caps and the labels were applied and the bottles packed into cases.

There were four separate lines of filling, corking,

labelling and capping machines, a capacity way beyond the jobs in hand. The machines themselves, like the vats and hoses, were new compared with the buildings. It all looked bright, clean, orderly, spacious and well run.

'I somehow expected something dark and Dickensian,' Gerard said. 'Where do we look?'

'Those big wooden slatted crates standing around probably contain empty bottles,' I said, 'but some might have full ones ready for labelling. Look in those.'

'What are those glass booth things?'

'The actual bottling machines and corking machines and automatic labellers are enclosed with glass for safety and they don't work unless the glass doors are shut. One set of the machines looks ready to go. See the corks in that transparent hopper up there? And up there,' I pointed, 'on that bridge, see those four vats? The wine or whatever is pumped along from those huge storage vats in the long hall through the hoses up into these vats on the bridge, then it feeds down again by gravity into the bottles. The pumps for those vats look as if they're up on the bridge. I'll go up and see if there's anything in those feeder vats, if you like.'

Gerard nodded and I went up the stairs. The bridge, stretching from side to side of the bottling hall, was about twelve feet wide, railed at the sides, with four feeder vats on it standing taller than my head, each with a ladder bolted to its side so that one could go up to the entry valves on top.

1109

There were four electric pumps on the bridge, one for each feeder vat, but only one was connected to hoses. In that one case a hose came up from the floor below and a second hose ran from the pump to the top of one of the feeder vats. In that vat I thought I might find more of the 'St Estèphe', and I squatted at the base of it and released a few drops through the small valve there.

Gerard was rattling bottles in the slatted wooden crates, looking for full ones. The crates were about five feet square, four feet high, very heavy, constructed of rows of timber rather like five barred gates. One could see the bottles inside glinting between the slats, hundreds in each crate.

I had become so at home in my more or less natural surroundings that I'd forgotten to be frightened for the past ten minutes: and that was a fundamental mistake because a voice suddenly spoke from directly beneath me, harsh, fortissimo and threatening.

'What the hell do you think you're doing? Back off, put your hands up and turn round.'

CHAPTER TWENTY-ONE

He was speaking not to me but to Gerard.

He advanced from below the bridge into my vision, young, bullish, dressed in jeans and padded jacket, carrying a short-barrelled shotgun. He had his back to me and he hadn't seen me, and I crouched on the bridge in a frozen state, incapable of movement, muscles locked, with the old clammy chill of abject fear sweeping over my skin and setting in my gut.

He was the one, I was intuitively certain, who had shot us before.

He was probably Denny. I called him Denny in my mind.

Gerard turned slowly towards him and raised one hand, the other being still in its sling. He didn't look up to the bridge. He could have seen me perhaps if he had, even though I was down behind the railings and between two vats. He did nothing, said nothing, then or later, to let Denny suspect I was there.

'Stand still,' Denny said, 'or I'll blast you.'

Another voice said, 'Who is it? Is it Beach?' and that was worse. I knew the voice too well.

Paul Young's voice. Stewart Naylor.

'That's not Beach,' he said.

He appeared from below me and stood beside Denny.

I could see the black hair, the heavy shoulders, the glint of glasses, the hearing aid behind his ear.

'Who is it, then?' Denny said.

'The one who was with him. Older, greyer, wearing a sling. That's him. Some name like Gregg, Lew said.'

Who was Lew . . .

'What's the sling for?' Stewart Naylor demanded.

Gerard didn't answer. After a silence Naylor said, 'You said you hit someone in a car at Beach's shop. Was this him?'

Denny said, 'I couldn't see who it was.'

'I don't want him shot in here,' Naylor said forcefully. 'Too much sodding mess. You just keep your sodding finger off the trigger. And you, Gregg, take your arm out of that sling and turn your back to me and put both your hands on the top rail of that bottle-container crate, and you do just what I tell you or you'll get shot again, mess or not.'

Gerard did as he was told. I've got to do something, I thought, and couldn't think what. Couldn't think. Listened in hopeless horror.

Stewart Naylor walked to Gerard and patted him all over, looking for weapons. Gerard didn't move. Naylor reached round into Gerard's jacket and pulled out his wallet, stepping back a few paces to look at the contents.

'Gerard McGregor,' Naylor said, reading. 'Where's your friend Beach?'

'Don't know,' Gerard said, shrugging.

'How the hell did he turn up here?' Denny said. 'I don't like it.'

With suddenly spurting alarm and anger Naylor viciously said, 'He'll sodding wish he hadn't!'

I watched in despair. He had found in the wallet the fake labels from upstairs. He was holding them out as if in disbelief.

'He's seen the press,' he said furiously. 'He knows too bloody much. We'll kill him and dump him. He'll have had no chance yet to tell what he's seen. We'll be all right.' He sounded convinced of it.

Gerard's apparently untroubled voice rose as if in courteous discussion. 'I did of course leave word of where I was going. If I don't return safely you'll find the police at your door.'

'They always say that in movies,' Denny said. 'It's never bloody true.'

After a pause Naylor said, 'Hold him there, Denny. I'll be straight back,' and he turned and walked under the bridge and out of the bottling hall, and I thought about trying to jump onto Denny . . . who was too far away for it to be practicable. He would whirl when he heard me move and he would shoot while I was

1113

climbing the railings to launch myself far enough out
to have a hope of reaching him in one jump ... he
would shoot either Gerard or me for sure before we
could overpower and disarm him. I didn't see what else
to do and I was certain that that jump would be literally
fatal perhaps for both of us, and I was worrying also
and cringing inside with fear that the reason I didn't
move was fear ... Not caution, just cowardice. One
could fling one's life away trying to prove to oneself
one was brave ... and maybe for some people it was
worth it, but not to me.

Stewart Naylor came back carrying a small package
which he zipped open as he walked.

The contents were wide white bandage.

I felt sick.

I should have jumped, I thought. I should have
risked it while I had the chance. Why hadn't I?

Common sense, emotion, logic, bravado ... they
could whirl through the mind in a jumbled mess, and
how could one tell which was right.

Naylor walked over to Gerard and with great speed
tied the wrist of his injured arm to the rail with the
bandage. A strong tremor ran visibly through Gerard's
body and he turned away from the crate, trying to tug
himself free, trying to escape. The lines of his face were
set rigid, the eyes hollowly dark.

He's afraid too, I thought. He knows what that
bandage is. He's as human as I am ... and he's terrified.

He didn't look up at the bridge.

Something, I thought. I must do something. I had no weapon. Nothing. Gerard. Plaster of Paris.

What did I have . . .

I had knowledge.

Naylor hit Gerard's face a swiping blow with his fist and when he had him off balance he tied the second wrist to the railing, and although I could then see only his back the desperation in Gerard's body was like a shout.

In my mind I was begging, 'No, don't do it, no, no . . .' and Naylor wound the bandage once round Gerard's neck.

Knowledge.

The bandage went round twice and three times. Naylor was intent on the work. So was Denny, his back to me, the barrel of the gun drooping.

Gerard was kicking backwards and not reaching Naylor's legs, yelling to him, screaming that what he was doing was useless, useless, people knew he was there and would come looking.

Neither Naylor nor Denny believed him. They were intent . . . enjoying . . . the wrapping of a living head . . . to turn it to rock.

The weapon I had was knowledge.

I moved. My muscles felt stiff. I slid jerkily round the vat I'd tested for St Estèphe and climbed its ladder.

Go on yelling, Gerard, I thought. Go on filling the hearing aid of the deaf man. Go on kicking. Keep them looking your way.

My hands grasped the locking nut which connected the hose to the valve at the top of the feeder vat. Usually I could turn them easily without a wrench. My hands slipped with sweat. I'd got to unlock it. Only chance. Had to have the hose off the vat.

Had to have the hose free at that end.

On top of the vat I strained with almost fury and felt the locking nut turn and turn again and come loose. I lifted the hose off the vat and carried the end of it with me down the short ladder, trying to do it all silently, making small noises that sounded frightful to me but brought no dreaded shouts from the floor.

I was down the ladder. By the pump. From the pump the main long hose ran down to the ground and away into the distance, going to the great storage vat in the main hall. Long hose, holding a good deal of wine.

I switched on the pump. Begging. Praying. Sick.

The pump went smoothly about its business, efficient beyond dream. Wine gushed out of the hose I held like red force-driven water out of a fire hose. I directed it straight at Naylor, drenching Denny on the way. I propped the spurting nozzle between the railings. I climbed over the railings myself and made the flying leap that had been so illogical, so impossible, so deadly. I landed on Denny who couldn't see for wine, and grabbed his shotgun from him and hit him hard with it on the head.

Naylor, totally surprised, tried to clutch me. I felt such anger for him that he would have needed twice his strength. I caught him by his clothes and pushed him until he was under the gushing wine, and I pulled his head back by the hair until the wine was running full onto his face, onto his glasses and up his nose and into his opening mouth until he was beginning to choke.

I was drowning him, I thought.

Perhaps I shouldn't.

He was gagging for breath. Waving his arms about. Helpless.

I half pulled, half pushed him back to the crate Gerard was tied to and propped him chest forwards against it, holding him there by leaning on his back.

He really was choking. Not breathing.

I hit him very hard with my palm below the shoulder blades and the air trapped in his lungs rushed out through the wine blockage in his trachea, and he began to breathe again in whooping gasps like whooping cough, air fighting against wine in all his bronchial tubes.

He had dropped the plaster of Paris bandage at Gerard's feet. I picked up the roll, wet and soggy and pink now with wine, and unwound the layers from Gerard's throat.

Naylor hadn't had any scissors. The bandage led from Gerard's neck down to one wrist and from there to the other. Tight knots on his wrists beyond undoing.

Something to cut with, to free him.

Old blunt penknife. I felt in my pocket for it and

with some astonishment came up with Flora's new sharp silver present. Blessed Flora.

I cut the roll of bandage off Gerard's wrist and then cut the bandages tying his wrists to the crate. Even when his wrists were no longer fixed there he held onto the rail for a few moments, and in that time I'd wound the end of the bandage roll about eight times around one of Naylor's wrists instead, and fastened it similarly to the crate.

Naylor leaned over the crate, retching, coughing, his glasses opaque with wine, his body jerking with the effort of drawing breath. He seemed hardly to notice, much less fight, when I fastened his other wrist to the rail.

Denny on the floor returned to life. I looked down from tying knots and watched fuzzy thoughts begin to straighten out in his eyes, and I took one of the empty bottles out of the crate and hit him again with it on the head.

The bottle broke. A claret bottle, I remotely noticed. The pieces fell into the wine that was still flooding out in a red lake all over the floor, curling round corners, making rivers, pulsating down from the open hose. The smell of it filled the senses; heavily sensuous, headily potent.

So much wine . . . The main valve on the huge storage vat must be open, I thought. The whole thing must be emptying through the pump. Fifteen hundred gallons . . .

Denny was lying face down in it. I hauled him over to the crate, turned him onto his back, pulled his arms up, and with soggy pink bandage tied each of his wrists separately to one of the sturdy lower slats.

Wine swirled through his hair. If there was blood there also, I couldn't see.

Gerard watched, leaning against the crate.

When I'd finished the essential tying there was still some bandage left in the roll. I wound some more of it round each of Naylor's wrists, joining them in more and more layers to the crate, and then used the last of it to do the same for Denny.

The gypsum in the bandage had been already released to some extent by the wine so that my fingers were covered with pale pink slime. I picked an empty bottle from the crate and held it under the spurting hose until it was half filled and then I carefully poured wine over each tied wrist until the bandages were soaked right through.

Gerard watched throughout, speechless.

Finally I went up the stairs and switched off the pump.

The gusher stopped. The only sound suddenly was the laboured wheezing of Naylor fighting for breath.

I looked down for a moment at the scene below: at so much floor redly awash, at Denny lying on his back with his hands tied above his head, at Naylor heaving over the crate, at the shotgun lying in the wine, and the broken claret bottle ... and the bottles in the crates.

The only thing that might cut through hardening plaster of Paris was broken glass.

I went down the stairs and carefully removed the broken bottle from anywhere near Denny, and took enough bottles out of the crate to make sure Naylor couldn't reach any.

I pushed the shotgun well out of their reach with my foot.

What else?

Nothing else.

I was myself, like Naylor and Denny, soaked from head to foot with wine: jacket, trousers, shirt, socks, shoes, all dark red against dark red skin. Gerard alone, though copiously splashed, was relatively dry.

I said to him, 'Could you fetch your car to the gate? I'll drive from there, but I'm not quite sure that I'm what they'd expect in this neighbourhood.'

'What about them?' he said, looking at our captives.

'We'll send the posse. I'd like to get away from here first. Denny has a partner somewhere.'

'Right. Yes, I'll get the car.' He sounded exhausted and very subdued, and looked anywhere but at my face.

Denny stirred and groaned. Naylor wheezed. In a very few minutes the bandages round their wrists would be pink rock, and it would take a saw to release them.

We left without locking anything. Gerard brought the car to the gates and I drove from there on, apologizing as I got in for the stains I would be leaving on the upholstery. He said stains were secondary. He said little else.

We stopped again as in the morning at a nearby public telephone and this time I got through myself to the priority number, reversing the charges. I said to the answering voice that I wanted an urgent message to reach Detective Chief Superintendent Wilson from Tony Beach.

Hold on, he said. I held. A smooth well-known voice came on the line and said, 'Mr Beach? Is that you?'

'Yes, Mr Wilson.'

'And was it you earlier, who directed us to Martineau Park?'

'Not exactly.'

'Mr McGregor, was it?'

'Yes. How do you know?'

'A man at the racecourse . . . the Deputy Clerk of the Course who is present there on Saturdays and Sundays while the gates and doors are unlocked . . . he told our men that a Mr Beach had been to the caterer's section yesterday and again today with a Mr McGregor.'

'What happened?' I asked.

'Paul Young hasn't gone there, Mr Beach.' He spoke partly regretfully, partly with faint reproof.

'Has anyone?' I asked.

'A man called Lew Smith arrived a short while ago

1121

in a van from Vintners Incorporated. Our men surrounded him, accompanied by the Deputy Clerk of the Course. Lew Smith could give no good reason for being there, but neither was he Paul Young. There seemed to be no grounds for detaining him on the basis of an anonymous telephone call, and our men let him go. And now Mr Beach, could you give me an explanation? Why did you expect Paul Young to go to Martineau Park?'

'Mr Wilson,' I said. 'I do know where Paul Young is now. Do you want him?'

'Don't be facetious, Mr Beach.'

I told him exactly where to find his quarry. I said, 'You'll find a printing press if you go upstairs, complete with Bell's labels and also the same fake wine labels found in the Silver Moondance. You'll find stolen whisky in the vats . . . if you apply to Rannoch whisky distillers you'll get a profile match. The Scotch was stolen from tankers belonging to a firm called Charter Carriers . . . you'll find another branch of the police investigating those thefts. You'll find plaster of Paris in Paul Young's office . . . and he's Larry Trent's half-brother and his name is Stewart Naylor.'

'Mr Beach . . .'

'Goodbye, Mr Wilson,' I said. 'Please don't waste time. Lew Smith might drive there and free him. And oh, yes, you remember Gerard McGregor and I were shot at by the robbers outside my shop? You'll find one of those thieves tied up with Naylor. Also his gun's there. I think his name's Denny. Lew Smith was probably his partner. Worth a try, anyway.'

I put the receiver down although I could hear him still talking and got back into the car with Gerard.

'There will be endless questions,' he said.

'Can't be helped.'

I restarted the engine and we angled our way sedately out of Ealing, crossed the hinterland, made it safely back to the high road home.

Neither of us talked again for a long way. There was none of the euphoria of the Sunday before with the pellets burning in our bodies and our spirits high with escape. Today had been grimmer, dark with real horror, dark as wine.

Gerard shifted in his seat and sighed and said eventually, 'I'm glad you were with me.'

'Mm.'

Five minutes later he said, 'I was afraid.'

'Yes, I know. Well, so was I.'

He turned his head, glanced finally at my face and then looked forward again through the windscreen.

'That plaster . . .' He shuddered. 'I was screaming . . . I've never been so craven in my life.'

'Fear in a fearful situation is normal. Absence of fear is not.'

He swallowed. 'I also feared you wouldn't rescue me.'

'Wouldn't? Do you mean couldn't, or wouldn't try?'

'Couldn't, of course.' He seemed surprised at the

1123

question. 'It would have been pointless to do anything useless like throwing your life away to make a gesture.'

'Die in the attempt?'

'Dying in the attempt,' he said sombrely, 'has always seemed to me the height of incompetence.'

'Or plain bad luck.'

'All right,' he said. 'I'll allow bad luck.'

Another silence lengthened. We turned off the motorway and would soon be back where we'd left my car.

'Are you all right to drive home?' I said.

'Yes, perfectly.'

He looked no better than when we'd set off, but not worse either. Still grey, still strained, but still also with apparently endless reserves of stamina.

I had known him for two weeks. Fifteen days, to be accurate, since we had made tunnels under the tent at Flora's party. With him and through him I had looked newly into many internal mirrors and was coming to understand what I saw there. I owed him a great deal and didn't know how to tell him.

I stopped his car beside mine. We both got out. We stood looking at each other, almost awkwardly. After such intensity there seemed to be no suitable farewell.

'I'm in your debt,' he said.

I shook my head. 'Other way round.'

He smiled faintly, ruefully. 'Call it quits.'

He stepped quietly into his wine-stained car, gave me the briefest of waves, drove away.

I watched him go until he was out of sight. Then in similar peace I unlocked my own door and motored ordinarily home.

The sun was breaking through clouds when I reached the cottage, shining with the heavy golden slant of a late October tea-time.

I went into the hall and looked into the real mirror there. My hair was spiky and sticky with wine. The stains all over my head and face had dried to purple, but in the sun's rays they still seemed to glow red. My eyes shone pale grey in a burnished landscape.

I smiled. My teeth gleamed. I looked like a red devil, I thought. A bloody red devil from the far side of terror.

I was filled quite suddenly with a sort of restless exultation.

I went through my sun-filled house shouting aloud, 'Emma... Emma... Emma... Emma...' and my voice bounced off the walls, reverberating.

I didn't shout for lack of her but from wanting to tell her... wanting to shout to her to make her hear... that for once I felt I had done what I should, that I hadn't been for ever a coward, that I knew I hadn't failed her memory... or myself... or anything I thought I ought to be... and that I felt comforted and whole and at one with her, and that if I wept for her from now on it would be for what she had missed . . . the whole of life . . . the unborn child . . . and not for my own loss, not from loneliness . . . not from guilt.

CHAPTER TWENTY-TWO

Fragments of information floated my way for days like debris from a shipwreck.

Chief Superintendent Wilson came to tell me the police had had to saw through the crate and transport Naylor and Denny to a hospital to get their unorthodox handcuffs removed. He seemed deeply amused and also content, and took away a bottle of wine for dinner.

Sergeant Ridger returned with a cut forehead from his scuffle with the pickets and told me that the racecourse bars at Martineau Park had been on the police list of whisky complaints. He said we would have gone there on the next raceday and our pub crawl would have been successful: and I didn't like to tell him that it already had been, thanks to Mrs Alexis.

Mrs Alexis asked me to lunch. I went, laughed a lot, and came away with a commission to choose and supply wine for her restaurant. Wilfred had survived the soot and the sweep got the sack.

Gerard fed me with constant news, mostly good.

The Scotch in the big storage tanks had been

profile-matched and had proved to be the third load stolen from the tanker. The Martineau Park and Silver Moondance Scotch was all from the second load. The first load had presumably been sold and drunk.

Rannoch's were refusing to collect or accept their Scotch because of the tap water. Customs and Excise were pressing all and sundry for the duty. Kenneth Charter's insurers were insisting that as the whisky was Rannoch's, Rannoch's should pay. Rannoch's said Naylor should pay. Kenneth Charter's suggestion that they run the stuff away down a drain and forget it was not being treated seriously.

The best news was that the insurers had agreed to reinstate Charter's policies in full: the tanker fleet would stay in business.

Kenneth Junior's part was so far unknown to the police and would with luck remain so. Kenneth Junior wrote to his father from Australia asking for more money, which Kenneth Senior sent him along with advice to stay far away until parental disgust had abated.

Mission accomplished, Gerard said with satisfaction. Deglet's were sending Charter their account.

Into Deglet's office came news also from the Californian bloodstock agent: he regularly sold the horses shipped by Larry Trent and paid the proceeds as instructed into three bank accounts in the name of Stewart Naylor.

He had met Mr Naylor, who had been over once to

open the accounts. The horses were good and had won races for their new owners. Everything was straightforward, he was sure.

Flora came to tell me she and Jack were going to Barbados for a month to lie in the sun.

'We go every year, dear, but you know Jack, never still for five minutes except that this time his leg will slow him up nicely, won't it? Of course half the racing world goes to Barbados in the winter . . . did you know they call it Newmarket-on-Sea?' And later she sent me a postcard saying Orkney Swayle and Isabella were staying in the same hotel and one couldn't have everything, dear, could one?

Miles Quigley telephoned, full of importance, to offer me Vernon's job, starting immediately, as liquor manager to his firm. Double Vernon's salary, he said, and managerial status and a seat on the board; and I reflected while politely declining that if he'd given Vernon those rewards Vernon might have stayed loyal for life.

Quigley said he was sticking to his agreement not to prosecute and Vernon was co-operating with the police. Co-operating? I asked. Vernon, Quigley said, would be a prosecution witness, chattering in return for immunity. Was I sure about the job?

I was sure. Perfectly certain, thanks all the same.

I would stay with my shop, I thought, because for me it was right. The scale of its life was my scale. We fitted.

I would stay with good-natured Mrs Palissey and maybe one day teach Brian to write his own name. I would eat Sung Li's dinners and bow to him; and I would listen to my customers and sell them comfort.

Ordinary life would go on.

I went home one night after closing at nine and found the postman had left a package from my mother.

She seldom wrote; mostly telephoned. The note inside the package was characteristically short.

Darling,
    Turned out some very old boxes. Found these oddments of your father's. If you don't want them, throw them away.

The oddments were from a long way back, I thought, looking through them. One of a pair of military gold cuff links. A bronze belt buckle with his regimental crest. A leather jotter with a slot for a pencil, but no pencil.

I riffled through the pages of the jotter. Nothing but memos about things like duty rosters; notes about the day-to-day running of the regiment. It was only by chance that I came upon the page where he had written something else.

I stared at the page, transfixed. It was a scrawl, a *cri de coeur*, hurried, barely punctuated, ending without a question mark. I knew my mother wouldn't have sent it, if she'd seen it. It too nearly destroyed the myth.

I felt nearer to him than ever before. I felt his true son.

He had written ... at not quite my present age, he had written:

The battle must be soon now. It is essential not to show fear to the men, but God, I fear
    Why can't I have the courage of my father

Somewhere in the battle, I thought, he had found it.